The Editor

THOMAS RECCHIO is associate professor of English at the University of Connecticut. He is an advising editor of the *Encyclopedia of British Writers: 19th Century* and of the *Encyclopedia of British Writers: 20th Century.* His articles on the Victorian novel have appeared in *Dickens Studies Annual, Victorian Studies,* the *Gaskell Society Journal,* and *Studies in English Literature,* among others. His current work, *The Cultural Uses of Cranford,* examines the various cultural uses that Elizabeth Gaskell's novel has found since its publication in 1853.

W. W. NORTON & COMPANY, INC.
Also Publishes

THE NORTON ANTHOLOGY OF AFRICAN AMERICAN LITERATURE
edited by Henry Louis Gates Jr. and Nellie Y. McKay et al.

THE NORTON ANTHOLOGY OF AMERICAN LITERATURE
edited by Nina Baym et al.

THE NORTON ANTHOLOGY OF CHILDREN'S LITERATURE
edited by Jack Zipes et al.

THE NORTON ANTHOLOGY OF CONTEMPORARY FICTION
edited by R. V. Cassill and Joyce Carol Oates

THE NORTON ANTHOLOGY OF ENGLISH LITERATURE
edited by M. H. Abrams and Stephen Greenblatt et al.

THE NORTON ANTHOLOGY OF LITERATURE BY WOMEN
edited by Sandra M. Gilbert and Susan Gubar

THE NORTON ANTHOLOGY OF MODERN AND CONTEMPORARY POETRY
edited by Jahan Ramazani, Richard Ellmann, and Robert O'Clair

THE NORTON ANTHOLOGY OF POETRY
edited by Margaret Ferguson, Mary Jo Salter, and Jon Stallworthy

THE NORTON ANTHOLOGY OF SHORT FICTION
edited by R. V. Cassill and Richard Bausch

THE NORTON ANTHOLOGY OF THEORY AND CRITICISM
edited by Vincent B. Leitch et al.

THE NORTON ANTHOLOGY OF WORLD LITERATURE
edited by Sarah Lawall et al.

THE NORTON FACSIMILE OF THE FIRST FOLIO OF SHAKESPEARE
prepared by Charlton Hinman

THE NORTON INTRODUCTION TO LITERATURE
edited by Alison Booth, J. Paul Hunter, and Kelly J. Mays

THE NORTON INTRODUCTION TO THE SHORT NOVEL
edited by Jerome Beaty

THE NORTON READER
edited by Linda H. Peterson and John C. Brereton

THE NORTON SAMPLER
edited by Thomas Cooley

THE NORTON SHAKESPEARE, BASED ON THE OXFORD EDITION
edited by Stephen Greenblatt et al.

For a complete list of Norton Critical Editions, visit
www.wwnorton.com/college/english/nce_home.htm

A NORTON CRITICAL EDITION

Elizabeth Gaskell

MARY BARTON

AUTHORITATIVE TEXT

CONTEXTS

CRITICISM

Edited by

THOMAS RECCHIO
UNIVERSITY OF CONNECTICUT

W • W • NORTON & COMPANY • *New York* • *London*

W. W. Norton & Company has been independent since its founding in 1923, when William Warder Norton and Mary D. Herter Norton first published lectures delivered at the People's Institute, the adult education division of New York City's Cooper Union. The Nortons soon expanded their program beyond the Institute, publishing books by celebrated academics from America and abroad. By midcentury, the two major pillars of Norton's publishing program—trade books and college texts—were firmly established. In the 1950s, the Norton family transferred control of the company to its employees, and today—with a staff of four hundred and a comparable number of trade, college, and professional titles published each year—W. W. Norton & Company stands as the largest and oldest publishing house owned wholly by its employees.

The text of this book is composed in Fairfield Medium with the display set in Bernhard Modern.
Book design by Antonina Krass.
Composition by Binghamton Valley Composition.
Manufacturing by the Courier Companies, Westford division.
Production manager: Benjamin Reynolds.

Library of Congress Cataloging-in-Publication Data

Gaskell, Elizabeth Cleghorn, 1810–1865.
Mary Barton : authoritative text, contexts, criticism / Elizabeth Gaskell ; edited by Thomas Recchio. — 1st ed.
p. cm. — (A Norton critical edition)
Includes bibliographical references.

ISBN 978-0-393-93063-4 (pbk.)

1. Working class families—Fiction.   2. Triangles (Interpersonal relations)—Fiction.   3. Fathers and daughters—Fiction.   4. Trials (Murder)—Fiction.
5. Manchester (England)—Fiction.   6. Political fiction.   7. Domestic fiction.
8. Gaskell, Elizabeth Cleghorn, 1810–1865. Mary Barton.   I. Recchio, Thomas.   II. Title.
PR4710.M3 2008
823'.8—dc22   2008010821

W. W. Norton & Company, Inc., 500 Fifth Avenue, New York, N.Y. 10110-0017
wwnorton.com
W. W. Norton & Company Ltd., Castle House,
75/76 Wells Street, London W1T 3QT

2 3 4 5 6 7 8 9 0

Contents

Criticism

Acknowledgments

This edition would not have been possible without the work of numerous Gaskell scholars who have edited editions of *Mary Barton*. Stephen Gill's 1970 Penguin edition, based on the first edition of the novel, was the first that I read when I was introduced to Gaskell's work as an undergraduate more than thirty years ago. What follows is a list of the seven other significant editions, year of publication, and the base text each used that have been published in the years since: Edgar Wright's 1987 Oxford World's Classic (third edition as base text); Angus Easson's 1993 Ryburn edition (fifth edition as base text); Alan Shelston's 1996 Everyman edition (based on the fifth edition with collations from the other early editions except the fourth); MacDonald Daly's 1996 Penguin edition (third edition as base text); Jennifer Foster's 2000 Broadview edition (fifth edition as base text); Joanne Wilkes's 2005 Pickering & Chatto edition (volume five of the new, definitive ten-volume complete works, fifth edition as base text); and Shirley Foster's 2006 Oxford World Classics edition (fifth edition as base text). Although I consulted each of those editions at various points, I am most indebted to Shirley Foster's, Angus Easson's, MacDonald Daly's, and Edgar Wright's editions, which I mined for much invaluable information.

This work would not have been possible without the assistance of many others. Katie Peel has been extraordinary in her support, from helping with permissions to providing critical responses to all the supporting material. Matthew Mroz assisted with the reproduction of illustrations. Richard Pickering provided information on early dramatic adaptations of the novel. The University of Connecticut Research Council provided assistance with a grant. And the Homer Babbidge Library at the University of Connecticut provided essential assistance in locating source materials.

Preface

The Royal Exchange Theatre located in St. Ann's Square, Manchester opened its thirtieth anniversary season in 2006 with the world premiere of Rona Munro's two-act dramatic adaptation of Elizabeth Gaskell's first novel *Mary Barton*. The play, which ran from September 6 through October 14, was subsequently published in book form (Nick Hern Books, London 2006) with a foreword by Munro, in which she writes:

> Elizabeth Gaskell's passion to write came from a need to hold up the world she saw every day in front of an audience who might choose never to see it [at] all. At the birth of the Industrial Revolution she showed the human cost of a world in which economic forces were treated as forces of nature which could not be controlled, inevitable disasters bringing starvation and death to thousands. She wrote not a piece of polemic, but a complicated human story which has compassion for all its characters but poses the most difficult moral questions—still relevant today. (v–vi)

Munro's claims evoke three key emphases that have surfaced in much of the critical work on *Mary Barton*: Gaskell's intention to show her educated, affluent, middle-class readership the horrific actualities for many working-class people during periods of low employment and slack trade in the first industrial city in the world, Manchester during "the hungry forties"; her desire to demonstrate the destructive power of economic practices, which are based on the assumption that the laws of economics invented by laissez-faire economic theorists have the same validity as the laws of physics; and her resistance to proposing specific legal and economic reforms, which would transform the novel from a medium for reflection into a tract for debate. In other words, Gaskell concerns herself in *Mary Barton* with our tendency to turn away from human suffering in order to preserve our own sense of well-being, with the ease with which we rationalize our willful blindness by attributing the causes of suffering to forces beyond our control or our influence; and she confronts us with

morally complex and unsettling social realities through the texture of
the narrative world she presents.

Written intermittently over the years from 1844 to 1847 but not
published until October 1848, *Mary Barton* appeared at a moment
that augured well for its success. There had been a flurry of publications dating roughly from 1832 through 1845 that began to constitute what came to be called the "industrial" (and sometimes
"social problem") novel. Such works as Harriet Martineau's "A Manchester Strike" in her *Illustrations of Political Economy* (1832),
Frances Trollope's *Michael Armstrong, the Factory Boy* (1840), Charlotte Elizabeth Tonna's *Helen Fleetwood* (1840), Elizabeth Stone's
William Langshawe, the Cotton Lord (1842), and Benjamin Disraeli's *Sybil* (1845) are the most noteworthy examples, and all suffer
from similar limitations: the subordination of characterization to
the work's explicit argument and the tendency for the narrative to
degenerate into anti-industrial polemic. In the context of such an
emergent genre, *Mary Barton* was welcomed for its complexity of
characterization, its linguistic richness, and the verisimilitude of its
detail. In addition, 1848 was the year of a resurgence of revolutionary activity in Europe, most notably in France with the overthrow of
King Louis Philippe and the establishment of the second republic.
One of the issues fueling that revolution was a drive for universal
suffrage. One of the six points of the English "People's Charter" (carried as petitions to Parliament in 1839 and 1842) was a call for universal male suffrage. Consequently, *Mary Barton* was read in the
context of renewed English anxieties that conflated the terror of the
French Revolution from 1789 with the emergence of working class
organization, a conflation that accounted in part for the suppression
of working-class organization that resulted in the Peterloo Massacre
in Manchester in 1819. Gaskell was, in fact, concerned about her
novel being read as simply opportunistic because of an unexplained
delay in its publication that pushed the date of its appearance to a
time when the political unrest in Europe had been widely reported
and discussed. In a letter to her publisher John Chapman dated July
10, 1848, in response to his request for an "explanatory preface" to
the novel, Gaskell wrote: "The only thing I should like to make clear
is that it is no catch-penny run up since the events on the Continent
have directed public attention to the consideration of the state of
affairs between the Employers [*sic*], & their work-people" (*Letters*
26, p. 58). Having written that to Chapman, however, did not prevent her from evoking the revolutionary climate in her "Preface,"
which concludes with this sentence: "To myself that idea which I
formed of the state of feeling among too many of the factory-people
in Manchester, and which I endeavoured to represent in this tale
(completed above a year ago), has received some confirmation from

the events which have so recently occurred among a similar class on the Continent."

Note how deftly Gaskell registers her idea "of the state of feeling" within the working classes having come to her before "the events which have so recently occurred," those events confirming her insights rather than her insights being a response to events. Thus she announces her novel as a warning to address a "state of feeling." How much that "state of feeling" results from policy or from attitude is not clear. What is clear through a reading of the novel, though, is that it results from the unambiguous quality of experience in working-class life. Suffering was clear; what to do about it was not. A necessary preliminary to action, however, is understanding, and that is what the novel enables: by presenting working-class experience as fully as she does (with an emphasis on mortality and family stability), and by working metaphorically to evoke comparable experience in the middle-class, Gaskell offers her novel as a stimulus to reflection. The focus of such reflection Gaskell suggests in a letter she wrote to a Miss Lamont dated January 5, 1849: " 'John Barton' was the original name [for the novel *Mary Barton*], as being the central figure to my mind; indeed I had so long felt that the bewildered life of an ignorant thoughtful man of strong power of sympathy, dwelling in a town so full of striking contrasts as this is, was a tragic poem, that in the writing he was my 'hero'; and it was a London thought coming through the publisher that it must be called *Mary B*" (*Letters*, 39, p. 70). Gaskell addresses the wavering focus of the novel as a whole in that passage, noting her central conception of "an ignorant thoughtful man of strong power of sympathy" as the heart of her novel while acknowledging the shift in emphasis required by her publisher for, we can assume, marketing considerations.[1]

Gaskell's "hero" was John Barton; the publishers wanted Mary Barton as heroine. As the history of critical discussion on this issue shows, Gaskell's writing problem was a formal one, a question of genre. Was she writing a realistic narrative of industrial suffering or a romantic narrative about the obstacles placed between two lovers? Gaskell was doing both, turning the life of her working-class hero into a "tragic poem." In other words, as she notes elsewhere in her "Preface," Gaskell wondered about "the romance in the lives of some of those who elbowed me daily in the busy streets of the town in which I resided." We might say, then, that for Gaskell, the possibilities of romance broadly construed—romance as love (Jem and Mary), romance as memory (Alice Wilson), romance as adventure (Will Wilson as sailor and Mary's quest to find him), romance as science (Job

---

1. Love stories are always marketable. In a BBC interview with Sarah Frankcom, the director of Rona Munro's adaptation, Frankcom replied to the question, "Why should the people of Manchester go and see [*Mary Barton*]?" with: "Because it is a good old-fashioned love story!"

Legh)—are what provide a core of meaning and a drive for fulfillment in the most ordinary of lives. What turns romance into tragedy are the social conditions that distort the drive for fulfillment into violence, indirect and social in the case of the mill owners, direct and personal on the part of Barton. The net effect of the tragedy is to blur the distinction between the personal and the social. And that may be what Gaskell's novel encourages readers to reflect upon.

Consider the following passage presented as a direct address to the reader. On an errand of mercy John Barton had just left the Davenports' cellar where Ben Davenport, lying on the feces-strewn damp stones of his family's dwelling, is raving in the last throes of a typhus fever before his death. Barton is forcibly struck by "the contrast between the well-filled, well-lighted shops and the dim gloomy cellar," the same contrast that struck him even more powerfully on the death of his son when he observed the wife of a mill owner buying provisions for a party as his son was dying of starvation:

> [. . .] But he could not, you cannot, read the lot of those who daily pass you by in the street. How do you know the wild romances of their lives: the trials, temptations they are now enduring, resisting, sinking under? You may be elbowed one instant by a girl desperate in her abandonment, laughing in sad merriment with her outward gesture, while her soul is longing for the rest of the dead, and bringing itself to think of the cold-flowing river as the only mercy of God remaining to her here. You may pass the criminal, meditating crimes at which you will to-morrow shudder with horror as you read them. You may push against one, humble and unnoticed, the last upon earth, who in heaven will be in the immediate light of God's countenance. (Chapter 6)

The "romances" of the girl and the criminal alluded to in the passage find extended and painful echoes in the story of Barton's sister-in-law Esther, who becomes a streetwalker out of economic necessity and contemplates suicide, and in Barton's own story, with Barton himself turning to crime. (The "humble and unnoticed" is played out in the life of Alice Wilson.) The effort to read the lot of others becomes a path toward reading our own social and personal circumstance. In this context, we can read the novel as an extended reflection on the particular social conditions that distort a normative drive for fulfill-ment into simultaneously self-destructive actions. Esther's turn to prostitution and the death of Harry Carson, rather than being exceptional actions that distort the internal social logic of the novel (as some critics have maintained), become weirdly normative in a world where what Friedrich Engels called "social murder" is the shadow reality. Davenport's death, the starvation of Barton's son Tom, and the death of Harry Carson are all morally equivalent events in the novel. The death of Carson's son becomes a mirror that reflects back to Carson an image of himself. That too may be what Gaskell's novel encourages readers, especially her mill-owning readers, to reflect on. As the Manchester working-class poet Samuel Bamford wrote to Gaskell in a letter included in this volume: "You have drawn a fearfully true picture: a mournfully beautiful one also have you placed on the tables of the drawing rooms of the great, and good it must there effect; good for themselves, and good also I hope for the poor of every occupation."

II

The genesis of *Mary Barton* has often been told. The first sentence in the "Preface" alludes to one of the circumstances that encouraged Gaskell to write: "Three years ago I became anxious (from circumstances that need not be more fully alluded to) to employ myself in writing a work of fiction." Those circumstances center on a specific event: the death of her son Willie from scarlet fever in 1845. As a retreat from her grief, the story goes, William Gaskell encouraged his wife to write a novel. Another circumstance is recounted in Jenny Uglow's 1993 biography: "Elizabeth allegedly told Travers Madge of the moment that inspired *Mary Barton*. One day, visiting a poor family, she was trying . . . to argue against their suspicion of the rich, 'when the head of the family took hold of her arm, and grasping it tightly said, "Ay, ma'am, have ye ever seen a child clemmed [starved] to death?"'" (193). And such a sight, having seen his child starve to death, haunts John Barton throughout the novel.

But although *Mary Barton* was Gaskell's first novel, it was not her first attempt to write. She and her husband William broke into print in 1831 with their co-authored poem "Sketches among the Poor," which they modeled on the poetry of working-class poets such as George Crabb and Samuel Bamford. In 1839 she contributed a short description of Clopton Hall (a place she had visited as schoolgirl in Stratford-upon-Avon) to William Howitt's volume *Visits to Remarkable Places*. Subsequently, Howitt published three of her short stories in his *Howitt's Journal*: "Libbie March's Three Eras" (a story about single women coping with hardship in Manchester, included in this volume) and "The Sexton's Hero" in 1847 and "Christmas Storms and Sunshine" on New Year's Day 1848. All three stories were published under the general title "Life in Manchester" and with the pseudonym Cotton Mather Mills. Howitt sent the manuscript of *Mary Barton* to John Forster (Charles Dickens's great friend and later his first biographer) who advised the publishers Chapman and Hall to publish it. After some confusion as to whether or how to identify the author (Gaskell suggested the pen-name Stephen Berwick in a letter to Chapman dated October 19, the day after the book was released), the novel was published anonymously.

Because Gaskell lived among and socialized with many mill owners in Manchester—some of whom attended her husband's Unitarian Chapel each Sunday—she welcomed the anonymity, knowing that some of her friends and neighbors might be offended by her depiction of Mr. Carson and the other mill owners in the novel. And, indeed, when her identity as the author became common knowledge early in 1849, her neighbors were offended, some refusing to speak with her in church, and her family friend W.R. Greg writing a long, detailed, negative review (excerpted in this volume). But Gaskell did want to be read and to be known. She asked Chapman to send copies of *Mary Barton* to Dickens and to Thomas Carlyle (whose letter in response is included in this volume). When the reviews of the novel began to appear, the Manchester press tended to be unkind, but the London reviews were enthusiastic, notably John Forster's and Charles Kingsley's (also included in this volume). Gaskell decided to travel to London, where her publisher arranged tickets to cultural events, and where she was wined and dined by the London literati. She became, in effect, a celebrity, a circumstance that did not take her completely by surprise. In a letter to an unknown correspondent dated March 8, 1849, she expressed concern that in traveling to London "it would ill become me to say that I might not be materially altered for the worse by this mysterious process of 'lionizing'" (*Letters* 40, p. 71), that is, the process of one newly famous being publicly acknowledged and celebrated in at times surprising and unsettling ways. She already had had a taste of that in Manchester, for in the same letter she asserts, "Oh dear! I wish poor Mary Barton could be annihilated this next month; and I then might go where I liked, & do & see what I liked naturally & simply." But the genie, in effect, was out of the bottle. The "authoress of *Mary Barton*" became an important figure in mid-Victorian literary life, publishing between 1848 and her death in 1865 six substantial and wide-ranging novels, the finest literary biography of the century in *The Life of Charlotte Brontë*, and numerous short stories and occasional pieces in the periodical press.

III

Although her novels were widely reviewed and admired in her life time, Gaskell's work received much less critical scrutiny after her death. As Robert Selig notes in his *Elizabeth Gaskell: A Reference*

Guide, "Too much criticism on Elizabeth Gaskell from 1867 to 1946 tends to freeze selected earlier opinions into dogma and, at the same time, to respond to less and less of her work" (ix). There are a number of reasons for this. First, the venues for publication for literary criticism were limited; the explosion of academic publication venues such as university presses and specialized journals of criticism (one notable exception being the *Publication of the Modern Language Association*) did not occur until after the second world war. Second, one publishing venue that kept nineteenth-century British novels in circulation, other than the commercial press that marketed pocket editions of many Victorian novels, was the schoolbook industry, which started producing school editions of Victorian novels both English and American in the 1880s. The introductions to those school editions defined the authors and their work in highly restrictive ways appropriate in the publishers' minds for the benefit of schoolchildren. While there were no school editions of *Mary Barton*, there were nine school editions of *Cranford*, all published in America, and almost all discussing that novel as representative of Gaskell's "charming" and "sane" sensibility. Third, for complex reasons related to the role literature played in the construction of national identities in England and America, Gaskell's *Cranford*, by the 1890s, became the novel most identified with her name.

Soon after her death, however, Gaskell was probably most remembered for *Mary Barton*. In the ninth edition of the *Encyclopedia Britannica* published in 1879, for example, Flora Masson ends her entry on Gaskell with this: Gaskell "was far more an artist than a reformer. Had it not been so, *Mary Barton* would not rank so high in the literature of fiction as it does. It is no work of occasion, the chief interest of which departs when the occasion itself is over. It is a thoroughly artistic production, and for power of treatment and intense interest of plot has seldom been surpassed. It is as the authoress of *Mary Barton* that Mrs. Gaskell will be remembered." And even during the years of critical neglect, *Mary Barton* was valued in some surprising ways. In 1907 the novel was banned in Manchester area schools for girls because it was considered to be too emotionally stimulating (*Manchester Evening Chronicle* of May 9 and June 19 and the *Manchester Guardian* of June 22, 1907). That same year the London County Council banned *Mary Barton* from London schools for similar reasons (*The Academy*, June 22, 1907). Both actions are a testament to the power of the novel, a power that was felt as far away as Russia in 1860 when Fyodor Dostoevsky chose to publish a Russian translation of *Mary Barton* in his magazine *Vremya* (Time) to inaugurate a series of translations of foreign literature. The centenary year of Gaskell's death, 1910, also produced a wave of appreciation as evidenced by the more than three-score publications listed in Clark Northrup's 1929 bibliography in Sanders's *Elizabeth Gaskell* (1929), the most characteristic title being, perhaps, "The Gentle Radiance of Mrs. Gaskell's Enduring Fame" (*Current Literature*, November 2, 1910). (That title also suggests something of the dogmatic reverence toward Gaskell and her work characteristic of the time.) Mrs. Esther Alice Chadwick's *Mrs. Gaskell: Haunts, Homes, and Stories* was also published in the centenary year as was the special commemorative number of *The Bookman*, which included a beautiful chalk drawing of George Richmond's famous 1851 portrait of Gaskell as an insert suitable, as the expression goes, for framing. And 1948, the centenary year of *Mary Barton*, saw the publication of Annette Hopkins's "*Mary Barton*: A Victorian Bestseller," an article coming at the end of Selig's "frozen" period of Gaskell criticism. Subsequently Hopkins published the first full-length literary biography of Gaskell in 1954. But it was not until the 1970s, as the bibliography appended to this volume suggests, that Elizabeth Gaskell and *Mary Barton* became subjects of serious, sustained critical and popular interest. The popular interest can be best illustrated by the number of theater, radio, and television adaptations offered of Gaskell's work in recent years. Selig notes that "[i]n late 1975 *Cranford* was made into a musical by Joan Littlewood and John Wells at London's Theatre Workshop, and a dramatized version of *North and South* was shown on BBC television in December of 1975" (x). In 2001 the BBC produced a lavish television adaptation of *Wives and Daughters* and an unabridged dramatic reading of *Mary Barton* that was broadcast again in 2006. Another critically acclaimed *North and South* television adaptation was released by the BBC in 2004, and at the moment of this writing, the BBC is working on an adaptation of *Cranford* (fused with two of Gaskell's short stories) called *The Cranford Chronicles* starring Judi Dench. There are rumors afloat that an adaptation of *Mary Barton* is on the BBC drawing board.

IV

The critical material appended to the main text of *Mary Barton* is organized under two headings: Contexts and Criticism. Under "Contexts" are included letters related to the publication of the novel and Gaskell's reactions to the criticism the novel received. The contemporary reviews offer a sampling of the range of critical responses, which tend to fall into two camps: one appreciates the moral energy of the novel's engagement with the particularity of working-class life while the other argues for the deceptive implications of such particularity. "Libbie Marsh's Three Eras" is included to provide added texture to Gaskell's sensitive rendering of how working-class women bond together in response to economic and personal hardship. The selections from Engels were chosen to highlight two aspects of Gaskell's novel: its verisimilitude in description and its meta-phoric/aesthetic engagement with what Engels defines as social mur-der and an incipient class warfare. The Faucher material both confirms and revises Engels's descriptions, providing a more nuanced perspective that is closer to the terms of understanding that circu-lated within Gaskell's social circle. The brief selection from *The Christian Teacher* adds another view of labor-management relations.

Within "Contexts," the "Adaptation" and "Illustration" sections have a mutually reinforcing function, for novels do not circulate in a culture strictly through the critical discourse that contextualizes and responds to them. Novels stimulate responses in other aesthetic forms, and those responses can be read as forms of critical interpre-tation. For a dramatist like Dion Boucicault to choose to adapt *Mary Barton* for the popular and often melodramatic theater shows that he recognized a quality in certain narrative trajectories of the novel that could serve the purposes of drama. The Richard Altick piece included in the "Criticism" section that compares the novel to Boucicault's drama explores what some of those purposes are. Illustrations pro-vide pictorial representation of what the illustrator finds significant, provocative, and/or essential in the form and content of the novel. The Randolf Caldecott illustration from the frontispiece of the Smith & Elder illustrated edition of *Mary Barton*, for instance, in the way it represents Mary as tall and full-figured, standing over her seated, emaciated, hunched-over father, renders in a single image the cen-tral dynamic in the narrative pattern associated with John and Mary: John's deterioration on the one hand (the loss of his moral stature and paternal authority) and Mary's elevation through her loyalty and physical struggle to save both her father and her future husband. The other images in the "Illustration" section—another frontispiece, two series of three and another series of seven—all offer opportunities to explore narrative emphases highlighted by the visual images. In some ways, the empty critical space that Selig identified in the history of Gaskell criticism, is filled by the implicit criticism of adaptation and the material form of editions of the works themselves. Taken as a whole, the "Contexts" section provides examples of a range of dis-courses and perceptions that animated the social, political, eco-nomic, and artistic dialogue about industrial life in Manchester in the 1840s.

The heart of the "Criticism" section is composed of selections from the most important critical work done on *Mary Barton* since Ray-mond Williams's seminal discussion in *Culture & Society* (1958). John Lucas, Rosemarie Bodenheimer, Catherine Gallagher, Patsy Stoneman, and Hilary Schor are the most important critics of *Mary*

Barton by the standard of the frequency of reference to their work, which is a mark of how their work has stimulated more thought, more exploration of the critical significance of the novel. In other words, their work continually broadens the contexts within which *Mary Barton* may be said to speak. Perhaps the most forceful testament to the notion that *Mary Barton* can be brought into a wider range of contexts to contribute to an understanding of broad historical and cultural processes in ways that only novels of high literary quality can is suggested by the topics addressed by Grossman, King, and Corley: the intersections between the novel and the law; between the novel and natural history and folk knowledge of healing; and between the novel, imperialism, and the international drug trade. As a novelist, Gaskell may not have been intentionally addressing any of those matters in a systematic way, but she was exploring the intersection between individual experience and the material realities of her contemporary world. Consequently, Barton's addiction is not merely a symptom of his personal condition, a mark of his deterioration and physical deformity; his addiction is made possible by international trade practices and domestic distribution networks. Alice Wilson's knowledge of "field simples" is not a mark of her peculiarity but a sign of her historical connection to a way of life associated with folk wisdom and healing. What constitutes evidence in law and novelistic demonstrations of local "truth" may both echo and depend on each other in the wider culture for their functional validity.

A Note on the Text

I have used the fifth edition of 1854, the last one Gaskell saw through the press, as my base text. That edition included "Two Lectures on the Lancashire Dialect" written by her husband William Gaskell. I have decided not to include those lectures in this edition for a couple of reasons. First, the lectures serve as an extended gloss on the footnotes William Gaskell provided on the Lancashire dialect in the main text. For example, when Job Legh recounts his London journey, he says this about his infant granddaughter's crying: "But when the coach stopped for dinner it was awake, and crying for its pobbies" (Chapter 9). "Pobbies" is footnoted thus: "pobbies, or pobs, child's porridge." In Lecture One, William adds this: "The word generally used by Lancashire people for young children's food, bread soaked in milk or water by the fire, is 'pobs' or 'pobbies'; and the most probable derivation of this which I have been able to find, is from the Welsh 'pob,' which means a baking; 'pobi' being to bake or to roast." While the lectures are of interest in their own right, and while Gaskell herself was anxious that the lectures be printed with the novel as a way to honor her husband, they do little more than extend what the footnotes amply demonstrate: the literary and historical roots of the local dialect, giving that dialect cultural authority. In an effort to honor William's role in the writing of the novel, however, I have identified the footnotes he provided with a [WG] throughout this text. There are a couple of short explanatory notes in the original text, however, that seem more likely to be Gaskell's. Those I have identified with [EG]. Second, since this is a critical edition, I needed to save space to capture the increasingly wide-ranging critical history of the novel. And third, the lectures are readily available in the 2005 Pickering & Chatto and the 2006 Oxford World Classics editions.

Following the advice of my students, I have tried to restrict my notes to essential information to enhance reading without too much disruption. Consequently, I have avoided interpretive glosses and geographical identifications. Easson's Ryburn edition provides comprehensive geographical references as, following his lead, does Shirley Foster's. Since mid-twentieth-century criticism has focused so much on the documentary quality of *Mary Barton*, I thought it

important to capture in the notes the range of its textual relations. I
identify many (not nearly all) explicit and implicit biblical allusions
and highlight the major literary references in an effort to suggest how
literary Gaskell's first novel is.

The Text of
MARY BARTON

" Nimm nur, Fährmann, nimm die Miethe,
Die ich gerne dreifach biete !
Zween, die mit nur überfuhren,
Waren giestige Naturen."[1]

1. From "Auf der Uberfahrt" ("On the Crossing") (1832) by Johan Ludwig Uhland
(1787–1862). "Take, good ferryman, I pray / Take a triple fare today; / The twain who with
me touched the strand / Were visitants from another land." (A. W. Ward, translation from the
Knutsford edition of Elizabeth Gaskell's complete works.)

MARY BARTON;

A Tale of Manchester Life.

" 'How knowest thou,' may the distressed Novel-wright exclaim, 'that
I, here where I sit, am the Foolishest of existing mortals; that this my
Long-ear of a fictitious Biography shall not find one and the other, into whose
still longer ears it may be the means, under Providence, of instilling somewhat? We answer, 'None knows, none can certainly know: therefore,
write on, worthy Brother, even as thou canst, even as it is given thee.' "

CARLYLE.[2]

FIFTH EDITION.

LONDON:
CHAPMAN AND HALL, 193, PICCADILLY.
1854.

2. From "Biography" by Thomas Carlyle (1795–1881) in *Fraser's Magazine* 5 (April 1832).

Preface.

Three years ago I became anxious (from circumstances that need not be more fully alluded to)[3] to employ myself in writing a work of fiction. Living in Manchester, but with a deep relish and fond admiration for the country, my first thought was to find a framework for my story in some rural scene; and I had already made a little progress in a tale, the period of which was more than a century ago, and the place on the borders of Yorkshire, when I bethought me how deep might be the romance in the lives of some of those who elbowed me daily in the busy streets of the town in which I resided. I had always felt a deep sympathy with the care-worn men, who looked as if doomed to struggle through their lives in strange alternations between work and want; tossed to and fro by circumstances, apparently in even a greater degree than other men. A little manifestation of this sympathy, and a little attention to the expression of feelings on the part of some of the work-people with whom I was acquainted, had laid open to me the hearts of one or two of the more thoughtful among them; I saw that they were sore and irritable against the rich, the even tenor of whose seeming happy lives appeared to increase the anguish caused by the lottery-like nature of their own. Whether the bitter complaints made by them, of the neglect which they experienced from the prosperous—especially from the masters whose fortunes they had helped to build up—were well-founded or no, it is not for me to judge. It is enough to say, that this belief of the injustice and unkindness which they endure from their fellow-creatures, taints what might be resignation to God's will, and turns it to revenge, in too many of the poor uneducated factory-workers of Manchester.

The more I reflected on this unhappy state of things between those so bound to each other by common interests,[4] as the employers and the employed must ever be, the more anxious I became to give some utterance to the agony which from time to time convulses this dumb people; the agony of suffering without the sympathy of the happy, or of erroneously believing that such is the case. If it be an error, that the woes, which come with ever-returning tide-like flood to over-whelm the workmen in our manufacturing towns, pass unregarded by all but the sufferers, it is at any rate an error so bitter in its consequences to all parties, that whatever public effort can do in the way of legislation, or private effort in the way of merciful deeds, or help-less love in the way of "widow's mites,"[5] should be done, and that

---

3. The death in 1845 of her son William at ten months old of scarlet fever.
4. See "The Mutual Dependence of Men in a Social State" (1844) in this volume.
5. See Mark 12:41–44 and Luke 21:1–4.

speedily, to disabuse the work-people of so miserable a misapprehension. At present they seem to me to be left in a state wherein lamentations and tears are thrown aside as useless, but in which the lips are compressed for curses, and the hands clenched and ready to smite.

I know nothing of Political Economy,[6] or the theories of trade. I have tried to write truthfully; and if my accounts agree or clash with any system, the agreement or disagreement is unintentional.

To myself the idea which I have formed of the state of feeling among too many of the factory-people in Manchester, and which I endeavoured to represent in this tale (completed above a year ago) has received some confirmation from the events which have so recently occurred among a similar class on the Continent.[7]

October, 1848.

---

6. Economics.
7. A reference to working-class revolutionary activity in France, Italy, Hungary, and elsewhere in Europe in 1848.

Mary Barton

A Tale of Manchester Life

Chapter I.

"Oh! 'tis hard, 'tis hard to be working
The whole of the live-long day,
When all the neighbours about one
Are off to their jaunts and play.
There's Richard he carries his baby,
And Mary takes little Jane,
And lovingly they'll be wandering
Through field and briery lane."
MANCHESTER SONG.[8]

There are some fields near Manchester, well known to the inhabitants as "Green Heys Fields," through which runs a public footpath to a little village about two miles distant. In spite of these fields being flat, and low, nay, in spite of the want of wood (the great and usual recommendation of level tracts of land), there is a charm about them which strikes even the inhabitant of a mountainous district, who sees and feels the effect of contrast in these commonplace but thoroughly rural fields, with the busy, bustling manufacturing town he left but half an hour ago. Here and there an old black and white farm-house, with its rambling outbuildings, speaks of other times and other occupations than those which now absorb the population of the neighbourhood. Here in their seasons may be seen the country business of haymaking, ploughing, &c., which are such pleasant mysteries for townspeople to watch; and here the artisan, deafened with noise of tongues and engines, may come to listen awhile to the delicious sounds of rural life: the lowing of cattle, the milkmaid's call, the clatter and cackle of poultry in the old farm-yards. You cannot wonder, then, that these fields are popular places of resort at every holiday time; and you would not wonder, if you could see, or I properly describe, the charm of one particular stile, that it should be, on such occasions, a crowded

---

8. Unidentified headnotes with a specifically Manchester content were most likely written by Gaskell's husband, William.

halting-place. Close by it is a deep, clear pond, reflecting in its dark green depths the shadowy trees that bend over it to exclude the sun. The only place where its banks are shelving is on the side next to a rambling farm-yard, belonging to one of those old-world, gabled, black and white houses I named above, overlooking the field through which the public foot-path leads. The porch of this farm-house is covered by a rose-tree; and the little garden surrounding it is crowded with a medley of old-fashioned herbs and flowers, planted long ago, when the garden was the only druggist's shop within reach, and allowed to grow in scrambling and wild luxuriance—roses, lavender, sage, balm (for tea), rosemary, pinks and wallflowers, onions and jessamine, in most republican and indiscriminate order. This farm-house and garden are within a hundred yards of the stile of which I spoke, leading from the large pasture field into a smaller one, divided by a hedge of hawthorn and black-thorn; and near this stile, on the further side, there runs a tale that primroses may often be found, and occasionally the blue sweet violet on the grassy hedge bank.

I do not know whether it was on a holiday granted by the masters, or a holiday seized in right of Nature and her beautiful spring time by the workmen, but one afternoon (now ten or a dozen years ago)[9] these fields were much thronged. It was an early May evening—the April of the poets;[1] for heavy showers had fallen all the morning, and the round, soft, white clouds which were blown by a west wind over the dark blue sky, were sometimes varied by one blacker and more threatening. The softness of the day tempted forth the young green leaves, which almost visibly fluttered into life; and the willows, which that morning had had only a brown reflection in the water below, were now of that tender gray-green which blends so delicately with the spring harmony of colours.

Groups of merry and somewhat loud-talking girls, whose ages might range from twelve to twenty, came by with a buoyant step. They were most of them factory girls, and wore the usual out-of-doors dress of that particular class of maidens; namely, a shawl, which at mid-day or in fine weather was allowed to be merely a shawl, but towards evening, or if the day were chilly, became a sort of Spanish mantilla or Scotch plaid, and was brought over the head and hung loosely down, or was pinned under the chin in no unpicturesque fashion.

Their faces were not remarkable for beauty; indeed, they were below the average, with one or two exceptions; they had dark hair,

<hr>

9. The mid-1830s. The main events in the novel take place between 1839 and 1842.
1. A reference to the opening line of Geoffrey Chaucer's (1345?–1400) *The Canterbury Tales* (*1387?*): "Whan that Aprill with his shoures soote / The droghte of March hath perced to the roote."

neatly and classically arranged, dark eyes, but sallow complexions and irregular features. The only thing to strike a passer-by was an acuteness and intelligence of countenance, which has often been noticed in a manufacturing population.

There were also numbers of boys, or rather young men, rambling among these fields, ready to bandy jokes with any one, and particularly ready to enter into conversation with the girls, who, however, held themselves aloof, not in a shy, but rather in an independent way, assuming an indifferent manner to the noisy wit or obstreperous compliments of the lads. Here and there came a sober quiet couple, either whispering lovers, or husband and wife, as the case might be; and if the latter, they were seldom unencumbered by an infant, carried for the most part by the father, while occasionally even three or four little toddlers had been carried or dragged thus far, in order that the whole family might enjoy the delicious May afternoon together.

Some time in the course of that afternoon, two working men met with friendly greeting at the stile so often named. One was a thorough specimen of a Manchester man; born of factory workers, and himself bred up in youth, and living in manhood, among the mills. He was below the middle size and slightly made; there was almost a stunted look about him; and his wan, colourless face, gave you the idea, that in his childhood he had suffered from the scanty living consequent upon bad times, and improvident habits. His features were strongly marked, though not irregular, and their expression was extreme earnestness; resolute either for good or evil, a sort of latent stern enthusiasm. At the time of which I write, the good predominated over the bad in the countenance, and he was one from whom a stranger would have asked a favour with tolerable faith that it would be granted. He was accompanied by his wife, who might, without exaggeration, have been called a lovely woman, although now her face was swollen with crying, and often hidden behind her apron. She had the fresh beauty of the agricultural districts; and somewhat of the deficiency of sense in her countenance, which is likewise characteristic of the rural inhabitants in comparison with the natives of the manufacturing towns. She was far advanced in pregnancy, which perhaps occasioned the overpowering and hysterical nature of her grief. The friend whom they met was more handsome and less sensible-looking than the man I have just described; he seemed hearty and hopeful, and although his age was greater, yet there was far more of youth's buoyancy in his appearance. He was tenderly carrying a baby in arms, while his wife, a delicate fragile-looking woman, limping in her gait, bore another of the same age; little, feeble twins, inheriting the frail appearance of their mother.

The last-mentioned man was the first to speak, while a sudden look of sympathy dimmed his gladsome face. "Well, John, how goes it with you?" and in a lower voice, he added, "any news of Esther, yet?" Meanwhile the wives greeted each other like old friends, the soft and plaintive voice of the mother of the twins seeming to call forth only fresh sobs from Mrs. Barton.

"Come women," said John Barton, "you've both walked far enough. My Mary expects to have her bed in three weeks; and as for you, Mrs. Wilson, you know you are but a cranky sort of a body at the best of times." This was said so kindly, that no offence could be taken. "Sit you down here; the grass is well nigh dry by this time; and you're neither of you nesh*² folk about taking cold. Stay," he added, with some tenderness, "here's my pocket handkerchief to spread under you to save the gowns, women always think so much on; and now, Mrs. Wilson, give me the baby, I may as well carry him, while you talk and comfort my wife; poor thing, she takes on sadly about Esther."

These arrangements were soon completed; the two women sat down on the blue cotton handkerchiefs of their husbands, and the latter, each carrying a baby, set off for a further walk; but as soon as Barton had turned his back upon his wife, his countenance fell back into an expression of gloom.

"Then you've heard nothing of Esther, poor lass!" asked Wilson.

"No, nor shan't, as I take it. My mind is, she's gone off with somebody. My wife frets and thinks she's drowned herself, but I tell her, folks don't care to put on their best clothes to drown themselves; and Mrs. Bradshaw (where she lodged, you know) says the last time she set eyes on her was last Tuesday, when she came down stairs, dressed in her Sunday gown, and with a new ribbon in her bonnet, and gloves on her hands, like the lady she was so fond of thinking herself."

"She was as pretty a creature as ever the sun shone on."

"Ay, she was a farrantly† lass; more's the pity now," added Barton, with a sigh. "You see them Buckinghamshire people as comes to work here has quite a different look with them to us Manchester folk. You'll not see among the Manchester wenches such fresh rosy cheeks, or such black lashes to grey eyes (making them look like black), as my

---

* "Nesh;" Anglo-Saxon, nesc, tender.
  "It semeth for love his herte is tendre and neshe."
            CHAUCER—"*Court of Love.*" [WG]

2. Gaskell's husband William provided notes that show the source of many working-class Lancashire dialect words in medieval and Renaissance English literary texts. The purpose of those notes was not to suggest a thematic or imagistic connection between the literature and the dialect; rather, it was to provide a history for working-class speech, illustrating it to be as English as middle-class standard English speech. All such dialect notes will be identified with [WG].

† "Farrantly," comely, pleasant-looking.
  "And hir hatir (attire) was wele *farand*."
            ROBERT DE BRUNNE. [WG]

wife and Esther had. I never seed two such pretty women for sisters; never. Not but what beauty is a sad snare. Here was Esther so puffed up, that there was no holding her in. Her spirit was always up, if I spoke ever so little in the way of advice to her; my wife spoiled her, it is true, for you see she was so much older than Esther, she was more like a mother to her, doing every thing for her."

"I wonder she ever left you," observed his friend.

"That's the worst of factory work for girls. They can earn so much when work is plenty, that they can maintain themselves any how. My Mary shall never work in a factory, that I'm determined on. You see Esther spent her money in dress, thinking to set off her pretty face; and got to come home so late at night, that at last I told her my mind; my missis thinks I spoke crossly, but I meant right, for I loved Esther, if it was only for Mary's sake. Says I, 'Esther, I see what you'll end at with your artificials,[3] and your fly-away veils, and stopping out when honest women are in their beds; you'll be a street-walker,[4] Esther, and then, don't you go to think I'll have you darken my door, though my wife is your sister.' So says she, 'Don't trouble yourself, John, I'll pack up and be off now, for I'll never stay to hear myself called as you call me.' She flushed up like a turkey-cock, and I thought fire would come out of her eyes; but when she saw Mary cry (for Mary can't abide words in a house), she went and kissed her, and said she was not so bad as I thought her. So we talked more friendly, for, as I said, I liked the lass well enough, and her pretty looks, and her cheery ways. But she said (and at that time I thought there was sense in what she said) we should be much better friends if she went into lodgings, and only came to see us now and then."

"Then you still were friendly. Folks said you'd cast her off, and said you'd never speak to her again."

"Folks always make one a deal worse than one is," said John Barton, testily. "She came many a time to our house after she left off living with us. Last Sunday se'nnight—no! it was this very last Sunday, she came to drink a cup of tea with Mary; and that was the last time we set eyes on her."

"Was she any ways different in her manner?" asked Wilson.

"Well, I don't know. I have thought several times since, that she was a bit quieter, and more womanly-like; more gentle, and more blushing, and not so riotous and noisy. She comes in towards four o'clock, when afternoon church was loosing, and she goes and hangs her bonnet up on the old nail we used to call hers, while she lived with us. I remember thinking what a pretty lass she was, as she sat on a low stool by Mary, who was rocking herself, and in rather a poor

3. Artifices.
4. Prostitute.

way. She laughed and cried by turns, but all so softly and gently, like a child, that I couldn't find in my heart to scold her, especially as Mary was fretting already. One thing I do remember I did say, and pretty sharply too. She took our little Mary by the waist and——"

"Thou must leave off calling her 'little' Mary, she's growing up into as fine a lass as one can see on a summer's day; more of her mother's stock than thine," interrupted Wilson.

"Well, well, I call her 'little,' because her mother's name is Mary. But, as I was saying, she takes Mary in a coaxing sort of way, and 'Mary,' says she, 'what should you think if I sent for you some day and made a lady of you!' So I could not stand such talk as that to my girl, and I said, 'Thou'd best not put that nonsense i' th' girl's head I can tell thee; I'd rather see her earning her bread by the sweat of her brow,[5] as the Bible tells her she should do, ay, though she never got butter to her bread, than be like a do-nothing lady, worrying shopmen all morning, and screeching at her pianny all afternoon, and going to bed without having done a good turn to any one of God's creatures but herself.'"

"Thou never could abide the gentlefolk," said Wilson, half amused at his friend's vehemence.

"And what good have they ever done me that I should like them?" asked Barton, the latent fire lighting up his eye: and bursting forth, he continued, "If I am sick, do they come and nurse me?[6] If my child lies dying, (as poor Tom lay, with his white wan lips quivering, for want of better food than I could give him), does the rich man bring the wine or broth that might save his life? If I am out of work for weeks in the bad times, and winter comes, with black frost, and keen east wind, and there is no coal for the grate, and no clothes for the bed, and the thin bones are seen through the ragged clothes, does the rich man share his plenty with me, as he ought to do, if his religion wasn't a humbug? When I lie on my death-bed, and Mary (bless her) stands fretting, as I know she will fret," and here his voice faltered a little, "will a rich lady come and take her to her own home if need be, till she can look round, and see what best to do? No, I tell you, it's the poor, and the poor only, as does such things for the poor. Don't think to come over me with th' old tale, that the rich know nothing of the trials of the poor; I say, if they don't know, they ought to know. We're their slaves as long as we can work; we pile up their fortunes with the sweat of our brows, and yet we are to live as separate as if we were in two worlds; ay, as separate as Dives and Lazarus,[7] with a great gulf betwixt us: but I know who was best off then," and he wound up his speech with a low chuckle that had no mirth in it.

5. Genesis 3:19.
6. Matthew 25:36.
7. Luke 16:19–26 This parable, alluded to frequently in the novel, is about the happy, poor man in heaven and the tormented rich one in hell.

"Well neighbour," said Wilson, "all that may be very true, but what I want to know now is about Esther—when did you last hear of her?"

"Why, she took leave of us that Sunday night in a very loving way, kissing both wife Mary, and daughter Mary (if I must not call her 'little'), and shaking hands with me; but all in a cheerful sort of manner, so we thought nothing about her kisses and shakes. But on Wednesday night comes Mrs. Bradshaw's son with Esther's box, and presently Mrs. Bradshaw follows with the key; and when we began to talk, we found Esther told her she was coming back to live with us, and would pay her week's money for not giving notice; and on Tuesday night she carried off a little bundle (her best clothes were on her back, as I said before) and told Mrs. Bradshaw not to hurry herself about the big box, but bring it when she had time. So, of course, she thought she should find Esther with us; and when she told her story, my missis set up such a screech, and fell down in a dead swoon. Mary ran up with water for her mother, and I thought so much about my wife, I did not seem to care at all for Esther. But the next day I asked all the neighbours (both our own and Brad-shaw's) and they'd none of 'em heard or seen nothing of her. I even went to a policeman,[8] a good enough sort of man, but a fellow I'd never spoken to before because of his livery, and I asks him if his 'cuteness[9] could find any thing out for us. So I believe he asks other policemen; and one on 'em had seen a wench, like our Esther, walk-ing very quickly with a bundle under her arm, on Tuesday night, toward eight o'clock, and get into a hackney coach,[1] near Hulme Church, and we don't know th' number, and can't trace it no fur-ther. I'm sorry enough for the girl, for bad's come over her, one way or another, but I'm sorrier for my wife. She loved her next to me and Mary, and she's never been the same body since poor Tom's death. However let's go back to them; your old woman may have done her good."

As they walked homewards with a brisker pace, Wilson expressed a wish that they still were the near neighbours they once had been.

"Still our Alice lives in the cellar under No. 14, in Barber Street, and if you'd only speak the word she'd be with you in five minutes to keep your wife company when she's lonesome. Though I'm Alice's brother, and perhaps ought not to say it, I will say there's none more ready to help with heart or hand than she is. Though she may have done a hard day's wash, there's not a child ill within the street, but Alice goes to offer to sit up, and does sit up too, though may be she's to be at her work by six next morning."

---

8. A professional, uniformed police force was established in Manchester in 1839, ten years after Sir Robert Peel had established the first uniformed police in England.
9. Acuteness.
1. A coach for hire drawn by two ordinary horses or "hackneys."

"She's a poor woman, and can feel for the poor, Wilson," was Barton's reply; and then he added, "Thank you kindly for your offer, and mayhap I may trouble her to be a bit with my wife, for while I'm at work, and Mary's at school, I know she frets above a bit. See, there's Mary!" and the father's eye brightened, as in the distance, among a group of girls, he spied his only daughter, a bonny lass of thirteen or so, who came bounding along to meet and to greet her father, in a manner that showed that the stern-looking man had a tender nature within. The two men had crossed the last stile, while Mary loitered behind to gather some buds of the coming hawthorn, when an overgrown lad came past her, and snatched a kiss, exclaiming, "For old acquaintance sake, Mary."

"Take that for old acquaintance sake, then," said the girl, blushing rosy red, more with anger than shame, as she slapped his face. The tones of her voice called back her father and his friend, and the aggressor proved to be the eldest son of the latter, the senior by eighteen years of his little brothers.

"Here, children, instead o' kissing and quarrelling, do ye each take a baby, for if Wilson's arms be like mine they are heartily tired."

Mary sprang forward to take her father's charge, with a girl's fondness for infants, and with some little foresight of the event soon to happen at home; while young Wilson seemed to lose his rough, cubbish nature as he crowed and cooed to his little brother.

"Twins is a great trial to a poor man, bless 'em," said the half-proud, half-weary father, as he bestowed a smacking kiss on the babe ere he parted with it.

Chapter II.

Polly, put the kettle on,
And let's have tea!
Polly, put the kettle on,
And we'll all have tea.[2]

"Here we are, wife; did'st thou think thou'd lost us?" quoth hearty-voiced Wilson, as the two women rose and shook themselves in preparation for their homeward walk. Mrs. Barton was evidently soothed, if not cheered, by the unburdening of her fears and thoughts to her friend; and her approving look went far to second her husband's invitation that the whole party should adjourn from Green Heys Fields to tea, at the Bartons' house. The only faint opposition was raised by Mrs. Wilson, on account of the lateness of the hour at which they would probably return, which she feared on her babies' account.

2. A nursery rhyme.

"Now, hold your tongue, missis, will you," said her husband, good-temperedly. "Don't you know them brats never goes to sleep till long past ten? and haven't you a shawl, under which you can tuck one lad's head, as safe as a bird's under its wing? And as for t'other one, I'll put it in my pocket rather than not stay, now we are this far away from Ancoats."[3]

"Or, I can lend you another shawl," suggested Mrs. Barton.

"Ay, anything rather than not stay."

The matter being decided the party proceeded home, through many half-finished streets, all so like one another, that you might have easily been bewildered and lost your way. Not a step, however, did our friends lose; down this entry, cutting off that corner, until they turned out of one of these innumerable streets into a little paved court, having the backs of houses at the end opposite to the opening, and a gutter running through the middle to carry off household slops, washing suds, &c. The women who lived in the court were busy taking in strings of caps, frocks, and various articles of linen, which hung from side to side, dangling so low, that if our friends had been a few minutes sooner, they would have had to stoop very much, or else the half-wet clothes would have flapped in their faces: but although the evening seemed yet early when they were in the open fields—among the pent-up houses, night, with its mists and its darkness, had already begun to fall.

Many greetings were given and exchanged between the Wilsons and these women, for not long ago they had also dwelt in this court.

Two rude lads, standing at a disorderly looking house-door, exclaimed, as Mary Barton (the daughter) passed, "Eh, look! Polly Barton's getten* a sweetheart."

Of course this referred to young Wilson, who stole a look to see how Mary took the idea. He saw her assume the air of a young fury, and to his next speech she answered not a word.

Mrs. Barton produced the key of the door from her pocket; and on entering the house-place it seemed as if they were in total darkness, except one bright spot, which might be a cat's eye, or might be, what it was, a red-hot fire, smouldering under a large piece of coal, which John Barton immediately applied himself to break up, and the effect instantly produced was warm and glowing light in every corner of the room. To add to this (although the coarse yellow glare seemed lost in the ruddy glow from the fire), Mrs. Barton lighted a dip[4] by sticking it in the fire, and having placed it satisfactorily in a tin candlestick, began to look further about her, on hospitable thoughts intent. The room was

3. A working-class neighborhood.
* "For he had *geten* him yet no benefice."
   Prologue to Canterbury Tales. [WG]
4. A candle.

tolerably large, and possessed many conveniences. On the right of the door, as you entered, was a longish window, with a broad ledge. On each side of this, hung blue-and-white check curtains, which were now drawn, to shut in the friends met to enjoy themselves. Two geraniums, unpruned and leafy, which stood on the sill, formed a further defence from out-door pryers. In the corner between the window and the fire-side was a cupboard, apparently full of plates and dishes, cups and saucers, and some more nondescript articles, for which one would have fancied their possessors could find no use—such as triangular pieces of glass to save carving knives and forks from dirtying tablecloths. However, it was evident Mrs. Barton was proud of her crockery and glass, for she left her cupboard door open, with a glance round of satisfaction and pleasure. On the opposite side to the door and window was the staircase, and two doors; one of which (the nearest to the fire) led into a sort of little back kitchen, where dirty work, such as washing up dishes, might be done, and whose shelves served as larder, and pantry, and store-room, and all. The other door, which was considerably lower, opened into the coal-hole—the slanting closet under the stairs; from which, to the fire-place, there was a gay-coloured piece of oil-cloth laid. The place seemed almost crammed with furniture (sure sign of good times among the mills). Beneath the window was a dresser, with three deep drawers. Opposite the fireplace was a table, which I should call a Pembroke,[5] only that it was made of deal, and I cannot tell how far such a name may be applied to such humble material. On it, resting against the wall, was a bright green japanned[6] tea-tray, having a couple of scarlet lovers embracing in the middle. The fire-light danced merrily on this, and really (setting all taste but that of a child's aside) it gave a richness of colouring to that side of the room. It was in some measure propped up by a crimson tea-caddy, also of japan ware. A round table on one branching leg, really for use, stood in the corresponding corner to the cupboard; and, if you can picture all this, with a washy, but clean stencilled pattern on the walls, you can form some idea of John Barton's home.

The tray was soon hoisted down, and before the merry clatter of cups and saucers began, the women disburdened themselves of their out-of-door things, and sent Mary up-stairs with them. Then came a long whispering, and chinking of money, to which Mr. and Mrs. Wilson were too polite to attend; knowing, as they did full well, that it all related to the preparations for hospitality; hospitality that, in their turn, they should have such pleasure in offering. So they tried to be busily occupied with the children, and not to hear Mrs. Barton's directions to Mary.

5. A table with two hinged drop leaves.
6. Black lacquer finish.

"Run, Mary dear, just round the corner, and get some fresh eggs at Tipping's (you may get one a-piece, that will be five-pence), and see if he has any nice ham cut, that he would let us have a pound of."

"Say two pounds, missis, and don't be stingy," chimed in the husband.

"Well, a pound and a half, Mary. And get it Cumberland ham, for Wilson comes from there-away, and it will have a sort of relish of home with it he'll like,—and Mary" (seeing the lassie fain to be off), "you must get a pennyworth of milk and a loaf of bread—mind you get it fresh and new—and, and—that's all, Mary."

"No, it's not all," said her husband. "Thou must get six-pennyworth of rum, to warm the tea; thou'll get it at the 'Grapes.' And thou just go to Alice Wilson; he says she lives just right round the corner, under 14, Barber Street" (this was addressed to his wife); "and tell her to come and take her tea with us; she'll like to see her brother, I'll be bound, let alone Jane and the twins."

"If she comes she must bring a tea-cup and saucer, for we have but half-a-dozen, and here's six of us," said Mrs. Barton.

"Pooh, pooh, Jem and Mary can drink out of one, surely."

But Mary secretly determined to take care that Alice brought her tea-cup and saucer, if the alternative was to be her sharing any thing with Jem.

Alice Wilson had but just come in. She had been out all day in the fields, gathering wild herbs for drinks and medicine, for in addition to her invaluable qualities as a sick nurse and her worldly occupations as a washerwoman, she added a considerable knowledge of hedge and field simples,[7] and on fine days, when no more profitable occupation offered itself, she used to ramble off into the lanes and meadows as far as her legs could carry her. This evening she had returned loaded with nettles,[8] and her first object was to light a candle and see to hang them up in bunches in every available place in her cellar room. It was the perfection of cleanliness; in one corner stood the modest-looking bed, with a check curtain at the head, the whitewashed wall filling up the place where the corresponding one should have been. The floor was bricked, and scrupulously clean, although so damp that it seemed as if the last washing would never dry up. As the cellar window looked into an area in the street, down which boys might throw stones, it was protected by an outside shutter, and was oddly festooned with all manner of hedge-row, ditch, and field plants, which we are accustomed to call valueless, but which have a powerful effect either for good or for evil, and are consequently much used among the poor. The room was strewed, hung, and darkened with these bunches, which emitted no

7. Medicinal herbs and plants.
8. Nettles could be made into a tea to soothe an irritated stomach.

very fragrant odour in their process of drying. In one corner was a sort of broad hanging shelf, made of old planks, where some old hoards of Alice's were kept. Her little bit of crockery-ware was ranged on the mantelpiece, where also stood her candlestick and box of matches. A small cupboard contained at the bottom coals, and at the top her bread and basin of oatmeal, her frying-pan, tea-pot, and a small tin saucepan, which served as a kettle, as well as for cooking the delicate little messes of broth which Alice was sometimes able to manufacture for a sick neighbour.

After her walk she felt chilly and weary, and was busy trying to light her fire with the damp coals, and half-green sticks, when Mary knocked.

"Come in," said Alice, remembering, however, that she had barred the door for the night, and hastening to make it possible for any one to come in.

"Is that you, Mary Barton?" exclaimed she, as the light from the candle streamed on the girl's face. "How you are grown since I used to see you at my brother's! Come in, lass, come in."

"Please," said Mary, almost breathless, "mother says you're to come to tea, and bring your cup and saucer, for George and Jane Wilson is with us, and the twins, and Jem. And you're to make haste, please."

"I'm sure it's very neighbourly and kind in your mother, and I'll come, with many thanks. Stay, Mary, has your mother got any nettles for spring drink? If she hasn't I'll take her some."

"No, I don't think she has."

Mary ran off like a hare to fulfil what, to a girl of thirteen, fond of power, was the more interesting part of her errand—the money-spending part. And well and ably did she perform her business, returning home with a little bottle of rum, and the eggs in one hand, while her other was filled with some excellent red-and-white, smoke-flavoured, Cumberland ham, wrapped up in paper.

She was at home, and frying ham, before Alice had chosen her nettles, put out her candle, locked her door, and walked in a very foot-sore manner as far as John Barton's. What an aspect of comfort did his house-place present, after her humble cellar! She did not think of comparing; but for all that she felt the delicious glow of the fire, the bright light that revelled in every corner of the room, the savoury smells, the comfortable sounds of a boiling kettle, and the hissing, frizzling ham. With a little old-fashioned curtsey she shut the door, and replied with a loving heart to the boisterous and surprised greeting of her brother.

And now all preparations being made, the party sat down; Mrs. Wilson in the post of honour, the rocking chair, on the right-hand side of the fire, nursing her baby, while its father, in an opposite arm-chair tried vainly to quieten the other with bread soaked in milk.

Mrs. Barton knew manners too well to do anything but sit at the tea-table and make tea, though in her heart she longed to be able to superintend the frying of the ham, and cast many an anxious look at Mary as she broke the eggs and turned the ham, with a very comfortable portion of confidence in her own culinary powers. Jem stood awkwardly leaning against the dresser, replying rather gruffly to his aunt's speeches, which gave him, he thought, the air of being a little boy; whereas he considered himself as a young man, and not so very young neither, as in two months he would be eighteen. Barton vibrated between the fire and the tea-table, his only draw-back being a fancy that every now and then his wife's face flushed and contracted as if in pain.

At length the business actually began. Knives and forks, cups and saucers made a noise, but human voices were still, for human beings were hungry and had no time to speak. Alice first broke silence; holding her tea-cup with the manner of one proposing a toast, she said, "Here's to absent friends. Friends may meet, but mountains never."

It was an unlucky toast or sentiment, as she instantly felt. Every one thought of Esther, the absent Esther; and Mrs. Barton put down her food, and could not hide the fast-dropping tears. Alice could have bitten her tongue out.

It was a wet blanket to the evening; for though all had been said and suggested in the fields that could be said or suggested, every one had a wish to say something in the way of comfort to poor Mrs. Barton, and a dislike to talk about anything else while her tears fell fast and scalding. So George Wilson, his wife, and children set off early home, not before (in spite of *mal-à-propos*[9] speeches) they had expressed a wish that such meetings might often take place, and not before John Barton had given his hearty consent; and declared that as soon as ever his wife was well again they would have just such another evening.

"I will take care not to come and spoil it," thought poor Alice, and going up to Mrs. Barton, she took her hand almost humbly, and said, "You don't know how sorry I am I said it."

To her surprise, a surprise that brought tears of joy into her eyes, Mary Barton put her arms round her neck, and kissed the self-reproaching Alice. "You didn't mean any harm, and it was me as was so foolish; only this work about Esther, and not knowing where she is, lies so heavy on my heart. Good night, and never think no more about it. God bless you, Alice."

Many and many a time, as Alice reviewed that evening in her after life, did she bless Mary Barton for these kind and thoughtful words. But just then all she could say was, "Good night, Mary, and may God bless *you*."

---

9. Inappropriate.

Chapter III.

"But when the morn came dim and sad,
   And chill with early showers,
Her quiet eyelids closed—she had
   Another morn than ours."

                              Hood.[1]

In the middle of that same night a neighbour of the Bartons was roused from her sound, well-earned sleep, by a knocking, which had at first made part of her dream; but starting up, as soon as she became convinced of its reality, she opened the window, and asked who was there?

"Me—John Barton," answered he, in a voice tremulous with agitation. "My missis is in labour, and, for the love of God, step in while I run for th' doctor, for she's fearful bad."

While the woman hastily dressed herself, leaving the window still open, she heard the cries of agony, which resounded in the little court in the stillness of the night. In less than five minutes she was standing by Mrs. Barton's bed-side, relieving the terrified Mary, who went about where she was told, like an automaton; her eyes tearless, her face calm, though deadly pale, and uttering no sound, except when her teeth chattered for very nervousness.

The cries grew worse.

The doctor was very long in hearing the repeated rings at his night-bell, and still longer in understanding who it was that made this sudden call upon his services; and then he begged Barton just to wait while he dressed himself, in order that no time might be lost in finding the court and house. Barton absolutely stamped with impatience, outside the doctor's door, before he came down; and walked so fast homewards, that the medical man several times asked him to go slower.

"Is she so very bad?" asked he.

"Worse, much worser than I ever saw her before," replied John.

No! she was not—she was at peace. The cries were still for ever. John had no time for listening. He opened the latched door, stayed not to light a candle for the mere ceremony of showing his companion up the stairs, so well known to himself; but, in two minutes, was in the room, where lay the dead wife, whom he had loved with all the power of his strong heart. The doctor stumbled up-stairs by the fire-light, and met the awe-struck look of the neighbour, which at once told him the state of things. The room was still, as he, with habitual tip-toe step, approached the poor frail body, that nothing now could

---

1. "The Death Bed" (1831) by Thomas Hood (1799–1845).

more disturb. Her daughter knelt by the bed-side, her face buried in the clothes, which were almost crammed into her mouth, to keep down the choking sobs. The husband stood like one stupified. The doctor questioned the neighbour in whispers, and then approaching Barton, said, "You must go down stairs. This is a great shock, but bear it like a man. Go down."

He went mechanically and sat down on the first chair. He had no hope. The look of death was too clear upon her face. Still, when he heard one or two unusual noises, the thought burst on him that it might only be a trance, a fit, a—he did not well know what,—but not death! Oh, not death! And he was starting up to go up-stairs again, when the doctor's heavy cautious creaking footstep was heard on the stairs. Then he knew what it really was in the chamber above.

"Nothing could have saved her—there has been some shock to the system—" and so he went on; but, to unheeding ears, which yet retained his words to ponder on; words not for immediate use in conveying sense, but to be laid by, in the store-house of memory, for a more convenient season. The doctor seeing the state of the case, grieved for the man; and, very sleepy, thought it best to go, and accordingly wished him good-night—but there was no answer, so he let himself out; and Barton sat on, like a stock or a stone, so rigid, so still. He heard the sounds above, too, and knew what they meant. He heard the stiff unseasoned drawer, in which his wife kept her clothes, pulled open. He saw the neighbour come down, and blunder about in search of soap and water. He knew well what she wanted, and *why* she wanted them, but he did not speak, nor offer to help. At last she went, with some kindly meant words (a text of comfort, which fell upon a deafened ear), and something about "Mary," but which Mary, in his bewildered state, he could not tell.

He tried to realise it—to think it possible. And then his mind wandered off to other days, to far different times. He thought of their courtship; of his first seeing her, an awkward beautiful rustic, far too shiftless[2] for the delicate factory work to which she was apprenticed; of his first gift to her, a bead necklace, which had long ago been put by, in one of the deep drawers of the dresser, to be kept for Mary. He wondered if it was there yet, and with a strange curiosity he got up to feel for it; for the fire by this time was well nigh out, and candle he had none. His groping hand fell on the piled-up tea-things, which at his desire she had left unwashed till morning—they were all so tired. He was reminded of one of the daily little actions, which acquire such power when they have been performed for the last time by one we love. He began to think over his wife's daily round of duties: and something in the remembrance that these would never more be done

2. Vulnerable, helpless.

by her, touched the source of tears, and he cried aloud. Poor Mary, meanwhile, had mechanically helped the neighbour in all the last attentions to the dead; and when she was kissed and spoken to soothingly, tears stole quietly down her cheeks: but she reserved the luxury of a full burst of grief till she should be alone. She shut the chamber-door softly, after the neighbour was gone, and then shook the bed by which she knelt with her agony of sorrow. She repeated, over and over again, the same words; the same vain, unanswered address to her who was no more. "Oh, mother! mother, are you really dead! Oh, mother, mother!"[3]

At last she stopped, because it flashed across her mind that her violence of grief might disturb her father. All was still below. She looked on the face so changed, and yet so strangely like. She bent down to kiss it. The cold, unyielding flesh struck a shudder to her heart, and hastily obeying her impulse, she grasped the candle, and opened the door. Then she heard the sobs of her father's grief; and quickly, quietly, stealing down the steps, she knelt by him, and kissed his hand. He took no notice at first, for his burst of grief would not be controlled. But when her shriller sobs, her terrified cries (which she could not repress), rose upon his ear, he checked himself.

"Child, we must be all to one another, now *she* is gone," whispered he.

"Oh, father, what can I do for you? Do tell me! I'll do anything."

"I know thou wilt. Thou must not fret thyself ill, that's the first thing I ask. Thou must leave me and go to bed now, like a good girl as thou art."

"Leave you, father! oh, don't say so."

"Ay, but thou must! thou must go to bed, and try and sleep; thou'lt have enough to do and to bear, poor wench, to-morrow."

Mary got up, kissed her father, and sadly went up-stairs to the little closet, where she slept. She thought it was of no use undressing, for that she could never, never sleep, so threw herself on her bed in her clothes, and before ten minutes had passed away, the passionate grief of youth had subsided into sleep.

Barton had been roused by his daughter's entrance, both from his stupor and from his incontrollable sorrow. He could think on what was to be done, could plan for the funeral, could calculate the necessity of soon returning to his work, as the extravagance of the past night would leave them short of money, if he long remained away from the mill. He was in a club,[4] so that money was provided for the burial. These things settled in his own mind, he recalled the doctor's

---

3. This moment is illustrated in the frontispiece of the Sir Walter Scott edition of *Mary Barton*. See illustration section to this volume.
4. A burial club in which members paid a weekly fee to save for funeral expenses for themselves and their families.

words, and bitterly thought of the shock his poor wife had so recently had, in the mysterious disappearance of her cherished sister. His feelings towards Esther almost amounted to curses. It was she who had brought on all this sorrow. Her giddiness, her lightness of conduct, had wrought this woe. His previous thoughts about her had been tinged with wonder and pity, but now he hardened his heart against her for ever.

One of the good influences over John Barton's life had departed that night. One of the ties which bound him down to the gentle humanities of earth was loosened, and henceforward the neighbours all remarked he was a changed man. His gloom and his sternness became habitual instead of occasional. He was more obstinate. But never to Mary. Between the father and the daughter there existed in full force that mysterious bond which unites those who have been loved by one who is now dead and gone. While he was harsh and silent to others, he humoured Mary with tender love; she had more of her own way than is common in any rank with girls of her age. Part of this was the necessity of the case; for of course all the money went through her hands, and the household arrangements were guided by her will and pleasure. But part was her father's indulgence, for he left her, with full trust in her unusual sense and spirit, to choose her own associates, and her own times for seeing them.

With all this, Mary had not her father's confidence in the matters which now began to occupy him, heart and soul; she was aware that he had joined clubs, and become an active member of the Trades' Union,[5] but it was hardly likely that a girl of Mary's age (even when two or three years had elapsed since her mother's death) should care much for the differences between the employers and the employed,— an eternal subject for agitation in the manufacturing districts, which, however it may be lulled for a time, is sure to break forth again with fresh violence at any depression of trade, showing that in its apparent quiet, the ashes had still smouldered in the breasts of a few.

Among these few was John Barton. At all times it is a bewildering thing to the poor weaver to see his employer removing from house to house, each one grander than the last, till he ends in building one more magnificent than all, or withdraws his money from the concern, or sells his mill, to buy an estate in the country, while all the time the weaver, who thinks he and his fellows are the real makers of this wealth, is struggling on for bread for his children, through the vicissitudes of lowered wages, short hours, fewer hands employed, &c. And when he knows trade is bad, and could understand (at least

---

5. Combination Acts passed in the eighteenth century outlawed labor unions. The acts were repealed in 1824, and in 1825 a law was passed granting limited rights for unions to organize.

partially) that there are not buyers enough in the market to purchase the goods already made, and consequently that there is no demand for more; when he would bear and endure much without complaining, could he also see that his employers were bearing their share; he is, I say, bewildered and (to use his own word) "aggravated" to see that all goes on just as usual with the mill-owners. Large houses are still occupied, while spinners' and weavers' cottages stand empty, because the families that once filled them are obliged to live in rooms or cellars. Carriages still roll along the streets, concerts are still crowded by subscribers, the shops for expensive luxuries still find daily customers, while the workman loiters away his unemployed time in watching these things, and thinking of the pale, uncomplaining wife at home, and the wailing children asking in vain for enough of food,—of the sinking health, of the dying life of those near and dear to him. The contrast is too great. Why should he alone suffer from bad times?

I know that this is not really the case; and I know what is the truth in such matters: but what I wish to impress is what the workman feels and thinks. True, that with child-like improvidence, good times will often dissipate his grumbling, and make him forget all prudence and foresight.

But there are earnest men among these people, men who have endured wrongs without complaining, but without ever forgetting or forgiving those whom (they believe) have caused all this woe.

Among these was John Barton. His parents had suffered; his mother had died from absolute want of the necessaries of life. He himself was a good, steady workman, and, as such, pretty certain of steady employment. But he spent all he got with the confidence (you may also call it improvidence) of one who was willing, and believed himself able, to supply all his wants by his own exertions. And when his master suddenly failed, and all hands in the mill were turned back, one Tuesday morning, with the news that Mr. Hunter had stopped, Barton had only a few shillings to rely on; but he had good heart of being employed at some other mill, and accordingly, before returning home, he spent some hours in going from factory to factory, asking for work. But at every mill was some sign of depression of trade! some were working short hours, some were turning off hands, and for weeks Barton was out of work, living on credit. It was during this time that his little son, the apple of his eye, the cynosure of all his strong power of love, fell ill of the scarlet fever.[6] They dragged him through the crisis, but his life hung on a gossamer thread. Every thing, the doctor said, depended on good nourishment, on generous living, to keep up the little fellow's strength, in the prostration in

---

6. The same disease that killed Gaskell's son William.

which the fever had left him. Mocking words! when the commonest food in the house would not furnish one little meal. Barton tried credit; but it was worn out at the little provision shops, which were now suffering in their turn. He thought it would be no sin to steal, and would have stolen; but he could not get the opportunity in the few days the child lingered. Hungry himself, almost to an animal pitch of ravenousness, but with the bodily pain swallowed up in anxiety for his little sinking lad, he stood at one of the shop windows where all edible luxuries are displayed; haunches of venison, Stilton cheeses, moulds of jelly—all appetising sights to the common passer-by. And out of this shop came Mrs. Hunter! She crossed to her carriage, followed by the shopman loaded with purchases for a party. The door was quickly slammed to, and she drove away; and Barton returned home with a bitter spirit of wrath in his heart, to see his only boy a corpse!

You can fancy, now, the hoards of vengeance in his heart against the employers. For there are never wanting those who, either in speech or in print, find it their interest to cherish such feelings in the working classes; who know how and when to rouse the dangerous power at their command; and who use their knowledge with unrelenting purpose to either party.

So while Mary took her own way, growing more spirited every day, and growing in her beauty too, her father was chairman at many a Trades' Union meeting; a friend of delegates, and ambitious of being a delegate himself; a Chartist,[7] and ready to do any thing for his order.

But now times were good; and all these feelings were theoretical, not practical. His most practical thought was getting Mary apprenticed to a dressmaker; for he had never left off disliking a factory life for a girl, on more accounts than one.

Mary must do something. The factories being, as I said, out of the question, there were two things open—going out to service, and the dressmaking business; and against the first of these, Mary set herself with all the force of her strong will. What that will might have been able to achieve had her father been against her, I cannot tell; but he disliked the idea of parting with her, who was the light of his hearth; the voice of his otherwise silent home. Besides, with his ideas and feelings towards the higher classes, he considered domestic servitude as a species of slavery; a pampering of artificial wants on the one side, a giving-up of every right of leisure by day and quiet rest by night on the other. How far his strong exaggerated feelings had any foundation

---

7. A working class movement, the Chartists proposed a six-point "People's Charter," which addressed questions of parliamentary representation for the working classes. The charter's six points include universal male suffrage, the secret ballot, payment for members of Parliament, and annual parliamentary sessions.

in truth, it is for you to judge. I am afraid that Mary's determination not to go to service arose from far less sensible thoughts on the subject than her father's. Three years of independence of action (since her mother's death such a time had now elapsed) had little inclined her to submit to rules as to hours and associates, to regulate her dress by a mistress's ideas of propriety, to lose the dear feminine privileges of gossiping with a merry neighbour, and working night and day to help one who was sorrowful. Besides all this, the sayings of her absent, the mysterious aunt Esther, had an unacknowledged influence over Mary. She knew she was very pretty; the factory people as they poured from the mills, and in their freedom told the truth (whatever it might be) to every passer-by, had early let Mary into the secret of her beauty. If their remarks had fallen on an unheeding ear, there were always young men enough, in a different rank from her own, who were willing to compliment the pretty weaver's daughter as they met her in the streets. Besides, trust a girl of sixteen for knowing it well if she is pretty; concerning her plainness she may be ignorant. So with this consciousness she had early determined that her beauty should make her a lady; the rank she coveted the more for her father's abuse; the rank to which she firmly believed her lost aunt Esther had arrived. Now, while a servant must often drudge and be dirty, must be known as her servant by all who visited at her master's house, a dressmaker's apprentice must (or so Mary thought) be always dressed with a certain regard to appearances; must never soil her hands, and need never redden or dirty her face with hard labour. Before my telling you so truly what folly Mary felt or thought, injures her without redemption in your opinion, think what are the silly fancies of sixteen years of age in every class, and under all circumstances. The end of all the thoughts of father and daughter was, as I said before, Mary was to be a dressmaker; and her ambition prompted her unwilling father to apply at all the first establishments, to know on what terms of painstaking and zeal his daughter might be admitted into ever so humble a workwoman's situation. But high premiums were asked at all; poor man! he might have known that without giving up a day's work to ascertain the fact. He would have been indignant, indeed, had he known that if Mary had accompanied him, the case might have been rather different, as her beauty would have made her desirable as a show-woman. Then he tried second-rate places; at all the payment of a sum of money was necessary, and money he had none. Disheartened and angry he went home at night, declaring it was time lost; that dressmaking was at all events a troublesome business, and not worth learning. Mary saw that the grapes were sour, and the next day she set out herself, as her father could not afford to lose another day's work; and before night (as yesterday's experience had considerably lowered her ideas) she had engaged herself as apprentice (so

called, though there were no deeds or indentures to the bond) to a
certain Miss Simmonds, milliner and dressmaker, in a respectable
little street leading off Ardwick Green, where her business was duly
announced in gold letters on a black ground, enclosed in a bird's-eye
maple frame, and stuck in the front parlour window; where the workwomen were called "her young ladies;" and where Mary was to work
for two years without any remuneration, on consideration of being
taught the business; and where afterwards she was to dine and have
tea, with a small quarterly salary (paid quarterly because so much
more genteel than by week), a *very* small one, divisible into a minute
weekly pittance. In summer she was to be there by six, bringing her
day's meals during the first two years; in winter she was not to come
till after breakfast. Her time for returning home at night must always
depend upon the quantity of work Miss Simmonds had to do.

And Mary was satisfied; and seeing this, her father was contented
too, although his words were grumbling and morose; but Mary knew
his ways, and coaxed and planned for the future so cheerily, that both
went to bed with easy if not happy hearts.

Chapter IV.

"To envy nought beneath the ample sky;
To mourn no evil deed, no hour misspent;
And like a living violet, silently
Return in sweets to Heaven what goodness lent,
Then bend beneath the chastening shower content."
                                        ELLIOTT.[8]

Another year passed on. The waves of time seemed long since to have
swept away all trace of poor Mary Barton. But her husband still
thought of her, although with a calm and quiet grief, in the silent
watches of the night: and Mary would start from her hard-earned
sleep, and think, in her half-dreamy, half-awakened state, she saw her
mother stand by her bed-side, as she used to do "in the days of long
ago;" with a shaded candle and an expression of ineffable tenderness,
while she looked on her sleeping child. But Mary rubbed her eyes and
sank back on her pillow, awake, and knowing it was a dream; and still,
in all her troubles and perplexities, her heart called on her mother for
aid, and she thought, "If mother had but lived, she would have helped
me." Forgetting that the woman's sorrows are far more difficult to

---

8. "Withered Wild Flowers" (1834) by Ebenezer Elliott (1781–1849). A working-class poet,
   Elliott was known as the "Corn-Law Rhymer" for his resistance to the high tariffs (i.e., corn
   laws) imposed on imported grain to keep domestic agricultural prices high. The increased
   cost of bread as a result of those laws was felt most forcefully by the working class in periods of unemployment.

mitigate than a child's, even by the mighty power of a mother's love; and unconscious of the fact, that she was far superior in sense and spirit to the mother she mourned. Aunt Esther was still mysteriously absent, and people had grown weary of wondering, and began to forget. Barton still attended his club, and was an active member of a Trades' Union; indeed, more frequently than ever, since the time of Mary's return in the evening was so uncertain; and, as she occasionally, in very busy times, remained all night. His chiefest friend was still George Wilson, although he had no great sympathy on the questions that agitated Barton's mind. But their hearts were bound by old ties to one another, and the remembrance of former things gave an unspoken charm to their meetings. Our old friend, the cub-like lad, Jem Wilson, had shot up into the powerful, well-made young man, with a sensible face enough; nay, a face that might have been hand-some, had it not been here and there marked by the smallpox. He worked with one of the great firms of engineers, who send from out their towns of workshops engines and machinery to the dominions of the Czar and the Sultan.[9] His father and mother were never weary of praising Jem, at all which commendation pretty Mary Barton would toss her head, seeing clearly enough that they wished her to under-stand what a good husband he would make, and to favour his love, about which he never dared to speak, whatever eyes and looks revealed.

One day, in the early winter time, when people were provided with warm substantial gowns, not likely soon to wear out, and when, accordingly, business was rather slack at Miss Simmonds', Mary met Alice Wilson, coming home from her half-day's work at some tradesman's house. Mary and Alice had always liked each other; indeed, Alice looked with particular interest on the mother-less girl, the daughter of her whose forgiving kiss had comforted her in many sleepless hours. So there was a warm greeting between the tidy old woman and the blooming young work-girl; and then Alice ventured to ask if she would come in and take her tea with her that very evening.

"You'll think it dull enough to come just to sit with an old woman like me, but there's a tidy young lass as lives in the floor above, who does plain work, and now and then a bit in your own line, Mary; she's grand-daughter to old Job Legh, a spinner, and a good girl she is. Do come, Mary; I've a terrible wish to make you known to each other. She's a genteel-looking lass, too."

At the beginning of this speech Mary had feared the intended vis-itor was to be no other than Alice's nephew; but Alice was too delicate-minded to plan a meeting, even for her dear Jem, when one

9. References to Russia and Turkey, respectively.

would have been an unwilling party; and Mary, relieved from her apprehension by the conclusion, gladly agreed to come. How busy Alice felt! it was not often she had any one to tea; and now her sense of the duties of a hostess were almost too much for her. She made haste home, and lighted the unwilling fire, borrowing a pair of bellows to make it burn the faster. For herself she was always patient; she let the coals take their time. Then she put on her pattens,[1] and went to fill her kettle at the pump in the next court, and on her way she borrowed a cup; of odd saucers she had plenty, serving as plates when occasion required. Half an ounce of tea and a quarter of a pound of butter went far to absorb her morning's wages; but this was an unusual occasion. In general, she used herb-tea for herself, when at home, unless some thoughtful mistress made a present of tea-leaves from her more abundant household. The two chairs drawn out for visitors, and duly swept and dusted; an old board arranged with some skill upon two old candle boxes set on end (rather ricketty to be sure, but she knew the seat of old, and when to sit lightly; indeed the whole affair was more for apparent dignity of position than for any real ease); a little, very little round table, put just before the fire, which by this time was blazing merrily; her unlackered, ancient, third-hand tea-tray arranged with a black tea-pot, two cups with a red and white pattern, and one with the old friendly willow pattern, and saucers, not to match (on one of the extra supply the lump of butter flourished away); all these preparations complete, Alice began to look about her with satisfaction, and a sort of wonder what more could be done to add to the comfort of the evening. She took one of the chairs away from its appropriate place by the table, and putting it close to the broad large hanging shelf I told you about when I first described her cellar-dwelling, and mounting on it, she pulled towards her an old deal box, and took thence a quantity of the oat bread of the north, the "clap-bread"[2] of Cumberland and Westmoreland, and descending carefully with the thin cakes, threatening to break to pieces in her hand, she placed them on the bare table, with the belief that her visitors would have an unusual treat in eating the bread of her childhood. She brought out a good piece of a four-pound loaf of common household bread as well, and then sat down to rest, really to rest, and not to pretend, on one of the rush-bottomed chairs. The candle was ready to be lighted, the kettle boiled, the tea was awaiting its doom in its paper parcel; all was ready.

A knock at the door! It was Margaret, the young workwoman who lived in the rooms above, who having heard the bustle, and the subsequent quiet, began to think it was time to pay her visit below. She

1. Wooden overshoes.
2. Thin oat cakes, baked brittle and hard.

was a sallow, unhealthy, sweet-looking young woman, with a care-worn look; her dress was humble and very simple, consisting of some kind of dark stuff gown, her neck being covered by a drab shawl or large handkerchief, pinned down behind and at the sides in front. The old woman gave her a hearty greeting, and made her sit down on the chair she had just left, while she balanced herself on the board seat, in order that Margaret might think it was quite her free and in-dependent choice to sit there.

"I cannot think what keeps Mary Barton. She's quite grand with her late hours," said Alice, as Mary still delayed.

The truth was, Mary was dressing herself; yes, to come to poor old Alice's—she thought it worth while to consider what gown she should put on. It was not for Alice, however, you may be pretty sure; no, they knew each other too well. But Mary liked making an impression, and in this it must be owned she was pretty often gratified—and there was this strange girl to consider just now. So she put on her pretty new blue merino,[3] made tight to her throat, her little linen collar and linen cuffs, and sallied forth to impress poor gentle Margaret. She certainly succeeded. Alice, who never thought much about beauty, had never told Margaret how pretty Mary was; and, as she came in half-blushing at her own self-consciousness, Margaret could hardly take her eyes off her, and Mary put down her long black lashes with a sort of dislike of the very observation she had taken such pains to secure. Can you fancy the bustle of Alice to make the tea, to pour it out, and sweeten it to their liking, to help and help again to clap-bread and bread-and-butter? Can you fancy the delight with which she watched her piled-up clap-bread disappear before the hungry girls, and lis-tened to the praises of her home-remembered dainty?

"My mother used to send me some clap-bread by any north-country person—bless her! She knew how good such things taste when far away from home. Not but what every one likes it. When I was in service my fellow-servants were always glad to share with me. Eh, it's a long time ago, yon."

"Do tell us about it, Alice," said Margaret.

"Why, lass, there's nothing to tell. There was more mouths at home than could be fed. Tom, that's Will's father (you don't know Will, but he's a sailor to foreign parts), had come to Manchester, and sent word what terrible lots of work was to be had, both for lads and lasses. So father sent George first (you know George, well enough, Mary), and then work was scarce out toward Burton, where we lived, and father said I maun try and get a place. And George wrote as how wages were far higher in Manchester than Milnthorpe or Lancaster; and, lasses, I was young and thoughtless, and thought it was a fine thing to go so

---

3. A fine, soft wool or wool/cotton blend resembling cashmere.

far from home. So, one day, th' butcher he brings us a letter fra
George, to say he'd heard on a place—and I was all agog to go, and
father was pleased like; but mother said little, and that little was very
quiet. I've often thought she was a bit hurt to see me so ready to go—
God forgive me! But she packed up my clothes, and some of the better end of her own as would fit me, in yon little paper box up
there—it's good for nought now, but I would liefer* live without fire
than break it up to be burnt; and yet it's going on for eighty years old,
for she had it when she was a girl, and brought all her clothes in it to
father's when they were married. But, as I was saying, she did not cry,
though the tears was often in her eyes; and I seen her looking after
me down the lane as long as I were in sight, with her hand shading
her eyes—and that were the last look I ever had on her."

Alice knew that before long she should go to that mother; and,
besides, the griefs and bitter woes of youth have worn themselves out
before we grow old; but she looked so sorrowful that the girls caught
her sadness, and mourned for the poor woman who had been dead
and gone so many years ago.

"Did you never see her again, Alice? Did you never go home while
she was alive?" asked Mary.

"No, nor since. Many a time and oft have I planned to go. I plan it
yet, and hope to go home again before it please God to take me.
I used to try and save money enough to go for a week when I was in
service; but first one thing came, and then another. First, missis's
children fell ill of the measles, just when the week I'd asked for came,
and I couldn't leave them, for one and all cried for me to nurse them.
Then missis herself fell sick, and I could go less than ever. For, you
see, they kept a little shop, and he drank, and missis and me was all
there was to mind children and shop and all, and cook and wash
besides."

Mary was glad she had not gone into service, and said so.

"Eh, lass! thou little knows the pleasure o' helping others; I was as
happy there as could be; almost as happy as I was at home. Well, but
next year I thought I could go at a leisure time, and missis told me
I should have a fortnight then, and I used to sit up all that winter
working hard at patchwork, to have a quilt of my own making to take
to my mother. But master died, and missis went away fra Manchester, and I'd to look out for a place again."

"Well, but," interrupted Mary, "I should have thought that was the
best time to go home."

"No, I thought not. You see it was a different thing going home for
a week on a visit, may be with money in my pocket to give father a

---

* Liefer, *rather*. A. S. leof, *dear*.
  "There n'is no thing, sauf bred, that me were *lever*."
  CHAUCER—*"Monk's Tale."* [WG]

lift, to going home to be a burden to him. Besides, how could I hear o' a place there? Anyways I thought it best to stay, though perhaps it might have been better to ha' gone, for then I should ha' seen mother again;" and the poor old woman looked puzzled.

"I'm sure you did what you thought right," said Margaret, gently.

"Ay, lass, that's it," said Alice, raising her head and speaking more cheerfully. "That's the thing, and then let the Lord send what he sees fit; not but that I grieved sore, oh, sore and sad, when toward spring next year, when my quilt were all done to th' lining, George came in one evening to tell me mother was dead. I cried many a night at after;* I'd no time for crying by day, for that missis was terrible strict; she would not hearken to my going to th' funeral; and indeed I would have been too late, for George set off that very night by th' coach, and the letter had been kept or summut (posts were not like th' posts now-a-days),[4] and he found the burial all over, and father talking o' flitting; for he couldn't abide the cottage after mother was gone."

"Was it a pretty place?" asked Mary.

"Pretty, lass! I never seed such a bonny bit anywhere. You see there are hills there as seem to go up into th' skies, not near may be, but that makes them all the bonnier. I used to think they were the golden hills of heaven, about which mother sang when I was a child:

> 'Yon are the golden hills o' heaven,
> Where ye sall never win.'[5]

Something about a ship and a lover that should hae been na lover, the ballad was. Well, and near our cottage were rocks. Eh, lasses! ye don't know what rocks are in Manchester! Gray pieces o' stone as large as a house, all covered over wi' mosses of different colours, some yellow, some brown; and the ground beneath them knee deep in purple heather, smelling sae sweet and fragrant, and the low music of the humming-bee for ever sounding among it. Mother used to send Sally and me out to gather ling[6] and heather for besoms,[7] and it was such pleasant work! We used to come home of an evening loaded so as you could not see us, for all that it was so light to carry. And then mother would make us sit down under the old hawthorn tree (where we used to make our house among the great roots as stood above th' ground), to pick and tie up the heather. It seems all like yesterday, and yet it's a long long time agone. Poor sister Sally has been in her grave this forty year and more. But I often wonder if the hawthorn is standing yet, and if the lasses still go to gather heather, as we did many and many a year

---

*   "Come to me, Tyrrel, soon, *at after* supper."
        Shakspeare—"*Richard III.*" [WG]
4. The penny post was introduced in England by Rowland Hill in 1840. Manchester itself had a local penny post dating from 1793.
5. From a ballad of various titles, including "The Daemon Lover" and "The Carpenter's Wife."
6. A heath plant.
7. Brooms made of twig bundles.

past and gone. I sicken at heart to see the old spot once again. May be next summer I may set off, if God spares me to see next summer."

"Why have you never been in all these many years?" asked Mary.

"Why, lass! first one wanted me and then another; and I couldn't go without money either, and I got very poor at times. Tom was a scapegrace, poor fellow, and always wanted help of one kind or another; and his wife (for I think scapegraces are always married long before steady folk) was but a helpless kind of body. She were always ailing, and he were always in trouble; so I had enough to do with my hands, and my money too, for that matter. They died within twelve-month of each other, leaving one lad (they had had seven, but the Lord had taken six to hisself), Will, as I was telling you on; and I took him myself, and left service to make a bit on a home-place for him, and a fine lad he was, the very spit of his father as to looks, only steadier. For he was steady, although nought would serve him but going to sea. I tried all I could to set him again a sailor's life. Says I, 'Folks is as sick as dogs all the time they're at sea. Your own mother told me (for she came from foreign parts, being a Manx woman[8]) that she'd ha' thanked any one for throwing her into the water.' Nay, I sent him a' the way to Runcorn by th' Duke's canal,[9] that he might know what th' sea were; and I looked to see him come back as white as a sheet wi' vomiting. But the lad went on to Liverpool and saw real ships, and came back more set than ever on being a sailor, and he said as how he had never been sick at all, and thought he could stand the sea pretty well. So I told him he mun do as he liked; and he thanked me and kissed me, for all I was very frabbit* with him; and now he's gone to South America, at t'other side of the sun, they tell me."

Mary stole a glance at Margaret to see what she thought of Alice's geography; but Margaret looked so quiet and demure, that Mary was in doubt if she were not really ignorant. Not that Mary's knowledge was very profound, but she had seen a terrestrial globe, and knew where to find France and the continents on a map.

After this long talking Alice seemed lost for a time in reverie; and the girls respecting her thoughts, which they suspected had wandered to the home and scenes of her childhood, were silent. All at once she recalled her duties as hostess, and by an effort brought back her mind to the present time.

"Margaret, thou must let Mary hear thee sing. I don't know about fine music myself, but folks say Marget is a rare singer, and I know she can make me cry at any time by singing 'Th' Owdham Weaver.' Do sing that, Marget, there's a good lass."

8. The Isle of Man.
9. A canal developed in the 1760s by the Duke of Bridgewater connecting, in part, Manchester and Liverpool.
* "Frabbit," peevish. [WG]

With a faint smile, as if amused at Alice's choice of a song, Margaret began.

Do you know "The Oldham Weaver?" Not unless you are Lancashire born and bred, for it is a complete Lancashire ditty. I will copy it for you.

The Oldham Weaver.

I.

Oi'm a poor cotton-weyver, as mony a one knoowas,
Oi've nowt for t' yeat, an' oi've worn eawt my clooas,
Yo'ad hardly gi' tuppence for aw as oi've on,
My clogs are both brosten, an' stuckings oi've none,
      Yo'd think it wur hard,
      To be browt into th' warld,
To be—clemmed,'* an' do th' best as yo con.

II.

Owd Dicky o' Billy's kept telling me lung,
Wee s'd ha' better toimes if I'd but howd my tung,
Oi've howden my tung, till oi've near stopped my breath,
Oi think i' my heeart oi'se soon clem to deeath,
      Owd Dicky's weel crammed,
      He never wur clemmed,
An' he ne'er picked ower i' his loife.†

III.

We tow'rt on six week—thinking aitch day wur th' last,
We shifted, an' shifted, till neaw we're quoite fast;
We lived upo' nettles, whoile nettles wur good,
An' Waterloo porridge the best o' eawr food,
      Oi'm tellin' yo' true,
      Oi can find folk enow,
As wur livin' na better nor me.

VI.

Owd Billy o' Dans sent th' baileys one day,
Fur a shop deebt oi eawd him, as oi could na pay,
But he wur too lat, fur owd Billy o' th' Bent,
Had sowd th' tit an' cart, an' ta'en goods for th' rent,
      We'd neawt left bo' th' owd stoo',
      That wur seeats fur two,
An' on it ceawred Marget an' me.

---

* "Clem," to starve with hunger. "Hard is the choice, when the valiant must eat their arms or *clem*."—BEN JONSON. [WG]
† To "pick ower," means to throw the shuttle in hand-loom weaving. [WG]

V.

Then t' baileys leuked reawnd as sloy as a meawse,
When they seed as aw t' goods were ta'en eawt o' t' heawse,
Says one chap to th' tother, "Aws gone, theaw may see;"
Says oi, "Ne'er freet, mon, yeaur welcome ta' me."
                    They made no moor ado
                    But whopped up th' eawd stoo',
An' we booath leet, whack—upo' t' flags!

VI.

Then oi said to eawr Marget, as we lay upo' t' floor,
"We's never be lower i' this warld, oi'm sure,
If ever things awtern, oi'm sure they mun mend,
For oi think i' my heart we're booath at t' far eend;
                    For meeat we ha' none,
                    Nor looms t' weyve on,—
Edad! they're as good lost as fund."

VII.

Eawr Marget declares had hoo clooas to put on,
Hoo'd goo up to Lunnon an' talk to th' greet mon;
An' if things were na awtered when there hoo had been,
Hoo's fully resolved t' sew up meawth an' eend;
                    Hoo's neawt to say again t' king,
                    But hoo loikes a fair thing,
An' hoo says hoo can tell when hoo's hurt.[1]

    The air to which this is sung is a kind of droning recitative, depending much on expression and feeling. To read it, it may, perhaps, seem humorous; but it is that humour which is near akin to pathos, and to those who have seen the distress it describes it is a powerfully pathetic song. Margaret had both witnessed the destitution, and had the heart to feel it, and withal, her voice was of that rich and rare order, which does not require any great compass of notes to make itself appreciated. Alice had her quiet enjoyment of tears. But Margaret, with fixed eye, and earnest, dreamy look, seemed to become more and more absorbed in realising to herself the woe she had been describing, and which she felt might at that very moment be suffering and hopeless within a short distance of their comparative comfort.

    Suddenly she burst forth with all the power of her magnificent voice, as if a prayer from her very heart for all who were in distress, in the grand supplication, "Lord remember David."[2] Mary held her

1. This dialect poem, composed from the first-person perspective of a Lancashire workman, was composed just after the Napoleonic wars during a time of hardship for handloom weavers. It is one of a series of "Jone o' Grinfilt" ballads.
2. "And all of his afflictions." Psalm 132:1.

breath, unwilling to lose a note, it was so clear, so perfect, so imploring. A far more correct musician than Mary might have paused with
equal admiration of the really scientific knowledge with which the
poor depressed-looking young needlewoman used her superb and
flexile voice. Deborah Travis[3] herself (once an Oldham factory girl,
and afterwards the darling of fashionable crowds as Mrs. Knyvett)
might have owned a sister in her art.

She stopped; and with tears of holy sympathy in her eyes, Alice
thanked the songstress, who resumed her calm, demure manner, much
to Mary's wonder, for she looked at her unweariedly, as if surprised that
the hidden power should not be perceived in the outward appearance.

When Alice's little speech of thanks was over, there was quiet
enough to hear a fine, though rather quavering, male voice, going
over again one or two strains of Margaret's song.

"That's grandfather!" exclaimed she. "I must be going, for he said
he should not be at home till past nine."

"Well, I'll not say nay, for I have to be up by four for a very heavy
wash at Mrs. Simpson's; but I shall be terrible glad to see you again
at any time, lasses; and I hope you'll take to one another."

As the girls ran up the cellar steps together, Margaret said: "Just
step in, and see grandfather. I should like him to see you."

And Mary consented.

Chapter V.

> "Learned he was; nor bird, nor insect flew,
> But he its leafy home and history knew:
> Nor wild-flower decked the rock, nor moss the well,
> But he its name and qualities could tell."
>
> ELLIOTT.[4]

There is a class of men in Manchester, unknown even to many of the
inhabitants, and whose existence will probably be doubted by many,
who yet may claim kindred with all the noble names that science recognises. I said in "Manchester," but they are scattered all over the manufacturing districts of Lancashire. In the neighbourhood of Oldham
there are weavers, common hand loom weavers, who throw the shuttle with unceasing sound, though Newton's "Principia"[5] lies open on
the loom, to be snatched at in work hours, but revelled over in meal
times, or at night. Mathematical problems are received with interest,

---

3. Travis was a handloom weaver from the Manchester area, who trained to be a professional
   singer in London. She specialized in works by Handel and performed in industrial cities.
   She went blind later in life.
4. "The Splendid Village" (1834), Part I, stanza ix by Ebenezer Elliott.
5. Sir Isaac Newton (1642–1727) describes his laws of motion and principles of gravity in the
   Principia Mathematica (1686–87).

and studied with absorbing attention by many a broad-spoken, common-looking factory-hand. It is perhaps less astonishing that the more popularly interesting branches of natural history have their warm and devoted followers among this class. There are botanists among them, equally familiar with either the Linnæan or the Natural system,[6] who know the name and habitat of every plant within a day's walk from their dwellings; who steal the holiday of a day or two when any particular plant should be in flower, and tying up their simple food in their pocket handkerchiefs, set off with single purpose to fetch home the humble-looking weed. There are entomologists, who may be seen with a rude-looking net, ready to catch any winged insect, or a kind of dredge, with which they rake the green and slimy pools; practical, shrewd, hard-working men, who pore over every new specimen with real scientific delight. Nor is it the common and more obvious divisions of Entomology and Botany that alone attract these earnest seekers after knowledge. Perhaps it may be owing to the great annual town-holiday of Whitsun-week[7] so often falling in May or June, that the two great beautiful families of Ephemeridæa and Phryganidæ[8] have been so much and so closely studied by Manchester workmen, while they have in a great measure escaped general observation. If you will refer to the preface to Sir J. E. Smith's Life[9] (I have it not by me, or I would copy you the exact passage), you will find that he names a little circumstance corroborative of what I have said. Being on a visit to Roscoe,[1] of Liverpool, he made some inquiries from him as to the habitat of a very rare plant, said to be found in certain places in Lancashire. Mr. Roscoe knew nothing of the plant; but stated, that if any one could give him the desired information, it would be a hand-loom weaver in Manchester, whom he named. Sir J. E. Smith proceeded by boat to Manchester, and on arriving at that town, he inquired of the porter who was carrying his luggage if he could direct him to So and So.

"Oh, yes," replied the man. "He does a bit in my way;" and, on further investigation, it turned out, that both the porter, and his friend the weaver, were skilful botanists; and able to give Sir J. E. Smith the very information which he wanted.

Such are the tastes and pursuits of some of the thoughtful, little understood, working men of Manchester.

And Margaret's grandfather was one of these. He was a little wiry-looking old man, who moved with a jerking motion, as if his limbs

6. Carl Linnaeus (1707–1778) developed an artificial system for classifying plants based on a limited set of characteristics in contrast to the later, "natural" system that relied on a wider range of characteristics for classification.
7. The week of Pentecost on the church calendar that begins on the seventh Sunday after Easter.
8. Families of insects.
9. Sir James Edward Smith (1759–1828), botanist and founder of the Linnaean Society in 1788. His memoirs and letters were published in 1832.
1. William Roscoe (1753–1831), an art historian from Liverpool and friend of Smith's.

were worked by a string like a child's toy, with dun-coloured hair lying thin and soft at the back and sides of his head; his forehead was so large it seemed to overbalance the rest of his face, which had, indeed, lost its natural contour by the absence of all the teeth. The eyes absolutely gleamed with intelligence; so keen, so observant, you felt as if they were almost wizard-like. Indeed, the whole room looked not unlike a wizard's dwelling. Instead of pictures were hung rude wooden frames of impaled insects; the little table was covered with cabalistic books; and beside them lay a case of mysterious instruments, one of which Job Legh was using when his grand-daughter entered.

On her appearance he pushed his spectacles up so as to rest midway on his forehead, and gave Mary a short, kind welcome. But Margaret he caressed as a mother caresses her first-born; stroking her with tenderness, and almost altering his voice as he spoke to her.

Mary looked round on the odd, strange things she had never seen at home, and which seemed to her to have a very uncanny look.

"Is your grandfather a fortune-teller?" whispered she to her new friend.

"No," replied Margaret, in the same voice; "but you are not the first as has taken him for such. He is only fond of such things as most folks know nothing about."

"And do you know aught about them too?"

"I know a bit about some of the things grandfather is fond on; just because he's fond on 'em, I tried to learn about them."

"What things are these?" said Mary, struck with the weird-looking creatures that sprawled around the room in their roughly-made glass cases.

But she was not prepared for the technical names which Job Legh pattered down on her ear, on which they fell like hail on a skylight; and the strange language only bewildered her more than ever. Margaret saw the state of the case, and came to the rescue.

"Look, Mary, at this horrid scorpion. He gave me such a fright: I am all of a twitter yet when I think of it. Grandfather went to Liverpool one Whitsun-week to go strolling about the docks and pick up what he could from the sailors, who often bring some queer thing or another from the hot countries they go to; and so he sees a chap with a bottle in his hand, like a druggist's physic-bottle; and says grandfather, 'What have ye gotten there?' So the sailor holds it up, and grandfather knew it was a rare kind o' scorpion, not common even in the East Indies where the man came from; and says he, 'How did you catch this fine fellow, for he wouldn't be taken for nothing, I'm thinking?' And the man said as how when they were unloading the ship he'd found him lying behind a bag of rice, and he thought the cold had killed him, for he was not squashed nor injured a bit. He did not like to part with any of the spirit out of his grog to put the scorpion in, but slipped him into the bottle, knowing there were folks enow who would give him something for him. So grandfather gives him a shilling."

"Two shillings," interrupted Job Legh; "and a good bargain it was."

"Well! grandfather came home as proud as Punch, and pulled the bottle out of his pocket. But you see th' scorpion were doubled up, and grandfather thought I couldn't fairly see how big he was. So he shakes him out right before the fire; and a good warm one it was, for I was ironing, I remember. I left off ironing and stooped down over him, to look at him better, and grandfather got a book, and began to read how this very kind were the most poisonous and vicious species, how their bite were often fatal, and then went on to read how people who were bitten got swelled, and screamed with pain. I was listening hard, but as it fell out, I never took my eyes off the creature, though I could not ha' told I was watching it. Suddenly it seemed to give a jerk, and before I could speak it gave another, and in a minute it was as wild as it could be, running at me just like a mad dog."

"What did you do?" asked Mary.

"Me! why, I jumped first on a chair, and then on all the things I'd been ironing on the dresser, and I screamed for grandfather to come up by me, but he did not hearken to me."

"Why, if I'd come up by thee, who'd ha' caught the creature, I should like to know?"

"Well, I begged grandfather to crush it, and I had the iron right over it once, ready to drop, but grandfather begged me not to hurt it in that way. So I couldn't think what he'd have, for he hopped round the room as if he were sore afraid, for all he begged me not to injure it. At last he goes to th' kettle, and lifts up the lid, and peeps in. What on earth is he doing that for, thinks I; he'll never drink his tea with a scorpion running free and easy about the room. Then he takes the tongs, and he settles his spectacles on his nose, and in a minute he had lifted the creature up by th' leg, and dropped him into the boiling water."

"And did that kill him?" said Mary.

"Ay, sure enough; he boiled for longer time than grandfather liked, though. But I was so afeard of his coming round again. I ran to the public-house for some gin, and grandfather filled the bottle, and then we poured off the water, and picked him out of the kettle, and dropped him into the bottle, and he were there above a twelvemonth."

"What brought him to life at first?" asked Mary.

"Why, you see, he were never really dead, only torpid—that is, dead asleep with the cold, and our good fire brought him round."

"I'm glad father does not care for such things," said Mary.

"Are you! Well, I'm often downright glad grandfather is so fond of

his books, and his creatures, and his plants. It does my heart good to
see him so happy, sorting them all at home, and so ready to go in
search of more, whenever he's a spare day. Look at him now! he's
gone back to his books, and he'll be as happy as a king, working away
till I make him go to bed. It keeps him silent, to be sure; but so long
as I see him earnest, and pleased, and eager, what does that matter?
Then, when he has his talking bouts, you can't think how much he
has to say. Dear grandfather! you don't know how happy we are!"

Mary wondered if the dear grandfather heard all this, for Margaret
did not speak in an under tone; but no! he was far too deep and eager
in solving a problem. He did not even notice Mary's leave-taking, and
she went home with the feeling that she had that night made the
acquaintance of two of the strangest people she ever saw in her life.
Margaret, so quiet, so commonplace, until her singing powers were
called forth; so silent from home, so cheerful and agreeable at home;
and her grandfather so very different to any one Mary had ever seen.
Margaret had said he was not a fortune-teller, but she did not know
whether to believe her.

To resolve her doubts, she told the history of the evening to her
father, who was interested by her account, and curious to see and
judge for himself. Opportunities are not often wanting where inclination goes before, and ere the end of that winter Mary looked upon
Margaret almost as an old friend. The latter would bring her work
when Mary was likely to be at home in the evenings and sit with her;
and Job Legh would put a book and his pipe in his pocket and just
step round the corner to fetch his grandchild, ready for a talk if he
found Barton in; ready to pull out pipe and book if the girls wanted
him to wait, and John was still at his club. In short, ready to do whatever would give pleasure to his darling Margaret.

I do not know what points of resemblance, or dissimilitude (for this
joins people as often as that) attracted the two girls to each other.
Margaret had the great charm of possessing good strong common
sense, and do you not perceive how involuntarily this is valued? It is
so pleasant to have a friend who possesses the power of setting a difficult question in a clear light; whose judgment can tell what is best
to be done; and who is so convinced of what is "wisest, best," that in
consideration of the end, all difficulties in the way diminish. People
admire talent, and talk about their admiration. But they value common sense without talking about it, and often without knowing it.

So Mary and Margaret grew in love one toward the other; and
Mary told many of her feelings in a way she had never done before to
any one. Most of her foibles also were made known to Margaret, but
not all. There was one cherished weakness still concealed from every
one. It concerned a lover, not beloved, but favoured by fancy. A gallant, handsome young man; but—not beloved. Yet Mary hoped to

meet him every day in her walks, blushed when she heard his name, and tried to think of him as her future husband, and above all, tried to think of herself as his future wife. Alas! poor Mary! Bitter woe did thy weakness work thee.

She had other lovers. One or two would gladly have kept her company, but she held herself too high, they said. Jem Wilson said nothing, but loved on and on, ever more fondly; he hoped against hope; he would not give up, for it seemed like giving up life to give up thought of Mary. He did not dare to look to any end of all this; the present, so that he saw her, touched the hem of her garment, was enough. Surely, in time, such deep love would beget love.

He would not relinquish hope, and yet her coldness of manner was enough to daunt any man; and it made Jem more despairing than he would acknowledge for a long time even to himself.

But one evening he came round by Barton's house, a willing messenger for his father, and opening the door saw Margaret sitting asleep before the fire. She had come in to speak to Mary; and worn out by a long, working, watching night, she fell asleep in the genial warmth.

An old fashioned saying about a pair of gloves came into Jem's mind,[2] and stepping gently up, he kissed Margaret with a friendly kiss.

She awoke, and perfectly understanding the thing, she said, "For shame of yourself, Jem! What would Mary say?"

Lightly said, lightly answered.

"She'd nobbut* say, practice makes perfect." And they both laughed. But the words Margaret had said rankled in Jem's mind. Would Mary care? Would she care in the very least? They seemed to call for an answer by night and by day; and Jem felt that his heart told him Mary was quite indifferent to any action of his. Still he loved on, and on, ever more fondly.

Mary's father was well aware of the nature of Jem Wilson's feelings for his daughter, but he took no notice of them to any one, thinking Mary full young yet for the cares of married life, and unwilling, too, to entertain the idea of parting with her at any time, however distant. But he welcomed Jem at his house, as he would have done his father's son, whatever were his motives for coming; and now and then admitted the thought, that Mary might do worse, when her time came, than marry Jem Wilson, a steady workman at a good trade, a good son to his parents, and a fine manly spirited chap—at least when Mary was not by; for when she was present he watched her too closely, and too anxiously, to have much of what John Barton called "spunk" in him.

---

2. A folk tradition that a man could claim a pair of gloves if he found a woman sleeping and kissed her.

* "Nobbut," none but, only. "No man sigh evere God no but the oon bigitun sone."—Wiclif's Version. [WG]

It was towards the end of February, in that year, and a bitter black frost had lasted for many weeks. The keen east wind had long since swept the streets clean, though on a gusty day the dust would rise like pounded ice, and make people's faces quite smart with the cold force with which it blew against them. Houses, sky, people, and everything looked as if a gigantic brush had washed them all over with a dark shade of Indian ink. There was some reason for this grimy appearance on human beings, whatever there might be for the dun looks of the landscape; for soft water had become an article not even to be purchased; and the poor washerwomen might be seen vainly trying to procure a little by breaking the thick gray ice that coated the ditches and ponds in the neighbourhood. People prophesied a long continuance to this already lengthened frost; said the spring would be very late; no spring fashions required; no summer clothing purchased for a short uncertain summer. Indeed, there was no end to the evil prophesied during the continuance of that bleak east wind.

Mary hurried home one evening, just as daylight was fading, from Miss Simmonds', with her shawl held up to her mouth, and her head bent as if in deprecation of the meeting wind. So she did not perceive Margaret till she was close upon her at the very turning into the court.

"Bless me, Margaret! is that you? Where are you bound to?"

"To nowhere but your own house (that is, if you'll take me in). I've a job of work to finish to-night; mourning, as must be in time for the funeral to-morrow; and grandfather has been out moss-hunting, and will not be home till late."

"Oh, how charming it will be! I'll help you if you're backward. Have you much to do?"

"Yes, I only got the order yesterday at noon; and there's three girls beside the mother; and what with trying on and matching the stuff (for there was not enough in the piece they chose first), I'm above a bit behindhand. I've the skirts all to make; I kept that work till candlelight; and the sleeves, to say nothing of little bits to the bodies; for the missis is very particular, and I could scarce keep from smiling while they were crying so, really taking on sadly I'm sure, to hear first one and then t'other clear up to notice the sit of her gown. They weren't to be misfits, I promise you, though they were in such trouble."

"Well, Margaret, you're right welcome, as you know, and I'll sit down and help you with pleasure, though I was tired enough of sewing to-night at Miss Simmonds'."

By this time Mary had broken up the raking coal, and lighted her candle; and Margaret settled herself to her work on one side of the table, while her friend hurried over her tea at the other. The things were then lifted *en masse* to the dresser; and dusting her side of the table with the apron she always wore at home, Mary took up some breadths and began to run them together.

"Who's it all for, for if you told me I've forgotten?"

"Why, for Mrs. Ogden as keeps the greengrocer's shop in Oxford Road. Her husband drank himself to death, and though she cried over him and his ways all the time he was alive, she's fretted sadly for him now he's dead."

"Has he left her much to go upon?" asked Mary, examining the texture of the dress. "This is beautifully fine soft bombazine."[3]

"No, I'm much afeard there's but little, and there's several young children, besides the three Miss Ogdens."

"I should have thought girls like them would ha' made their own gowns," observed Mary.

"So I dare say they do, many a one, but now they seem all so busy getting ready for the funeral; for it's to be quite a grand affair, well-nigh twenty people to breakfast, as one of the little ones told me; the little thing seemed to like the fuss, and I do believe it comforted poor Mrs. Ogden to make all the piece o' work. Such a smell of ham boiling and fowls roasting while I waited in the kitchen; it seemed more like a wedding nor* a funeral. They said she'd spend a matter o' sixty pound on th' burial."

"I thought you said she was but badly off," said Mary.

"Ay, I know she's asked for credit at several places, saying her husband laid hands on every farthing he could get for drink. But th' undertakers urge her on, you see, and tell her this thing's usual, and that thing's only a common mark of respect, and that every body has t'other thing, till the poor woman has no will o' her own. I dare say, too, her heart strikes her (it always does when a person's gone) for many a word and many a slighting deed to him who's stiff and cold; and she thinks to make up matters, as it were, by a grand funeral, though she and all her children, too, may have to pinch many a year to pay the expenses, if ever they pay them at all."

"This mourning, too, will cost a pretty penny," said Mary. "I often wonder why folks wear mourning; it's not pretty or becoming; and it costs a deal of money just when people can spare it least; and if what the Bible tells us be true, we ought not to be sorry when a friend, who's been good, goes to his rest; and as for a bad man, one's glad enough to get shut† on him. I cannot see what good comes out o' wearing mourning."

"I'll tell you what I think the fancy was sent for (Old Alice calls everything 'sent for,' and I believe she's right). It does do good, though

---

3. A heavy wool fabric popular for mourning dress.
* "Nor," generally used in Lancashire for "than."
  "They had lever sleep *nor* be in laundery."—*Dunbar*. [WG]
† "Shut," quit. [WG]

not as much as it costs, that I do believe, in setting people (as is cast down by sorrow and feels themselves unable to settle to anything but crying) something to do. Why now I told you how they were grieving; for, perhaps, he was a kind husband and father, in his thoughtless way, when he wasn't in liquor. But they cheered up wonderful while I was there, and I asked 'em for more directions than usual, that they might have something to talk over and fix about; and I left 'em my fashion-book (though it were two months old) just a purpose."

"I don't think every one would grieve a that way. Old Alice wouldn't."

"Old Alice is one in a thousand. I doubt, too, if she would fret much, however sorry she might be. She would say it were sent, and fall to trying to find out what good it were to do. Every sorrow in her mind is sent for good. Did I ever tell you, Mary, what she said one day when she found me taking on about something?"

"No; do tell me. What were you fretting about, first place?"

"I can't tell you, just now; perhaps I may some time."

"When?"

"Perhaps this very evening, if it rises in my heart; perhaps never. It's a fear that sometimes I can't abide to think about, and sometimes I don't like to think on any thing else. Well, I was fretting about this fear, and Alice comes in for something, and finds me crying. I would not tell her no more than I would you, Mary; so she says, 'Well, dear, you must mind this, when you're going to fret and be low about any thing—An anxious mind is never a holy mind.' Oh, Mary, I have so often checked my grumbling sin'* she said that."

The weary sound of stitching was the only sound heard for a little while, till Mary inquired,

"Do you expect to get paid for this mourning?"

"Why, I do not much think I shall. I've thought it over once or twice, and I mean to bring myself to think I shan't, and to like to do it as my bit towards comforting them. I don't think they can pay, and yet they're just the sort of folk to have their minds easier for wearing mourning. There's only one thing I dislike making black for, it does so hurt the eyes."

Margaret put down her work with a sigh, and shaded her eyes. Then she assumed a cheerful tone, and said,

"You'll not have to wait long, Mary, for my secret's on the tip of my tongue. Mary, do you know I sometimes think I'm growing a little blind, and then what would become of grandfather and me? Oh, God help me, Lord help me!"

---

* "Sin'," since.
  "*Sin* that his lord was twenty yere of age."
  Prologue to Canterbury Tales. [WG]

She fell into an agony of tears, while Mary knelt by her, striving to soothe and to comfort her; but, like an inexperienced person, striving rather to deny the correctness of Margaret's fear, than helping her to meet and overcome the evil.

"No," said Margaret, quietly fixing her tearful eyes on Mary; "I know I'm not mistaken. I have felt one going some time, long before I ever thought what it would lead to; and last autumn I went to a doctor; and he did not mince the matter, but said unless I sat in a darkened room, with my hands before me, my sight would not last me many years longer. But how could I do that, Mary? For one thing, grandfather would have known there was somewhat the matter; and, oh! it will grieve him sore whenever he's told, so the later the better; and besides, Mary, we've sometimes little enough to go upon, and what I earn is a great help. For grandfather takes a day here, and a day there, for botanising or going after insects, and he'll think little enough of four or five shillings for a specimen; dear grandfather! and I'm so loath to think he should be stinted of what gives him such pleasure. So I went to another doctor to try and get him to say something different, and he said, 'Oh, it was only weakness,' and gived me a bottle of lotion; but I've used three bottles (and each of 'em cost two shillings), and my eye is so much worse, not hurting so much, but I can't see a bit with it. There now Mary," continued she, shutting one eye, "now you only look like a great black shadow, with the edges dancing and sparkling."

"And can you see pretty well with th' other?"

"Yes, pretty near as well as ever. Th' only difference is, that if I sew a long time together, a bright spot like th' sun comes right where I'm looking; all the rest is quite clear but just where I want to see. I've been to both doctors again, and now they're both o' the same story; and I suppose I'm going dark as fast as may be. Plain work pays so bad, and mourning has been so plentiful this winter, that I were tempted to take in any black work I could; and now I'm suffering from it."

"And yet, Margaret, you're going on taking it in; that's what you'd call foolish in another."

"It is, Mary! and yet what can I do? Folk mun live; and I think I should go blind any way, and I darn't tell grandfather, else I would leave it off; but he will so fret."

Margaret rocked herself backward and forward to still her emotion.

"Oh Mary!" she said, "I try to get his face off by heart, and I stare at him so when he's not looking, and then shut my eyes to see if I can remember his dear face. There's one thing, Mary, that serves a bit to comfort me. You'll have heard of old Jacob Butterworth, the singing weaver?[4] Well, I know'd him a bit, so I went to him, and said how I

---

4. A common Lancashire name rather than a reference to a known teacher.

wished he'd teach me the right way o' singing; and he says I've a rare fine voice, and I go once a week, and take a lesson fra' him. He's been a grand singer in his day. He led the choruses at the Festivals, and got thanked many a time by London folk; and one foreign singer, Madame Catalani,[5] turned round and shook him by th' hand before the Oud Church* full o' people. He says I may gain ever so much money by singing; but I don't know. Any rate, it's sad work, being blind."

She took up her sewing, saying her eyes were rested now, and for some time they sewed on in silence.

Suddenly there were steps heard in the little paved court; person after person ran past the curtained window.

"Something's up," said Mary. She went to the door, and stopping the first person she saw, inquired the cause of the commotion.

"Eh, wench! donna ye see the fire-light? Carsons' mill is blazing away like fun;" and away her informant ran.

"Come, Margaret, on wi' your bonnet, and let's go to see Carsons' mill; it's afire, and they say a burning mill is such a grand sight. I never saw one."

"Well, I think it's a fearful sight. Besides, I've all this work to do."

But Mary coaxed in her sweet manner, and with her gentle caresses, promising to help with the gowns all night long if necessary, nay, saying she should quite enjoy it.

The truth was, Margaret's secret weighed heavily and painfully on her mind, and she felt her inability to comfort; besides, she wanted to change the current of Margaret's thoughts; and in addition to these unselfish feelings, came the desire she had honestly expressed, of seeing a factory on fire.

So in two minutes they were ready. At the threshold of the house they met John Barton, to whom they told their errand.

"Carsons' mill! Ay, there is a mill on fire somewhere, sure enough by the light, and it will be a rare blaze, for there's not a drop o' water to be got. And much Carsons will care, for they're well insured, and the machines are a' th' oud-fashioned kind. See if they don't think it a fine thing for themselves. They'll not thank them as tries to put it out."

He gave way for the impatient girls to pass. Guided by the ruddy light more than by any exact knowledge of the streets that led to the mill, they scampered along with bent heads, facing the terrible east wind as best they might.

Carsons' mill ran lengthways from east to west. Along it went one of the oldest thoroughfares in Manchester. Indeed, all that part of the

---

5. The Italian soprano Angelica Catalani (1780–1849) performed in Manchester in 1828 and 1836.
* "Old Church;" now the Cathedral of Manchester. [WG]

town was comparatively old; it was there that the first cotton mills were built, and the crowded alleys and back streets of the neighbourhood made a fire there particularly to be dreaded. The staircase of the mill ascended from the entrance at the western end, which faced into a wide, dingy-looking street, consisting principally of public-houses, pawnbrokers' shops, rag and bone warehouses, and dirty provision shops. The other, the east end of the factory, fronted into a very narrow back street, not twenty feet wide, and miserably lighted and paved. Right against this end of the factory were the gable ends of the last house in the principal street—a house which from its size, its handsome stone facings, and the attempt at ornament in the front, had probably been once a gentleman's house; but now the light which streamed from its enlarged front windows made clear the interior of the splendidly fitted up room, with its painted walls, its pillared recesses, its gilded and gorgeous fittings-up, its miserable squalid inmates. It was a gin palace.[6]

Mary almost wished herself away, so fearful (as Margaret had said) was the sight when they joined the crowd assembled to witness the fire. There was a murmur of many voices whenever the roaring of the flames ceased for an instant. It was easy to perceive the mass were deeply interested.

"What do they say?" asked Margaret of a neighbour in the crowd, as she caught a few words, clear and distinct from the general murmur.

"There never is anyone in the mill, surely!" exclaimed Mary, as the sea of upward-turned faces moved with one accord to the eastern end, looking into Dunham Street, the narrow back lane already mentioned.

The western end of the mill, whither the raging flames were driven by the wind, was crowned and turreted with triumphant fire. It sent forth its infernal tongues from every window hole, licking the black walls with amorous fierceness; it was swayed or fell before the mighty gale, only to rise higher and yet higher, to ravage and roar yet more wildly. This part of the roof fell in with an astounding crash, while the crowd struggled more and more to press into Dunham Street, for what were magnificent terrible flames—what were falling timbers or tottering walls, in comparison with human life?

There, where the devouring flames had been repelled by the yet more powerful wind, but where yet black smoke gushed out from every aperture—there, at one of the windows on the fourth story, or rather a doorway where a crane was fixed to hoist up goods, might occasionally be seen, when the thick gusts of smoke cleared partially away for an instant, the imploring figures of two men. They had

6. A pub that also offered entertainment.

remained after the rest of the workmen for some reason or other, and, owing to the wind having driven the fire in the opposite direction, had perceived no sight or sound of alarm, till long after (if anything could be called long in that throng of terrors which passed by in less than half an hour) the fire had consumed the old wooden staircase at the other end of the building. I am not sure whether it was not the first sound of the rushing crowd below that made them fully aware of their awful position.

"Where are the engines?" asked Margaret of her neighbour.

"They're coming, no doubt; but bless you, I think it's bare ten minutes since we first found out th' fire; it rages so wi' this wind, and all so dry-like."

"Is no one gone for a ladder?" gasped Mary, as the men were perceptibly, though not audibly, praying the great multitude below for help.

"Ay, Wilson's son and another man were off like a shot, well-nigh five minutes ago. But th' masons, and slaters, and such like, have left their work, and locked up the yards."

Wilson, then, was that man whose figure loomed out against the ever-increasing dull hot light behind, whenever the smoke was clear,—was that George Wilson? Mary sickened with terror. She knew he worked for Carsons; but at first she had had no idea that any lives were in danger; and since she had become aware of this, the heated air, the roaring flames, the dizzy light, and the agitated and murmuring crowd, had bewildered her thoughts.

"Oh! let us go home, Margaret; I cannot stay."

"We cannot go! See how we are wedged in by folks. Poor Mary! ye won't hanker after a fire again. Hark! listen!"

For through the hushed crowd pressing round the angle of the mill, and filling up Dunham Street, might be heard the rattle of the engine, the heavy, quick tread of loaded horses.

"Thank God!" said Margaret's neighbour, "the engine's come."

Another pause; the plugs were stiff, and water could not be got.

Then there was a pressure through the crowd, the front rows bearing back on those behind, till the girls were sick with the close ramming confinement. Then a relaxation, and a breathing freely once more.

" 'Twas young Wilson and a fireman wi' a ladder," said Margaret's neighbour, a tall man who could overlook the crowd.

"Oh, tell us what you see?" begged Mary.

"They've getten it fixed against the gin-shop wall. One o' the men i' the factory has fell back; dazed wi' the smoke, I'll warrant. The floor's not given way there. God!" said he, bringing his eye lower down, "the ladder's too short! It's a' over wi' them, poor chaps. Th' fire's coming slow and sure to that end, and afore they've either getten water, or another ladder, they'll be dead out and out. Lord have mercy on them!"

A sob, as if of excited women, was heard in the hush of the crowd. Another pressure like the former! Mary clung to Margaret's arm with a pinching grasp, and longed to faint, and be insensible, to escape from the oppressing misery of her sensations. A minute or two.

"They've taken th' ladder into th' Temple of Apollor.[7] Can't press back with it to the yard it came from."

A mighty shout arose; a sound to wake the dead. Up on high, quivering in the air, was seen the end of the ladder, protruding out of a garret window, in the gable end of the gin palace, nearly opposite to the door-way where the men had been seen. Those in the crowd nearest the factory, and consequently best able to see up to the garret window, said that several men were holding one end, and guiding by their weight its passage to the doorway. The garret window-frame had been taken out before the crowd below were aware of the attempt.

At length—for it seemed long, measured by beating hearts, though scarce two minutes had elapsed—the ladder was fixed, an aërial bridge at a dizzy height, across the narrow street.

Every eye was fixed in unwinking anxiety, and people's very breathing seemed stilled in suspense. The men were nowhere to be seen, but the wind appeared, for the moment, higher than ever, and drove back the invading flames to the other end.

Mary and Margaret could see now: right above them danced the ladder in the wind. The crowd pressed back from under; firemen's helmets appeared at the window, holding the ladder firm, when a man, with quick, steady tread, and unmoving head, passed from one side to the other. The multitude did not even whisper while he crossed the perilous bridge, which quivered under him; but when he was across, safe comparatively in the factory, a cheer arose for an instant, checked, however, almost immediately, by the uncertainty of the result, and the desire not in any way to shake the nerves of the brave fellow who had cast his life on such a die.

"There he is again!" sprung to the lips of many, as they saw him at the doorway, standing as if for an instant to breathe a mouthful of the fresher air, before he trusted himself to cross. On his shoulders he bore an insensible body.

"It's Jem Wilson and his father," whispered Margaret; but Mary knew it before.

The people were sick with anxious terror. He could no longer balance himself with his arms; every thing must depend on nerve and eye. They saw the latter was fixed, by the position of the head, which never wavered; the ladder shook under the double weight; but still he

---

7. The name of the gin palace.

never moved his head—he dared not look below. It seemed an age before the crossing was accomplished. At last the window was gained; the bearer relieved from his burden; both had disappeared.

Then the multitude might shout; and above the roaring flames, louder than the blowing of the mighty wind, arose that tremendous burst of applause at the success of the daring enterprise. Then a shrill cry was heard, asking,

"Is the oud man alive, and likely to do?"

"Ay," answered one of the firemen to the hushed crowd below. "He's coming round finely, now he's had a dash of cowd water."

He drew back his head; and the eager inquiries, the shouts, the sea-like murmurs of the moving rolling mass began again to be heard—but only for an instant. In far less time than even that in which I have endeavoured briefly to describe the pause of events, the same bold hero stepped again upon the ladder, with evident purpose to rescue the man yet remaining in the burning mill.

He went across in the same quick steady manner as before, and the people below, made less acutely anxious by his previous success, were talking to each other, shouting out intelligence of the progress of the fire at the other end of the factory, telling of the endeavours of the firemen at that part to obtain water, while the closely-packed body of men heaved and rolled from side to side. It was different from the former silent breathless hush. I do not know if it were from this cause, or from the rec-ollection of peril past, or that he looked below, in the breathing moment before returning with the remaining person (a slight little man) slung across his shoulders, but Jem Wilson's step was less steady, his tread more uncertain; he seemed to feel with his foot for the next round of the ladder, to waver, and finally to stop half-way. By this time the crowd was still enough; in the awful instant that intervened no one durst speak, even to encourage. Many turned sick with terror, and shut their eyes to avoid seeing the catastrophe they dreaded. It came. The brave man swayed from side to side, at first as slightly as if only balancing himself; but he was evidently losing nerve, and even sense; it was only wonder-ful how the animal instinct of self-preservation did not overcome every generous feeling, and impel him at once to drop the helpless, inanimate body he carried; perhaps the same instinct told him, that the sudden loss of so heavy a weight would of itself be a great and imminent danger.

"Help me; she's fainted," cried Margaret. But no one heeded. All eyes were directed upwards. At this point of time a rope, with a run-ning noose, was dexterously thrown by one of the firemen, after the manner of a lasso, over the head and round the bodies of the two men. True, it was with rude and slight adjustment: but slight as it was, it served as a steadying guide; it encouraged the sinking heart, the dizzy head. Once more Jem stepped onwards. He was not hurried by any jerk or pull. Slowly and gradually the rope was hauled in, slowly and gradually did he make the four or five paces between him and safety. The window was gained, and all were saved. The multitude in the street absolutely danced with triumph, and huzzaed and yelled till you would have fancied their very throats would crack; and then, with all the fickleness of interest characteristic of a large body of people, pressed and stumbled, and cursed and swore, in the hurry to get out of Dunham Street, and back to the immediate scene of the fire, the mighty diapason[8] of whose roaring flames formed an awful accompaniment to the screams, and yells, and imprecations, of the struggling crowd.

As they pressed away, Margaret was left, pale and almost sinking under the weight of Mary's body, which she had preserved in an upright position by keeping her arms tight round Mary's waist, dreading, with reason, the trampling of unheeding feet.

Now, however, she gently let her down on the cold clean pavement; and the change of posture, and the difference in temperature, now that the people had withdrawn from their close neighbourhood, speedily restored her to consciousness.

Her first glance was bewildered and uncertain. She had forgotten where she was. Her cold, hard bed felt strange; the murky glare in the sky affrighted her. She shut her eyes to think, to recollect.

Her next look was upwards. The fearful bridge had been withdrawn; the window was unoccupied.

"They are safe," said Margaret.

"All? Are all safe, Margaret?" asked Mary.

"Ask yon fireman, and he'll tell you more about it than I can. But I know they're all safe."

The fireman hastily corroborated Margaret's words.

"Why did you let Jem Wilson go twice?" asked Margaret.

"Let?—why, we could not hinder him. As soon as ever he'd heard his father speak (which he was na long a doing), Jem were off like a shot; only saying he knowed better nor us where to find t'other man. We'd all ha' gone, if he had na been in such a hurry, for no one can say as Manchester firemen is ever backward when there's danger."

So saying, he ran off; and the two girls, without remark or discussion, turned homewards. They were overtaken by the elder Wilson, pale, grimy, and blear-eyed, but apparently as strong and well as ever. He loitered a minute or two alongside of them, giving an account of his detention in the mill; he then hastily wished good-night, saying he must go home and tell his missis he was all safe and well: but after he had gone a few steps, he turned back, came on Mary's side of the pavement, and in an earnest whisper, which Margaret could not avoid hearing, he said,

"Mary, if my boy comes across you to-night, give him a kind word or two for my sake. Do! bless you, there's a good wench."

8. Deep, full outburst of harmonious sound.

Mary hung her head and answered not a word, and in an instant he was gone.

When they arrived at home, they found John Barton smoking his pipe, unwilling to question; yet very willing to hear all the details they could give him. Margaret went over the whole story, and it was amusing to watch his gradually increasing interest and excitement. First, the regular puffing abated, then ceased. Then the pipe was fairly taken out of his mouth, and held suspended. Then he rose, and at every further point he came a step nearer to the narrator.

When it was ended he swore (an unusual thing for him) that if Jem Wilson wanted Mary he should have her to-morrow, if he had not a penny to keep her.

Margaret laughed, but Mary, who was now recovered from her agitation, pouted and looked angry.

The work which they had left was resumed: but with full hearts fingers never go very quickly; and I am sorry to say, that owing to the fire, the two younger Miss Ogdens were in such grief for the loss of their excellent father, that they were unable to appear before the little circle of sympathising friends gathered together to comfort the widow, and see the funeral set off.

Chapter VI.

"How little can the rich man know
    Of what the poor man feels,
When Want, like some dark demon foe,
    Nearer and nearer steals!

He never tramp'd the weary round,
    A stroke of work to gain,
And sicken'd at the dreaded sound
    Which tells he seeks in vain.

Foot-sore, heart-sore, *he* never came
    Back through the winter's wind,
To a dank cellar, there no flame,
    No light, no food, to find.

He never saw his darlings lie
    Shivering, the flags their bed;
He never heard that maddening cry,
    'Daddy, a bit of bread!'"
                        MANCHESTER SONG.[9]

John Barton was not far wrong in his idea that the Messrs. Carson would not be over-much grieved for the consequences of the fire

9. By William Gaskell.

in their mill. They were well insured; the machinery lacked the improvements of late years, and worked but poorly in comparison with that which might now be procured. Above all, trade was very slack; cottons could find no market, and goods lay packed and piled in many a warehouse. The mills were merely worked to keep the machinery, human and metal, in some kind of order and readiness for better times. So this was an excellent opportunity, Messrs. Carson thought, for refitting their factory with first-rate improvements, for which the insurance-money would amply pay. They were in no hurry about the business, however. The weekly drain of wages given for labour, useless in the present state of the market, was stopped. The partners had more leisure than they had known for years; and promised wives and daughters all manner of pleasant excursions, as soon as the weather should become more genial. It was a pleasant thing to be able to lounge over breakfast with a review or newspaper in hand; to have time for becoming acquainted with agreeable and accomplished daughters, on whose education no money had been spared, but whose fathers, shut up during a long day with calicoes and accounts, had so seldom had leisure to enjoy their daughters' talents. There were happy family evenings, now that the men of business had time for domestic enjoyments. There is another side to the picture. There were homes over which Carsons' fire threw a deep, terrible gloom; the homes of those who would fain work, and no man gave unto them—the homes of those to whom leisure was a curse. There, the family music was hungry wails, when week after week passed by, and there was no work to be had, and consequently no wages to pay for the bread the children cried aloud for in their young impatience of suffering. There was no breakfast to lounge over; their lounge was taken in bed, to try and keep warmth in them that bitter March weather, and, by being quiet, to deaden the gnawing wolf within. Many a penny that would have gone little way enough in oatmeal or potatoes, bought opium to still the hungry little ones,[1] and make them forget their uneasiness in heavy troubled sleep. It was mother's mercy. The evil and the good of our nature came out strongly then. There were desperate fathers; there were bitter-tongued mothers (Oh God! what wonder!); there were reckless children; the very closest bonds of nature were snapt in that time of trial and distress. There was Faith such as the rich can never imagine on earth; there was "Love strong as death;"[2] and self-

---

1. Opium (also called laudanum) was legally sold in liquid form (the form used to pacify children) and in solid form. Both forms were consumed by adults. Its addictive qualities were known, but it was nonetheless unregulated.
2. Song of Solomon 8:6

denial, among rude, coarse men, akin to that of Sir Philip Sidney's most glorious deed.[3] The vices of the poor sometimes astound us *here;* but when the secrets of all hearts shall be made known, their virtues will astound us in far greater degree. Of this I am certain.

As the cold, bleak spring came on (spring, in name alone), and consequently as trade continued dead, other mills shortened hours, turned off hands, and finally stopped work altogether.

Barton worked short hours; Wilson, of course, being a hand in Carsons' factory, had no work at all. But his son, working at an engineer's, and a steady man, obtained wages enough to maintain all the family in a careful way. Still it preyed on Wilson's mind to be so long indebted to his son. He was out of spirits, and depressed. Barton was morose, and soured towards mankind as a body, and the rich in particular. One evening, when the clear light at six o'clock contrasted strangely with the Christmas cold, and when the bitter wind piped down every entry, and through every cranny, Barton sat brooding over his stinted fire, and listening for Mary's step, in unacknowledged trust that her presence would cheer him. The door was opened, and Wilson came breathless in.

"You've not got a bit o' money by you, Barton?" asked he.

"Not I; who has now, I'd like to know. Whatten you want it for?"

"I donnot* want it for mysel', tho' we've none to spare. But don ye know Ben Davenport as worked at Carsons'? He's down wi' the fever, and ne'er a stick o' fire nor a cowd† potato in the house."

"I han got no money, I tell ye," said Barton. Wilson looked disappointed. Barton tried not to be interested, but he could not help it in spite of his gruffness. He rose, and went to the cupboard (his wife's pride long ago). There lay the remains of his dinner, hastily put by ready for supper. Bread, and a slice of cold fat boiled bacon. He wrapped them in his handkerchief, put them in the crown of his hat, and said—"Come, let us be going."

"Going—art thou going to work this time o' day?"

"No stupid, to be sure not. Going to see the chap thou spoke on." So they put on their hats and set out. On the way Wilson said Davenport was a good fellow, though too much of the Methodee,[4] that his children were too young to work, but not too young to be cold and hungry; that they had sunk lower and lower, and pawned thing after

---

3. The legend that Sir Philip Sydney (1554–1586) refused water while dying on the battlefield, directing it instead to an injured, lower-ranking soldier whose need, Sydney was reported to have said, "is greater than mine."

* "Don" is constantly used in Lancashire for "do;" as it was by our older writers. "And that may non Hors *don*."—*Sir J. Mandeville.*
  "But for th' entent to *don* this sinne."—*Chaucer.* [WG]

† "Cowd," cold. Teut. *kaud.* Dutch, *koud.* [WG]

4. Methodist, a dissenting sect (later to become a mainstream, Protestant denomination) characterized by overt piety and earnestness that developed in response to the evangelical work of John Wesley.

thing, and that they now lived in a cellar in Berry Street, off Store Street. Barton growled inarticulate words of no benevolent import to a large class of mankind, and so they went along till they arrived in Berry Street. It was unpaved: and down the middle a gutter forced its way, every now and then forming pools in the holes with which the street abounded. Never was the old Edinburgh cry of "Gardez l'eau!"[5] more necessary than in this street. As they passed, women from their doors tossed household slops of *every* description into the gutter; they ran into the next pool, which overflowed and stagnated. Heaps of ashes[6] were the stepping-stones, on which the passer-by, who cared in the least for cleanliness, took care not to put his foot. Our friends were not dainty, but even they picked their way, till they got to some steps leading down to a small area, where a person standing would have his head about one foot below the level of the street, and might at the same time, without the least motion of his body, touch the window of the cellar and the damp muddy wall right opposite. You went down one step even from the foul area into the cellar in which a family of human beings lived. It was very dark inside. The window-panes many of them were broken and stuffed with rags, which was reason enough for the dusky light that pervaded the place even at mid-day. After the account I have given of the state of the street, no one can be surprised that on going into the cellar inhabited by Davenport, the smell was so fœtid as almost to knock the two men down. Quickly recovering themselves, as those inured to such things do, they began to penetrate the thick darkness of the place, and to see three or four little children rolling on the damp, nay wet brick floor, through which the stagnant, filthy moisture of the street oozed up; the fireplace was empty and black; the wife sat on her husband's lair,[7] and cried in the dark loneliness.

"See, missis, I'm back again.—Hold your noise, children, and don't mither* your mammy for bread; here's a chap as has got some for you."

In that dim light, which was darkness to strangers, they clustered round Barton, and tore from him the food he had brought with him. It was a large hunch of bread, but it vanished in an instant.

"We mun do summut for 'em," said he, to Wilson. "Yo stop here, and I'll be back in half-an-hour."

So he strode, and ran, and hurried home. He emptied into the ever-useful pocket handkerchief the little meal remaining in the mug.

---

5. An incorrect French phrase meaning "beware of the water," a reference to the emptying of chamber pots into the streets.
6. A euphemism for human excrement.
7. A place where one sleeps, usually used in reference to animals. Perhaps a misprint for "chair."
* "Mither," to trouble and perplex. "I'm welly mithered"—I'm well-nigh crazed. [WG]

Mary would have her tea at Miss Simmonds'; her food for the day was safe. Then he went up-stairs for his better coat, and his one, gay red-and-yellow silk pocket-handkerchief—his jewels, his plate, his valu-ables, these were. He went to the pawn-shop; he pawned them for five shillings; he stopped not, nor stayed, till he was once more in London Road, within five minutes' walk of Berry Street—then he loi-tered in his gait, in order to discover the shops he wanted. He bought meat, and a loaf of bread, candles, chips, and from a little retail yard he purchased a couple of hundredweights[8] of coal. Some money still remained—all destined for them, but he did not yet know how best to spend it. Food, light, and warmth, he had instantly seen were nec-essary; for luxuries he would wait. Wilson's eyes filled with tears when he saw Barton enter with his purchases. He understood it all, and longed to be once more in work that he might help in some of these material ways, without feeling that he was using his son's money. But though "silver and gold he had none,"[9] he gave heart-service, and love-works of far more value. Nor was John Barton behind in these. "The fever"[1] was (as it usually is in Manchester) of a low, putrid, typhoid kind; brought on by miserable living, filthy neighbourhood, and great depression of mind and body. It is virulent, malignant, and highly infectious. But the poor are fatalists with regard to infection; and well for them it is so, for in their crowded dwellings no invalid can be isolated. Wilson asked Barton if he thought he should catch it, and was laughed at for his idea.

The two men, rough, tender nurses as they were, lighted the fire, which smoked and puffed into the room as if it did not know the way up the damp, unused chimney. The very smoke seemed purifying and healthy in the thick clammy air. The children clamoured again for bread; but this time Barton took a piece first to the poor, helpless, hopeless woman, who still sat by the side of her husband, listening to his anxious miserable mutterings. She took the bread, when it was put into her hand, and broke a bit, but could not eat. She was past hunger. She fell down on the floor with a heavy unresisting bang. The men looked puzzled. "She's well-nigh clemmed," said Barton. "Folk do say one mustn't give clemmed people much to eat; but, bless us, she'll eat nought."

"I'll tell yo what I'll do," said Wilson. "I'll take these two big lads, as does nought but fight, home to my missis for to-night, and I'll get a jug o' tea. Them women always does best with tea, and such-like slop."

So Barton was now left alone with a little child, crying (when it had done eating) for mammy; with a fainting, dead-like woman; and with

8. A unit of measure for coal equal to 112 lbs.
9. Acts 3:6.
1. A reference to the series of typhoid fever epidemics in the 1830s.

the sick man, whose mutterings were rising up to screams and shrieks of agonized anxiety. He carried the woman to the fire, and chafed her hands. He looked around for something to raise her head. There was literally nothing but some loose bricks. However, those he got; and taking off his coat he covered them with it as well as he could. He pulled her feet to the fire, which now began to emit some faint heat. He looked round for water, but the poor woman had been too weak to drag herself out to the distant pump, and water there was none. He snatched the child, and ran up the area-steps to the room above, and borrowed their only saucepan with some water in it. Then he began, with the useful skill of a working man, to make some gruel;[2] and when it was hastily made, he seized a battered iron table-spoon (kept when many other little things had been sold in a lot), in order to feed baby, and with it he forced one or two drops between her clenched teeth. The mouth opened mechanically to receive more, and gradually she revived. She sat up and looked round; and recollecting all, fell down again in weak and passive despair. Her little child crawled to her, and wiped with its fingers the thick-coming tears which she now had strength to weep. It was now high time to attend to the man. He lay on straw, so damp and mouldy, no dog would have chosen it in preference to flags:[3] over it was a piece of sacking, coming next to his worn skeleton of a body; above him was mustered every article of clothing that could be spared by mother or children this bitter weather; and in addition to his own, these might have given as much warmth as one blanket, could they have been kept on him; but as he restlessly tossed to and fro, they fell off and left him shivering in spite of the burning heat of his skin. Every now and then he started up in his naked madness, looking like the prophet of woe in the fearful plague-picture,[4] but he soon fell again in exhaustion, and Barton found he must be closely watched, lest in these falls he should injure himself against the hard brick floor. He was thankful when Wilson re-appeared, carrying in both hands a jug of steaming tea, intended for the poor wife; but when the delirious husband saw drink, he snatched at it with animal instinct, with a selfishness he had never shown in health.

Then the two men consulted together. It seemed decided, without a word being spoken on the subject, that both should spend the night with the forlorn couple; that was settled. But could no doctor be had? In all probability, no; the next day an Infirmary order[5] must be begged, but meanwhile the only medical advice they could have must

2. Thin, watery porridge.
3. Stones for flooring.
4. Paul Falconer Poole's (1807–1879) "Solomon Eagle Exhorting the People to Repentance during the Plague of the Year 1665," exhibited at the Royal Academy in 1843. The subject is from Daniel Defoe's *Journal of the Plague Year* (1722).
5. Patrons of hospitals had the authority to issue orders for both in-patient and out-patient treatment.

be from a druggist's. So Barton (being the moneyed man) set out to find a shop in London Road.

It is a pretty sight to walk through a street with lighted shops; the gas is so brilliant, the display of goods so much more vividly shown than by day, and of all shops a druggist's looks the most like the tales of our childhood, from Aladdin's garden of enchanted fruits[6] to the charming Rosamond with her purple jar.[7] No such associations had Barton; yet he felt the contrast between the well-filled, well-lighted shops and the dim gloomy cellar, and it made him moody that such contrasts should exist. They are the mysterious problem of life to more than him. He wondered if any in all the hurrying crowd had come from such a house of mourning. He thought they all looked joyous, and he was angry with them. But he could not, you cannot, read the lot of those who daily pass you by in the street. How do you know the wild romances of their lives; the trials, the temptations they are even now enduring, resisting, sinking under? You may be elbowed one instant by the girl desperate in her abandonment, laughing in mad merriment with her outward gesture, while her soul is longing for the rest of the dead, and bringing itself to think of the cold-flowing river as the only mercy of God remaining to her here. You may pass the criminal, meditating crimes at which you will to-morrow shudder with horror as you read them. You may push against one, humble and unnoticed, the last upon earth,[8] who in heaven will for ever be in the immediate light of God's countenance. Errands of mercy—errands of sin—did you ever think where all the thousands of people you daily meet are bound? Barton's was an errand of mercy; but the thoughts of his heart were touched by sin, by bitter hatred of the happy, whom he, for the time, confounded with the selfish.

He reached a druggist's shop, and entered. The druggist (whose smooth manners seemed to have been salved over with his own spermaceti)[9] listened attentively to Barton's description of Davenport's illness; concluded it was typhus fever, very prevalent in that neighbourhood; and proceeded to make up a bottle of medicine, sweet spirits of nitre, or some such innocent potion, very good for slight colds, but utterly powerless to stop, for an instant, the raging fever of the poor man it was intended to relieve. He recommended the same course they had previously determined to adopt, applying the next morning for an Infirmary order; and Barton left the shop with comfortable faith in the physic given him; for men of his class, if they believe in physic at all, believe that every description is equally efficacious.

6. In *The Thousand and One Nights* Aladdin discovers a garden where the fruits on the trees are precious stones.
7. From a story called "The Purple Jar" by Maria Edgeworth (1767–1849).
8. Matthew 19:30.
9. A waxy substance obtained from sperm whales and used in cosmetics and salves.

Meanwhile, Wilson had done what he could at Davenport's home. He had soothed, and covered the man many a time; he had fed and hushed the little child, and spoken tenderly to the woman, who lay still in her weakness and her weariness. He had opened a door, but only for an instant; it led into a back cellar, with a grating instead of a window, down which dropped the moisture from pigsties, and worse abominations. It was not paved; the floor was one mass of bad smelling mud. It had never been used, for there was not an article of furniture in it; nor could a human being, much less a pig, have lived there many days. Yet the "back apartment" made a difference in the rent. The Davenports paid threepence more for having two rooms. When he turned round again, he saw the woman suckling the child from her dry, withered breast.

"Surely the lad is weaned!" exclaimed he, in surprise. "Why, how old is he?"

"Going on two year," she faintly answered. "But, oh! it keeps him quiet when I've nought else to gi' him, and he'll get a bit of sleep lying there, if he's getten nought beside. We han done our best to gi' the childer* food, howe'er we pinch ourselves."

"Han† ye had no money fra' th' town?"

"No; my master is Buckinghamshire born; and he's feared the town would send him back to his parish, if he went to th' board;¹ so we've just borne on in hope o' better times. But I think they'll never come in my day," and the poor woman began her weak high-pitched cry again.

"Here, sup‡ this drop o' gruel, and then try and get a bit o' sleep. John and I will watch by your master to-night."

"God's blessing be on you."

She finished the gruel, and fell into a deep sleep. Wilson covered her with his coat as well as he could, and tried to move lightly for fear of disturbing her; but there need have been no such dread, for her sleep was profound and heavy with exhaustion. Once only she roused to pull the coat round her little child.

And now Wilson's care, and Barton's to boot, was wanted to restrain the wild mad agony of the fevered man. He started up, he yelled, he seemed infuriated by overwhelming anxiety. He cursed and swore, which surprised Wilson, who knew his piety in health, and who did not know the unbridled tongue of delirium. At length he seemed exhausted, and fell asleep; and Barton and Wilson drew near the fire, and talked together in whispers. They sat on the floor,

---

* Wickliffe uses "childre" in his Apology, page 26. [WG]
† "What concord han light and dark."—Spenser. [WG]
1. The New Poor Law Act of 1834 designated a Board of Poor Law Guardians which had the authority to send urban applicants for relief back to their own home rural villages.
‡ And they soupe the brothe thereof."—Sir J. Mandeville. [WG]

for chairs there were none; the sole table was an old tub turned upside down. They put out the candle and conversed by the flickering fire-light.

"Han yo known this chap long?" asked Barton.

"Better nor three year. He's worked wi' Carsons that long, and were always a steady, civil-spoken fellow, though, as I said afore, somewhat of a Methodee. I wish I'd getten a letter he'd sent his missis, a week or two agone, when he were on tramp for work. It did my heart good to read it; for, yo see, I were a bit grumbling mysel; it seemed hard to be spunging on Jem, and taking a' his flesh-meat money to buy bread for me and them as I ought to be keeping. But, yo know, though I can earn nought, I mun eat summut. Well, as I telled ye, I were grumbling, when she (indicating the sleeping woman by a nod) brought me Ben's letter, for she could na' read hersel. It were as good as Bible-words; ne'er a word o' repining; a' about God being our father, and that we mun bear patiently whate'er he sends."

"Don ye think he's th' masters' father, too? I'd be loth to have 'em for brothers."

"Eh, John! donna talk so; sure there's many and many a master as good or better nor us."

"If you think so, tell me this. How comes it they're rich, and we're poor? I'd like to know that. Han they done as they'd be done by for us?"

But Wilson was no arguer; no speechifier, as he would have called it. So Barton, seeing he was likely to have it his own way, went on.

"You'll say (at least many a one does), they'n* getten capital an' we'n getten none. I say, our labour's our capital, and we ought to draw interest on that. They get interest on their capital somehow a' this time, while ourn is lying idle, else how could they all live as they do? Besides, there's many on 'em has had nought to begin wi'; there's Carsons, and Duncombes, and Mengies, and many another, as comed into Manchester with clothes to their back, and that were all, and now they're worth their tens of thousands, a' getten out of our labour; why the very land as fetched but sixty pound twenty year agone is now worth six hundred, and that, too, is owing to our labour: but look at yo, and see me, and poor Davenport yonder; whatten better are we? They'n screwed us down to th' lowest peg, in order to make their great big fortunes, and build their great big houses, and we, why we're just clemming, many and many of us. Can you say there's nought wrong in this?"

"Well, Barton, I'll not gainsay ye. But Mr. Carson spoke to me after th' fire, and says he, 'I shall ha' to retrench, and be very careful in my expenditure during these bad times, I assure ye;' so yo see th' masters suffer too."

---

* "They'n," contraction of "they han," they have. [WG]

"Han they ever seen a child o' their'n die for want o' food?" asked Barton, in a low, deep voice.

"I donnot mean," continued he, "to say as I'm so badly off. I'd scorn to speak for mysel; but when I see such men as Davenport there dying away, for very clemming, I cannot stand it. I've but gotten Mary, and she keeps herself pretty much. I think we'll ha' to give up house-keeping; but that I donnot mind."

And in this kind of talk the night, the long heavy night of watch-ing, wore away. As far as they could judge, Davenport continued in the same state, although the symptoms varied occasionally. The wife slept on, only roused by the cry of her child now and then, which seemed to have power over her, when far louder noises failed to dis-turb her. The watchers agreed, that as soon as it was likely Mr. Car-son would be up and visible, Wilson should go to his house, and beg for an Infirmary order. At length the gray dawn penetrated even into the dark cellar; Davenport slept, and Barton was to remain there until Wilson's return; so, stepping out into the fresh air, brisk and reviving, even in that street of abominations, Wilson took his way to Mr. Carson's.

Wilson had about two miles to walk before he reached Mr. Car-son's house, which was almost in the country. The streets were not yet bustling and busy. The shopmen were lazily taking down the shut-ters, although it was near eight o'clock; for the day was long enough for the purchases people made in that quarter of the town, while trade was so flat. One or two miserable-looking women were setting off on their day's begging expedition. But there were few people abroad. Mr. Carson's was a good house, and furnished with disregard to expense. But, in addition to lavish expenditure, there was much taste shown, and many articles chosen for their beauty and elegance adorned his rooms. As Wilson passed a window which a housemaid had thrown open, he saw pictures and gilding, at which he was tempted to stop and look; but then he thought it would not be respectful. So he hastened on to the kitchen door. The servants seemed very busy with preparations for breakfast; but good-naturedly, though hastily, told him to step in, and they could soon let Mr. Car-son know he was there. So he was ushered into a kitchen hung round with glittering tins, where a roaring fire burnt merrily, and where numbers of utensils hung round, at whose nature and use Wilson amused himself by guessing. Meanwhile, the servants bustled to and fro; an out-door man-servant came in for orders, and sat down near Wilson. The cook broiled steaks, and the kitchen-maid toasted bread, and boiled eggs.

The coffee steamed upon the fire, and altogether the odours were so mixed and appetising, that Wilson began to yearn for food to break his fast, which had lasted since dinner the day before. If the servants had known this, they would have willingly given him meat and bread in abundance; but they were like the rest of us, and not feeling hunger themselves, forgot it was possible another might. So Wilson's craving turned to sickness, while they chatted on, making the kitchen's free and keen remarks upon the parlour.

"How late you were last night, Thomas!"

"Yes, I was right weary of waiting; they told me to be at the rooms by twelve; and there I was. But it was two o'clock before they called me."

"And did you wait all that time in the street?" asked the housemaid, who had done her work for the present, and come into the kitchen for a bit of gossip.

"My eye as like! you don't think I'm such a fool as to catch my death of cold, and let the horses catch their death too, as we should ha' done if we'd stopped there. No! I put th' horses up in th' stables at th' Spread Eagle, and went mysel, and got a glass or two by th' fire. They're driving a good custom, them, wi' coachmen. There were five on us, and we'd many a quart o' ale, and gin wi' it, to keep out th' cold."

"Mercy on us, Thomas; you'll get a drunkard at last!"

"If I do, I know whose blame it will be. It will be missis's, and not mine. Flesh and blood can't sit to be starved to death on a coach-box, waiting for folks as don't know their own mind."

A servant, semi-upper-housemaid, semi-lady's-maid, now came down with orders from her mistress.

"Thomas, you must ride to the fishmonger's, and say missis can't give above half-a-crown a pound for salmon for Tuesday; she's grumbling because trade's so bad. And she'll want the carriage at three to go to the lecture, Thomas; at the Royal Execution,[2] you know."

"Ay, ay, I know."

"And you'd better all of you mind your P's and Q's for she's very black this morning. She's got a bad headache."

"It's a pity Miss Jenkins is not here to match her. Lord! how she and missis did quarrel which had got the worst headaches; it was that Miss Jenkins left for; she would not give up having bad headaches, and missis could not abide any one to have 'em but herself."

"Missis will have her breakfast up-stairs, cook, and the cold partridge as was left yesterday, and put plenty of cream in her coffee, and she thinks there's a roll left, and she would like it well buttered."

So saying, the maid left the kitchen to be ready to attend to the young ladies' bell when they chose to ring, after their late assembly the night before.

---

2. The Royal Institution, founded in 1823, for the promotion of fine arts and culture through exhibitions and lectures.

In the luxurious library, at the well-spread breakfast-table, sat the two Mr. Carsons, father and son. Both were reading—the father a newspaper, the son a review—while they lazily enjoyed their nicely prepared food. The father was a prepossessing-looking old man; perhaps self-indulgent you might guess. The son was strikingly handsome, and knew it. His dress was neat and well appointed, and his manners far more gentlemanly than his father's. He was the only son, and his sisters were proud of him; his father and mother were proud of him: he could not set up his judgment against theirs; he was proud of himself.

The door opened and in bounded Amy, the sweet youngest daughter of the house, a lovely girl of sixteen, fresh and glowing, and bright as a rosebud.[3] She was too young to go to assemblies, at which her father rejoiced, for he had little Amy with her pretty jokes, and her bird-like songs, and her playful caresses all the evening to amuse him in his loneliness; and she was not too much tired like Sophy and Helen, to give him her sweet company at breakfast the next morning.

He submitted willingly while she blinded him with her hands, and kissed his rough red face all over. She took his newspaper away after a little pretended resistance, and would not allow her brother Harry to go on with his review.

"I'm the only lady this morning, papa, so you know you must make a great deal of me."

"My darling, I think you have your own way always, whether you're the only lady or not."

"Yes, papa, you're pretty good and obedient, I must say that; but I'm sorry to say Harry is very naughty, and does not do what I tell him; do you, Harry?"

"I'm sure I don't know what you mean to accuse me of, Amy; I expected praise and not blame; for did not I get you that eau de Portugal[4] from town, that you could not meet with at Hughes', you little ungrateful puss?"

"Did you? Oh, sweet Harry; you're as sweet as eau de Portugal yourself; you're almost as good as papa; but still you know you did go and forget to ask Bigland for that rose, that new rose they say he has got."

"No, Amy, I did not forget. I asked him, and he has got the Rose, *sans réproche*;[5] but do you know little Miss Extravagance, a very small one is half a guinea?"[6]

---

3. Illustrated in the frontispiece of the Collins edition illustrated by Ivor Symes. See the illustrations in this volume.
4. Toilet water.
5. Without reproach.
6. Gold coin equal to one pound one shilling.

"Oh, I don't mind. Papa will give it me, won't you, dear father? He knows his little daughter can't live without flowers and scents?"

Mr. Carson tried to refuse his darling, but she coaxed him into acquiescence, saying she must have it, it was one of her necessaries. Life was not worth having without flowers.

"Then, Amy," said her brother, "try and be content with peonies and dandelions."

"Oh you wretch! I don't call them flowers. Besides, you're every bit as extravagant. Who gave half-a-crown for a bunch of lilies of the valley at Yates', a month ago, and then would not let his poor little sister have them, though she went on her knees to beg them? Answer me that, Master Hal."

"Not on compulsion,"[7] replied her brother, smiling with his mouth, while his eyes had an irritated expression, and he went first red, then pale, with vexed embarrassment.

"If you please, sir," said a servant, entering the room, "here's one of the mill people wanting to see you; his name is Wilson, he says."

"I'll come to him directly; stay, tell him to come in here."

Amy danced off into the conservatory which opened out of the room, before the gaunt, pale, unwashed, unshaven weaver was ushered in. There he stood at the door, sleeking his hair with old country habit, and every now and then stealing a glance round at the splendour of the apartment.

"Well, Wilson, and what do you want to-day, man?"

"Please, sir, Davenport's ill of the fever, and I'm come to know if you've got an Infirmary order for him?"

"Davenport—Davenport; who is the fellow? I don't know the name?"

"He's worked in your factory better nor three years, sir."

"Very likely; I don't pretend to know the names of the men I employ; that I leave to the overlooker. So he's ill, eh?"

"Ay, sir, he's very bad; we want to get him in at the Fever Wards."

"I doubt if I've an in-patient's order to spare at present; but I'll give you an out-patient's, and welcome."

So saying, he rose up, unlocked a drawer, pondered a minute, and then gave Wilson an out-patient's order.

Meanwhile, the younger Mr. Carson had ended his review, and began to listen to what was going on. He finished his breakfast, got up, and pulled five shillings out of his pocket, which he gave to Wilson as he passed him, for the "poor fellow." He went past quickly, and calling for his horse, mounted gaily, and rode away. He was anxious to be in time to have a look and a smile from lovely Mary Barton, as

---

7. From Shakespeare's *I Henry IV* 2.4 when Falstaff refuses to answer Prince Hal's questions about his part in a robbery.

she went to Miss Simmonds'. But to-day he was to be disappointed. Wilson left the house, not knowing whether to be pleased or grieved. They had all spoken kindly to him, and who could tell if they might not inquire into Davenport's case, and do something for him and his family. Besides, the cook, who, when she had had time to think, after breakfast was sent in, had noticed his paleness, had had meat and bread ready to put in his hand when he came out of the parlour; and a full stomach makes every one of us more hopeful.

When he reached Berry Street, he had persuaded himself he bore good news, and felt almost elated in his heart. But it fell when he opened the cellar-door, and saw Barton and the wife both bending over the sick man's couch with awe-struck, saddened look.

"Come here," said Barton. "There's a change comed over him sin' yo left, is there not?"

Wilson looked. The flesh was sunk, the features prominent, bony, and rigid. The fearful clay-colour of death was over all. But the eyes were open and sensitive, though the films of the grave were setting upon them.

"He wakened fra' his sleep, as yo left him in, and began to mutter and moan; but he soon went off again, and we never knew he were awake till he called his wife, but now she's here he's gotten nought to say to her."

Most probably, as they all felt, he could not speak, for his strength was fast ebbing. They stood round him still and silent; even the wife checked her sobs, though her heart was like to break. She held her child to her breast, to try and keep him quiet. Their eyes were all fixed on the yet living one, whose moments of life were passing so rapidly away. At length he brought (with jerking convulsive effort) his two hands into the attitude of prayer. They saw his lips move, and bent to catch the words, which came in gasps, and not in tones.

"Oh, Lord God! I thank thee, that the hard struggle of living is over."

"Oh, Ben! Ben!" wailed forth his wife, "have you no thought for me? Oh, Ben! Ben! do say one word to help me through life."

He could not speak again. The trump of the archangel[8] would set his tongue free; but not a word more would it utter till then. Yet he heard, he understood, and though sight failed, he moved his hand gropingly over the covering. They knew what he meant, and guided it to her head, bowed and hidden in her hands, when she had sunk in her woe. It rested there with a feeble pressure of endearment. The face grew beautiful, as the soul neared God. A peace beyond understanding came over it.[9] The hand was a heavy stiff weight on the

---

8. I Thessalonians 4:16.
9. Philippians 4:7.

wife's head. No more grief or sorrow for him. They reverently laid out
the corpse—Wilson fetching his only spare shirt to array it in. The
wife still lay hidden in the clothes, in a stupor of agony.

There was a knock at the door, and Barton went to open it. It was
Mary, who had received a message from her father, through a neighbour, telling her where he was; and she had set out early to come and
have a word with him before her day's work; but some errands she
had to do for Miss Simmonds had detained her until now.

"Come in, wench!" said her father. "Try if thou canst comfort yon
poor, poor woman, kneeling down there. God help her!" Mary did not
know what to say, or how to comfort; but she knelt down by her, and
put her arm round her neck, and in a little while fell to crying herself
so bitterly that the source of tears was opened by sympathy in the
widow, and her full heart was, for a time, relieved.

And Mary forgot all purposed meeting with her gay lover, Harry
Carson; forgot Miss Simmonds' errands, and her anger, in the anxious desire to comfort the poor lone woman. Never had her sweet
face looked more angelic, never had her gentle voice seemed so musical as when she murmured her broken sentences of comfort.

"Oh, don't cry so, dear Mrs. Davenport, pray don't take on so. Sure
he's gone where he'll never know care again. Yes, I know how lonesome you must feel; but think of your children. Oh! we'll all help to
earn food for 'em. Think how sorry *he'd* be, if he sees you fretting so.
Don't cry so, please don't."

And she ended by crying herself as passionately as the poor widow.

It was agreed the town must bury him; he had paid to a burial club
as long as he could, but by a few weeks' omission, he had forfeited his
claim to a sum of money now. Would Mrs. Davenport and the little
child go home with Mary? The latter brightened up as she urged this
plan; but no! where the poor, fondly loved remains were, there would
the mourner be; and all that they could do was to make her as comfortable as their funds would allow, and to beg a neighbour to look in
and say a word at times. So she was left alone with her dead, and they
went to work that had work, and he who had none, took upon him
the arrangements for the funeral.

Mary had many a scolding from Miss Simmonds that day for her
absence of mind. To be sure Miss Simmonds was much put out by
Mary's non-appearance in the morning with certain bits of muslin,
and shades of silk which were wanted to complete a dress to be worn
that night; but it was true enough that Mary did not mind what she
was about; she was too busy planning how her old black gown (her
best when her mother died) might be spunged, and turned, and
lengthened into something like decent mourning for the widow. And
when she went home at night (though it was very late, as a sort of retribution for her morning's negligence), she set to work at once, and

was so busy and so glad over her task, that she had, every now and then, to check herself in singing merry ditties, which she felt little accorded with the sewing on which she was engaged.

So when the funeral day came, Mrs. Davenport was neatly arrayed in black, a satisfaction to her poor heart in the midst of her sorrow. Barton and Wilson both accompanied her, as she led her two elder boys, and followed the coffin. It was a simple walking funeral, with nothing to grate on the feelings of any; far more in accordance with its purpose, to my mind, than the gorgeous hearses, and nodding plumes, which form the grotesque funeral pomp of respectable people. There was no "rattling the bones over the stones," of the pauper's funeral.[1] Decently and quietly was he followed to the grave by one determined to endure her woe meekly for his sake. The only mark of pauperism attendant on the burial concerned the living and joyous, far more than the dead, or the sorrowful. When they arrived in the churchyard, they halted before a raised and handsome tombstone; in reality a wooden mockery of stone respectabilities which adorned the burial-ground. It was easily raised in a very few minutes, and below was the grave in which pauper bodies were piled until within a foot or two of the surface; when the soil was shovelled over, and stamped down, and the wooden cover went to do temporary duty over another hole.* But little recked they of this who now gave up their dead.

Chapter VII.

> "How infinite the wealth of love and hope
> Garnered in these same tiny treasure-houses!
> And oh! what bankrupts in the world we feel,
> When Death, like some remorseless creditor,
> Seizes on all we fondly thought our own."
> "THE TWINS."[2]

The ghoul-like fever was not to be braved with impunity, and baulked of its prey. The widow had reclaimed her children; her neighbours, in the good-Samaritan sense of the word, had paid her little arrears of rent, and made her a few shillings beforehand with the world. She determined to flit from that cellar to another less full of painful associations, less haunted by mournful memories. The board, not so formidable as she had imagined, had inquired into her case; and, instead of sending her to Stoke Claypole, her husband's Buckinghamshire parish, as she had dreaded, had agreed to pay her rent. So food for

1. From "The Pauper's Drive" in *Rhymes and Roundelays* by Thomas Noel (1799–1861).
* The case, to my certain knowledge, in one churchyard in Manchester. There may be more. [EG]
2. William Gaskell.

four mouths was all she was now required to find; only for three she would have said; for herself and the unweaned child were but reckoned as one in her calculation.

She had a strong heart, now her bodily strength had been recruited by a week or two of food, and she would not despair. So she took in some little children to nurse, who brought their daily food with them, which she cooked for them, without wronging their helplessness of a crumb; and when she had restored them to their mothers at night, she set to work at plain sewing, "seam, and gusset, and band,"[3] and sat thinking how she might best cheat the factory inspector, and persuade him that her strong, big, hungry Ben, was above thirteen. Her plan of living was so far arranged, when she heard, with keen sorrow, that Wilson's twin lads were ill of the fever.

They had never been strong. They were like many a pair of twins, and seemed to have but one life divided between them. One life, one strength, and in this instance, I might almost say, one brain; for they were helpless, gentle, silly children, but not the less dear to their parents and to their strong, active, manly, elder brother. They were late on their feet, late in talking, late every way; had to be nursed and cared for when other lads of their age were tumbling about in the street, and losing themselves, and being taken to the police-office miles away from home.

Still want had never yet come in at the door to make love for these innocents fly out of the window. Nor was this the case even now, when Jem Wilson's earnings, and his mother's occasional charings, were barely sufficient to give all the family their fill of food.

But when the twins, after ailing many days, and caring little for their meat, fell sick on the same afternoon, with the same heavy stupor of suffering, the three hearts that loved them so, each felt, though none acknowledged to the other, that they had little chance for life. It was nearly a week before the tale of their illness spread as far as the court where the Wilsons had once dwelt, and the Bartons yet lived.

Alice had heard of the sickness of her little nephews several days before, and had locked her cellar door, and gone off straight to her brother's house, in Ancoats; but she was often absent for days, sent for, as her neighbours knew, to help in some sudden emergency of illness or distress, so that occasioned no surprise.

Margaret met Jem Wilson several days after his brothers were seriously ill, and heard from him the state of things at his home. She told Mary of it as she entered the court late that evening; and Mary listened with saddened heart to the strange contrast which such woful tidings

3. From Thomas Hood's "The Song of the Shirt" (1843).

presented to the gay and loving words she had been hearing on her walk home. She blamed herself for being so much taken up with visions of the golden future, that she had lately gone but seldom on Sunday afternoons, or other leisure time, to see Mrs. Wilson, her mother's friend; and with hasty purpose of amendment she only stayed to leave a message for her father with the next-door neighbour, and then went off at a brisk pace on her way to the house of mourning.

She stopped with her hand on the latch of the Wilsons' door, to still her beating heart, and listened to the hushed quiet within. She opened the door softly: there sat Mrs. Wilson in the old rocking-chair, with one sick, death-like boy lying on her knee, crying without let or pause, but softly, gently, as fearing to disturb the troubled gasping child; while behind her, old Alice let her fast-dropping tears fall down on the dead body of the other twin, which she was laying out on a board placed on a sort of sofa-settee in a corner of the room. Over the child, which yet breathed, the father bent, watching anxiously for some ground of hope, where hope there was none. Mary stepped slowly and lightly across to Alice.

"Ay, poor lad! God has taken him early, Mary."

Mary could not speak; she did not know what to say; it was so much worse than she had expected. At last she ventured to whisper,

"Is there any chance for the other one, think you?"

Alice shook her head, and told with a look that she believed there was none. She next endeavoured to lift the little body, and carry it to its old-accustomed bed in its parents' room. But earnest as the father was in watching the yet-living, he had eyes and ears for all that concerned the dead, and sprang gently up, and took his dead son on his hard couch in his arms with tender strength, and carried him upstairs as if afraid of wakening him.

The other child gasped longer, louder, with more of effort.

"We mun get him away from his mother. He cannot die while she's wishing him."

"Wishing him?" said Mary, in a tone of inquiry.

"Ay; donno' ye know what 'wishing' means? There's none can die in the arms of those who are wishing them sore to stay on earth. The soul o' them as holds them won't let the dying soul go free; so it has a hard struggle for the quiet of death. We mun get him away fra' his mother, or he'll have a hard death, poor lile* fellow."

So without circumlocution she went and offered to take the sinking child. But the mother would not let him go, and looking in Alice's face with brimming and imploring eyes, declared, in earnest whispers, that she was not wishing him, that she would fain have him

---

* "Lile," a north-country word for "little."
  "Wit *leil* labour to live."—*Piers Ploughman*. [WG]

released from his suffering. Alice and Mary stood by with eyes fixed on the poor child, whose struggles seemed to increase, till at last his mother said, with a choking voice,

"May happen† yo'd better take him, Alice; I believe my heart's wishing him a' this while, for I cannot, no, I cannot bring mysel to let my two childer go in one day; I cannot help longing to keep him, and yet he sha'n't suffer longer for me."

She bent down, and fondly, oh! with what passionate fondness, kissed her child, and then gave him up to Alice, who took him with tender care. Nature's struggles were soon exhausted, and he breathed his little life away in peace.

Then the mother lifted up her voice and wept. Her cries brought her husband down to try with his aching heart to comfort hers. Again Alice laid out the dead, Mary helping with reverent fear. The father and mother carried him up-stairs to the bed, where his little brother lay in calm repose.

Mary and Alice drew near the fire, and stood in quiet sorrow for some time. Then Alice broke the silence by saying,

"It will be bad news for Jem, poor fellow, when he comes home."

"Where is he?" asked Mary.

"Working over-hours at th' shop. They'n getten a large order fra' forrin parts; and yo know, Jem mun work, though his heart's well nigh breaking for these poor laddies."

Again they were silent in thought, and again Alice spoke first.

"I sometimes think the Lord is against planning. Whene'er I plan over-much, He is sure to send and mar all my plans, as if He would ha' me put the future into His hands. Afore Christmastime I was as full as full could be, of going home for good and all; yo han heard how I've wished it this terrible long time. And a young lass from behind Burton came into place in Manchester last Martinmas;[4] so after awhile she had a Sunday out, and she comes to me, and tells me some cousins o' mine bid her find me out, and say how glad they should be to ha' me to bide wi' em, and look after th' childer, for they'n getten a big farm, and she's a deal to do among th' cows. So many a winter's night did I lie awake and think, that please God, come summer, I'd bid George and his wife good-bye, and go home at last. Little did I think how God Almighty would baulk me, for not leaving my days in His hands, who had led me through the wilderness hitherto. Here's George out of work, and more cast down than ever I seed him; wanting every chip o' comfort he can get, e'en afore this last heavy stroke; and now I'm thinking the Lord's finger points very clear to my fit abiding place; and I'm sure if George and Jane can say 'His will be done,' it's no more than what I'm beholden to do."

† "May happen," perhaps. [WG]
4. The Feast of St. Martin on November 11.

So saying, she fell to tidying the room, removing as much as she could every vestige of sickness; making up the fire, and setting on the kettle for a cup of tea for her sister-in-law, whose low moans and sobs were occasionally heard in the room below.

Mary helped her in all these little offices. They were busy in this way when the door was softly opened, and Jem came in, all grimed and dirty from his night-work, his soiled apron wrapped round his middle, in guise and apparel in which he would have been sorry at another time to have been seen by Mary. But just now he hardly saw her; he went straight up to Alice, and asked how the little chaps were. They had been a shade better at dinner-time, and he had been working away through the long afternoon, and far into the night, in the belief that they had taken the turn. He had stolen out during the half-hour allowed at the works for tea, to buy them an orange or two, which now puffed out his jacket-pocket.

He would make his aunt speak: he would not understand her shake of the head and fast coursing tears.

"They're both gone," said she.

"Dead!"

"Ay! poor fellows. They took worse about two o'clock. Joe went first, as easy as a lamb, and Will died harder like."

"Both!"

"Ay, lad! both. The Lord has ta'en them from some evil to come, or He would na ha' made choice o' them. Ye may rest sure o' that."

Jem went to the cupboard, and quietly extricated from his pocket the oranges he had bought. But he stayed long there, and at last his sturdy frame shook with his strong agony. The two women were frightened, as women always are, on witnessing a man's overpowering grief. They cried afresh in company. Mary's heart melted within her as she witnessed Jem's sorrow, and she stepped gently up to the corner where he stood, with his back turned to them, and putting her hand softly on his arm, said,

"O, Jem, don't give way so; I cannot bear to see you."

Jem felt a strange leap of joy in his heart, and knew the power she had of comforting him. He did not speak, as though fearing to destroy by sound or motion the happiness of that moment, when her soft hand's touch thrilled through his frame, and her silvery voice was whispering tenderness in his ear. Yes! it might be very wrong; he could almost hate himself for it; with death and woe so surrounding him, it yet was happiness, was bliss, to be so spoken to by Mary.

"Don't Jem, please don't," whispered she again, believing that his silence was only another form of grief.

He could not contain himself. He took her hand in his firm yet trembling grasp, and said, in tones that instantly produced a revulsion in her mood,

"Mary, I almost loathe myself when I feel I would not give up this minute, when my brothers lie dead, and father and mother are in such trouble, for all my life that's past and gone. And, Mary (as she tried to release her hand), you know what makes me feel so blessed."

She did know—he was right there. But as he turned to catch a look at her sweet face, he saw that it expressed unfeigned distress, almost amounting to vexation; a dread of him, that he thought was almost repugnance.

He let her hand go, and she quickly went away to Alice's side.

"Fool that I was—nay, wretch that I was—to let myself take this time of trouble to tell her how I loved her; no wonder that she turns away from such a selfish beast."

Partly to relieve her from his presence, and partly from natural desire, and partly, perhaps, from a penitent wish to share to the utmost his parents' sorrow, he soon went up-stairs to the chamber of death.

Mary mechanically helped Alice in all the duties she performed through the remainder of that long night, but she did not see Jem again. He remained up-stairs until after the early dawn showed Mary that she need have no fear of going home through the deserted and quiet streets, to try and get a little sleep before work-hour. So leaving kind messages to George and Jane Wilson, and hesitating whether she might dare to send a few kind words to Jem, and deciding that she had better not, she stepped out into the bright morning light, so fresh a contrast to the darkened room where death had been.

> "They had
> Another morn than ours."[5]

Mary lay down on her bed in her clothes; and whether it was this, or the broad daylight that poured in through the sky window, or whether it was over-excitement, it was long before she could catch a wink of sleep. Her thoughts ran on Jem's manner and words; not but what she had known the tale they told for many a day; but still she wished he had not put it so plainly.

"Oh dear," said she to herself, "I wish he would not mistake me so; I never dare to speak a common word o' kindness, but his eye brightens and his cheek flushes. It's very hard on me; for father and George Wilson are old friends; and Jem and I ha' known each other since we were quite children. I cannot think what possesses me, that I must always be wanting to comfort him when he's downcast, and that I must go meddling wi' him to-night, when sure enough it was his aunt's place to speak to him. I don't care for him, and yet, unless I'm always watching myself, I'm speaking to him in a loving voice. I think I cannot go right, for I either check myself till I'm downright cross to

---

5. Thomas Hood's "The Death Bed" (1831). See motto to Chapter 3.

him, or else I speak just natural, and that's too kind and tender by half. And I'm as good as engaged to be married to another; and another far handsomer than Jem; only I think I like Jem's face best for all that; liking's liking, and there's no help for it. Well, when I'm Mrs. Harry Carson, may happen I can put some good fortune in Jem's way. But will he thank me for it? He's rather savage at times, that I can see, and perhaps kindness from me, when I'm another's, will only go against the grain. I'll not plague myself wi' thinking any more about him, that I won't."

So she turned on her pillow, and fell asleep, and dreamt of what was often in her waking thoughts; of the day when she should ride from church in her carriage, with wedding-bells ringing, and take up her astonished father, and drive away from the old dim work-a-day court for ever, to live in a grand house, where her father should have newspapers, and pamphlets, and pipes, and meat dinners, every day,—and all day long if he liked.

Such thoughts mingled in her predilection for the handsome young Mr. Carson, who, unfettered by work-hours, let scarcely a day pass without contriving a meeting with the beautiful little milliner he had first seen while lounging in a shop where his sisters were making some purchases, and afterwards never rested till he had freely, though respectfully, made her acquaintance in her daily walks. He was, to use his own expression to himself, quite infatuated by her, and was restless each day till the time came when he had a chance, and, of late, more than a chance of meeting her. There was something of keen practical shrewdness about her, which contrasted very bewitchingly with the simple, foolish, unworldly ideas she had picked up from the romances which Miss Simmonds' young ladies were in the habit of recommending to each other.

Yes! Mary was ambitious, and did not favour Mr. Carson the less because he was rich and a gentleman. The old leaven,[6] infused years ago by her aunt Esther, fermented in her little bosom, and perhaps all the more, for her father's aversion to the rich and the gentle. Such is the contrariness of the human heart, from Eve downwards, that we all, in our old Adam state, fancy things forbidden sweetest. So Mary dwelt upon and enjoyed the idea of some day becoming a lady, and doing all the elegant nothings appertaining to ladyhood. It was a comfort to her, when scolded by Miss Simmonds, to think of the day when she would drive up to the door in her own carriage, to order her gowns from the hasty-tempered yet kind dressmaker. It was a pleasure to her to hear the general admiration of the two elder Miss Carsons, acknowledged beauties in ball-room and street, on horseback and on foot, and to think of the time when she should ride and walk

6. I Corinthians 5:7–8.

with them in loving sisterhood. But the best of her plans, the holiest, that which in some measure redeemed the vanity of the rest, were those relating to her father; her dear father, now oppressed with care, and always a disheartened, gloomy person. How she would surround him with every comfort she could devise (of course, he was to live with them), till he should acknowledge riches to be very pleasant things, and bless his lady-daughter! Every one who had shown her kindness in her low estate should then be repaid a hundred-fold.

Such were the castles in air, the Alnaschar-visions[7] in which Mary indulged, and which she was doomed in after days to expiate with many tears.

Meanwhile, her words—or, even more, her tones—would maintain their hold on Jem Wilson's memory. A thrill would yet come over him when he remembered how her hand had rested on his arm. The thought of her mingled with all his grief, and it was profound, for the loss of his brothers,

Chapter VIII.

"Deal gently with them, they have much endured;
Scoff not at their fond hopes and earnest plans,
Though they may seem to thee wild dreams and fancies.
Perchance, in the rough school of stern Experience,
They've something learned which Theory does not teach;
Or if they greatly err, deal gently still,
And let their error but the stronger plead
'Give us the light and guidance that we need!'"
                                        "LOVE THOUGHTS."[8]

One Sunday afternoon, about three weeks after that mournful night, Jem Wilson set out with the ostensible purpose of calling on John Barton. He was dressed in his best, his Sunday suit of course; while his face glittered with the scrubbing he had bestowed on it. His dark black hair had been arranged and re-arranged before the household looking-glass, and in his button-hole he stuck a narcissus (a sweet Nancy is its pretty Lancashire name), hoping it would attract Mary's notice, so that he might have the delight of giving it her.

It was a bad beginning of his visit of happiness that Mary saw him some minutes before he came into her father's house. She was sitting at the end of the dresser, with the little window-blind drawn on one side, in order that she might see the passers-by, in the intervals of reading her Bible, which lay open before her. So she watched all the greeting a friend gave Jem; she saw the face of condolence, the sym-

7. From *The Thousand and One Nights* where Alnascharr's visions of wealth come to nothing.
8. William Gaskell.

pathetic shake of the hand, and had time to arrange her own face and manner before Jem came in, which he did, as if he had eyes for no one but her father, who sat smoking his pipe by the fire, while he read an old "Northern Star,"[9] borrowed from a neighbouring public-house.

Then he turned to Mary, who, he felt through the sure instinct of love, by which almost his body thought,[1] was present. Her hands were busy adjusting her dress; a forced and unnecessary movement Jem could not help thinking. Her accost was quiet and friendly, if grave; she felt that she reddened like a rose, and wished she could prevent it, while Jem wondered if her blushes arose from fear, or anger, or love.

She was very cunning, I am afraid. She pretended to read diligently, and not to listen to a word that was said, while in fact she heard all sounds, even to Jem's long, deep sighs, which wrung her heart. At last she took up her Bible, and as if their conversation disturbed her, went up-stairs to her little room. And she had scarcely spoken a word to Jem; scarcely looked at him; never noticed his beautiful sweet Nancy, which only awaited her least word of praise to be hers! He did not know—that pang was spared—that in her little dingy bedroom stood a white jug, filled with a luxuriant bunch of early spring roses, making the whole room fragrant and bright. They were the gift of her richer lover. So Jem had to go on sitting with John Barton, fairly caught in his own trap, and had to listen to his talk, and answer him as best he might.

"There's the right stuff in this here 'Star,' and no mistake. Such a right-down piece for short hours."

"At the same rate of wages as now?" asked Jem.

"Ay, ay! else where's the use? It's only taking out o' the masters' pocket what they can well afford. Did I ever tell yo what th' Infirmary chap let me into, many a year agone?"

"No," said Jem, listlessly.

"Well! yo must know I were in th' Infirmary for a fever, and times were rare and bad, and there be good chaps there to a man, while he's wick,* whate'er they may be about cutting him up at after.† So when I were better o' th' fever, but weak as water, they says to me, says they, 'If yo can write, you may stay in a week longer, and help our surgeon wi' sorting his papers; and we'll take care yo've your bellyful of meat and drink. Yo'll be twice as strong in a week.' So there wanted but one

9. Militantly Chartist, radical newspaper established in 1837 by the Irish MP (Member of Parliament) Fergus O'Connor.

1. An echo of John Donne's (1571–1631) "That one might almost say, her body thought" from "Of the Progress of the Soul: The Second Anniversary" line 246.

*   "Wick," alive. Anglo-Saxon, cwic. "The *quick* and the dead."—*Book of Common Prayer*. [WG]
†   "At after."
    "*At after* souper goth this noble king."
       Chaucer; 'The Squire's Tale.' [WG]

word to that bargain. So I were set to writing and copying; th' writing I could do well enough, but they'd such queer ways o' spelling, that I'd ne'er been used to, that I'd to look first at th' copy and then at my letters, for all the world like a cock picking up grains o' corn. But one thing startled me e'en then, and I thought I'd make bold to ask the surgeon the meaning o't. I've getten no head for numbers, but this I know, that by *far th' greater part o' the accidents as comed in, happened in th' last two hours o' work*, when folk getten tired and careless. Th' surgeon said it were all true, and that he were going to bring that fact to light."

Jem was pondering Mary's conduct; but the pause made him aware he ought to utter some civil listening noise; so he said,

"Very true."

"Ay, its true enough, my lad, that we're sadly over-borne, and worse will come of it afore long. Block-printers is going to strike; they'n getten a bang-up Union, as won't let 'em be put upon. But there's many a thing will happen afore long, as folk don't expect. Yo may take my word for that, Jem."

Jem was very willing to take it, but did not express the curiosity he should have done, So John Barton thought he'd try another hint or two.

"Working folk won't be ground to the dust much longer. We'n a' had as much to bear as human nature can bear. So, if th' masters can't do us no good, and they say they can't, we mun try higher folk."

Still Jem was not curious. He gave up hope of seeing Mary again by her own good free will; and the next best thing would be, to be alone to think of her. So muttering something which he meant to serve as an excuse for his sudden departure, he hastily wished John good afternoon, and left him to resume his pipe and his politics.

For three years past trade had been getting worse and worse, and the price of provisions higher and higher. This disparity between the amount of the earnings of the working classes and the price of their food, occasioned, in more cases than could well be imagined, disease and death. Whole families went through a gradual starvation. They only wanted a Dante to record their sufferings.[2] And yet even his words would fall short of the awful truth; they could only present an outline of the tremendous facts of the destitution that surrounded thousands upon thousands in the terrible years 1839, 1840, and 1841. Even philanthropists who had studied the subject, were forced to own themselves perplexed in their endeavour to ascertain the real causes of the misery; the whole matter was of so complicated a nature, that it became next to impossible to understand it thoroughly.

2. A reference to the Ugolino in the Tower of Hunger story in Dante Alighieri's (1265–1321) *Divine Comedy*.

It need excite no surprise, then, to learn that a bad feeling between working men and the upper classes became very strong in this season of privation. The indigence and sufferings of the operatives induced a suspicion in the minds of many of them, that their legislators, their magistrates, their employers, and even the ministers of religion, were, in general, their oppressors and enemies; and were in league for their prostration and enthralment. The most deplorable and enduring evil that arose out of the period of commercial depression to which I refer, was this feeling of alienation between the different classes of society. It is so impossible to describe, or even faintly to picture, the state of distress which prevailed in the town at that time, that I will not attempt it; and yet I think again that surely, in a Christian land, it was not known even so feebly as words could tell it, or the more happy and fortunate would have thronged with their sympathy and their aid. In many instances the sufferers wept first, and then they cursed. Their vindictive feelings exhibited themselves in rabid politics. And when I hear, as I have heard, of the sufferings and privations of the poor, of provision shops where ha'porths[3] of tea, sugar, butter, and even flour, were sold to accommodate the indigent,— of parents sitting in their clothes by the fireside during the whole night for seven weeks together, in order that their only bed and bedding might be reserved for the use of their large family,—of others sleeping upon the cold hearthstone for weeks in succession, without adequate means of providing themselves with food or fuel (and this in the depth of winter),—of others being compelled to fast for days together, uncheered by any hope of better fortune, living, moreover, or rather starving, in a crowded garret, or damp cellar, and gradually sinking under the pressure of want and despair into a premature grave; and when this has been confirmed by the evidence of their careworn looks, their excited feelings, and their desolate homes,— can I wonder that many of them, in such times of misery and destitution, spoke and acted with ferocious precipitation?

An idea was now springing up among the operatives, that originated with the Chartists, but which came at last to be cherished as a darling child by many and many a one. They could not believe that government knew of their misery: they rather chose to think it possible that men could voluntarily assume the office of legislators for a nation who were ignorant of its real state; as who should make domestic rules for the pretty behaviour of children without caring to know that those children had been kept for days without food. Besides, the starving multitudes had heard, that the very existence of their distress had been denied in Parliament; and though they felt this strange and inexplicable, yet the idea that their misery had still

3. Half-penny worth.

to be revealed in all its depths, and that then some remedy would be found, soothed their aching hearts, and kept down their rising fury.

So a petition was framed, and signed by thousands in the bright spring days of 1839, imploring Parliament to hear witnesses who could testify to the unparalleled destitution of the manufacturing districts. Nottingham, Sheffield, Glasgow, Manchester, and many other towns, were busy appointing delegates to convey this petition, who might speak, not merely of what they had seen, and had heard, but from what they had borne and suffered. Life-worn, gaunt, anxious, hunger-stamped men, were those delegates.

One of them was John Barton. He would have been ashamed to own the flutter of spirits his appointment gave him. There was the childish delight of seeing London—that went a little way, and but a little way. There was the vain idea of speaking out his notions before so many grand folk—that went a little further; and last, there was the really pure gladness of heart arising from the idea that he was one of those chosen to be instruments in making known the distresses of the people, and consequently in procuring them some grand relief, by means of which they should never suffer want or care any more. He hoped largely, but vaguely, of the results of his expedition. An argosy of the precious hopes of many otherwise despairing creatures, was that petition to be heard concerning their sufferings.

The night before the morning on which the Manchester delegates were to leave for London, Barton might be said to hold a levée,[4] so many neighbours came dropping in. Job Legh had early established himself and his pipe by John Barton's fire, not saying much, but puffing away, and imagining himself of use in adjusting the smoothing-irons that hung before the fire, ready for Mary when she should want them. As for Mary, her employment was the same as that of Beau Tibbs' wife, "Just washing her father's two shirts," in the pantry back-kitchen; for she was anxious about his appearance in London.[5] (The coat had been redeemed, though the silk handkerchief was forfeited.) The door stood open, as usual, between the houseplace and back-kitchen, so she gave her greeting to their friends as they entered.

"So, John, yo're bound for London, are yo?" said one.

"Ay, I suppose I mun go," answered John, yielding to necessity as it were.

"Well, there's many a thing I'd like yo to speak on to the Parliament people. Thou'lt not spare 'em, John, I hope. Tell 'em our minds; how we're thinking we'n been clemmed long enough, and we donnot see whatten good they'n been doing, if they can't give us what we're all crying for sin' the day we were born."

4. A reception.
5. From Oliver Goldsmith's (1730?–1774) *The Citizen of the World* (1760).

"Ay, ay! I'll tell 'em that, and much more to it, when it gets to my turn; but thou knows there's many will have their word afore me."

"Well, thou'lt speak at last. Bless thee, lad, do ask 'em to make th' masters to break th' machines.[6] There's never been good times sin' spinning-jennies came up."[7]

"Machines is th' ruin of poor folk," chimed in several voices.

"For my part," said a shivering, half-clad man, who crept near the fire, as if ague-stricken, "I would like thee to tell 'em to pass th' short-hours' bill. Flesh and blood gets wearied wi' so much work; why should factory hands work so much longer nor other trades? Just ask 'em that, Barton, will ye?"

Barton was saved the necessity of answering, by the entrance of Mrs. Davenport, the poor widow he had been so kind to; she looked half-fed, and eager, but was decently clad. In her hand she brought a little newspaper parcel, which she took to Mary, who opened it, and then called out, dangling a shirt collar from her soapy fingers:

"See, father, what a dandy you'll be in London! Mrs. Davenport has brought you this; made new cut, all after the fashion.—Thank you for thinking on him."

"Eh, Mary!" said Mrs. Davenport, in a low voice, "whatten's all I can do, to what he's done for me and mine? But, Mary, sure I can help ye, for you'll be busy wi' this journey."

"Just help me wring these out, and then I'll take 'em to the mangle."[8]

So Mrs. Davenport became a listener to the conversation; and after a while joined in.

"I'm sure, John Barton, if yo are taking messages to the Parliament folk, yo'll not object to telling 'em what a sore trial it is, this law o' theirs, keeping childer fra' factory work, whether they be weakly or strong. There's our Ben; why, porridge seems to go no way wi' him, he eats so much; and I han gotten no money to send him t' school, as I would like; and there he is, rampaging about the streets a' day, getting hungrier and hungrier, and picking up a' manner o' bad ways; and th' inspector won't let him in to work in th' factory, because he's not right age; though he's twice as strong as Sankey's little ritling* of a lad, as works till he cries for his legs aching so, though he is right age, and better."

"I've one plan I wish to tell John Barton," said a pompous, careful-speaking man, "and I should like him for to lay it afore the

6. A reference to the Luddite uprisings against the introduction of power looms to replace hand-loom weaving. The Luddites were famous for "breaking the machines."
7. A machine used to wind yarn on more than one spindle at a time.
8. A crank driven roller press for ironing laundry.
* "Ritling," probably a corruption of "ricketling," a child that suffers from the rickets—a weakling. [WG]

Honourable House. My mother comed out o' Oxfordshire, and were under-laundry-maid in Sir Francis Dashwood's family[9]; and when we were little ones, she'd tell us stories of their grandeur: and one thing she named were, that Sir Francis wore two shirts a day. Now he were all as one as a Parliament man; and many on 'em, I han no doubt, are like extravagant. Just tell 'em, John, do, that they'd be doing the Lancashire weavers a great kindness, if they'd ha' their shirts a' made o' calico; 'twould make trade brisk, that would, wi' the power o' shirts they wear."

Job Legh now put in his word. Taking the pipe out of his mouth, and addressing the last speaker, he said:

"I'll tell ye what, Bill, and no offence, mind ye; there's but hundreds of them Parliament folk as wear so many shirts to their back; but there's thousands and thousands o' poor weavers as han only gotten one shirt i' the world; ay, and don't know where t' get another when that rag's done, though they're turning out miles o' calico every day; and many a mile o't is lying in warehouses, stopping up trade for want o' purchasers. Yo take my advice, John Barton, and ask Parliament to set trade free, so as workmen can earn a decent wage, and buy their two, ay and three, shirts a-year; that would make weaving brisk."

He put his pipe in his mouth again, and redoubled his puffing, to make up for lost time.

"I'm afeard, neighbours," said John Barton, "I've not much chance o' telling 'em all yo say; what I think on, is just speaking out about the distress that they say is nought. When they hear o'children born on wet flags, without a rag t' cover 'em or a bit o' food for th' mother; when they hear of folk lying down to die i' th' streets, or hiding their want i' some hole o' a cellar till death come to set 'em free; and when they hear o' all this plague, pestilence, and famine, they'll surely do somewhat wiser for us than we can guess at now. Howe'er, I han no objection, if so be there's an opening, to speak up for what yo say; anyhow, I'll do my best, and yo see now, if better times don't come after Parliament knows all."

Some shook their heads, but more looked cheery: and then one by one dropped off, leaving John and his daughter alone.

"Didst thou mark how poorly Jane Wilson looked?" asked he, as they wound up their hard day's work by a supper eaten over the fire, which glowed and glimmered through the room, and formed their only light.

"No, I can't say as I did. But she's never rightly held up her head since the twins died; and all along she has never been a strong woman."

9. Baron Le Despenser (1708–1781), a notorious rake in his youth, later Chancellor of the Exchequer.

"Never sin' her accident. Afore that I mind her looking as fresh and likely a girl as e'er a one in Manchester."

"What accident, father?"

"She cotched* her side again a wheel. It were afore wheels were boxed up.[1] It were just when she were to have been married, and many a one thought George would ha' been off his bargain; but I knew he wern't the chap for that trick. Pretty near the first place she went to when she were able to go about again, was th' Oud Church; poor wench, all pale and limping she went up the aisle, George holding her up as tender as a mother, and walking as slow as e'er he could, not to hurry her, though there were plenty enow of rude lads to cast their jests at him and her. Her face were white like a sheet when she came in church, but afore she got to th' altar she were all one flush. But for a' that it's been a happy marriage, and George has stuck by me through life like a brother. He'll never hold up his head again if he loses Jane. I didn't like her looks to-night."

And so he went to bed, the fear of forthcoming sorrow to his friend mingling with his thoughts of to-morrow, and his hopes for the future. Mary watched him set off, with her hands over her eyes to shade them from the bright slanting rays of the morning sun, and then she turned into the house to arrange its disorder before going to her work. She wondered if she should like or dislike the evening and morning solitude; for several hours when the clock struck she thought of her father, and wondered where he was; she made good resolutions according to her lights; and by-and-by came the distractions and events of the broad full day to occupy her with the present, and to deaden the memory of the absent.

One of Mary's resolutions was, that she would not be persuaded or induced to see Mr. Harry Carson during her father's absence. There was something crooked in her conscience after all; for this very resolution seemed an acknowledgment that it was wrong to meet him at any time; and yet she had brought herself to think her conduct quite innocent and proper, for although unknown to her father, and certain, even did he know it, to fail of obtaining his sanction, she esteemed her love-meetings with Mr. Carson as sure to end in her father's good and happiness. But now that he was away, she would do nothing that he would disapprove of; no, not even though it was for his own good in the end.

Now, amongst Miss Simmonds' young ladies was one who had been from the beginning a confidante in Mary's love affair, made so by Mr. Carson himself. He had felt the necessity of some third person to carry letters and messages, and to plead his cause when he

* "Cotched," caught. [WG]
1. The Factory Act of 1844 mandated fencing off dangerously exposed machinery.

was absent. In a girl named Sally Leadbitter he had found a willing advocate. She would have been willing to have embarked in a love-affair herself (especially a clandestine one), for the mere excitement of the thing; but her willingness was strengthened by sundry half-sovereigns,[2] which from time to time Mr. Carson bestowed upon her.

Sally Leadbitter was vulgar-minded to the last degree; never easy unless her talk was of love and lovers; in her eyes it was an honour to have had a long list of wooers. So constituted, it was a pity that Sally herself was but a plain, red-haired, freckled girl; never likely, one would have thought, to become a heroine on her own account. But what she lacked in beauty she tried to make up for by a kind of witty boldness, which gave her what her betters would have called piquancy. Considerations of modesty or propriety never checked her utterance of a good thing. She had just talent enough to corrupt others. Her very good-nature was an evil influence. They could not hate one who was so kind; they could not avoid one who was so willing to shield them from scrapes by any exertion of her own; whose ready fingers would at any time make up for their deficiencies, and whose still more convenient tongue would at any time invent for them. The Jews, or Mohammedans (I forget which), believe that there is one little bone of our body,—one of the vertebræ, if I remember rightly,—which will never decay and turn to dust, but will lie incorrupt and indestructible in the ground until the Last Day: this is the Seed of the Soul. The most depraved have also their Seed of the Holiness that shall one day overcome their evil. Their one good quality, lurking hidden, but safe, among all the corrupt and bad.

Sally's seed of the future soul was her love for her mother, an aged bedridden woman. For her she had self-denial; for her, her good-nature rose into tenderness; to cheer her lonely bed, her spirits, in the evenings, when her body was often wofully tired, never flagged, but were ready to recount the events of the day, to turn them into ridicule, and to mimic, with admirable fidelity, any person gifted with an absurdity who had fallen under her keen eye. But the mother was lightly principled like Sally herself; nor was there need to conceal from her the reason why Mr. Carson gave her so much money. She chuckled with pleasure, and only hoped that the wooing would be long a-doing.

Still neither she, nor her daughter, nor Harry Carson liked this resolution of Mary, not to see him during her father's absence.

One evening (and the early summer evenings were long and bright now), Sally met Mr. Carson by appointment, to be charged with a let-

2. Gold coins worth ten shillings.

ter for Mary, imploring her to see him, which Sally was to back with all her powers of persuasion. After parting from him she determined, as it was not so very late, to go at once to Mary's, and deliver the message and letter.

She found Mary in great sorrow. She had just heard of George Wilson's sudden death: her old friend, her father's friend, Jem's father—all his claims came rushing upon her. Though not guarded from unnecessary sight or sound of death, as the children of the rich are, yet it had so often been brought home to her this last three or four months. It was so terrible thus to see friend after friend depart. Her father, too, who had dreaded Jane Wilson's death the evening before he set off. And she, the weakly, was left behind, while the strong man was taken. At any rate the sorrow her father had so feared for him was spared. Such were the thoughts which came over her.

She could not go to comfort the bereaved, even if comfort were in her power to give; for she had resolved to avoid Jem; and she felt that this of all others was not the occasion on which she could keep up a studiously cold manner.

And in this shock of grief, Sally Leadbitter was the last person she wished to see. However, she rose to welcome her, betraying her tear-swollen face.

"Well, I shall tell Mr. Carson to-morrow how you're fretting for him; it's no more nor he's doing for you, I can tell you."

"For him, indeed!" said Mary, with a toss of her pretty head.

"Ay, miss, for him! You've been sighing as if your heart would break now for several days, over your work; now, arn't you a little goose not to go and see one who I am sure loves you as his life, and whom you love; 'How much, Mary?' 'This much,' as the children say" (opening her arms very wide).

"Nonsense," said Mary pouting; "I often think I don't love him at all."

"And I'm to tell him that, am I, next time I see him?" asked Sally.

"If you like," replied Mary. "I'm sure I don't care for that or anything else now;" weeping afresh.

But Sally did not like to be the bearer of any such news. She saw she had gone on the wrong tack, and that Mary's heart was too full to value either message or letter as she ought. So she wisely paused in their delivery, and said, in a more sympathetic tone than she had hitherto used,

"Do tell me, Mary, what's fretting you so? You know I never could abide to see you cry."

"George Wilson's dropped down dead this afternoon," said Mary, fixing her eyes for one minute on Sally, and the next hiding her face in her apron as she sobbed anew.

"Dear, dear! All flesh is grass; here to-day and gone tomorrow, as the Bible says.[3] Still he was an old man, and not good for much; there's better folk than him left behind. Is th' canting[4] old maid as was his sister alive yet?"

"I don't know who you mean," said Mary, sharply; for she did know, and did not like to have her dear, simple Alice so spoken of.

"Come, Mary, don't be so innocent. Is Miss Alice Wilson alive, then; will that please you? I haven't seen her hereabouts lately."

"No, she's left living here. When the twins died, she thought she could, may be, be of use to her sister, who was sadly cast down, and Alice thought she could cheer her up; at any rate she could listen to her when her heart grew overburdened; so she gave up her cellar and went to live with them."

"Well, good go with her. I'd no fancy for her, and I'd no fancy for her making my pretty Mary into a Methodee."

"She wasn't a Methodee; she was Church o' England."

"Well, well, Mary, you're very particular. You know what I meant. Look, who is this letter from?" holding up Henry Carson's letter.

"I don't know, and don't care," said Mary, turning very red.

"My eye! as if I didn't know you did know and did care."

"Well, give it me," said Mary, impatiently, and anxious in her present mood for her visitor's departure.

Sally relinquished it unwillingly. She had, however, the pleasure of seeing Mary dimple and blush as she read the letter, which seemed to say the writer was not indifferent to her.

"You must tell him I can't come," said Mary, raising her eyes at last. "I have said I won't meet him while father is away, and I won't."

"But, Mary, he does so look for you. You'd be quite sorry for him, he's so put out about not seeing you. Besides, you go when your father's at home, without letting on[*] to him, and what harm would there be in going now?"

"Well, Sally, you know my answer, I won't; and I won't."

"I'll tell him to come and see you himself some evening, instead o' sending me; he'd may be find you not so hard to deal with."

Mary flashed up.

"If he dares to come here while father's away, I'll call the neighbours in to turn him out, so don't be putting him up to that."

"Mercy on us! one would think you were the first girl that ever had a lover; have you never heard what other girls do and think no shame of?"

"Hush, Sally! that's Margaret Jennings at the door."

And in an instant Margaret was in the room. Mary had begged Job

3. Isaiah 40:6 and I Peter 1:24.
4. Jargon associated with specific religious or social groups.
* "Letting on," informing. [WG]

Legh to let her come and sleep with her. In the uncertain fire-light you could not help noticing that she had the groping walk of a blind person.

"Well, I must go, Mary," said Sally. "And that's your last word?"

"Yes, yes; good night." She shut the door gladly on her unwelcome visitor—unwelcome at that time at least.

"Oh, Margaret, have ye heard this sad news about George Wilson?"

"Yes, that I have. Poor creatures, they've been sore tried lately. Not that I think sudden death so bad a thing; it's easy, and there's no terrors for him as dies. For them as survives it's very hard. Poor George! he were such a hearty-looking man."

"Margaret," said Mary who had been closely observing her friend, "thou'rt very blind to night, arn't thou? Is it wi' crying? Your eyes are so swollen and red."

"Yes, dear! but not crying for sorrow. Han ye heard where I was last night?"

"No; where?"

"Look here." She held up a bright golden sovereign. Mary opened her large gray eyes with astonishment.

"I'll tell you all and how about it. You see there's a gentleman lecturing on music at th' Mechanics',[5] and he wants folk to sing his songs. Well, last night the counter[6] got a sore throat and couldn't make a note. So they sent for me. Jacob Butterworth had said a good word for me, and they asked me would I sing? You may think I was frightened, but I thought, Now or never, and said I'd do my best. So I tried o'er the songs wi' th' lecturer, and then th' managers told me I were to make myself decent and be there by seven."

"And what did you put on?" asked Mary. "Oh, why didn't you come in for my pretty pink gingham?"

"I did think on't; but you had na come home then. No! I put on my merino, as was turned last winter, and my white shawl, and did my hair pretty tidy; it did well enough. Well, but as I was saying, I went at seven. I couldn't see to read my music, but I took th' paper in wi' me, to ha' something to do wi' my fingers. Th' folks' heads danced, as I stood as right afore 'em all as if I'd been going to play at ball wi' 'em. You may guess I felt squeamish, but mine weren't the first song, and th' music sounded like a friend's voice telling me to take courage. So, to make a long story short, when it were all o'er th' lecturer thanked me, and th' managers said as how there never was a new singer so applauded (for they'd clapped and stamped after I'd done, till I began to wonder how many pair o' shoes they'd get through a week at that

5. The Mechanics' Institute, founded in 1824, provided a library, lectures, and other support for working-class culture and recreation. The Manchester Institute was one of many in major English cities.
6. Counter-tenor.

rate, let alone their hands). So I'm to sing again o' Thursday; and I got a sovereign last night, and am to have half-a-sovereign every night th' lecturer is at th' Mechanics'."

"Well, Margaret, I'm right glad to hear it."

"And I don't think you've heard the best bit yet. Now that a way seemed open to me, of not being a burden to any one, though it did please God to make me blind, I thought I'd tell grandfather. I only tell'd him about the singing and the sovereign last night, for I thought I'd not send him to bed wi' a heavy heart; but this morning I told him all."

"And how did he take it?"

"He's not a man of many words; and it took him by surprise like."

"I wonder at that; I've noticed it in your ways ever since you telled me."

"Ay, that's it! If I'd not telled you, and you'd seen me every day, you'd not ha' noticed the little mite o' difference fra' day to day."

"Well, but what did your grandfather say?"

"Why, Mary," said Margaret, half smiling, "I'm a bit loth to tell yo, for unless yo knew grandfather's ways like me, yo'd think it strange. He was taken by surprise, and he said: 'Damn yo!' Then he began looking at his book as it were, and were very quiet, while I telled him all about it; how I'd feared, and how downcast I'd been; and how I were now reconciled to it, if it were th' Lord's will; and how I hoped to earn money by singing; and while I were talking, I saw great big tears come dropping on th' book; but in course I never let on that I saw 'em. Dear grandfather! and all day long he's been quietly moving things out o' my way, as he thought might trip me up, and putting things in my way as he thought I might want; never knowing I saw and felt what he were doing; for, yo see, he thinks I'm out and out blind, I guess—as I shall be soon."

Margaret sighed in spite of her cheerful and relieved tone.

Though Mary caught the sigh, she felt it was better to let it pass without notice, and began, with the tact which true sympathy rarely fails to supply, to ask a variety of questions respecting her friend's musical debut, which tended to bring out more distinctly how successful it had been.

"Why, Margaret," at length she exclaimed, "thou'lt become as famous, may be, as that grand lady fra' London, as we see'd one night driving up to th' concert-room door in her carriage."

"It looks very like it," said Margaret, with a smile. "And be sure, Mary, I'll not forget to give thee a lift now an' then when that comes about. Nay, who knows, if thou'rt a good girl, but mayhappen I may make thee my lady's maid! Wouldn't that be nice? So I e'en sing to mysel' th' beginning o' one o' my songs,

> " 'An' ye shall walk in silk attire,
>   An' siller hae to spare.' "[7]

"Nay, don't stop; or else give me something rather more new, for somehow I never quite liked that part about thinking o' Donald mair."

"Well, though I'm a bit tir'd, I don't care if I do. Before I come, I were practising well-nigh upon two hours this one which I'm to sing o' Thursday. The lecturer said he were sure it would just suit me, and I should do justice to it; and I should be right sorry to disappoint him, he were so nice and encouraging like to me. Eh! Mary, what a pity there isn't more o' that way, and less scolding and rating i' th' world! It would go a vast deal further. Beside, some o' th' singers said, they were a'most certain that it were a song o' his own, because he were so fidgety and particular about it, and so anxious I should give it th' proper expression. And that makes me care still more. Th' first verse, he said, were to be sung 'tenderly, but joyously!' I'm afraid I don't quite hit that, but I'll try.

> 'What a single word can do!
> Thrilling all the heart-strings through,
> Calling forth fond memories,
> Raining round hope's melodies,
> Steeping all in one bright hue—
> What a single word can do!'

Now it falls into th' minor key, and must be very sad-like. I feel as if I could do that better than t'other.

> 'What a single word can do!
> Making life seem all untrue,
> Driving joy and hope away,
> Leaving not one cheering ray,
> Blighting every flower that grew—
> What a single word can do!' "[8]

Margaret certainly made the most of this little song. As a factory worker, listening outside, observed, "She spun it reet* fine!" And if she only sang it at the Mechanics' with half the feeling she put into it that night, the lecturer must have been hard to please, if he did not admit that his expectations were more than fulfilled.

When it was ended, Mary's looks told more than words could have done what she thought of it; and partly to keep in a tear which would fain have rolled out, she brightened into a laugh, and said, "For certain, th' carriage is coming. So let us go and dream on it."

---

7. From "The Silver Crown" by Susanna Blamire (1747–1794).
8. By William Gaskell.
* "Reet," right; often used for "very." [WG]

Chapter IX.

"A life of self-indulgence is for us,
A life of self-denial is for them;
For us the streets, broad-built and populous,
For them unhealthy corners, garrets dim,
And cellars where the water-rat may swim!
For us green paths refreshed by frequent rain,
For them dark alleys where the dust lies grim!
Not doomed by us to this appointed pain—
God made us rich and poor—of what do these complain?"
                    MRS. NORTON'S "CHILD OF THE ISLANDS."[9]

The next evening it was a warm, pattering, incessant rain—just the rain to waken up the flowers. But in Manchester, where, alas! there are no flowers, the rain had only a disheartening and gloomy effect; the streets were wet and dirty, the drippings from the houses were wet and dirty, and the people were wet and dirty. Indeed, most kept within doors; and there was an unusual silence of footsteps in the little paved courts.

Mary had to change her clothes after her walk home; and had hardly settled herself before she heard some one fumbling at the door. The noise continued long enough to allow her to get up, and go and open it. There stood—could it be? yes it was, her father!

Drenched and wayworn, there he stood! He came in with no word to Mary in return for her cheery and astonished greeting. He sat down by the fire in his wet things, unheeding. But Mary would not let him so rest. She ran up and brought down his working-day clothes, and went into the pantry to rummage up their little bit of provision while he changed by the fire, talking all the while as gaily as she could, though her father's depression hung like lead on her heart.

For Mary, in her seclusion at Miss Simmonds',—where the chief talk was of fashions, and dress, and parties to be given, for which such and such gowns would be wanted, varied with a slight-whispered interlude occasionally about love and lovers,—had not heard the political news of the day: that Parliament had refused to listen to the working men,[1] when they petitioned, with all the force of their rough, untutored words, to be heard concerning the distress which was riding, like the Conqueror on his Pale Horse,[2] among the people; which was crushing their lives out of them, and stamping woe-marks over the land.

9. Caroline Norton (1808–1877) became a friend of Gaskell's in the 1850s. She published *The Child of the Islands* in 1845 and in later years worked to reform the Divorce Laws to gain more rights for women.
1. The first Chartist petition was presented to Parliament in May but not taken up until July when Parliament voted 235 to 46 against even discussing it.
2. Reference to one of the four horsemen of the apocalypse: Revelation 6:8.

When he had eaten and was refreshed, they sat for some time in silence; for Mary wished him to tell her what oppressed him so, yet durst not ask. In this she was wise; for when we are heavy-laden in our hearts it falls in better with our humour to reveal our case in our own way, and our own time.

Mary sat on a stool at her father's feet in old childish guise, and stole her hand into his, while his sadness infected her, and she "caught the trick of grief, and sighed,"[3] she knew not why.

"Mary, we mun speak to our God to hear us, for man will not hearken; no, not now, when we weep tears o' blood."

In an instant Mary understood the fact, if not the details, that so weighed down her father's heart. She pressed his hand with silent sympathy. She did not know what to say, and was so afraid of speaking wrongly, that she was silent. But when his attitude had remained unchanged for more than half-an-hour, his eyes gazing vacantly and fixedly at the fire, no sound but now and then a deep-drawn sigh to break the weary ticking of the clock, and the drip-drop from the roof without, Mary could bear it no longer. Any thing to rouse her father. Even bad news.

"Father, do you know George Wilson's dead?" (Her hand was suddenly and almost violently compressed.) "He dropped down dead in Oxford Road yester morning. It's very sad, isn't it, father?"

Her tears were ready to flow as she looked up in her father's face for sympathy. Still the same fixed look of despair, not varied by grief for the dead.

"Best for him to die," he said, in a low voice.

This was unbearable. Mary got up under pretence of going to tell Margaret that she need not come to sleep with her to-night, but really to ask Job Legh to come and cheer her father.

She stopped outside the door. Margaret was practising her singing, and through the still night air her voice rang out, like that of an angel:

"Comfort ye, comfort ye, my people, saith your God."[4]

The old Hebrew prophetic words fell like dew on Mary's heart. She could not interrupt. She stood listening and "comforted," till the little buzz of conversation again began, and then entered and told her errand.

Both grandfather and granddaughter rose instantly to fulfil her request.

"He's just tired out, Mary," said old Job. "He'll be a different man to-morrow."

There is no describing the looks and tones that have power over an aching, heavy-laden heart; but in an hour or so John Barton was talking

3. From William Wordsworth's *The Excursion*, Bk. I, lines. 831–32.
4. From Handel's *Messiah* based on Isaiah 40:1.

away as freely as ever, though all his talk ran, as was natural, on the disappointment of his fond hope, of the forlorn hope of many.

"Ay, London's a fine place," said he, "and finer folk live in it than I ever thought on, or ever heerd tell on except in th' storybooks. They are having their good things now, that afterwards they may be tormented."

Still at the old parable of Dives and Lazarus! Does it haunt the minds of the rich as it does those of the poor?

"Do tell us all about London, dear father," asked Mary, who was sitting at her old post by her father's knee.

"How can I tell yo a' about it, when I never see'd one-tenth of it. It's as big as six Manchesters, they told me. One-sixth may be made up o' grand palaces, and three-sixth's o' middling kind, and th' rest o' holes o' iniquity and filth, such as Manchester knows nought on, I'm glad to say."

"Well, father, but did you see the Queen?"

"I believe I didn't, though one day I thought I'd seen her many a time. You see," said he, turning to Job Legh, "there were a day appointed for us to go to Parliament House. We were most on us bidding at a public-house in Holborn, where they did very well for us. Th' morning of taking our petition we had such a spread for breakfast as th' Queen hersel might ha' sitten down to. I suppose they thought we wanted putting in heart. There were mutton kidneys, and sausages, and broiled ham, and fried beef and onions; more like a dinner nor a breakfast. Many on our chaps though, I could see, could eat but little. Th' food stuck in their throats when they thought o' them at home, wives and little ones, as had, may be at that very time, nought to eat. Well, after breakfast, we were all set to walk in procession, and a time it took to put us in order, two and two, and the petition, as was yards long, carried by th' foremost pairs. The men looked grave enough, yo may be sure; and such a set of thin, wan, wretched-looking chaps as they were!"

"Yourself is none to boast on."

"Ay, but I were fat and rosy to many a one. Well, we walked on and on through many a street, much the same as Deansgate. We had to walk slowly, slowly, for th' carriages an' cabs as thronged th' streets. I thought by-and-by we should may be get clear on 'em, but as the streets grew wider they grew worse, and at last we were fairly blocked up at Oxford Street. We getten across at after a while though, and my eyes! the grand streets we were in then! They're sadly puzzled how to build houses though in London; there'd be an opening for a good steady master builder there, as know'd his business. For yo see the houses are many on 'em built without any proper shape for a body to live in; some on 'em they've after thought would fall down, so they've stuck great ugly pillars out before 'em. And some on 'em (we thought they must be th' tailors' sign) had getten stone men and women as wanted clothes stuck on 'em. I were like a child, I forgot a' my errand in looking about me. By this it were dinner-time, or better, as we could tell by the sun, right above our heads, and we were dusty and tired, going a step now and a step then. Well, at last we getten into a street grander nor all, leading to th' Queen's palace, and there it were I thought I saw th' Queen. Yo've seen th' hearses wi' white plumes. Job?"

Job assented.

"Well, them undertaker folk are driving a pretty trade in London. Wellnigh every lady we saw in a carriage had hired one o' them plumes for the day, and had it niddle noddling on her head. It were th' Queen's drawing-room, they said, and th' carriages went bowling along toward her house, some wi' dressed up gentlemen like circus folk in 'em, and rucks* o' ladies in others. Carriages themselves were great shakes too. Some o' th' gentlemen as couldn't get inside hung on behind, wi' nosegays to smell at, and sticks to keep off folk as might splash their silk stockings. I wondered why they didn't hire a cab rather than hang on like a whip-behind boy; but I suppose they wished to keep wi' their wives, Darby and Joan like.[5] Coachmen were little squat men, wi' wigs like th' oud-fashioned parsons'. Well, we could na get on for these carriages, though we waited and waited. Th' horses were too fat to move quick; they never known want o' food, one might tell by their sleek coats; and police pushed us back when we tried to cross. One or two of 'em struck wi' their sticks, and coachmen laughed, and some officers as stood nigh put their spy-glasses in their eye, and left 'em sticking there like mountebanks. One o' th' police struck me. 'Whatten business have you to do that?' said I.

" 'You're frightening them horses,' says he, in his mincing way (for Londoners are mostly all tongue-tied, and can't say their a's and i's properly), 'and it's our business to keep you from molesting the ladies and gentlemen going to her Majesty's drawing-room.'

"And why are we to be molested," asked I, "going decently about our business, which is life and death to us, and many a little one clemming at home in Lancashire? Which business is of most consequence i' the sight o' God, think yo, our'n or them grand ladies and gentlemen as yo think so much on?

"But I might as well ha' held my peace, for he only laughed."

John ceased. After waiting a little, to see if he would go on himself, Job said,

"Well, but that's not a' your story, man. Tell us what happened when you got to th' Parliament House."

---

* "Rucks," a great quantity. "Rycian," to collect. [WG]
5. Expression for elderly, devoted married couple.

After a little pause, John answered,

"If you please, neighbour, I'd rather say nought about that. It's not to be forgotten, or forgiven either, by me or many another; but I canna tell of our down-casting just as a piece of London news. As long as I live, our rejection of that day will abide in my heart; and as long as I live I shall curse them as so cruelly refused to hear us; but I'll not speak of it no[†] more."

So, daunted in their inquiries, they sat silent for a few minutes.

Old Job, however, felt that some one must speak, else all the good they had done in dispelling John Barton's gloom was lost. So after a while he thought of a subject, neither sufficiently dissonant from the last to jar on the full heart, nor too much the same to cherish the continuance of the gloomy train of thought.

"Did you ever hear tell," said he to Mary, "that I were in London once?"

"No!" said she, with surprise, and looking at Job with increased respect.

"Ay, but I were though, and Peg there too, though she minds nought about it, poor wench! You must know I had but one child, and she were Margaret's mother. I loved her above a bit, and one day when she came (standing behind me for that I should not see her blushes, and stroking my cheeks in her own coaxing way), and told me she and Frank Jennings (as was a joiner lodging near us) should be so happy if they were married, I could not find in my heart t' say her nay, though I went sick at the thought of losing her away from my home. However, she was my only child, and I never said nought of what I felt, for fear o' grieving her young heart. But I tried to think o' the time when I'd been young mysel, and had loved her blessed mother, and how we'd left father and mother, and gone out into th' world together, and I'm now right thankful I held my peace, and didna fret her wi' telling her how sore I was at parting wi' her that were the light o' my eyes."

"But," said Mary, "you said the young man were a neighbour."

"Ay, so he were, and his father afore him. But work were rather slack in Manchester, and Frank's uncle sent him word o' London work and London wages, so he were to go there, and it were there Margaret was to follow him. Well, my heart aches yet at thought of those days. She so happy, and he so happy; only the poor father as fretted sadly behind their backs. They were married and stayed some days wi' me afore setting off; and I've often thought sin', Margaret's heart failed her many a time those few days, and she would fain ha' spoken; but I knew fra' mysel it were better to keep it pent up, and I

---

† A similar use of a double negative is frequent in Chaucer; as in the "Miller's Tale:"
"That of no wife toke he non offering
For curtesie, he sayd, he n'old non." [WG]

never let on what I were feeling; I knew what she meant when she came kissing, and holding my hand, and all her old childish ways o' loving me. Well, they went at last. You know them two letters, Margaret?"

"Yes, sure," replied his granddaughter.

"Well, them two were the only letters I ever had fra' her, poor lass. She said in them she were very happy, and I believe she were. And Frank's family heard he were in good work. In one o' her letters, poor thing, she ends wi' saying, 'Farewell, Grandad!' wi' a line drawn under grandad, and fra' that an' other hints I knew she were in th' family way; and I said nought, but I screwed up a little money, thinking come Whitsuntide I'd take a holiday and go and see her an' th' little one. But one day towards Whitsuntide, comed Jennings wi' a grave face, and says he, 'I hear our Frank and your Margaret's both getten the fever.' You might ha' knocked me down wi' a straw, for it seemed as if God told me what th' upshot would be. Old Jennings had gotten a letter, you see, fra' the landlady they lodged wi'; a well-penned letter, asking if they'd no friends to come and nurse them. She'd caught it first, and Frank, who was as tender o'er her as her own mother could ha' been, had nursed her till he'd caught it himsel; and she expecting her down-lying* every day. Well, t' make a long story short, old Jennings and I went up by that night's coach. So you see, Mary, that was the way I got to London."

"But how was your daughter when you got there?" asked Mary, anxiously.

"She were at rest, poor wench, and so were Frank. I guessed as much when I see'd th' landlady's face, all swelled wi' crying, when she opened th' door to us. We said, 'Where are they?' and I knew they were dead, fra' her look; but Jennings didn't, as I take it; for when she showed us into a room wi' a white sheet on th' bed, and underneath it, plain to be seen, two still figures, he screeched out as if he'd been a woman.

"Yet he'd other children and I'd none. There lay my darling, my only one. She were dead, and there were no one to love me, no not one. I disremember† rightly what I did; but I know I were very quiet, while my heart were crushed within me.

"Jennings could na' stand being in the room at all, so the landlady took him down, and I were glad to be alone. It grew dark while I sat there; and at last th' landlady came up again, and said, 'Come here.' So I got up, and walked into the light, but I had to hold by th' stair-rails, I were so weak and dizzy. She led me into a room, where Jennings lay on a sofa fast asleep, wi' his pocket handkerchief over his

---

* "Down-lying," lying in. [WG]
† "Disremember," forget. [WG]

head for a night-cap. She said he'd cried himself fairly off to sleep. There were tea on th' table all ready; for she were a kind-hearted body. But she still said, 'Come here,' and took hold o' my arm. So I went round the table, and there were a clothes-basket by th' fire, wi' a shawl put o'er it. 'Lift that up,' says she, and I did; and there lay a little wee babby fast asleep. My heart gave a leap, and th' tears comed rushing into my eyes first time that day. 'Is it hers?' said I, though I knew it were. 'Yes,' said she. 'She were getting a bit better o' the fever, and th' babby were born; and then the poor young man took worse and died, and she were not many hours behind.'

"Little mite of a thing! and yet it seemed her angel come back to comfort me. I were quite jealous o' Jennings, whenever he went near the babby. I thought it were more my flesh and blood than his'n, and yet I were afraid he would claim it. However, that were far enough fra' his thoughts; he'd plenty other childer, and, as I found out after, he'd all along been wishing me to take it. Well, we buried Margaret and her husband in a big, crowded, lonely churchyard in London. I were loath to leave them there, as I thought, when they rose again, they'd feel so strange at first away fra' Manchester, and all old friends; but it could na be helped. Well, God watches o'er their graves there as well as here. That funeral cost a mint o' money, but Jennings and I wished to do th' thing decent. Then we'd the stout little babby to bring home. We'd not overmuch money left; but it were fine weather, and we thought we'd take th' coach to Brummagem,[6] and walk on. It were a bright May morning when I last saw London town, looking back from a big hill a mile or two off. And in that big mass o' a place I were leaving my blessed child asleep—in her last sleep. Well, God's will be done! She's gotten to heaven afore me; but I shall get there at last, please God, though it's a long while first.

"The babby had been fed afore we set out, and th' coach moving kept it asleep, bless its little heart! But when th' coach stopped for dinner it were awake, and crying for its pobbies.* So we asked for some bread and milk, and Jennings took it first for to feed it; but it made its mouth like a square, and let it run out at each o' the four corners. 'Shake it, Jennings,' says I; 'that's the way they make water run through a funnel, when it's o'er full; and a child's mouth is broad end o' th' funnel, and th' gullet the narrow one.' So he shook it, but it only cried th' more. 'Let me have it,' says I, thinking he were an awkward oud chap. But it were just as bad wi' me. By shaking th' babby we got better nor a gill[7] into its mouth, but more nor that came up again, wetting a' th' nice dry clothes landlady had put on. Well, just as we'd

6. Birmingham.
* "Pobbies," or "pobs," child's porridge. [WG]
7. Four ounces.

gotten to th' dinner-table, and helped oursels, and eaten two mouthful, came in th' guard, and a fine chap wi' a sample o' calico flourishing in his hand. 'Coach is ready!' says one; 'Half-a-crown your dinner!'
says the other. Well, we thought it a deal for both our dinners, when
we'd hardly tasted 'em; but, bless your life, it were half-a-crown
apiece, and a shilling for th' bread and milk as were possetted all over
babby's clothes. We spoke up again'† it; but everybody said it were the
rule, so what could two poor oud chaps like us do again' it? Well, poor
babby cried without stopping to take breath, fra' that time till we got
to Brummagem for the night. My heart ached for th' little thing. It
caught wi' its wee mouth at our coat sleeves and at our mouths, when
we tried t' comfort it by talking to it. Poor little wench! it wanted its
mammy, as were lying cold in th' grave. 'Well,' says I, 'it'll be clemmed
to death, if it lets out its supper as it did its dinner. Let's get some
woman to feed it; it comes natural to women to do for babbies.' So
we asked th' chambermaid at the inn, and she took quite kindly to it;
and we got a good supper, and grew rare and sleepy, what wi' th'
warmth and wi' our long ride i' the open air. Th' chambermaid said
she would like t' have it t' sleep wi' her, only missis would scold so; but
it looked so quiet and smiling like, as it lay in her arms, that we
thought 'twould be no trouble to have it wi' us. I says: 'See, Jennings,
how women folk do quieten babbies; its just as I said.' He looked
grave; he were always thoughtful-looking, though I never heard him
say anything very deep. At last says he—

"'Young woman! have you gotten a spare nightcap?'

"'Missis always keeps nightcaps for gentlemen as does not like to
unpack,' says she, rather quick.

"'Ay, but young woman, it's one of your nightcaps I want. Th' babby
seems to have taken a mind to yo; and may be in th' dark it might take
me for yo if I'd gotten your nightcap on.'

"The chambermaid smirked and went for a cap, but I laughed outright at th' oud bearded chap thinking he'd make hissel like a woman
just by putting on a woman's cap. Howe'er he'd not be laughed out
on't, so I held th' babby till he were in bed. Such a night as we had
on it! Babby began to scream o' th' oud fashion, and we took it turn
and turn about to sit up and rock it. My heart were very sore for the
little one, as it groped about wi' its mouth; but for a' that I could
scarce keep fra' smiling at th' thought o' us two oud chaps, th' one wi'
a woman's nightcap on, sitting on our hinder ends for half the night,
hushabying a babby as wouldn't be hushabied. Toward morning, poor
little wench! it fell asleep, fairly tired out wi' crying, but even in its
sleep it gave such pitiful sobs, quivering up fra' the very bottom of its
little heart, that once or twice I almost wished it lay on its mother's

† "Again," for against. "He that is not with me, he is ageyn me."—*Wickliffe's Version.* [WG]

breast, at peace for ever. Jennings fell asleep too; but I began for to reckon up our money. It were little enough we had left, our dinner the day afore had ta'en so much. I didn't know what our reckoning would be for that night lodging, and supper, and breakfast. Doing a sum always sent me asleep ever sin' I were a lad; so I fell sound in a short time, and were only wakened by chambermaid tapping at th' door, to say she'd dress the babby before her missis were up if we liked. But bless yo, we'd never thought o' undressing it the night afore, and now it were sleeping so sound, and we were so glad o' the peace and quietness, that we thought it were no good to waken it up to screech again.

"Well! (there's Mary asleep for a good listener!) I suppose you're getting weary of my tale, so I'll not be long over ending it. Th' reckoning left us very bare, and we thought we'd best walk home, for it were only sixty mile, they telled us, and not stop again for nought, save victuals. So we left Brummagem (which is as black a place as Manchester, without looking so like home), and walked a' that day, carrying babby turn and turn about: It were well fed by chambermaid afore we left, and th' day were fine, and folk began to have some knowledge o' th' proper way o' speaking, and we were more cheery at thought o' home (though mine, God knows, were lonesome enough). We stopped none for dinner, but at baggin-time* we getten a good meal at a public house, an' fed th' babby as well as we could, but that were but poorly. We got a crust too for it to suck—chambermaid put us up to that. That night, whether we were tired or whatten, I don't know, but it were dree† work, and th' poor little wench had slept out her sleep, and began th' cry as wore my heart out again. Says Jennings, says he,

"'We should na ha' set out so like gentlefolk a top o' the coach yesterday.'

"'Nay, lad! We should ha' had more to walk if we had na ridden, and I'm sure both you and I'se‡ weary o' tramping.'

"So he were quiet a bit. But he were one o' them as were sure to find out somewhat had been done amiss when there were no going back to undo it. So presently he coughs, as if he were going to speak, and I says to myself, 'At it again, my lad.' Says he,

"'I ax pardon, neighbour, but it strikes me it would ha' been better for my son if he had never begun to keep company wi' your daughter.'

"Well! that put me up, and my heart got very full, and but that I were carrying *her* babby, I think I should ha' struck him. At last I could hold in no longer, and says I,

---

* "Baggin-time," time of the evening meal. [WG]
† "Dree," long and tedious. Anglo-Saxon, "dreogan," to suffer, to endure. [WG]
‡ "I have not been, nor *is*, nor never schal."—*Wickliffe's "Apology*," p. 1. [WG]

" 'Better say at once it would ha' been better for God never to ha' made th' world, for then we'd never ha' been in it, to have had th' heavy hearts we have now.'

"Well! he said that were rank blasphemy; but I thought his way of casting up again th' events God had pleased to send, were worse blasphemy. Howe'er, I said nought more angry, for th' little babby's sake, as were th' child o' his dead son, as well as o' my dead daughter.

"Th' longest lane will have a turning, and that night came to an end at last; and we were footsore and tired enough, and to my mind the babby were getting weaker and weaker, and it wrung my heart to hear its little wail! I'd ha' given my right hand for one of yesterday's hearty cries. We were wanting our breakfasts, and so were it too, motherless babby! We could see no public-houses, so about six o'clock (only we thought it were later) we stopped at a cottage, where a woman were moving about near th' open door. Says I, 'Good woman, may we rest us a bit?' 'Come in,' says she, wiping a chair, as looked bright enough afore, wi' her apron. It were a cheery, clean room; and we were glad to sit down again, though I thought my legs would never bend at th' knees. In a minute she fell a noticing th' babby, and took it in her arms, and kissed it again and again. 'Missis,' says I 'we're not without money, and if yo'd give us somewhat for breakfast, we'd pay yo honest, and if yo would wash and dress that poor babby, and get some pobbies down its throat, for its well-nigh clemmed, I'd pray for you till my dying day.' So she said nought but gived me th' babby back, and afore you could say Jack Robinson, she'd a pan on th' fire, and bread and cheese on th' table. When she turned round, her face looked red, and her lips were tight pressed together. Well! we were right down glad on our breakfast, and God bless and reward that woman for her kindness that day! she fed th' poor babby as gently and softly, and spoke to it as tenderly as its own poor mother could ha' done. It seemed as if that stranger and it had known each other afore, may be in heaven, where folk's spirits come from, they say; th' babby looked up so lovingly in her eyes, and made little noises more like a dove than aught else. Then she undressed it (poor darling! it were time), touching it so softly; and washed it from head to foot; and as many on its clothes were dirty, and what bits o' things its mother had gotten ready for it had been sent by th' carrier fra' London, she put 'em aside; and wrapping little naked babby in her apron, she pulled out a key, as were fastened to a black ribbon, and hung down her breast, and unlocked a drawer in th' dresser. I were sorry to be prying, but I could na help seeing in that drawer some little child's clothes, all strewed wi' lavender, and lying by 'em a little whip an' a broken rattle. I began to have an insight into that woman's heart then. She took out a thing or two, and locked the drawer, and went on dressing babby. Just about then come her husband down, a great big fellow as didn't look half awake, though it were getting late; but he'd heard all as had been said down stairs, as were plain to be seen; but he were a gruff chap. We'd finished our breakfast, and Jennings were looking hard at th' woman as she were getting the babby to sleep wi' a sort of rocking way. At length says he, 'I ha' learnt th' way now; it's two jiggits and a shake, two jiggits and a shake. I can get that babby asleep now mysel.'

"The man had nodded cross enough to us, and had gone to th' door, and stood there whistling wi' his hands in his breeches-pockets, looking abroad. But at last he turns and says, quite sharp,

"'I say, missis, I'm to have no breakfast to-day, I 'spose.'

"So wi' that she kissed th' child, a long, soft kiss; and looking in my face to see if I could take her meaning, gave me th' babby without a word. I were loath to stir, but I saw it were better to go. So giving Jennings a sharp nudge (for he'd fallen asleep), I says, 'Missis, what's to pay?' pulling out my money wi' a jingle that she might na guess we were at all bare o' cash. So she looks at her husband, who said ne'er a word, but were listening with all his ears nevertheless; and when she saw he would na say, she said, hesitating, as if pulled two ways, by her fear o' him, 'Should you think sixpence over much?' It were so different to public-house reckoning, for we'd eaten a main deal afore the chap came down. So says I, 'And, missis, what should we gie you for the babby's bread and milk?' (I had it once in my mind to say 'and for a' your trouble with it,' but my heart would na let me say it, for I could read in her ways how it had been a work o' love). So says she, quite quick, and stealing a look at her husband's back, as looked all ear, if ever a back did, 'Oh, we could take nought for the little babby's food, if it had eaten twice as much, bless it.' Wi' that he looked at her; such a scowling look! She knew what he meant, and stepped softly across the floor to him, and put her hand on his arm. He seem'd as though he'd shake it off by a jerk on his elbow, but she said quite low, 'For poor little Johnnie's sake, Richard.' He did not move or speak again, and after looking in his face for a minute, she turned away, swallowing deep in her throat. She kissed th' sleeping babby as she passed, when I paid her. To quieten th' gruff husband, and stop him if he rated her, I could na help slipping another sixpence under th' loaf, and then we set off again. Last look I had o' that woman she were quietly wiping her eyes wi' the corner of her apron, as she went about her husband's breakfast. But I shall know her in heaven."

He stopped to think of that long-ago May morning, when he had carried his granddaughter under the distant hedge-rows and beneath the flowering sycamores.

"There's nought more to say, wench," said he to Margaret, as she begged him to go on. "That night we reached Manchester, and I'd found out that Jennings would be glad enough to give up babby to me, so I took her home at once, and a blessing she's been to me."

They were all silent for a few minutes; each following out the current of their thoughts. Then, almost simultaneously, their attention fell upon Mary. Sitting on her little stool, her head resting on her father's knee, and sleeping as soundly as any infant, her breath (still like an infant's) came and went as softly as a bird steals to her leafy nest. Her half-open mouth was as scarlet as the winter-berries, and contrasted finely with the clear paleness of her complexion, where the eloquent blood[8] flushed carnation at each motion. Her black eyelashes lay on the delicate cheek, which was still more shaded by the masses of her golden hair, that seemed to form a nest-like pillar for her as she lay. Her father in fond pride straightened one glossy curl, for an instant, as if to display its length and silkiness. The little action awoke her, and, like nine out of ten people in similar circumstances, she exclaimed, opening her eyes to their fullest extent,

"I'm not asleep. I've been awake all the time."

Even her father could not keep from smiling, and Job Legh and Margaret laughed outright.

"Come, wench," said Job, "don't look so gloppened* because thou'st fallen asleep while an oud chap like me was talking on oud times. It were like enough to send thee to sleep. Try if thou canst keep thine eyes open while I read thy father a bit on a poem as is written by a weaver like oursel. A rare chap I'll be bound is he who could weave verse like this."

So adjusting his spectacles on nose, cocking his chin, crossing his legs, and coughing to clear his voice, he read aloud a little poem of Samuel Bamford's[†] he had picked up somewhere.

> God help the poor, who, on this wintry morn,
>   Come forth from alleys dim and courts obscure.
> God help yon poor pale girl, who droops forlorn,
>   And meekly her affliction doth endure;
> God help her, outcast lamb; she trembling stands,
> All wan her lips, and frozen red her hands;
> Her sunken eyes are modestly down-cast,
> Her night-black hair streams on the fitful blast;
> Her bosom, passing fair, is half revealed,
> And oh! so cold, the snow lies there congealed;
> Her feet benumbed, her shoes all rent and worn,
> God help thee, outcast lamb, who standst forlorn!
>   God help the poor!
>
> God help the poor! An infant's feeble wail
>   Comes from yon narrow gateway, and behold!

---

8. From John Donne's "Of the Progress of the Soul: The Second Anniversary," line 244.
* "Gloppened," amazed, frightened. [WG]
† The fine-spirited author of "Passages in the Life of a Radical"—a man who illustrates his order, and shows what nobility may be in a cottage. [WG]

A female crouching there, so deathly pale,
　　Huddling her child, to screen it from the cold;
Her vesture scant, her bonnet crushed and torn;
　　A thin shawl doth her baby dear enfold:
And so she 'bides the ruthless gale of morn,
　　Which almost to her heart hath sent its cold,
And now she, sudden, darts a ravening look,
As one, with new hot bread, goes past the nook;
And, as the tempting load is onward borne,
She weeps. God help thee, helpless one, forlorn!
　　　　　　　　　　　　　　　God help the poor!

God help the poor! Behold yon famished lad,
　　No shoes, nor hose, his wounded feet protect;
With limping gait, and looks so dreamy sad,
　　He wanders onward, stopping to inspect
Each window, stored with articles of food.
　　He yearns but to enjoy one cheering meal;
Oh! to the hungry palate viands rude,
　　Would yield a zest the famished only feel!
He now devours a crust of mouldy bread;
　　With teeth and hands the precious boon is torn;
Unmindful of the storm that round his head
　　Impetuous sweeps. God help thee, child forlorn!
　　　　　　　　　　　　　　　God help the poor!

God help the poor! Another have I found—
　　A bowed and venerable man is he;
His slouched hat with faded crape is bound;
　　His coat is grey, and threadbare too, I see.
"The rude winds" seem "to mock his hoary hair;"
His shirtless bosom to the blast is bare.
Anon he turns and casts a wistful eye,
　　And with scant napkin wipes the blinding spray,
And looks around, as if he fain would spy
　　Friends he had feasted in his better day:
Ah! some are dead; and some have long forborne
To know the poor; and he is left forlorn!
　　　　　　　　　　　　　　　God help the poor!

God help the poor, who in lone valleys dwell,
　　Or by far hills, where whin and heather grow;
Theirs is a story sad indeed to tell;
　　Yet little cares the world, and less 'twould know
　　About the toil and want men undergo.
The wearying loom doth call them up at morn;
　　They work till worn-out nature sinks to sleep;
　　They taste, but are not fed. The snow drifts deep

Around the fireless cot, and blocks the door;
    The night-storm howls a dirge across the moor;
And shall they perish thus—oppressed and lorn?
Shall toil and famine, hopeless, still be borne?
    No! God will yet arise and help the poor![9]

"Amen!" said Barton, solemnly and sorrowfully. "Mary! wench, couldst thou copy me them lines, dost think?—that's to say, if Job there has no objection."

"Not I. More they're heard and read and the better, say I."

So Mary took the paper. And the next day, on a blank half sheet of a valentine, all bordered with hearts and darts—a valentine she had once suspected to come from Jem Wilson—she copied Bamford's beautiful little poem.

Chapter X.

"My heart, once soft as woman's tear, is gnarled
    With gloating on the ills I cannot cure."
                                    ELLIOTT.[1]

"Then guard and shield her innocence,
    Let her not fall like me;
'Twere better, oh! a thousand times,
    She in her grave should be."
                                "THE OUTCAST."

Despair settled down like a heavy cloud; and now and then, through the dead calm of sufferings, came pipings of stormy winds, foretelling the end of these dark prognostics. In times of sorrowful or fierce endurance, we are often soothed by the mere repetition of old proverbs which tell the experience of our forefathers; but now, "it's a long lane that has no turning," "the weariest day draws to an end," &c., seemed false and vain sayings, so long and so weary was the pressure of the terrible times. Deeper and deeper still sank the poor; it showed how much lingering suffering it takes to kill men, that so few (in comparison) died during those times. But remember! we only miss those who do men's work in their humble sphere; the aged, the feeble, the children, when they die, are hardly noted by the world; and yet to many hearts, their deaths make a blank which long years will never fill up. Remember, too, that though it may take much suffering to kill the able-bodied and effective members of society, it does *not* take much to reduce them to worn, listless, diseased creatures, who thenceforward crawl through life with moody hearts and pain-stricken bodies.

9. Gaskell's friend and working-class poet, Samuel Bamford (1788–1872) wrote two memoirs, most notably *Passages in the Life of a Radical* (1844). Bamford, however, was not a Chartist.
1. "The Village Patriarch" (1829) Bk. III. Sect. II. 11. 31–22.

The people had thought the poverty of the preceding years hard to bear, and had found its yoke heavy; but this year added sorely to its weight. Former times had chastised them with whips, but this chastised them with scorpions.[2]

Of course, Barton had his share of mere bodily sufferings. Before he had gone up to London on his vain errand, he had been working short time. But in the hopes of speedy redress by means of the interference of Parliament, he had thrown up his place; and now, when he asked leave to resume his work he was told they were diminishing their number of hands every week, and he was made aware, by the remarks of fellow-workmen, that a Chartist delegate, and a leading member of a Trades' Union, was not likely to be favoured in his search after employment. Still he tried to keep up a brave heart concerning himself. He knew he could bear hunger; for that power of endurance had been called forth when he was a little child, and had seen his mother hide her daily morsel to share it among her children, and when he, being the eldest, had told the noble lie, that "he was not hungry, could not eat a bit more," in order to imitate his mother's bravery, and still the sharp wail of the younger infants. Mary, too, was secure of two meals a day at Miss Simmonds'; though, by the way, the dressmaker too, feeling the effect of bad times, had left off giving tea to her apprentices, setting them the example of long abstinence by putting off her own meal till work was done for the night, however late that might be.

But the rent! It was half-a-crown a week—nearly all Mary's earnings—and much less room might do for them, only two.—(Now came the time to be thankful that the early dead were saved from the evil to come.)—The agricultural labourer generally has strong local attachments; but they are far less common, almost obliterated, among the inhabitants of a town. Still there are exceptions, and Barton formed one. He had removed to his present house just after the last bad times, when little Tom had sickened and died. He had then thought the bustle of a removal would give his poor stunned wife something to do, and he had taken more interest in the details of the proceeding than he otherwise would have done, in the hope of calling her forth to action again. So he seemed to know every brass-headed nail driven up for her convenience. Only one had been displaced. It was Esther's bonnet nail, which in his deep revengeful anger against her, after his wife's death, he had torn out of the wall, and cast into the street. It would be hard work to leave the house, which yet seemed hallowed by his wife's presence in the happy days of old. But he was a law unto himself, though sometimes a bad, fierce law; and he resolved to give the rent-collector notice, and look out for

2. I Kings 12:11.

a cheaper abode, and tell Mary they must flit. Poor Mary! she loved the house, too. It was wrenching up her natural feelings of home, for it would be long before the fibres of her heart would gather themselves about another place.

This trial was spared. The collector (of himself), on the very Monday, when Barton planned to give him notice of his intention to leave, lowered the rent threepence a week, just enough to make Barton compromise and agree to stay on a little longer.

But by degrees the house was stripped of all its little ornaments. Some were broken; and the odd twopences and threepences, wanted to pay for their repairs, were required for the far sterner necessity of food. And by-and-by Mary began to part with other superfluities at the pawn-shop. The smart tea-tray, and tea-caddy, long and carefully kept, went for bread for her father. He did not ask for it, or complain, but she saw hunger in his shrunk, fierce, animal look. Then the blankets went, for it was summer time, and they could spare them; and their sale made a fund, which Mary fancied would last till better times came. But it was soon all gone; and then she looked around the room to crib it of its few remaining ornaments. To all these proceedings her father said never a word. If he fasted, or feasted (after the sale of some article) on an unusual meal of bread and cheese, he took all with a sullen indifference, which depressed Mary's heart. She often wished he would apply for relief from the Guardians' relieving office; often wondered the Trades' Union did nothing for him. Once, when she asked him as he sat, grimed, unshaven, and gaunt, after a day's fasting, over the fire, why he did not get relief from the town, he turned round, with grim wrath, and said, "I don't want money, child! D—n their charity and their money! I want work, and it is my right. I want work."

He would bear it all, he said to himself. And he did bear it, but not meekly; that was too much to expect. Real meekness of character is called out by experience of kindness. And few had been kind to him. Yet through it all, with stern determination he refused the assistance his Trades' Union would have given him. It had not much to give, but, with worldly wisdom, thought it better to propitiate an active, useful member, than to help those who were more unenergetic, though they had large families to provide for. Not so thought John Barton. With him, need was right.

"Give it to Tom Darbyshire," he said. "He's more claim on it than me, for he's more need of it, with his seven children."

Now Tom Darbyshire was, in his listless, grumbling way, a back-biting enemy of John Barton's. And he knew it; but he was not to be influenced by that in a matter like this.

Mary went early to her work; but her cheery laugh over it was now missed by the other girls. Her mind wandered over the present distress, and then settled, as she stitched, on the visions of the future, where yet her thoughts dwelt more on the circumstances of ease, and the pomps and vanities awaiting her, than on the lover with whom she was to share them. Still she was not insensible to the pride of having attracted one so far above herself in station; not insensible to the secret pleasure of knowing that he, whom so many admired, had often said he would give any thing for one of her sweet smiles. Her love for him was a bubble, blown out of vanity; but it looked very real and very bright. Sally Leadbitter, meanwhile, keenly observed the signs of the times; she found out that Mary had begun to affix a stern value to money as the "Purchaser of Life," and many girls had been dazzled and lured by gold, even without the betraying love which she believed to exist in Mary's heart. So she urged young Mr. Carson, by representations of the want she was sure surrounded Mary, to bring matters more to a point. But he had a kind of instinctive dread of hurting Mary's pride of spirit, and durst not hint his knowledge in any way of the distress that many must be enduring. He felt that for the present he must still be content with stolen meetings and summer evening strolls, and the delight of pouring sweet honeyed words into her ear, while she listened with a blush and a smile that made her look radiant with beauty. No; he would be cautious in order to be certain; for Mary, one way or another, he must make his. He had no doubt of the effect of his own personal charms in the long run; for he knew he was handsome, and believed himself fascinating.

If he had known what Mary's home was, he would not have been so much convinced of his increasing influence over her, by her being more and more ready to linger with him in the sweet summer air. For when she returned for the night her father was often out, and the house wanted the cheerful look it had had in the days when money was never wanted to purchase soap and brushes, black-lead and pipe-clay. It was dingy and comfortless; for, of course, there was not even the dumb familiar home-friend, a fire. And Margaret, too, was now very often from home, singing at some of those grand places. And Alice; oh, Mary wished she had never left her cellar to go and live at Ancoats with her sister-in-law. For in that matter Mary felt very guilty; she had put off and put off going to see the widow, after George Wilson's death, from dread of meeting Jem, or giving him reason to think she wished to be as intimate with him as formerly; and now she was so much ashamed of her delay that she was likely never to go at all.

If her father was at home it was no better; indeed, it was worse. He seldom spoke, less than ever; and often when he did speak, they were sharp angry words, such as he had never given her formerly. Her temper was high, too, and her answers not overmild; and once in his passion he had even beaten her. If Sally Leadbitter or Mr. Carson had been at hand at that moment, Mary would have been ready to leave home for ever. She sat alone, after her father had flung out of the house, bitterly thinking on the days that were gone; angry with her own hastiness, and believing that her father did not love her; striving to heap up one painful thought on another. Who cared for her? Mr. Carson might, but in this grief that seemed no comfort. Mother dead! Father so often angry, so lately cruel (for it was a hard blow, and blistered and reddened Mary's soft white skin with pain): and then her heart turned round, and she remembered with self-reproach how provokingly she had looked and spoken, and how much her father had to bear; and oh, what a kind and loving parent he had been, till these days of trial. The remembrance of one little instance of his fatherly love thronged after another into her mind, and she began to wonder how she could have behaved to him as she had done.

Then he came home; and but for very shame she would have confessed her penitence in words. But she looked sullen, from her effort to keep down emotion; and for some time her father did not know how to begin to speak. At length he gulped down pride, and said:

"Mary, I'm not above saying I'm very sorry I beat thee. Thou wert a bit aggravating, and I'm not the man I was. But it were wrong, and I'll try never to lay hands on thee again."

So he held out his arms, and in many tears she told him her repentance for her fault. He never struck her again.

Still, he often was angry. But that was almost better than being silent. Then he sat near the fireplace (from habit), smoking, or chewing opium. Oh, how Mary loathed that smell! And in the dusk, just before it merged into the short summer night, she had learned to look with dread towards the window, which now her father would have kept uncurtained; for there were not seldom seen sights which haunted her in her dreams. Strange faces of pale men, with dark glaring eyes, peered into the inner darkness, and seemed desirous to ascertain if her father was at home. Or, a hand and arm (the body hidden) was put within the door, and beckoned him away. He always went. And once or twice, when Mary was in bed, she heard men's voices below, in earnest, whispered talk.

They were all desperate members of Trades' Unions, ready for any thing; made ready by want.

While all this change for gloom yet struck fresh and heavy on Mary's heart, her father startled her out of a reverie one evening, by asking her when she had been to see Jane Wilson. From his manner of speaking, she was made aware that he had been; but at the time of his visit he had never mentioned any thing about it. Now, however, he gruffly told her to go next day without fail, and added some abuse of her for not having been before. The little outward impulse of her father's speech gave Mary the push which she in this instance required; and accordingly, timing her visit so as to avoid Jem's hours at home, she went the following afternoon to Ancoats.

The outside of the well-known house struck her as different; for the door was closed, instead of open, as it once had always stood. The window-plants, George Wilson's pride and especial care, looked withering and drooping. They had been without water for a long time, and now, when the widow had reproached herself severely for neglect, in her ignorant anxiety she gave them too much. On opening the door, Alice was seen, not stirring about in her habitual way, but knitting by the fire-side. The room felt hot, although the fire burnt gray and dim, under the bright rays of the afternoon sun. Mrs. Wilson was "siding"* the dinner things, and talking all the time, in a kind of whining, shouting voice, which Mary did not at first understand. She understood, at once, however, that her absence had been noted, and talked over; she saw a con-strained look on Mrs. Wilson's sorrow-stricken face, which told her a scolding was to come.

"Dear! Mary, is that you?" she began. "Why, who would ha' dreamt of seeing you! We thought you'd clean forgotten us; and Jem has often wondered if he should know you, if he met you in the street."

Now, poor Jane Wilson had been sorely tried; and at present her trials had had no outward effect, but that of increased acerbity of temper. She wished to show Mary how much she was offended, and meant to strengthen her cause, by putting some of her own sharp speeches into Jem's mouth.

Mary felt guilty, and had no good reason to give as an apology; so for a minute she stood silent, looking very much ashamed, and then turned to speak to aunt Alice, who, in her surprised, hearty greeting to Mary, had dropped her ball of worsted, and was busy, trying to set the thread to rights, before the kitten had entangled it past redemp-tion, once round every chair, and twice round the table.

"You mun speak louder than that, if you mean her to hear; she's become as deaf as a post this last few weeks. I'd ha' told you, if I'd remembered how long it were sin' you'd seen her."

"Yes, my dear, I'm getting very hard o' hearing of late," said Alice, catching the state of the case, with her quick glancing eyes. "I sup-pose it's the beginning of th' end."

"Don't talk o' that way," screamed her sister-in-law. "We've had enow of ends and deaths without forecasting more." She covered her face with her apron, and sat down to cry.

"He was such a good husband," said she, in a less excited tone, to Mary, as she looked up with tear-streaming eyes from behind her

* To "side," to put aside, or in order. [WG]

apron. "No one can tell what I've lost in him, for no one knew his worth like me."

Mary's listening sympathy softened her, and she went on to unburden her heavy-laden heart.

"Eh, dear, dear! No one knows what I've lost. When my poor boys went, I thought the Almighty had crushed me to th' ground, but I never thought o' losing George; I did na' think I could ha' borne to ha' lived without him. And yet I'm here, and he's——" A fresh burst of crying interrupted her speech.

"Mary,"—beginning to speak again,—"did you ever hear what a poor creature I were when he married me? And he such a handsome fellow! Jem's nothing to what his father were at his age."

Yes! Mary had heard, and so she said. But the poor woman's thoughts had gone back to those days, and her little recollections came out, with many interruptions of sighs, and tears, and shakes of the head.

"There were nought about me for him to choose me. I were just well enough afore that accident, but at after I were downright plain. And there was Bessy Witter as would ha' given her eyes for him; she as is Mrs. Carson now, for she were a handsome lass, although I never could see her beauty then; and Carson warn't so much above her, as they're both above us all now."

Mary went very red, and wished she could help doing so, and wished also that Mrs. Wilson would tell her more about the father and mother of her lover; but she durst not ask, and Mrs. Wilson's thoughts soon returned to her husband, and their early married days.

"If you'll believe me, Mary, there never was such a born goose at house-keeping as I were; and yet he married me! I had been in a factory sin' five years old a'most, and I knew nought about cleaning, or cooking, let alone washing and such like work. The day after we were married, he went to his work at after breakfast, and says he, 'Jenny, we'll ha' th' cold beef, and potatoes, and that's a dinner for a prince.' I were anxious to make him comfortable, God knows how anxious. And yet I'd no notion how to cook a potato. I know'd they were boiled, and know'd their skins were taken off, and that were all. So I tidied my house in a rough kind o' way, then I looked at that very clock up yonder," pointing at one that hung against the wall, "and I seed it were nine o'clock, so, thinks I, th' potatoes shall be well boiled at any rate, and I gets 'em on th' fire in a jiffy (that's to say, as soon as I could peel 'em, which were a tough job at first), and then I fell to unpacking my boxes! and at twenty minutes past twelve, he comes home, and I had the beef ready on th' table, and I went to take the potatoes out o' th' pot; but oh! Mary, th' water had boiled away, and they were all a nasty brown mess, as smelt through all the house. He said nought, and were very gentle; but, oh, Mary, I cried so that afternoon. I shall

ne'er forget it; no, never. I made many a blunder at after, but none
that fretted me like that."

"Father does not like girls to work in factories," said Mary.

"No, I know he does not; and reason good. They oughtn't to go at
after they're married, that I'm very clear about. I could reckon up"
(counting with her finger), "ay, nine men, I know, as has been driven
to th' public-house by having wives as worked in factories; good
folk, too, as thought there was no harm in putting their little ones
out at nurse, and letting their house go all dirty, and their fires all
out; and that was a place as was tempting for a husband to stay in,
was it? He soon finds out gin-shops, where all is clean and bright,
and where th' fire blazes cheerily, and gives a man a welcome as it
were."

Alice, who was standing near for the convenience of hearing, had
caught much of this speech, and it was evident the subject had previously been discussed by the women, for she chimed in.

"I wish our Jem could speak a word to th' Queen, about factory
work for married women. Eh! but he comes it strong, when once yo
get him to speak about it. Wife o' his'n will never work away fra'
home."

"I say it's Prince Albert[3] as ought to be asked how he'd like his missis to be from home when he comes in, tired and worn, and wanting
some one to cheer him; and maybe, her to come in by-and-by, just as
tired and down in th' mouth; and how he'd like for her never to be at
home to see to th' cleaning of his house, or to keep a bright fire in his
grate. Let alone his meals being all hugger-mugger and comfortless.
I'd be bound, prince as he is, if his missis served him so, he'd be off
to a gin-palace, or summut o' that kind. So why can't he make a law
again poor folks' wives working in factories?"

Mary ventured to say that she thought the Queen and Prince
Albert could not make laws, but the answer was,

"Pooh! don't tell me it's not the Queen as makes laws; and isn't she
bound to obey Prince Albert? And if he said they mustn't, why she'd
say they mustn't, and then all folk would say, oh, no, we never shall
do any such thing no more."

"Jem's getten on rarely," said Alice, who had not heard her sister's
last burst of eloquence, and whose thoughts were still running on her
nephew, and his various talents. "He's found out summut about a
crank or tank, I forget rightly which it is, but th' master's made him
foreman, and he all the while turning off hands; but he said he could
na' part wi' Jem, nohow. He's good wage now; I tell him he'll be thinking of marrying soon, and he deserves a right down good wife, that
he does."

3. Prince Albert married Queen Victoria on February 10, 1840.

Mary went very red, and looked annoyed, although there was a secret spring of joy deep down in her heart, at hearing Jem so spoken of. But his mother only saw the annoyed look, and was piqued accordingly. She was not over and above desirous that her son should marry. His presence in the house seemed a relic of happier times, and she had some little jealousy of his future wife, whoever she might be. Still she could not bear any one not to feel gratified and flattered by Jem's preference, and full well she knew how above all others he preferred Mary. Now she had never thought Mary good enough for Jem, and her late neglect in coming to see her still rankled a little in her breast. So she determined to invent a little, in order to do away with any idea Mary might have that Jem would choose her for "his right down good wife," as aunt Alice called it.

"Ay, he'll be for taking a wife soon," and then, in a lower voice, as if confidentially, but really to prevent any contradiction or explanation from her simple sister-in-law, she added,

"It'll not be long afore Molly Gibson[4] (that's her at th' provision shop round the corner) will hear a secret as will not displease her, I'm thinking. She's been casting sheep's eyes at our Jem this many a day, but he thought her father would not give her to a common working man; but now he's good as her, every bit. I thought once he'd a fancy for thee, Mary, but I donnot think yo'd ever ha' suited, so it's best as it is."

By an effort Mary managed to keep down her vexation, and to say, "She hoped he'd be happy with Molly Gibson. She was very handsome, for certain."

"Ay, and a notable body, too. I'll just step up-stairs and show you the patchwork quilt she gave me but last Saturday."

Mary was glad she was going out of the room. Her words irritated her; perhaps not the less because she did not fully believe them. Besides, she wanted to speak to Alice, and Mrs. Wilson seemed to think that she, as the widow, ought to absorb all the attention.

"Dear Alice," began Mary, "I'm so grieved to find you so deaf; it must have come on very rapid."

"Yes, dear, it's a trial; I'll not deny it. Pray God give me strength to find out its teaching. I felt it sore one fine day when I thought I'd go gather some meadow-sweet to make tea for Jane's cough; and the fields seemed so dree and still; and at first I could na' make out what was wanting; and then it struck me it were th' song o' the birds, and that I never should hear their sweet music no more, and I could na' help crying a bit. But I've much to be thankful for. I think I'm a comfort to Jane, if I'm only some one to scold now and then; poor body!

---

4. The name of the heroine of Gaskell's last novel *Wives and Daughters* (1866).

It takes off her thoughts from her sore losses when she can scold a bit. If my eyes are left I can do well enough; I can guess at what folk are saying."

The splendid red and yellow patch quilt now made its appearance, and Jane Wilson would not be satisfied unless Mary praised it all over, border, centre, and ground-work, right side and wrong; and Mary did her duty, saying all the more, because she could not work herself up to any very hearty admiration of her rival's present. She made haste, however, with her commendations, in order to avoid encountering Jem. As soon as she was fairly away from the house and street, she slackened her pace, and began to think. Did Jem really care for Molly Gibson? Well, if he did, let him. People seemed all to think he was much too good for her (Mary's own self). Perhaps some one else, far more handsome, and far more grand, would show him one day that she was good enough to be Mrs. Henry Carson. So temper, or what Mary called "spirit," led her to encourage Mr. Carson more than ever she had done before.

Some weeks after this there was a meeting of the Trades' Union to which John Barton belonged. The morning of the day on which it was to take place he had lain late in bed, for what was the use of getting up? He had hesitated between the purchase of meal or opium, and had chosen the latter, for its use had become a necessity with him. He wanted it to relieve him from the terrible depression its absence occasioned. A large lump seemed only to bring him into a natural state, or what had been his natural state formerly. Eight o'clock was the hour fixed for the meeting; and at it were read letters, filled with details of woe, from all parts of the country. Fierce, heavy gloom brooded over the assembly; and fiercely and heavily did the men separate, towards eleven o'clock, some irritated by the opposition of others to their desperate plans.

It was not a night to cheer them, as they quitted the glare of the gas-lighted room, and came out into the street. Unceasing, soaking rain was falling; the very lamps seemed obscured by the damp upon the glass, and their light reached but to a little distance from the posts. The streets were cleared of passers-by; not a creature seemed stirring, except here and there a drenched policeman in his oil-skin cape. Barton wished the others good night, and set off home. He had gone through a street or two, when he heard a step behind him; but he did not care to stop and see who it was. A little further, and the person quickened step, and touched his arm very lightly. He turned, and saw, even by the darkness visible[5] of that badly-lighted street, that the woman who stood by him was of no doubtful profession. It was told by her faded finery, all unfit to meet the pelting of that pitiless

5. From John Milton's (1608–1674) *Paradise Lost* (1667), Bk. I, line 63.

storm; the gauze bonnet, once pink, now dirty white, the muslin gown, all draggled, and soaking wet up to the very knees; the gay-coloured barège shawl, closely wrapped round the form, which yet shivered and shook, as the woman whispered: "I want to speak to you."

He swore an oath, and bade her begone.

"I really do. Don't send me away. I'm so out of breath, I cannot say what I would all at once." She put her hand to her side, and caught her breath with evident pain.

"I tell thee I'm not the man for thee," adding an opprobrious name. "Stay," said he, as a thought suggested by her voice flashed across him. He griped her arm—the arm he had just before shaken off, and dragged her, faintly resisting, to the nearest lamp-post. He pushed the bonnet back, and roughly held the face she would fain have averted, to the light, and in her large, unnaturally bright grey eyes, her lovely mouth, half open, as if imploring the forbearance she could not ask for in words, he saw at once the long-lost Esther; she who had caused his wife's death. Much was like the gay creature of former years; but the glaring paint, the sharp features, the changed expression of the whole! But most of all, he loathed the dress; and yet the poor thing, out of her little choice of attire, had put on the plainest she had, to come on that night's errand.

"So it's thee, is it? It's thee!" exclaimed John, as he ground his teeth, and shook her with passion. "I've looked for thee long at corners o' streets, and such like places. I knew I should find thee at last. Thee'll maybe bethink thee o' some words I spoke, which put thee up at th' time; summut about street-walkers; but oh no! thou art none o' them naughts; no one thinks thou art, who sees thy fine draggle-tailed dress, and thy pretty pink cheeks!" stopping for very want of breath.

"Oh, mercy! John, mercy! listen to me for Mary's sake!"

She meant his daughter, but the name only fell on his ear as belonging to his wife; and it was adding fuel to the fire. In vain did her face grow deadly pale around the vivid circle of paint, in vain did she gasp for mercy,—he burst forth again.

"And thou names that name to me! and thou thinks the thought of her will bring thee mercy! Dost thou know it was thee who killed her, as sure as ever Cain killed Abel.[6] She'd loved thee as her own, and she trusted thee as her own, and when thou wert gone she never held head up again, but died in less than a three week; and at her judgment-day she'll rise, and point to thee as her murderer; or if she don't, I will."

He flung her, trembling, sinking, fainting, from him, and strode away. She fell with a feeble scream against the lamppost, and lay

6. Genesis 4:8.

there in her weakness, unable to rise. A policeman came up in time to see the close of these occurrences, and concluding from Esther's unsteady, reeling fall, that she was tipsy, he took her in her half-unconscious state to the lock-ups for the night. The superintendent of that abode of vice and misery was roused from his dozing watch through the dark hours, by half-delirious wails and moanings, which he reported as arising from intoxication. If he had listened, he would have heard these words, repeated in various forms, but always in the same anxious, muttering way:

"He would not listen to me; what can I do? He would not listen to me, and I wanted to warn him! Oh, what shall I do to save Mary's child! What shall I do? How can I keep her from being such a one as I am; such a wretched, loathsome creature! She was listening just as I listened, and loving just as I loved, and the end will be just like my end. How shall I save her? She won't hearken to warning, or heed it more than I did; and who loves her well enough to watch over her as she should be watched? God keep her from harm! And yet I won't pray for her; sinner that I am! Can my prayers be heard? No! they'll only do harm. How shall I save her? He would not listen to me."

So the night wore away. The next morning she was taken up to the New Bailey.[7] It was a clear case of disorderly vagrancy, and she was committed to prison for a month. How much might happen in that time!

Chapter XI.

> "Oh Mary, canst thou wreck his peace,
>   Wha for thy sake wad gladly die?
> Or canst thou break that heart of his,
>   Whase only fault is loving thee?"
>   BURNS.[8]

> "I can like of the wealth, I must confess,
> Yet more I prize the man though moneyless;
> I am not of their humour yet that can
> For title or estate affect a man;
> Or of myself one body deign to make
> With him I loath, for his possessions' sake."
>   WITHER'S 'FIDELIA.'

Barton returned home after his encounter with Esther, uneasy and dissatisfied. He had said no more than he had been planning to say

---

7. The New Bailey prison was built in 1790.
8. From Robert Burns's (1759–1796) "Mary Morison." The second epigraph is from George Wither's (1588–1667) "An Elegiacal Epistle of Fidelia to Her Inconstant Friend" (1615), lines 1037–42.

for years, in case she was ever thrown in his way, in the character in which he felt certain he should meet her. He believed she deserved it all, and yet he now wished he had not said it. Her look, as she asked for mercy, haunted him through his broken and disordered sleep; her form, as he last saw her, lying prostrate in helplessness, would not be banished from his dreams. He sat up in bed to try and dispel the vision. Now, too late, his conscience smote him with harshness. It would have been all very well, he thought, to have said what he did, if he had added some kind words, at last. He wondered if his dead wife was conscious of that night's occurrence; and he hoped not, for with her love for Esther he believed it would embitter heaven to have seen her so degraded and repulsed. For he now recalled her humility, her tacit acknowledgment of her lost character; and he began to marvel if there was power in the religion he had often heard of, to turn her from her ways. He felt that no earthly power that he knew of could do it, but there glimmered on his darkness the idea that religion might save her. Still, where to find her again? In the wilderness of a large town, where to meet with an individual of so little value or note to any?

And evening after evening he paced the same streets in which he had heard those footsteps following him, peering under every fantastic, discreditable bonnet, in the hopes of once more meeting Esther, and addressing her in a far different manner from what he had done before. But he returned, night after night, disappointed in his search, and at last gave it up in despair, and tried to recall his angry feelings towards her, in order to find relief from his present self-reproach.

He often looked at Mary, and wished she were not so like her aunt, for the very bodily likeness seemed to suggest the possibility of a similar likeness in their fate; and then this idea enraged his irritable mind, and he became suspicious and anxious about Mary's conduct. Now hitherto she had been so remarkably free from all control, and almost from all inquiry concerning her actions, that she did not brook this change in her father's behaviour very well. Just when she was yielding more than ever to Mr. Carson's desire of frequent meetings, it was hard to be so questioned concerning her hours of leaving off work, whether she had come straight home, &c. She could not tell lies; though she could conceal much if she were not questioned. So she took refuge in obstinate silence, alleging as a reason for it her indignation at being so cross-examined. This did not add to the good feeling between father and daughter, and yet they dearly loved each other; and in the minds of each, one principal reason for maintaining such behaviour as displeased the other, was the believing that this conduct would insure that person's happiness.

Her father now began to wish Mary was married. Then this terrible superstitious fear suggested by her likeness to Esther would be done away with. He felt that he could not resume the reins he had once slackened. But with a husband it would be different. If Jem Wilson would but marry her! With his character for steadiness and talent! But he was afraid Mary had slighted him, he came so seldom now to the house. He would ask her.

"Mary, what's come o'er thee and Jem Wilson? Yo were great friends at one time."

"Oh, folk say he is going to be married to Molly Gibson, and of course courting takes up a deal o' time," answered Mary as indifferently as she could.

"Thou'st played thy cards badly, then," replied her father, in a surly tone. "At one time he were desperate fond o' thee, or I'm much mistaken. Much fonder of thee than thou deservedst."

"That's as people think," said Mary, pertly, for she remembered that the very morning before she had met Mr. Carson, who had sighed, and swore, and protested all manner of tender vows that she was the loveliest, sweetest, best, &c. And when she had seen him afterwards riding with one of his beautiful sisters, had he not evidently pointed her out as in some way or other an object worthy of attention and interest, and then lingered behind his sister's horse for a moment to kiss his hand repeatedly. So, as for Jem Wilson, she could whistle him down the wind.

But her father was not in the mood to put up with pertness, and he upbraided her with the loss of Jem Wilson till she had to bite her lips till the blood came, in order to keep down the angry words that would rise in her heart. At last her father left the house, and then she might give way to her passionate tears.

It so happened that Jem, after much anxious thought, had determined that day to "put his fortune to the touch, to win or lose all."[9] He was in a condition to maintain a wife in comfort. It was true his mother and aunt must form part of the household; but such is not an uncommon case among the poor, and if there were the advantages of previous friendship between the parties, it was not, he thought, an obstacle to matrimony. Both mother and aunt, he believed, would welcome Mary. And oh! what a certainty of happiness the idea of that welcome implied.

He had been absent and abstracted all day long with the thought of the coming event of the evening. He almost smiled at himself for his care in washing and dressing in preparation for his visit to Mary; as if one waistcoat or another could decide his fate in so passionately momentous a thing. He believed he only delayed before his little looking-glass for cowardice, for absolute fear of a girl. He

9. From James Graham's (1612–1650) "My Dear and Only Love."

would try not to think so much about the affair, and he thought the more.

Poor Jem! it is not an auspicious moment for thee!

"Come in," said Mary, as some one knocked at the door, while she sat sadly at her sewing, trying to earn a few pence by working over hours at some mourning.

Jem entered, looking more awkward and abashed than he had ever done before. Yet here was Mary all alone, just as he had hoped to find her. She did not ask him to take a chair, but after standing a minute or two he sat down near her.

"Is your father at home, Mary?" said he, by way of making an open-ing, for she seemed determined to keep silence, and went on stitch-ing away.

"No, he's gone to his Union, I suppose." Another silence. It was no use waiting, thought Jem. The subject would never be led to by any talk he could think of in his anxious, fluttered state. He had better begin at once.

"Mary!" said he, and the unusual tone of his voice made her look up for an instant, but in that time she understood from his counte-nance what was coming, and her heart beat so suddenly and violently she could hardly sit still. Yet one thing she was sure of; nothing he could say should make her have him. She would show them all *who* would be glad to have her. She was not yet calm after her father's irri-tating speeches. Yet her eyes fell veiled before that passionate look fixed upon her.

"Dear Mary! (for how dear you are, I cannot rightly tell you in words). It's no new story I'm going to speak about. You must ha' seen and known it long; for since we were boy and girl, I ha' loved you above father and mother and all; and all I've thought on by day and dreamt on by night, has been something in which you've had a share. I'd no way of keeping you for long, and I scorned to try and tie you down; and I lived in terror lest some one else should take you to him-self. But now, Mary, I'm foreman in th' works, and, dear Mary! listen," as she, in her unbearable agitation, stood up and turned away from him. He rose too, and came nearer, trying to take hold of her hand; but this she would not allow. She was bracing herself up to refuse him, for once and for all.

"And now, Mary, I've a home to offer you, and a heart as true as ever man had to love you and cherish you; we shall never be rich folk. I dare say; but if a loving heart and a strong right arm can shield you from sorrow, or from want, mine shall do it. I cannot speak as I would like; my love won't let itself be put in words. But oh! darling, say you'll believe me, and that you'll be mine."

She could not speak at once; her words would not come.

"Mary, they say silence gives consent; is it so?" he whispered.

Now or never the effort must be made.

"No! it does not with me." Her voice was calm, although she trembled from head to foot. "I will always be your friend, Jem, but I can never be your wife."

"Not my wife," said he, mournfully. "Oh, Mary, think awhile! you cannot be my friend if you will not be my wife. At least I can never be content to be only your friend. Do think awhile! If you say No, you will make me hopeless, desperate. It's no love of yesterday. It has made the very groundwork of all that people call good in me. I don't know what I shall be if you won't have me. And, Mary! think how glad your father would be! It may sound vain, but he's told me more than once how much he should like to see us two married!"

Jem intended this for a powerful argument, but in Mary's present mood it told against him more than anything; for it suggested the false and foolish idea, that her father, in his evident anxiety to promote her marriage with Jem, had been speaking to him on the subject with some degree of solicitation.

"I tell you, Jem, it cannot be. Once for all, I will never marry you."

"And is this the end of all my hopes and fears? the end of my life, I may say, for it is the end of all worth living for!" His agitation rose and carried him into passion. "Mary, you'll hear, maybe, of me as a drunkard, and may be as a thief, and may be as a murderer. Remember! when all are speaking ill of me, you will have no right to blame me, for it's your cruelty that will have made me what I feel I shall become. You won't even say you'll try and like me; will you, Mary!" said he, suddenly changing his tone from threatening despair to fond, passionate entreaty, as he took her hand and held it forcibly between both of his, while he tried to catch a glimpse of her averted face. She was silent, but it was from deep and violent emotion. He could not bear to wait; he would not hope, to be dashed away again; he rather in his bitterness of heart chose the certainty of despair, and before she could resolve what to answer, he flung away her hand and rushed out of the house.

"Jem! Jem!" cried she, with faint and choking voice. It was too late; he left street after street behind him with his almost winged speed, as he sought the fields, where he might give way unobserved to all the deep despair he felt.

It was scarcely ten minutes since he had entered the house, and found Mary at comparative peace, and now she lay half across the dresser, her head hidden in her hands, and every part of her body shaking with the violence of her sobs. She could not have told at first (if you had asked her, and she could have commanded voice enough to answer) why she was in such agonised grief. It was too sudden for her to analyse, or think upon it. She only felt, that by her own doing her life would be hereafter blank and dreary. By-and-by her sorrow exhausted her body by its power, and she seemed to have no strength left for crying. She sat down; and now thoughts crowded on her mind. One little hour ago, and all was still unsaid, and she had her fate in her own power. And yet, how long ago had she determined to say pretty much what she did, if the occasion ever offered.

It was as if two people were arguing the matter; that mournful, desponding communion between her former self, and her present self. Herself, a day, an hour ago; and herself now. For we have every one of us felt how a very few minutes of the months and years called life, will sometimes suffice to place all time past and future in an entirely new light; will make us see the vanity or the criminality of the by-gone, and so change the aspect of the coming time that we look with loathing on the very thing we have most desired. A few moments may change our character for life, by giving a totally different direction to our aims and energies.

To return to Mary. Her plan had been, as we well know, to marry Mr. Carson, and the occurrence an hour ago was only a preliminary step. True; but it had unveiled her heart to her; it had convinced her that she loved Jem above all persons or things. But Jem was a poor mechanic, with a mother and aunt to keep; a mother, too, who had shown her pretty clearly that she did not desire her for a daughter-in-law: while Mr. Carson was rich; and prosperous, and gay, and (she believed) would place her in all circumstances of ease and luxury, where want could never come. What were these hollow vanities to her, now she had discovered the passionate secret of her soul? She felt as if she almost hated Mr. Carson, who had decoyed her with his baubles. She now saw how vain, how nothing to her, would be all gaieties and pomps, all joys and pleasures, unless she might share them with Jem; yes, with him she had harshly rejected so short a time ago. If he were poor, she loved him all the better. If his mother did think her unworthy of him, what was it but the truth? as she now owned with bitter penitence. She had hitherto been walking in grope-light[1] towards a precipice; but in the clear revelation of that past hour, she saw her danger, and turned away resolutely, and for ever.

That was some comfort: I mean her clear perception of what she ought not to do; of what no luring temptation should ever again induce her to hearken to. How she could best undo the wrong she had done to Jem and herself by refusing his love, was another anxious question. She wearied herself by proposing plans, and rejecting them.

She was roused to a consciousness of time, by hearing the neighbouring church clock strike twelve. Her father she knew might be expected home any minute, and she was in no mood for a meeting

1. Semi-darkness.

with him. So she hastily gathered up her work, and went to her own little bedroom, leaving him to let himself in.

She put out her candle, that her father might not see its light under the door; and sat down on her bed to think. But again, turning things over in her mind again and again, she could only determine at once to put an end to all further communication with Mr. Carson, in the most decided way she could. Maidenly modesty (and true love is ever modest) seemed to oppose every plan she could think of, for showing Jem how much she repented her decision against him, and how dearly she had now discovered that she loved him. She came to the unusual wisdom of resolving to do nothing, but strive to be patient, and improve circumstances as they might turn up. Surely, if Jem knew of her remaining unmarried, he would try his fortune again. He would never be content with one rejection; she believed she could not in his place. She had been very wrong, but now she would endeavour to do right, and have womanly patience, until he saw her changed and repentant mind in her natural actions. Even if she had to wait for years, it was no more than now it was easy to look forward to, as a penance for her giddy flirting on the one hand, and her cruel mistake concerning her feelings on the other.[2] So anticipating a happy ending to the course of her love, however distant it might be, she fell asleep just as the earliest factory bells were ringing. She had sunk down in her clothes, and her sleep was unrefreshing. She wakened up shivery and chill in body, and sorrow-stricken in mind, though she could not at first rightly tell the cause of her depression.

She recalled the events of the night before, and still resolved to adhere to the determinations she had then formed. But patience seemed a far more difficult virtue this morning.

She hastened down stairs, and in her earnest, sad desire to do right, now took much pains to secure a comfortable though scanty breakfast for her father; and when he dawdled into the room, in an evidently irritable temper, she bore all with the gentleness of penitence, till at last her mild answers turned away wrath.

She loathed the idea of meeting Sally Leadbitter at her daily work; yet it must be done, and she tried to nerve herself for the encounter, and to make it at once understood, that having determined to give up having anything further to do with Mr. Carson, she considered the bond of intimacy broken between them.

But Sally was not the person to let these resolutions be carried into effect too easily. She soon became aware of the present state of Mary's feelings, but she thought they merely arose from the change-

---

2. This sentence, which is the same in all editions, seems to have had a part deleted from manuscript to printing. Shirley Foster glosses the sentence this way: "Even if she had to wait for years, it was no more than [she could expect or deserved, and] now it was easy to look forward to."

ableness of girlhood, and that the time would come when Mary would thank her for almost forcing her to keep up her meetings and communications with her rich lover.

So, when two days had passed over in rather too marked avoidance of Sally on Mary's part, and when the former was made aware by Mr. Carson's complaints that Mary was not keeping her appointments with him, and that unless he detained her by force, he had no chance of obtaining a word as she passed him in the street on her rapid walk home, she resolved to compel Mary to what she called her own good.

She took no notice during the third day of Mary's avoidance as they sat at work; she rather seemed to acquiesce in the coolness of their intercourse. She put away her sewing early, and went home to her mother, who, she said, was more ailing than usual. The other girls soon followed her example, and Mary, casting a rapid glance up and down the street, as she stood last on Miss Simmonds' doorstep, darted homewards, in hopes of avoiding the person whom she was fast learning to dread. That night she was safe from any encounter on her road, and she arrived at home, which she found, as she expected, empty; for she knew it was a club night, which her father would not miss. She sat down to recover breath, and to still her heart, which panted more from nervousness than from over-exertion, although she had walked so quickly. Then she arose, and taking off her bonnet, her eye caught the form of Sally Leadbitter passing the window with a lingering step, and looking into the darkness with all her might, as if to ascertain if Mary were returned. In an instant she repassed and knocked at the house-door; but without awaiting an answer, she entered.

"Well, Mary, dear," (knowing well how little "dear" Mary considered her just then); "it's so difficult to get any comfortable talk at Miss Simmonds', I thought I'd just step up and see you at home."

"I understood, from what you said, your mother was ailing, and that you wanted to be with her," replied Mary, in no welcoming tone.

"Ay, but mother's better now," said the unabashed Sally. "Your father's out, I suppose?" looking round as well as she could; for Mary made no haste to perform the hospitable offices of striking a match, and lighting a candle.

"Yes, he's out," said Mary, shortly, and busying herself at last about the candle, without ever asking her visitor to sit down.

"So much the better," answered Sally; "for to tell you the truth, Mary, I've a friend at th' end of the road, as is anxious to come and see you at home, since you're grown so particular as not to like to speak to him in the street. He'll be here directly."

"Oh, Sally, don't let him," said Mary, speaking at last heartily; and running to the door, she would have fastened it, but Sally held her hands, laughing meanwhile at her distress.

"Oh, please, Sally," struggling, "dear Sally! don't let him come here, the neighbours will so talk, and father'll go mad if he hears; he'll kill me, Sally, he will. Besides, I don't love him—I never did. Oh, let me go," as footsteps approached; and then, as they passed the house, and seemed to give her a respite, she continued, "Do, Sally, dear Sally, go and tell him I don't love him, and that I don't want to have anything more to do with him. It was very wrong, I dare say, keeping company with him at all, but I'm very sorry, if I've led him to think too much of me; and I don't want him to think any more. Will you tell him this, Sally? and I'll do anything for you, if you will."

"I'll tell you what I'll do," said Sally, in a more relenting mood; "I'll go back with you to where he's waiting for us; or rather, I should say, where I told him to wait for a quarter of an hour, till I seed if your father was at home; and if I didn't come back in that time, he said he'd come here, and break the door open but he'd see you."

"Oh, let us go, let us go," said Mary, feeling that the interview must be, and had better be anywhere than at home, where her father might return at any minute. She snatched up her bonnet, and was at the end of the court in an instant; but then, not knowing whether to turn to the right or to the left, she was obliged to wait for Sally, who came leisurely up, and put her arm through Mary's with a kind of decided hold, intended to prevent the possibility of her changing her mind, and turning back. But this, under the circumstances, was quite different to Mary's plan. She had wondered more than once if she must not have another interview with Mr. Carson; and had then determined, while she expressed her resolution that it should be the final one, to tell him how sorry she was if she had thoughtlessly given him false hopes. For be it remembered, she had the innocence, or the ignorance, to believe his intentions honourable; and he, feeling that at any price he must have her, only that he would obtain her as cheaply as he could, had never undeceived her; while Sally Leadbitter laughed in her sleeve at them both, and wondered how it would all end,—whether Mary would gain her point of marriage, with her sly affectation of believing such to be Mr. Carson's intention in courting her.

Not very far from the end of the street, into which the court where Mary lived opened, they met Mr. Carson, his hat a good deal slouched over his face, as if afraid of being recognised. He turned when he saw them coming, and led the way without uttering a word (although they were close behind) to a street of half-finished houses.

The length of the walk gave Mary time to recoil from the interview which was to follow; but even if her own resolve to go through with it had failed, there was the steady grasp of Sally Leadbitter, which she could not evade without an absolute struggle.

At last he stopped in the shelter and concealment of a wooden fence, put up to keep the building rubbish from intruding on the foot-pavement. Inside this fence, a minute afterwards, the girls were standing by him; Mary now returning Sally's detaining grasp with interest, for she had determined on the way to make her a witness, willing, or unwilling, to the ensuing conversation. But Sally's curiosity led her to be a very passive prisoner in Mary's hold.

With more freedom than he had ever used before, Mr. Carson put his arm firmly round Mary's waist, in spite of her indignant resistance.

"Nay, nay! you little witch! Now I have caught you, I shall keep you prisoner. Tell me now what has made you run away from me so fast these few days—tell me, you sweet little coquette!"

Mary ceased struggling, but turned so as to be almost opposite to him, while she spoke out calmly, and boldly.

"Mr. Carson! I want to speak to you for once and for all. Since I met you last Monday evening, I have made up my mind to have nothing more to do with you. I know I've been wrong in leading you to think I liked you; but I believe I didn't rightly know my own mind; and I humbly beg your pardon, sir, if I've led you to think too much of me."

For an instant he was surprised; the next, vanity came to his aid, and convinced him that she could only be joking. He, young, agreeable, rich, handsome! No! she was only showing a little womanly fondness for coquetting.

"You're a darling little rascal to go on in this way! 'Humbly begging my pardon if you've made me think too much of you.' As if you didn't know I think of you from morning till night. But you want to be told it again and again, do you?"

"No, indeed, sir, I don't. I would far liefer* that you should say you would never think of me again, than that you should speak of me in this way. For indeed, sir, I never was more in earnest than I am, when I say to-night is the last night I will ever speak to you."

"Last night, you sweet little equivocator, but not last day. Ha, Mary, I've caught you, have I?" as she, puzzled by his perseverance in thinking her joking, hesitated in what form she could now put her meaning.

"I mean, sir," she said sharply, "that I will never speak to you again, at any time, after to-night."

"And what's made this change, Mary?" said he, seriously enough now. "Have I done anything to offend you?" added he, earnestly.

---

* "Liefer," rather.
  "Yet had I *levre* unwist for sorrow die."
       Chaucer; 'Troilus and Creseide.' [WG]

"No, sir," she answered gently, but yet firmly. "I cannot tell you exactly why I've changed my mind; but I shall not alter it again; and, as I said before, I beg your pardon if I've done wrong by you. And now, sir, if you please, good night."

"But I do not please. You shall not go. What have I done, Mary? Tell me. You must not go without telling me how I have vexed you. What would you have me do?"

"Nothing, sir, but" (in an agitated tone), "oh! let me go! You cannot change my mind; it's quite made up. Oh, sir! why do you hold me so tight? If you *will* know why I won't have anything more to do with you, it is that I cannot love you. I have tried, and I really cannot."

This naïve and candid avowal served her but little. He could not understand how it could be true. Some reason lurked behind. He was passionately in love. What should he do to tempt her? A thought struck him.

"Listen! Mary. Nay, I cannot let you go till you have heard me. I do love you dearly; and I won't believe but what you love me a very little, just a very little. Well, if you don't like to own it, never mind! I only want now to tell you how much I love you, by what I am ready to give up for you. You know (or perhaps you are not fully aware) how little my father and mother would like me to marry you. So angry would they be, and so much ridicule should I have to brave, that of course I have never thought of it till now. I thought we could be happy enough without marriage." (Deep sank those words into Mary's heart.) "But now, if you like, I'll get a licence to-morrow morning— nay, to-night, and I'll marry you in defiance of all the world, rather than give you up. In a year or two my father will forgive me, and meanwhile you shall have every luxury money can purchase, and every charm that love can devise to make your life happy. After all, my mother was but a factory girl." (This was said to himself, as if to reconcile himself to this bold step.) "Now, Mary, you see how willing I am to—to sacrifice a good deal for you; I even offer you marriage, to satisfy your little ambitious heart; so now, won't you say, you can love me a little, little bit?"

He pulled her towards him. To his surprise, she still resisted. Yes! though all she had pictured to herself for so many months in being the wife of Mr. Carson was now within her grasp, she resisted. His speech had given her but one feeling, that of exceeding great relief. For she had dreaded, now she knew what true love was, to think of the attachment she might have created; the deep feeling her flirting conduct might have called out. She had loaded herself with reproaches for the misery she might have caused. It was a relief, to gather that the attachment was of that low, despicable kind which can plan to seduce the object of its affection; that the feeling she had caused was shallow enough, for it only pretended to embrace self, at the expense of the misery, the ruin, of one falsely termed beloved. She need not be penitent to such a plotter! That was the relief.

"I am obliged to you, sir, for telling me what you have. You may think I am a fool; but I did think you meant to marry me all along; and yet, thinking so, I felt I could not love you. Still I felt sorry I had gone so far in keeping company with you. Now, sir, I tell you, if I had loved you before, I don't think I should have loved you now you have told me you meant to ruin me; for that's the plain English of not meaning to marry me till just this minute. I said I was sorry, and humbly begged your pardon; that was before I knew what you were. Now I scorn you, sir, for plotting to ruin a poor girl. Good night."

And with a wrench, for which she had reserved all her strength, she flew off like a bolt. They heard her flying footsteps echo down the quiet street. The next sound was Sally's laugh, which grated on Mr. Carson's ears, and keenly irritated him.

"And what do you find so amusing, Sally?" asked he.

"Oh, sir, I beg your pardon. I humbly beg your pardon, as Mary says, but I can't help laughing to think how she's outwitted us." (She was going to have said, "outwitted you," but changed the pronoun.)

"Why, Sally, had you any idea she was going to fly out in this style?"

"No, I hadn't, to be sure. But if you did think of marrying her, why (if I may be so bold as to ask) did you go and tell her you had no thought of doing otherwise by her? That was what put her up at last!"

"Why, I had repeatedly before led her to infer that marriage was not my object. I never dreamed she could have been so foolish as to have mistaken me, little provoking romancer though she be! So I naturally wished her to know what a sacrifice of prejudice, of—of myself, in short, I was willing to make for her sake; yet I don't think she was aware of it after all. I believe I might have any lady in Manchester if I liked, and yet I was willing and ready to marry a poor dressmaker. Don't you understand me now? and don't you see what a sacrifice I was making to humour her? and all to no avail."

Sally was silent, so he went on:

"My father would have forgiven any temporary connexion, far sooner than my marrying one so far beneath me in rank."

"I thought you said, sir, your mother was a factory girl," remarked Sally, rather maliciously.

"Yes, yes!—but then my father was in much such a station; at any rate, there was not the disparity there is between Mary and me."

Another pause.

"Then you mean to give her up, sir? She made no bones of saying she gave you up."

"No; I do not mean to give her up, whatever you and she may please to think. I am more in love with her than ever; even for this charming capricious ebullition of hers. She'll come round, you may depend upon it. Women always do. They always have second thoughts, and find out that they are best in casting off a lover. Mind, I don't say I shall offer her the same terms again."

With a few more words of no importance, the allies parted.

Chapter XII.

> "I lov'd him not; and yet, now he is gone,
>   I feel I am alone.
> I check'd him while he spoke; yet could he speak,
>   Alas! I would not check.
> For reasons not to love him once I sought,
>   And wearied all my thought."
>   W. S. LANDOR.[3]

AND now Mary had, as she thought, dismissed both her lovers. But they looked on their dismissals with very different eyes. He who loved her with all his heart and with all his soul, considered his rejection final. He did not comfort himself with the idea, which would have proved so well founded in his case, that women have second thoughts about casting off their lovers. He had too much respect for his own heartiness of love to believe himself unworthy of Mary; that mock humble conceit did not enter his head. He thought he did "not hit Mary's fancy;" and though that may sound a trivial every-day expression, yet the reality of it cut him to the heart. Wild visions of enlistment, of drinking himself into forgetfulness, of becoming desperate in some way or another, entered his mind; but then the thought of his mother stood like an angel with a drawn sword in the way to sin.[4] For, you know, "he was the only son of his mother, and she was a widow;"[5] dependent on him for daily bread. So he could not squander away health and time, which were to him money wherewith to support her failing years. He went to his work, accordingly, to all outward semblance just as usual; but with a heavy, heavy heart within.

Mr. Carson, as we have seen, persevered in considering Mary's rejection of him as merely a "charming caprice." If she were at work, Sally Leadbitter was sure to slip a passionately loving note into her hand, and then so skilfully move away from her side, that Mary could not all at once return it, without making some sensation among the workwomen. She was even forced to take several home with her. But after reading one, she determined on her plan. She made no great resistance to receiving them from Sally, but kept them unopened, and

---

3. From Walter Savage Landor's (1775–1864) "The Maid's Lament" in his *Examination of Shakespeare* (1834).
4. Numbers 22:31.
5. Luke 7:12.

occasionally returned them in a blank half-sheet of paper. But far worse than this, was the being so constantly waylaid as she went home by her persevering lover; who had been so long acquainted with all her habits, that she found it difficult to evade him. Late or early, she was never certain of being free from him. Go this way or that, he might come up some cross street when she had just congratulated herself on evading him for that day. He could not have taken a surer mode of making himself odious to her.

And all this time Jem Wilson never came! Not to see her—that she did not expect—but to see her father; to—she did not know what, but she had hoped he would have come on some excuse, just to see if she hadn't changed her mind. He never came. Then she grew weary and impatient, and her spirits sank. The persecution of the one lover, and the neglect of the other, oppressed her sorely. She could not now sit quietly through the evening at her work; or, if she kept, by a strong effort, from pacing up and down the room, she felt as if she must sing to keep off thought while she sewed. And her songs were the maddest, merriest, she could think of. "Barbara Allen,"[6] and such sorrowful ditties, did well enough for happy times; but now she required all the aid that could be derived from external excitement to keep down the impulse of grief.

And her father, too—he was a great anxiety to her, he looked so changed and so ill. Yet he would not acknowledge to any ailment. She knew, that be it as late as it would, she never left off work until (if the poor servants paid her pretty regularly for the odd jobs of mending she did for them) she had earned a few pence, enough for one good meal for her father on the next day. But very frequently all she could do in the morning, after her late sitting up at night, was to run with the work home, and receive the money from the person for whom it was done. She could not stay often to make purchases of food, but gave up the money at once to her father's eager clutch; sometimes prompted by a savage hunger it is true, but more frequently by a craving for opium.

On the whole he was not so hungry as his daughter. For it was a long fast from the one o'clock dinner-hour at Miss Simmonds' to the close of Mary's vigil, which was often extended to midnight. She was young, and had not yet learned to bear "clemming."

One evening, as she sang a merry song over her work, stopping occasionally to sigh, the blind Margaret came groping in. It had been one of Mary's additional sorrows that her friend had been absent from home, accompanying the lecturer on music in his round among the manufacturing towns of Yorkshire and Lancashire. Her grandfather, too, had seen this a good time for going his expeditions in search of specimens; so that the house had been shut up for several weeks.

6. An old folk ballad about dying from unrequited love.

"Oh! Margaret, Margaret! how glad I am to see you. Take care. There, now, you're all right, that's father's chair. Sit down."—She kissed her over and over again.

"It seems like the beginning o' brighter times, to see you again, Margaret. Bless you! And how well you look!"

"Doctors always send ailing folk for change of air: and you know I've had plenty o' that same lately."

"You've been quite a traveller for sure! Tell us all about it, do, Margaret. Where have you been to, first place?"

"Eh, lass, that would take a long time to tell. Half o'er the world I sometimes think. Bolton and Bury, and Owdham, and Halifax, and— but Mary, guess who I saw there? Maybe you know though, so it's not fair guessing."

"No, I donnot. Tell me, Margaret, for I cannot abide waiting, and guessing."

"Well, one night as I were going fra' my lodgings wi' the help on a lad as belonged to th' landlady, to find the room where I were to sing, I heard a cough before me, walking along. Thinks I, that's Jem Wilson's cough, or I'm much mistaken. Next time came a sneeze and cough, and then I were certain. First I hesitated whether I should speak, thinking if it were a stranger he'd maybe think me forrard.* But I knew blind folks must not be nesh about using their tongues, so says I, 'Jem Wilson, is that you?' And sure enough it was, and nobody else. Did you know he were in Halifax, Mary?"

"No," she answered faintly and sadly; for Halifax was all the same to her heart as the Antipodes; equally inaccessible by humble penitent looks and maidenly tokens of love.

"Well, he's there, however: he's putting up an engine for some folks there, for his master. He's doing well, for he's gotten four or five men under him; we'd two or three meetings, and he told me all about his invention for doing away wi' the crank, or somewhat. His master's bought it from him, and ta'en out a patent, and Jem's a gentleman for life wi' the money his master gied him. But you'll ha' heard all this, Mary?"

No! she had not.

"Well, I thought it all happened afore he left Manchester, and then in course you'd ha' known. But maybe it were all settled after he got to Halifax; however, he's gotten two or three hunder pounds for his invention. But what's up with you, Mary? you're sadly out of sorts. You've never been quarrelling wi' Jem, surely."

Now Mary cried outright; she was weak in body, and unhappy in mind, and the time was come when she might have the relief of telling her grief. She could not bring herself to confess how much of her sor-

---

* "Forrard," forward. [WG]

row was caused by her having been vain and foolish; she hoped that need never be known, and she could not bear to think of it.

"Oh, Margaret; do you know Jem came here one night when I were put out, and cross. Oh, dear! dear! I could bite my tongue out when I think on it. And he told me how he loved me, and I thought I did not love him, and I told him I didn't; and, Margaret,—he believed me, and went away so sad, and so angry; and now I'd do any thing,—I would indeed," her sobs choked the end of her sentence. Margaret looked at her with sorrow, but with hope; for she had no doubt in her own mind, that it was only a temporary estrangement.

"Tell me, Margaret," said Mary, taking her apron down from her eyes, and looking at Margaret with eager anxiety, "What can I do to bring him back to me? Should I write to him?"

"No," replied her friend, "that would not do. Men are so queer, they like to have a' the courting to themselves."

"But I did not mean to write him a courting letter," said Mary, somewhat indignantly.

"If you wrote at all, it would be to give him a hint you'd taken the rue,[7] and would be very glad to have him now. I believe now he'd rather find that out himself."

"But he won't try," said Mary, sighing. "How can he find it out when he's at Halifax?"

"If he's a will he's a way, depend upon it. And you would not have him if he's not a will to you, Mary! No, dear!" changing her tone from the somewhat hard way in which sensible people too often speak, to the soft accents of tenderness which come with such peculiar grace from them, "you must just wait and be patient. You may depend upon it, all will end well, and better than if you meddled in it now."

"But it's so hard to be patient," pleaded Mary.

"Ay, dear; being patient is the hardest work we, any on us, have to do through life, I take it. Waiting is far more difficult than doing. I've known that about my sight, and many a one has known it in watching the sick; but it's one of God's lessons we all must learn, one way or another." After a pause. "Have ye been to see his mother of late?"

"No; not for some weeks. When last I went she was so frabbit* with me, that I really thought she wish'd I'd keep away."

"Well! if I were you I'd go. Jem will hear on't, and it will do you far more good in his mind than writing a letter, which, after all, you would find a tough piece of work when you came to settle to it. 'Twould be hard to say neither too much nor too little. But I must be going, grandfather is at home, and it's our first night together, and he must not be sitting wanting me any longer."

7. Repented.
* "Frabbit," ill-tempered. [WG]

She rose up from her seat, but still delayed going.

"Mary! I've somewhat else I want to say to you, and I don't rightly know how to begin. You see, grandfather and I know what bad times is, and we know your father is out of work, and I'm getting more money than I can well manage; and dear, would you just take this bit o' gold, and pay me back in good times." The tears stood in Margaret's eyes as she spoke.

"Dear Margaret, we're not so bad pressed as that." (The thought of her father and his ill looks, and his one meal a day, rushed upon Mary.) "And yet, dear, if it would not put you out o' your way,—I would work hard to make it up to you;—but would not your grandfather be vexed?"

"Not he, wench! It were more his thought than mine, and we have gotten ever so many more at home, so don't hurry yourself about paying. It's hard to be blind, to be sure, else money comes in so easily now to what it used to do; and it's downright pleasure to earn it, for I do so like singing."

"I wish I could sing," said Mary, looking at the sovereign.

"Some has one kind of gifts, and some another. Many's the time when I could see, that I longed for your beauty, Mary! We're like childer, ever wanting what we han not got. But now I must say just one more word. Remember, if you're sore pressed for money, we shall take it very unkind if you donnot let us know. Good-bye to ye."

In spite of her blindness she hurried away, anxious to rejoin her grandfather, and desirous also to escape from Mary's expressions of gratitude.

Her visit had done Mary good in many ways. It had strengthened her patience and her hope; it had given her confidence in Margaret's sympathy; and last, and really least in comforting power (of so little value are silver and gold in comparison to love, that gift in every one's power to bestow), came the consciousness of the money-value of the sovereign she held in her hand. The many things it might purchase! First of all came the thought of a comfortable supper for her father that very night; and acting instantly upon the idea, she set off in hopes that all the provision shops might not yet be closed, although it was so late.

That night the cottage shone with unusual light and fire gleam; and the father and daughter sat down to a meal they thought almost extravagant. It was so long since they had had enough to eat.

"Food gives heart," say the Lancashire people; and the next day Mary made time to go and call on Mrs. Wilson, according to Margaret's advice. She found her quite alone, and more gracious than she had been the last time Mary had visited her. Alice was gone out, she said.

"She would just step up to the post-office, all for no earthly use. For it were to ask if they hadn't a letter lying there for her from her foster-son, Will Wilson, the sailor-lad."

"What made her think there were a letter?" asked Mary.

"Why yo see, a neighbour as has been in Liverpool, told us Will's ship were come in. Now he said last time he were in Liverpool, he'd ha' come to ha' seen Alice, but his ship had but a week holiday, and hard work for the men in that time, too. So Alice makes sure he'll come this, and has had her hand behind her ear at every noise in th' street, thinking it were him. And to-day she were neither to have nor to hold, but off she would go to th' post, and see if he had na' sent her a line to th' old house near yo. I tried to get her to give up going, for let alone her deafness she's getten so dark, she cannot see five yards afore her; but no, she would go, poor old body."

"I did not know her sight failed her; she used to have good eyes enough when she lived near us."

"Ay, but it's gone lately a good deal. But you never ask after Jem"— anxious to get in a word on the subject nearest her heart.

"No," replied Mary, blushing scarlet. "How is he?"

"I cannot justly say how he is, seeing he's at Halifax; but he were very well when he wrote last Tuesday. Han ye heard o' his good luck?"

Rather to her disappointment, Mary owned she had heard of the sum his master had paid him for his invention.

"Well! and did not Margaret tell you what he'd done wi' it. It's just like him, though, ne'er to say a word about it. Why, when he were paid, what does he do but get his master to help him to buy an income for me and Alice. He had her name put down for her life; but, poor thing, she'll not be long to the fore, I'm thinking. She's sadly failed of late. And so, Mary, yo see, we're two ladies o' property. It's a matter o' twenty pound a year, they tell me. I wish the twins had lived, bless 'em," said she, dropping a few tears. "They should ha' had the best o' schooling, and their bellyfuls o' food. I suppose they're better off in heaven, only I should so like to see 'em."

Mary's heart filled with love at this new proof of Jem's goodness; but she could not talk about it. She took Jane Wilson's hand, and pressed it with affection; and then turned the subject to Will, her sailor nephew. Jane was a little bit sorry, but her prosperity had made her gentler, and she did not resent what she felt as Mary's indifference to Jem and his merits.

"He's been in Africa, and that neighbourhood, I believe. He's a fine chap, but he's not getten Jem's hair. His has too much o' the red in it. He sent Alice (but, maybe, she told you) a matter o' five pound when he were over before; but that were nought to an income, yo know."

"It's not every one that can get a hundred or two at a time," said Mary.

"No! no! that's true enough. There's not many a one like Jem. That's Alice's step," said she, hastening to open the door to her sister-in-law. Alice looked weary, and sad, and dusty. The weariness and the dust would not have been noticed either by her, or the others, if it had not been for the sadness.

"No letters!" said Mrs. Wilson.

"No, none! I must just wait another day to hear fra' my lad. It's very dree work, waiting," said Alice.

Margaret's words came into Mary's mind. Every one has their time and kind of waiting.

"If I but knew he were safe, and not drowned!" spoke Alice. "If I but knew he *were* drowned, I would ask grace to say, Thy will be done. It's the waiting."

"It's hard work to be patient to all of us," said Mary; "I know I find it so, but I did not know one so good as you did, Alice; I shall not think so badly of myself for being a bit impatient, now I've heard you say you find it difficult."

The idea of reproach to Alice was the last in Mary's mind; and Alice knew it was. Nevertheless, she said,

"Then, my dear, I beg your pardon, and God's pardon, too, if I've weakened your faith, by showing you how feeble mine was. Half our life's spent in waiting, and it ill becomes one like me, wi' so many mercies, to grumble. I'll try and put a bridle o'er my tongue, and my thoughts too." She spoke in a humble and gentle voice, like one asking forgiveness.

"Come, Alice," interposed Mrs. Wilson, "don't fret yoursel for e'er a trifle wrong said here or there. See! I've put th' kettle on, and you and Mary shall ha' a dish o' tea in no time."

So she bustled about, and brought out a comfortable-looking substantial loaf, and set Mary to cut bread and butter, while she rattled out the tea-cups—always a cheerful sound.

Just as they were sitting down, there was a knock heard at the door, and without waiting for it to be opened from the inside, some one lifted the latch, and in a man's voice asked, if one George Wilson lived there?

Mrs. Wilson was entering on a long and sorrowful explanation of his having once lived there, but of his having dropped down dead; when Alice, with the instinct of love (for in all usual and common instances sight and hearing failed to convey impressions to her until long after other people had received them), arose, and tottered to the door.

"My bairn!—my own dear bairn!" she exclaimed, falling on Will Wilson's neck.

You may fancy the hospitable and welcoming commotion that ensued; how Mrs. Wilson laughed, and talked, and cried, all together, if such a thing can be done; and how Mary gazed with wondering pleasure at her old playmate; now, a dashing, bronzed-looking, ringleted sailor, frank, and hearty, and affectionate.

But it was something different from common to see Alice's joy at once more having her foster-child with her. She did not speak, for she really could not; but the tears came coursing down hor old withered cheeks, and dimmed the horn spectacles she had put on, in order to pry lovingly into his face. So what with her failing sight, and her tear-blinded eyes, she gave up the attempt of learning his face by heart through the medium of that sense, and tried another. She passed her sodden, shrivelled hands, all trembling with eagerness, over his manly face, bent meekly down in order that she might more easily make her strange inspection. At last, her soul was satisfied.

After tea, Mary feeling sure there was much to be said on both sides, at which it would be better none should be present, not even an intimate friend like herself, got up to go away. This seemed to arouse Alice from her dreamy consciousness of exceeding happiness, and she hastily followed Mary to the door. There, standing outside, with the latch in her hand, she took hold of Mary's arm, and spoke nearly the first words she had uttered since her nephew's return.

"My dear! I shall never forgive mysel, if my wicked words to-night are any stumbling-block in your path. See how the Lord has put coals of fire on my head! Oh! Mary, don't let my being an unbelieving Thomas weaken your faith. Wait patiently on the Lord, whatever your trouble may be."[8]

Chapter XIII.

"The mermaid sat upon the rocks
    All day long,
Admiring her beauty and combing her locks
    And singing a mermaid song.

And hear the mermaid's song you may,
    As sure as sure can be,
If you will but follow the sun all day,
    And souse with him into the sea."
                    W. S. LANDOR.[9]

It was perhaps four or five days after the events mentioned in the last chapter, that one evening, as Mary stood lost in reverie at the window, she saw Will Wilson enter the court, and come quickly up to her door. She was glad to see him, for he had always been a friend of hers, perhaps too much like her in character ever to become anything nearer or dearer. She opened the door in readiness to receive his frank greeting, which she as frankly returned.

8. A sequence of biblical paraphrases: Romans 12:20, John 20:24–29, and Psalms 37:7.
9. From Walter Savage Landor's "The Mermaid" in *The Examination of Shakespeare*.

"Come Mary! on with bonnet and shawl, or whatever rigging you women require before leaving the house. I'm sent to fetch you, and I can't lose time when I'm under orders."

"Where am I to go to?" asked Mary, as her heart leaped up at the thought of who might be waiting for her.

"Not very far," replied he. "Only to old Job Legh's round the corner there. Aunt would have me come and see these new friends of hers, and then we meant to ha' come on here to see you and your father, but the old gentleman seems inclined to make a night of it, and have you all there. Where is your father? I want to see him. He must come too."

"He's out, but I'll leave word next door for him to follow me; that's to say, if he comes home afore long." She added, hesitatingly, "Is any one else at Job's?"

"No! My aunt Jane would not come, for some maggot[1] or other; and as for Jem! I don't know what you've all been doing to him, but he's as down-hearted a chap as I'd wish to see. He's had his sorrows sure enough, poor lad! But it's time for him to be shaking off his dull looks, and not go moping like a girl."

"Then he's come fra' Halifax, is he?" asked Mary.

"Yes! his body's come, but I think he's left his heart behind him. His tongue I'm sure he has, as we used to say to childer, when they would not speak. I try to rouse him up a bit, and I think he likes having me with him, but still he's as gloomy and as dull as can be. 'Twas only yesterday he took me to the works, and you'd ha' thought us two Quakers as the spirit hadn't moved,[2] all the way down we were so mum. It's a place to craze a man, certainly; such a noisy black hole! There were one or two things worth looking at, the bellows for instance, or the gale they called a bellows. I could ha' stood near it a whole day; and if I'd a berth in that place, I should like to be bellows-man, if there is such a one. But Jem weren't diverted even with that; he stood as grave as a judge while it blew my hat out o' my hand. He's lost all relish for his food, too, which frets my aunt sadly. Come! Mary, ar'n't you ready?"

She had not been able to gather if she were to see Jem at Job Legh's; but when the door was opened, she at once saw and felt he was not there. The evening then would be a blank; at least so she thought for the first five minutes; but she soon forgot her disappointment in the cheerful meeting of old friends, all, except herself, with some cause for rejoicing at that very time. Margaret, who could not be idle, was knitting away, with her face looking full into the room, away from her work. Alice sat meek and patient with her

---

1. Whim.
2. It was the practice in Quaker (The Society of Friends) church meetings for no one to speak unless "moved by the spirit."

dimmed eyes and gentle look, trying to see and to hear, but never complaining; indeed, in her inner self she was blessing God for her happiness; for the joy of having her nephew, her child, near her, was far more present to her mind, than her deprivations of sight and hearing.

Job was in the full glory of host and hostess too, for by a tacit agreement he had roused himself from his habitual abstraction, and had assumed many of Margaret's little household duties. While he moved about he was deep in conversation with the young sailor, trying to extract from him any circumstances connected with the natural history of the different countries he had visited.

"Oh! if you are fond of grubs, and flies, and beetles, there's no place for 'em like Sierra Leone. I wish you'd had some of ours; we had rather too much of a good thing; we drank them with our drink, and could scarcely keep from eating them with our food. I never thought any folk could care for such fat green beasts as those, or I would ha' brought you them by the thousand. A plate full o' peas soup would ha' been full enough for you, I dare say; it were often too full for us."

"I would ha' given a good deal for some on 'em," said Job.

"Well, I knew folk at home liked some o' the queer things one meets with abroad; but I never thought they'd care for them nasty slimy things. I were always on the look out for a mermaid, for that, I knew, were a curiosity."

"You might ha' looked long enough," said Job, in an under tone of contempt, which, however, the quick ears of the sailor caught.

"Not so long, master, in some latitudes, as you think. It stands to reason th' sea hereabouts is too cold for mermaids; for women here don't go half naked on account o' climate. But I've been in lands where muslin were too hot to wear on land, and where the sea were more than milk-warm; and though I'd never the good luck to see a mermaid in that latitude, I know them that has."

"Do tell us about it," cried Mary.

"Pooh, pooh!" said Job, the naturalist.

Both speeches determined Will to go on with his story. What could a fellow who had never been many miles from home know about the wonders of the deep, that he should put him down in that way?

"Well, it were Jack Harris, our third mate, last voyage, as many and many a time telled us all about it. You see he were becalmed off Chatham Island (that's in the Great Pacific, and a warm enough latitude for mermaids, and sharks, and such like perils). So some of the men took the long-boat, and pulled for the island to see what it were like; and when they got near, they heard a puffing, like a creature come up to take breath; you've never heard a diver? No! Well; you've heard folks in th' asthma, and it were for all the world like that. So they looked around, and what should they see but a mermaid, sitting on a rock, and sunning herself. The water is always warmer when it's rough, you know, so I suppose in the calm she felt it rather chilly, and had come up to warm herself."

"What was she like?" asked Mary, breathlessly.

Job took his pipe off the chimney-piece, and began to smoke with very audible puffs, as if the story were not worth listening to.

"Oh! Jack used to say she was for all the world as beautiful as any of the wax ladies in the barbers' shops; only, Mary, there were one little difference: her hair was bright grass green."

"I should not think that was pretty," said Mary, hesitatingly; as if not liking to doubt the perfection of any thing belonging to such an acknowledged beauty.

"Oh! but it is when you're used to it. I always think when first we get sight of land, there's no colour so lovely as grass green. However, she had green hair sure enough; and were proud enough of it, too; for she were combing it out full length when first they saw her. They all thought she were a fair prize, and may be as good as a whale in ready money (they were whale-fishers, you know). For some folk think a deal of mermaids, whatever other folk do." This was a hit at Job, who retaliated in a series of sonorous spittings and puffs.

"So, as I were saying, they pulled towards her, thinking to catch her. She were all the while combing her beautiful hair, and beckoning to them, while with the other hand she held a looking-glass."

"How many hands had she?" asked Job.

"Two, to be sure, just like any other woman," answered Will, indignantly.

"Oh! I thought you said she beckoned with one hand, and combed her hair with another, and held a looking-glass with her third," said Job, with provoking quietness.

"No! I didn't! at least, if I did, I meant she did one thing after another, as any one but" (here he mumbled a word or two) "could understand. Well, Mary," turning very decidedly towards her, "when she saw them coming near, whether it were she grew frightened at their fowling-pieces, as they had on board for a bit o' shooting on the island, or whether it were she were just a fickle jade as did not rightly know her own mind (which, seeing one half of her was woman, I think myself was most probable), but when they were only about two oars' length from the rock where she sat, down she plopped into the water, leaving nothing but her hinder end of a fish tail sticking up for a minute, and then that disappeared too."

"And did they never see her again?" asked Mary.

"Never so plain; the man who had the second watch one night declared he saw her swimming round the ship, and holding up her glass for him to look in; and then he saw the little cottage near Aber in Wales (where his wife lived) as plain as ever he saw it in life, and his wife standing outside, shading her eyes as if she were looking for him. But Jack Harris gave him no credit, for he said he were always a bit of a romancer, and beside that, were a home-sick, down-hearted chap."

"I wish they had caught her," said Mary, musing.

"They got one thing as belonged to her," replied Will, "and that I've often seen with my own eyes, and I reckon it's a sure proof of the truth of their story, for them that wants proof."

"What was it?" asked Margaret, almost anxious her grandfather should be convinced.

"Why, in her hurry she left her comb on the rock, and one o' the men spied it; so they thought that were better than nothing, and they rowed there and took it, and Jack Harris had it on board the *John Cropper*, and I saw him comb his hair with it every Sunday morning."

"What was it like?" asked Mary, eagerly; her imagination running on coral combs, studded with pearls.

"Why, if it had not had such a strange yarn belonging to it, you'd never ha' noticed it from any other small-tooth comb."

"I should rather think not," sneered Job Legh.

The sailor bit his lips to keep down his anger against an old man. Margaret felt very uneasy, knowing her grandfather so well, and not daring to guess what caustic remark might come next to irritate the young sailor guest.

Mary, however, was too much interested by the wonders of the deep to perceive the incredulity with which Job Legh received Wilson's account of the mermaid, and when he left off, half offended, and very much inclined not to open his lips again through the evening, she eagerly said,

"Oh, do tell us something more of what you hear and see on board ship. Do, Will!"

"What's the use, Mary, if folk won't believe one. There are things I saw with my own eyes, that some people would pish and pshaw at, as if I were a baby to be put down by cross noises. But I'll tell you, Mary," with an emphasis on *you*, "some more of the wonders of the sea, sin' you're not too wise to believe me. I have seen a fish fly."

This did stagger Mary. She had heard of mermaids as signs of inns and as sea-wonders, but never of flying fish. Not so Job. He put down his pipe, and nodding his head as a token of approbation, he said,

"Ay! ay! young man. Now you're speaking truth."

"Well, now, you'll swallow that, old gentleman. You'll credit me when I say I've seen a critter half fish, half bird, and you won't credit me when I say there be such beasts as mermaids, half fish, half woman. To me, one's just as strange as t'other."

"You never saw the mermaid yoursel'," interposed Margaret, gently. But "love me, love my dog," was Will Wilson's motto, only his version was, "Believe me, believe Jack Harris;" and the remark was not so soothing to him as it was intended to have been.

"It's the Exocetus; one of the Malacopterygii Abdominales,"[3] said Job, much interested.

"Ay, there you go! You're one o' them folks as never knows beasts unless they're called out o'their names. Put 'em in Sunday clothes, and you know 'em, but in their work-a-day English you never know nought about 'em. I've met wi' many o' your kidney; and if I'd ha' known it, I'd ha' christened poor Jack's mermaid wi' some grand gibberish of a name. Mermaidicus Jack Harrisensis; that's just like their new-fangled words. D'ye believe there's such a thing as the Mermaidicus, master?" asked Will, enjoying his own joke uncommonly, as most people do.

"Not I! tell me about the——"

"Well!" said Will, pleased at having excited the old gentleman's faith and credit at last, "it were on this last voyage, about a day's sail from Madeira, that one of our men——"

"Not Jack Harris, I hope," murmured Job.

"Called me," continued Will, not noticing the interruption, "to see the what d'ye call it—flying fish I say it is. It were twenty feet out o' water, and it flew near on to a hundred yards. But I say, old gentleman, I ha' gotten one dried, and if you'll take it, why I'll give it you; only," he added, in a lower tone, "I wish you'd just gie me credit for the Mermaidicus."

I really believe, if the assuming faith in the story of the mermaid had been made the condition of receiving the flying fish, Job Legh, sincere man as he was, would have pretended belief; he was so much delighted at the idea of possessing this specimen. He won the sailor's heart by getting up to shake both his hands in his vehement gratitude, puzzling poor old Alice, who yet smiled through her wonder: for she understood the action to indicate some kindly feeling towards her nephew.

Job wanted to prove his gratitude, and was puzzled how to do it. He feared the young man would not appreciate any of his duplicate Araneides;[4] not even the great American Mygale,[5] one of his most precious treasures; or else he would gladly have bestowed any duplicate on the donor of a real dried Exocetus. What could he do for him? He could ask Margaret to sing. Other folks beside her old doating grandfather thought a deal of her songs. So Margaret began some of her noble old-fashioned songs. She knew no modern music (for which her auditors might have been thankful), but she poured her

---

3. Latin classification for a type of flying fish.
4. Spiders.
5. Tarantula.

rich voice out in some of the old canzonets[6] she had lately learnt while accompanying the musical lecturer on his tour.

Mary was amused to see how the young sailor sat entranced; mouth, eyes, all open, in order to catch every breath of sound. His very lids refused to wink, as if afraid in that brief proverbial interval to lose a particle of the rich music that floated through the room. For the first time the idea crossed Mary's mind that it was possible the plain little sensible Margaret, so prim and demure, might have power over the heart of the handsome, dashing, spirited Will Wilson.

Job, too, was rapidly changing his opinion of his new guest. The flying fish went a great way, and his undisguised admiration for Margaret's singing carried him still further.

It was amusing enough to see these two, within the hour so barely civil to each other, endeavouring now to be ultra-agreeable. Will, as soon as he had taken breath (a long, deep gasp of admiration) after Margaret's song, sidled up to Job, and asked him in a sort of doubting tone,

"You wouldn't like a live Manx cat, would ye, master?"

"A what?" exclaimed Job.

"I don't know its best name," said Will, humbly. "But we call 'em just Manx cats. They're cats without tails."

Now Job, in all his natural history, had never heard of such animals; so Will continued,

"Because I'm going, afore joining my ship, to see mother's friends in the island, and would gladly bring you one, if so be you'd like to have it. They look as queer and out o' nature as flying fish, or"—he gulped the words down that should have followed. "Especially when you see 'em walking a roof-top, right again the sky, when a cat, as is a proper cat, is sure to stick her tail stiff out behind, like a slack rope dancer a-balancing; but these cats having no tail, cannot stick it out, which captivates some people uncommonly. If yo'll allow me, I'll bring one for Miss there," jerking his head at Margaret. Job assented with grateful curiosity, wishing much to see the tail-less phenomenon.

"When are you going to sail?" asked Mary.

"I cannot justly say; our ship's bound for America next voyage, they tell me. A messmate will let me know when her sailing-day is fixed; but I've got to go to th' Isle o' Man first. I promised uncle last time I were in England to go this next time. I may have to hoist the blue Peter[7] any day; so, make much of me while you have me, Mary."

Job asked him if he had been in America.

"Haven't I? North and South both! This time we're bound to North. Yankee-Land, as we call it, where Uncle Sam lives."

"Uncle who?" said Mary.

---

6. A light song characterized by repeated lines.
7. A blue flag with a white square in the center raised to signal that the ship is about to sail.

"Oh it's a way sailors have of speaking. I only mean I'm going to Boston, U.S., that's Uncle Sam."

Mary did not understand, so she left him and went to sit by Alice, who could not hear conversation unless expressly addressed to her. She had sat patiently silent the greater part of the night, and now greeted Mary with a quiet smile.

"Where's yo'r father?" asked she.

"I guess he's at his Union! he's there most evenings."

Alice shook her head; but whether it were that she did not hear, or that she did not quite approve of what she heard, Mary could not make out. She sat silently watching Alice, and regretting over her dimmed and veiled eyes, formerly so bright and speaking. As if Alice understood by some other sense what was passing in Mary's mind, she turned suddenly round, and answered Mary's thought.

"Yo're mourning for me, my dear! and there's no need, Mary. I'm as happy as a child. I sometimes think I am a child, whom the Lord is hushabying to my long sleep. For when I were a nurse-girl, my missis always telled me to speak very soft and low, and to darken the room that her little one might go to sleep; and now all noises are hushed and still to me, and the bonny earth seems dim and dark, and I know it's my Father lulling me away to my long sleep. I'm very well content, and yo mustn't fret for me. I've had well-nigh every blessing in life I could desire."

Mary thought of Alice's long-cherished, fond wish to revisit the home of her childhood, so often and often deferred, and now probably never to take place. Or if it did, how changed from the fond anticipation of what it was to have been! It would be a mockery to the blind and deaf Alice.

The evening came quickly to an end. There was the humble cheerful meal, and then the bustling, merry farewell, and Mary was once more in the quietness and solitude of her own dingy, dreary-looking home; her father still out, the fire extinguished, and her evening's task of work lying all undone upon the dresser. But it had been a pleasant little interlude to think upon. It had distracted her attention for a few hours from the pressure of many uneasy thoughts, of the dark, heavy, oppressive times, when sorrow and want seemed to surround her on every side; of her father, his changed and altered looks, telling so plainly of broken health, and an embittered heart; of the morrow, and the morrow beyond that, to be spent in that close monotonous workroom, with Sally Leadbitter's odious whispers hissing in her ear; and of the hunted look, so full of dread, from Miss Simmonds' door-step up and down the street, lest her persecuting lover should be near; for he lay in wait for her with wonderful perseverance, and of late had made himself almost hateful, by the unmanly force which he had used to detain her to listen to him, and the indifference with which he exposed her to the remarks of the passers-by, any one of whom might circulate reports which it would be terrible for her father to hear—and worse than death should they reach Jem Wilson. And all this she had drawn upon herself by her giddy flirting. Oh! how she loathed the recollection of the hot summer evening, when, worn out by stitching and sewing, she had loitered homewards with weary languor, and first listened to the voice of the tempter.

And Jem Wilson! Oh, Jem, Jem, why did you not come to receive some of the modest looks and words of love which Mary longed to give you, to try and make up for the hasty rejection which you as hastily took to be final, though both mourned over it with many tears. But day after day passed away, and patience seemed of no avail; and Mary's cry was ever the old moan of the Moated Grange,

> " 'Why comes he not,' she said,
> 'I am aweary, aweary.
>   I would that I were dead.' "[8]

Chapter XIV.

> 'Know the temptation ere you judge the crime!
> Look on this tree—'twas green, and fair and graceful;
> Yet now, save these few shoots, how dry and rotten!
> Thou canst not tell the cause. Not long ago,
> A neighbour oak, with which its roots were twined,
> In falling wrenched them with such cruel force,
> That though we covered them again with care,
> Its beauty withered, and it pined away.
> So, could we look into the human breast,
> How oft the fatal blight that meets our view,
> Should we trace down to the torn, bleeding fibres
> Of a too trusting heart—where it were shame,
> For pitying tears, to give contempt or blame."
>   "STREET WALKS."[9]

The month was over;—the honeymoon to the newly-married; the exquisite convalescence to the "living mother of a living child;" "the first dark days of nothingness"[1] to the widow and the child-bereaved; the term of penance, of hard labour, and of solitary confinement, to the shrinking, shivering, hopeless prisoner.

"Sick, and in prison, and ye visited me."[2] Shall you, or I, receive such blessing? I know one who will. An overseer of a foundry, an aged man, with hoary hair, has spent his Sabbaths, for many years, in visiting the

---

8. Misquoted from Alfred Tennyson's (1809–1892) "Mariana" (1830). The poem refers to Shakespeare's *Measure for Measure* (specifically, 3. 1. 270–71).
9. By William Gaskell.
1. From Lord Byron's (1788–1824) *The Giaour* (1813), line 170.
2. Matthew 25:36.

prisoners and the afflicted, in Manchester New Bailey; not merely advising, and comforting, but putting means into their power of regaining the virtue and the peace they had lost; becoming himself their guarantee in obtaining employment, and never deserting those who have once asked help from him. *³

Esther's term of imprisonment was ended. She received a good character in the governor's books; she had picked her daily quantity of oakum,⁴ had never deserved the extra punishment of the treadmill,⁵ and had been civil and decorous in her language. And once more she was out of prison. The door closed behind her with a ponderous clang, and in her desolation she felt as if shut out of home—from the only shelter she could meet with, houseless and penniless as she was, on that dreary day.

But it was but for an instant that she stood there doubting. One thought had haunted her both by night and by day, with monomaniacal incessancy; and that thought was how to save Mary (her dead sister's only child, her own little pet in the days of her innocence) from following in the same downward path to vice. To whom could she speak and ask for aid? She shrank from the idea of addressing John Barton again; her heart sank within her, at the remembrance of his fierce repulsing action, and far fiercer words. It seemed worse than death to reveal her condition to Mary, else she sometimes thought that this course would be the most terrible, the most efficient warning. She must speak; to that she was soul-compelled; but to whom? She dreaded addressing any of her former female acquaintance, even supposing they had sense, or spirit, or interest enough to undertake her mission.

To whom shall the outcast prostitute tell her tale! Who will give her help in the day of need? Hers is the leper-sin, and all stand aloof dreading to be counted unclean.

In her wild night wanderings, she had noted the haunts and habits of many a one who little thought of a watcher in the poor forsaken woman. You may easily imagine that a double interest was attached by her to the ways and companionships of those with whom she had been acquainted in the days which, when present, she had considered hardly-worked and monotonous, but which now in retrospection seemed so happy and unclouded. Accordingly, she had, as we have seen, known where to meet with John Barton on that unfortunate night, which had only produced irritation in him, and a month's

---

*   Vide *Manchester Guardian*, of Wednesday, March 18, 1846; and also the Reports of Captain Williams, prison inspector. [EG]

3. A reference to Thomas Wright (1789–1876), a foundry worker, who after a religious conversion, visited prisoners and assisted them on their release.

4. Picking fibers of old ropes for reuse.

5. Being compelled to walk on a treadmill was a form of punishment.

imprisonment to her. She had also observed that he was still intimate with the Wilsons. She had seen him walking and talking with both father and son; her old friends too; and she had shed unregarded, unvalued tears, when some one had casually told her of George Wilson's sudden death. It now flashed across her mind that to the son, to Mary's playfellow, her elder brother in the days of childhood, her tale might be told, and listened to with interest by him, and some mode of action suggested by which Mary might be guarded and saved.

All these thoughts had passed through her mind while yet she was in prison; so when she was turned out, her purpose was clear, and she did not feel her desolation of freedom as she would otherwise have done.

That night she stationed herself early near the foundry where she knew Jem worked; he stayed later than usual, being detained by some arrangements for the morrow. She grew tired and impatient; many workmen had come out of the door in the long, dead, brick wall, and eagerly had she peered into their faces, deaf to all insult or curse. He must have gone home early; one more turn in the street, and she would go.

During that turn he came out, and in the quiet of that street of workshops and warehouses, she directly heard his steps. How her heart failed her for an instant! but still she was not daunted from her purpose, painful as its fulfilment was sure to be. She laid her hand on his arm. As she expected, after a momentary glance at the person who thus endeavoured to detain him, he made an effort to shake it off, and pass on. But, trembling as she was, she had provided against this by a firm and unusual grasp.

"You must listen to me, Jem Wilson," she said, with almost an accent of command.

"Go away, missis; I've nought to do with you, either in hearkening or talking."

He made another struggle.

"You must listen," she said again, authoritatively, "for Mary Barton's sake."

The spell of her name was as potent as that of the mariner's glittering eye. "He listened like a three-year child."[6]

"I know you care enough for her to wish to save her from harm."

He interrupted his earnest gaze into her face, with the exclamation—

"And who can yo be to know Mary Barton, or to know that she's aught to me?"

---

6. From Samuel Taylor Coleridge's (1772–1834) "The Rime of the Ancient Mariner" (1798), Part I, slightly misquoted.

There was a little strife in Esther's mind for an instant, between the shame of acknowledging herself, and the additional weight to her revelation which such acknowledgment would give. Then she spoke,

"Do you remember Esther, the sister of John Barton's wife? the aunt to Mary? And the Valentine I sent you last February ten years?"

"Yes, I mind her well! But yo are not Esther, are you?" He looked again into her face, and seeing that indeed it was his boyhood's friend, he took her hand, and shook it with a cordiality that forgot the present in the past.

"Why, Esther! Where han ye been this many a year? Where han ye been wandering that we none of us could find you out?"

The question was asked thoughtlessly, but answered with fierce earnestness.

"Where have I been? What have I been doing? Why do you torment me with questions like these? Can you not guess? But the story of my life is wanted to give force to my speech, afterwards I will tell it you. Nay! don't change your fickle mind now, and say you don't want to hear it. You must hear it, and I must tell it; and then see after Mary, and take care she does not become like me. As she is loving now, so did I love once: one above me far." She remarked not, in her own absorption, the change in Jem's breathing, the sudden clutch at the wall which told the fearfully vivid interest he took in what she said. "He was so handsome, so kind! Well, the regiment was ordered to Chester (did I tell you he was an officer?), and he could not bear to part from me, nor I from him, so he took me with him. I never thought poor Mary[7] would have taken it so to heart! I always meant to send for her to pay me a visit when I was married; for, mark you! he promised me marriage. They all do. Then came three years of happiness. I suppose I ought not to have been happy, but I was. I had a little girl, too. Oh! the sweetest darling that ever was seen! But I must not think of her," putting her hand wildly up to her forehead, "or I shall go mad; I shall."

"Don't tell me any more about yoursel," said Jem, soothingly.

"What! you're tired already, are you? but I will tell you; as you've asked for it, you shall hear it. I won't recal the agony of the past for nothing. I will have the relief of telling it.[8] Oh, how happy I was!"— sinking her voice into a plaintive, child-like manner. "It went like a shot through me when one day he came to me and told me he was ordered to Ireland, and must leave me behind; at Bristol we then were."

Jem muttered some words; she caught their meaning, and in a pleading voice continued,

7. Esther's sister.
8. Another echo of "The Rime of the Ancient Mariner."

"Oh, don't abuse him; don't speak a word against him! You don't know how I love him yet; yet, when I am sunk so low. You don't guess how kind he was. He gave me fifty pounds before we parted, and I knew he could ill spare it. Don't, Jem, please," as his muttered indignation rose again. For her sake he ceased. "I might have done better with the money; I see now. But I did not know the value of it then. Formerly I had earned it easily enough at the factory, and as I had no more sensible wants, I spent it on dress and on eating. While I lived with him, I had it for asking; and fifty pounds would, I thought, go a long way. So I went back to Chester, where I'd been so happy, and set up a small-ware shop, and hired a room near. We should have done well, but alas! alas! my little girl fell ill, and I could not mind my shop and her too: and things grew worse and worse. I sold my goods any how to get money to buy her food and medicine; I wrote over and over again to her father for help, but he must have changed his quarters, for I never got an answer. The landlord seized the few bobbins and tapes I had left, for shop-rent; and the person to whom the mean little room, to which we had been forced to remove, belonged, threatened to turn us out unless his rent was paid; it had run on many weeks, and it was winter, cold bleak winter; and my child was so ill, so ill, and I was starving. And I could not bear to see her suffer, and forgot how much better it would be for us to die together;—oh, her moans, her moans, which money could give the means of relieving! So I went out into the street one January night—Do you think God will punish me for that?" she asked with wild vehemence, almost amounting to insanity, and shaking Jem's arm in order to force an answer from him.

But before he could shape his heart's sympathy into words, her voice had lost its wildness, and she spoke with the quiet of despair.

"But it's no matter! I've done that since, which separates us as far asunder as heaven and hell can be." Her voice rose again to the sharp pitch of agony. "My darling! my darling! even after death I may not see thee, my own sweet one! she was so good—like a little angel. What is that text, I don't remember,—the text mother used to teach me when I sat on her knee long ago; it begins 'Blessed are the pure——' "

"Blessed are the pure in heart, for they shall see God."[9]

"Ay, that's it! It would break mother's heart if she knew what I am now—it did break Mary's heart, you see. And now I recollect it was about her child I wanted to see you, Jem. You know Mary Barton, don't you?" said she, trying to collect her thoughts.

Yes, Jem knew her. How well, his beating heart could testify!

"Well, there's something to do for her; I forget what; wait a minute! She is so like my little girl;" said she, raising her eyes, glistening with unshed tears, in search of the sympathy of Jem's countenance.

9. Matthew 5:8.

He deeply pitied her; but oh! how he longed to recal her mind to the subject of Mary, and the lover above her in rank, and the service to be done for her sake. But he controlled himself to silence. After awhile, she spoke again, and in a calmer voice.

"When I came to Manchester (for I could not stay in Chester after her death), I found you all out very soon. And yet I never thought my poor sister was dead. I suppose I would not think so. I used to watch about the court where John lived, for many and many a night, and gather all I could about them from the neighbours' talk; for I never asked a question. I put this and that together, and followed one, and listened to another; many's the time I've watched the policeman off his beat, and peeped through the chink of the window-shutter to see the old room, and sometimes Mary or her father sitting up late for some reason or another. I found out Mary went to learn dressmaking, and I began to be frightened for her; for it's a bad life for a girl to be out late at night in the streets, and after many an hour of weary work, they're ready to follow after any novelty that makes a little change. But I made up my mind, that bad as I was, I could watch over Mary, and perhaps keep her from harm. So I used to wait for her at nights, and follow her home, often when she little knew any one was near her. There was one of her companions I never could abide, and I'm sure that girl is at the bottom of some mischief. By-and-by Mary's walks homewards were not alone. She was joined soon after she came out by a man; a gentleman. I began to fear for her, for I saw she was light-hearted, and pleased with his attentions; and I thought worse of him for having such long talks with that bold girl I told you of. But I was laid up for a long time with spitting of blood; and could do nothing. I'm sure it made me worse, thinking about what might be happening to Mary. And when I came out, all was going on as before, only she seemed fonder of him than ever; and oh! Jem, her father won't listen to me, and it's you must save Mary! You're like a brother to her, and maybe could give her advice and watch over her, and at any rate John will hearken to you; only he's so stern, and so cruel." She began to cry a little at the remembrance of his harsh words; but Jem cut her short by his hoarse, stern inquiry,

"Who is this spark that Mary loves? Tell me his name!"

"It's young Carson, old Carson's son, that your father worked for."
There was a pause. She broke the silence.

"Oh! Jem, I charge you with the care of her! I suppose it would be murder to kill her, but it would be better for her to die than to live to lead such a life as I do. Do you hear me, Jem!"

"Yes! I hear you. It would be better. Better we were all dead." This was said as if thinking aloud; but he immediately changed his tone and continued,

"Esther, you may trust to my doing all I can for Mary. That I have determined on. And now listen to me. You loathe the life you lead, else you would not speak of it as you do. Come home with me. Come to my mother. She and my aunt Alice live together. I will see that they give you a welcome. And to-morrow I will see if some honest way of living cannot be found for you. Come home with me."

She was silent for a minute, and he hoped he had gained his point. Then she said,

"God bless you, Jem, for the words you have just spoken. Some years ago you might have saved me, as I hope and trust you will yet save Mary. But it is too late now;—too late," she added, with accents of deep despair.

Still he did not relax his hold. "Come home," he said.

"I tell you, I cannot. I could not lead a virtuous life if I would. I should only disgrace you. If you will know all," said she, as he still seemed inclined to urge her, "I must have drink. Such as live like me could not bear life if they did not drink. It's the only thing to keep us from suicide. If we did not drink, we could not stand the memory of what we have been, and the thought of what we are, for a day. If I go without food, and without shelter, I must have my dram. Oh! you don't know the awful nights I have had in prison for want of it;" said she, shuddering, and glaring round with terrified eyes, as if dreading to see some spiritual creature, with dim form, near her.

"It is so frightful to see them," whispering in tones of wildness, although so low spoken. "There they go round and round my bed the whole night through. My mother, carrying little Annie (I wonder how they got together) and Mary—and all looking at me with their sad, stony eyes; oh Jem! it is so terrible! They don't turn back either, but pass behind the head of the bed, and I feel their eyes on me everywhere. If I creep under the clothes I still see them; and what is worse," hissing out her words with fright, "they see me. Don't speak to me of leading a better life—I must have drink. I cannot pass to-night without a dram; I dare not."

Jem was silent from deep sympathy. O! could he, then, do nothing for her! She spoke again, but in a less excited tone, although it was thrillingly earnest.

"You are grieved for me! I know it better than if you told me in words. But you can do nothing for me. I am past hope. You can yet save Mary. You must. She is innocent, except for the great error of loving one above her in station. Jem! you *will* save her?"

With heart and soul, though in few words, Jem promised that if aught earthly could keep her from falling, he would do it. Then she blessed him, and bade him good night.

"Stay a minute," said he, as she was on the point of departure. "I may want to speak to you again. I mun know where to find you—where do you live?"

She laughed strangely. "And do you think one sunk so low as I am has a home? Decent, good people have homes. We have none. No; if you want me, come at night, and look at the corners of the streets about here. The colder, the bleaker, the more stormy the night, the more certain you will be to find me. For then," she added, with a plaintive fall in her voice, "it is so cold sleeping in entries, and on door-steps, and I want a dram more than ever."

Again she rapidly turned off, and Jem also went on his way. But before he reached the end of the street, even in the midst of the jealous anguish that filled his heart, his conscience smote him. He had not done enough to save her. One more effort, and she might have come. Nay, twenty efforts would have been well rewarded by her yielding. He turned back, but she was gone. In the tumult of his other feelings, his self-reproach was deadened for the time. But many and many a day afterwards he bitterly regretted his omission of duty; his weariness of well-doing.[1]

Now, the great thing was to reach home, and solitude. Mary loved another! Oh! how should he bear it? He had thought her rejection of him a hard trial, but that was nothing now. He only remembered it, to be thankful that he had not yielded to the temptation of trying his fate again, not in actual words, but in a meeting, where her manner should tell far more than words, that her sweet smiles, her dainty movements, her pretty household ways, were all to be reserved to gladden another's eyes and heart. And he must live on; that seemed the strangest. That a long life (and he knew men did live long, even with deep, biting sorrow corroding at their hearts) must be spent without Mary; nay, with the consciousness she was another's! That hell of thought he would reserve for the quiet of his own room, the dead stillness of night. He was on the threshold of home now.

He entered. There were the usual faces, the usual sights. He loathed them, and then he cursed himself because he loathed them. His mother's love had taken a cross turn, because he had kept the tempting supper she had prepared for him waiting until it was nearly spoilt. Alice, her dulled senses deadening day by day, sat mutely near the fire; her happiness bounded by the consciousness of the presence of her foster-child, knowing that his voice repeated what was passing to her deafened ear, that his arm removed each little obstacle to her tottering steps. And Will, out of the very kindness of his heart, talked more and more merrily than ever. He saw Jem was downcast, and fancied his rattling might cheer him; at any rate, it drowned his aunt's muttered grumblings, and in some measure concealed the blank of the evening. At last, bed-time came; and Will withdrew to his neighbouring lodging; and Jane and Alice Wilson had raked the fire, and

1. II Thessalonians 3:13.

fastened doors and shutters, and pattered up-stairs, with their tottering footsteps and shrill voices. Jem, too, went to the closet termed his bedroom. There was no bolt to the door; but by one strong effort of his right arm, a heavy chest was moved against it, and he could sit down on the side of his bed, and think.

Mary loved another! That idea would rise uppermost in his mind, and had to be combated in all its forms of pain. It was, perhaps, no great wonder that she should prefer one so much above Jem in the external things of life. But the gentleman; why did he, with his range of choice among the ladies of the land, why did he stoop down to carry off the poor man's darling? With all the glories of the garden at his hand, why did he prefer to cull the wild-rose,—Jem's own fragrant wild-rose?

His *own!* Oh! never now his own!—Gone for evermore!

Then uprose the guilty longing for blood!—The frenzy of jealousy!—Some one should die. He would rather Mary were dead, cold in her grave, than that she were another's. A vision of her pale, sweet face, with her bright hair all bedabbled with gore, seemed to float constantly before his aching eyes. But hers were ever open, and contained, in their soft, deathly look, such mute reproach! What had she done to deserve such cruel treatment from him? She had been wooed by one whom Jem knew to be handsome, gay, and bright, and she had given him her love. That was all! It was the wooer who should die. Yes, die, knowing the cause of his death. Jem pictured him (and gloated on the picture), lying smitten, yet conscious; and listening to the upbraiding accusation of his murderer. How he had left his own rank, and dared to love a maiden of low degree! and oh! stinging agony of all—how she, in return, had loved him! Then the other nature spoke up, and bade him remember the anguish he should so prepare for Mary! At first he refused to listen to that better voice; or listened only to pervert. He would glory in her wailing grief! he would take pleasure in her desolation of heart!

No! he could not, said the still small voice.[2] It would be worse, far worse, to have caused such woe, than it was now to bear his present heavy burden.

But it was too heavy, too grievous to be borne, and live. He would slay himself and the lovers should love on, and the sun shine bright, and he with his burning, woful heart would be at rest. "Rest that is reserved for the people of God."[3]

Had he not promised with such earnest purpose of soul, as makes words more solemn than oaths, to save Mary from becoming such as Esther? Should he shrink from the duties of life, into the cowardliness of death? Who would then guard Mary, with her love and her

2. I Kings 19:12.
3. Hebrews 4:9, misquoted.

innocence? Would it not be a goodly thing to serve her, although she loved him not; to be her preserving angel, through the perils of life; and she, unconscious all the while?

He braced up his soul, and said to himself, that with God's help he would be that earthly keeper.

And now the mists and the storms seemed clearing away from his path, though it still was full of stinging thorns. Having done the duty nearest to him (of reducing the tumult of his own heart to something like order), the second became more plain before him.[4]

Poor Esther's experience had led her, perhaps too hastily, to the conclusion that Mr. Carson's intentions were evil towards Mary; at least she had given no just ground for the fears she entertained that such was the case. It was possible, nay, to Jem's heart very probable, that he might only be too happy to marry her. She was a lady by right of nature, Jem thought; in movement, grace, and spirit. What was birth to a Manchester manufacturer, many of whom glory, and justly too, in being the architects of their own fortunes? And, as far as wealth was concerned, judging another by himself, Jem could only imagine it a great privilege to lay it at the feet of the loved one. Harry Carson's mother had been a factory girl; so, after all, what was the great reason for doubting his intentions towards Mary?

There might probably be some little awkwardness about the affair at first: Mary's father having such strong prejudices on the one hand; and something of the same kind being likely to exist on the part of Mr. Carson's family. But Jem knew he had power over John Barton's mind; and it would be something to exert that power in promoting Mary's happiness, and to relinquish all thought[5] of self in so doing.

Oh! why had Esther chosen him for this office? It was beyond his strength to act rightly! Why had she singled him out?

The answer came when he was calm enough to listen for it, Because Mary had no other friend capable of the duty required of him; the duty of a brother, as Esther imagined him to be in feeling, from his long friendship. He would be unto her as a brother.

As such, he ought to ascertain Harry Carson's intentions towards her in winning her affections. He would ask him straight-forwardly, as became man speaking to man, not concealing, if need were, the interest he felt in Mary.

Then, with the resolve to do his duty to the best of his power, peace came into his soul; he had left the windy storm and tempest behind.[6]

Two hours before day-dawn he fell asleep.

4. Echo from Thomas Carlyle's (1795–1881) *Sartor Resartus* (1833–1834) in which the spiritual crisis of the philosopher Diogenes Teufelsdröckh is resolved, in part, through these words: "'Do the duty which lies nearest thee,' which thou knowest to be a Duty! Thy second Duty will already have become clearer."
5. Echoes Carlyle's notion of "self annihilation" in *Sartor Resartus*.
6. Another echo from *Sartor Resartus*.

149

Chapter XV.

"What thoughtful heart can look into this gulf
That darkly yawns 'twixt rich and poor,
And not find food for saddest meditation!
Can see, without a pang of keenest grief,
Them fiercely battling (like some natural foes)
Whom God had made, with help and sympathy,
To stand as brothers, side by side, united!
Where is the wisdom that shall bridge this gulf,
And bind them once again in trust and love?"
"LOVE-TRUTHS."[7]

We must return to John Barton. Poor John! He never got over his disappointing journey to London. The deep mortification he then experienced (with, perhaps, as little selfishness for its cause as mortification ever had) was of no temporary nature; indeed, few of his feelings were.

Then came a long period of bodily privation; of daily hunger after food; and though he tried to persuade himself he could bear want himself with stoical indifference, and did care about it as little as most men, yet the body took its revenge for its uneasy feelings. The mind became soured and morose, and lost much of its equipoise. It was no longer elastic, as in the days of youth, or in times of comparative happiness; it ceased to hope. And it is hard to live on when one can no longer hope.

The same state of feeling which John Barton entertained, if belonging to one who had had leisure to think of such things, and physicians to give names to them, would have been called monomania; so haunting, so incessant, were the thoughts that pressed upon him. I have somewhere read a forcibly described punishment among the Italians, worthy of a Borgia.[8] The supposed or real criminal was shut up in a room, supplied with every convenience and luxury; and at first mourned little over his imprisonment. But day by day he became aware that the space between the walls of his apartment was narrowing, and then he understood the end. Those painted walls would come into hideous nearness, and at last crush the life out of him.

And so day by day, nearer and nearer, came the diseased thoughts of John Barton. They excluded the light of heaven, the cheering sounds of earth. They were preparing his death.

It is true much of their morbid power might be ascribed to the use of opium. But before you blame too harshly this use, or rather abuse, try a hopeless life, with daily cravings of the body for food. Try, not

7. By William Gaskell.
8. The Borgia family in fifteenth- and sixteenth-century Rome were famous for their ruthlessness and cruelty.

alone being without hope yourself, but seeing all around you reduced to the same despair, arising from the same circumstances; all around you telling (though they use no words or language), by their looks and feeble actions, that they are suffering and sinking under the pressure of want. Would you not be glad to forget life, and its burdens? And opium gives forgetfulness for a time.

It is true they who thus purchase it pay dearly for their oblivion; but can you expect the uneducated to count the cost of their whistle? Poor wretches! They pay a heavy price. Days of oppressive weariness and languor, whose realities have the feeble sickliness of dreams; nights, whose dreams are fierce realities of agony; sinking health, tottering frames, incipient madness, and worse, the *consciousness* of incipient madness; this is the price of their whistle. But have you taught them the science of consequences?

John Barton's overpowering thought, which was to work out his fate on earth, was rich and poor; why are they so separate, so distinct, when God has made them all? It is not His will that their interests are so far apart. Whose doing is it?

And so on into the problems and mysteries of life, until, bewildered and lost, unhappy and suffering, the only feeling that remained clear and undisturbed in the tumult of his heart, was hatred to the one class, and keen sympathy with the other.

But what availed his sympathy? No education had given him wisdom; and without wisdom, even love, with all its effects, too often works but harm. He acted to the best of his judgment, but it was a widely-erring judgment.

The actions of the uneducated seem to me typified in those of Frankenstein, that monster of many human qualities, ungifted with a soul, a knowledge of the difference between good and evil.[9]

The people rise up to life; they irritate us, they terrify us, and we become their enemies. Then, in the sorrowful moment of our triumphant power, their eyes gaze on us with mute reproach. Why have we made them what they are; a powerful monster, yet without the inner means for peace and happiness?

John Barton became a Chartist, a Communist,[1] all that is commonly called wild and visionary. Ay! but being visionary is something. It shows a soul, a being not altogether sensual; a creature who looks forward for others, if not for himself.

And with all his weakness he had a sort of practical power, which made him useful to the bodies of men to whom he belonged. He had

---

9. In Mary Shelley's (1797–1851) novel, *Frankenstein, or the Modern Prometheus* (1818) the monster is not named. Gaskell confuses the monster with Victor Frankenstein, his creator.
1. Communism here refers to the doctrines of Robert Owen (1771–1858) who tried to establish utopian communities at New Lanark in Scotland and New Harmony, Indiana, in the United States. His emphasis was on communal living rather than class struggle.

a ready kind of rough Lancashire eloquence, arising out of the fulness of his heart, which was very stirring to men similarly circumstanced, who liked to hear their feelings put into words. He had a pretty clear head at times, for method and arrangement; a necessary talent to large combinations of men. And what perhaps more than all made him relied upon and valued, was the consciousness which every one who came in contact with him felt, that he was actuated by no selfish motives; that his class, his order, was what he stood by, not the rights of his own paltry self. For even in great and noble men, as soon as self comes into prominent existence, it becomes a mean and paltry thing.

A little time before this, there had come one of those occasions for deliberation among the employed, which deeply interested John Barton, and the discussions concerning which had caused his frequent absence from home of late.

I am not sure if I can express myself in the technical terms of either masters or workmen, but I will try simply to state the case on which the latter deliberated.

An order for coarse goods came in from a new foreign market. It was a large order, giving employment to all the mills engaged in that species of manufacture; but it was necessary to execute it speedily, and at as low prices as possible, as the masters had reason to believe that a duplicate order had been sent to one of the continental manufacturing towns, where there were no restrictions on food, no taxes on building or machinery, and where consequently they dreaded that the goods could be made at a much lower price than they could afford them for; and that, by so acting and charging, the rival manufactures would obtain undivided possession of the market. It was clearly their interest to buy cotton as cheaply, and to beat down wages as low as possible. And in the long run the interests of the workmen would have been thereby benefited. Distrust each other as they may, the employers and the employed must rise or fall together. There may be some difference as to chronology, none as to fact.

But the masters did not choose to make all these circumstances known. They stood upon being the masters, and that they had a right to order work at their own prices, and they believed that in the present depression of trade, and unemployment of hands, there would be no great difficulty in getting it done.

Now let us turn to the workmen's view of the question. The masters (of the tottering foundation of whose prosperity they were ignorant) seemed doing well, and, like gentlemen, "lived at home in ease," while they were starving, gasping on from day to day; and there was a foreign order to be executed, the extent of which, large as it was, was greatly exaggerated; and it was to be done speedily. Why were the masters offering such low wages under these circumstances? Shame upon them! It was taking advantage of their workpeople being almost starved; but they would starve entirely rather than come into such terms. It was bad enough to be poor, while by the labour of their thin hands, the sweat of their brows, the masters were made rich; but they would not be utterly ground down to dust. No! they would fold their hands and sit idle, and smile at the masters, whom even in death they could baffle. With Spartan endurance they determined to let the employers know their power, by refusing to work.

So class distrusted class, and their want of mutual confidence wrought sorrow to both. The masters would not be bullied, and compelled to reveal why they felt it wisest and best to offer only such low wages; they would not be made to tell that they were even sacrificing capital to obtain a decisive victory over the continental manufacturers. And the workmen sat silent and stern with folded hands refusing to work for such pay. There was a strike in Manchester.

Of course it was succeeded by the usual consequences. Many other Trades' Unions, connected with different branches of business, supported with money, countenance, and encouragement of every kind, the stand which the Manchester power-loom weavers were making against their masters. Delegates from Glasgow, from Nottingham, and other towns, were sent to Manchester, to keep up the spirit of resistance; a committee was formed, and all the requisite officers elected; chairman, treasurer, honorary secretary:—among them was John Barton.

The masters, meanwhile, took their measures. They placarded the walls with advertisements for power-loom weavers. The workmen replied by a placard in still larger letters, stating their grievances. The masters met daily in town, to mourn over the time (so fast slipping away) for the fulfilment of the foreign orders; and to strengthen each other in their resolution not to yield. If they gave up now, they might give up always. It would never do. And amongst the most energetic of the masters, the Carsons, father and son, took their places. It is well known, that there is no religionist so zealous as a convert; no masters so stern, and regardless of the interests of their workpeople, as those who have risen from such a station themselves. This would account for the elder Mr. Carson's determination not to be bullied into yielding; not even to be bullied into giving reasons for acting as the masters did. It was the employers' will, and that should be enough for the employed. Harry Carson did not trouble himself much about the grounds for his conduct. He liked the excitement of the affair. He liked the attitude of resistance. He was brave, and he liked the idea of personal danger, with which some of the more cautious tried to intimidate the violent among the masters.

Meanwhile, the power-loom weavers living in the more remote parts of Lancashire, and the neighbouring counties, heard of the

masters' advertisements for workmen; and in their solitary dwellings
grew weary of starvation, and resolved to come to Manchester. Foot-
sore, way-worn, half-starved looking men they were, as they tried to
steal into town in the early dawn, before people were astir, or in the
dusk of the evening. And now began the real wrong-doing of the
Trades' Unions. As to their decision to work, or not, at such a particular rate of wages, that was either wise or unwise; all error of judgment at the worst. But they had no right to tyrannise over others, and
tie them down to their own Procrustean bed.[2] Abhorring what they
considered oppression in the masters, why did they oppress others?
Because, when men get excited, they know not what they do.[3] Judge,
then, with something of the mercy of the Holy One, whom we all
love.

In spite of policemen, set to watch over the safety of the poor country weavers—in spite of magistrates, and prisons, and severe
punishments—the poor depressed men tramping in from Burnley,
Padiham, and other places, to work at the condemned "Starvation
Prices," were waylaid, and beaten, and left by the road-side almost for
dead. The police broke up every lounging knot of men:—they separated quietly, to reunite half-a-mile out of town.

Of course the feeling between the masters and workmen did not
improve under these circumstances.

Combination is an awful power. It is like the equally mighty agency
of steam; capable of almost unlimited good or evil. But to obtain a
blessing on its labours, it must work under the direction of a high and
intelligent will; incapable of being misled by passion or excitement.
The will of the operatives had not been guided to the calmness of
wisdom.

So much for generalities. Let us now return to individuals.

A note, respectfully worded, although its tone of determination
was strong, had been sent by the power-loom weavers, requesting
that a "deputation" of them might have a meeting with the masters,
to state the conditions they must have fulfilled before they would end
the turn-out. They thought they had attained a sufficiently commanding position to dictate. John Barton was appointed one of the
deputation.

The masters agreed to this meeting, being anxious to end the strife,
although undetermined among themselves how far they should yield,
or whether they should yield at all. Some of the old, whose experience
had taught them sympathy, were for concession. Others, white-
headed men too, had only learnt hardness and obstinacy from the

2. A Greek legend in which Procrustes forces his victims to lie in his bed; he either stretches
   them or cuts off their limbs to make them fit. The reference is to the dangers of an inflexible system.
3. Luke 23:34.

days of the years of their lives, and sneered at the more gentle and yielding. The younger men were one and all for an unflinching resistance to claims urged with so much violence. Of this party Harry Carson was the leader.

But like all energetic people, the more he had to do the more time he seemed to find. With all his letter-writing, his calling, his being present at the New Bailey when investigations of any case of violence against knob-sticks* was going on, he beset Mary more than ever. She was weary of her life for him. From blandishments he had even gone to threats—threats that whether she would or not she should be his; he showed an indifference that was almost insulting to everything which might attract attention and injure her character.

And still she never saw Jem. She knew he had returned home. She heard of him occasionally through his cousin, who roved gaily from house to house, finding and making friends everywhere. But she never saw him. What was she to think? Had he given her up? Were a few hasty words, spoken in a moment of irritation, to stamp her lot through life? At times she thought that she could bear this meekly, happy in her own constant power of loving. For of change or of forgetfulness she did not dream. Then at other times her state of impatience was such, that it required all her self-restraint to prevent her from going and seeking him out, and (as man would do to man, or woman to woman) begging him to forgive her hasty words, and allow her to retract them, and bidding him accept of the love that was filling her whole heart. She wished Margaret had not advised her against such a manner of proceeding; she believed it was her friend's words that seemed to make such a simple action impossible, in spite of all the internal urgings. But a friend's advice is only thus powerful, when it puts into language the secret oracle of our souls. It was the whisperings of her womanly nature that caused her to shrink from any unmaidenly action, not Margaret's counsel.

All this time, this ten days or so, of Will's visit to Manchester, there was something going on which interested Mary even now, and which, in former times, would have exceedingly amused and excited her. She saw as clearly as if told in words, that the merry, random, boisterous sailor had fallen deeply in love with the quiet, prim, somewhat plain Margaret: she doubted if Margaret was aware of it, and yet, as she watched more closely, she began to think some instinct made the blind girl feel whose eyes were so often fixed upon her pale face; that some inner feeling made the delicate and becoming rose-flush steal over her countenance. She did not speak so decidedly as before; there was a hesitation in her manner, that seemed to make her very attractive; as if something softer, more loveable than excellent sense, were

---

* "Knob-sticks," those who consent to work at lower wages. [WG]

coming in as a motive for speech; her eyes had always been soft, and were in no ways disfigured by her blindness, and now seemed to have a new charm, as they quivered under their white downcast lids. She must be conscious, thought Mary,—heart answering to heart.

Will's love had no blushings, no downcast eyes, no weighing of words; it was as open and undisguised as his nature; yet he seemed afraid of the answer its acknowledgment might meet with. It was Margaret's angelic voice that had entranced him, and which made him think of her as a being of some other sphere, that he feared to woo. So he tried to propitiate Job in all manner of ways. He went over to Liverpool to rummage in his great sea-chest for the flying-fish (no very odorous present, by the way). He hesitated over a child's caul[4] for some time, which was, in his eyes, a far greater treasure than any Exocetus. What use could it be of to a landsman? Then Margaret's voice rang in his ears; and he determined to sacrifice it, his most precious possession, to one whom she loved as she did her grandfather.

It was rather a relief to him, when, having put it and the flying-fish together in a brown paper parcel, and sat upon them for security all the way in the railroad, he found that Job was so indifferent to the precious caul, that he might easily claim it again. He hung about Margaret, till he had received many warnings and reproaches from his conscience in behalf of his dear aunt Alice's claims upon his time. He went away, and then he bethought him of some other little word with Job. And he turned back, and stood talking once more in Margaret's presence, door in hand, only waiting for some little speech of encouragement to come in and sit down again. But as the invitation was not given, he was forced to leave at last, and go and do his duty.

Four days had Jem Wilson watched for Mr. Harry Carson without success; his hours of going and returning to his home were so irregular, owing to the meetings and consultations among the masters, which were rendered necessary by the turn-out. On the fifth, without any purpose on Jem's part, they met.

It was the workman's dinner hour, the interval between twelve and one; when the streets of Manchester are comparatively quiet, for a few shopping ladies, and lounging gentlemen, count for nothing in that busy, bustling, living place. Jem had been on an errand for his master, instead of returning to his dinner; and in passing along a lane, a road (called, in compliment to the intentions of some future builder, a street), he encountered Harry Carson, the only person, as far as he saw, beside himself, treading the unfrequented path. Along one side ran a high broad fence, blackened over by coal-tar, and spiked and stuck with pointed nails at the top, to prevent any one

4. Residue from the membrane enclosing the fetus, which sometimes survived as loose skin on a baby's head at birth, was prized by sailors as a charm against drowning.

from climbing over into the garden beyond. By this fence was the footpath. The carriage-road was such as no carriage, no, not even a cart, could possibly have passed along, without Hercules to assist in lifting it out of the deep clay ruts. On the other side of the way was a dead brick wall; and a field after that, where there was a sawpit, and joiner's shed.

Jem's heart beat violently, when he saw the gay, handsome young man approaching, with a light buoyant step. This, then, was he whom Mary loved. It was, perhaps, no wonder; for he seemed to the poor smith so elegant, so well appointed, that he felt the superiority in externals, strangely and painfully, for an instant. Then something uprose within him, and told him, that "a man's a man for a' that, for a' that, and twice as much as a' that."[5] And he no longer felt troubled by the outward appearance of his rival.

Harry Carson came on, lightly bounding over the dirty places with almost a lad's buoyancy. To his surprise the dark, sturdy-looking artisan stopped him, by saying respectfully,

"May I speak a word wi' you, sir?"

"Certainly, my good man," looking his astonishment; then finding that the promised speech did not come very quickly, he added, "But make haste, for I'm in a hurry."

Jem had cast about for some less abrupt way of broaching the subject uppermost in his mind than he now found himself obliged to use. With a husky voice that trembled as he spoke, he said,

"I think, sir, yo're keeping company wi' a young woman called Mary Barton?"

A light broke in upon Henry Carson's mind, and he paused before he gave the answer for which the other waited.

Could this man be a lover of Mary's? And (strange stinging thought) could he be beloved by her, and so have caused her obstinate rejection of himself? He looked at Jem from head to foot, a black, grimy mechanic, in dirty fustian clothes, strongly built, and awkward (according to the dancing master); then he glanced at himself, and recalled the reflection he had so lately quitted in his bedroom. It was impossible. No woman with eyes could choose the one when the other wooed. It was Hyperion to a Satyr.[6] That quotation came aptly; he forgot, "That a man's a man for a' that." And yet here was a clue, which he had often wanted, to her changed conduct towards him. If she loved this man. If——he hated the fellow, and longed to strike him. He would know all.

"Mary Barton! let me see. Ay, that is the name of the girl. An arrant flirt the little hussy is; but very pretty. Ay, Mary Barton is her name."

---

5. From Robert Burns's "For A' That and A' That."
6. From Shakespeare's *Hamlet* 1.2.140 comparing the God of the sun to a half-man/half-goat.

Jem bit his lips. Was it then so; that Mary was a flirt; the giddy creature of whom he spoke? He would not believe it, and yet how he
wished the suggestive words unspoken. That thought must keep now,
though. Even if she were, the more reason for there being some one
to protect her; poor faulty darling.

"She's a good girl, sir, though maybe a bit set up with her beauty;
but she's her father's only child, sir, and——" he stopped; he did not
like to express suspicion, and yet he was determined he would be certain there was ground for none. What should he say?

"Well, my fine fellow, and what have I to do with that! It's but loss
of my time, and yours, too, if you've only stopped me to tell me Mary
Barton is very pretty; I know that well enough."

He seemed as though he would have gone on, but Jem put his
black, working, right hand upon his arm to detain him. The haughty
young man shook it off, and with his glove pretended to brush away
the sooty contamination that might be left upon his light great-coat
sleeve. The little action aroused Jem.

"I will tell you, in plain words, what I have got to say to you, young
man. It's been telled me by one as knows, and has seen, that you walk
with this same Mary Barton, and are known to be courting her; and
her as spoke to me about it, thinks as how Mary loves you. That may
be, or may not. But I'm an old friend of hers and her father's; and I
just wished to know if you mean to marry the girl. Spite of what you
said of her lightness, I ha' known her long enough to be sure she'll
make a noble wife for any one, let him be what he may; and I mean
to stand by her like a brother; and if you mean rightly, you'll not think
the worse on me for what I've now said; and if—but no, I'll not say
what I'll do to the man who wrongs a hair of her head. He shall rue
it to the longest day he lives, that's all. Now, sir, what I ask of you is
this. If you mean fair and honourable by her, well and good; but if
not, for your own sake as well as hers, leave her alone, and never
speak to her more." Jem's voice quivered with the earnestness with
which he spoke, and he eagerly waited for some answer.

Harry Carson, meanwhile, instead of attending very particularly to
the purpose the man had in addressing him, was trying to gather from
his speech what was the real state of the case. He succeeded so far
as to comprehend that Jem inclined to believe that Mary loved his
rival; and consequently, that if the speaker were attached to her himself, he was not a favoured admirer. The idea came into Mr. Carson's
mind, that perhaps, after all, Mary loved him in spite of her frequent
and obstinate rejections; and that she had employed this person
(whoever he was) to bully him into marrying her. He resolved to try
and ascertain more correctly the man's relation to her. Either he was
a lover, and if so, not a favoured one (in which case Mr. Carson could
not at all understand the man's motives for interesting himself in

securing her marriage); or he was a friend, an accomplice, whom she had employed to bully him. So little faith in goodness have the mean and selfish!

"Before I make you into my confidant, my good man," said Mr. Carson, in a contemptuous tone, "I think it might be as well to inquire your right to meddle with our affairs. Neither Mary nor I, as I conceive, called you in as a mediator." He paused: he wanted a distinct answer to this last supposition. None came; so he began to imagine he was to be threatened into some engagement, and his angry spirit rose.

"And so, my fine fellow, you will have the kindness to leave us to ourselves, and not to meddle with what does not concern you. If you were a brother or father of hers, the case might have been different. As it is, I can only consider you an impertinent meddler."

Again he would have passed on, but Jem stood in a determined way before him, saying,

"You say if I had been her brother, or her father, you'd have answered me what I ask. Now, neither father nor brother could love her as I have loved her—ay, and as I love her still; if love gives a right to satisfaction, it's next to impossible any one breathing can come up to my right. Now, sir, tell me! do you mean fair by Mary or not? I've proved my claim to know, and, by G—, I will know."

"Come, come, no impudence," replied Mr. Carson, who, having discovered what he wanted to know (namely, that Jem was a lover of Mary's, and that she was not encouraging his suit), wished to pass on.

"Father, brother, or rejected lover" (with an emphasis on the word rejected), "no one has a right to interfere between my little girl and me. No one shall. Confound you, man! get out of my way, or I'll make you," as Jem still obstructed his path with dogged determination.

"I won't then, till you've given me your word about Mary," replied the mechanic, grinding his words out between his teeth, and the livid paleness of the anger he could no longer keep down covering his face till he looked ghastly.

"Won't you?" (with a taunting laugh), "then I'll make you." The young man raised his slight cane, and smote the artisan across the face with a stinging stroke. An instant afterwards he lay stretched in the muddy road, Jem standing over him, panting with rage. What he would have done next in his moment of ungovernable passion, no one knows; but a policeman from the main street, into which this road led, had been sauntering about for some time, unobserved by either of the parties, and expecting some kind of conclusion like the present to the violent discussion going on between the two young men. In a minute he had pinioned Jem, who sullenly yielded to the surprise.

Mr. Carson was on his feet directly, his face glowing with rage or shame.

"Shall I take him to the lock-ups for assault, sir?" said the policeman.

"No, no," exclaimed Mr. Carson; "I struck him first. It was no assault on his side: though," he continued, hissing out his words to Jem, who even hated freedom procured for him, however justly, at the intervention of his rival, "I will never forgive or forget your insult. Trust me," he gasped the words in excess of passion, "Mary shall fare no better for your insolent interference." He laughed, as if with the consciousness of power.

Jem replied with equal excitement—

"And if you dare to injure her in the least, I will await you where no policeman can step in between. And God shall judge between us two."

The policeman now interfered with persuasions and warnings. He locked his arm in Jem's to lead him away in an opposite direction to that in which he saw Mr. Carson was going. Jem submitted, gloomily, for a few steps, then wrenched himself free. The policeman shouted after him.

"Take care, my man! there's no girl on earth worth what you'll be bringing on yourself, if you don't mind."

But Jem was out of hearing.

Chapter XVI.

> "Not for a moment take the scorner's chair;
> While seated there, thou know'st not how a word,
> A tone, a look, may gall thy brother's heart,
> And make him turn in bitterness against thee."
> 'LOVE-TRUTHS.'[7]

The day arrived on which the masters were to have an interview with a deputation of the workpeople. The meeting was to take place in a public room, at an hotel; and there, about eleven o'clock, the mill-owners, who had received the foreign orders, began to collect.

Of course, the first subject, however full their minds might be of another, was the weather. Having done their duty by all the showers and sunshine which had occurred during the past week, they fell to talking about the business which brought them together. There might be about twenty gentlemen in the room, including some by courtesy, who were not immediately concerned in the settlement of

7. By William Gaskell.

the present question; but who, nevertheless, were sufficiently interested to attend. These were divided into little groups, who did not
seem by any means unanimous. Some were for a slight concession,
just a sugar-plum to quieten the naughty child, a sacrifice to peace
and quietness. Some were steadily and vehemently opposed to the
dangerous precedent of yielding one jot or one tittle to the outward
force of a turn-out. It was teaching the workpeople how to become
masters, said they. Did they want the wildest thing hereafter, they
would know that the way to obtain their wishes would be to strike
work. Besides, one or two of those present had only just returned
from the New Bailey, where one of the turn-outs had been tried for
a cruel assault on a poor north-country weaver, who had attempted
to work at the low price. They were indignant, and justly so, at the
merciless manner in which the poor fellow had been treated; and
their indignation at wrong, took (as it often does) the extreme form
of revenge. They felt as if, rather than yield to the body of men who
were resorting to such cruel measures towards their fellow-workmen,
they, the masters, would sooner relinquish all the benefits to be
derived from the fulfilment of the commission, in order that the
workmen might suffer keenly. They forgot that the strike was in this
instance the consequence of want and need, suffered unjustly, as the
endurers believed; for, however insane, and without ground of reason, such was their belief, and such was the cause of their violence.
It is a great truth that you cannot extinguish violence by violence. You
may put it down for a time; but while you are crowing over your imag-
inary success, see if it does not return with seven devils worse than
its former self![8]

No one thought of treating the workmen as brethren and friends,
and openly, clearly, as appealing to reasonable men, stating exactly
and fully the circumstances which led the masters to think it was the
wise policy of the time to make sacrifices themselves, and to hope for
them from the operatives.

In going from group to group in the room, you caught such a medley of sentences as the following:

"Poor devils! they're near enough to starving, I'm afraid. Mrs.
Aldred makes two cows' heads into soup every week, and people come
many miles to fetch it; and if these times last, we must try and do
more. But we must not be bullied into any thing!"

"A rise of a shilling or so won't make much difference, and they will
go away thinking they've gained their point."

"That's the very thing I object to. They'll think so, and whenever
they've a point to gain, no matter how unreasonable, they'll strike
work."

8. Matthew 12:43–45 and Luke 11:24–26.

"It really injures them more than us."

"I don't see how our interests can be separated."

"The d——d brute had thrown vitriol[9] on the poor fellow's ankles, and you know what a bad part that is to heal. He had to stand still with the pain, and that left him at the mercy of the cruel wretch, who beat him about the head till you'd hardly have known he was a man. They doubt if he'll live."

"If it were only for that, I'll stand out against them, even if it is the cause of my ruin."

"Ay, I for one won't yield one farthing to the cruel brutes; they're more like wild beasts than human beings."

(Well, who might have made them different?)

"I say, Carson, just go and tell Duncombe of this fresh instance of their abominable conduct. He's wavering, but I think this will decide him."

The door was now opened, and the waiter announced that the men were below, and asked if it were the pleasure of the gentlemen that they should be shown up.

They assented, and rapidly took their places round the official table; looking, as like as they could, to the Roman senators who awaited the irruption of Brennus and his Gauls.[1]

Tramp, tramp, came the heavy clogged feet up the stairs; and in a minute five wild, earnest-looking men, stood in the room. John Barton, from some mistake as to time, was not among them Had they been larger boned men, you would have called them gaunt; as it was, they were little of stature, and their fustian clothes hung loosely upon their shrunk limbs. In choosing their delegates, too, the operatives had had more regard to their brains, and power of speech, than to their wardrobes; they might have read the opinions of that worthy Professor Teufelsdreck, in Sartor Resartus, to judge from the dilapidated coats and trousers, which yet clothed men of parts and of power.[2] It was long since many of them had known the luxury of a new article of dress; and air-gaps were to be seen in their garments. Some of the masters were rather affronted at such a ragged detachment coming between the wind and their nobility[3]; but what cared they?

At the request of a gentleman hastily chosen to officiate as chair-

9. Sulphuric acid used as a weapon by being thrown onto a victim's skin.
1. When the Gauls, under Brennus's leadership, attacked Rome in the fourth century, the Roman senators sacrificed themselves by refusing to retreat and being subsequently slaughtered.
2. Reference to the Thomas Carlyle's *Sartor Resartus* (the tailor re-tailored) in which Diogenes Teufelsdrockh articulates a philosophy of clothes, which, in part, emphasizes the difference between outer appearance and essential reality.
3. Another echo of Falstaff's description of his conscripted troops in Shakespeare's *I Henry IV* 4.2.12–.

man, the leader of the delegates read, in a high-pitched, psalm-singing voice, a paper, containing the operatives statement of the case at issue, their complaints, and their demands, which last were not remarkable for moderation.

He was then desired to withdraw for a few minutes, with his fellow-delegates, to another room, while the masters considered what should be their definitive answer.

When the men had left the room, a whispered earnest consultation took place, every one re-urging his former arguments. The conceders carried the day, but only by a majority of one. The minority haughtily and audibly expressed their dissent from the measures to be adopted, even after the delegates re-entered the room; their words and looks did not pass unheeded by the quick-eyed operatives; their names were registered in bitter hearts.

The masters could not consent to the advance demanded by the workmen. They would agree to give one shilling per week more than they had previously offered. Were the delegates empowered to accept such offer?

They were empowered to accept or decline any offer made that day by the masters.

Then it might be as well for them to consult among themselves as to what should be their decision. They again withdrew.

It was not for long. They came back, and positively declined any compromise of their demands.

Then up sprang Mr. Henry Carson, the head and voice of the violent party among the masters, and addressing the chairman, even before the scowling operatives, he proposed some resolutions, which he, and those who agreed with him, had been concocting during this last absence of the deputation.

They were, firstly, withdrawing the proposal just made, and declaring all communication between the masters and that particular Trades' Union at an end; secondly, declaring that no master would employ any workman in future, unless he signed a declaration that he did not belong to any Trades' Union, and pledged himself not to assist or subscribe to any society, having for its object interference with the masters' powers; and, thirdly, that the masters should pledge themselves to protect and encourage all workmen willing to accept employment on those conditions, and at the rate of wages first offered. Considering that the men who now stood listening with lowering brows of defiance were all of them leading members of the Union, such resolutions were in themselves sufficiently provocative of animosity: but not content with simply stating them, Harry Carson went on to characterise the conduct of the workmen in no measured terms; every word he spoke rendering their looks more livid, their glaring eyes more fierce. One among them would have spoken, but checked himself, in obedience to the stern glance and pressure on his arm, received from the leader. Mr. Carson sat down, and a friend instantly got up to second the motion. It was carried, but far from unanimously. The chairman announced it to the delegates (who had been once more turned out of the room for a division). They received it with deep brooding silence, but spake never a word, and left the room without even a bow.

Now there had been some by-play at this meeting, not recorded in the Manchester newspapers, which gave an account of the more regular part of the transaction.

While the men had stood grouped near the door, on their first entrance, Mr. Harry Carson had taken out his silver pencil, and had drawn an admirable caricature of them—lank, ragged, dispirited, and famine-stricken. Underneath he wrote a hasty quotation from the fat knight's well-known speech in Henry IV.[4] He passed it to one of his neighbours, who acknowledged the likeness instantly, and by him it was sent round to others, who all smiled and nodded their heads. When it came back to its owner he tore the back of the letter on which it was drawn in two, twisted them up, and flung them into the fireplace; but, careless whether they reached their aim or not, he did not look to see that they fell just short of any consuming cinders.

This proceeding was closely observed by one of the men.

He watched the masters as they left the hotel (laughing, some of them were, at passing jokes), and when all had gone, he re-entered. He went to the waiter, who recognised him.

"There's a bit on a picture up yonder, as one o' the gentlemen threw away; I've a little lad at home as dearly loves a picture; by your leave I'll go up for it."

The waiter, good-natured and sympathetic, accompanied him up-stairs; saw the paper picked up and untwisted, and then being convinced, by a hasty glance at its contents, that it was only what the man had called it, "a bit of a picture," he allowed him to bear away his prize.

Towards seven o'clock that evening, many operatives began to assemble in a room in the Weavers' Arms' public-house, a room appropriated for "festive occasions," as the landlord, in his circular, on opening the premises, had described it. But, alas! it was on no festive occasion that they met there this night. Starved, irritated, despairing men, they were assembling to hear the answer that morning given by the masters to their delegates; after which, as was stated in the notice, a gentleman from London would have the honour of addressing the meeting on the present state of affairs between the employers and the employed, or (as he chose to term them) the idle

4. Especially 4.2.38, "No eye hath seen such scarecrows."

and the industrious classes. The room was not large, but its bareness
of furniture made it appear so. Unshaded gas flared down upon the
lean and unwashed artisans as they entered, their eyes blinking at the
excess of light.

They took their seats on benches, and awaited the deputation. The
latter, gloomily and ferociously, delivered the masters' ultimatum,
adding thereto not one word of their own; and it sank all the deeper
into the sore hearts of the listeners for their forbearance.

Then the "gentleman from London" (who had been previously
informed of the masters' decision) entered. You would have been
puzzled to define his exact position, or what was the state of his mind
as regarded education. He looked so self-conscious, so far from
earnest, among the group of eager, fierce, absorbed men, among
whom he now stood. He might have been a disgraced medical student of the Bob Sawyer class,[5] or an unsuccessful actor, or a flashy
shopman. The impression he would have given you would have been
unfavourable, and yet there was much about him that could only be
characterised as doubtful.

He smirked in acknowledgment of their uncouth greetings, and sat
down; then glancing round, he inquired whether it would not be
agreeable to the gentlemen present to have pipes and liquor handed
round, adding, that he would stand treat.

As the man who has had his taste educated to love reading, falls
devouringly upon books after a long abstinence, so these poor fellows, whose tastes had been left to educate themselves into a liking
for tobacco, beer, and similar gratifications, gleamed up at the proposal of the London delegate. Tobacco and drink deaden the pangs
of hunger, and make one forget the miserable home, the desolate
future.

They were now ready to listen to him with approbation. He felt it;
and rising like a great orator, with his right arm outstretched, his left
in the breast of his waistcoat, he began to declaim, with a forced theatrical voice.

After a burst of eloquence, in which he blended the deeds of the
elder and the younger Brutus,[6] and magnified the resistless might of
the "millions of Manchester," the Londoner descended to matter-of-
fact business, and in his capacity this way he did not belie the good
judgment of those who had sent him as delegate. Masses of people,
when left to their own free choice, seem to have discretion in distinguishing men of natural talent; it is a pity they so little regard
temper and principles. He rapidly dictated resolutions, and suggested measures. He wrote out a stirring placard for the walls. He

5. Medical student in Dickens's *The Pickwick Papers* (1836–1837).
6. The elder Brutus founded the Roman republic and killed his two sons when they tried to
   restore the Roman monarchy; the younger Brutus helped assassinate Juluis Caesar.

proposed sending delegates to entreat the assistance of other Trades' Unions in other towns. He headed the list of subscribing Unions, by a liberal donation from that with which he was especially connected in London; and what was more, and more uncommon, he paid down the money in real, clinking, blinking, golden sovereigns! The money, alas! was cravingly required; but before alleviating any private necessities on the morrow, small sums were handed to each of the delegates, who were in a day or two to set out on their expeditions to Glasgow, Newcastle, Nottingham, &c. These men were most of them members of the deputation who had that morning waited upon the masters. After he had drawn up some letters, and spoken a few more stirring words, the gentleman from London withdrew, previously shaking hands all round; and many speedily followed him out of the room, and out of the house.

The newly-appointed delegates, and one or two others, remained behind to talk over their respective missions, and to give and exchange opinions in more homely and natural language than they dared to use before the London orator.

"He's a rare chap, yon," began one, indicating the departed delegate by a jerk of his thumb towards the door. "He's getten the gift of the gab, anyhow!"

"Ay! ay! he knows what he's about. See how he poured it into us about that there Brutus. He were pretty hard, too, to kill his own son!"

"I could kill mine if he took part with the masters; to be sure, he's but a step-son, but that makes no odds," said another.

But now tongues were hushed, and all eyes were directed towards the member of the deputation who had that morning returned to the hotel to obtain possession of Harry Carson's clever caricature of the operatives.

The heads clustered together, to gaze at and detect the likenesses.

"That's John Slater! I'd ha' known him anywhere, by his big nose. Lord! how like; that's me, by G—d, it's the very way I'm obligated to pin my waistcoat up, to hide that I've getten no shirt. That *is* a shame, and I'll not stand it."

"Well!" said John Slater, after having acknowledged his nose and his likeness; "I could laugh at a jest as well as e'er the best on 'em, though it did tell agen mysel, if I were not clemming" (his eyes filled with tears; he was a poor, pinched, sharp-featured man, with a gentle and melancholy expression of countenance), "and if I could keep from thinking of them at home, as is clemming; but with their cries for food ringing in my ears, and making me afeard of going home, and wonder if I should hear 'em wailing out, if I lay cold and drowned at th' bottom o' th' canal, there,—why, man, I cannot laugh at aught. It seems to make me sad that there is any as can make game on what they've never knowed; as can make such laughable pictures on men, whose very hearts within 'em are so raw and sore as ours were and are, God help us."

John Barton began to speak; they turned to him with great attention. "It makes me more than sad, it makes my heart burn within me, to see that folk can make a jest of striving men; of chaps who comed to ask for a bit o' fire for th' old granny, as shivers i' th' cold; for a bit o' bedding, and some warm clothing to the poor wife who lies in labour on th' damp flags; and for victuals for the childer, whose little voices are getting too faint and weak to cry aloud wi' hunger. For, brothers, is not them the things we ask for when we ask for more wage? We donnot want dainties, we want bellyfuls; we donnot want gimcrack[7] coats and waistcoats, we want warm clothes; and so that we get 'em, we'd not quarrel wi' what they're made on. We donnot want their grand houses, we want a roof to cover us from the rain, and the snow, and the storm; ay, and not alone to cover us, but the helpless ones that cling to us in the keen wind, and ask us with their eyes why we brought 'em into th' world to suffer?" He lowered his deep voice almost to a whisper:

"I've seen a father who had killed his child rather than let it clem before his eyes; and he were a tender-hearted man."

He began again in his usual tone. "We come to th' masters wi' full hearts, to ask for them things I named afore. We know that they've getten money, as we've earned for 'em; we know trade is mending, and they've large orders, for which they'll be well paid; we ask for our share o' th' payment; for, say we, if th' masters get our share of payment it will only go to keep servants and horses—to more dress and pomp. Well and good, if yo choose to be fools we'll not hinder you, so long as you're just; but our share we must and will have; we'll not be cheated. *We* want it for daily bread, for life itself; and not for our own lives neither (for there's many a one here, I know by mysel, as would be glad and thankful to lie down and die out o' this weary world), but for the lives of them little ones, who don't yet know what life is, and are afeard of death. Well, we come before th' masters to state what we want, and what we must have, afore we'll set shoulder to their work; and they say, 'No.' One would think that would be enough of hard-heartedness, but it isn't. They go and make jesting pictures on us! I could laugh at mysel, as well as poor John Slater there; but then I must be easy in my mind to laugh. Now I only know that I would give the last drop of my blood to avenge us on yon chap, who had so little feeling in him as to make game on earnest, suffering men!"

7. Cheap and showy.

A low angry murmur was heard among the men, but it did not yet take form or words. John continued—

"You'll wonder, chaps, how I came to miss the time this morning; I'll just tell you what I was a-doing. Th' chaplain at the New Bailey sent and gived me an order to see Jonas Higginbotham; him as was taken up last week for throwing vitriol in a knob-stick's face. Well, I couldn't help but go; and I didn't reckon it would ha' kept me so late. Jonas were like one crazy when I got to him; he said he could na' get rest night or day for th' face of the poor fellow he had damaged; then he thought on his weak, clemmed look, as he tramped, footsore, into town; and Jonas thought, maybe, he had left them at home as would look for news, and hope and get none, but, haply, tidings of his death. Well, Jonas had thought on these things till he could not rest, but walked up and down continually like a wild beast in his cage. At last he bethought him on a way to help a bit, and he got the chaplain to send for me; and he tell'd me this; and that th' man were lying in the Infirmary, and he bade me go (to-day's the day as folk may be admitted into th' Infirmary) and get his silver watch, as was his mother's, and sell it as well as I could, and take the money, and bid the poor knob-stick send it to his friends beyond Burnley; and I were to take him Jonas's kind regards, and he humbly axed him to forgive him. So I did what Jonas wished. But bless your life, none on us would ever throw vitriol again (at least at a knob-stick) if they could see the sight I saw to-day. The man lay, his face all wrapped in cloths, so I didn't see *that:* but not a limb, nor a bit of a limb, could keep from quivering with pain. He would ha' bitten his hand to keep down his moans, but couldn't, his face hurt him so if he moved it e'er so little. He could scarce mind me when I telled him about Jonas; he did squeeze my hand when I jingled the money, but when I axed his wife's name, he shrieked out, 'Mary, Mary, shall I never see you again? Mary, my darling, they've made me blind because I wanted to work for you and our own baby; oh, Mary, Mary!' Then the nurse came, and said he were raving, and that I had made him worse. And I'm afeard it was true; yet I were loth to go without knowing where to send the money. . . . . So that kept me beyond my time, chaps."

"Did you hear where the wife lived at last?" asked many anxious voices.

"No! he went on talking to her, till his words cut my heart like a knife. I axed th' nurse to find out who she was, and where she lived. But what I'm more especial naming it now for is this,—for one thing I wanted you all to know why I weren't at my post this morning; for another, I wish to say, that I, for one, ha' seen enough of what comes of attacking knob-sticks, and I'll ha' nought to do with it no more."

There were some expressions of disapprobation, but John did not mind them.

"Nay! I'm no coward," he replied, "and I'm true to th' backbone. What I would like, and what I would do, would be to fight the masters. There's one among yo called me a coward. Well! every man has a right to his opinion; but since I've thought on th' matter to-day, I've thought we han all on us been more like cowards in attacking the poor like ourselves; them as has none to help, but mun choose between vitriol and starvation. I say we're more cowardly in doing that than in leaving them alone. No! what I would do is this. Have at the masters!" Again he shouted, "Have at the masters!" He spoke lower; all listened with hushed breath:

"It's the masters as has wrought this woe; it's the masters as should pay for it. Him as called me coward just now, may try if I am one or not. Set me to serve out the masters, and see if there's aught I'll stick at."

"It would give the masters a bit on a fright if one of them were beaten within an inch of his life," said one.

"Ay! or beaten till no life were left in him," growled another.

And so with words, or looks that told more than words, they built up a deadly plan. Deeper and darker grew the import of their speeches, as they stood hoarsely muttering their meaning out, and glaring, with eyes that told the terror their own thoughts were to them, upon their neighbours. Their clenched fists, their set teeth, their livid looks, all told the suffering which their minds were voluntarily undergoing in the contemplation of crime, and in familiarising themselves with its details.

Then came one of those fierce terrible oaths which bind members of Trades' Unions to any given purpose. Then under the flaring gaslight, they met together to consult further. With the distrust of guilt, each was suspicious of his neighbour; each dreaded the treachery of another. A number of pieces of paper (the identical letter on which the caricature had been drawn that very morning) were torn up, and *one was marked*. Then all were folded up again, looking exactly alike. They were shuffled together in a hat. The gas was extinguished; each drew out a paper. The gas was re-lighted. Then each went as far as he could from his fellows, and examined the paper he had drawn without saying a word, and with a countenance as stony and immovable as he could make it.

Then, still rigidly silent, they each took up their hats and went every one his own way.

He who had drawn the marked paper had drawn the lot of the assassin! and he had sworn to act according to his drawing! But no one, save God and his own conscience, knew who was the appointed murderer.

Chapter XVII.

"Mournful is't to say Farewell,
  Though for few brief hours we part;
In that absence, who can tell
  What may come to wring the heart!"

ANONYMOUS.

The events recorded in the last chapter took place on a Tuesday. On Thursday afternoon Mary was surprised, in the midst of some little bustle in which she was engaged, by the entrance of Will Wilson. He looked strange, at least it was strange to see any different expression on his face to his usual joyous beaming appearance. He had a paper parcel in his hand. He came in, and sat down, more quietly than usual.

"Why, Will! what's the matter with you? You seem quite cut up about something!"

"And I am, Mary! I'm come to say good-bye; and few folk like to say good-bye to them they love."

"Good-bye! Bless me, Will, that's sudden, isn't it?"

Mary left off ironing, and came and stood near the fireplace. She had always liked Will; but now it seemed as if a sudden spring of sisterly love had gushed up in her heart, so sorry did she feel to hear of his approaching departure.

"It's very sudden, isn't it?" said she, repeating the question.

"Yes, it's very sudden," said he, dreamily. "No, it isn't;" rousing himself, to think of what he was saying. "The captain told me in a fortnight he would be ready to sail again; but it comes very sudden on me, I had got so fond of you all."

Mary understood the particular fondness that was thus generalised. She spoke again.

"But it's not a fortnight since you came. Not a fortnight since you knocked at Jane Wilson's door, and I was there, you remember. Nothing like a fortnight!"

"No; I know it's not. But, you see, I got a letter this afternoon from Jack Harris, to tell me our ship sails on Tuesday next; and it's long since I promised my uncle (my mother's brother, him that lives at Kirk-Christ, beyond Ramsay, in the Isle of Man) that I'd go and see him and his, this time of coming ashore. I must go. I'm sorry enough; but I mustn't slight poor mother's friends. I must go. Don't try to keep me," said he, evidently fearing the strength of his own resolution, if hard pressed by entreaty.

"I'm not a-going, Will. I dare say you're right; only I can't help feeling sorry you're going away. It seems so flat to be left behind. When do you go?"

"To-night. I shan't see you again."

"To-night! and you go to Liverpool! Maybe you and father will go together. He's going to Glasgow, by way of Liverpool."

"No! I'm walking; and I don't think your father will be up to walking."

"Well! and why on earth are you walking? You can get by railway for three-and-sixpence."

"Ay, but Mary! (thou mustn't let out what I'm going to tell thee) I haven't got three shillings, no, nor even a sixpence left, at least not here; before I came I gave my landlady enough to carry me to the island and back, and maybe a trifle for presents, and I brought the rest here; and it's all gone but this," jingling a few coppers in his hand.

"Nay, never fret over my walking a matter of thirty mile," added he, as he saw she looked grave and sorry. "It's a fine clear night, and I shall set off betimes, and get in afore the Manx packet[8] sails. Where's your father going? To Glasgow did you say? Perhaps he and I may have a bit of a trip together then, for, if the Manx boat has sailed when I get into Liverpool, I shall go by a Scotch packet. What's he going to do in Glasgow?—Seek for work? Trade is as bad there as here, folk say."

"No; he knows that," answered Mary sadly. "I sometimes think he'll never get work again, and that trade will never mend. It's very hard to keep up one's heart. I wish I were a boy, I'd go to sea with you. It would be getting away from bad news at any rate; and now, there's hardly a creature that crosses the door-step, but has something sad and unhappy to tell one. Father is going as a delegate from his Union, to ask help from the Glasgow folk. He's starting this evening."

Mary sighed, for the feeling again came over her that it was very flat to be left alone.

"You say no one crosses the threshold but has something sad to say; you don't mean that Margaret Jennings has any trouble?" asked the young sailor, anxiously.

"No!" replied Mary, smiling a little; "she's the only one I know, I believe, who seems free from care. Her blindness almost appears a blessing sometimes; she was so downhearted when she dreaded it, and now she seems so calm and happy when it's downright come. No! Margaret's happy, I do think."

"I could almost wish it had been otherwise," said Will, thoughtfully. "I could have been so glad to comfort her, and cherish her, if she had been in trouble."

"And why can't you cherish her, even though she is happy?" asked Mary.

"Oh! I don't know. She seems so much better than I am! And her voice! When I hear it, and think of the wishes that are in my heart, it

8. Cargo boat.

seems as much out of place to ask her to be my wife, as it would be to ask an angel from heaven."

Mary could not help laughing outright, in spite of her depression, at the idea of Margaret as an angel; it was so difficult (even to her dressmaking imagination) to fancy where, and how, the wings would be fastened to the brown stuff gown, or the blue and yellow print.

Will laughed, too, a little, out of sympathy with Mary's pretty merry laugh. Then he said—

"Ay, you may laugh, Mary; it only shows you've never been in love."

In an instant Mary was carnation colour, and the tears sprang to her soft grey eyes. She that was suffering so much from the doubts arising from love! It was unkind of him. He did not notice her change of look and of complexion. He only noticed that she was silent, so he continued:

"I thought—I think, that when I come back from this voyage, I will speak. It's my fourth voyage in the same ship and with the same captain, and he's promised he'll make me a second mate after this trip; then I shall have something to offer Margaret; and her father, and Aunt Alice, shall live with her, and keep her from being lonesome while I'm at sea. I'm speaking as if she cared for me, and would marry me; d'ye think she does care at all for me, Mary?" asked he anxiously.

Mary had a very decided opinion of her own on the subject, but she did not feel as if she had any right to give it. So she said—

"You must ask Margaret, not me, Will; she's never named your name to me." His countenance fell. "But I should say that was a good sign from a girl like her; I've no right to say what I think; but, if I was you, I would not leave her now without speaking."

"No! I cannot speak! I have tried. I've been in to wish them good-bye, and my voice stuck in my throat. I could say nought of what I'd planned to say; and I never thought of being so bold as to offer her marriage till I'd been my next trip, and been made mate. I could not even offer her this box," said he, undoing his paper parcel and displaying a gaudily ornamented accordion; "I longed to buy her something, and I thought, if it were something in the music line, she would maybe fancy it more. So, will you give it to her, Mary, when I'm gone? and, if you can slip in something tender,—something, you know, of what I feel,—maybe she would listen to you, Mary."

Mary promised that she would do all that he asked.

"I shall be thinking on her many and many a night, when I'm keeping my watch in mid-sea; I wonder if she will ever think on me, when the wind is whistling, and the gale rising. You'll often speak of me to her, Mary? And if I should meet with any mischance, tell her how dear, how very dear, she was to me, and bid her, for the sake of one who loved her well, try and comfort my poor aunt Alice. Dear old aunt! you and Margaret will often go and see her, won't you? She's

sadly failed since I was last ashore. And so good as she has been!
When I lived with her, a little wee chap, I used to be wakened by the
neighbours knocking her up; this one was ill, and that body's child
was restless; and for as tired as ever she might be, she would be up
and dressed in a twinkling, never thinking of the hard day's wash
afore her next morning. Them were happy times! How pleased I used
to be when she would take me into the fields with her to gather herbs!
I've tasted tea in China since then, but it wasn't half so good as the
herb tea she used to make for me o' Sunday nights. And she knew
such a deal about plants and birds, and their ways. She used to tell
me long stories about her childhood, and we used to plan how we
would go some time, please God (that was always her word), and live
near her old home beyond Lancaster; in the very cottage where she
was born, if we could get it. Dear! and how different it is! Here is she
still in a back street o' Manchester, never likely to see her own home
again; and I, a sailor, off for America next week. I wish she had been
able to go to Burton once afore she died."

"She would maybe have found all sadly changed," said Mary,
though her heart echoed Will's feeling.

"Ay! ay! I dare say it's best. One thing I do wish though, and I have
often wished it when out alone on the deep sea, when even the most
thoughtless can't choose but think on th' past and th' future; and that
is, that I'd never grieved her. Oh Mary! many a hasty word comes
sorely back on the heart, when one thinks one shall never see the person whom one has grieved again!"

They both stood thinking. Suddenly Mary started.

"That's father's step. And his shirt's not ready!"

She hurried to her irons, and tried to make up for lost time.

John Barton came in. Such a haggard and wildly anxious-looking
man, Will thought he had never seen. He looked at Will, but spoke
no word of greeting or welcome.

"I'm come to bid you good-bye," said the sailor, and would in his
sociable friendly humour have gone on speaking. But John answered
abruptly,

"Good-bye to ye, then."[9]

There was that in his manner which left no doubt of his desire to
get rid of the visitor, and Will accordingly shook hands with Mary, and
looked at John, as if doubting how far to offer to shake hands with
him. But he met with no answering glance or gesture, so he went his
way, stopping for an instant at the door to say,

"You'll think on me on Tuesday, Mary. That's the day we shall hoist
our blue Peter, Jack Harris says."

---

9. This scene was illustrated by C. M. Relyea in 1907. See the illustrations section of this
volume.

Mary was heartily sorry when the door closed; it seemed like shutting out a friendly sunbeam. And her father! what could be the matter with him? He was so restless; not speaking (she wished he would), but starting up and then sitting down, and meddling with her irons; he seemed so fierce, too, to judge from his face. She wondered if he disliked Will being there; or if he were vexed to find that she had not got further on with her work. At last she could bear his nervous way no longer, it made her equally nervous and fidgety. She would speak.

"When are you going, father? I don't know the time o' the trains."

"And why shouldst thou know?" replied he, gruffly. "Meddle with thy ironing, but donnot be asking questions about what doesn't concern thee."

"I wanted to get you something to eat first," answered she, gently.

"Thou dost not know that I'm larning to do without food," said he.

Mary looked at him to see if he spoke jestingly. No! he looked savagely grave.

She finished her bit of ironing, and began preparing the food she was sure her father needed; for by this time her experience in the degrees of hunger had taught her that his present irritability was increased, if not caused, by want of food.

He had had a sovereign given him to pay his expenses as delegate to Glasgow, and out of this he had given Mary a few shillings in the morning; so she had been able to buy a sufficient meal, and now her care was to cook it so as to tempt him.

"If thou'rt doing that for me, Mary, thou mayst spare thy labour. I told thee I were not for eating."

"Just a little bit, father, before starting," coaxed Mary, perseveringly.

At that instant who should come in but Job Legh. It was not often he came, but when he did pay visits, Mary knew from past experience they were anything but short. Her father's countenance fell back into the deep gloom from which it was but just emerging at the sound of Mary's sweet voice, and pretty pleading. He became again restless and fidgety, scarcely giving Job Legh the greeting necessary for a host in his own house. Job, however, did not stand upon ceremony. He had come to pay a visit, and was not to be daunted from his purpose. He was interested in John Barton's mission to Glasgow, and wanted to hear all about it; so he sat down, and made himself comfortable, in a manner that Mary saw was meant to be stationary.

"So thou'rt off to Glasgow, art thou?" he began his catechism.

"Ay."

"When art starting?"

"To-night."

"That I knowed. But by what train?"

That was just what Mary wanted to know; but what apparently her father was in no mood to tell. He got up without speaking, and went up-stairs. Mary knew from his step, and his way, how much he was put out, and feared Job would see it too. But no! Job seemed imperturbable. So much the better, and perhaps she could cover her father's rudeness by her own civility to so kind a friend.

So, half listening to her father's movements up-stairs (passionate, violent, restless motions they were), and half attending to Job Legh, she tried to pay him all due regard.

"When does thy father start, Mary?"

That plaguing question again.

"Oh! very soon. I'm just getting him a bit of supper. Is Margaret very well?"

"Yes, she's well enough. She's meaning to go and keep Alice Wilson company for an hour or so this evening; as soon as she thinks her nephew will have started for Liverpool; for she fancies the old woman will feel a bit lonesome. Th' Union is paying for your father, I suppose?"

"Yes, they've giv'n him a sovereign. You're one of th' Union, Job?"

"Ay! I'm one, sure enough; but I'm but a sleeping partner in the concern. I were obliged to become a member for peace, else I don't go along with 'em. Yo see they think themselves wise, and me silly, for differing with them! Well! there's no harm in that. But then they won't let me be silly in peace and quietness, but will force me to be as wise as they are; now that's not British liberty, I say. I'm forced to be wise according to their notions, else they parsecute me, and sarve me out."

What could her father be doing up-stairs? Tramping and banging about. Why did he not come down? Or why did not Job go? The supper would be spoilt.

But Job had no notion of going.

"You see my folly is this, Mary. I would take what I could get; I think half a loaf is better than no bread. I would work for low wages rather than sit idle and starve. But, comes the Trades' Union, and says, 'Well, if you take the half-loaf, we'll worry you out of your life. Will you be clemmed, or will you be worried?' Now clemming is a quiet death, and worrying isn't, so I choose clemming, and come into th' Union. But I'd wish they'd leave me free, if I am a fool."

Creak, creak, went the stairs. Her father was coming down at last.

Yes, he came down, but more doggedly fierce than before, and made up for his journey, too; with his little bundle on his arm. He went up to Job, and, more civilly than Mary expected, wished him good-bye. He then turned to her, and in a short cold manner, bade her farewell.

"Oh! father, don't go yet. Your supper is all ready. Stay one moment."

But he pushed her away, and was gone. She followed him to the door, her eyes blinded by sudden tears; she stood there looking after him. He was so strange, so cold, so hard. Suddenly, at the end of the court, he turned, and saw her standing there; he came back quickly, and took her in his arms.

"God bless thee, Mary!—God in heaven bless thee, poor child!" She threw her arms round his neck.

"Don't go yet, father; I can't bear you to go yet. Come in, and eat some supper; you look so ghastly; dear father, do!"

"No," he said, faintly and mournfully. "It's best as it is. I couldn't eat, and it's best to be off. I cannot be still at home. I must be moving."

So saying, he unlaced her soft twining arms, and kissing her once more, set off on his fierce errand.

And he was out of sight! She did not know why, but she had never before felt so depressed, so desolate. She turned in to Job, who sat there still. Her father, as soon as he was out of sight, slackened his pace, and fell into that heavy listless step, which told as well as words could do, of hopelessness and weakness. It was getting dark, but he loitered on, returning no greeting to any one.

A child's cry caught his ear. His thoughts were running on little Tom; on the dead and buried child of happier years. He followed the sound of wail, that might have been *his*, and found a poor little mortal, who had lost his way, and whose grief had choked up his thoughts to the single want, "Mammy, mammy." With tender address, John Barton soothed the little laddie, and with beautiful patience he gathered fragments of meaning from the half-spoken words which came mingled with sobs from the terrified little heart. So, aided by inquiries here and there from a passer-by, he led and carried the little fellow home, where his mother had been too busy to miss him, but now received him with thankfulness, and with an eloquent Irish blessing. When John heard the words of blessing, he shook his head mournfully, and turned away to retrace his steps.

Let us leave him.

Mary took her sewing after he had gone, and sat on, and sat on, trying to listen to Job, who was more inclined to talk than usual. She had conquered her feeling of impatience towards him so far as to be able to offer him her father's rejected supper; and she even tried to eat herself. But her heart failed her. A leaden weight seemed to hang over her; a sort of presentiment of evil, or perhaps only an excess of low-spirited feeling in consequence of the two departures which had taken place that afternoon.

She wondered how long Job Legh would sit. She did not like putting down her work, and crying before him, and yet she had never in her life longed so much to be alone in order to indulge a good hearty burst of tears.

"Well, Mary," she suddenly caught him saying, "I thought you'd be a bit lonely to-night; and as Margaret were going to cheer th' old woman, I said I'd go and keep th' young 'un company; and a very pleasant chatty evening we've had; very. Only I wonder as Margaret is not come back."

"But perhaps she is," suggested Mary.

"No, no, I took care o' that. Look ye here!" and he pulled out the great house-key. She'll have to stand waiting i' th' street, and that I'm sure she wouldn't do, when she knew where to find me."

"Will she come back by hersel?" asked Mary.

"Ay. At first I were afraid o' trusting her, and I used to follow her a bit behind; never letting on, of course. But, bless you! she goes along as steadily as can be; rather slow to be sure, and her head a bit on one side, as if she were listening. And it's real beautiful to see her cross the road. She'll wait above a bit to hear that all is still; not that she's so dark as not to see a coach or a cart like a big black thing, but she can't rightly judge how far off it is by sight, so she listens. Hark! that's her!"

Yes; in she came with her usually calm face, all tear-stained and sorrow-marked.

"What's the matter, my wench?" said Job, hastily.

"Oh, grandfather! Alice Wilson's so bad!" She could say no more for her breathless agitation. The afternoon, and the parting with Will, had weakened her nerves for any aftershock.

"What is it? Do tell us Margaret!" said Mary, placing her in a chair, and loosening her bonnet-strings.

"I think it's a stroke o' the palsy. Any rate she has lost the use of one side."

"Was it afore Will had set off?" asked Mary.

"No, he were gone before I got there," said Margaret; "and she were much about as well as she has been for many a day. She spoke a bit, but not much; but that were only natural, for Mrs. Wilson likes to have the talk to hersel, you know. She got up to go across the room, and then I heard a drag wi' her leg, and presently a fall, and Mrs. Wilson came running, and set up such a cry! I stopped wi' Alice, while she fetched a doctor; but she could not speak, to answer me, though she tried, I think."

"Where was Jem? Why didn't he go for the doctor?"

"He were out when I got there, and he never came home while I stopped."

"Thou'st never left Mrs. Wilson alone wi' poor Alice?" asked Job, hastily.

"No, no," said Margaret. "But oh! grandfather, it's now I feel how hard it is to have lost my sight. I should have so loved to nurse her; and I did try, until I found I did more harm than good. Oh, grandfather; if I could but see!"

She sobbed a little; and they let her give that ease to her heart. Then she went on—

"No! I went round by Mrs. Davenport's, and she were hard at work; but, the minute I told my errand, she were ready and willing to go to Jane Wilson, and stop up all night with Alice."

"And what does the doctor say?" asked Mary.

"Oh! much what all doctors say: he puts a fence on this side, and a fence on that, for fear he should be caught tripping in his judgment. One moment he does not think there's much hope—but while there is life there is hope; th' next he says he should think she might recover partial—but her age is again her. He's ordered her leeches to her head."[1]

Margaret having told her tale, leant back with weariness, both of body and mind. Mary hastened to make her a cup of tea; while Job, lately so talkative, sat quiet and mournfully silent.

"I'll go first thing to-morrow morning, and learn how she is; and I'll bring word back before I go to work," said Mary.

"It's a bad job Will's gone," said Job.

"Jane does not think she knows any one," replied Margaret. "It's perhaps as well he shouldn't see her now, for they say her face is sadly drawn. He'll remember her with her own face better, if he does not see her again."

With a few more sorrowful remarks they separated for the night, and Mary was left alone in her house, to meditate on the heavy day that had passed over her head. Every thing seemed going wrong. Will gone; her father gone—and so strangely too! And to a place so mysteriously distant as Glasgow seemed to be to her! She had felt his presence as a protection against Harry Carson and his threats; and now she dreaded lest he should learn she was alone. Her heart began to despair, too, about Jem. She feared he had ceased to love her; and she—she only loved him more and more for his seeming neglect. And, as if all this aggregate of sorrowful thoughts was not enough, here was this new woe, of poor Alice's paralytic stroke.

---

1. Leeches were applied to the skin to draw blood. This practice was a standard treatment for a range of medical conditions.

Chapter XVIII.

"But in his pulse there was no throb,
Nor on his lips one dying sob;
Sigh, nor word, nor struggling breath
Heralded his way to death."
                    SIEGE OF CORINTH.[2]

"My brain runs this way and that way; 'twill not fix
On aught but vengeance."
                    DUKE OF GUISE.[3]

I must now go back to an hour or two before Mary and her friends parted for the night. It might be about eight o'clock that evening, and the three Miss Carsons were sitting in their father's drawing-room. He was asleep in the dining-room, in his own comfortable chair. Mrs. Carson was (as was usual with her, when no particular excitement was going on) very poorly, and sitting up-stairs in her dressing-room, indulging in the luxury of a head-ache. She was not well, certainly. "Wind in the head," the servants called it. But it was but the natural consequence of the state of mental and bodily idleness in which she was placed. Without education enough to value the resources of wealth and leisure, she was so circumstanced as to command both. It would have done her more good than all the ether and sal-volatile[4] she was daily in the habit of swallowing, if she might have taken the work of one of her own housemaids for a week; made beds, rubbed tables, shaken carpets, and gone out into the fresh morning air, without all the paraphernalia of shawl, cloak, boa, fur boots, bonnet, and veil, in which she was equipped before setting out for an "airing," in the closely shut-up carriage.

So the three girls were by themselves in the comfortable, elegant, well-lighted drawing-room; and, like many similarly situated young ladies, they did not exactly know what to do to while away the time until the tea-hour. The elder two had been at a dancing-party the night before, and were listless and sleepy in consequence. One tried to read "Emerson's Essays,"[5] and fell asleep in the attempt; the other was turning over a parcel of new songs, in order to select what she liked. Amy, the youngest, was copying some manuscript music. The air was heavy with the fragrance of strongly-scented flowers, which sent out their night odours from an adjoining conservatory.

---

2. Byron's *The Siege of Corinth* (1816), xxvi, lines 889–92.
3. John Dryden's (1631–1679) and Nathaniel Lee's (?1653–1692) *The Duke of Guise* (1683), III, I.
4. Ether (alcohol and sulphuric acid) was taken as a sedative; sal-volatile (ammonia) was used as smelling salts and taken with water for restorative purposes.
5. The American essayist and poet Ralph Waldo Emerson (1803–1882) lectured in Manchester in 1847. His essays were published in 1841 and 1844.

The clock on the chimney-piece chimed eight. Sophy (the sleeping sister) started up at the sound.

"What o'clock is that?" she asked.

"Eight," said Amy.

"Oh, dear! how tired I am! Is Harry come in? Tea will rouse one up a little. Are you not worn out, Helen?"

"Yes; I am tired enough. One is good for nothing the day after a dance. Yet I don't feel weary at the time; I suppose it is the lateness of the hours."

"And yet, how could it be managed otherwise? So many don't dine till five or six, that one cannot begin before eight or nine; and then it takes a long time to get into the spirit of the evening. It is always more pleasant after supper than before."

"Well, I'm too tired to-night to reform the world in the matter of dances or balls. What are you copying, Amy?"

"Only that little Spanish air you sing, 'Quien quiera.'"[6]

"What are you copying it for?" asked Helen.

"Harry asked me to do it for him this morning at breakfast-time—for Miss Richardson, he said."

"For Jane Richardson!" said Sophy, as if a new idea were receiving strength in her mind.

"Do you think Harry means anything by his attention to her?" asked Helen.

"Nay, I do not know anything more than you do; I can only observe and conjecture. What do you think, Helen?"

"Harry always likes to be of consequence to the belle of the room. If one girl is more admired than another, he likes to flutter about her, and seem to be on intimate terms with her. That is his way, and I have not noticed anything beyond that in his manner to Jane Richardson."

"But I don't think she knows it's only his way. Just watch her the next time we meet her when Harry is there, and see how she crimsons, and looks another way when she feels he is coming up to her. I think he sees it, too, and I think he is pleased with it."

"I dare say Harry would like well enough to turn the head of such a lovely girl as Jane Richardson. But I'm not convinced that he's in love, whatever she may be."

"Well, then!" said Sophy, indignantly, "though it is our own brother, I do think he is behaving very wrongly. The more I think of it, the more sure I am that she thinks he means something, and that he intends her to think so. And then, when he leaves off paying her attention——"

"Which will be as soon as a prettier girl makes her appearance," interrupted Helen.

---

6. Whoever, or what are you seeking?

"As soon as he leaves off paying her attention," resumed Sophy, "she will have many and many a heart-ache, and then she will harden herself into being a flirt, a feminine flirt, as he is a masculine flirt. Poor girl!"

"I don't like to hear you speak so of Harry," said Amy, looking up at Sophy.

"And I don't like to have to speak so, Amy, for I love him dearly. He is a good, kind brother, but I do think him vain, and I think he hardly knows the misery, the crime, to which indulged vanity may lead him."

Helen yawned.

"Oh! do you think we may ring for tea. Sleeping after dinner makes me so feverish."

"Yes, surely. Why should not we?" said the more energetic Sophy, pulling the bell with some determination.

"Tea, directly, Parker," said she, authoritatively, as the man entered the room.

She was too little in the habit of reading expressions on the faces of others to notice Parker's countenance.

Yet it was striking. It was blanched to a dead whiteness; the lips compressed as if to keep within some tale of horror; the eyes distended and unnatural. It was a terror-stricken face.

The girls began to put away their music and books, in preparation for tea. The door slowly opened again, and this time it was the nurse who entered. I call her nurse, for such had been her office in bygone days, though now she held rather an anomalous situation in the family. Seamstress, attendant on the young ladies, keeper of the stores; only "Nurse" was still her name. She had lived longer with them than any other servant, and to her their manner was far less haughty than to the other domestics. She occasionally came into the drawing-room to look for things belonging to their father or mother, so it did not excite any surprise when she advanced into the room. They went on arranging their various articles of employment.

She wanted them to look up. She wanted them to read something in her face—her face so full of woe, of horror. But they went on without taking any notice. She coughed; not a natural cough; but one of those coughs which asks so plainly for remark.

"Dear nurse, what is the matter?" asked Amy. "Are not you well?"

"Is mamma ill?" asked Sophy, quickly.

"Speak, speak, nurse!" said they all, as they saw her efforts to articulate choked by the convulsive rising in her throat. They clustered round her with eager faces, catching a glimpse of some terrible truth to be revealed.

"My dear young ladies! my dear girls!" she gasped out at length, and then she burst into tears.

"Oh! do tell us what it is, nurse!" said one. "Anything is better than this. Speak!"

"My children! I don't know how to break it to you. My dears, poor Mr. Harry is brought home——"

"Brought home—*brought* home—how?" Instinctively they sank their voices to a whisper; but a fearful whisper it was. In the same low tone, as if afraid lest the walls, the furniture, the inanimate things which told of preparation for life and comfort, should hear, she answered,

"Dead!"

Amy clutched her nurse's arm, and fixed her eyes on her as if to know if such a tale could be true; and when she read its confirmation in those sad, mournful, unflinching eyes, she sank, without word or sound, down in a faint upon the floor. One sister sat down on an ottoman, and covered her face, to try and realise it. That was Sophy. Helen threw herself on the sofa, and burying her head in the pillows, tried to stifle the screams and moans which shook her frame.

The nurse stood silent. She had not told *all*.

"Tell me," said Sophy, looking up, and speaking in a hoarse voice, which told of the inward pain, "tell me, nurse! Is he *dead*, did you say? Have you sent for a doctor? Oh! send for one, send for one," continued she, her voice rising to shrillness, and starting to her feet. Helen lifted herself up, and looked, with breathless waiting, towards nurse.

"My dears, he is dead! But I have sent for a doctor. I have done all I could."

"When did he—when did they bring him home?" asked Sophy.

"Perhaps ten minutes ago. Before you rang for Parker."

"How did he die? Where did they find him? He looked so well. He always seemed so strong. Oh! are you sure he is dead?"

She went towards the door. Nurse laid her hand on her arm.

"Miss Sophy, I have not told you all. Can you bear to hear it? Remember, master is in the next room, and he knows nothing yet. Come, you must help me to tell him. Now, be quiet, dear! It was no common death he died!" She looked in her face as if trying to convey her meaning by her eyes.

Sophy's lips moved, but nurse could hear no sound.

"He has been shot as he was coming home along Turner-street to-night."

Sophy went on with the motion of her lips, twitching them almost convulsively.

"My dear, you must rouse yourself, and remember your father and mother have yet to be told. Speak! Miss Sophy!"

But she could not; her whole face worked involuntarily. The nurse left the room, and almost immediately brought back some sal-volatile and water. Sophy drank it eagerly, and gave one or two deep gasps. Then she spoke in a calm, unnatural voice.

"What do you want me to do, nurse? Go to Helen, and poor Amy. See, they want help."

"Poor creatures! we must let them alone for a bit. You must go to master; that's what I want you to do, Miss Sophy. You must break it to him, poor old gentleman! Come, he's asleep in the dining-room, and the men are waiting to speak to him."

Sophy went mechanically to the dining-room door.

"Oh! I cannot go in. I cannot tell him. What must I say?"

"I'll come with you, Miss Sophy. Break it to him by degrees."

"I can't, nurse. My head throbs so, I shall be sure to say the wrong thing."

However, she opened the door. There sat her father, the shaded light of the candle-lamp falling upon, and softening his marked features, while his snowy hair contrasted well with the deep crimson morocco of the chair. The newspaper he had been reading had dropped on the carpet by his side. He breathed regularly and deeply.

At that instant the words of Mrs. Hemans's song came full in Sophy's mind:—

> "Ye know not what ye do,
>   That call the slumberer back
> From the realms unseen by you,
>   To life's dim weary track."[7]

But this life's track would be to the bereaved father something more than dim and weary, hereafter.

"Papa," said she, softly. He did not stir.

"Papa!" she exclaimed somewhat louder.

He started up, half awake.

"Tea is ready, is it?" and he yawned.

"No! papa, but something very dreadful—very sad, has happened!"

He was gaping so loud that he did not catch the words she uttered, and did not see the expression of her face.

"Master Henry has not come back," said nurse. Her voice, heard in unusual speech to him, arrested his attention, and rubbing his eyes, he looked at the servant.

"Harry! oh no! he had to attend a meeting of the masters about these cursed turn-outs. I don't expect him yet. What are you looking at me so strangely for, Sophy?"

"Oh, papa, Harry is come back," said she, bursting into tears.

"What do you mean?" said he, startled into an impatient consciousness that something was wrong. "One of you says he is not come home, and the other says he is. Now, that's nonsense! Tell me

---

7. From Felicia Dorothea Hemans's (1793–1835) "The Sleeper" (1830).

at once what's the matter. Did he go on horseback to town? Is he thrown? Speak, child, can't you?"

"No! he's not been thrown, papa," said Sophy, sadly.

"But he's badly hurt," put in the nurse, desirous to be drawing his anxiety to a point.

"Hurt? Where? How? Have you sent for a doctor?" said he, hastily rising, as if to leave the room.

"Yes, papa, we've sent for a doctor—but I'm afraid—I believe it's of no use."

He looked at her for a moment, and in her face he read the truth. His son, his only son, was dead.

He sank back in his chair, and hid his face in his hands, and bowed his head upon the table. The strong mahogany dining-table shook and rattled under his agony.

Sophy went and put her arms round his bowed neck.

"Go! you are not Harry," said he; but the action roused him.

"Where is he? where is the——" said he, with his strong face set into the lines of anguish, by two minutes of such intense woe.

"In the servants' hall," said nurse. "Two policemen and another man brought him home. They would be glad to speak to you when you are able, sir."

"I am now able," replied he. At first when he stood up he tottered. But steadying himself, he walked, as firmly as a soldier on drill, to the door. Then he turned back and poured out a glass of wine from the decanter which yet remained on the table. His eye caught the wine-glass which Harry had used but two or three hours before. He sighed a long quivering sigh, and then mastering himself again, he left the room.

"You had better go back to your sisters, Miss Sophy," said nurse.

Miss Carson went. She could not face death yet.

The nurse followed Mr. Carson to the servants' hall. There on their dinner-table lay the poor dead body. The men who had brought it were sitting near the fire, while several of the servants stood round the table, gazing at the remains.

The remains!

One or two were crying; one or two were whispering; awed into a strange stillness of voice and action by the presence of the dead. When Mr. Carson came in they all drew back and looked at him with the reverence due to sorrow.

He went forward and gazed long and fondly on the calm, dead face; then he bent down and kissed the lips yet crimson with life. The policeman had advanced, and stood ready to be questioned. But at first the old man's mind could only take in the idea of death; slowly, slowly came the conception of violence, of murder. "How did he die?" he groaned forth.

The policemen looked at each other. Then one began, and stated that having heard the report of a gun in Turner-street, he had turned down that way (a lonely unfrequented way Mr. Carson knew, but a short cut to his garden door, of which Harry had a key); that as he (the policeman) came nearer, he had heard footsteps as of a man running away; but the evening was so dark (the moon not having yet risen) that he could see no one twenty yards off. That he had even been startled when close to the body by seeing it lying across the path at his feet. That he had sprung his rattle;[8] and when another policeman came up, by the light of the lantern they had discovered who it was that had been killed. That they believed him to be dead when they first took him up, as he had never moved, spoken, or breathed. That intelligence of the murder had been sent to the superintendent, who would probably soon be here. That two or three policemen were still about the place where the murder was committed, seeking out for some trace of the murderer. Having said this, they stopped speaking.

Mr. Carson had listened attentively, never taking his eyes off the dead body. When they had ended, he said,

"Where was he shot?"

They lifted up some of the thick chestnut curls, and showed a blue spot (you could hardly call it a hole, the flesh had closed so much over it) in the left temple. A deadly aim! And yet it was so dark a night!

"He must have been close upon him," said one policeman.

"And have had him between him and the sky," added the other.

There was a little commotion at the door of the room, and there stood poor Mrs. Carson, the mother.

She had heard unusual noises in the house, and had sent down her maid (much more a companion to her than her highly educated daughters) to discover what was going on. But the maid either forgot, or dreaded, to return; and with nervous impatience Mrs. Carson came down herself, and had traced the hum and buzz of voices to the servants' hall.

Mr. Carson turned round. But he could not leave the dead for any one living.

"Take her away, nurse. It is no sight for her. Tell Miss Sophy to go to her mother." His eyes were again fixed on the dead face of his son.

Presently Mrs. Carson's hysterical cries were heard all over the house. Her husband shuddered at the outward expression of the agony which was rending his heart.

Then the police superintendent came, and after him the doctor. The latter went through all the forms of ascertaining death, without uttering a word, and when at the conclusion of the operation of open-

8. Device for making a rattling noise; used like a police whistle.

ing a vein, from which no blood flowed, he shook his head, all present understood the confirmation of their previous belief. The superintendent asked to speak to Mr. Carson in private.

"It was just what I was going to request of you," answered he; so he led the way into the dining-room, with the wine-glass still on the table.

The door was carefully shut, and both sat down, each apparently waiting for the other to begin.

At last Mr. Carson spoke.

"You probably have heard that I am a rich man."

The superintendent bowed in assent.

"Well, sir, half—nay, if necessary, the whole of my fortune I will give to have the murderer brought to the gallows."

"Every exertion, you may be sure, sir, shall be used on our part; but probably offering a handsome reward might accelerate the discovery of the murderer. But what I wanted particularly to tell you, sir, is that one of my men has already got some clue, and that another (who accompanied me here) has within this quarter of an hour found a gun in the field which the murderer crossed, and which he probably threw away when pursued, as encumbering his flight. I have not the smallest doubt of discovering the murderer."

"What do you call a handsome reward?" said Mr. Carson.

"Well, sir, three, or five hundred pounds is a munificent reward: more than will probably be required as a temptation to any accomplice."

"Make it a thousand," said Mr. Carson, decisively. "It's the doing of those damned turn-outs."

"I imagine not," said the superintendent. "Some days ago the man I was naming to you before, reported to the inspector when he came on his beat, that he had to separate your son from a young man, who by his dress he believed to be employed in a foundry; that the man had thrown Mr. Carson down, and seemed inclined to proceed to more violence, when the policeman came up and interfered. Indeed, my man wished to give him in charge for an assault, but Mr. Carson would not allow that to be done."

"Just like him!—noble fellow!" murmured the father.

"But after your son had left, the man made use of some pretty strong threats. And it's rather a curious coincidence that this scuffle took place in the very same spot where the murder was committed; in Turner-street."

There was some one knocking at the door of the room. It was Sophy, who beckoned her father out, and then asked him, in an awe-struck whisper, to come up-stairs and speak to her mother.

"She will not leave Harry, and talks so strangely. Indeed—indeed—papa, I think she has lost her senses."

And the poor girl sobbed bitterly.

"Where is she?" asked Mr. Carson.

"In his room."

They went up-stairs rapidly, and silently. It was a large comfortable bedroom; too large to be well lighted by the flaring, flickering kitchen-candle which had been hastily snatched up, and now stood on the dressing-table.

On the bed, surrounded by its heavy, pall-like green curtains, lay the dead son. They had carried him up, and laid him down, as tenderly as though they feared to waken him; and, indeed, it looked more like sleep than death, so very calm and full of repose was the face. You saw, too, the chiselled beauty of the features much more perfectly than when the brilliant colouring of life had distracted your attention. There was a peace about him which told that death had come too instantaneously to give any previous pain.

In a chair, at the head of the bed, sat the mother,—smiling. She held one of the hands (rapidly stiffening, even in her warm grasp), and gently stroked the back of it, with the endearing caress she had used to all her children when young.

"I am glad you are come," said she, looking up at her husband, and still smiling. "Harry is so full of fun, he always has something new to amuse us with; and now he pretends he is asleep, and that we can't waken him. Look! he is smiling now; he hears I have found him out. Look!"

And, in truth, the lips, in the rest of death, did look as though they wore a smile, and the waving light of the unsnuffed candle almost made them seem to move.

"Look, Amy," said she to her youngest child, who knelt at her feet, trying to soothe her, by kissing her garments.

"Oh, he was always a rogue! You remember, don't you, love? how full of play he was as a baby; hiding his face under my arm, when you wanted to play with him. Always a rogue, Harry!"

"We must get her away, sir," said nurse; "you know there is much to be done, before——"

"I understand, nurse," said the father, hastily interrupting her in dread of the distinct words which would tell of the changes of mortality.

"Come love," said he to his wife. "I want you to come with me. I want to speak to you down stairs."

"I'm coming," said she, rising; "perhaps, after all, nurse, he's really tired, and would be glad to sleep. Don't let him get cold, though,— he feels rather chilly," continued she, after she had bent down, and kissed the pale lips.

Her husband put his arm around her waist, and they left the room. Then the three sisters burst into unrestrained wailings. They were

startled into the reality of life and death. And yet in the midst of
shrieks and moans, of shivering and chattering of teeth, Sophy's eye
caught the calm beauty of the dead; so calm amidst such violence,
and she hushed her emotion.

"Come," said she to her sisters, "nurse wants us to go; and besides,
we ought to be with mamma. Papa told the man he was talking to,
when I went for him, to wait, and she must not be left."

Meanwhile, the superintendent had taken a candle, and was examining the engravings that hung round the dining-room. It was so common to him to be acquainted with crime, that he was far from feeling
all his interest absorbed in the present case of violence, although he
could not help having much anxiety to detect the murderer. He was
busy looking at the only oil-painting in the room (a youth of eighteen
or so, in a fancy dress), and conjecturing its identity with the young
man so mysteriously dead, when the door opened, and Mr. Carson
returned. Stern as he had looked before leaving the room, he looked
far sterner now. His face was hardened into deep-purposed wrath.

"I beg your pardon, sir, for leaving you." The superintendent
bowed. They sat down, and spoke long together. One by one the
policemen were called in, and questioned.

All through the night there was bustle and commotion in the
house. Nobody thought of going to bed. It seemed strange to Sophy
to hear nurse summoned from her mother's side to supper, in the
middle of the night, and still stranger that she could go. The necessity of eating and drinking seemed out of place in the house of death.

When night was passing into morning, the dining-room door
opened, and two persons' steps were heard along the hall. The superintendent was leaving at last. Mr. Carson stood on the front-door
step, feeling the refreshment of the caller[9] morning air, and seeing
the starlight fade away into dawn.

"You will not forget," said he. "I trust to you." The policeman bowed.

"Spare no money. The only purpose for which I now value wealth
is to have the murderer arrested, and brought to justice. My hope in
life now is to see him sentenced to death. Offer any rewards. Name
a thousand pounds in the placards. Come to me at any hour, night or
day, if that be required. All I ask of you is, to get the murderer hanged.
Next week, if possible—to-day is Friday. Surely with the clues you
already possess, you can muster up evidence sufficient to have him
tried next week."

"He may easily request an adjournment of his trial, on the ground
of the shortness of the notice," said the superintendent.

"Oppose it, if possible. I will see that the first lawyers are employed.
I shall know no rest while he lives."

9. Fresh.

"Everything shall be done, sir."

"You will arrange with the coroner. Ten o'clock if convenient."

The superintendent took leave.

Mr. Carson stood on the step, dreading to shut out the light and air, and return into the haunted, gloomy house.

"My son! my son!" he said, at last. "But you shall be avenged, my poor murdered boy."

Ay! to avenge his wrongs the murderer had singled out his victim, and with one fell action had taken away the life that God had given. To avenge his child's death, the old man lived on; with the single purpose in his heart of vengeance on the murderer. True, his vengeance was sanctioned by law, but was it the less revenge?

Are ye worshippers of Christ? or of Alecto?[1]

Oh! Orestes,[2] you would have made a very tolerable Christian of the nineteenth century!

Chapter XIX.

> "Deeds to be hid which were not hid,
> Which, all confused, I could not know,
> Whether I suffered or I did,
> For all seemed guilt, remorse, or woe."
>
> COLERIDGE.[3]

I left Mary, on that same Thursday night which left its burden of woe at Mr. Carson's threshold, haunted with depressing thoughts. All through the night she tossed restlessly about, trying to get quit of the ideas that harassed her, and longing for the light when she could rise, and find some employment. But just as dawn began to appear, she became more quiet, and fell into a sound heavy sleep, which lasted till she was sure it was late in the morning, by the full light that shone in.

She dressed hastily, and heard the neighbouring church clock strike eight. It was far too late to do as she had planned (after inquiring how Alice was, to return and tell Margaret), and she accordingly went in to inform the latter of her change of purpose, and the cause of it; but on entering the house she found Job sitting alone, looking sad enough. She told him what she came for.

"Margaret, wench! why she's been gone to Wilson's these two hours. Ay! sure, you did say last night you would go; but she could na rest in her bed, so was off betimes this morning."

Mary could do nothing but feel guilty of her long morning nap, and

---

1. One of the Greek furies or avenging deities.
2. Killed his mother, who had murdered his father. Pursued by Alecto.
3. From Coleridge's "The Pains of Sleep" (1816), lines 27–30.

hasten to follow Margaret's steps; for late as it was, she felt she could not settle well to her work, unless she learnt how kind good Alice Wilson was going on.

So, eating her crust-of-bread breakfast, she passed rapidly along the street. She remembered afterwards the little groups of people she had seen, eagerly hearing, and imparting news; but at the time her only care was to hasten on her way, in dread of a reprimand from Miss Simmonds.

She went into the house at Jane Wilson's, her heart at the instant giving a strange knock, and sending the rosy flush into her face, at the thought that Jem might possibly be inside the door. But I do assure you, she had not thought of it before. Impatient and loving as she was, her solicitude about Alice on that hurried morning had not been mingled with any thought of him.

Her heart need not have leaped, her colour need not have rushed so painfully to her cheeks, for he was not there. There was the round table, with a cup and saucer, which had evidently been used, and there was Jane Wilson sitting on the other side, crying quietly, while she ate her breakfast with a sort of unconscious appetite. And there was Mrs. Davenport washing away at a night-cap or so, which, by their simple, old-world make, Mary knew at a glance were Alice's. But nothing—no one else.

Alice was much the same, or rather better of the two, they told her; at any rate she could speak, though it was sad rambling talk. Would Mary like to see her?

Of course she would. Many are interested by seeing their friends under the new aspect of illness: and among the poor there is no wholesome fear of injury or excitement to restrain this wish.

So Mary went up-stairs, accompanied by Mrs. Davenport, wringing the suds off her hands, and speaking in a loud whisper far more audible than her usual voice.

"I mun be hastening home, but I'll come again to-night, time enough to iron her cap; 'twould be a sin and a shame if we let her go dirty now she's ill, when she's been so rare and clean all her life long. But she's sadly forsaken, poor thing! She'll not know you, Mary; she knows none of us."

The room up-stairs held two beds, one superior in the grandeur of four posts and checked curtains to the other, which had been occupied by the twins in their brief lifetime. The smaller had been Alice's bed since she had lived there; but with the natural reverence to one "stricken of God and afflicted,"[4] she had been installed, since her paralytic stroke the evening before, in the larger and grander bed; while Jane Wilson had taken her short broken rest on the little pallet.

4. Isaiah 54:3.

Margaret came forwards to meet her friend, whom she half expected, and whose step she knew. Mrs. Davenport returned to her washing.

The two girls did not speak; the presence of Alice awed them into silence. There she lay with the rosy colour, absent from her face since the days of childhood, flushed once more into it by her sickness nigh unto death. She lay on the affected side, and with her other arm she was constantly sawing the air, not exactly in a restless manner, but in a monotonous, incessant way, very trying to a watcher. She was talking away, too, almost as constantly, in a low indistinct tone. But her face, her profiled countenance, looked calm and smiling, even interested by the ideas that were passing through her clouded mind.

"Listen!" said Margaret, as she stooped her head down to catch the muttered words more distinctly.

"What will mother say? The bees are turning homeward for th' last time, and we've a terrible long bit to go yet. See! here's a linnet's nest in this gorse bush. Th' hen bird is on it. Look at her bright eyes, she won't stir. Ay! we mun hurry home. Won't mother be pleased with the bonny lot of heather we've got! Make haste, Sally, maybe we shall have cockles for supper. I saw th' cockle-man's donkey turn up our way fra' Arnside."

Margaret touched Mary's hand, and the pressure in return told her that they understood each other; that they knew how in this illness to the old, world-weary woman, God had sent her a veiled blessing: she was once more in the scenes of her childhood, unchanged and bright as in those long departed days; once more with the sister of her youth, the playmate of fifty years ago, who had for nearly as many years slept in a grassy grave in the little churchyard beyond Burton.

Alice's face changed; she looked sorrowful, almost penitent.

"Oh, Sally! I wish we'd told her. She thinks we were in church all morning, and we've gone on deceiving her. If we'd told her at first how it was—how sweet th' hawthorn smelt through the open church door, and how we were on th' last bench in the aisle, and how it were the first butterfly we'd seen this spring, and how it flew into th' very church itself; oh! mother is so gentle, I wish we'd told her. I'll go to her next time she comes in sight, and say, 'Mother, we were naughty last Sabbath.'"

She stopped, and a few tears came stealing down the old withered cheek, at the thought of the temptation and deceit of her childhood. Surely, many sins could not have darkened that innocent child-like spirit since. Mary found a red-spotted pocket-handkerchief, and put it into the hand which sought about for something to wipe away the trickling tears. She took it with a gentle murmur.

"Thank you, mother."

Mary pulled Margaret away from the bed.

"Don't you think she's happy, Margaret?"

"Ay! that I do, bless her. She feels no pain, and knows nought of her present state. Oh! that I could see, Mary! I try and be patient with her afore me, but I'd give aught I have to see her, and see what she wants. I am so useless! I mean to stay here as long as Jane Wilson is alone; and I would fain be here all to-night, but——"

"I'll come," said Mary, decidedly.

"Mrs. Davenport said she'd come again, but she's hard-worked all day——"

"I'll come," repeated Mary.

"Do!" said Margaret, "and I'll be here till you come. Maybe, Jem and you could take th' night between you, and Jane Wilson might get a bit of sound sleep in his bed; for she were up and down the better part of last night, and just when she were in a sound sleep this morning, between two and three, Jem came home, and th' sound o' his voice roused her in a minute."

"Where had he been till that time o' night?" asked Mary.

"Nay! it were none of my business; and, indeed, I never saw him till he came in here to see Alice. He were in again this morning, and seemed sadly downcast. But you'll, maybe, manage to comfort him to-night, Mary," said Margaret, smiling, while a ray of hope glimmered in Mary's heart, and she almost felt glad, for an instant, of the occasion which would at last bring them together. Oh! happy night! when would it come? Many hours had yet to pass.

Then she saw Alice, and repented, with a bitter self-reproach. But she could not help having gladness in the depths of her heart, blame herself as she would. So she tried not to think, as she hurried along to Miss Simmonds', with a dancing step of lightness.

She was late—that she knew she should be. Miss Simmonds was vexed and cross. That also she had anticipated, and had intended to smooth her raven down[5] by extraordinary diligence and attention. But there was something about the girls she did not understand—had not anticipated. They stopped talking when she came in; or rather, I should say, stopped listening, for Sally Leadbitter was the talker to whom they were hearkening with deepest attention. At first they eyed Mary, as if she had acquired some new interest to them since the day before. Then they began to whisper; and, absorbed as Mary had been in her own thoughts, she could not help becoming aware that it was of her they spoke.

At last Sally Leadbitter asked Mary if she had heard the news?

"No! What news?" answered she.

The girls looked at each other with gloomy mystery. Sally went on.

5. Adapted from Milton's *Comus* (1634): "smoothing the raven down/Of darkness till it smiled" (lines 250–51).

"Have you not heard that young Mr. Carson was murdered last night?"

Mary's lips could not utter a negative, but no one who looked at her pale and terror-stricken face could have doubted that she had not heard before of the fearful occurrence.

Oh, it is terrible, that sudden information, that one you have known has met with a bloody death! You seem to shrink from the world where such deeds can be committed, and to grow sick with the idea of the violent and wicked men of earth. Much as Mary had learned to dread him lately, now he was dead (and dead in such a manner) her feeling was that of oppressive sorrow for him.

The room went round and round, and she felt as though she should faint; but Miss Simmonds came in, bringing a waft of fresher air as she opened the door, to refresh the body, and the certainty of a scolding for inattention to brace the sinking mind. She, too, was full of the morning's news.

"Have you heard any more of this horrid affair, Miss Barton?" asked she, as she settled to her work.

Mary tried to speak; at first she could not, and when she succeeded in uttering a sentence, it seemed as though it were not her own voice that spoke.

"No, ma'am, I never heard of it till this minute."

"Dear! that's strange, for every one is up about it. I hope the murderer will be found out, that I do. Such a handsome young man to be killed as he was. I hope the wretch that did it may be hanged as high as Haman."[6]

One of the girls reminded them that the assizes[7] came on next week.

"Ay," replied Miss Simmonds, "and the milkman told me they will catch the wretch, and have him tried and hung in less than a week. Serve him right, whoever he is. Such a handsome young man as he was."

Then each began to communicate to Miss Simmonds the various reports they had heard.

Suddenly she burst out—

"Miss Barton! as I live, dropping tears on that new silk gown of Mrs. Hawkes'! Don't you know they will stain, and make it shabby for ever? Crying like a baby, because a handsome young man meets with an untimely end. For shame of yourself, miss! Mind your character and your work, if you please. Or if you must cry" (seeing her scolding rather increased the flow of Mary's tears, than otherwise), "take this print to cry over. That won't be marked like this beautiful silk,"

6. Esther 7:9–10 where Haman is hanged on the gallows he had built for Mordecai.
7. Courts held periodically to try serious crimes.

rubbing it, as if she loved it, with a clean pocket-handkerchief, in order to soften the edges of the hard round drops.

Mary took the print, and, naturally enough, having had leave given her to cry over it, rather checked the inclination to weep.

Everybody was full of the one subject. The girl sent out to match silk, came back with the account gathered at the shop, of the coroner's inquest then sitting; the ladies who called to speak about gowns first began about the murder, and mingled details of that, with directions for their dresses. Mary felt as though the haunting horror were a nightmare, a fearful dream, from which awakening would relieve her. The picture of the murdered body, far more ghastly than the reality, seemed to swim in the air before her eyes. Sally Leadbitter looked and spoke of her, almost accusingly, and made no secret now of Mary's conduct, more blameable to her fellow-workwomen for its latter changeableness, than for its former giddy flirting.

"Poor young gentleman," said one, as Sally recounted Mary's last interview with Mr. Carson.

"What a shame!" exclaimed another, looking indignantly at Mary.

"That's what I call regular jilting," said a third. "And he lying cold and bloody in his coffin now!"

Mary was more thankful than she could express, when Miss Simmonds returned, to put a stop to Sally's communications, and to check the remarks of the girls.

She longed for the peace of Alice's sick room. No more thinking with infinite delight of her anticipated meeting with Jem; she felt too much shocked for that now; but longing for peace and kindness, for the images of rest and beauty, and sinless times long ago, which the poor old woman's rambling presented, she wished to be as near death as Alice; and to have struggled through this world, whose sufferings she had early learnt, and whose crimes now seemed pressing close upon her. Old texts from the Bible, that her mother used to read (or rather spell out) aloud in the days of childhood, came up to her memory. "Where the wicked cease from troubling, and the weary are at rest." "And God shall wipe away all tears from their eyes,"[8] &c. And it was to that world Alice was hastening! Oh! that she were Alice!

I must return to the Wilsons' house, which was far from being the abode of peace that Mary was picturing it to herself. You remember the reward Mr. Carson offered for the apprehension of the murderer of his son? It was in itself a temptation, and to aid its efficacy came the natural sympathy for the aged parents mourning for their child, for the young man cut off in the flower of his days; and besides this, there is always a pleasure in unravelling a mystery, in catching at the gossamer clue which will guide to certainty. This feeling, I am sure,

8. Job 3:17 and Revelation 7:17.

gives much impetus to the police. Their senses are ever and always on the qui-vive,[9] and they enjoy the collecting and collating evidence, and the life of adventure they experience; a continual unwinding of Jack Sheppard romances,[1] always interesting to the vulgar and uneducated mind, to which the outward signs and tokens of crime are ever exciting.

There was no lack of clue or evidence at the coroner's inquest that morning. The shot, the finding of the body, the subsequent discovery of the gun, were rapidly deposed to; and then the policeman who had interrupted the quarrel between Jem Wilson and the murdered young man was brought forward, and gave his evidence, clear, simple, and straightforward. The coroner had no hesitation, the jury had none, but the verdict was cautiously worded. "Wilful murder against some person unknown."

This very cautiousness, when he deemed the thing so sure as to require no caution, irritated Mr. Carson. It did not soothe him that the superintendent called the verdict a mere form,—exhibited a warrant empowering him to seize the body of Jem Wilson committed on suspicion,—declared his intention of employing a well-known officer in the Detective Service to ascertain the ownership of the gun, and to collect other evidence especially as regarded the young woman, about whom the policeman deposed that the quarrel had taken place; Mr. Carson was still excited and irritable; restless in body and mind. He made every preparation for the accusation of Jem the following morning before the magistrates: he engaged attorneys skilled in criminal practice to watch the case and prepare briefs; he wrote to celebrated barristers coming the Northern circuit, to bespeak their services. A speedy conviction, a speedy execution, seemed to be the only things that would satisfy his craving thirst for blood. He would have fain been policeman, magistrate, accusing speaker, all; but most of all, the judge, rising with full sentence of death on his lips.

That afternoon, as Jane Wilson had begun to feel the effect of a night's disturbed rest, evinced in frequent droppings off to sleep while she sat by her sister-in-law's bed-side, lulled by the incessant crooning of the invalid's feeble voice, she was startled by a man speaking in the house-place below, who, wearied of knocking at the door, without obtaining any answer, had entered and was calling lustily for

"Missis! missis!"

When Mrs. Wilson caught a glimpse of the intruder through the stair-rails, she at once saw he was a stranger, a working man, it might

---

9. On the look-out.
1. A Newgate (crime) novel written in 1839 by William Harrison Ainsworth that romanticized the life of an eighteenth-century criminal.

be a fellow-labourer with her son, for his dress was grimy enough for the supposition. He held a gun in his hand.

"May I make bold to ask if this gun belongs to your son?"

She first looked at the man, and then, weary and half asleep, not seeing any reason for refusing to answer the enquiry, she moved forward to examine it, talking while she looked for certain old-fashioned ornaments on the stock. "It looks like his; ay, it is his, sure enough. I could speak to it anywhere by these marks. You see it were his grandfather's as were gamekeeper to some one up in th' north; and they don't make guns so smart now-a-days. But, how comed you by it? He sets great store on it. Is he bound for th' shooting gallery? He is not, for sure, now his aunt is so ill, and me left all alone;" and the immediate cause of her anxiety being thus recalled to her mind, she entered on a long story of Alice's illness, interspersed with recollections of her husband's and her children's deaths.

The disguised policeman listened for a minute or two, to glean any further information he could; and then, saying he was in a hurry, he turned to go away. She followed him to the door, still telling him her troubles, and was never struck, until it was too late to ask the reason, with the unaccountableness of his conduct, in carrying the gun away with him. Then, as she heavily climbed the stairs, she put away the wonder and the thought about his conduct, by determining to believe he was some workman with whom her son had made some arrangement about shooting at the gallery; or mending the old weapon; or something or other. She had enough to fret her, without moidering[2] herself about old guns. Jem had given it to him to bring to her; so it was safe enough; or, if it was not, why she should be glad never to set eyes on it again, for she could not abide fire-arms, they were so apt to shoot people.

So, comforting herself for the want of thought in not making further inquiry, she fell off into another doze, feverish, dream-haunted, and unrefreshing.

Meanwhile, the policeman walked off with his prize, with an odd mixture of feelings; a little contempt, a little disappointment, and a good deal of pity. The contempt and the disappointment were caused by the widow's easy admission of the gun being her son's property, and her manner of identifying it by the ornaments. He liked an attempt to baffle him; he was accustomed to it; it gave some exercise to his wits and his shrewdness. There would be no fun in fox-hunting, if Renard[3] yielded himself up without any effort to escape. Then, again, his mother's milk was yet in him, policeman, officer of the Detective Service though he was; and he felt sorry for the old woman, whose "softness" had given such material assistance

2. Worrying, troubling.
3. A fox notorious for cunning in medieval tales.

in identifying her son as the murderer. However, he conveyed the gun, and the intelligence he had gained, to the superintendent; and the result was, that, in a short time afterwards, three policemen went to the works at which Jem was foreman, and announced their errand to the astonished overseer, who directed them to the part of the foundry where Jem was then superintending a casting.

Dark, black were the walls, the ground, the faces around them, as they crossed the yard. But, in the furnace-house, a deep and lurid red glared over all; the furnace roared with mighty flame. The men, like demons, in their fire-and-soot colouring, stood swart[4] around, awaiting the moment when the tons of solid iron should have melted down into fiery liquid, fit to be poured, with still, heavy sound, into the delicate moulding of fine black sand, prepared to receive it. The heat was intense, and the red glare grew every instant more fierce; the policemen stood awed with the novel sight. Then, black figures, holding strange-shaped bucket-shovels, came athwart the deep-red furnace light, and clear and brilliant flowed forth the iron into the appropriate mould. The buzz of voices rose again; there was time to speak, and gasp, and wipe the brows; and then, one by one, the men dispersed to some other branch of their employment.

No. B 72 pointed out Jem as the man he had seen engaged in a scuffle with Mr. Carson, and then the other two stepped forward and arrested him, stating of what he was accused, and the grounds of the accusation. He offered no resistance, though he seemed surprised; but calling a fellow-workman to him, he briefly requested him to tell his 'mother he had got into trouble, and could not return home at present. He did not wish her to hear more at first.

So Mrs. Wilson's sleep was next interrupted in almost an exactly similar way to the last, like a recurring nightmare.

"Missis! missis!" some one called out from below.

Again it was a workman, but this time a blacker-looking one than before.

"What don ye want?" said she, peevishly.

"Only, nothing but——" stammered the man, a kind-hearted matter-of-fact person, with no invention, but a great deal of sympathy.

"Well, speak out, can't ye, and ha' done with it?"

"Jem's in trouble," said he, repeating Jem's very words, as he could think of no others.

"Trouble?" said the mother, in a high-pitched voice of distress. "Trouble! God help me, trouble will never end, I think. What d'ye mean by trouble? Speak out man, can't ye? Is he ill? My boy! tell me, is he ill?" in a hurried voice of terror.

---

4. Dark from soot.

"Na, na, that's not it. He's well enough. All he bade me say was, 'Tell mother I'm in trouble, and can't come home tonight.'"

"Not come home to-night! And what am I to do with Alice? I can't go on, wearing my life out wi' watching. He might come and help me."

"I tell you he can't," said the man.

"Can't, and he is well, you say? Stuff! It's just that he's getten like other young men, and wants to go a-larking. But I'll give it him when he comes back."

The man turned to go; he durst not trust himself to speak in Jem's justification. But she would not let him off.

She stood between him and the door, as she said,

"Yo shall not go till yo've told me what he's after. I can see plain enough you know, and I'll know, too, before I've done."

"You'll know soon enough, missis!"

"I'll know now, I tell ye. What's up that he can't come home and help me nurse? Me, as never got a wink o' sleep last night wi' watching."

"Well, if you will have it out," said the poor badgered man, "the police have got hold on him."

"On my Jem!" said the enraged mother. "You're a downright liar, and that's what you are. My Jem, as never did harm to any one in his life. You're a liar, that's what you are."

"He's done harm enough now," said the man, angry in his turn, "for there's good evidence he murdered young Carson, as was shot last night."

She staggered forward to strike the man for telling the terrible truth; but the weakness of old age, of motherly agony, overcame her, and she sank down on a chair, and covered her face. He could not leave her.

When next she spoke, it was in an imploring, feeble, child-like voice.

"Oh, master, say you're only joking. I ax your pardon if I have vexed ye, but please say you're only joking. You don't know what Jem is to me."

She looked humbly, anxiously up at him.

"I wish I were only joking, missis; but it's true as I say. They've taken him up on charge of murder. It were his gun as were found near th' place; and one o' the police heard him quarrelling with Mr. Carson a few days back, about a girl."

"About a girl!" broke in the mother, once more indignant, though too feeble to show it as before. "My Jem was as steady as——" she hesitated for a comparison wherewith to finish, and then repeated, "as steady as Lucifer, and he were an angel, you know. My Jem was not one to quarrel about a girl."

"Ay, but it was that, though. They'd got her name quite pat. The man had heard all they said. Mary Barton was her name, whoever she may be."

"Mary Barton! the dirty hussy! to bring my Jem into trouble of this kind. I'll give it her well when I see her: that I will. Oh! my poor Jem!" rocking herself to and fro. "And what about the gun? What did ye say about that?"

"His gun were found on th' spot where the murder were done."

"That's a lie for one, then. A man has got the gun now, safe and sound. I saw it not an hour ago."

The man shook his head.

"Yes, he has indeed. A friend o' Jem's, as he'd lent it to."

"Did you know the chap?" asked the man, who was really anxious for Jem's exculpation, and caught a gleam of hope from her last speech.

"No! I can't say as I did. But he were put on as a workman."

"It's maybe only one of them policemen, disguised."

"Nay; they'd never go for to do that, and trick me into telling on my own son. It would be like seething a kid in its mother's milk; and that th' Bible forbids."[5]

"I don't know," replied the man.

Soon afterwards he went away, feeling unable to comfort, yet distressed at the sight of sorrow; she would fain have detained him, but go he would. And she was alone.

She never for an instant believed Jem guilty: she would have doubted if the sun were fire, first: but sorrow, desolation, and at times, anger, took possession of her mind. She told the unconscious Alice, hoping to rouse her to sympathy; and then was disappointed, because, still smiling and calm, she murmured of her mother, and the happy days of infancy.

Chapter XX.

"I saw where stark and cold he lay,
        Beneath the gallows-tree,
And every one did point and say,
        ' 'Twas there he died for thee!'

"Oh! weeping heart! Oh! bleeding heart!
        What boots thy pity now?
Bid from his eyes that shade depart,
        That death-damp from his brow!"

'THE BIRTLE TRAGEDY.'[6]

So there was no more peace in the house of sickness except to Alice, the dying Alice.

5. Exodus 23:19
6. Unknown.

But Mary knew nothing of the afternoon's occurrences; and gladly did she breathe in the fresh air, as she left Miss Simmonds' house, to hasten to the Wilsons'. The very change, from the in-door to the out-door atmosphere, seemed to alter the current of her thoughts. She thought less of the dreadful subject which had so haunted her all day; she cared less for the upbraiding speeches of her fellow-workwomen; the old association of comfort and sympathy received from Alice gave her the idea that, even now, her bodily presence would soothe and compose those who were in trouble, changed, unconscious, and absent though her spirit might be.

Then, again, she reproached herself a little for the feeling of pleasure she experienced, in thinking that he whom she dreaded could never more beset her path; in the security with which she could pass each street corner—each shop, where he used to lie in ambush. Oh! beating heart! was there no other little thought of joy lurking within, to gladden the very air without? Was she not going to meet, to see, to hear Jem; and could they fail at last to understand each other's loving hearts!

She softly lifted the latch, with the privilege of friendship. *He* was not there, but his mother was standing by the fire, stirring some little mess or other. Never mind! he would come soon: and with an unmixed desire to do her grateful duty to all belonging to him, she stepped lightly forwards, unheard by the old lady, who was partly occupied by the simmering, bubbling sound of her bit of cookery; but more with her own sad thoughts, and wailing, half-uttered murmurings.

Mary took off bonnet and shawl with speed, and advancing, made Mrs. Wilson conscious of her presence, by saying,

"Let me do that for you. I'm sure you mun be tired."

Mrs. Wilson slowly turned round, and her eyes gleamed like those of a pent-up wild beast, as she recognised her visitor.

"And is it thee that dares set foot in this house, after what has come to pass? Is it not enough to have robbed me of my boy with thy arts and thy profligacy, but thou must come here to crow over me—me—his mother? Dost thou know where he is, thou bad hussy, with thy great blue eyes and yellow hair, to lead men on to ruin? Out upon thee with thy angel's face, thou whited sepulchre![7] Dost thou know where Jem is, all through thee?"

"No!" quivered out poor Mary, scarcely conscious that she spoke, so daunted, so terrified was she by the indignant mother's greeting.

"He's lying in th' New Bailey," slowly and distinctly spoke the mother, watching the effect of her words, as if believing in their infinite power to pain. "There he lies, waiting to take his trial for murdering young Mr. Carson."

7. Beautiful on the outside, rotten within. Matthew 23:27.

There was no answer; but such a blanched face, such wild, distended eyes, such trembling limbs, instinctively seeking support!

"Did you know Mr. Carson as now lies dead?" continued the merciless woman. "Folk say you did, and knew him but too well. And that for the sake of such as you, my precious child shot yon chap. But he did not. I know he did not. They may hang him, but his mother will speak to his innocence with her last dying breath."

She stopped more from exhaustion than want of words. Mary spoke, but in so changed and choked a voice that the old woman almost started. It seemed as if some third person must be in the room, the voice was so hoarse and strange.

"Please say it again. I don't quite understand you. What has Jem done? Please to tell me."

"I never said he had done it. I said, and I'll swear that he never did do it. I don't care who heard 'em quarrel, or if it is his gun as were found near the body. It's not my own Jem as would go for to kill any man, choose how a girl had jilted him. My own good Jem, as was a blessing sent upon the house where he was born." Tears came into the mother's burning eyes as her heart recurred to the days when she had rocked the cradle of her "first-born;" and then, rapidly passing over events, till the full consciousness of his present situation came upon her, and perhaps annoyed at having shown any softness of character in the presence of the Dalilah[8] who had lured him to his danger, she spoke again, and in a sharp tone.

"I told him, and told him to leave off thinking on thee; but he wouldn't be led by me. Thee! wench! thou wert not good enough to wipe the dust off his feet. A vile, flirting quean[9] as thou art. It's well thy mother does not know (poor body) what a good-for-nothing thou art."

"Mother! oh mother!" said Mary, as if appealing to the merciful dead. "But I was not good enough for him! I know I was not," added she, in a voice of touching humility.

For through her heart went tolling the ominous, prophetic words he had used when he had last spoken to her:

"Mary! you'll maybe hear of me as a drunkard, and maybe as a thief, and maybe as a murderer. Remember! when all are speaking ill of me, yo will have no right to blame me, for it's your cruelty that will have made me what I feel I shall become."

And she did not blame him, though she doubted not his guilt; she felt how madly she might act if once jealous of him, and how much cause had she not given him for jealousy, miserable guilty wretch that she was! Speak on, desolate mother. Abuse her as you will. Her broken spirit feels to have merited all.

8. The woman who cut off Samson's hair, depriving him of all his strength. Judges 16.
9. Young woman (with hints of immorality).

But her last humble, self-abased words had touched Mrs. Wilson's heart, sore as it was; and she looked at the snow-pale girl with those piteous eyes, so hopeless of comfort, and she relented in spite of herself.

"Thou seest what comes of light conduct, Mary! It's thy doing that suspicion has lighted on him, who is as innocent as the babe unborn. Thou'lt have much to answer for if he's hung. Thou'lt have my death too at thy door!"

Harsh as these words seem, she spoke them in a milder tone of voice than she had yet used. But the idea of Jem on the gallows, Jem dead, took possession of Mary, and she covered her eyes with her wan hands, as if indeed to shut out the fearful sight.

She murmured some words, which, though spoken low, as if choked up from the depths of agony, Jane Wilson caught. "My heart is breaking," said she, feebly. "My heart is breaking."

"Nonsense!" said Mrs. Wilson. "Don't talk in that silly way. My heart has a better right to break than yours, and yet I hold up, you see. But, oh dear! oh dear!" with a sudden revulsion of feeling, as the reality of the danger in which her son was placed pressed upon her. "What am I saying? How could I hold up if thou wert gone, Jem? Though I'm as sure as I stand here of thy innocence, if they hang thee, my lad, I will lie down and die!"

She wept aloud with bitter consciousness of the fearful chance awaiting her child. She cried more passionately still.

Mary roused herself up.

"Oh, let me stay with you, at any rate, till we know the end. Dearest Mrs. Wilson, mayn't I stay?"

The more obstinately and upbraidingly Mrs. Wilson refused, the more Mary pleaded, with ever the same soft entreating cry, "Let me stay with you." Her stunned soul seemed to bound its wishes, for the hour at least, to remaining with one who loved and sorrowed for the same human being that she did.

But no. Mrs. Wilson was inflexible.

"I've, maybe, been a bit hard on you, Mary, I'll own that. But I cannot abide you yet with me. I cannot but remember it's your giddiness as has wrought this woe. I'll stay with Alice, and perhaps Mrs. Davenport may come help a bit. I cannot put up with you about me. Good night. To-morrow I may look on you different, maybe. Good night."

And Mary turned out of the house, which had been *his* home, where *he* was loved, and mourned for, into the busy, desolate, crowded street, where they were crying halfpenny broadsides,[1] giving an account of the bloody murder, the coroner's inquest, and a raw-head-and-bloody-bones picture of the suspected murderer, James Wilson.

---

1. Crude accounts of crimes, popular ballads, and general interest stories printed on large, single sheets of newsprint.

But Mary heard not; she heeded not. She staggered on like one in a dream. With hung head and tottering steps, she instinctively chose the shortest cut to that home which was to her, in her present state of mind, only the hiding-place of four-walls, where she might vent her agony, unseen and unnoticed by the keen unkind world without, but where no welcome, no love, no sympathising tears awaited her.

As she neared that home, within two minutes' walk of it, her impetuous course was arrested by a light touch on her arm, and turning hastily, she saw a little Italian boy, with his humble show-box,— a white mouse, or some such thing. The setting sun cast its red glow on his face, otherwise the olive complexion would have been very pale; and the glittering tear-drops hung on the long curled eyelashes. With his soft voice, and pleading looks, he uttered, in his pretty broken English, the word—

"Hungry! so hungry."

And as if to aid by gesture the effect of the solitary word, he pointed to his mouth, with its white quivering lips.

Mary answered him impatiently, "Oh, lad, hunger is nothing— nothing!"

And she rapidly passed on. But her heart upbraided her the next minute with her unrelenting speech, and she hastily entered her door and seized the scanty remnant of food which the cupboard contained, and she retraced her steps to the place where the little hopeless stranger had sunk down by his mute companion in loneliness and starvation, and was raining down tears as he spoke in some foreign tongue, with low cries for the far distant "Mamma mia!"[2]

With the elasticity of heart belonging to childhood he sprang up as he saw the food the girl brought; she whose face, lovely in its woe, had tempted him first to address her; and, with the graceful courtesy of his country, he looked up and smiled while he kissed her hand, and then poured forth his thanks, and shared her bounty with his little pet companion. She stood an instant, diverted from the thought of her own grief by the sight of his infantine gladness; and then bending down and kissing his smooth forehead, she left him, and sought to be alone with her agony once more.

She re-entered the house, locked the door, and tore off her bonnet, as if greedy of every moment which took her from the full indulgence of painful, despairing thought.

Then she threw herself on the ground, yes, on the hard flags she threw her soft limbs down; and the comb fell out of her hair, and those bright tresses swept the dusty floor, while she pillowed and hid her face on her arms, and burst forth into loud, suffocating sobs.

Oh, earth! thou didst seem but a dreary dwelling-place for thy poor

---

2. Mother of mine.

child that night. None to comfort, none to pity! And self-reproach gnawing at her heart.

Oh, why did she ever listen to the tempter? Why did she ever give ear to her own suggestions, and cravings after wealth and grandeur? Why had she thought it a fine thing to have a rich lover?

She—she had deserved it all: but he was the victim,—he, the beloved. She could not conjecture, she could not even pause to think who had revealed, or how he had discovered her acquaintance with Harry Carson. It was but too clear, some way or another, he had learnt all; and what would he think of her? No hope of his love,—oh, that she would give up, and be content: it was his life, his precious life, that was threatened! Then she tried to recal the particulars, which, when Mrs. Wilson had given them, had fallen but upon a deafened ear,— something about a gun, a quarrel, which she could not remember clearly. Oh, how terrible to think of his crime, his blood-guiltiness; he who had hitherto been so good, so noble, and now an assassin! And then she shrank from him in thought; and then, with bitter remorse, clung more closely to his image with passionate self-upbraiding. Was it not she who had led him to the pit into which he had fallen? Was she to blame him? She to judge him? Who could tell how maddened he might have been by jealousy; how one moment's uncontrollable passion might have led him to become a murderer! And she had blamed him in her heart after his last deprecating, imploring, prophetic speech!

Then she burst out crying afresh; and when weary of crying, fell to thinking again. The gallows! The gallows! Black it stood against the burning light which dazzled her shut eyes, press on them as she would. Oh! she was going mad; and for awhile she lay outwardly still, but with the pulses careering through her head with wild vehemence.

And then came a strange forgetfulness of the present, in thought of the long-past times;—of those days when she hid her face on her mother's pitying, loving bosom, and heard tender words of comfort, be her grief or her error what it might;—of those days when she had felt as if her mother's love was too mighty not to last for ever;—of those days when hunger had been to her (as to the little stranger she had that evening relieved) something to be thought about, and mourned over;— when Jem and she had played together; he, with the condescension of an older child, and she, with unconscious earnestness, believing that he was as much gratified with important trifles as she was;—when her father was a cheery-hearted man, rich in the love of his wife, and the companionship of his friend;—when (for it still worked round to that), when mother was alive, and *he* was not a murderer.

And then Heaven blessed her unaware, and she sank from remembering, to wandering, unconnected thought, and thence to sleep. Yes! it was sleep, though in that strange posture, on that hard cold bed; and she dreamt of the happy times of long ago, and her mother came to her, and kissed her as she lay, and once more the dead were alive again in that happy world of dreams. All was restored to the gladness of childhood, even to the little kitten which had been her playmate and bosom friend then, and which had been long forgotten in her waking hours. All the loved ones were there!

She suddenly wakened! Clear and wide awake! Some noise had startled her from sleep. She sat up, and put her hair (still wet with tears) back from her flushed cheeks, and listened. At first she could only hear her beating heart. All was still without, for it was after midnight, such hours of agony had passed away; but the moon shone clearly in at the unshuttered window, making the room almost as light as day, in its cold ghastly radiance. There was a low knock at the door! A strange feeling crept over Mary's heart, as if something spiritual were near; as if the dead, so lately present in her dreams, were yet gliding and hovering round her, with their dim, dread forms. And yet, why dread? Had they not loved her?—and who loved her now? Was she not lonely enough to welcome the spirits of the dead, who had loved her while here? If her mother had conscious being, her love for her child endured. So she quieted her fears, and listened—listened still.

"Mary! Mary! open the door!" as a little movement on her part seemed to tell the being outside of her wakeful, watchful state. They were the accents of her mother's voice; the very south-country pronunciation, that Mary so well remembered; and which she had sometimes tried to imitate when alone, with the fond mimicry of affection.

So, without fear, without hesitation, she rose and unbarred the door. There, against the moonlight, stood a form, so closely resembling her dead mother, that Mary never doubted the identity, but exclaiming (as if she were a terrified child, secure of safety when near the protecting care of its parent)—

"Oh! mother! mother! You are come at last?" she threw herself, or rather fell, into the trembling arms of her long-lost, unrecognised aunt, Esther.

Chapter XXI.

"My rest is gone,
   My heart is sore,
Peace find I never,
   And never more."
            MARGARET'S SONG IN 'FAUST.'[3]

I must go back a little to explain the motives which caused Esther to seek an interview with her niece.

3. From Johann Wolfgang von Goethe's (1749–1832) *Faust* (1808), Part I.

The murder had been committed early on Thursday night, and between then and the dawn of the following day there was ample time for the news to spread far and wide among all those whose duty, or whose want, or whose errors, caused them to be abroad in the streets of Manchester.

Among those who listened to the tale of violence was Esther.

A craving desire to know more took possession of her mind. Far away as she was from Turner Street, she immediately set off to the scene of the murder, which was faintly lighted by the grey dawn as she reached the spot. It was so quiet and still that she could hardly believe it to be the place. The only vestige of any scuffle or violence was a trail on the dust, as if somebody had been lying there, and then been raised by extraneous force. The little birds were beginning to hop and twitter in the leafless hedge, making the only sound that was near and distinct. She crossed into the field where she guessed the murderer to have stood; it was easy of access, for the worn, stunted hawthorn-hedge had many gaps in it. The night-smell of bruised grass came up from under her feet, as she went towards the saw-pit and carpenter's shed which as I have said before, were in a corner of the field near the road, and where one of her informants had told her it was supposed by the police that the murderer had lurked while waiting for his victim. There was no sign, however, that any one had been about the place. If the grass had been bruised or bent where he had trod, it had had enough of the elasticity of life to raise itself under the dewy influences of night. She hushed her breath in involuntary awe, but nothing else told of the violent deed by which a fellow-creature had passed away. She stood still for a minute, imagining to herself the position of the parties, guided by the only circumstance which afforded any evidence, the trailing mark on the dust in the road.

Suddenly (it was before the sun had risen above the horizon) she became aware of something white in the hedge. All other colours wore the same murky hue, though the forms of objects were perfectly distinct. What was it? It could not be a flower;—that, the time of year made clear. A frozen lump of snow, lingering late in one of the gnarled tufts of the hedge? She stepped forward to examine. It proved to be a little piece of stiff writing-paper compressed into a round shape. She understood it instantly; it was the paper that had served as wadding for the murderer's gun. Then she had been standing just where the murderer must have been but a few hours before; probably (as the rumour had spread through the town, reaching her ears) one of the poor maddened turn-outs, who hung about everywhere, with black, fierce looks, as if contemplating some deed of violence. Her sympathy was all with them, for she had known what they suffered; and besides this, there was her own individual dislike of Mr. Carson, and dread of him for Mary's sake. Yet, poor Mary! Death was a terrible, though sure, remedy for the evil Esther had dreaded for her; and how would she stand the shock, loving as her aunt believed her to do? Poor Mary! who would comfort her? Esther's thoughts began to picture her sorrow, her despair, when the news of her lover's death should reach her; and she longed to tell her there might have been a keener grief yet had he lived.

Bright, beautiful came the slanting rays of the morning sun. It was time for such as she to hide themselves, with the other obscene things of night, from the glorious light of day, which was only for the happy. So she turned her steps towards town, still holding the paper. But in getting over the hedge it encumbered her to hold it in her clasped hand, and she threw it down. She passed on a few steps, her thoughts still of Mary, till the idea crossed her mind, could it (blank as it appeared to be) give any clue to the murderer? As I said before, her sympathies were all on that side, so she turned back and picked it up; and then feeling as if in some measure an accessory, she hid it unexamined in her hand, and hastily passed out of the street at the opposite end to that by which she had entered it.

And what do you think she felt, when, having walked some distance from the spot, she dared to open the crushed paper, and saw written on it Mary Barton's name, and not only that, but the street in which she lived! True, a letter or two was torn off, but, nevertheless, there was the name clear to be recognised. And oh! what terrible thought flashed into her mind; or was it only fancy? But it looked very like the writing which she had once known well—the writing of Jem Wilson, who, when she lived at her brother-in-law's, and he was a near neighbour, had often been employed by her to write her letters to people, to whom she was ashamed of sending her own misspelt scrawl. She remembered the wonderful flourishes she had so much admired in those days, while she sat by dictating, and Jem, in all the pride of newly-acquired penmanship, used to dazzle her eyes by extraordinary graces and twirls.

If it were his!

Oh! perhaps it was merely that her head was running so on Mary, that she was associating every trifle with her. As if only one person wrote in that flourishing, meandering style!

It was enough to fill her mind to think from what she might have saved Mary by securing the paper. She would look at it just once more, and see if some very dense and stupid policeman could have mistaken the name, or if Mary would certainly have been dragged into notice in the affair.

No! no one could have mistaken the "ry Barton," and it *was* Jem's handwriting!

Oh! if it was so, she understood it all, and she had been the cause! With her violent and unregulated nature, rendered morbid by the course of life she led, and her consciousness of her degradation, she cursed herself for the interference which she believed had led to this; for the information and the warning she had given to Jem, which had roused him to this murderous action. How could she, the abandoned and polluted outcast, ever have dared to hope for a blessing, even on her efforts to do good? The black curse of Heaven rested on all her doings, were they for good or for evil.

Poor, diseased mind! and there were none to minister to thee![4]

So she wandered about, too restless to take her usual heavy morning's sleep, up and down the streets, greedily listening to every word of the passers-by, and loitering near each group of talkers, anxious to scrape together every morsel of information, or conjecture, or suspicion, though without possessing any definite purpose in all this. And ever and always she clenched the scrap of paper which might betray so much, until her nails had deeply indented the palm of her hand; so fearful was she in her nervous dread, lest unawares she should let it drop.

Towards the middle of the day she could no longer evade the body's craving want of rest and refreshment; but the rest was taken in a spirit vault, and the refreshment was a glass of gin.

Then she started up from the stupor she had taken for repose; and suddenly driven before the gusty impulses of her mind, she pushed her way to the place where at that very time the police were bringing the information they had gathered with regard to the all-engrossing murder. She listened with painful acuteness of comprehension to dropped words, and unconnected sentences, the meaning of which became clearer, and yet more clear to her. Jem was suspected. Jem was ascertained to be the murderer.

She saw him (although he, absorbed in deep sad thought, saw her not), she saw him brought handcuffed, and guarded out of the coach. She saw him enter the station,—she gasped for breath till he came out, still handcuffed, and still guarded, to be conveyed to the New Bailey.

He was the only one who had spoken to her with hope that she might win her way back to virtue. His words had lingered in her heart with a sort of call to Heaven, like distant Sabbath bells, although in her despair she had turned away from his voice. He was the only one who had spoken to her kindly. The murder, shocking though it was, was an absent, abstract thing, on which her thoughts could not, and would not dwell: all that was present in her mind was Jem's danger, and his kindness.

Then Mary came to remembrance. Esther wondered till she was sick of wondering, in what way she was taking the affair. In some

4. Echo of Macbeth's words to his raving wife in Shakespeare's *Macbeth* 5.3.40–42.

manner it would be a terrible blow for the poor, motherless girl; with her dreadful father, too, who was to Esther a sort of accusing angel.

She set off towards the court where Mary lived, to pick up what she could there of information. But she was ashamed to enter in where once she had been innocent, and hung about the neighbouring streets, not daring to question, so she learnt but little; nothing, in fact, but the knowledge of John Barton's absence from home.

She went up a dark entry to rest her weary limbs on a doorstep and think. Her elbows on her knees, her face hidden in her hands, she tried to gather together and arrange her thoughts. But still every now and then she opened her hand to see if the paper were yet there.

She got up at last. She had formed a plan, and had a course of action to look forward to that would satisfy one craving desire at least. The time was long gone by when there was much wisdom or consistency in her projects.

It was getting late, and that was so much the better. She went to a pawnshop, and took off her finery in a back room. She was known by the people, and had a character for honesty, so she had no very great difficulty in inducing them to let her have a suit of outer clothes, befitting the wife of a working man, a black silk bonnet, a printed gown, a plaid shawl, dirty and rather worn to be sure, but which had a sort of sanctity to the eyes of the streetwalker, as being the appropriate garb of that happy class to which she could never, never more belong.

She looked at herself in the little glass which hung against the wall, and sadly shaking her head, thought how easy were the duties of that Eden of innocence from which she was shut out; how she would work, and toil, and starve, and die, if necessary, for a husband, a home,—for children,—but that thought she could not bear; a little form rose up, stern in its innocence, from the witches' caldron of her imagination, and she rushed into action again.

You know now how she came to stand by the threshold of Mary's door, waiting, trembling, until the latch was lifted, and her niece, with words that spoke of such desolation among the living, fell into her arms.

She had felt as if some holy spell would prevent her (even as the unholy Lady Geraldine was prevented, in the abode of Christabel) from crossing the threshold of that home of her early innocence;[5] and she had meant to wait for an invitation. But Mary's helpless action did away with all reluctant feeling, and she bore or dragged her to her seat, and looked on her bewildered eyes, as, puzzled with the likeness, which was not identity, she gazed on her aunt's features.

In pursuance of her plan, Esther meant to assume the manners

---

5. Coleridge's "Christabel" (1816), in which the Lady Geraldine, a spirit of evil, cannot enter Christabel's home except by invitation.

and character, as she had done the dress, of a mechanic's wife; but then, to account for her long absence, and her long silence towards all that ought to have been dear to her, it was necessary that she should put on an indifference far distant from her heart, which was loving and yearning, in spite of all its faults. And, perhaps, she over-acted her part, for certainly Mary felt a kind of repugnance to the changed and altered aunt, who so suddenly reappeared on the scene; and it would have cut Esther to the very core, could she have known how her little darling of former days was feeling towards her.

"You don't remember me, I see, Mary!" she began. "It's a long while since I left you all, to be sure; and I, many a time, thought of coming to see you, and—and your father. But I live so far off, and am always so busy, I cannot do just what I wish. You recollect aunt Esther, don't you, Mary?"

"Are you aunt Hetty?" asked Mary, faintly, still looking at the face which was so different from the old recollections of her aunt's fresh dazzling beauty.

"Yes! I am aunt Hetty. Oh! it's so long since I heard that name," sighing forth the thoughts it suggested; then, recovering herself, and striving after the hard character she wished to assume, she contin-ued: "and to-day I heard a friend of yours, and of mine too, long ago, was in trouble, and I guessed you would be in sorrow, so I thought I would just step this far and see you."

Mary's tears flowed afresh, but she had no desire to open her heart to her strangely-found aunt, who had, by her own confession, kept aloof from and neglected them for so many years. Yet she tried to feel grateful for kindness (however late) from any one, and wished to be civil. Moreover, she had a strong disinclination to speak on the terri-ble subject uppermost in her mind. So, after a pause, she said,

"Thank you. I daresay you mean very kind. Have you had a long walk? I'm so sorry," said she, rising with a sudden thought, which was as suddenly checked by recollection, "but I've nothing to eat in the house, and I'm sure you must be hungry, after your walk."

For Mary concluded that certainly her aunt's residence must be far away on the other side of the town, out of sight or hearing. But, after all, she did not think much about her; her heart was so aching-full of other things, that all besides seemed like a dream. She received feel-ings and impressions from her conversation with her aunt, but did not, could not, put them together, or think or argue about them.

And Esther! How scanty had been her food for days and weeks, her thinly-covered bones and pale lips might tell, but her words should never reveal! So, with a little unreal laugh, she replied,

"Oh! Mary, my dear! don't talk about eating. We've the best of everything, and plenty of it, for my husband is in good work. I'd such a supper before I came out. I couldn't touch a morsel if you had it."

Her words shot a strange pang through Mary's heart. She had always remembered her aunt's loving and unselfish disposition; how was it changed, if, living in plenty, she had never thought it worth while to ask after relations who were all but starving! She shut up her heart instinctively against her aunt.

And all the time poor Esther was swallowing her sobs, and over-acting her part, and controlling herself more than she had done for many a long day, in order that her niece might not be shocked and revolted, by the knowledge of what her aunt had become:—a prostitute; an outcast.

She had longed to open her wretched, wretched heart, so hopeless, so abandoned by all living things, to one who had loved her once; and yet she refrained, from dread of the averted eye, the altered voice, the internal loathing, which she feared such disclosure might create. She would go straight to the subject of the day. She could not tarry long, for she felt unable to support the character she had assumed for any length of time.

They sat by the little round table, facing each other. The candle was placed right between them, and Esther moved it in order to have a clearer view of Mary's face, so that she might read her emotions, and ascertain her interests. Then she began:

"It's a bad business, I'm afraid, this of Mr. Carson's murder."

Mary winced a little.

"I hear Jem Wilson is taken up for it."

Mary covered her eyes with her hands, as if to shade them from the light, and Esther herself, less accustomed to self-command, was getting too much agitated for calm observation of another.

"I was taking a walk near Turner Street, and I went to see the spot," continued Esther, "and, as luck would have it, I spied this bit of paper in the hedge," producing the precious piece still folded in her hand. "It has been used as wadding for the gun, I reckon; indeed, that's clear enough, from the shape it's crammed into. I was sorry for the murderer, whoever he might be (I didn't then know of Jem's being suspected), and I thought I would never leave a thing about, as might help, ever so little, to convict him; the police are so 'cute about straws. So I carried it a little way, and then I opened it, and saw your name, Mary."

Mary took her hands away from her eyes, and looked with surprise at her aunt's face, as she uttered these words. She *was* kind after all, for was she not saving her from being summoned, and from being questioned and examined; a thing to be dreaded above all others: as she felt sure that her unwilling answers, frame them how she might, would add to the suspicions against Jem; her aunt was indeed kind, to think of what would spare her this.

Esther went on, without noticing Mary's look. The very action of speaking was so painful to her, and so much interrupted by the hard, raking little cough, which had been her constant annoyance for months, that she was too much engrossed by the physical difficulty of utterance, to be a very close observer.

"There could be no mistake if they had found it. Look at your name, together with the very name of this court! And in Jem's handwriting too, or I'm much mistaken. Look, Mary!"

And now she did watch her.

Mary took the paper and flattened it: then suddenly stood stiff up, with irrepressible movement, as if petrified by some horror abruptly disclosed; her face, strung and rigid; her lips compressed tight, to keep down some rising exclamation. She dropped on her seat, as suddenly as if the braced muscles had in an instant given way. But she spoke no word.

"It is his handwriting—isn't it?" asked Esther, though Mary's manner was almost confirmation enough.

"You will not tell. You never will tell," demanded Mary, in a tone so sternly earnest, as almost to be threatening.

"Nay, Mary," said Esther, rather reproachfully, "I am not so bad as that. Oh! Mary, you cannot think I would do that, whatever I may be."

The tears sprang to her eyes at the idea that she was suspected of being one who would help to inform against an old friend.

Mary caught her sad and upbraiding look.

"No! I know you would not tell, aunt. I don't know what I say, I am so shocked. But say you will not tell. Do."

"No, indeed I will not tell, come what may."

Mary sat still looking at the writing, and turning the paper round with careful examination, trying to hope, but her very fears belying her hopes.

"I thought you cared for the young man that's murdered," observed Esther, half-aloud; but feeling that she could not mistake this strange interest in the suspected murderer, implied by Mary's eagerness to screen him from anything which might strengthen suspicion against him. She had come, desirous to know the extent of Mary's grief for Mr. Carson, and glad of the excuse afforded her by the important scrap of paper. Her remark about its being Jem's handwriting, she had, with this view of ascertaining Mary's state of feeling, felt to be most imprudent the instant after she had uttered it; but Mary's anxiety that she should not tell, was too great, and too decided, to leave a doubt as to her interest for Jem. She grew more and more bewildered, and her dizzy head refused to reason. Mary never spoke. She held the bit of paper firmly, determined to retain possession of it, come what might; and anxious, and impatient, for her aunt to go. As she sat, her face bore a likeness to Esther's dead child.

"You are so like my little girl, Mary!" said Esther, weary of the one subject on which she could get no satisfaction, and recurring, with full heart, to the thought of the dead.

Mary looked up. Her aunt had children, then. That was all the idea she received. No faint imagination of the love and the woe of that poor creature crossed her mind, or she would have taken her, all guilty and erring, to her bosom, and tried to bind up the broken heart. No! it was not to be. Her aunt had children, then; and she was on the point of putting some question about them, but before it could be spoken another thought turned it aside, and she went back to her task of unravelling the mystery of the paper, and the handwriting. Oh! how she wished her aunt would go!

As if, according to the believers in mesmerism, the intenseness of her wish gave her power over another, although the wish was unexpressed, Esther felt herself unwelcome, and that her absence was desired.

She felt this some time before she could summon up resolution to go. She was so much disappointed in this longed-for, dreaded interview with Mary; she had wished to impose upon her with her tale of married respectability, and yet she had yearned and craved for sympathy in her real lot. And she had imposed upon her well. She should perhaps be glad of it afterwards; but her desolation of hope seemed for the time redoubled. And she must leave the old dwelling-place, whose very walls, and flags, dingy and sordid as they were, had a charm for her. Must leave the abode of poverty, for the more terrible abodes of vice. She must—she would go.

"Well, good-night, Mary. That bit of paper is safe enough with you, I see. But you made me promise I would not tell about it, and you must promise me to destroy it before you sleep."

"I promise," said Mary, hoarsely, but firmly. "Then you are going?"

"Yes. Not if you wish me to stay. Not if I could be of any comfort to you, Mary;" catching at some glimmering hope.

"Oh, no," said Mary, anxious to be alone. "Your husband will be wondering where you are. Some day you must tell me all about yourself. I forget what your name is?"

"Fergusson," said Esther, sadly.

"Mrs. Fergusson," repeated Mary, half unconsciously. "And where did you say you lived?"

"I never did say," muttered Esther; then aloud, "In Angel's Meadow, 145, Nicholas Street."

"145, Nicholas Street, Angel Meadow. I shall remember."

As Esther drew her shawl around her, and prepared to depart, a thought crossed Mary's mind that she had been cold and hard in her manner towards one, who had certainly meant to act kindly in bringing her the paper (that dread, terrible piece of paper!), and thus saving her from——she could not rightly think how much, or how little she was spared. So, desirous of making up for her previous indifferent manner, she advanced to kiss her aunt before her departure.

But, to her surprise, her aunt pushed her off with a frantic kind of gesture, and saying the words,

"Not me. You must never kiss me. You!"

She rushed into the outer darkness of the street, and there wept long and bitterly.

Chapter XXII.

> "There was a listening fear in her regard,
> As if calamity had but begun;
> As if the vanward clouds of evil days
> Had spent their malice, and the sullen rear
> Was, with its stored thunder, labouring up."
>   KEATS' 'HYPERION.'[6]

No sooner was Mary alone than she fastened the door, and put the shutters up against the window, which had all this time remained shaded only by the curtains hastily drawn together on Esther's entrance, and the lighting of the candle.

She did all this with the same compressed lips, and the same stony look that her face had assumed on the first examination of the paper. Then she sat down for an instant to think; and, rising directly, went, with a step rendered firm by inward resolution of purpose, up the stairs; passed her own door, two steps, into her father's room. What did she want there?

I must tell you; I must put into words the dreadful secret which she believed that bit of paper had revealed to her.

Her father was the murderer!

That corner of stiff, shining, thick, writing paper, she recognised as a part of the sheet on which she had copied Samuel Bamford's beautiful lines so many months ago—copied (as you perhaps remember) on the blank part of a valentine sent to her by Jem Wilson, in those days when she did not treasure and hoard up everything he had touched, as she would do now.

That copy had been given to her father for whom it was made, and she had occasionally seen him reading it over, not a fortnight ago she was sure. But she resolved to ascertain if the other part still remained in his possession. He might,—it was just possible he *might*, have given it away to some friend; and if so, that person was the guilty one, for she could swear to the paper anywhere.

6. From John Keat's (1795–1821) *Hyperion: A Fragment* (1819), Bk. I, lines 37–41.

First of all she pulled out every article from the little old chest of drawers. Amongst them were some things which had belonged to her mother, but she had no time now to examine and try and remember them. All the reverence she could pay them was to carry them and lay them on the bed carefully, while the other things were tossed impatiently out upon the floor.

The copy of Bamford's lines was not there. Oh! perhaps he might have given it away; but then must it not have been to Jem? It was his gun.

And she set to with redoubled vigour to examine the deal box which served as chair, and which had once contained her father's Sunday clothes, in the days when he could afford to have Sunday clothes.

He had redeemed his better coat from the pawn-shop before he left, that she had noticed. Here was his old one. What rustled under her hand in the pocket?

The paper! "Oh! Father!"

Yes, it fitted; jagged end to jagged end, letter to letter; and even the part which Esther had considered blank had its tallying mark with the larger piece, its tails of *y*s and *g*s. And then, as if that were not damning evidence enough, she felt again, and found some little bullets or shot (I don't know which you would call them) in that same pocket, along with a small paper parcel of gunpowder. As she was going to replace the jacket, having abstracted the paper, and bullets, &c., she saw a woollen guncase, made of that sort of striped horse-cloth you must have seen a thousand times appropriated to such a purpose. The sight of it made her examine still further, but there was nothing else that could afford any evidence, so she locked the box, and sat down on the floor to contemplate the articles; now with a sickening despair, now with a kind of wondering curiosity, how her father had managed to evade observation. After all it was easy enough. He had evidently got possession of some gun (was it really Jem's? was he an accomplice? No! she did not believe it; he never, never would deliberately plan a murder with another, however he might be wrought up to it by passionate feeling at the time. Least of all would he accuse her to her father, without previously warning her; it was out of his nature).

Then having obtained possession of the gun, her father had loaded it at home, and might have carried it away with him some time when the neighbours were not noticing, and she was out, or asleep; and then he might have hidden it somewhere to be in readiness when he should want it. She was sure he had no such thing with him when he went away the last time.

She felt it was of no use to conjecture his motives. His actions had become so wild and irregular of late, that she could not reason upon them. Besides, was it not enough to know that he was guilty of this terrible offence? Her love for her father seemed to return with painful force, mixed up as it was with horror at his crime. That dear father who was once so kind, so warm-hearted, so ready to help either man or beast in distress, to murder! But in the desert of misery with which these thoughts surrounded her, the arid depths of whose gloom she dared not venture to contemplate, a little spring of comfort was gushing up at her feet, unnoticed at first, but soon to give her strength and hope.

And *that* was the necessity for exertion on her part which this discovery enforced.

Oh! I do think that the necessity for exertion, for some kind of action (bodily or mentally) in time of distress, is a most infinite blessing, although the first efforts at such seasons are painful. Something to be done implies that there is yet hope of some good thing to be accomplished, or some additional evil that may be avoided; and by degrees the hope absorbs much of the sorrow.

It is the woes that cannot in any earthly way be escaped that admit least earthly comforting. Of all trite, worn-out, hollow mockeries of comfort that were ever uttered by people who will not take the trouble of sympathising with others, the one I dislike the most is the exhortation not to grieve over an event, "for it cannot be helped." Do you think if I could help it, I would sit still with folded hands, content to mourn? Do you not believe that as long as hope remained I would be up and doing? I mourn because what has occurred cannot be helped. The reason you give me for not grieving, is the very and sole reason of my grief. Give me nobler and higher reasons for enduring meekly what my Father sees fit to send, and I will try earnestly and faithfully to be patient; but mock me not, or any other mourner, with the speech, "Do not grieve, for it cannot be helped. It is past remedy."

But some remedy to Mary's sorrow came with thinking. If her father was guilty, Jem was innocent. If innocent, there was a possibility of saving him. He must be saved. And she must do it; for, was not she the sole depository of the terrible secret? Her father was not suspected; and never should be, if by any foresight or any exertions of her own she could prevent it.

She did not know how Jem was to be saved, while her father was also to be considered innocent. It would require much thought, and much prudence. But with the call upon her exertions, and her various qualities of judgment and discretion, came the answering consciousness of innate power to meet the emergency. Every step now, nay, the employment of every minute, was of consequence; for you must remember she had learnt at Miss Simmonds' the probability that the murderer would be brought to trial the next week. And you must remember, too, that never was so young a girl so friendless, or so penniless, as Mary was at this time. But the lion accompanied Una through the wilderness and the danger;[7] and so will a high, resolved purpose of right doing ever guard and accompany the helpless.

It struck two; deep, mirk, night.

It was of no use bewildering herself with plans this weary, endless night. Nothing could be done before morning: and, at first in her impatience, she began to long for day; but then she felt in how unfit a state her body was for any plan of exertion, and she resolutely made up her mind to husband her physical strength.

First of all she must burn the tell-tale paper. The powder, bullets, and gun-case, she tied into a bundle, and bid in the sacking of the bed for the present, although there was no likelihood of their affording evidence against any one. Then she carried the paper down-stairs, and burned it on the hearth, powdering the very ashes with her fingers, and dispersing the fragments of fluttering black films among the cinders of the grate. Then she breathed again.

Her head ached with dizzying violence; she must get quit of the pain or it would incapacitate her for thinking and planning. She looked for food, but there was nothing but a little raw oatmeal in the house: still, although it almost choked her, she ate some of this, knowing from experience, how often headaches were caused by long fasting. Then she sought for some water to bathe her throbbing temples, and quench her feverish thirst. There was none in the house, so she took the jug and went out to the pump at the other end of the court, whose echoes resounded her light footsteps in the quiet stillness of the night. The hard, square outlines of the houses cut sharply against the cold bright sky, from which myriads of stars were shining down in eternal repose. There was little sympathy in the outward scene, with the internal trouble. All was so still, so motionless, so hard! Very different to this lovely night in the country in which I am now writing, where the distant horizon is soft and undulating in the moonlight, and the nearer trees sway gently to and fro in the night-wind with something of almost human motion; and the rustling air makes music among their branches, as if speaking soothingly to the weary ones, who lie awake in heaviness of heart. The sights and sounds of such a night lull pain and grief to rest.

But Mary re-entered her home after she had filled her pitcher, with a still stronger sense of anxiety, and a still clearer conviction of how much rested upon her unassisted and friendless self, alone with her terrible knowledge, in the hard, cold, populous world.

She bathed her forehead, and quenched her thirst, and then, with wise deliberation of purpose, went up-stairs, and undressed herself, as if for a long night's slumber, although so few hours intervened

7. Reference to Edmund Spenser's *The Faerie Queene* (1590), Bk. I, Canto iii.

before day-dawn. She believed she never could sleep, but she lay down, and shut her eyes; and before many minutes she was in as deep and sound a slumber as if there was no sin or sorrow in the world.

She woke up, as it was natural, much refreshed in body; but with a consciousness of some great impending calamity. She sat up in bed to recollect, and when she did remember, she sank down again with all the helplessness of despair. But it was only the weakness of an instant; for were not the very minutes precious, for deliberation if not for action?

Before she had finished the necessary morning business of dressing, and setting her house in some kind of order, she had disentangled her ravelled ideas, and arranged some kind of a plan for action. If Jem was innocent (and now, of his guilt, even his slightest participation in, or knowledge of, the murder, she acquitted him with all her heart and soul), he must have been somewhere else when the crime was committed; probably with some others, who might bear witness to the fact, if she only knew where to find them. Every thing rested on her. She had heard of an *alibi*, and believed it might mean the deliverance she wished to accomplish; but she was not quite sure, and determined to apply to Job, as one of the few among her acquaintance gifted with the knowledge of hard words, for to her, all terms of law, or natural history, were alike many-syllabled mysteries.

No time was to be lost. She went straight to Job Legh's house, and found the old man and his grand-daughter sitting at breakfast; as she opened the door she heard their voices speaking in a grave, hushed, subdued tone, as if something grieved their hearts. They stopped talking on her entrance, and then she knew they had been conversing about the murder; about Jem's probable guilt; and (it flashed upon her for the first time) on the new light they would have obtained regarding herself: for until now they had never heard of her giddy flirting with Mr. Carson; not in all her confidential talk with Margaret had she ever spoken of him. And now, Margaret would hear her conduct talked of by all, as that of a bold, bad girl; and even if she did not believe everything that was said, she could hardly help feeling wounded, and disappointed in Mary.

So it was in a timid voice that Mary wished her usual goodmorrow, and her heart sunk within her a little, when Job, with a form of civility, bade her welcome in that dwelling, where, until now, she had been too well assured to require to be asked to sit down.

She took a chair. Margaret continued silent.

"I'm come to speak to you about this—about Jem Wilson."

"It's a bad business, I'm afeard," replied Job, sadly.

"Ay, it's bad enough anyhow. But Jem's innocent. Indeed he is; I'm as sure as sure can be."

"How can you know, wench? Facts bear strong again him, poor

fellow, though he'd a deal to put him up, and aggravate him, they say. Ay, poor lad, he's done for himself, I'm afeard."

"Job," said Mary, rising from her chair in her eagerness, "you must not say he did it. He didn't; I'm sure and certain he didn't. Oh! why do you shake your head? Who is to believe me,—who is to think him innocent, if you, who know'd him so well, stick to it he's guilty?"

"I'm loth enough to do it, lass," replied Job; "but I think he's been ill-used, and—jilted (that's plain truth, Mary, bare as it may seem), and his blood has been up—many a man has done the like afore, from like causes."

"Oh, God! Then you won't help me, Job, to prove him innocent? Oh! Job, Job; believe me, Jem never did harm to no one."

"Not afore;—and mind, wench! I don't over-blame him for this." Job relapsed into silence.

Mary thought a moment.

"Well, Job, you'll not refuse me this, I know. I won't mind what you think, if you'll help me as if he was innocent. Now suppose I know— I knew, he was innocent,—it's only supposing, Job,—what must I do to prove it? Tell me, Job! Isn't it called an *alibi*, the getting folk to swear to where he really was at the time."

"Best way, if you know'd him innocent, would be to find out the real murderer. Some one did it, that's clear enough. If it wasn't Jem, who was it?"

"How can I tell?" answered Mary, in agony of terror, lest Job's question was prompted by any suspicion of the truth.

But he was far enough from any such thought. Indeed, he had no doubt in his own mind that Jem had, in some passionate moment, urged on by slighted love and jealousy, been the murderer. And he was strongly inclined to believe, that Mary was aware of this, only that, too late repentant of her light conduct which had led to such fatal consequences, she was now most anxious to save her old playfellow, her early friend, from the doom awaiting the shedder of blood.

"If Jem's not done it, I don't see as any on us can tell who did it. We might find out something if we'd time; but they say he's to be tried on Tuesday. It's no use hiding it, Mary; things looks strong against him."

"I know they do! I know they do! But, oh! Job! isn't an *alibi* a proving where he really was at th' time of the murder; and how must I set about an *alibi*?"

"An *alibi* is that, sure enough." He thought a little. "You mun ask his mother his doings, and his whereabouts that night; the knowledge of that will guide you a bit."

For he was anxious that on another should fall the task of enlightening Mary on the hopelessness of the case, and he felt that her own sense would be more convinced by inquiry and examination than any mere assertion of his.

Margaret had sat silent and grave all this time. To tell the truth, she was surprised and disappointed by the disclosure of Mary's conduct, with regard to Mr. Henry Carson. Gentle, reserved, and prudent herself, never exposed to the trial of being admired for her personal appearance, and unsusceptible enough to be in doubt even yet, whether the fluttering, tender, infinitely-joyous feeling, she was for the first time experiencing, at sight or sound, or thought of Will Wilson, was love or not,—Margaret had no sympathy with the temptations to which loveliness, vanity, ambition, or the desire of being admired, exposes so many; no sympathy with flirting girls, in short. Then, she had no idea of the strength of the conflict between will and principle in some who were differently constituted from herself. With her, to be convinced that an action was wrong, was tantamount to a determination not to do so again; and she had little or no difficulty in carrying out her determination. So she could not understand how it was that Mary had acted wrongly, and had felt too much ashamed, in spite of internal sophistry, to speak of her actions. Margaret considered herself deceived; felt aggrieved; and, at the time of which I am now telling you, was strongly inclined to give Mary up altogether, as a girl devoid of the modest proprieties of her sex, and capable of gross duplicity, in speaking of one lover as she had done of Jem, while she was encouraging another in attentions, at best of a very doubtful character.

But now Margaret was drawn into the conversation. Suddenly it flashed across Mary's mind, that the night of the murder was the very night, or rather the same early morning, that Margaret had been with Alice. She turned sharp round, with—

"Oh! Margaret, you can tell me; you were there when he came back that night; were you not? No! you were not; but you were there not many hours after. Did not you hear where he'd been? He was away the night before, too, when Alice was first taken; when you were there for your tea. Oh! where was he, Margaret?"

"I don't know," she answered. "Stay! I do remember something about his keeping Will company, in his walk to Liverpool. I can't justly say what it was, so much happened that night."

"I'll go to his mother's," said Mary resolutely.

They neither of them spoke, either to advise or dissuade. Mary felt she had no sympathy from them, and braced up her soul to act without such loving aid of friendship. She knew that their advice would be willingly given at her demand, and that was all she really required for Jem's sake. Still her courage failed a little as she walked to Jane Wilson's, alone in the world with her secret.

Jane Wilson's eyes were swelled with crying; and it was sad to see the ravages which intense anxiety and sorrow had made on her appearance in four-and-twenty hours. All night long she and Mrs. Davenport had crooned over their sorrows, always recurring, like the burden of an old song, to the dreadest sorrow of all, which was now impending over Mrs. Wilson. She had grown—I hardly know what word to use—but, something like proud of her martyrdom; she had grown to hug her grief; to feel an excitement in her agony of anxiety about her boy.

"So, Mary, you're here! Oh! Mary, lass! He's to be tried on Tuesday."

She fell to sobbing, in the convulsive breath-catching manner which tells so of much previous weeping.

"Oh! Mrs. Wilson, don't take on so! We'll get him off, you'll see. Don't fret; they can't prove him guilty!"

"But I tell thee they will," interrupted Mrs. Wilson, half-irritated at the light way, as she considered it, in which Mary spoke; and a little displeased that another could hope when she had almost brought herself to find pleasure in despair.

"It may suit thee well," continued she, "to make light o' the misery thou hast caused; but I shall lay his death at thy door, as long as I live, and die I know he will; and all for what he never did—no, he never did; my own blessed boy!"

She was too weak to be angry long; her wrath sank away to feeble sobbing and worn-out moans.

Mary was most anxious to soothe her from any violence of either grief or anger; she did so want her to be clear in her recollection; and, besides, her tenderness was great towards Jem's mother. So she spoke in a low gentle tone the loving sentences, which sound so broken and powerless in repetition, and which yet have so much power, when accompanied with caressing looks and actions, fresh from the heart; and the old woman insensibly gave herself up to the influence of those sweet, loving blue eyes, those tears of sympathy, those words of love and hope, and was lulled into a less morbid state of mind.

"And now, dear Mrs. Wilson, can you remember where he said he was going on Thursday night? He was out when Alice was taken ill; and he did not come home till early in the morning, or, to speak true, in the night: did he?"

"Ay! he went out near upon five; he went out with Will; he said he were going to set* him a part of the way, for Will were hot upon walking to Liverpool, and wouldn't hearken to Jem's offer of lending him five shillings for his fare. So the two lads set off together. I mind it all now: but, thou seest, Alice's illness, and this business of poor Jem's, drove it out of my head; they went off together, to walk to Liverpool; that's to say, Jem were to go a part o' th' way. But, who knows" (falling back into the old desponding tone) "if he really went? He might be led off on the road. Oh! Mary, wench! they'll hang him for what he's never done."

---

* "To set," to accompany. [WG]

"No, they won't, they shan't! I see my way a-bit now. We mun get Will to help; there'll be time. He can swear that Jem were with him. Where is Jem?"

"Folk said he were taken to Kirkdale, i' th' prison van this morning; without my seeing him, poor chap! Oh! wench! but they've hurried on the business at a cruel rate."

"Ay! they've not let grass grow under their feet, in hunting out the man that did it," said Mary, sorrowfully and bitterly. "But keep up your heart. They got on the wrong scent when they took to suspecting Jem. Don't be afeard. You'll see it will end right for Jem."

"I should mind it less if I could do aught," said Jane Wilson: "but I'm such a poor weak old body, and my head's so gone, and I'm so daz'd like, what with Alice and all, that I think and think, and can do nought to help my child. I might ha' gone and seen him last night, they tell me now, and then I missed it. Oh! Mary, I missed it; and I may never see the lad again."

She looked so piteously in Mary's face with her miserable eyes, that Mary felt her heart giving way, and, dreading the weakness of her powers, which the burst of crying she longed for would occasion, hastily changed the subject to Alice; and Jane, in her heart, feeling that there was no sorrow like a mother's sorrow, replied,

"She keeps on much the same, thank you. She's happy, for she knows nothing of what's going on; but th' doctor says she grows weaker and weaker. Thou'lt maybe like to see her?"

Mary went up-stairs: partly because it is the etiquette in humble life, to offer to friends a last opportunity of seeing the dying or the dead, while the same etiquette forbids a refusal of the invitation; and partly because she longed to breathe, for an instant, the atmosphere of holy calm, which seemed ever to surround the pious good old woman. Alice lay, as before, without pain, or at least any outward expression of it; but totally unconscious of all present circumstances, and absorbed in recollections of the days of her girlhood, which were vivid enough to take the place of reality to her. Still she talked of green fields, and still she spoke to the long-dead mother and sister, low-lying in their graves this many a year, as if they were with her and about her, in the pleasant places where her youth had passed.

But the voice was fainter, the motions were more languid; she was evidently passing away; but *how* happily!

Mary stood for a time in silence, watching and listening. Then she bent down and reverently kissed Alice's cheek; and drawing Jane Wilson away from the bed, as if the spirit of her who lay there were yet cognisant of present realities, she whispered a few words of hope to the poor mother, and kissing her over and over again in a warm, loving manner, she bade her good-bye, went a few steps, and then once more came back to bid her keep up her heart.

And when she had fairly left the house, Jane Wilson felt as if a sun-beam had ceased shining into the room.

Yet oh! how sorely Mary's heart ached; for more and more the fell certainty came on her that her father was the murderer! She struggled hard not to dwell on this conviction; to think alone on the means of proving Jem's innocence; that was her first duty, and that should be done.

Chapter XXIII.

"And must it then depend on this poor eye
And this unsteady hand, whether the bark,
That bears my all of treasured hope and love,
Shall find a passage through these frowning rocks
To some fair port where peace and safety smile,—
Or whether it shall blindly dash against them,
And miserably sink? Heaven be my help;
And clear my eye and nerve my trembling hand!"
                                    'THE CONSTANT WOMAN.[8]

Her heart beating, her head full of ideas, which required time and solitude to be reduced into order, Mary hurried home. She was like one who finds a jewel of which he cannot all at once ascertain the value, but who hides his treasure until some quiet hour when he may ponder over the capabilities its possession unfolds. She was like one who discovers the silken clue which guides to some bower of bliss, and secure of the power within his grasp, has to wait for a time before he may thread the labyrinth.

But no jewel, no bower of bliss was ever so precious to miser or lover as was the belief which now pervaded Mary's mind, that Jem's innocence might be proved, without involving any suspicion of that other—that dear one, so dear, although so criminal—on whose part in this cruel business she dared not dwell even in thought. For if she did, there arose the awful question,—if all went against Jem the innocent, if judge and jury gave the verdict forth which had the looming gallows in the rear, what ought she to do, possessed of her terrible knowledge? Surely not to inculpate her father—and yet—and yet—she almost prayed for the blessed unconsciousness of death or madness, rather than that awful question should have to be answered by her.

But now a way seemed opening, opening yet more clear. She was thankful she had thought of the *alibi*, and yet more thankful to have so easily obtained the clue to Jem's whereabouts that miserable night. The bright light that her new hope threw over all, seemed also

8. Unknown.

to make her thankful for the early time appointed for the trial. It would be easy to catch Will Wilson on his return from the Isle of Man, which he had planned should be on the Monday; and on the Tuesday all would be made clear—all that she dared to wish to be made clear.

She had still to collect her thoughts and freshen her memory enough to arrange how to meet with Will—for to the chances of a letter she would not trust; to find out his lodgings when in Liverpool; to try and remember the name of the ship in which he was to sail: and the more she considered these points, the more difficulty she found there would be in ascertaining these minor but important facts. For you are aware that Alice, whose memory was clear and strong on all points in which her heart was interested, was lying in a manner senseless: that Jane Wilson was (to use her own word, so expressive to a Lancashire ear) "dazed,"* that is to say, bewildered, lost in the confusion of terrifying and distressing thoughts; incapable of concentrating her mind; and at the best of times Will's proceedings were a matter of little importance to her (or so she pretended), she was so jealous of aught which distracted attention from her pearl of price, her only son Jem. So Mary felt hopeless of obtaining any intelligence of the sailor's arrangements from her.

Then, should she apply to Jem himself? No! she knew him too well. She felt how thoroughly he must ere now have had it in his power to exculpate himself at another's expense. And his tacit refusal so to do, had assured her of what she had never doubted, that the murderer was safe from any impeachment of his. But then neither would he consent, she feared, to any steps which might tend to prove himself innocent. At any rate, she could not consult him. He was removed to Kirkdale, and time pressed. Already it was Saturday at noon. And even if she could have gone to him, I believe she would not. She longed to do all herself; to be his liberator, his deliverer; to win him life, though she might never regain his lost love by her own exertions. And oh! how could she see him to discuss a subject in which both knew who was the blood-stained man; and yet whose name might not be breathed by either, so dearly with all his faults, his sins, was he loved by both.

All at once, when she had ceased to try and remember, the name of Will's ship flashed across her mind. The *John Cropper*.

He had named it, she had been sure, all along. He had named it in his conversation with her that last, that fatal Thursday evening. She repeated it over and over again, through a nervous dread of again forgetting it. The *John Cropper*.

---

* "They make him so amazed,
    And his eyes so dazed."—*Skelton*. [WG]

And then, as if she were rousing herself out of some strange stupor, she bethought her of Margaret. Who so likely as Margaret to treasure every little particular respecting Will, now Alice was dead to all the stirring purposes of life?

She had gone thus far in her process of thought, when a neighbour stepped in; she with whom they had usually deposited the house-key, when both Mary and her father were absent from home, and who consequently took upon herself to answer all inquiries, and receive all messages which any friends might make, or leave, on finding the house shut up.

"Here's somewhat for you, Mary! A policeman left it."

A bit of parchment.

Many people have a dread of those mysterious pieces of parchment. I am one. Mary was another. Her heart misgave her as she took it, and looked at the unusual appearance of the writing, which, though legible enough, conveyed no idea to her, or rather her mind shut itself up against receiving any idea, which after all was rather a proof she had some suspicion of the meaning that awaited her.

"What is it?" asked she, in a voice from which all the pith and marrow seemed extracted.

"Nay! how should I know? Policeman said he'd call again towards evening, and see if you'd getten it. He were loth to leave it, though I told him who I was, and all about my keeping th' key, and taking messages."

"What is it about?" asked Mary again, in the same hoarse, feeble voice, and turning it over in her fingers, as if she dreaded to inform herself of its meaning.

"Well! yo can read word of writing and I cannot, so it's queer I should have to tell you. But my master says it's a summons for yo to bear witness again Jem Wilson, at th' trial at Liverpool Assize."

"God pity me!" said Mary, faintly, as white as a sheet.

"Nay, wench, never take on so. What yo can say will go little way either to help or hinder, for folk say he's certain to be hung, and sure enough, it was t'other one as was your sweetheart."

Mary was beyond any pang this speech would have given at another time. Her thoughts were all busy picturing to herself the terrible occasion of their next meeting—not as lovers meet should they meet!

"Well!" said the neighbour, seeing no use in remaining with one who noticed her words or her presence so little; "thou'lt tell policeman thou'st getten his precious bit of paper. He seemed to think I should be keeping it for mysel; he's the first as has ever misdoubted me about giving messages, or notes. Good day."

She left the house, but Mary did not know it. She sat still with the parchment in her hand.

All at once she started up. She would take it to Job Legh, and ask him to tell her the true meaning, for it could not be *that*.

So she went, and choked out her words of inquiry.

"It's a sub-pœna," he replied, turning the parchment over with the air of a connoisseur; for Job loved hard words, and lawyer-like forms, and even esteemed himself slightly qualified for a lawyer, from the smattering of knowledge he had picked up from an odd volume of Blackstone[9] that he had once purchased at a book-stall.

"A sub-pœna—what is that?" gasped Mary, still in suspense.

Job was struck with her voice, her changed miserable voice, and peered at her countenance from over his spectacles.

"A sub-pœna is neither more nor less than this, my dear. It's a summonsing you to attend, and answer such questions as may be asked of you regarding the trial of James Wilson, for the murder of Henry Carson; that's the long and short of it, only more elegantly put, for the benefit of them who knows how to value the gift of language. I've been a witness before-time myself; there's nothing much to be afeard on; if they are impudent, why, just you be impudent, and give 'em tit for tat."

"Nothing much to be afeard on!" echoed Mary, but in such a different tone.

"Ay, poor wench, I see how it is. It'll go hard with thee a bit, I dare say; but keep up thy heart. Yo cannot have much to tell 'em, that can go either one way or th' other. Nay! maybe thou may do him a bit o'good, for when they set eyes on thee, they'll see fast enough how he came to be so led away by jealousy; for thou'r a pretty creature, Mary, and one look at thy face will let 'em into th' secret of a young man's madness, and make 'em more ready to pass it over."

"Oh! Job, and won't you ever believe me when I tell you he's innocent? Indeed, and indeed I can prove it; he was with Will all that night; he was, indeed, Job!"

"My wench! whose word hast thou for that?" said Job, pityingly.

"Why! his mother told me, and I'll get Will to bear witness to it. But, oh! Job" (bursting into tears), "it is hard if you won't believe me. How shall I clear him to strangers, when those who know him, and ought to love him, are so set against his being innocent?"

"God knows, I'm not against his being innocent," said Job, solemnly. "I'd give half my remaining days on earth,—I'd give them all, Mary (and but for the love I bear to my poor blind girl, they'd be no great gift), if I could save him. You've thought me hard, Mary, but I'm not hard at bottom, and I'll help you if I can; that I will, right or wrong," he added; but in a low voice, and coughed the uncertain words away the moment afterwards.

9. *Commentaries on the Laws of England* (1765–1769) by William Blackstone (1723–1780) was the standard work on the English legal system.

"Oh, Job! if you will help me," exclaimed Mary, brightening up (though it was but a wintry gleam after all), "tell me what to say, when they question me; I shall be so gloppened,* I sha'n't know what to answer."

"Thou canst do nought better than tell the truth. Truth's best at all times, they say; and for sure it is when folk have to do with lawyers; for they're 'cute and cunning enough to get it out sooner or later, and it makes folk look like Tom Noddies,[1] when truth follows falsehood, against their will."

"But I don't know the truth; I mean—I can't say rightly what I mean; but I'm sure, if I were pent up, and stared at by hundreds of folk, and asked ever so simple a question, I should be for answering it wrong; if they asked me if I had seen you on a Saturday, or a Tuesday, or any day, I should have clean forgotten all about it, and say the very thing I should not."

"Well, well, don't go for to get such notions into your head; they're what they call 'narvous,' and talking on 'em does no good. Here's Margaret! bless the wench! Look Mary, how well she guides hersel."

Job fell to watching his grand-daughter, as with balancing, measured steps, timed almost as if to music, she made her way across the street.

Mary shrank as if from a cold blast—shrank from Margaret! The blind girl, with her reserve, her silence, seemed to be a severe judge; she, listening, would be such a check to the trusting earnestness of confidence, which was beginning to unlock the sympathy of Job. Mary knew herself to blame; felt her errors in every fibre of her heart; but yet she would rather have had them spoken about, even in terms of severest censure, than have been treated in the icy manner in which Margaret had received her that morning.

"Here's Mary," said Job, almost as if he wished to propitiate his grand-daughter, "come to take a bit of dinner with us, for I'll warrant she's never thought of cooking any for herself to-day; and she looks as wan and pale as a ghost."

It was calling out the feeling of hospitality, so strong and warm in most of those who have little to offer, but whose heart goes eagerly and kindly with that little. Margaret came towards Mary with a welcoming gesture, and a kinder manner by far than she had used in the morning.

"Nay, Mary, thou know'st thou'st getten nought at home," urged Job.

And Mary, faint and weary, and with a heart too aching-full of other matters to be pertinacious in this, withdrew her refusal.

---

* "Gloppened," terrified. [WG]
1. Fools.

They ate their dinner quietly; for to all it was an effort to speak: and after one or two attempts they had subsided into silence.

When the meal was ended Job began again on the subject they all had at heart.

"Yon poor lad at Kirkdale will want a lawyer to see they don't put on him, but do him justice. Hast thought of that?"

Mary had not, and felt sure his mother had not.

Margaret confirmed this last supposition.

"I've but just been there, and poor Jane is like one dateless;[2] so many griefs come on her at once. One time she seems to make sure he'll be hung; and if I took her in that way, she flew out (poor body!) and said, that in spite of what folks said, there were them as could, and would prove him guiltless. So I never knew where to have her. The only thing she was constant in, was declaring him innocent."

"Mother-like!" said Job.

"She meant Will, when she spoke of them that could prove him innocent. He was with Will on Thursday night; walking a part of the way with him to Liverpool; now the thing is to lay hold on Will, and get him to prove this." So spoke Mary, calm, from the earnestness of her purpose.

"Don't build too much on it, my dear," said Job.

"I do build on it," replied Mary, "because I know it's the truth, and I mean to try and prove it, come what may. Nothing you can say will daunt me, Job, so don't you go and try. You may help, but you cannot hinder me doing what I'm resolved on."

They respected her firmness of determination, and Job almost gave into her belief, when he saw how steadfastly she was acting upon it. Oh! surest way of conversion to our faith, whatever it may be,— regarding either small things, or great,—when it is beheld as the actuating principle, from which we never swerve! When it is seen that, instead of over-much profession, it is worked into the life, and moves every action!

Mary gained courage as she instinctively felt she had made way with one at least of her companions.

"Now I'm clear about this much," she continued, "he was with Will when the——shot was fired (she could not bring herself to say, when the murder was committed, when she remembered *who* it was that, she had every reason to believe, was the taker-away of life). Will can prove this, I must find Will. He wasn't to sail till Tuesday. There's time enough. He was to come back from his uncle's, in the Isle of Man, on Monday. I must meet him in Liverpool, on that day, and tell him what has happened, and how poor Jem is in trouble, and that he must prove an *alibi*, come Tuesday. All this I can and will do, though per-

2. Crazed.

haps I don't clearly know how, just at present. But surely God will help me. When I know I'm doing right, I will have no fear, but put my trust in Him; for I'm acting for the innocent and good, and not for my own self, who have done so wrong. I have no fear when I think of Jem, who is so good."

She stopped, oppressed with the fullness of her heart. Margaret began to love her again; to see in her the same, sweet, faulty, impulsive, loveable creature she had known in the former Mary Barton, but with more of dignity, self-reliance, and purpose.

Mary spoke again.

"Now I know the name of Will's vessel—the *John Cropper;* and I know that she is bound to America. That is something to know. But I forgot, if I ever heard, where he lodges in Liverpool. He spoke of his landlady, as a good, trustworthy woman; but if he named her name, it has slipped my memory. Can you help me, Margaret?"

She appealed to her friend calmly and openly, as if perfectly aware of, and recognising the unspoken tie which bound her and Will together; she asked her in the same manner in which she would have asked a wife where her husband dwelt. And Margaret replied in the like calm tone, two spots of crimson on her cheeks alone bearing witness to any internal agitation.

"He lodges at a Mrs. Jones', Milk-House Yard, out of Nicholas Street. He has lodged there ever since he began to go to sea; she is a very decent kind of woman, I believe."

"Well, Mary! I'll give you my prayers," said Job. "It's not often I pray regular, though I often speak a word to God, when I'm either very happy, or very sorry; I've catched myself thanking him at odd hours when I've found a rare insect, or had a fine day for an out; but I cannot help it, no more than I can talking to a friend. But this time I'll pray regular for Jem, and for you. And so will Margaret, I'll be bound. Still, wench! what think yo of a lawyer? I know one, Mr. Cheshire, who's rather given to th' insect line—and a good kind o'chap. He and I have swopped specimens many's the time, when either of us had a duplicate. He'll do me a kind turn, I'm sure. I'll just take my hat, and pay him a visit."

No sooner said, than done.

Margaret and Mary were left alone. And this seemed to bring back the feeling of awkwardness, not to say estrangement.

But Mary, excited to an unusual pitch of courage, was the first to break silence.

"Oh, Margaret!" said she, "I see—I feel how wrong you think I have acted; you cannot think me worse than I think myself, now my eyes are opened." Here her sobs came choking up her voice.

"Nay," Margaret began, "I have no right to—"

"Yes, Margaret, you have a right to judge; you cannot help it; only in your judgment remember mercy, as the Bible says. You, who have been always good, cannot tell how easy it is at first to go a little wrong, and then how hard it is to go back. Oh! I little thought when I was first pleased with Mr. Carson's speeches, how it would all end; perhaps in the death of him I love better than life."

She burst into a passion of tears. The feelings pent up through the day would have vent. But checking herself with a strong effort, and looking up at Margaret as piteously as if those calm, stony eyes could see her imploring face, she added,

"I must not cry; I must not give way; there will be time enough for that hereafter, if—I only wanted you to speak kindly to me, Margaret, for I am very, very wretched; more wretched than any one can ever know; more wretched, I sometimes fancy, than I have deserved,—but that's wrong, isn't it, Margaret? Oh! I have done wrong, and I am punished: you cannot tell how much."

Who could resist her voice, her tones of misery, of humility? Who would refuse the kindness for which she begged so penitently? Not Margaret. The old friendly manner came back. With it, maybe, more of tenderness.

"Oh! Margaret, do you think he can be saved; do you think they can find him guilty, if Will comes forward as a witness? Won't that be a good *alibi?*"

Margaret did not answer for a moment.

"Oh, speak! Margaret," said Mary, with anxious impatience.

"I know nought about law, or *alibis*," replied Margaret, meekly; "but, Mary, as grandfather says, aren't you building too much on what Jane Wilson has told you about his going with Will? Poor soul, she's gone dateless, I think, with care, and watching, and overmuch trouble; and who can wonder? Or Jem may have told her he was going, by way of a blind."

"You don't know Jem," said Mary, starting from her seat in a hurried manner, "or you would not say so."

"I hope I may be wrong! but think, Mary, how much there is against him. The shot was fired with his gun; he it was as threatened Mr. Carson not many days before; he was absent from home at that very time, as we know, and, as I'm much afeard, some one will be called on to prove, and there's no one else to share suspicion with him."

Mary heaved a deep sigh.

"But, Margaret, he did not do it," Mary again asserted.

Margaret looked unconvinced.

"I can do no good, I see, by saying so, for none on you believe me, and I won't say so again till I can prove it. Monday morning I'll go to Liverpool. I shall be at hand for the trial. Oh dear! dear! And I will find Will; and then, Margaret, I think you'll be sorry for being so stubborn about Jem."

"Don't fly off, dear Mary, I'd give a deal to be wrong. And now I'm going to be plain spoken. You'll want money. Them lawyers is no better than a sponge for sucking up money; let alone your hunting out Will, and your keep in Liverpool, and what not. You must take some of the mint I've got laid by in the old teapot. You have no right to refuse, for I offer it to Jem, not to you; it's for his purposes you're to use it."

"I know—I see. Thank you, Margaret; you're a kind one at any rate. I take it for Jem; and I'll do my very best with it for him. Not all, though; don't think I'll take all. They'll pay me for my keep. I'll take this," accepting a sovereign from the hoard which Margaret produced out of its accustomed place in the cupboard. "Your grandfather will pay the lawyer, I'll have nought to do with him," shuddering as she remembered Job's words, about lawyers' skill in always discovering the truth, sooner or later; and knowing what was the secret she had to hide.

"Bless you! don't make such ado about it," said Margaret, cutting short Mary's thanks. "I sometimes think there's two sides to the commandment; and that we may say, 'Let others do unto you, as you would do unto them,' for pride often prevents our giving others a great deal of pleasure, in not letting them be kind, when their hearts are longing to help; and when we ourselves should wish to do just the same, if we were in their place. Oh! how often I've been hurt, by being coldly told by persons not to trouble myself about their care, or sorrow, when I saw them in great grief, and wanted to be of comfort. Our Lord Jesus was not above letting folk minister to Him, for he knew how happy it makes one to do aught for another. It's the happiest work on earth."

Mary had been too much engrossed by watching what was passing in the street to attend very closely to that which Margaret was saying. From her seat she could see out of the window pretty plainly, and she caught sight of a gentleman walking alongside of Job, evidently in earnest conversation with him, and looking keen and penetrating enough to be a lawyer. Job was laying down something to be attended to she could see, by his uplifted forefinger, and his whole gesture; then he pointed and nodded across the street to his own house, as if inducing his companion to come in. Mary dreaded lest he should, and she be subjected to a closer cross-examination than she had hitherto undergone, as to why she was so certain that Jem was innocent. She feared he was coming; he stepped a little towards the spot. No! it was only to make way for a child, tottering along, whom Mary had overlooked. Now Job took him by the button, so earnestly familiar had he grown. The gentleman looked "fidging fain"[3] to be gone, but

3. Impatient and eager.

submitted in a manner that made Mary like him in spite of his profession. Then came a volley of last words, answered by briefest nods,
and monosyllables; and then the stranger went off with redoubled
quickness of pace, and Job crossed the street with a little satisfied air
of importance on his kindly face.

"Well! Mary," said he, on entering, "I've seen the lawyer, not Mr.
Cheshire though; trials for murder, it seems, are not his line o' business. But he gave me a note to another 'torney; a fine fellow enough,
only too much of a talker; I could hardly get a word in, he cut me so
short. However, I've just been going over the principal points again
to him; maybe you saw us! I wanted him just come over and speak to
you himsel, Mary, but he was pressed for time; and he said your evidence would not be much either here or there. He's going to the 'sizes
first train on Monday morning, and will see Jem, and hear the ins and
outs from him, and he's gived me his address, Mary, and you and Will
are to call on him (Will 'special) on Monday, at two o'clock. Thou'rt
taking it in, Mary; thou'rt to call on him in Liverpool at two, Monday
afternoon?"

Job had reason to doubt if she fully understood him; for all this
minuteness of detail, these satisfactory arrangements, as he considered them, only seemed to bring the circumstances in which she was
placed more vividly home to Mary. They convinced her that it was
real, and not all a dream, as she had sunk into fancying it for a few
minutes, while sitting in the old accustomed place, her body enjoying the rest, and her frame sustained by food, and listening to Margaret's calm voice. The gentleman she had just beheld would see and
question Jem in a few hours, and what would be the result?

Monday: that was the day after to-morrow, and on Tuesday, life and
death would be tremendous realities to her lover; or else death would
be an awful certainty to her father.

No wonder Job went over his main points again:—

"Monday; at two o'clock, mind; and here's his card. 'Mr. Bridgnorth, 41, Renshaw Street, Liverpool.' He'll be lodging there."

Job ceased talking, and the silence roused Mary up to thank him.

"You're very kind, Job; very. You and Margaret won't desert me,
come what will."

"Pooh! pooh! wench; don't lose heart, just as I'm beginning to get
it. He seems to think a deal on Will's evidence. You're sure, girls,
you're under no mistake about Will?"

"I'm sure," said Mary, "he went straight from here, purposing to go
to see his uncle at the Isle of Man, and be back Sunday night, ready
for the ship sailing on Tuesday."

"So am I," said Margaret. "And the ship's name was the *John Cropper*, and he lodged where I told Mary before. Have you got it down,
Mary?" Mary wrote it on the back of Mr. Bridgnorth's card.

"He was not over willing to go," said she, as she wrote, "for he knew little about his uncle, and said he didn't care if he never know'd more. But he said kinsfolk was kinsfolk, and promises was promises, so he'd go for a day or so, and then it would be over."

Margaret had to go and practise some singing in town; so, though loth to depart and be alone, Mary bade her friends good-bye.

Chapter XXIV.

"O sad and solemn is the trembling watch
Of those who sit and count the heavy hours,
Beside the fevered sleep of one they love!
O awful is it in the hushed mid-night,
While gazing on the pallid, moveless form,
To start and ask, 'Is it now sleep—or death?'"
ANONYMOUS.

Mary could not be patient in her loneliness; so much painful thought weighed on her mind, the very house was haunted with memories and foreshadowings.

Having performed all duties to Jem, as far as her weak powers, yet loving heart could act; and a black veil being drawn over her father's past, present, and future life, beyond which she could not penetrate to judge of any filial service she ought to render; her mind unconsciously sought after some course of action in which she might engage. Any thing, any thing, rather than leisure for reflection.

And then came up the old feeling which first bound Ruth to Naomi;[4] the love they both held towards one object; and Mary felt that her cares would be most lightened by being of use, or of comfort to his mother. So she once more locked up the house, and set off towards Ancoats; rushing along with down-cast head, for fear lest any one should recognise her and arrest her progress.

Jane Wilson sat quietly in her chair as Mary entered; so quietly, as to strike one by the contrast it presented to her usual, bustling, and nervous manner.

She looked very pale and wan; but the quietness was the thing that struck Mary most. She did not rise as Mary came in, but sat still and said something in so gentle, so feeble a voice, that Mary did not catch it.

Mrs. Davenport, who was there, plucked Mary by the gown, and whispered, "Never heed her; she's worn out, and best let alone. I'll tell you all about it, up-stairs."

But Mary, touched by the anxious look with which Mrs. Wilson

4. Ruth 1:16.

gazed at her, as if waiting the answer to some question, went forward to listen to the speech she was again repeating.

"What is this? will you tell me?"

Then Mary looked, and saw another ominous slip of parchment in the mother's hand, which she was rolling up and down in a tremulous manner between her fingers.

Mary's heart sickened within her; and she could not speak.

"What is it?" she repeated. "Will you tell me?" She still looked at Mary, with the same child-like gaze of wonder and patient entreaty.

What could she answer?

"I told ye not to heed her," said Mrs. Davenport, a little angrily. "She knows well enough what it is,—too well, belike. I was not in when they sarved it; but Mrs. Heming (her as lives next door) was, and she spelled out the meaning, and made it all clear to Mrs. Wilson. It's a summons to be a witness on Jem's trial—Mrs. Heming thinks, to swear to the gun; for yo see, there's nobbut* her as can testify to its being his, and she let on so easily to the policeman that it was his, that there's no getting off her word now. Poor body; she takes it very hard, I dare say!"

Mrs. Wilson had waited patiently while this whispered speech was being uttered, imagining, perhaps, that it would end in some explanation addressed to her. But when both were silent, though their eyes without speech or language, told their heart's pity, she spoke again in the same unaltered gentle voice (so different from the irritable impatience she had been ever apt to show to every one except her husband—he who had wedded her, broken down, and injured) in a voice so different, I say, from the old, hasty manner, she spoke now the same anxious words.

"What is this? Will you tell me?"

"Yo'd better give it me at once, Mrs. Wilson, and let me put it out of your sight. Speak to her, Mary, wench, and ask for a sight on it; I've tried and better-tried to get it from her, and she takes no heed of words, and I'm loth to pull it by force out of her hands."

Mary drew the little "cricket"† out from under the dresser, and sat down at Mrs. Wilson's knee, and, coaxing one of her tremulous ever moving hands into hers, began to rub it soothingly; there was a little resistance—a very little, but that was all; and presently, in the nervous movement of the imprisoned hand, the parchment fell to the ground.

Mary calmly and openly picked it up, without any attempt at concealment, and quietly placing it in sight of the anxious eyes that followed it with a kind of spell-bound dread, went on with her soothing caresses.

---

*   "Nobbut," none-but. "No man sigh evere God *no but* the oon bigetun sone."—*Wiclif's Version*. [WG]
†   "Cricket," a stool. [WG]

"She has had no sleep for many nights," said the girl to Mrs. Davenport, "and all this woe and sorrow,—it's no wonder."

"No, indeed!" Mrs. Davenport answered.

"We must get her fairly to bed; we must get her undressed, and all; and trust to God in His mercy, to send her to sleep, or else,—"

For, you see, they spoke before her as if she were not there; her heart was so far away.

Accordingly they almost lifted her from the chair, in which she sat motionless, and taking her up as gently as a mother carries her sleeping baby, they undressed her poor, worn form, and laid her in the little bed up-stairs. They had once thought of placing her in Jem's bed, to be out of sight or sound of any disturbance of Alice's; but then again they remembered the shock she might receive in awakening in so unusual a place, and also that Mary, who intended to keep vigil that night in the house of mourning, would find it difficult to divide her attention in the possible cases that might ensue.

So they laid her, as I said before, on that little pallet-bed; and, as they were slowly withdrawing from the bed-side, hoping and praying that she might sleep, and forget for a time her heavy burden, she looked wistfully after Mary, and whispered,

"You haven't told me what it is. What is it?"

And gazing in her face for the expected answer, her eye-lids slowly closed, and she fell into a deep, heavy sleep, almost as profound a rest as death.

Mrs. Davenport went her way, and Mary was alone,—for I cannot call those who sleep allies against the agony of thought which solitude sometimes brings up.

She dreaded the night before her. Alice might die; the doctor had that day declared her case hopeless, and not far from death; and at times, the terror so natural to the young, not of death, but of the remains of the dead, came over Mary; and she bent and listened anxiously for the long-drawn, pausing breath of the sleeping Alice.

Or Mrs. Wilson might awake in a state which Mary dreaded to anticipate, and anticipated while she dreaded;—in a state of complete delirium. Already her senses had been severely stunned by the full explanation of what was required of her,—of what she had to prove against her son, her Jem, her only child,—which Mary could not doubt the officious Mrs. Heming had given; and what if in dreams (that land into which no sympathy nor love can penetrate with another, either to share its bliss or its agony,—that land whose scenes are unspeakable terrors, are hidden mysteries, are priceless treasures to one alone,—that land where alone I may see, while yet I tarry here, the sweet looks of my dear child),—what if, in the horrors of her dreams, her brain should go still more astray, and she should waken crazy with her visions, and the terrible reality that begot them?

How much worse is anticipation sometimes than reality! How Mary dreaded that night, and how calmly it passed by! Even more so than if Mary had not had such claims upon her care!

Anxiety about them deadened her own peculiar anxieties. She thought of the sleepers whom she was watching, till overpowered herself by the want of rest, she fell off into short slumbers in which the night wore imperceptibly away. To be sure, Alice spoke, and sang during her waking moments, like the child she deemed herself; but so happily with the dearly-loved ones around her, with the scent of the heather, and the song of the wild bird hovering about her in imagination—with old scraps of ballads, or old snatches of primitive versions of the Psalms (such as are sung in country churches half draperied over with ivy, and where the running brook, or the murmuring wind among the trees makes fit accompaniment to the chorus of human voices uttering praise and thanksgiving to their God)—that the speech and the song gave comfort and good cheer to the listener's heart, and the gray dawn began to dim the light of the rush-candle, before Mary thought it possible that day was already trembling in the horizon.

Then she got up from the chair where she had been dozing, and went, half-asleep, to the window to assure herself that morning was at hand. The streets were unusually quiet with a Sabbath stillness. No factory bells that morning; no early workmen going to their labours; no slip-shod girls cleaning the windows of the little shops which broke the monotony of the street; instead, you might see here and there some operative sallying forth for a breath of country air, or some father leading out his wee toddling bairns for the unwonted pleasure of a walk with "Daddy," in the clear frosty morning. Men with more leisure on week days would perhaps have walked quicker than they did through the fresh sharp air of this Sunday morning; but to them there was a pleasure, an absolute refreshment in the dawdling gait they, one and all of them, had.

There were, indeed, one or two passengers on that morning whose objects were less innocent and less praiseworthy than those of the people I have already mentioned, and whose animal state of mind and body clashed jarringly on the peacefulness of the day, but upon them I will not dwell; as you and I, and almost every one, I think, may send up our individual cry of self-reproach that we have not done all that we could for the stray and wandering ones of our brethren.

When Mary turned from the window, she went to the bed of each sleeper, to look and listen. Alice looked perfectly quiet and happy in her slumber, and her face seemed to have become much more youthful during the painless approach to death.

Mrs. Wilson's countenance was stamped with the anxiety of the last few days, although she, too, appeared sleeping soundly; but as

Mary gazed on her, trying to trace a likeness to her son in her face, she awoke and looked up into Mary's eyes, while the expression of consciousness came back into her own.

Both were silent for a minute or two. Mary's eyes had fallen beneath that penetrating gaze, in which the agony of memory seemed every minute to find fuller vent.

"Is it a dream?" the mother asked at last in a low voice.

"No!" replied Mary, in the same tone.

Mrs. Wilson hid her face in the pillow.

She was fully conscious of everything this morning; it was evident that the stunning effect of the subpœna, which had affected her so much last night in her weak, worn-out state, had passed away. Mary offered no opposition when she indicated by languid gesture and action that she wished to rise. A sleepless bed is a haunted place.

When she was dressed with Mary's aid, she stood by Alice for a minute or two looking at the slumberer.

"How happy she is!" said she, quietly and sadly.

All the time that Mary was getting breakfast ready, and performing every other little domestic office she could think of, to add to the comfort of Jem's mother, Mrs. Wilson sat still in the arm-chair, watching her silently. Her old irritation of temper and manner seemed to have suddenly disappeared, or perhaps she was too depressed in body and mind to show it.

Mary told her all that had been done with regard to Mr. Bridgenorth; all her own plans for seeking out Will; all her hopes; and concealed as well as she could all the doubts and fears that would arise unbidden. To this Mrs. Wilson listened without much remark, but with deep interest and perfect comprehension. When Mary ceased, she sighed and said, "Oh wench! I am his mother, and yet I do so little, I can do so little! That's what frets me! I seem like a child a sees its mammy ill, and moans and cries its little heart out, yet does nought to help. I think my sense has left me all at once, and I can't even find strength to cry like the little child."

Hereupon she broke into a feeble wail of self-reproach, that her outward show of misery was not greater; as if any cries, or tears, or loud-spoken words could have told of such pangs at the heart as that look, and that thin, piping, altered voice!

But think of Mary and what she was enduring. Picture to yourself (for I cannot tell you) the armies of thoughts that met and clashed in her brain; and then imagine the effort it cost her to be calm, and quiet, and even in a faint way, cheerful and smiling at times.

After a while she began to stir about in her own mind for some means of sparing the poor mother the trial of appearing as a witness in the matter of the gun. She had made no allusion to her summons this morning, and Mary almost thought she must have forgotten it;

and surely some means might be found to prevent that additional sorrow. She must see Job about it; nay, if necessary, she must see Mr. Bridgenorth, with all his truth-compelling powers; for, indeed, she had so struggled and triumphed (though a sadly-bleeding victor at heart) over herself these two last days, had so concealed agony, and hidden her inward woe and bewilderment, that she began to take confidence, and to have faith in her own powers of meeting any one with a passably fair show, whatever might be rending her life beneath the cloak of her deception.

Accordingly, as soon as Mrs. Davenport came in after morning church, to ask after the two lone women, and she had heard the report Mary had to give (so much better as regarded Mrs. Wilson than what they had feared the night before it would have been)—as soon as this kind-hearted, grateful woman came in, Mary, telling her her purpose, went off to fetch the doctor who attended Alice.

He was shaking himself after his morning's round, and happy in the anticipation of his Sunday's dinner; but he was a good-tempered man, who found it difficult to keep down his jovial easiness even by the bed of sickness or death. He had mischosen his profession; for it was his delight to see every one around him in full enjoyment of life.

However, he subdued his face to the proper expression of sympathy, befitting a doctor listening to a patient, or a patient's friend (and Mary's sad, pale, anxious face, might be taken for either the one, or the other).

"Well, my girl! and what brings you here?" said he, as he entered his surgery. "Not on your own account, I hope."

"I wanted you to come and see Alice Wilson,—and then I thought you would maybe take a look at Mrs. Wilson."

He bustled on his hat and coat, and followed Mary, instantly.

After shaking his head over Alice (as if it was a mournful thing for one so pure and good, so true, although so humble a Christian, to be nearing her desired heaven), and muttering the accustomed words intended to destroy hope, and prepare anticipation, he went in compliance with Mary's look to ask the usual questions of Mrs. Wilson, who sat passively in her arm-chair.

She answered his questions, and submitted to his examination.

"How do you think her?" asked Mary, eagerly.

"Why—a," began he, perceiving that he was desired to take one side in his answer, and unable to find out whether his listener was anxious for a favourable verdict or otherwise; but thinking it most probable that she would desire the former, he continued,

"She is weak, certainly; the natural result of such a shock as the arrest of her son would be,—for I understand this James Wilson, who murdered Mr. Carson, was her son. Sad thing to have such a reprobate in the family."

"You say '*who murdered*,' sir!" said Mary, indignantly. "He is only taken up on suspicion, and many have no doubt of his innocence—those who know him, sir."

"Ah, well, well! doctors have seldom time to read newspapers, and I dare say I'm not very correct in my story. I dare say he's innocent; I'm sure I had no right to say otherwise,—only words slip out.—No! indeed, young woman, I see no cause for apprehension about this poor creature in the next room;—weak—certainly; but a day or two's good nursing will set her up, and I'm sure you're a good nurse, my dear, from your pretty kindhearted face,—I'll send a couple of pills and a draught, but don't alarm yourself—there's no occasion, I assure you."

"But you don't think her fit to go to Liverpool?" asked Mary, still in the anxious tone of one who wishes earnestly for some particular decision.

"To Liverpool—yes," replied he. "A short journey like that couldn't fatigue, and might distract her thoughts. Let her go by all means,—it would be the very thing for her."

"Oh, sir!" burst out Mary, almost sobbing; "I did so hope you would say she was too ill to go."

"Whew—" said he, with a prolonged whistle, trying to understand the case; but, being, as he said, no reader of newspapers, utterly unaware of the peculiar reasons there might be for so apparently unfeeling a wish,—"Why did you not tell me so sooner? It might certainly do her harm in her weak state! there is always some risk attending journeys—draughts, and what not. To her, they might prove very injurious,—very. I disapprove of journeys, or excitement, in all cases where the patient is in the low, fluttered state in which Mrs. Wilson is. If you take *my* advice, you will certainly put a stop to all thoughts of going to Liverpool." He really had completely changed his opinion, though quite unconsciously; so desirous was he to comply with the wishes of others.

"Oh, sir, thank you! And will you give me a certificate of her being unable to go, if the lawyer says we must have one? The lawyer, you know," continued she, seeing him look puzzled, "who is to defend Jem,—it was as a witness against him——"

"My dear girl!" said he, almost angrily, "why did you not state the case fully at first? one minute would have done it,—and my dinner waiting all this time. To be sure, she can't go,—it would be madness to think of it; if her evidence could have done good, it would have been a different thing. Come to me for the certificate any time; that is to say, if the lawyer advises you. I second the lawyer; take counsel with both the learned professions—ha, ha, ha."

And laughing at his own joke, he departed, leaving Mary, accusing herself of stupidity in having imagined that every one was as well acquainted with the facts concerning the trial as she was herself; for indeed she had never doubted that the doctor would have been aware of the purpose of poor Mrs. Wilson's journey to Liverpool.

Presently she went to Job (the ever ready Mrs. Davenport keeping watch over the two old women), and told him her fears, her plans, and her proceedings.

To her surprise he shook his head, doubtfully.

"It may have an awkward look, if we keep her back. Lawyers is up to tricks."

"But it is no trick," said Mary. "She is so poorly, she was last night so, at least; and to-day she's so faded and weak."

"Poor soul! I dare say. I only mean for Jem's sake; and so much is known, it won't do now to hang back. But I'll ask Mr. Bridgenorth. I'll e'en take your doctor's advice. Yo tarry at home, and I'll come to yo in an hour's time. Go thy ways, wench."

Chapter XXV.

"Something there was, what, none presumed to say,
Clouds lightly passing on a smiling day,—
Whispers and hints which went from ear to ear,
And mixed reports no judge on earth could clear."

CRABBE.

"Curious conjectures he may always make,
And either side of dubious questions take."

IB.[5]

Mary went home. Oh! how her head did ache, and how dizzy her brain was growing! But there would be time enough she felt for giving way hereafter.

So she sat quiet and still by an effort; sitting near the window, and looking out of it, but seeing nothing, when all at once she caught sight of something which roused her up, and made her draw back.

But it was too late. She had been seen.

Sally Leadbitter flaunted into the little dingy room, making it gaudy with the Sunday excess of colouring in her dress.

She was really curious to see Mary; her connection with a murderer seemed to have made her into a sort of *lusus naturæ*,[6] and was almost, by some, expected to have made a change in her personal appearance, so earnestly did they stare at her. But Mary had been too much absorbed the last day or two to notice this.

---

5. From George Crabbe's (1754–1832) *The Borough* (1810) Letter XV, lines 39–42 and Letter VII, lines 37–38.
6. Freak of nature.

Now Sally had a grand view, and looked her over and over (a very different thing from looking her through and through), and almost learnt her off by heart:—"Her every-day gown (Hoyle's print you know, that lilac thing with the high body) she was so fond of; a little black silk handkerchief just knotted round her neck, like a boy; her hair all taken back from her face, as if she wanted to keep her head cool—she would always keep that hair of hers so long; and her hands twitching continually about——"

Such particulars would make Sally into a Gazette Extraordinary[7] the next morning at the work-room, and were worth coming for, even if little else could be extracted from Mary.

"Why, Mary!" she began. "Where have you hidden yourself? You never showed your face all yesterday at Miss Simmonds's. You don't fancy we think any the worse of you for what's come and gone. Some on us, indeed, were a bit sorry for the poor young man, as lies stiff and cold for your sake, Mary; but we shall ne'er cast it up against you. Miss Simmonds, too, will be mighty put out if you don't come, for there's a deal of mourning, agait."

"I can't," Mary said, in a low voice. "I don't mean ever to come again."

"Why, Mary!" said Sally, in unfeigned surprise. "To be sure, you'll have to be in Liverpool, Tuesday, and maybe Wednesday; but after that you'll surely come, and tell us all about it. Miss Simmonds knows you'll have to be off those two days. But between you and me, she's a bit of a gossip, and will like hearing all how and about the trial, well enough to let you off very easy for your being absent a day or two. Besides, Betsy Morgan was saying yesterday, she shouldn't wonder but you'd prove quite an attraction to customers. Many a one would come and have their gowns made by Miss Simmonds just to catch a glimpse at you, at after the trial's over. Really, Mary, you'll turn out quite a heroine."

The little fingers twitched worse than ever; the large soft eyes looked up pleadingly into Sally's face; but she went on in the same strain, not from any unkind or cruel feeling towards Mary, but solely because she was incapable of comprehending her suffering.

She had been shocked, of course, at Mr. Carson's death, though at the same time the excitement was rather pleasant than otherwise; and dearly now would she have enjoyed the conspicuous notice which Mary was sure to receive.

"How shall you like being cross-examined, Mary?"

"Not at all," answered Mary, when she found she must answer.

"La! what impudent fellows those lawyers are! And their clerks, too, not a bit better. I shouldn't wonder" (in a comforting tone, and

---

7. A journal of notable events and personalities.

really believing she was giving comfort) "if you picked up a new sweetheart in Liverpool. What gown are you going in, Mary?"

"Oh, I don't know and don't care," exclaimed Mary, sick and weary of her visitor.

"Well, then! take my advice, and go in that blue merino. It's old to be sure, and a bit worn at elbows, but folk won't notice that, and th' colour suits you. Now mind, Mary. And I'll lend you my black-watered[8] scarf," added she, really good-naturedly, according to her sense of things, and withal, a little bit pleased at the idea of her pet article of dress figuring away on the person of a witness at a trial for murder.

"I'll bring it to-morrow before you start."

"No, don't!" said Mary; "thank you, but I don't want it."

"Why, what can you wear? I know all your clothes as well as I do my own, and what is there you can wear? Not your old plaid shawl, I do hope? You would not fancy this I have on, more nor the scarf, would you?" said she, brightening up at the thought, and willing to lend it, or anything else.

"Oh, Sally! don't go on talking a-that-ns; how can I think on dress at such a time? When it's a matter of life and death to Jem?"

"Bless the girl! It's Jem, is it? Well, now I thought there was some sweetheart in the back-ground, when you flew off so with Mr. Carson. Then what, in the name of goodness, made him shoot Mr. Harry? After you had given up going with him, I mean? Was he afraid you'd be on again?"

"How dare you say he shot Mr. Harry?" asked Mary, firing up from the state of languid indifference into which she had sunk while Sally had been settling about her dress. "But it's no matter what you think, as did not know him. What grieves me is, that people should go on thinking him guilty as did know him," she said, sinking back into her former depressed tone and manner.

"And don't you think he did it?" asked Sally.

Mary paused; she was going on too fast with one so curious and so unscrupulous. Besides she remembered how even she herself had, at first, believed him guilty; and she felt it was not for her to cast stones at those who, on similar evidence, inclined to the same belief. None had given him much benefit of a doubt. None had faith in his innocence. None but his mother; and there the heart loved more than the head reasoned, and her yearning affection had never for an instant entertained the idea that her Jem was a murderer. But Mary disliked the whole conversation; the subject, the manner in which it was treated, were all painful, and she had a repugnance to the person with whom she spoke.

---

8. A process in which textiles are soaked and pressed into a lustrous finish.

She was thankful, therefore, when Job Legh's voice was heard at the door, as he stood with the latch in his hand, talking to a neighbour, and when Sally jumped up in vexation and said, "There's that old fogey coming in here, as I'm alive! Did your father set him to look after you while he was away? or what brings the old chap here? However, I'm off; I never could abide either him or his prim granddaughter. Good-bye, Mary."

So far in a whisper, then louder, "If you think better of my offer about the scarf, Mary, just step in to-morrow before nine, and you're quite welcome to it."

She and Job passed each other at the door, with mutual looks of dislike, which neither took any pains to conceal.

"Yon's a bold, bad girl," said Job to Mary.

"She's very good-natured," replied Mary, too honourable to abuse a visitor who had only that instant crossed her threshold, and gladly dwelling on the good quality most apparent in Sally's character.

"Ay, ay! good-natured, generous, jolly, full of fun; there are a number of other names for the good qualities the devil leaves his children, as baits to catch gudgeons[9] with. D'ye think folk could be led astray by one who was every way bad? Howe'er, that's not what I came to talk about. I've seen Mr. Bridgnorth, and he is in a manner of the same mind as we; he thinks it would have an awkward look, and might tell against the poor lad on his trial; still if she's ill she's ill, and it can't be helped."

"I don't know if she's so bad as all that," said Mary, who began to dread her part in doing anything which might tell against her poor lover.

"Will you come and see her, Job? The doctor seemed to say as I liked, not as he thought."

"That's because he had no great thought on the subject, either one way or t'other," replied Job, whose contempt for medical men pretty nearly equalled his respect for lawyers. "But I'll go and welcome. I han not seen th' ould ladies since their sorrows, and it's but manners to go and ax after them. Come along."

The room at Mrs. Wilson's had that still, changeless look you must have often observed in the house of sickness or mourning. No particular employment going on; people watching and waiting rather than acting, unless in the more sudden and violent attacks: what little movement is going on, so noiseless and hushed; the furniture all arranged and stationary, with a view to the comfort of the afflicted; the window-blinds drawn down, to keep out the disturbing variety of a sunbeam; the same saddened serious look on the faces of the indwellers: you fall back into the same train of thought with all these

9. Small, European, freshwater fish.

associations, and forget the street, the outer world, in the contemplation of the one stationary, absorbing interest within.

Mrs. Wilson sat quietly in her chair, with just the same look Mary
had left on her face; Mrs. Davenport went about with creaking shoes
which made all the more noise from her careful and lengthened
tread, annoying the ears of those who were well, in this instance, far
more than the dull senses of the sick and the sorrowful. Alice's voice
still was going on cheerfully in the upper room with incessant talking and little laughs to herself, or perhaps in sympathy with her
unseen companions; "unseen," I say, in preference to "fancied," for
who knows whether God does not permit the forms of those who
were dearest when living, to hover round the bed of the dying?

Job spoke, and Mrs. Wilson answered.

So quietly that it was unnatural under the circumstances. It made
a deeper impression on the old man than any token of mere bodily
illness could have done. If she had raved in delirium, or moaned in
fever, he could have spoken after his wont, and given his opinion, his
advice, and his consolation: now he was awed into silence.

At length he pulled Mary aside into a corner of the house-place,
where Mrs. Wilson was sitting, and began to talk to her.

"Yo're right, Mary! She's no ways fit to go to Liverpool, poor soul.
Now I've seen her I only wonder the doctor could ha' been unsettled
in his mind at th' first. Choose how it goes wi' poor Jem, she cannot
go. One way or another it will soon be over, the best to leave her in
the state she is till then."

"I was sure you would think so," said Mary.

But they were reckoning without their host. They esteemed her
senses gone, while, in fact, they were only inert, and could not convey impressions rapidly to the over-burdened, troubled brain. They
had not noticed that her eyes had followed them (mechanically it
seemed at first) as they had moved away to the corner of the room;
that her face, hitherto so changeless, had begun to work with one or
two of the old symptoms of impatience.

But when they were silent she stood up, and startled them almost
as if a dead person had spoken, by saying clearly and decidedly—"I
go to Liverpool. I hear you and your plans; and I tell you I shall go to
Liverpool. If my words are to kill my son, they have already gone forth
out of my mouth, and nought can bring them back. But I will have
faith. Alice (up above) has often told me I wanted faith, and now I
will have it. They cannot—they will not kill my child, my only child.
I will not be afeared. Yet oh! I am so sick with terror. But if he is to
die, think ye not that I will see him again; ay! see him at his trial?
When all are hating him, he shall have his poor mother near him, to
give him all the comfort, eyes, and looks, and tears, and a heart that
is dead to all but him, can give; his poor old mother, who knows how

free he is from sin—in the sight of man at least. They'll let me go to him, maybe, the very minute it's over; and I know many Scripture texts (though you would not think it), that may keep up his heart. I missed seeing him ere he went to yon prison, but nought shall keep me away again one minute when I can see his face; for maybe the minutes are numbered, and the count but small. I know I can be a comfort to him, poor lad. You would not think it now, but he'd always speak as kind and soft to me as if he were courting me, like. He loved me above a bit; and I am to leave him now to dree* all the cruel slander they'll put upon him? I can pray for him at each hard word they say against him, if I can do nought else; and he'll know what his mother is doing for him, poor lad, by the look on my face."

Still they made some look, or gesture of opposition to her wishes. She turned sharp round on Mary, the old object of her pettish attacks, and said, "Now wench! once for all, I tell you this. *He* could never guide me; and he'd sense enough not to try. What he could na do, don't you try. I shall go to Liverpool to-morrow, and find my lad, and stay with him through thick and thin; and if he dies, why, perhaps, God of His mercy will take me too. The grave is a sure cure for an aching heart!"

She sank back in her chair, quite exhausted by the sudden effort she had made; but if they even offered to speak, she cut them short (whatever the subject might be), with the repetition of the same words, "I shall go to Liverpool."

No more could be said, the doctor's opinion had been so undecided; Mr. Bridgenorth had given his legal voice in favour of her going, and Mary was obliged to relinquish the idea of persuading her to remain at home, if, indeed, under all the circumstances, it could be thought desirable.

"Best way will be," said Job, "for me to hunt out Will, early to-morrow morning, and yo, Mary, come at after with Jane Wilson. I know a decent woman where yo two can have a bed, and where we may meet together when I've found Will, afore going to Mr. Bridgenorth's at two o'clock; for, I can tell him, I'll not trust none of his clerks for hunting up Will, if Jem's life's to depend on it."

Now Mary disliked this plan inexpressibly; her dislike was partly grounded on reason, and partly on feeling. She could not bear the idea of deputing to any one the active measures necessary to be taken in order to save Jem. She felt as if they were her duty, her right. She durst not trust to any one the completion of her plan: they might not have energy, or perseverance, or desperation enough to follow out the slightest chance; and her love would endow her with all these qualities, independently of the terrible alternative which awaited her in

---

* A. S. dreogan, to suffer, endure. [WG]

case all failed and Jem was condemned. No one could have her motives; and consequently no one could have her sharpened brain, her despairing determination. Beside (only that was purely selfish), she could not endure the suspense of remaining quiet, and only knowing the result when all was accomplished.

So with vehemence and impatience she rebutted every reason Job adduced for his plan; and, of course, thus opposed, by what appeared to him wilfulness, he became more resolute, and angry words were exchanged, and a feeling of estrangement rose up between them, for a time, as they walked homewards.

But then came in Margaret with her gentleness, like an angel of peace, so calm and reasonable, that both felt ashamed of their irritation, and tacitly left the decision to her (only, by the way, I think Mary could never have submitted if it had gone against her, penitent and tearful as was her manner now to Job, the good old man who was helping her to work for Jem, although they differed as to the manner).

"Mary had better go," said Margaret to her grandfather, in a low tone, "I know what she's feeling, and it will be a comfort to her soon, maybe, to think she did all she could herself. She would perhaps fancy it might have been different; do, grandfather, let her."

Margaret had still, you see, little or no belief in Jem's innocence; and besides she thought if Mary saw Will, and heard herself from him that Jem had not been with him that Thursday night, it would in a measure break the force of the blow which was impending.

"Let me lock up house, grandfather, for a couple of days, and go and stay with Alice. It's but little one like me can do, I know" (she added softly); "but, by the blessing o' God, I'll do it and welcome; and here comes one kindly use o' money, I can hire them as will do for her what I cannot. Mrs. Davenport is a willing body, and one who knows sorrow and sickness, and I can pay her for her time, and keep her there pretty near altogether. So let that be settled. And you take Mrs. Wilson, dear grandad, and let Mary go find Will, and you can all meet together at after, and I'm sure I wish you luck."

Job consented with only a few dissenting grunts; but on the whole with a very good grace for an old man who had been so positive only a few minutes before.

Mary was thankful for Margaret's interference. She did not speak, but threw her arms round Margaret's neck, and put up her rosy-red mouth to be kissed; and even Job was attracted by the pretty, child-like gesture; and when she drew near him, afterwards, like a little creature sidling up to some person whom it feels to have offended, he bent down and blessed her, as if she had been a child of his own.

To Mary the old man's blessing came like words of power.

Chapter XXVI.

"Like a bark upon the sea,
  Life is floating over death;
Above, below, encircling thee,
  Danger lurks in every breath.

Parted art thou from the grave
  Only by a plank most frail;
Tossed upon the restless wave,
  Sport of every fickle gale.

Let the skies be e'er so clear,
  And so calm and still the sea,
Shipwreck yet has he to fear
  Who life's voyager will be."

RÜCKERT.[1]

The early trains for Liverpool, on Monday morning, were crowded by attorneys, attorneys' clerks, plaintiffs, defendants, and witnesses, all going to the Assizes. They were a motley assembly, each with some cause for anxiety stirring at his heart; though, after all, that is saying little or nothing, for we are all of us in the same predicament through life; each with a fear and a hope from childhood to death. Among the passengers there was Mary Barton, dressed in the blue gown and obnoxious plaid shawl.

Common as railroads are now in all places as a means of transit, and especially in Manchester, Mary had never been on one before; and she felt bewildered by the hurry, the noise of people, and bells, and horns; the whiz and the scream of the arriving trains.

The very journey itself seemed to her a matter of wonder. She had a back seat, and looked towards the factory-chimneys, and the cloud of smoke which hovers over Manchester, with a feeling akin to the "Heimweh."[2] She was losing sight of the familiar objects of her childhood for the first time; and unpleasant as those objects are to most, she yearned after them with some of the same sentiment which gives pathos to the thoughts of the emigrant.

The cloud-shadows which give beauty to Chat-Moss, the picturesque old houses of Newton, what were they to Mary, whose heart was full of many things? Yet she seemed to look at them earnestly as they glided past; but she neither saw nor heard.

She neither saw nor heard till some well-known names fell upon her ear.

Two lawyers' clerks were discussing the cases to come on that

1. Poetic paraphrase from Friedrich Ruckert's (1788–1866) "Schiffahrt" ("Voyage") or from his "Liebesfruhling" ("Springtime") or from his "Maileider" ("May-songs").
2. Homesickness.

Assizes; of course, "the murder case," as it had come to be termed, held a conspicuous place in their conversation.

They had no doubt of the result.

"Juries are always very unwilling to convict on circumstantial evidence, it is true," said one, "but here there can hardly be any doubt."

"If it had not been so clear a case," replied the other, "I should have said they were injudicious in hurrying on the trial so much. Still more evidence might have been collected."

"They tell me," said the first speaker—"the people in Gardener's office, I mean—that it was really feared the old gentleman would have gone out of his mind, if the trial had been delayed. He was with Mr. Gardener as many as seven times on Saturday, and called him up at night to suggest that some letter should be written, or something done to secure the verdict."

"Poor old man," answered his companion, "who can wonder?—an only son,—such a death,—the disagreeable circumstances attending it; I had not time to read the *Guardian* on Saturday,[3] but I understand it was some dispute about a factory girl?"

"Yes, some such person. Of course she'll be examined, and Williams will do it in style. I shall slip out from our court to hear him, if I can hit the nick of time."

"And if you can get a place, you mean, for depend upon it the court will be crowded."

"Ay, ay, the ladies (sweet souls) will come in shoals to hear a trial for murder, and see the murderer, and watch the judge put on his black cap."[4]

"And then go home and groan over the Spanish ladies who take delight in bull-fights—'such unfeminine creatures!'"

Then they went on to other subjects.

It was but another drop to Mary's cup; but she was nearly in that state which Crabbe describes:

> "For when so full the cup of sorrows flows,
> Add but a drop it instantly o'erflows."[5]

And now they were in the tunnel!—and now they were in Liverpool; and she must rouse herself from the torpor of mind and body which was creeping over her; the result of much anxiety and fatigue, and several sleepless nights.

She asked a policeman the way to Milk House Yard, and following his directions with the *savoir faire* of a town-bred girl, she reached a little court leading out of a busy, thronged street, not far from the Docks.

---

3. The *Manchester Guardian*.
4. Judges wore black caps when pronouncing death sentences.
5. Crabbe's "The Parish Register" (1807), II "Marriages," lines 209–10.

When she entered the quiet little yard, she stopped to regain her breath, and to gather strength, for her limbs trembled, and her heart beat violently.

All the unfavourable contingencies she had, until now, forbidden herself to dwell upon, came forward to her mind—the possibility, the bare possibility, of Jem being an accomplice in the murder—the still greater possibility that he had not fulfilled his intention of going part of the way with Will, but had been led off by some little accidental occurrence from his original intention; and that he had spent the evening with those whom it was now too late to bring forward as witnesses.

But sooner or later she must know the truth; so, taking courage, she knocked at the door of a house.

"Is this Mrs. Jones's?" she inquired.

"Next door but one," was the curt answer.

And even this extra minute was a reprieve.

Mrs. Jones was busy washing, and would have spoken angrily to the person who knocked so gently at the door, if anger had been in her nature; but she was a soft, helpless kind of woman, and only sighed over the many interruptions she had had to her business that unlucky Monday morning.

But the feeling which would have been anger in a more impatient temper, took the form of prejudice against the disturber, whoever he or she might be.

Mary's fluttered and excited appearance strengthened this prejudice in Mrs. Jones's mind, as she stood, stripping the soap-suds off her arms, while she eyed her visitor, and waited to be told what her business was.

But no words would come. Mary's voice seemed choaked up in her throat.

"Pray what do you want, young woman?" coldly asked Mrs. Jones at last.

"I want—Oh! is Will Wilson here?"

"No, he is not," replied Mrs. Jones, inclining to shut the door in her face.

"Is he not come back from the Isle of Man?" asked Mary, sickening.

"He never went; he stayed in Manchester too long; as perhaps you know, already."

And again the door seemed closing.

But Mary bent forwards with suppliant action (as some young tree bends, when blown by the rough, autumnal wind), and gasped out,

"Tell me—tell me—where is he?"

Mrs. Jones suspected some love affair, and, perhaps, one of not the most creditable kind; but the distress of the pale young creature before her was so obvious and so pitiable, that were she ever so sinful, Mrs. Jones could no longer uphold her short, reserved manner.

"He's gone this very morning, my poor girl. Step in, and I'll tell you about it."

"Gone!" cried Mary. "How gone? I must see him,—it's a matter of life and death: he can save the innocent from being hanged,—he cannot be gone,—how gone?"

"Sailed, my dear! sailed in the *John Cropper* this very blessed morning."

"Sailed!"

Chapter XXVII.

"Yon is our quay!
Hark to the clamour in that miry road,
Bounded and narrowed by yon vessel's load;
The lumbering wealth she empties round the place,
Package and parcel, hogshead, chest, and case;
While the loud seaman and the angry hind,
Mingling in business, bellow to the wind."

CRABBE.[6]

Mary staggered into the house. Mrs. Jones placed her tenderly in a chair, and there stood bewildered by her side.

"Oh, father! father!" muttered she, "what have you done!—What must I do? must the innocent die?—or he—whom I fear—I fear—oh! what am I saying?" said she, looking round affrighted, and, seemingly reassured by Mrs. Jones's countenance, "I am so helpless, so weak,— but a poor girl after all. How can I tell what is right? Father! you have always been so kind to me,—and you to be—never mind—never mind, all will come right in the grave."

"Save us, and bless us!" exclaimed Mrs. Jones, "if I don't think she's gone out of her wits!"

"No, I am not!" said Mary, catching at the words, and with a strong effort controlling the mind she felt to be wandering, while the red blood flushed to scarlet the heretofore white cheek,—"I'm not out of my senses; there is so much to be done—so much—and no one but me to do it, you know,—though I can't rightly tell what it is," looking up with bewilderment into Mrs. Jones's face. "I must not go mad whatever comes—at least not yet. No!" (bracing herself up), "something may yet be done, and I must do it. Sailed! did you say? The *John Cropper*? Sailed?"

6. From Crabbe's *The Borough*, Letter I, lines 69, 73–78.

"Ay! she went out of dock last night, to be ready for the morning's tide."

"I thought she was not to sail till to-morrow," murmured Mary.

"So did Will (he's lodged here long, so we all call him 'Will')" replied Mrs. Jones. "The mate had told him so, I believe, and he never knew different till he got to Liverpool on Friday morning; but as soon as he heard, he gave up going to the Isle o' Man, and just ran over to Rhyl with the mate, one John Harris, as has friends a bit beyond Abergele; you may have heard him speak on him, for they are great chums, though I've my own opinion of Harris."

"And he's sailed?" repeated Mary, trying by repetition to realise the fact to herself.

"Ay, he went on board last night to be ready for the morning's tide, as I said afore, and my boy went to see the ship go down the river, and came back all agog with the sight. Here Charley, Charley!" She called out loudly for her son; but Charley was one of those boys who are never "far to seek," as the Lancashire people say, when anything is going on; a mysterious conversation, an unusual event, a fire, or a riot, anything in short; such boys are the little omnipresent people of this world.

Charley had, in fact, been spectator and auditor all this time; though for a little while he had been engaged in "dollying"[7] and a few other mischievous feats in the washing line, which had prevented his attention from being fully given to his mother's conversation with the strange girl who had entered.

"Oh, Charley! there you are! Did you not see the *John Cropper* sail down the river this morning? Tell the young woman about it, for I think she hardly credits me."

"I saw her tugged down the river by a steam-boat, which comes to same thing," replied he.

"Oh! if I had but come last night!" moaned Mary. "But I never thought of it. I never thought but what he knew right when he said he would be back from the Isle of Man on Monday morning, and not afore—and now some one must die for my negligence!"

"Die!" exclaimed the lad. "How?"

"Oh! Will would have proved an *alibi*,—but he's gone,—and what am I to do?"

"Don't give it up yet," cried the energetic boy, interested at once in the case; "let's have a try for him. We are but where we were, if we fail."

Mary roused herself. The sympathetic "we" gave her heart and hope. "But what can be done? You say he's sailed; what can be done?" But she spoke louder, and in a more life-like tone.

---

7. Stirring clothes in a tub with a wooden device with protruding arms (a dolly).

"No! I did not say he'd sailed; mother said that, and women know nought about such matters. You see" (proud of his office of instructor, and insensibly influenced, as all about her were, by Mary's sweet, earnest, lovely countenance), "there's sand-banks at the mouth of the river, and ships can't get over them but at high water; especially ships of heavy burden, like the *John Cropper*. Now she was tugged down the river at low water, or pretty near, and will have to lie some time before the water will be high enough to float her over the banks. So hold up your head,—you've a chance yet, though, maybe, but a poor one."

"But what must I do?" asked Mary, to whom all this explanation had been a vague mystery.

"Do!" said the boy, impatiently, "why, have not I told you? Only women (begging your pardon) are so stupid at understanding about any thing belonging to the sea;—you must get a boat, and make all haste, and sail after him,—after the *John Cropper*. You may overtake her, or you may not. It's just a chance; but she's heavy laden, and that's in your favour. She'll draw many feet of water."

Mary had humbly and eagerly (oh, how eagerly!) listened to this young Sir Oracle's speech,[8] but try as she would, she could only understand that she must make haste, and sail—somewhere.

"I beg your pardon" (and her little acknowledgment of inferiority in this speech pleased the lad, and made him her still more zealous friend). "I beg your pardon," said she, "but I don't know where to get a boat. Are there boat-stands?"

The lad laughed outright.

"You're not long in Liverpool, I guess. Boat-stands! No; go down to the pier,—any pier will do, and hire a boat,—you'll be at no loss when once you are there. Only make haste."

"Oh, you need not tell me that, if I but knew how," said Mary, trembling with eagerness. "But you say right,—I never was here before, and I don't know my way to the place you speak on; only tell me, and I'll not lose a minute."

"Mother!" said the wilful lad, "I'm going to show her the way to the pier; I'll be back in an hour,—or so," he added in a lower tone.

And before the gentle Mrs. Jones could collect her scattered wits sufficiently to understand half of the hastily formed plan, her son was scudding down the street, closely followed by Mary's half-running steps.

Presently he slackened his pace sufficiently to enable him to enter into conversation with Mary, for once escaped from the reach of his mother's recalling voice, he thought he might venture to indulge his curiosity.

"Ahem!—What's your name? It's so awkward to be calling you young woman."

8. Reference to a young man of bogus gravity in Shakespeare's *The Merchant of Venice* 1.1.93.

"My name is Mary,—Mary Barton," answered she, anxious to propitiate one who seemed so willing to exert himself in her behalf, or
else she grudged every word which caused the slightest relaxation in
her speed, although her chest seemed tightened, and her head throbbing, from the rate at which they were walking.

"And you want Will Wilson to prove an *alibi*—is that it?"

"Yes—oh, yes—can we not cross now?"

"No, wait a minute; it's the teagle[9] hoisting above your head I'm
afraid of;—and who is it that's to be tried?"

"Jem; oh, lad! can't we get past?"

They rushed under the great bales quivering in the air above their
heads and pressed onward for a few minutes, till Master Charley
again saw fit to walk a little slower, and ask a few more questions.

"Mary, is Jem your brother, or your sweetheart, that you're so set
upon saving him?"

"No—no," replied she, but with something of hesitation, that
made the shrewd boy yet more anxious to clear up the mystery.

"Perhaps he's your cousin, then? Many a girl has a cousin who has
not a sweetheart."

"No, he's neither kith nor kin to me. What's the matter? What are
you stopping for?" said she, with nervous terror, as Charley turned
back a few steps, and peered up a side street.

"Oh, nothing to flurry you so, Mary. I heard you say to mother you
had never been in Liverpool before, and if you'll only look up this
street you may see the back windows of our Exchange.[1] Such a building as yon is! with 'natomy hiding under a blanket, and Lord Admiral
Nelson,[2] and a few more people in the middle of the court! No! come
here," as Mary, in her eagerness, was looking at any window that
caught her eye first, to satisfy the boy. "Here then, now you can see
it. You can say, now, you've seen Liverpool Exchange."

"Yes, to be sure—it's a beautiful window, I'm sure. But are we near
the boats? I'll stop as I come back, you know; only I think we'd better get on now."

"Oh! if the wind's in your favour you'll be down the river in no time,
and catch Will, I'll be bound; and if it's not, why, you know the minute
it took you to look at the Exchange will be neither here nor there."

Another rush onwards, till one of the long crossings near the Docks
caused a stoppage, and gave Mary time for breathing, and Charley
leisure to ask another question.

"You've never said where you come from?"

"Manchester," replied she.

9. Tackle for hoisting.
1. Town Hall built in 1809.
2. Statue built in 1813 to Admiral Nelson who died in 1805 at the end of a naval battle at
   Trafalgar during the Napoleonic Wars.

"Eh, then! you've a power of things to see. Liverpool beats Manchester hollow, they say. A nasty, smoky hole, bean't it? Are you bound to live there?"

"Oh, yes! it's my home."

"Well, I don't think I could abide a home in the middle of smoke. Look there! now you see the river! That's something now you'd give a deal for in Manchester. Look!"

And Mary did look, and saw down an opening made in the forest of masts belonging to the vessels in dock, the glorious river, along which white-sailed ships were gliding with the ensigns of all nations, not "braving the battle,"[3] but telling of the distant lands, spicy or frozen, that sent to that mighty mart for their comforts or their luxuries; she saw small boats passing to and fro on that glittering highway, but she also saw such puffs and clouds of smoke from the countless steamers, that she wondered at Charley's intolerance of the smoke of Manchester. Across the swing-bridge, along the pier,—and they stood breathless by a magnificent dock, where hundreds of ships lay motionless during the process of loading and unloading. The cries of the sailors, the variety of languages used by the passers-by, and the entire novelty of the sight compared with anything which Mary had ever seen, made her feel most helpless and forlorn; and she clung to her young guide as to one who alone by his superior knowledge could interpret between her and the new race of men by whom she was surrounded,—for a new race sailors might reasonably be considered, to a girl who had hitherto seen none but inland dwellers, and those for the greater part factory people.

In that new world of sight and sound, she still bore one prevailing thought, and though her eye glanced over the ships and the wide-spreading river, her mind was full of the thought of reaching Will.

"Why are we here?" asked she, of Charley. "There are no little boats about, and I thought I was to go in a little boat; those ships are never meant for short distances, are they?"

"To be sure not," replied he, rather contemptuously. "But the *John Cropper* lay in this dock, and I know many of the sailors; and if I could see one I knew, I'd ask him to run up the mast, and see if he could catch a sight of her in the offing.[4] If she's weighed her anchor, no use for your going, you know."

Mary assented quietly to this speech, as if she were as careless as Charley seemed now to be about her overtaking Will; but in truth her heart was sinking within her, and she no longer felt the energy which had hitherto upheld her. Her bodily strength was giving way, and she stood cold and shivering, although the noonday sun beat down with considerable power on the shadeless spot where she was standing.

3. Evokes Thomas Campbell's (1777–1824) "Ye Mariners of England."
4. Still visible from shore but out beyond the harbor.

"Here's Tom Bourne!" said Charley; and altering his manner from the patronising key in which he had spoken to Mary, he addressed a weather-beaten old sailor who came rolling along the pathway where they stood, his hands in his pockets, and his quid[5] in his mouth, with very much the air of one who had nothing to do but look about him, and spit right and left; addressing this old tar, Charley made known to him his wish in slang, which to Mary was almost inaudible, and quite unintelligible, and which I am too much of a land-lubber to repeat correctly.

Mary watched looks and actions with a renovated keenness of perception.

She saw the old man listen attentively to Charley; she saw him eye her over from head to foot, and wind up his inspection with a little nod of approbation (for her very shabbiness and poverty of dress were creditable signs to the experienced old sailor), and then she watched him leisurely swing himself on to a ship in the basin, and, borrowing a glass, run up the mast with the speed of a monkey.

"He'll fall!" said she, in affright, clutching at Charley's arm, and judging the sailor, from his storm-marked face and unsteady walk on land, to be much older than he really was.

"Not he!" said Charley. "He's at the mast-head now. See! he's looking through his glass, and using his arms as steady as if he were on dry land. Why, I've been up the mast, many and many a time; only don't tell mother. She thinks I'm to be a shoemaker, but I've made up my mind to be a sailor; only there's no good arguing with a woman. You'll not tell her, Mary?"

"Oh, see!" exclaimed she (his secret was very safe with her, for, in fact, she had not heard it); see! he's coming down; he's down. Speak to him, Charley."

But, unable to wait another instant, she called out herself,

"Can you see the *John Cropper?* Is she there yet?"

"Ay, ay," he answered, and coming quickly up to them, he hurried them away to seek for a boat, saying the bar was already covered, and in an hour the ship would hoist her sails, and be off. "You've the wind right against you, and must use oars. No time to lose."

They ran to some steps leading down to the water. They beckoned to some watermen, who, suspecting the real state of the case, appeared in no hurry for a fare, but leisurely brought their boat alongside the stairs, as if it were a matter of indifference to them whether they were engaged or not, while they conversed together in few words, and in an under tone, respecting the charge they should make.

"Oh, pray make haste," called Mary. "I want you to take me to the *John Cropper*. Where is she, Charley? Tell them—I don't rightly know the words,—only make haste!"

5. Lump of chewing tobacco.

"In the offing she is, sure enough, miss," answered one of the men, shoving Charley on one side, regarding him as too young to be a principal in the bargain.

"I don't think we can go, Dick," said he, with a wink to his companion; "there's the gentleman over at New Brighton as wants us."

"But, mayhap, the young woman will pay us handsome for giving her a last look at her sweetheart," interposed the other.

"Oh, how much do you want? Only make haste—I've enough to pay you, but every moment is precious," said Mary.

"Ay, that it is. Less than an hour won't take us to the mouth of the river, and she'll be off by two o'clock!"

Poor Mary's ideas of "plenty of money," however, were different to those entertained by the boatmen. Only fourteen or fifteen shillings remained out of the sovereign Margaret had lent her, and the boatmen imagining "plenty" to mean no less than several pounds, insisted upon receiving a sovereign (an exorbitant fare by-the-by, although reduced from their first demand of thirty shillings).

While Charley, with a boy's impatience of delay, and disregard to money, kept urging,

"Give it 'em, Mary; they'll none of them take you for less. It's your only chance. There's St. Nicholas ringing one!"

"I've only got fourteen and ninepence," cried she, in despair, after counting over her money; "but I'll give you my shawl, and you can sell it for four or five shillings,—oh! won't that much do?" asked she, in such a tone of voice, that they must indeed have had hard hearts who could refuse such agonised entreaty.

They took her on board.

And in less than five minutes she was rocking and tossing in a boat for the first time in her life, alone with two rough, hard-looking men.

Chapter XXVIII.

"A wet sheet and a flowing sea,
    A wind that follows fast
And fills the white and rustling sail,
    And bends the gallant mast!
And bends the gallant mast, my boys,
    While, like the eagle free,
Away the good ship flies, and leaves
    Old England on the lee."

ALLAN CUNNINGHAM.[6]

Mary had not understood that Charley was not coming with her. In fact, she had not thought about it, till she perceived his absence, as

6. From Allan Cunningham's (1784–1842) "A Wet Sheet and a Flowing Sea" (1825).

they pushed off from the landing-place, and remembered that she had never thanked him for all his kind interest in her behalf; and now his absence made her feel most lonely—even his, the little mushroom friend of an hour's growth.

The boat threaded her way through the maze of larger vessels which surrounded the shore, bumping against one, kept off by the oars from going right against another, overshadowed by a third, until at length they were fairly out on the broad river, away from either shore; the sights and sounds of land being heard in the distance.

And then came a sort of pause.

Both wind and tide were against the two men, and labour as they would they made but little way. Once Mary in her impatience had risen up to obtain a better view of the progress they had made; but the men had roughly told her to sit down immediately, and she had dropped on her seat like a chidden child, although the impatience was still at her heart.

But now she grew sure they were turning off from the straight course which they had hitherto kept on the Cheshire side of the river, whither they had gone to avoid the force of the current, and after a short time she could not help naming her conviction, as a kind of nightmare dread and belief came over her, that every thing animate and inanimate was in league against her one sole aim and object of overtaking Will.

They answered gruffly. They saw a boatman whom they knew, and were desirous of obtaining his services as a steersman, so that both might row with greater effect. They knew what they were about. So she sat silent with clenched hands while the parley went on, the explanation was given, the favour asked and granted. But she was sickening all the time with nervous fear.

They had been rowing a long, long time—half a day it seemed, at least—yet Liverpool appeared still close at hand, and Mary began almost to wonder that the men were not as much disheartened as she was, when the wind, which had been hitherto against them, dropped, and thin clouds began to gather over the sky, shutting out the sun, and casting a chilly gloom over everything.

There was not a breath of air, and yet it was colder than when the soft violence of the westerly wind had been felt.

The men renewed their efforts. The boat gave a bound forwards at every pull of the oars. The water was glassy and motionless, reflecting tint by tint of the Indian-ink sky above. Mary shivered, and her heart sank within her. Still now they evidently were making progress. Then the steersman pointed to a rippling line in the river only a little way off, and the men disturbed Mary, who was watching the ships that lay in what appeared to her the open sea, to get at their sails.

She gave a little start, and rose. Her patience, her grief, and perhaps her silence, had begun to win upon the men.

"Yon second to the norrard[7] is the *John Cropper*. Wind's right now, and sails will soon carry us alongside of her."

He had forgotten (or perhaps he did not like to remind Mary), that the same wind which now bore their little craft along with easy, rapid motion, would also be favourable to the *John Cropper*.

But as they looked with straining eyes, as if to measure the decreasing distance that separated them from her, they saw her sails unfurled and flap in the breeze, till, catching the right point, they bellied forth into white roundness, and the ship began to plunge and heave, as if she were a living creature, impatient to be off.

"They're heaving anchor!" said one of the boatmen to the other, as the faint musical cry of the sailors came floating over the waters that still separated them.

Full of the spirit of the chase, though as yet ignorant of Mary's motives, the men sprung to hoist another sail. It was fully as much as the boat could bear, in the keen, gusty east wind which was now blowing, and she bent, and laboured, and ploughed, and creaked upbraidingly as if tasked beyond her strength; but she sped along with a gallant swiftness.

They drew nearer, and they heard the distant "ahoy" more clearly. It ceased. The anchor was up, and the ship was away.

Mary stood up, steadying herself by the mast, and stretched out her arms, imploring the flying vessel to stay its course, by that mute action, while the tears streamed down her cheeks. The men caught up their oars, and hoisted them in the air, and shouted to arrest attention.

They were seen by the men aboard the larger craft; but they were too busy with all the confusion prevalent in an outward-bound vessel to pay much attention. There were coils of ropes and seamen's chests to be stumbled over at every turn; there were animals, not properly secured, roaming bewildered about the deck, adding their pitiful lowings and bleatings to the aggregate of noises. There were carcases not cut up, looking like corpses of sheep and pigs rather than like mutton and pork; there were sailors running here and there and everywhere, having had no time to fall into method, and with their minds divided between thoughts of the land and the people they had left, and the present duties on board ship; while the captain strove hard to procure some kind of order by hasty commands given, in a loud, impatient voice, to right and left, starboard and larboard, cabin and steerage.

As he paced the deck with a chafed step, vexed at one or two little mistakes on the part of the mate, and suffering himself from the pain

7. Northwards.

of separation from wife and children, but showing his suffering only by his outward irritation, he heard a hail from the shabby little river boat that was striving to overtake his winged ship. For the men fearing that, as the ship was now fairly over the bar, they should only increase the distance between them, and being now within shouting range, had asked of Mary her more particular desire.

Her throat was dry, all musical sound had gone out of her voice; but in a loud, harsh whisper she told the men her errand of life and death, and they hailed the ship.

"We're come for one William Wilson, who is wanted to prove an *alibi* in Liverpool Assize Courts to-morrow. James Wilson is to be tried for a murder done on Thursday night when he was with William Wilson. Any thing more, missus?" asked the boatmen of Mary, in a lower voice, and taking his hands down from his mouth.

"Say I'm Mary Barton. Oh, the ship is going on! Oh, for the love of Heaven, ask them to stop."

The boatman was angry at the little regard paid to his summons, and called out again; repeating the message with the name of the young woman who sent it, and interlarding it with sailors' oaths.

The ship flew along—away,—the boat struggled after.

They could see the captain take his speaking-trumpet. And oh! and alas! they heard his words.

He swore a dreadful oath; he called Mary a disgraceful name; and he said he would not stop his ship for any one, nor could he part with a single hand, whoever swung for it.

The words came in unpitying clearness with their trumpet-sound. Mary sat down looking like one who prays in the death agony. For her eyes were turned up to that Heaven, where mercy dwelleth, while her blue lips quivered, though no sound came. Then she bowed her head and hid it in her hands.

"Hark! yon sailor hails us."

She looked up. And her heart stopped its beating to listen.

William Wilson stood as near the stern of the vessel as he could get; and unable to obtain the trumpet from the angry captain, made a tube of his own hands.

"So help me God, Mary Barton, I'll come back in the pilot-boat, time enough to save the life of the innocent."

"What does he say?" asked Mary, wildly, as the voice died away in the increasing distance, while the boatmen cheered, in their kindled sympathy with their passenger.

"What does he say?" repeated she. "Tell me. I could not hear."

She had heard with her ears, but her brain refused to recognise the sense.

They repeated his speech, all three speaking at once, with many comments; while Mary looked at them and then at the vessel far away.

"I don't rightly know about it," said she, sorrowfully. "What is the pilot-boat?"

They told her, and she gathered the meaning out of the sailors' slang which enveloped it. There was a hope still, although so slight and faint.

"How far does the pilot go with the ship?"

To different distances they said. Some pilots would go as far as Holyhead for the chance of the homeward-bound vessels; others only took the ships over the Banks. Some captains were more cautious than others, and the pilots had different ways. The wind was against the homeward-bound vessels, so perhaps the pilot aboard the *John Cropper* would not care to go far out.

"How soon would he come back?"

There were three boatmen, and three opinions, varying from twelve hours to two days. Nay, the man who gave his vote for the longest time, on having his judgment disputed, grew stubborn, and doubled the time, and thought it might be the end of the week before the pilot-boat came home.

They began disputing, and urging reasons; and Mary tried to understand them; but independently of their nautical language, a veil seemed drawn over her mind, and she had no clear perception of anything that passed. Her very words seemed not her own, and beyond her power of control, for she found herself speaking quite differently to what she meant.

One by one her hopes had fallen away, and left her desolate; and though a chance yet remained, she could no longer hope. She felt certain it, too, would fade and vanish. She sank into a kind of stupor. All outward objects harmonised with her despair,—the gloomy leaden sky,—the deep, dark waters below, of a still heavier shade of colour,—the cold, flat, yellow shore in the distance, which no ray lightened up,—the nipping cutting wind.

She shivered with her depression of mind and body.

The sails were taken down, of course, on the return to Liverpool, and the progress they made, rowing and tacking, was very slow. The men talked together, disputing about the pilots at first, and then about matters of local importance, in which Mary would have taken no interest at any time, and she gradually became drowsy; irrepressibly so, indeed, for in spite of her jerking efforts to keep awake she sank away to the bottom of the boat, and there lay couched on a rough heap of sails, ropes, and tackle of various kinds.

The measured beat of the waters against the sides of the boat, and the musical boom of the more distant waves, were more lulling than silence, and she slept sound.

Once she opened her eyes heavily, and dimly saw the old gray, rough boatman (who had stood out the most obstinately for the full fare) covering her with his thick pea-jacket. He had taken it off on purpose, and was doing it tenderly in his way, but before she could rouse herself up to thank him she had dropped off to sleep again.

At last, in the dusk of evening, they arrived at the landing-place from which they had started some hours before. The men spoke to Mary, but though she mechanically replied, she did not stir; so, at length, they were obliged to shake her. She stood up, shivering and puzzled as to her whereabouts.

"Now tell me where you are bound to, missus," said the gray old man, "and maybe I can put you in the way."

She slowly comprehended what he said, and went through the process of recollection; but very dimly, and with much labour. She put her hand into her pocket and pulled out her purse, and shook its contents into the man's hand; and then began meekly to unpin her shawl, although they had turned away without asking for it.

"No, no!" said the old man, who lingered on the step before springing into the boat, and to whom she mutely offered the shawl.

"Keep it! we donnot want it. It were only for to try you,—some folks say they've no more blunt,[8] when all the while they've getten a mint."

"Thank you," said she, in a dull, low tone.

"Where are you bound to? I axed that question afore," said the gruff old fellow.

"I don't know. I'm a stranger," replied she, quietly, with a strange absence of anxiety under the circumstances.

"But you mun find out, then," said he, sharply; "pier-head's no place for a young woman to be standing on, gape-seying."[9]

"I've a card somewhere as will tell me," she answered, and the man partly relieved, jumped into the boat, which was now pushing off to make way for the arrivals from some steamer.

Mary felt in her pocket for the card, on which was written the name of the street where she was to have met Mr. Bridgenorth at two o'clock; where Job and Mrs. Wilson were to have been, and where she was to have learnt from the former the particulars of some respectable lodging. It was not to be found.

She tried to brighten her perceptions, and felt again, and took out the little articles her pocket contained, her empty purse, her pocket-handkerchief, and such little things, but it was not there.

In fact she had dropped it when, so eager to embark, she had pulled out her purse to reckon up her money.

She did not know this, of course. She only knew it was gone.

It added but little to the despair that was creeping over her. But she tried a little more to help herself, though every minute her mind

---

8. Ready money.
9. Silent and staring without purpose.

became more cloudy. She strove to remember where Will had lodged, but she could not; name, street, everything had passed away, and it did not signify; better she were lost than found.

She sat down quietly on the top step of the landing, and gazed down into the dark, dank water below. Once or twice a spectral thought loomed among the shadows of her brain; a wonder whether beneath that cold dismal surface there would not be rest from the troubles of earth. But she could not hold an idea before her for two consecutive moments; and she forgot what she thought about before she could act upon it.

So she continued sitting motionless, without looking up, or regarding in any way the insults to which she was subjected.

Through the darkening light the old boatman had watched her: interested in her in spite of himself, and his scoldings of himself.

When the landing-place was once more comparatively clear, he made his way towards it, across boats, and along planks, swearing at himself while he did so for an old fool.

He shook Mary's shoulder violently.

"D—you, I ask you again where you're bound to? Don't sit there, stupid. Where are you going to?"

"I don't know," sighed Mary.

"Come, come; avast[1] with that story. You said a bit ago you'd a card, which was to tell you where to go."

"I had, but I've lost it. Never mind."

She looked again down upon the black mirror below.

He stood by her, striving to put down his better self; but he could not. He shook her again. She looked up, as if she had forgotten him.

"What do you want?" asked she, wearily.

"Come with me and be d—d to you!" replied he, clutching her arm to pull her up.

She arose and followed him, with the unquestioning docility of a little child.

Chapter XXIX.

> "There are who, living by the legal pen,
> Are held in honour—honourable men."
>
> CRABBE.[2]

At five minutes before two, Job Legh stood upon the door-step of the house where Mr. Bridgenorth lodged at Assize time. He had left Mrs. Wilson at the dwelling of a friend of his, who had offered him a room

---

1. Stop.
2. From Crabbe's *The Borough*, Letter VI "The Profession—Law," lines 83–84.

for the old woman and Mary: a room which had frequently been his, on his occasional visits to Liverpool, but which he was thankful now to have obtained for them, as his own sleeping place was a matter of indifference to him, and the town appeared crowded and disorderly on the eve of the Assizes.

He was shown in to Mr. Bridgenorth, who was writing. Mary and Will Wilson had not yet arrived, being, as you know, far away on the broad sea; but of this Job of course knew nothing, and he did not as yet feel much anxiety about their non-appearance; he was more curious to know the result of Mr. Bridgenorth's interview that morning with Jem.

"Why, yes," said Mr. Bridgenorth, putting down his pen, "I have seen him, but to little purpose, I'm afraid. He's very impracticable— very. I told him, of course, that he must be perfectly open with me, or else I could not be prepared for the weak points. I named your name with the view of unlocking his confidence, but——"

"What did he say?" asked Job, breathlessly.

"Why, very little. He barely answered me. Indeed, he refused to answer some questions—positively refused. I don't know what I can do for him."

"Then you think him guilty, sir," said Job, despondingly.

"No, I don't," replied Mr. Bridgenorth, quickly and decisively. "Much less than I did before I saw him. The impression (mind, 'tis only impression; I rely upon your caution, not to take it for fact)— the impression," with an emphasis on the word, "he gave me is, that he knows something about the affair, but what, he will not say; and so, the chances are, if he persists in his obstinacy, he'll be hung. That's all."

He began to write again, for he had no time to lose.

"But he must not be hung," said Job, with vehemence.

Mr. Bridgenorth looked up, smiled a little, but shook his head.

"What did he say, sir, if I may be so bold as to ask?" continued Job.

"His words were few enough, and he was so reserved and short, that, as I said before, I can only give you the impression they conveyed to me. I told him, of course, who I was, and for what I was sent. He looked pleased, I thought,—at least his face (sad enough when I went in, I assure ye) brightened a little; but he said he had nothing to say, no defence to make. I asked him if he was guilty, then; and, by way of opening his heart, I said I understood he had had provocation enough, inasmuch as I heard that the girl was very lovely, and had jilted him to fall desperately in love with that handsome young Carson (poor fellow!). But James Wilson did not speak one way or another. I then went to particulars. I asked him if the gun was his, as his mother had declared. He had not heard of her admission, it was evident, from his quick way of looking up, and the glance of his eye;

but when he saw I was observing him, he hung down his head again, and merely said she was right; it was his gun."

"Well!" said Job, impatiently, as Mr. Bridgenorth paused.

"Nay! I have little more to tell you," continued that gentleman. "I asked him to inform me, in all confidence, how it came to be found there. He was silent for a time, and then refused. Not only refused to answer that question, but candidly told me he would not say another word on the subject, and, thanking me for my trouble and interest in his behalf, he all but dismissed me. Ungracious enough on the whole, was it not, Mr. Legh? And yet, I assure ye, I am twenty times more inclined to think him innocent than before I had the interview."

"I wish Mary Barton would come," said Job, anxiously. "She and Will are a long time about it."

"Ay, that's our only chance, I believe," answered Mr. Bridgenorth, who was writing again. "I sent Johnson off before twelve to serve him with his subpœna, and to say I wanted to speak with him; he'll be here soon, I've no doubt."

There was a pause. Mr. Bridgenorth looked up again, and spoke.

"Mr. Duncombe promised to be here to speak to his character. I sent him a subpœna on Saturday night. Though, after all, juries go very little by such general and vague testimony as that to character. It is very right that they should not often; but in this instance unfortunate for us, as we must rest our case on the *alibi*."

The pen went again, scratch, scratch over the paper.

Job grew very fidgety. He sat on the edge of his chair, the more readily to start up when Will and Mary should appear. He listened intently to every noise and every step on the stair.

Once he heard a man's footstep, and his old heart gave a leap of delight. But it was only Mr. Bridgenorth's clerk, bringing him a list of those cases in which the grand jury had found true bills. He glanced it over and pushed it to Job, merely saying,

"Of course we expected this," and went on with his writing.

There was a true bill against James Wilson. Of course. And yet Job felt now doubly anxious and sad. It seemed the beginning of the end. He had got, by imperceptible degrees, to think Jem innocent. Little by little this persuasion had come upon him.

Mary (tossing about in the little boat on the broad river) did not come, nor did Will.

Job grew very restless. He longed to go and watch for them out of the window, but feared to interrupt Mr. Bridgenorth. At length his desire to look out was irresistible, and he got up and walked carefully and gently across the room, his boots creaking at every cautious step. The gloom which had overspread the sky, and the influence of which had been felt by Mary on the open water, was yet more perceptible in

the dark, dull street. Job grew more and more fidgety. He was obliged
to walk about the room, for he could not keep still; and he did so,
regardless of Mr. Bridgenorth's impatient little motions and noises,
as the slow, stealthy, creaking movements were heard, backwards and
forwards, behind his chair.

He really liked Job, and was interested for Jem, else his nervousness would have overcome his sympathy long before it did. But he
could hold out no longer against the monotonous, grating sound; so
at last he threw down his pen, locked his portfolio, and taking up his
hat and gloves, he told Job he must go to the courts.

"But Will Wilson is not come," said Job, in dismay. "Just wait while
I run to his lodgings. I would have done it before, but I thought they'd
be here every minute, and I were afraid of missing them. I'll be back
in no time."

"No, my good fellow, I really must go. Besides, I begin to think
Johnson must have made a mistake, and have fixed with this William
Wilson to meet me at the courts. If you like to wait for him here, pray
make use of my room; but I've a notion I shall find him there: in
which case, I'll send him to your lodgings; shall I? You know where
to find me. I shall be here again by eight o'clock, and with the evidence of this witness that's to prove the *alibi*, I'll have the brief drawn
out, and in the hands of counsel to-night."

So saying, he shook hands with Job, and went his way. The old man
considered for a minute as he lingered at the door, and then bent his
steps towards Mrs. Jones's, where he knew (from reference to queer,
odd, heterogeneous memoranda, in an ancient black-leather pocket-
book) that Will lodged, and where he doubted not he should hear
both of him and of Mary.

He went there, and gathered what intelligence he could out of
Mrs. Jones's slow replies.

He asked if a young woman had been there that morning, and if
she had seen Will Wilson. "No!"

"Why not?"

"Why, bless you, 'cause he had sailed some hours before she came
asking for him."

There was a dead silence, broken only by the even, heavy sound of
Mrs. Jones's ironing.

"Where is the young woman now?" asked Job.

"Somewhere down at the docks," she thought. "Charley would
know, if he was in, but he wasn't. He was in mischief, somewhere or
other, she had no doubt. Boys always were. He would break his neck
some day, she knew;" so saying, she quietly spat upon her fresh iron,
to test its heat, and then went on with her business.

Job could have boxed her, he was in such a state of irritation. But
he did not, and he had his reward. Charley came in, whistling with

an air of indifference, assumed to carry off his knowledge of the lateness of the hour to which he had lingered about the docks.

"Here's an old man come to know where the young woman is, who went out with thee this morning," said his mother, after she had bestowed on him a little motherly scolding.

"Where she is now, I don't know. I saw her last sailing down the river after the *John Cropper*. I'm afeard she won't reach her; wind changed, and she would be under weigh, and over the bar in no time. She would have been back by now."

It took Job some little time to understand this, from the confused use of the feminine pronoun. Then he inquired how he could best find Mary.

"I'll run down again to the pier," said the boy;" "I'll warrant I'll find her."

"Thou shalt do no such a thing," said his mother, setting her back against the door. The lad made a comical face at Job, which met with no responsive look from the old man, whose sympathies were naturally in favour of the parent; although he would thankfully have availed himself of Charley's offer; for he was weary, and anxious to return to poor Mrs. Wilson, who would be wondering what had become of him.

"How can I best find her? Who did she go with, lad?"

But Charley was sullen at his mother's exercise of authority before a stranger, and at that stranger's grave looks when he meant to have made him laugh.

"They were river boatmen;—that's all I know," said he.

"But what was the name of their boat?" persevered Job.

"I never took no notice;—the *Anne*, or *William*,—or some of them common names, I'll be bound."

"What pier did she start from?" asked Job, despairingly.

"Oh, as for that matter, it were the stairs on the Prince's Pier she started from; but she'll not come back to the same, for the American steamer came up with the tide, and anchored close to it, blocking up the way for all the smaller craft. It's a rough evening, too, to be out on," he maliciously added.

"Well, God's will be done! I did hope we could have saved the lad," said Job, sorrowfully; "but I'm getten very doubtful again. I'm uneasy about Mary, too,—very. She's a stranger in Liverpool."

"So she told me," said Charley. "There's traps about for young women at every corner. It's a pity she's no one to meet her when she lands."

"As for that," replied Job, "I don't see how any one could meet her when we can't tell where she would come to. I must trust to her coming right. She's getten spirit and sense. She'll most likely be for coming here again. Indeed, I don't know what else she can do, for she knows no other place in Liverpool. Missus, if she comes, will you give your son leave to bring her to No. 8, Back Garden Court, where there's friends waiting for her? I'll give him sixpence for his trouble."

Mrs. Jones, pleased with the reference to her, gladly promised. And even Charley, indignant as he was at first at the idea of his motions being under the control of his mother, was mollified at the prospect of the sixpence, and at the probability of getting nearer to the heart of the mystery.

But Mary never came.

Chapter XXX.

> "Oh! sad is the night-time,
>   The night-time of sorrow,
> When through the deep gloom, we catch but the boom
>   Of the waves that may whelm us to-morrow."[3]

JOB found Mrs. Wilson pacing about in a restless way; not speaking to the woman at whose house she was staying, but occasionally heaving such deep oppressive sighs as quite startled those around her.

"Well!" said she, turning sharp round in her tottering walk up and down, as Job came in.

"Well, speak!" repeated she, before he could make up his mind what to say; for, to tell the truth, he was studying for some kind-hearted lie which might soothe her for a time. But now the real state of the case came blurting forth in answer to her impatient questioning.

"Will's not to the fore. But he'll maybe turn up yet, time enough."

She looked at him steadily for a minute, as if almost doubting if such despair could be in store for her as his words seemed to imply. Then she slowly shook her head, and said, more quietly than might have been expected from her previous excited manner,

"Don't go for to say that! Thou dost not think it. Thou'rt well-nigh hopeless, like me. I seed all along my lad would be hung for what he never did. And better he were, and were shut* of this weary world, where there's neither justice nor mercy left."

She looked up with tranced eyes as if praying, and then sat down.

"Nay, now thou'rt off at a gallop," said Job. "Will has sailed this morning, for sure; but that brave wench, Mary Barton, is after him, and will bring him back, I'll be bound, if she can but get speech on him. She's not back yet. Come, come, hold up thy head. It will all end right."

"It will all end right," echoed she; "but not as thou tak'st it. Jem will

---

3. Unknown.
* "Shut," quit. [WG]

be hung, and will go to his father and the little lads; where the Lord God wipes away all tears, and where the Lord Jesus speaks kindly to the little ones, who look about for the mothers they left upon earth. Eh, Job, yon's a blessed land, and I long to go to it, and yet I fret because Jem is hastening there. I would not fret if he and I could lie down to-night to sleep our last sleep; not a bit would I fret if folk would but know him to be innocent—as I do."

"They'll know it sooner or later, and repent sore if they've hanged him for what he never did," replied Job.

"Ay, that they will. Poor souls! May God have mercy on them when they find out their mistake."

Presently Job grew tired of sitting waiting, and got up, and hung about the door and window, like some animal wanting to go out. It was pitch dark, for the moon had not yet risen.

"You just go to bed," said he, to the widow; "you'll want your strength for to-morrow. Jem will be sadly off, if he sees you so cut up as you look to-night. I'll step down again and find Mary. She'll be back by this time. I'll come and tell you everything, never fear. But, now, you go to bed."

"Thou'rt a kind friend, Job Legh, and I'll go, as thou wishest me. But, oh! mind thou com'st straight off to me, and bring Mary as soon as thou'st lit on her." She spoke low, but very calmly.

"Ay, ay!" replied Job, slipping out of the house.

He went first to Mr. Bridgenorth's, where it had struck him that Will and Mary might be all this time waiting for him.

They were not there, however. Mr. Bridgenorth had just come in, and Job went breathlessly up-stairs to consult with him as to the state of the case.

"It's a bad job," said the lawyer, looking very grave, while he arranged his papers. "Johnson told me how it was; the woman that Wilson lodged with told him. I doubt it's but a wildgoose chase of the girl Barton. Our case must rest on the uncertainty of circumstantial evidence, and the goodness of the prisoner's previous character. A very vague and weak defence. However, I've engaged Mr. Clinton as counsel, and he'll make the best of it. And now, my good fellow, I must wish you good-night, and turn you out of doors. As it is, I shall have to sit up into the small hours. Did you see my clerk, as you came up-stairs. You did? Then may I trouble you to ask him to step up immediately."

After this Job could not stay, and, making his humble bow, he left the room.

Then he went to Mrs. Jones's. She was in, but Charley had slipped off again. There was no holding that boy. Nothing kept him but lock and key, and they did not always; for, once, she had him locked up in the garret, and he had got off through the skylight. Perhaps, now he was gone to see after the young woman down at the docks. He never wanted an excuse to be there.

Unasked, Job took a chair, resolved to await Charley's reappearance.

Mrs. Jones ironed and folded her clothes, talking all the time of Charley and her husband, who was a sailor in some ship bound for India, and who, in leaving her their boy, had evidently left her rather more than she could manage. She moaned and croaked over sailors, and seaport towns, and stormy weather, and sleepless nights, and trousers all over tar and pitch, long after Job had left off attending to her, and was only trying to hearken to every step, and every voice in the street.

At last Charley came in, but he came alone.

"Yon Mary Barton has getten into some scrape or another," said he, addressing himself to Job. "She's not to be heard of at any of the piers; and Bourne says it were a boat from the Cheshire side as she went aboard of. So there's no hearing of her till to-morrow morning."

"To-morrow morning she'll have to be in court at nine o'clock, to bear witness on a trial," said Job, sorrowfully.

"So she said; at least somewhat of the kind," said Charley, looking desirous to hear more. But Job was silent.

He could not think of anything further that could be done; so he rose up, and, thanking Mrs. Jones for the shelter she had given him, he went out into the street; and there he stood still, to ponder over probabilities and chances.

After some little time he slowly turned towards the lodging where he had left Mrs. Wilson. There was nothing else to be done; but he loitered on the way, fervently hoping that her weariness and her woes might have sent her to sleep before his return, that he might be spared her questionings.

He went very gently into the house-place where the sleepy landlady awaited his coming and his bringing the girl, who, she had been told, was to share the old woman's bed.

But in her sleepy blindness she knocked things so about in lighting the candle (she could see to have a nap by fire-light, she said), that the voice of Mrs. Wilson was heard from the little back-room, where she was to pass the night.

"Who's there?"

Job gave no answer, and kept down his breath, that she might think herself mistaken. The landlady, having no such care, dropped the snuffers with a sharp metallic sound, and then, by her endless apologies, convinced the listening woman that Job had returned.

"Job! Job Legh!" she cried out nervously.

"Eh, dear!" said Job, to himself, going reluctantly to her bed-room door. "I wonder if one little lie would be a sin, as things stand? It would happen give her sleep, and she won't have sleep for many and many a night (not to call sleep), if things goes wrong to-morrow. I'll chance it, any way."

"Job! art thou there?" asked she again, with a trembling impatience that told in every tone of her voice.

"Ay! sure! I thought thou'd ha' been asleep by this time."

"Asleep! How could I sleep till I know'd if Will were found?"

"Now for it," muttered Job to himself. Then in a louder voice, "Never fear! he's found, and safe, ready for to-morrow."

"And he'll prove that thing for my poor lad, will he? He'll bear witness that Jem were with him? Oh, Job, speak! tell me all!"

"In for a penny, in for a pound," thought Job. "Happen one prayer will do for the sum total. Any rate, I must go on now. Ay, ay," shouted he, through the door. "He can prove all; and Jem will come off as clear as a new-born babe."

He could hear Mrs. Wilson's rustling movements, and in an instant guessed she was on her knees, for he heard her trembling voice uplifted in thanksgiving and praise to God, stopped at times by sobs of gladness and relief.

And when he heard this, his heart misgave him; for he thought of the awful enlightening, the terrible revulsion of feeling that awaited her in the morning. He saw the short-sightedness of falsehood; but what could he do now?

While he listened, she ended her grateful prayers.

"And Mary? Thou'st found her at Mrs. Jones's, Job?" said she, continuing her inquiries.

He gave a great sigh.

"Yes, she was there, safe enough, second time of going. God forgive me!" muttered he, "who'd ha' thought of my turning out such an arrant liar in my old days."

"Bless the wench! Is she here? Why does not she come to bed? I'm sure she's need."

Job coughed away his remains of conscience, and made answer,

"She was a bit weary, and o'erdone with her sail; and Mrs. Jones axed her to stay there all night. It was nigh at hand to the courts, where she will have to be in the morning."

"It comes easy enough after a while," groaned out Job. "The father of lies helps one, I suppose, for now my speech comes as natural as truth. She's done questioning now, that's one good thing. I'll be off, before Satan and she are at me again."

He went to the house-place, where the landlady stood, wearily waiting. Her husband was in bed, and asleep long ago.

But Job had not yet made up his mind what to do. He could not go to sleep, with all his anxieties, if he were put into the best bed in Liverpool.

"Thou'lt let me sit up in this arm-chair," said he at length, to the woman, who stood, expecting his departure.

He was an old friend, so she let him do as he wished. But, indeed, she was too sleepy to have opposed him. She was too glad to be released, and go to bed.

Chapter XXXI.

"To think
That all this long interminable night,
Which I have passed in thinking on two words—
'Guilty'—'Not Guilty!'——like one happy moment
O'er many a head hath flown unheeded by;
O'er happy sleepers dreaming in their bliss
Of bright to-morrows—or far happier still,
With deep breath buried in forgetfulness.
O all the dismallest images of death
Did swim before my eyes!"

WILSON.[4]

And now, where was Mary?

How Job's heart would have been relieved of one of its cares if he could have seen her: for he was in a miserable state of anxiety about her; and many and many a time through that long night, he scolded her and himself; her for her obstinacy, and himself for his weakness in yielding to her obstinacy, when she insisted on being the one to follow and find out Will.

She did not pass that night in bed any more than Job; but she was under a respectable roof, and among kind, though rough people.

She had offered no resistance to the old boatman, when he had clutched her arm, in order to insure her following him, as he threaded the crowded dock-ways, and dived up strange by-streets. She came on meekly after him, scarcely thinking in her stupor where she was going, and glad (in a dead, heavy way) that some one was deciding things for her.

He led her to an old-fashioned house, almost as small as house could be, which had been built long ago, before all the other part of the street, and had a country-town look about it in the middle of that bustling back street. He pulled her into the house-place; and relieved to a certain degree of his fear of losing her on the way, he exclaimed,

"There!" giving a great slap of one hand on her back.

The room was light and bright, and roused Mary (perhaps the slap on her back might help a little, too), and she felt the awkwardness of accounting for her presence to a little bustling old woman who had

---

4. From John Wilson's (aka Christopher North) (1785–1854) "The Convict," I. i, 8–17.

been moving about the fireplace on her entrance. The boatman took it very quietly, never deigning to give any explanation, but sitting down in his own particular chair, and chewing tobacco, while he looked at Mary with the most satisfied air imaginable, half triumphantly, as if she were the captive of his bow and spear, and half defying, as if daring her to escape.

The old woman, his wife, stood still, poker in hand, waiting to be told who it was that her husband had brought home so unceremoniously; but, as she looked in amazement, the girl's cheek flushed, and then blanched to a dead whiteness; a film came over her eyes, and catching at the dresser for support in that hot whirling room, she fell in a heap on the floor.

Both man and wife came quickly to her assistance. They raised her up, still insensible, and he supported her on one knee, while his wife pattered away for some cold fresh water. She threw it straight over Mary; but though it caused a great sob, the eyes still remained closed, and the face as pale as ashes.

"Who is she, Ben?" asked the woman as she rubbed her unresisting, powerless hands.

"How should I know?" answered her husband, gruffly.

"Well-a-well" (in a soothing tone, such as you use to irritated children), and as if half to herself, "I only thought you might, you know, as you brought her home. Poor thing! we must not ask aught about her, but that she needs help. I wish I'd my salts at home, but I lent 'em to Mrs. Burton, last Sunday in church, for she could not keep awake through the sermon. Dear-a-me, how white she is!"

"Here! you hold her up a bit," said her husband.

She did as he desired, still crooning to herself, not caring for his short, sharp interruptions as she went on; and, indeed, to her old, loving heart, his crossest words fell like pearls and diamonds, for he had been the husband of her youth; and even he, rough and crabbed as he was, was secretly soothed by the sound of her voice, although not for worlds, if he could have helped it, would he have shown any of the love that was hidden beneath his rough outside.

"What's the old fellow after?" said she, bending over Mary, so as to accommodate the drooping head. "Taking my pen, as I've had for better nor five year. Bless us, and save us! he's burning it! Ay, I see now, he's his wits about him; burnt feathers is always good for a faint. But they don't bring her round, poor wench! Now what's he after next? Well! he is a bright one, my old man! That I never thought of that, to be sure!" exclaimed she, as he produced a square bottle of smuggled spirits, labelled "Golden Wasser,"[5] from a corner cupboard in their little room.

"That'll do!" said she, as the dose he poured into Mary's open

---

5. Golden water in German. A richly spiced liqueur with small flakes of gold leaf in it.

mouth made her start and cough. "Bless the man! It's just like him to be so tender and thoughtful!"

"Not a bit!" snarled he, as he was relieved by Mary's returning colour, and opened eyes, and wondering, sensible gaze; "not a bit! I never was such a fool afore."

His wife helped Mary to rise, and placed her in a chair.

"All's right, now, young woman?" asked the boatman, anxiously.

"Yes, sir, and thank you. I'm sure, sir, I don't know rightly how to thank you," faltered Mary softly forth.

"Be hanged to you and your thanks." And he shook himself, took his pipe, and went out without deigning another word; leaving his wife sorely puzzled as to the character and history of the stranger within her doors.

Mary watched the boatman leave the house, and then, turning her sorrowful eyes to the face of her hostess, she attempted feebly to rise, with the intention of going away,—where she knew not.

"Nay! nay! whoe'er thou be'st, thou'rt not fit to go out into the street. Perhaps" (sinking her voice a little) "thou'rt a bad one; I almost misdoubt thee, thou'rt so pretty. Well-a-well! it's the bad ones as have the broken hearts, sure enough; good folk never get utterly cast down, they've always getten hope in the Lord; it's the sinful as bear the bitter, bitter grief in their crushed hearts, poor souls; it's them we ought, most of all, to pity and to help. She shanna leave the house to-night, choose who she is,—worst woman in Liverpool, she shanna. I wished I knew where th' old man picked her up, that I do."

Mary had listened feebly to this soliloquy, and now tried to satisfy her hostess, in weak, broken sentences.

"I'm not a bad one, missis, indeed. Your master took me out to sea after a ship as had sailed. There was a man in it as might save a life at the trial to-morrow. The captain would not let him come, but he says he'll come back in the pilot-boat." She fell to sobbing at the thought of her waning hopes, and the old woman tried to comfort her, beginning with her accustomed,

"Well-a-well! and he'll come back, I'm sure. I know he will; so keep up your heart. Don't fret about it. He's sure to be back."

"Oh! I'm afraid! I'm sore afraid he won't," cried Mary, consoled, nevertheless, by the woman's assertions, all groundless as she knew them to be.

Still talking half to herself and half to Mary, the old woman prepared tea, and urged her visitor to eat and refresh herself. But Mary shook her head at the proffered food, and only drank a cup of tea with thirsty eagerness. For the spirits had thrown her into a burning heat, and rendered each impression received through her senses of the most painful distinctness and intensity, while her head ached in a terrible manner.

She disliked speaking, her power over her words seemed so utterly gone. She used quite different expressions to those she intended. So she kept silent, while Mrs. Sturgis (for that was the name of her hostess) talked away, and put her tea-things by, and moved about incessantly, in a manner that increased the dizziness in Mary's head. She felt as if she ought to take leave for the night, and go. But where?

Presently the old man came back; crosser and gruffer than when he went away. He kicked aside the dry shoes his wife had prepared for him, and snarled at all she said. Mary attributed this to his finding her still there, and gathered up her strength for an effort to leave the house. But she was mistaken. By-and-by, he said (looking right into the fire, as if addressing it) "Wind's right against them!"

"Ay, ay, and is it so?" said his wife, who, knowing him well, knew that his surliness proceeded from some repressed sympathy. "Well-a-well, wind changes often at night. Time enough before morning. I'd bet a penny it has changed sin' thou looked."

She looked out of her little window at a weathercock near, glittering in the moonlight; and as she was a sailor's wife, she instantly recognised the unfavourable point at which the indicator seemed stationary, and giving a heavy sigh, turned into the room, and began to beat about in her own mind for some other mode of comfort.

"There's no one else who can prove what you want at the trial tomorrow, is there?" asked she.

"No one!" answered Mary.

"And you've no clue to the one as is really guilty, if t'other is not?"

Mary did not answer, but trembled all over.

Sturgis saw it.

"Don't bother her with thy questions," said he to his wife. "She mun go to bed, for she's all in a shiver with the sea air. I'll see after the wind, hang it, and the weatheroock too. Tide will help 'em when it turns."

Mary went up-stairs murmuring thanks and blessings on those who took the stranger in. Mrs. Sturgis led her into a little room redolent of the sea and foreign lands. There was a small bed for one son, bound for China; and a hammock slung above for another, who was now tossing in the Baltic. The sheets looked made out of sail-cloth, but were fresh and clean in spite of their brownness.

Against the wall were wafered two rough drawings of vessels with their names written underneath, on which the mother's eyes caught, and gazed until they filled with tears. But she brushed the drops away with the back of her hand; and in a cheerful tone went on to assure Mary the bed was well aired.

"I cannot sleep, thank you. I will sit here, if you please," said Mary, sinking down on the window-seat.

"Come, now," said Mrs. Sturgis, "my master told me to see you to

bed, and I mun. What's the use of watching? A watched pot never
boils, and I see you are after watching that weathercock. Why now, I
try never to look at it, else I could do nought else. My heart many a
time goes sick when the wind rises, but I turn away and work away,
and try never to think on the wind, but on what I ha' getten to do."

"Let me stay up a little," pleaded Mary, as her hostess seemed so
resolute about seeing her to bed. Her looks won her suit.

"Well, I suppose I mun. I shall catch it down stairs, I know. He'll
be in a fidget till you're getten to bed, I know; so you mun be quiet if
you are so bent upon staying up."

And quietly, noiselessly, Mary watched the unchanging weathercock through the night. She sat on the little window-seat, her hand
holding back the curtain which shaded the room from the bright
moonlight without; her head resting its weariness against the corner
of the window-frame; her eyes burning, and stiff with the intensity of
her gaze.

The ruddy morning stole up the horizon, casting a crimson glow
into the watcher's room.

It was the morning of the day of trial!

Chapter XXXII.

> "Thou stand'st here arraign'd,
> That with presumption impious and accurs'd,
> Thou hast usurp'd God's high prerogative,
> Making thy fellow mortal's life and death
> Wait on thy moody and diseased passions;
> That with a violent and untimely steel
> Hath set abroach the blood, that should have ebbed
> In calm and natural current: to sum all
> In one wild name—a name the pale air freezes at,
> And every cheek of man sinks in with horror—
> Thou art a cold and midnight murderer."
>
> MILMAN'S 'FAZIO.'[6]

Of all the restless people who found that night's hours agonising from
excess of anxiety, the poor father of the murdered man was perhaps
the most restless. He had slept but little since the blow had fallen; his
waking hours had been too full of agitated thought, which seemed to
haunt and pursue him through his unquiet slumbers.

And this night of all others was the most sleepless. He turned over
and over again in his mind the wonder if everything had been done,
that could be done, to insure the conviction of Jem Wilson. He
almost regretted the haste with which he had urged forward the pro-

6. From Henry Hart Milman's (1791–1868) *Fazio* (1815), III, ii, lines 89–99.

ceedings, and yet, until he had obtained vengeance, he felt as if there were no peace on earth for him (I don't know that he exactly used the term vengeance in his thoughts; he spoke of justice, and probably thought of his desired end as such); no peace, either bodily or mental, for he moved up and down his bedroom with the restless incessant tramp of a wild beast in a cage, and if he compelled his aching limbs to cease for an instant, the twitchings which ensued almost amounted to convulsions, and he recommenced his walk as the lesser evil, and the more bearable fatigue.

With daylight, increased power of action came; and he drove off to arouse his attorney, and worry him with further directions and inquiries; and when that was ended, he sat, watch in hand, until the courts should be opened, and the trial begin.

What were all the living,—wife or daughters,—what were they in comparison with the dead,—the murdered son who lay unburied still, in compliance with his father's earnest wish, and almost vowed purpose, of having the slayer of his child sentenced to death, before he committed the body to the rest of the grave?

At nine o'clock they all met at their awful place of rendezvous.

The judge, the jury, the avenger of blood, the prisoner, the witnesses—all were gathered together within one building. And besides these were many others, personally interested in some part of the proceedings, in which, however, they took no part; Job Legh, Ben Sturgis, and several others were there, amongst whom was Charley Jones.

Job Legh had carefully avoided any questioning from Mrs. Wilson that morning. Indeed, he had not been much in her company, for he had risen up early to go out once more to make inquiry for Mary; and when he could hear nothing of her, he had desperately resolved not to undeceive Mrs. Wilson, as sorrow never came too late; and if the blow were inevitable, it would be better to leave her in ignorance of the impending evil as long as possible. She took her place in the witness-room, worn and dispirited, but not anxious.

As Job struggled through the crowd into the body of the court, Mr. Bridgenorth's clerk beckoned to him.

"Here's a letter for you from our client!"

Job sickened as he took it. He did not know why, but he dreaded a confession of guilt, which would be an overthrow of all hope.

The letter ran as follows:

"DEAR FRIEND,—I thank you heartily for your goodness in finding me a lawyer, but lawyers can do no good to me, whatever they may do to other people. But I am not the less obliged to you, dear friend. I foresee things will go against me—and no wonder. If I was a juryman I should say the man was guilty as had as much evidence brought against him as may be brought against me to-morrow. So it's no blame to them if they do. But, Job Legh, I think I need not tell you I am as guiltless in this matter as the babe unborn, although it is not in my power to prove it. If I did not believe that you thought me innocent, I could not write as I do now to tell you my wishes. You'll not forget they are the words of a man shortly to die. Dear friend, you must take care of my mother. Not in the money way, for she will have enough for her and Aunt Alice; but you must let her talk to you of me; and show her that (whatever others may do) you think I died innocent. I don't reckon she'll stay long behind when we are all gone. Be tender with her, Job, for my sake; and if she is a bit fractious at times, remember what she has gone through. I know mother will never doubt me, God bless her.

"There is one other whom I fear I have loved too dearly; and yet, the loving her has made the happiness of my life. She will think I have murdered her lover: she will think I have caused the grief she must be feeling. And she must go on thinking so. It is hard upon me to say this; but she *must*. It will be best for her, and that's all I ought to think on. But, dear Job, you are a hearty fellow for your time of life, and may live many years to come; and perhaps you could tell her, when you felt sure you were drawing near your end, that I solemnly told you (as I do now) that I was innocent of this thing. You must not tell her for many years to come; but I cannot well bear to think on her living through a long life, and hating the thought of me as the murderer of him she loved, and dying with that hatred to me in her heart. It would hurt me sore in the other world to see the look of it in her face, as it would be, till she was told. I must not let myself think on how she must be viewing me now.

"So God bless you, Job Legh; and no more from

"Yours to command,

"JAMES WILSON."

Job turned the letter over and over when he had read it; sighed deeply; and then wrapping it carefully up in a bit of newspaper he had about him, he put it in his waistcoat pocket, and went off to the door of the witness-room to ask if Mary Barton was there.

As the door opened he saw her sitting within, against a table on which her folded arms were resting, and her head was hidden within them. It was an attitude of hopelessness, and would have served to strike Job dumb in sickness of heart, even without the sound of Mrs. Wilson's voice in passionate sobbing, and sore lamentations, which told him as well as words could do (for she was not within view of the door, and he did not care to go in), that she was at any rate partially undeceived as to the hopes he had given her last night.

Sorrowfully did Job return into the body of the court; neither Mrs.

Wilson nor Mary having seen him as he had stood at the witness-room door.

As soon as he could bring his distracted thoughts to bear upon the present scene, he perceived that the trial of James Wilson for the murder of Henry Carson was just commencing. The clerk was gabbling over the indictment, and in a minute or two there was the accustomed question, "How say you, Guilty or Not Guilty?"

Although but one answer was expected,—was customary in all cases,—there was a pause of dead silence, an interval of solemnity even in this hackneyed part of the proceeding; while the prisoner at the bar stood with compressed lips, looking at the judge with his outward eyes, but with far other and different scenes presented to his mental vision; a sort of rapid recapitulation of his life,—remembrances of his childhood,—his father (so proud of him, his first-born child),—his sweet little playfellow, Mary,—his hopes, his love—his despair, yet still, yet ever and ever, his love,—the blank, wide world it had been without her love,—his mother,—his childless mother,—but not long to be so,— not long to be away from all she loved,—nor during that time to be oppressed with doubt as to his innocence, sure and secure of her darling's heart;—he started from his instant's pause, and said in a low firm voice,

"Not guilty, my lord."

The circumstances of the murder, the discovery of the body, the causes of suspicion against Jem, were as well known to most of the audience as they are to you, so there was some little buzz of conversation going on among the people while the leading counsel for the prosecution made his very effective speech.

"That's Mr. Carson, the father, sitting behind Serjeant Wilkinson!"

"What a noble-looking old man he is! so stern and inflexible, with such classical features! Does he not remind you of some of the busts of Jupiter?"[7]

"I am more interested by watching the prisoner. Criminals always interest me. I try to trace in the features common to humanity some expression of the crimes by which they have distinguished themselves from their kind. I have seen a good number of murderers in my day, but I have seldom seen one with such marks of Cain[8] on his countenance as the man at the bar."

"Well, I am no physiognomist,[9] but I don't think his face strikes me as bad. It certainly is gloomy and depressed, and not unnaturally so, considering his situation."

"Only look at his low, resolute brow, his downcast eye, his white compressed lips. He never looks up,—just watch him."

---

7. Roman version of the Greek god Zeus, chief of the gods.
8. Cain killed his brother Abel. Genesis 4:8–15.
9. One who reads a person's character through facial features.

"His forehead is not so low if he had that mass of black hair removed, and is very square, which some people say is a good sign. If others are to be influenced by such trifles as you are, it would have been much better if the prison barber had cut his hair a little previous to the trial; and as for downcast eye, and compressed lip, it is all part and parcel of his inward agitation just now; nothing to do with character, my good fellow."

Poor Jem! His raven hair (his mother's pride, and so often fondly caressed by her fingers), was that, too, to have its influence against him?

The witnesses were called. At first they consisted principally of policemen; who, being much accustomed to giving evidence, knew what were the material points they were called on to prove, and did not lose the time of the court in listening to anything unnecessary.

"Clear as day against the prisoner," whispered one attorney's clerk to another.

"Black as night, you mean," replied his friend; and they both smiled.

"Jane Wilson! who's she? some relation, I suppose, from the name."

"The mother,—she that is to prove the gun part of the case."

"Oh, ay—I remember! Rather hard on her, too, I think."

Then both were silent, as one of the officers of the court ushered Mrs. Wilson into the witness-box. I have often called her "the old woman," and "an old woman," because, in truth, her appearance was so much beyond her years, which could not be many above fifty. But partly owing to her accident in early life, which left a stamp of pain upon her face, partly owing to her anxious temper, partly to her sorrows, and partly to her limping gait, she always gave me the idea of age. But now she might have seemed more than seventy; her lines were so set and deep, her features so sharpened, and her walk so feeble. She was trying to check her sobs into composure, and (unconsciously) was striving to behave as she thought would best please her poor boy, whom she knew she had often grieved by her uncontrolled impatience. He had buried his face in his arms, which rested on the front of the dock (an attitude he retained during the greater part of his trial, and which prejudiced many against him).

The counsel began the examination.

"Your name is Jane Wilson, I believe?"

"Yes, sir."

"The mother of the prisoner at the bar?"

"Yes, sir," with quivering voice, ready to break out into weeping, but earning respect by the strong effort at self-control, prompted, as I have said before, by her earnest wish to please her son by her behaviour.

The barrister now proceeded to the important part of the examination, tending to prove that the gun found on the scene of the murder was the prisoner's. She had committed herself so fully to the policeman, that she could not well retract; so without much delay in bringing the question round to the desired point, the gun was produced in court, and the inquiry made—

"That gun belongs to your son, does it not?"

She clenched the sides of the witness-box in her efforts to make her parched tongue utter words. At last she moaned forth,

"Oh! Jem, Jem! what mun I say?"

Every one bent forward to hear the prisoner's answer; although, in fact, it was of little importance to the issue of the trial. He lifted up his head; and with a face brimming full of pity for his mother, yet resolved into endurance, said,

"Tell the truth, mother!"

And so she did, with the fidelity of a little child. Every one felt that she did; and the little colloquy between mother and son, did them some slight service in the opinion of the audience. But the awful judge sat unmoved; and the jurymen changed not a muscle of their countenances; while the counsel for the prosecution went triumphantly through this part of the case, including the fact of Jem's absence from home on the night of the murder, and bringing every admission to bear right against the prisoner.

It was over. She was told to go down. But she could no longer compel her mother's heart to keep silence, and suddenly turning towards the judge (with whom she imagined the verdict to rest), she thus addressed him with her choking voice:

"And now, sir, I've telled you the truth, and the whole truth, as *he* bid me; but don't ye let what I have said go for to hang him; oh, my lord judge, take my word for it, he's as innocent as the child as has yet to be born. For sure, I, who am his mother, and have nursed him on my knee, and been gladdened by the sight of him every day since, ought to know him better than yon pack of fellows" (indicating the jury, while she strove against her heart to render her words distinct and clear for her dear son's sake) "who, I'll go bail, never saw him before this morning in all their born days. My lord judge, he's so good I often wondered what harm there was in him; many is the time when I've been fretted (for I'm frabbit enough at times), when I've scold't myself, and said, 'You ungrateful thing, the Lord God has given you Jem, and isn't that blessing enough for you.' But He has seen fit to punish me. If Jem is—if Jem is—taken from me, I shall be a childless woman; and very poor, having nought left to love on earth, and I cannot say 'His will be done.' I cannot, my lord judge, oh, I cannot."

While sobbing out these words she was led away by the officers of the court, but tenderly, and reverently, with the respect which great sorrow commands.

The stream of evidence went on and on, gathering fresh force from every witness who was examined, and threatening to overwhelm poor Jem. Already they had proved that the gun was his, that he had been heard not many days before the commission of the deed to threaten the deceased; indeed, that the police had, at that time, been obliged to interfere, to prevent some probable act of violence. It only remained to bring forward a sufficient motive for the threat and the murder. The clue to this had been furnished by the policeman, who had overheard Jem's angry language to Mr. Carson; and his report in the first instance had occasioned the subpœna to Mary.

And now she was to be called on to bear witness. The court was by this time almost as full as it could hold; but fresh attempts were being made to squeeze in at all the entrances, for many were anxious to see and hear this part of the trial.

Old Mr. Carson felt an additional beat at his heart at the thought of seeing the fatal Helen,[1] the cause of all,—a kind of interest and yet repugnance, for was not she beloved by the dead; nay, perhaps in her way, loving and mourning for the same being that he himself was so bitterly grieving over? And yet he felt as if he abhorred her and her rumoured loveliness, as if she were the curse against him; and he grew jealous of the love with which she had inspired his son, and would fain have deprived her of even her natural right of sorrowing over her lover's untimely end: for you see it was a fixed idea in the minds of all, that the handsome, bright, gay, rich young gentleman must have been beloved in preference to the serious, almost stern-looking smith, who had to toil for his daily bread.

Hitherto the effect of the trial had equalled Mr. Carson's most sanguine hopes, and a severe look of satisfaction came over the face of the avenger,—over that countenance whence the smile had departed, never more to return.

All eyes were directed to the door through which the witnesses entered. Even Jem looked up to catch one glimpse, before he hid his face from her look of aversion. The officer had gone to fetch her.

She was in exactly the same attitude as when Job Legh had seen her two hours before through the half-open door. Not a finger had moved. The officer summoned her, but she did not stir. She was so still, he thought she had fallen asleep, and he stepped forward and touched her. She started up in an instant, and followed him with a kind of rushing rapid motion into the court, into the witness-box.

And amid all that sea of faces, misty and swimming before her eyes, she saw but two clear bright spots, distinct and fixed: the judge, who might have to condemn; and the prisoner, who might have to die.

The mellow sunlight streamed down that high window on her

---

1. Helen of Troy whose abduction by Paris caused the Trojan wars.

head, and fell on the rich treasure of her golden hair, stuffed away in masses under her little bonnet-cap; and in those warm beams the motes kept dancing up and down. The wind had changed—had changed almost as soon as she had given up her watching; the wind had changed, and she heeded it not.

Many who were looking for mere flesh and blood beauty, mere colouring, were disappointed; for her face was deadly white, and almost set in its expression, while a mournful bewildered soul looked out of the depths of those soft, deep, grey eyes. But others recognised a higher and a stranger kind of beauty; one that would keep its hold on the memory for many after years.

I was not there myself; but one who was, told me that her look, and indeed her whole face, was more like the well-known engraving from Guido's picture of "Beatrice Cenci"[2] than anything else he could give me an idea of. He added, that her countenance haunted him, like the remembrance of some wild sad melody, heard in childhood; that it would perpetually recur with its mute imploring agony.

With all the court reeling before her (always save and except those awful two), she heard a voice speak, and answered the simple inquiry (something about her name) mechanically, as if in a dream. So she went on for two or three more questions, with a strange wonder in her brain, at the reality of the terrible circumstances in which she was placed.

Suddenly she was roused, she knew not how or by what. She was conscious that all was real, that hundreds were looking at her, that true-sounding words were being extracted from her; that that figure, so bowed down, with the face concealed with both hands, was really Jem. Her face flashed scarlet, and then, paler than before. But in dread of herself, with the tremendous secret imprisoned within her, she exerted every power she had to keep in the full understanding of what was going on, of what she was asked, and of what she answered. With all her faculties preternaturally alive and sensitive, she heard the next question from the pert young barrister, who was delighted to have the examination of this witness.

"And pray, may I ask, which was the favoured lover? You say you knew both these young men. Which was the favoured lover? Which did you prefer?"

And who was he, the questioner, that he should dare so lightly to ask of her heart's secrets? That he should dare to ask her to tell, before that multitude assembled there, what woman usually whispers with blushes and tears, and many hesitations, to one ear alone?

So, for an instant, a look of indignation contracted Mary's brow, as

---

2. The portrait of Beatrice Cenci (1577–1599), who was beheaded for having killed her father after he raped her, was attributed to Guido Reni (1575–1642). The portrait, however, is not of Beatrice, and it was painted by Gian-Francesco Barbieri ("Guercino") (1591–1666).

she steadily met the eyes of the impertinent counsellor. But, in that instant, she saw the hands removed from a face beyond, behind; and a countenance revealed of such intense love and woe,—such a deprecating dread of her answer; and suddenly her resolution was taken. The present was everything; the future, that vast shroud, it was maddening to think upon; but *now* she might own her fault, but *now* she might even own her love. Now, when the beloved stood thus, abhorred of men, there would be no feminine shame to stand between her and her avowal. So she also turned towards the judge, partly to mark that her answer was not given to the monkeyfied man who questioned her, and likewise that the face might be averted from, and her eyes not gaze upon, the form that contracted with the dread of the words he anticipated.

"He asks me which of them two I liked best. Perhaps I liked Mr. Harry Carson once—I don't know—I've forgotten; but I loved James Wilson, that's now on trial, above what tongue can tell—above all else on earth put together; and I love him now better than ever, though he has never known a word of it till this minute. For you see, sir, mother died before I was thirteen, before I could know right from wrong about some things; and I was giddy and vain, and ready to listen to any praise of my good looks; and this poor young Mr. Carson fell in with me, and told me he loved me; and I was foolish enough to think he meant me marriage: a mother is a pitiful loss to a girl, sir; and so I used to fancy I could like to be a lady, and rich, and never know want any more. I never found out how dearly I loved another till one day, when James Wilson asked me to marry him, and I was very hard and sharp in my answer (for, indeed, sir, I'd a deal to bear just then), and he took me at my word and left me; and from that day to this I've never spoken a word to him, or set eyes on him; though I'd fain have done so, to try and show him we had both been too hasty; for he'd not been gone out of my sight above a minute before I knew I loved—far above my life," said she, dropping her voice as she came to this second confession of the strength of her attachment. "But, if the gentleman asks me which I loved the best, I make answer, I was flattered by Mr. Carson, and pleased with his flattery; but James Wilson I——"

She covered her face with her hands, to hide the burning scarlet blushes, which even dyed her fingers.

There was a little pause; still, though her speech might inspire pity for the prisoner, it only strengthened the supposition of his guilt. Presently the counsellor went on with his examination.

"But you have seen young Mr. Carson since your rejection of the prisoner?"

"Yes, often."

"You have spoken to him, I conclude, at these times."

"Only once, to call speaking."

"And what was the substance of your conversation? Did you tell him you found you preferred his rival?"

"No, sir, I don't think as I've done wrong in saying, now as things stand, what my feelings are; but I never would be so bold as to tell one young man I cared for another. I never named Jem's name to Mr. Carson. Never."

"Then what did you say when you had this final conversation with Mr. Carson? You can give me the substance of it, if you don't remember the words."

"I'll try, sir; but I'm not very clear. I told him I could not love him, and wished to have nothing more to do with him. He did his best to over-persuade me, but I kept steady, and at last I ran off."

"And you never spoke to him again?"

"Never!"

"Now, young woman, remember you are upon your oath. Did you ever tell the prisoner at the bar of Mr. Henry Carson's attentions to you? of your acquaintance, in short? Did you ever try to excite his jealousy by boasting of a lover so far above you in station?"

"Never. I never did," said she, in so firm and distinct a manner as to leave no doubt.

"Were you aware that he knew of Mr. Henry Carson's regard for you? Remember you are on your oath!"

"Never, sir. I was not aware until I heard of the quarrel between them, and what Jem had said to the policeman, and that was after the murder. To this day I can't make out who told Jem. Oh, sir, may not I go down?"

For she felt the sense, the composure, the very bodily strength which she had compelled to her aid for a time, suddenly giving way, and was conscious that she was losing all command over herself. There was no occasion to detain her longer; she had done her part. She might go down. The evidence was still stronger against the prisoner; but now he stood erect and firm, with self-respect in his attitude, and a look of determination on his face, which almost made it appear noble. Yet he seemed lost in thought.

Job Legh had all this time been trying to sooth and comfort Mrs. Wilson, who would first be in the court, in order to see her darling, and then, when her sobs became irrepressible, had to be led out into the open air, and sat there weeping, on the steps of the court-house. Who would have taken charge of Mary, on her release from the witness-box, I do not know, if Mrs. Sturgis, the boatman's wife, had not been there, brought by her interest in Mary, towards whom she now pressed, in order to urge her to leave the scene of the trial.

"No! no!" said Mary, to this proposition. "I must be here. I must watch that they don't hang him, you know I must."

"Oh! they'll not hang him! never fear! Besides, the wind has changed, and that's in his favour. Come away. You're so hot, and first white and then red; I'm sure you're ill. Just come away."

"Oh! I don't know about any thing but that I must stay," replied Mary, in a strange hurried manner, catching hold of some rails as if she feared some bodily force would be employed to remove her. So Mrs. Sturgis just waited patiently by her, every now and then peeping among the congregation of heads in the body of the court, to see if her husband were still there. And there he always was to be seen, looking and listening with all his might. His wife felt easy that he would not be wanting her at home until the trial was ended.

Mary never let go her clutched hold on the rails. She wanted them to steady her, in that heaving, whirling court. She thought the feeling of something hard compressed within her hand would help her to listen, for it was such pain, such weary pain in her head, to strive to attend to what was being said. They were all at sea, sailing away on billowy waves, and every one speaking at once, and no one heeding her father, who was calling on them to be silent, and listen to him. Then again, for a brief second, the court stood still, and she could see the judge, sitting up there like an idol, with his trappings, so rigid and stiff; and Jem, opposite, looking at her, as if to say, am I to die for what you know your——. Then she checked herself, and by a great struggle brought herself round to an instant's sanity. But the round of thought never stood still; and off she went again; and every time her power of struggling against the growing delirium grew fainter and fainter. She muttered low to herself, but no one heard her except her neighbour, Mrs. Sturgis; all were too closely attending to the case for the prosecution, which was now being wound up.

The counsel for the prisoner had avoided much cross-examination, reserving to himself the right of calling the witnesses forward again; for he had received so little, and such vague instructions, and understood that so much depended on the evidence of one who was not forthcoming, that in fact he had little hope of establishing anything like a show of a defence, and contented himself with watching the case, and lying in wait for any legal objections that might offer themselves. He lay back on the seat, occasionally taking a pinch of snuff, in a manner intended to be contemptuous; now and then elevating his eyebrows, and sometimes exchanging a little note with Mr. Bridgenorth behind him. The attorney had far more interest in the case than the barrister, to which he was perhaps excited by his poor old friend Job Legh; who had edged and wedged himself through the crowd close to Mr. Bridgenorth's elbow, sent thither by Ben Sturgis, to whom he had been "introduced" by Charley Jones, and who had accounted for Mary's disappearance on the preceding day, and spoken of their chase, their fears, their hopes.

All this was told in a few words to Mr. Bridgenorth—so few, that they gave him but a confused idea, that time was of value; and this he named to his counsel, who now rose to speak for the defence.

Job Legh looked about for Mary, now he had gained, and given, some idea of the position of things. At last he saw her, standing by a decent looking woman, looking flushed and anxious, and moving her lips incessantly, as if eagerly talking; her eyes never resting on any object, but wandering about as if in search of something. Job thought it was for him she was seeking, and he struggled to get round to her. When he had succeeded, she took no notice of him, although he spoke to her, but still kept looking round and round in the same wild, restless manner. He tried to hear the low quick mutterings of her voice; he caught the repetition of the same words over and over again:

"I must not go mad. I must not, indeed. They say people tell the truth when they're mad; but I don't. I was always a liar. I was, indeed; but I'm not mad. I must not go mad. I must not, indeed."

Suddenly she seemed to become aware how earnestly Job was listening (with mournful attention) to her words, and turning sharp round upon him, with upbraiding, for his eaves-dropping, on her lips, she caught sight of something,—or some one,—who, even in that state, had power to arrest her attention; and throwing up her arms with wild energy, she shrieked aloud,

"Oh, Jem! Jem! you're saved; and I *am* mad——" and was instantly seized with convulsions. With much commiseration she was taken out of court, while the attention of many was diverted from her, by the fierce energy with which a sailor forced his way over rails and seats, against turnkeys and policemen. The officers of the court opposed this forcible manner of entrance, but they could hardly induce the offender to adopt any quieter way of attaining his object, and telling his tale in the witness-box, the legitimate place. For Will had dwelt so impatiently on the danger in which his absence would place his cousin, that even yet he seemed to fear that he might see the prisoner carried off, and hung, before he could pour out the narrative which would exculpate him. As for Job Legh, his feelings were all but uncontrollable; as you may judge by the indifference with which he saw Mary borne, stiff and convulsed, out of the court, in the charge of the kind Mrs. Sturgis, who, you will remember, was an utter stranger to him.

"She'll keep! I'll not trouble myself about her," said he to himself, as he wrote with trembling hands a little note of information to Mr. Bridgenorth, who had conjectured, when Will had first disturbed the awful tranquillity of the life-and-death court, that the witness had arrived (better late than never) on whose evidence rested all the slight chance yet remaining to Jem Wilson of escaping death. During the commotion in the court, among all the cries and commands, the dismay and the directions, consequent upon Will's entrance, and poor Mary's fearful attack of illness, Mr. Bridgenorth had kept his lawyer-like presence of mind; and long before Job Legh's almost illegible note was poked at him, he had recapitulated the facts on which Will had to give evidence, and the manner in which he had been pursued, after his ship had taken her leave of the land.

The barrister who defended Jem took new heart when he was put in possession of these striking points to be adduced, not so much out of earnestness to save the prisoner, of whose innocence he was still doubtful, as because he saw the opportunities for the display of forensic eloquence which were presented by the facts; "a gallant tar brought back from the pathless ocean by a girl's noble daring," "the dangers of too hastily judging from circumstantial evidence," &c. &c.; while the counsellor for the prosecution prepared himself by folding his arms, elevating his eyebrows, and putting his lips in the form in which they might best whistle down the wind such evidence as might be produced by a suborned witness, who dared to perjure himself. For, of course, it is etiquette to suppose that such evidence as may be given against the opinion which lawyers are paid to uphold, is any thing but based on truth; and "perjury," "conspiracy," and "peril of your immortal soul," are light expressions to throw at the heads of those who may prove (not the speaker, there would then be some excuse for the hasty words of personal anger, but) the hirer of the speaker to be wrong, or mistaken.

But when once Will had attained his end, and felt that his tale, or part of a tale, would be heard by judge and jury; when once he saw Jem standing safe and well before him (even though he saw him pale and care-worn at the felons' bar), his courage took the shape of presence of mind, and he awaited the examination with a calm, unflinching intelligence, which dictated the clearest and most pertinent answers. He told the story you know so well: how his leave of absence being nearly expired, he had resolved to fulfil his promise, and go to see an uncle residing in the Isle of Man; how his money (sailor-like) was all expended in Manchester, and how, consequently, it had been necessary for him to walk to Liverpool, which he had accordingly done on the very night of the murder, accompanied as far as Hollins Green by his friend and cousin, the prisoner at the bar. He was clear and distinct in every corroborative circumstance, and gave a short account of the singular way in which he had been recalled from his outward-bound voyage, and the terrible anxiety he had felt, as the pilot-boat had struggled home against the wind. The jury felt that their opinion (so nearly decided half an hour ago) was shaken and disturbed in a very uncomfortable and perplexing way, and were almost grateful to the counsel for the prosecution, when he got up, with a brow of thunder, to demolish the evidence, which was so bewildering when taken in connexion with every thing previously adduced. But if such, without looking to the consequences, was the first impulsive feeling of some among the jury, how shall I describe the vehemence of passion which possessed the mind of poor Mr. Carson, as he saw the effect of the young sailor's statement? It never shook his belief in Jem's guilt in the least, that attempt at an *alibi*; his hatred, his longing for vengeance, having once defined an object to itself, could no more bear to be frustrated and disappointed, than the beast of prey can submit to have his victim taken from his hungry jaws. No more likeness to the calm stern power of Jupiter was there in that white eager face, almost distorted by its fell anxiety of expression.

The counsel to whom etiquette assigned the cross-examination of Will, caught the look on Mr. Carson's face, and in his desire to further the intense wish there manifested, he over-shot his mark even in his first insulting question:

"And now, my man, you've told the court a very good and very convincing story; no reasonable man ought to doubt the unstained innocence of your relation at the bar. Still there is one circumstance you have forgotten to name; and I feel that without it your evidence is rather incomplete. Will you have the kindness to inform the gentlemen of the jury what has been your charge for repeating this very plausible story? How much good coin of her Majesty's realm have you received, or are you to receive, for walking up from the Docks, or some less creditable place, and uttering the tale you have just now repeated,—very much to the credit of your instructor, I must say? Remember, sir, you are upon oath."

It took Will a minute to extract the meaning from the garb of unaccustomed words in which it was invested, and during this time he looked a little confused. But the instant the truth flashed upon him he fixed his bright clear eyes, flaming with indignation, upon the counsellor, whose look fell at last before that stern unflinching gaze. Then, and not till then, Will made answer:

"Will you tell the judge and jury how much money you've been paid for your impudence towards one who has told God's blessed truth, and who would scorn to tell a lie, or blackguard any one, for the biggest fee as ever lawyer got for doing dirty work? Will you tell, sir?— But I'm ready, my lord judge, to take my oath as many times as your lordship or the jury would like, to testify to things having happened just as I said. There's O'Brien, the pilot, in court now. Would somebody with a wig on please to ask him how much he can say for me?"

It was a good idea, and caught at by the counsel for the defence. O'Brien gave just such testimony as was required to clear Will from all suspicion. He had witnessed the pursuit, he had heard the conversation which took place between the boat and the ship; he had given Will a homeward passage in his boat. And the character of an accredited pilot, appointed by the Trinity House,[3] was known to be above suspicion.

Mr. Carson sank back on his seat in sickening despair. He knew enough of courts to be aware of the extreme unwillingness of juries to convict, even where the evidence is most clear, when the penalty of such conviction is death. At the period of the trial most condemnatory to the prisoner, he had repeated this fact to himself, in order to damp his too certain expectation of a conviction. Now it needed not repetition, for it forced itself upon his consciousness, and he seemed to *know*, even before the jury retired to consult, that by some trick, some negligence, some miserable hocus-pocus, the murderer of his child, his darling, his Absalom,[4] who had never rebelled,—the slayer of his unburied boy would slip through the fangs of justice, and walk free and unscathed over that earth where his son would never more be seen.

It was even so. The prisoner hid his face once more to shield the expression of an emotion he could not control, from the notice of the over-curious; Job Legh ceased his eager talking to Mr. Bridgenorth; Charley looked grave and earnest; for the jury filed one by one back into their box, and the question was asked to which such an awful answer might be given.

The verdict they had come to was unsatisfactory to themselves at last; neither being convinced of his innocence, nor yet quite willing to believe him guilty in the teeth of the *alibi*. But the punishment that awaited him, if guilty, was so terrible, and so unnatural a sentence for man to pronounce on man, that the knowledge of it had weighed down the scale on the side of innocence, and "Not Guilty" was the verdict that thrilled through the breathless court.

One moment of silence, and then the murmurs rose, as the verdict was discussed by all with lowered voice. Jem stood motionless, his head bowed; poor fellow, he was stunned with the rapid career of events during the last few hours.

He had assumed his place at the bar with little or no expectation of an acquittal; and with scarcely any desire for life, in the complication of occurrences tending to strengthen the idea of Mary's more than indifference to him; she had loved another, and in her mind Jem believed that he himself must be regarded as the murderer of him she loved. And suddenly, athwart this gloom which made Life seem such a blank expanse of desolation, there flashed the exquisite delight of hearing Mary's avowal of love, making the future all glorious, if a future in this world he might hope to have. He could not dwell on any

---

3. The licensing agency for the shipping industry in England named after its London office building.
4. King David's son who was killed after rebelling against his father. 2 Samuel 18:33.

thing but her words, telling of her passionate love; all else was indistinct, nor could he strive to make it otherwise. She loved him.

And Life, now full of tender images, suddenly bright with all exquisite promises, hung on a breath, the slenderest gossamer chance. He tried to think that the knowledge of her love would soothe him even in his dying hours; but the phantoms of what life with her might be, would obtrude, and made him almost gasp and reel under the uncertainty he was enduring. Will's appearance had only added to the intensity of this suspense.

The full meaning of the verdict could not at once penetrate his brain. He stood dizzy and motionless. Some one pulled his coat. He turned, and saw Job Legh, the tears stealing down his brown furrowed cheeks, while he tried in vain to command voice enough to speak. He kept shaking Jem by the hand, as the best and necessary expression of his feeling.

"Here, make yourself scarce! I should think you'd be glad to get out of that!" exclaimed the gaoler, as he brought up another livid prisoner, from out whose eyes came the anxiety which he would not allow any other feature to display.

Job Legh pressed out of court, and Jem followed unreasoningly.

The crowd made way, and kept their garments tight about them, as Jem passed, for about him there still hung the taint of the murderer.

He was in the open air, and free once more! Although many looked on him with suspicion, faithful friends closed round him; his arm was unresistingly pumped up and down by his cousin and Job; when one was tired, the other took up the wholesome exercise, while Ben Sturgis was working off his interest in the scene by scolding Charley for walking on his head round and round Mary's sweetheart, for a sweetheart he was now satisfactorily ascertained to be, in spite of her assertion to the contrary. And all this time Jem himself felt bewildered and dazzled; he would have given any thing for an hour's uninterrupted thought on the occurrences of the past week, and the new visions raised up during the morning; ay, even though that tranquil hour were to be passed in the hermitage of his quiet prison cell. The first question sobbed out by his choking voice, oppressed with emotion, was,

"Where is she?"

They led him to the room where his mother sat. They had told her of her son's acquittal, and now she was laughing, and crying, and talking, and giving way to all those feelings which she had restrained with such effort during the last few days. They brought her son to her, and she threw herself upon his neck, weeping there. He returned her embrace, but looked around, beyond. Excepting his mother, there was no one in the room but the friends who had entered with him.

"Eh, lad!" she said, when she found voice to speak. "See what it is to have behaved thysel! I could put in a good word for thee, and the jury could na go and hang thee in the face of th' character I gave thee. Was na it a good thing they did na keep me from Liverpool? But I would come; I knew I could do thee good, bless thee, my lad. But thou'rt very white, and all of a tremble."

He kissed her again and again, but looking round as if searching for some one he could not find, the first words he uttered were still—

"Where is she?"

Chapter XXXIII.

"Fear no more the heat o' th' sun,
    Nor the furious winter's rages;
Thou thy worldly task hast done,
    Home art gone and ta'en thy wages."

CYMBELINE.[5]

"While day and night can bring delight,
    Or nature aught of pleasure give;
While joys above my mind can move
    For thee, and thee alone I live:

"When that grim foe of joy below
    Comes in between to make us part,
The iron hand that breaks our band,
    It breaks my bliss—it breaks my heart."

BURNS.[6]

She was where no words of peace, no soothing hopeful tidings could reach her; in the ghastly spectral world of delirium. Hour after hour, day after day, she started up with passionate cries on her father to save Jem; or rose wildly, imploring the winds and waves, the pitiless winds and waves, to have mercy; and over and over again she exhausted her feverish fitful strength in these agonised entreaties, and fell back powerless, uttering only the wailing moans of despair. They told her Jem was safe, they brought him before her eyes; but sight and hearing were no longer channels of information to that poor distracted brain, nor could human voice penetrate to her understanding.

Jem alone gathered the full meaning of some of her strange sentences, and perceived that, by some means or other, she, like himself, had divined the truth of her father being the murderer.

Long ago (reckoning time by events and thoughts, and not by clock or dial-plate), Jem had felt certain that Mary's father was Harry Carson's murderer; and although the motive was in some measure a mys-

---

5. Shakespeare's *Cymbeline* 4.2.259–62.
6. Robert Burns's "The Day Returns" (1788) slightly misquoted; "foe of joy" should read "foe of life."

tery, yet a whole train of circumstances (the principal of which was that John Barton had borrowed the fatal gun only two days before) had left no doubt in Jem's mind. Sometimes he thought that John had discovered, and thus bloodily resented, the attentions which Mr. Carson had paid to his daughter; at others, he believed the motive to exist in the bitter feuds between the masters and their workpeople, in which Barton was known to take so keen an interest. But if he had felt himself pledged to preserve this secret, even when his own life was the probable penalty, and he believed he should fall execrated by Mary as the guilty destroyer of her lover, how much more was he bound now to labour to prevent any word of hers from inculpating her father, now that she was his own; now that she had braved so much to rescue him; and now that her poor brain had lost all guiding and controlling power over her words.

All that night long Jem wandered up and down the narrow precincts of Ben Sturgis's house. In the little bedroom where Mrs. Sturgis alternately tended Mary, and wept over the violence of her illness, he listened to her ravings; each sentence of which had its own peculiar meaning and reference, intelligible to his mind, till her words rose to the wild pitch of agony, that no one could alleviate, and he could bear it no longer, and stole, sick and miserable, down-stairs, where Ben Sturgis thought it his duty to snore away in an arm-chair instead of his bed, under the idea that he should thus be more ready for active service, such as fetching the doctor to revisit his patient.

Before it was fairly light, Jem (wide awake, and listening with an earnest attention he could not deaden, however painful its results proved) heard a gentle subdued knock at the house door; it was no business of his, to be sure, to open it, but as Ben slept on, he thought he would see who the early visitor might be, and ascertain if there was any occasion for disturbing either host or hostess. It was Job Legh who stood there, distinct against the outer light of the street.

"How is she? Eh! poor soul! is that her? No need to ask! How strange her voice sounds! Screech! screech! and she so low, sweet-spoken, when she's well! Thou must keep up heart, old boy, and not look so dismal, thysel."

"I can't help it, Job; it's past a man's bearing to hear such a one as she is, going on as she is doing; even if I did not care for her, it would cut me sore to see one so young, and—I can't speak of it, Job, as a man should do," said Jem, his sobs choking him.

"Let me in, will you?" said Job, pushing past him, for all this time Jem had stood holding the door, unwilling to admit Job where he might hear so much that would be suggestive to one acquainted with the parties that Mary named.

"I'd more than one reason for coming betimes. I wanted to hear how yon poor wench was;—that stood first. Late last night I got a letter from Margaret, very anxious-like. The doctor says the old lady yonder can't last many days longer, and it seems so lonesome for her to die with no one but Margaret and Mrs. Davenport about her. So I thought I'd just come and stay with Mary Barton, and see as she's well done to, and you and your mother and Will go and take leave of old Alice."

Jem's countenance, sad at best just now, fell lower and lower. But Job went on with his speech.

"She still wanders, Margaret says, and thinks she's with her mother at home; but for all that, she should have some kith and kin near her to close her eyes, to my thinking."

"Could not you and Will take mother home? I'd follow when——" Jem faltered out thus far, when Job interrupted,

"Lad! if thou knew what thy mother has suffered for thee, thou'd not speak of leaving her just when she's got thee from the grave as it were. Why, this very night she roused me up, and 'Job,' says she, 'I ask your pardon for wakening you, but tell me, am I awake or dreaming? Is Jem proved innocent? Oh, Job Legh! God send I've not been only dreaming it!' For thou see'st she can't rightly understand why thou'rt with Mary, and not with her. Ay, ay! I know why; but a mother only gives up her son's heart inch by inch to his wife, and then she gives it up with a grudge. No, Jem! thou must go with thy mother just now, if ever thou hopest for God's blessing. She's a widow, and has none but thee. Never fear for Mary! She's young, and will struggle through. They are decent people, these folk she is with, and I'll watch o'er her as though she was my own poor girl, that lies cold enough in London-town. I grant ye, it's hard enough for her to be left among strangers. To my mind, John Barton would be more in the way of his duty, look-ing after his daughter, than delegating it up and down the country, looking after every one's business but his own."

A new idea and a new fear came into Jem's mind. What if Mary should implicate her father?

"She raves terribly," said he. "All night long she's been speaking of her father, and mixing up thoughts of him with the trial she saw yes-terday. I should not wonder if she'll speak of him as being in court next thing."

"I should na wonder, either," answered Job. "Folk in her way say many and many a strange thing; and th' best way is never to mind them. Now you take your mother home, Jem, and stay by her till old Alice is gone, and trust me for seeing after Mary."

Jem felt how right Job was, and could not resist what he knew to be his duty, but I cannot tell you how heavy and sick at heart he was as he stood at the door to take a last fond, lingering look at Mary. He saw her sitting up in bed, her golden hair, dimmed with her one day's illness, floating behind her, her head bound round with wetted cloths, her features all agitated, even to distortion, with the pangs of her anxiety.

Her lover's eyes filled with tears. He could not hope. The elasticity of his heart had been crushed out of him by early sorrows; and now, especially, the dark side of everything seemed to be presented to him. What if she died, just when he knew the treasure, the untold treasure he possessed in her love! What if (worse than death) she remained a poor gibbering maniac all her life long (and mad people do live to be old sometimes, even under all the pressure of their burden), terror-distracted as she was now, and no one able to comfort her!

"Jem!" said Job, partly guessing the other's feelings by his own. "Jem!" repeated he, arresting his attention before he spoke. Jem turned round, the little motion causing the tears to overflow and trickle down his cheeks. "Thou must trust in God, and leave her in his hands." He spoke hushed, and low; but the words sank all the more into Jem's heart, and gave him strength to tear himself away.

He found his mother (notwithstanding that she had but just regained her child through Mary's instrumentality) half inclined to resent his having passed the night in anxious devotion to the poor invalid. She dwelt on the duties of children to their parents (above all others), till Jem could hardly believe the relative positions they had held only yesterday, when she was struggling with and controlling every instinct of her nature, only because *he* wished it. However, the recollection of that yesterday, with its hair's breadth between him and a felon's death, and the love that had lightened the dark shadow, made him bear with the meekness and patience of a true-hearted man all the worrying little acerbities of to-day; and he had no small merit in doing so; for in him, as in his mother, the re-action after intense excitement had produced its usual effect in increased irritability of the nervous system.

They found Alice alive, and without pain. And that was all. A child of a few weeks old would have had more bodily strength; a child of a very few months old, more consciousness of what was passing before her. But even in this state she diffused an atmosphere of peace around her. True, Will, at first, wept passionate tears at the sight of her, who had been as a mother to him, so standing on the confines of life. But even now, as always, loud passionate feeling could not long endure in the calm of her presence. The firm faith which her mind had no longer power to grasp, had left its trail of glory; for by no other word can I call the bright happy look which illumined the old earth-worn face. Her talk, it is true, bore no more that constant earnest reference to God and His holy word which it had done in health, and there were no deathbed words of exhortation from the lips of one so habitually pious. For still she imagined herself once again in the happy, happy realms of child-hood; and again dwelling in the lovely northern haunts where she had so often longed to be. Though earthly sight was gone away, she beheld again the scenes she had loved from long years ago! she saw them without a change to dim the old radiant hues. The long dead were with her, fresh and blooming as in those bygone days. And death came to her as a welcome blessing, like as evening comes to the weary child. Her work here was finished, and faithfully done.

What better sentence can an emperor wish to have said over his bier? In second childhood (that blessing clouded by a name), she said her "Nunc Dimittis,"[7]—the sweetest canticle to the holy.

"Mother, good night! Dear mother! bless me once more! I'm very tired, and would fain go to sleep." She never spoke again on this side heaven.

She died the day after their return from Liverpool. From that time, Jem became aware that his mother was jealously watching for some word or sign which should betoken his wish to return to Mary. And yet go to Liverpool he must and would, as soon as the funeral was over, if but for a simple glimpse of his darling. For Job had never written; indeed, any necessity for his so doing had never entered his head. If Mary died, he would announce it personally; if she recovered, he meant to bring her home with him. Writing was to him little more than an auxiliary to natural history; a way of ticketing specimens, not of expressing thoughts.

The consequence of this want of intelligence as to Mary's state was, that Jem was constantly anticipating that every person and every scrap of paper was to convey to him the news of her death. He could not endure this state long; but he resolved not to disturb the house by announcing to his mother his purposed intention of returning to Liverpool, until the dead had been carried forth.

On Sunday afternoon they laid her low with many tears. Will wept as one who would not be comforted.

The old childish feeling came over him, the feeling of loneliness at being left among strangers.

By-and-by, Margaret timidly stole near him, as if waiting to console; and soon his passion sank down to grief, and grief gave way to melancholy, and though he felt as if he never could be joyful again, he was all the while unconsciously approaching nearer to the full happiness of calling Margaret his own, and a golden thread was interwoven even now with the darkness of his sorrow. Yet it was on his arm that Jane Wilson leant on her return homewards. Jem took charge of Margaret.

"Margaret, I'm bound for Liverpool by the first train to-morrow; I must set your grandfather at liberty."

---

7. Latin translation of Luke 2:29–32, "The Song of Simeon": "Lord, now lettest thou thy servant depart in peace."

"I'm sure he likes nothing better than watching over poor Mary; he loves her nearly as well as me. But let me go! I have been so full of poor Alice, I've never thought of it before; I can't do so much as many a one, but Mary will like to have a woman about her that she knows. I'm sorry I waited to be reminded, Jem," replied Margaret, with some little self-reproach.

But Margaret's proposition did not at all agree with her companion's wishes. He found he had better speak out, and put his intention at once to the right motive; the subterfuge about setting Job Legh at liberty had done him harm instead of good.

"To tell truth, Margaret, it's I that must go, and that for my own sake, not your grandfather's. I can rest neither by night nor day for thinking on Mary. Whether she lives or dies, I look on her as my wife before God, as surely and solemnly as if we were married. So being, I have the greatest right to look after her, and I cannot yield it even to——"

"Her father," said Margaret, finishing his interrupted sentence. "It seems strange that a girl like her should be thrown on the bare world to struggle through so bad an illness. No one seems to know where John Barton is, else I thought of getting Morris to write him a letter telling him about Mary. I wish he was home, that I do!"

Jem could not echo this wish.

"Mary's not bad off for friends where she is," said he. "I call them friends, though a week ago we none of us knew there were such folks in the world. But being anxious and sorrowful about the same thing makes people friends quicker than anything, I think. She's like a mother to Mary in her ways; and he bears a good character, as far as I could learn just in that hurry. We're drawing near home, and I've not said my say, Margaret. I want you to look after mother a bit. She'll not like my going, and I've got to break it to her yet. If she takes it very badly, I'll come back to-morrow night; but if she's not against it very much, I mean to stay till it's settled about Mary, one way or the other. Will, you know, will be there, Margaret, to help a bit in doing for mother."

Will's being there made the only objection Margaret saw to this plan. She disliked the idea of seeming to throw herself in his way, and yet she did not like to say anything of this feeling to Jem, who had all along seemed perfectly unconscious of any love-affair, besides his own, in progress.

So Margaret gave a reluctant consent.

"If you can just step up to our house to night, Jem, I'll put up a few things as may be useful to Mary, and then you can say when you'll likely be back. If you come home to-morrow night, and Will's there, perhaps I need not step up?"

"Yes, Margaret, do! I shan't leave easy unless you go some time in the day to see mother. I'll come to-night, though; and now good-by. Stay! do you think you could just coax poor Will to walk a bit home with you, that I might speak to mother by myself?"

No! that Margaret could not do. That was expecting too great a sacrifice of bashful feeling.

But the object was accomplished by Will's going upstairs immediately on their return to the house, to indulge his mournful thoughts alone. As soon as Jem and his mother were left by themselves, he began on the subject uppermost in his mind.

"Mother!"

She put her handkerchief from her eyes, and turned quickly round so as to face him where he stood, thinking what best to say. The little action annoyed him, and he rushed at once into the subject.

"Mother! I am going back to Liverpool to-morrow morning to see how Mary Barton is."

"And what's Mary Barton to thee, that thou shouldst be running after her in that-a-way?"

"If she lives, she shall be my wedded wife. If she dies—mother, I can't speak of what I shall feel if she dies." His voice was choked in his throat.

For an instant his mother was interested by his words; and then came back the old jealousy of being supplanted in the affections of that son, who had been, as it were, newly born to her, by the escape he had so lately experienced from danger. So she hardened her heart against entertaining any feeling of sympathy; and turned away from the face, which recalled the earnest look of his childhood, when he had come to her in some trouble, sure of help and comfort.

And coldly she spoke, in those tones which Jem knew and dreaded, even before the meaning they expressed was fully shaped. "Thou'rt old enough to please thysel. Old mothers are cast aside, and what they've borne forgotten as soon as a pretty face comes across. I might have thought of that last Tuesday, when I felt as if thou wert all my own, and the judge were some wild animal trying to rend thee from me. I spoke up for thee then; but it's all forgotten now, I suppose."

"Mother! you know all this while, *you know* I can never forget any kindness you've ever done for me; and they've been many. Why should you think I've only room for one love in my heart? I can love you as dearly as ever, and Mary too, as much as man ever loved woman."

He awaited a reply. None was vouchsafed.

"Mother, answer me!" said he, at last.

"What mun I answer? You asked me no question."

"Well! I ask you this now. To-morrow morning I go to Liverpool to see her who is as my wife. Dear mother! will you bless me on my errand? If it please God she recovers, will you take her to you as you would a daughter?"

She could neither refuse nor assent.

"Why need you go?" said she querulously, at length. "You'll be getting in some mischief or another again. Can't you stop at home quiet with me?"

Jem got up, and walked about the room in despairing impatience. She would not understand his feelings. At last he stopped right before the place where she was sitting, with an air of injured meekness on her face.

"Mother! I often think what a good man father was! I've often heard you tell of your courting days; and of the accident that befel you, and how ill you were. How long is it ago?"

"Near upon five-and-twenty years," said she, with a sigh.

"You little thought when you were so ill you should live to have such a fine strapping son as I am, did you now?"

She smiled a little, and looked up at him, which was just what he wanted.

"Thou'rt not so fine a man as thy father was, by a deal;" said she, looking at him with much fondness, notwithstanding her depreciatory words.

He took another turn or two up and down the room. He wanted to bend the subject round to his own case.

"Those were happy days when father was alive!"

"You may say so, lad! Such days as will never come again to me, at any rate." She sighed sorrowfully.

"Mother!" said he, at last, stopping short, and taking her hand in his with tender affection, "you'd like me to be as happy a man as my father was before me, would not you? You'd like me to have some one to make me as happy as you made father? Now, would not you, dear mother?"

"I did not make him as happy as I might ha' done," murmured she, in a low, sad voice of self-reproach. "Th' accident gave a jar to my temper it's never got the better of; and now he's gone, where he can never know how I grieve for having frabbed[8] him as I did."

"Nay, mother, we don't know that!" said Jem, with gentle soothing. "Any how, you and father got along with as few rubs as most people. But for *his* sake, dear mother, don't say me nay, now that I come to you to ask your blessing before setting out to see her, who is to be my wife, if ever woman is; for *his* sake, if not for mine, love her who I shall bring home to be to me all you were to him: and, mother! I do not ask for a truer or a tenderer heart than yours is, in the long run."

The hard look left her face; though her eyes were still averted from Jem's gaze, it was more because they were brimming over with tears, called forth by his words, than because any angry feeling yet

8. Nagged, worried.

remained. And when his manly voice died away in low pleadings, she lifted up her hands, and bent down her son's head below the level of her own; and then she solemnly uttered a blessing.

"God bless thee, Jem, my own dear lad. And may He bless Mary Barton for thy sake."

Jem's heart leapt up, and from this time hope took the place of fear in his anticipations with regard to Mary.

"Mother! you show your own true self to Mary, and she'll love you as dearly as I do."

So with some few smiles, and some few tears, and much earnest talking, the evening wore away.

"I must be off to see Margaret. Why, it's near ten o'clock! Could you have thought it? Now don't you stop up for me, mother. You and Will go to bed, for you've both need of it. I shall be home in an hour."

Margaret had felt the evening long and lonely; and was all but giving up the thoughts of Jem's coming that night, when she heard his step at the door.

He told her of his progress with his mother; he told her his hopes, and was silent on the subject of his fears.

"To think how sorrow and joy are mixed up together. You'll date your start in life as Mary's acknowledged lover from poor Alice Wilson's burial day. Well! the dead are soon forgotten!"

"Dear Margaret! But you're worn out with your long evening waiting for me. I don't wonder. But never you, nor any one else, think because God sees fit to call up new interests, perhaps right out of the grave, that therefore the dead are forgotten. Margaret, you yourself can remember our looks, and fancy what we're like."

"Yes! but what has that to do with remembering Alice?"

"Why, just this. You're not always trying to think on our faces, and making a labour of remembering; but often, I'll be bound, when you're sinking off to sleep, or when you're very quiet and still, the faces you knew so well when you could see, come smiling before you with loving looks. Or you remember them, without striving after it, and without thinking it's your duty to keep recalling them. And so it is with them that are hidden from our sight. If they've been worthy to be heartily loved while alive, they'll not be forgotten when dead; it's against nature. And we need no more be upbraiding ourselves for letting in God's rays of light upon our sorrow, and no more be fearful of forgetting them, because their memory is not always haunting and taking up our minds, than you need to trouble yourself about remembering your grandfather's face, or what the stars were like,—you can't forget if you would, what it's such a pleasure to think about. Don't fear my forgetting aunt Alice."

"I'm not, Jem; not now, at least; only you seemed so full about Mary."

"I've kept it down so long, remember. How glad aunt Alice would have been to know that I might hope to have her for my wife! that's to say if God spares her!"

"She would not have known it, even if you could have told her this last fortnight,—ever since you went away she's been thinking always that she was a little child at her mother's apron-string. She must have been a happy little thing; it was such a pleasure to her to think about those early days, when she lay old and gray on her deathbed."

"I never knew any one seem more happy all her life long."

"Ay! and how gentle and easy her death was! She thought her mother was near her."

They fell into calm thought about those last peaceful, happy hours. It struck eleven. Jem started up.

"I should have been gone long ago. Give me the bundle. You'll not forget my mother. Good night Margaret."

She let him out and bolted the door behind him. He stood on the steps to adjust some fastening about the bundle. The court, the street, was deeply still. Long ago all had retired to rest on that quiet Sabbath evening. The stars shone down on the silent deserted streets, and the clear soft moonlight fell in bright masses, leaving the steps on which Jem stood in shadow.

A foot-fall was heard along the pavement; slow and heavy was the sound. Before Jem had ended his little piece of business, a form had glided into sight; a wan, feeble figure, bearing with evident and painful labour a jug of water from the neighbouring pump. It went before Jem, turned up the court at the corner of which he was standing, passed into the broad, calm light; and there, with bowed head, sinking and shrunk body, Jem recognised John Barton.

No haunting ghost could have had less of the energy of life in its involuntary motions than he, who, nevertheless, went on with the same measured clockwork tread until the door of his own house was reached. And then he disappeared, and the latch fell feebly to, and made a faint and wavering sound, breaking the solemn silence of the night. Then all again was still.

For a minute or two Jem stood motionless, stunned by the thoughts which the sight of Mary's father had called up.

Margaret did not know he was at home: had he stolen like a thief by dead of night into his own dwelling? Depressed as Jem had often and long seen him, this night there was something different about him still; beaten down by some inward storm, he seemed to grovel along, all self-respect lost and gone.

Must he be told of Mary's state? Jem felt he must not; and this for many reasons. He could not be informed of her illness without many other particulars being communicated at the same time, of which it were better he should be kept in ignorance; indeed, of which Mary

herself could alone give the full explanation. No suspicion that he
was the criminal seemed hitherto to have been excited in the mind of
any one. Added to these reasons was Jem's extreme unwillingness to
face him, with the belief in his breast that he, and none other, had
done the fearful deed.

It was true that he was Mary's father, and as such had every right
to be told of all concerning her; but supposing he were, and that he
followed the impulse so natural to a father, and wished to go to her,
what might be the consequences? Among the mingled feelings she
had revealed in her delirium, ay, mingled even with the most tender
expressions of love for her father, was a sort of horror of him; a dread
of him as a blood-shedder, which seemed to separate him into two
persons,—one, the father who had dandled her on his knee, and
loved her all her life long; the other, the assassin, the cause of all her
trouble and woe.

If he presented himself before her while this idea of his character
was uppermost, who might tell the consequence?

Jem could not, and would not, expose her to any such fearful
chance: and to tell the truth, I believe he looked upon her as more
his own, to guard from all shadow of injury with most loving care,
than as belonging to any one else in this world, though girt with the
reverend name of Father, and guiltless of aught that might have less-
ened such reverence.

If you think this account of mine confused, of the half-feelings,
half-reasons, which passed through Jem's mind, as he stood gazing on
the empty space, where that crushed form had so lately been seen,—
if you are perplexed to disentangle the real motives, I do assure you
it was from just such an involved set of thoughts that Jem drew the
resolution to act as if he had not seen that phantom likeness of John
Barton; himself, yet not himself.

Chapter XXXIV.

> "*Dixwell.* Forgiveness! Oh, forgiveness, and a grave!
> *Mary.* God knows thy heart, my father! and I shudder
>   To think what thou perchance hast acted.
> *Dixwell.* Oh!
> *Mary.* No common load of woe is thine, my father."
>   Elliott's "KERHONAH."[9]

Mary still hovered between life and death when Jem arrived at the
house where she lay; and the doctors were as yet unwilling to compromise their wisdom by allowing too much hope to be entertained.

9. From Act I of Ebenezer Elliott's *Kerhonah* (1835).

But the state of things, if not less anxious, was less distressing than when Jem had quitted her. She lay now in a stupor, which was partly disease, and partly exhaustion after the previous excitement.

And now Jem found the difficulty which every one who has watched by a sick bed knows full well; and which is perhaps more insurmountable to men than it is to women,—the difficulty of being patient, and trying not to expect any visible change for long, long hours of sad monotony.

But after awhile the reward came. The laboured breathing became lower and softer, the heavy look of oppressive pain melted away from the face, and a languor that was almost peace took the place of suffering. She slept a natural sleep; and they stole about on tip-toe, and spoke low, and softly, and hardly dared to breathe, however much they longed to sigh out their thankful relief.

She opened her eyes. Her mind was in the tender state of a lately-born infant's. She was pleased with the gay but not dazzling colours of the paper; soothed by the subdued light; and quite sufficiently amused by looking at all the objects in the room—the drawing of the ships, the festoons of the curtain, the bright flowers on the painted backs of the chairs—to care for any stronger excitement. She wondered at the ball of glass, containing various-coloured sands from the Isle of Wight, or some other place, which hung suspended from the middle of the little valance over the window. But she did not care to exert herself to ask any questions, although she saw Mrs. Sturgis standing at the bedside with some tea, ready to drop it into her mouth by spoonfuls.

She did not see the face of honest joy, of earnest thankfulness, — the clasped hands,—the beaming eyes,—the trembling eagerness of gesture, of one who had long awaited her wakening, and who now stood behind the curtains watching through some little chink her every faint motion; or if she had caught a glimpse of that loving, peeping face, she was in too exhausted a state to have taken much notice, or have long retained the impression that he she loved so well was hanging about her, and blessing God for every conscious look which stole over her countenance.

She fell softly into slumber, without a word having been spoken by any one during that half hour of inexpressible joy. And again the stillness was enforced by sign and whispered word, but with eyes that beamed out their bright thoughts of hope. Jem sat by the side of the bed, holding back the little curtain, and gazing as if he could never gaze his fill at the pale, wasted face, so marbled and so chiselled in its wan outline.

She wakened once more; her soft eyes opened, and met his over-bending look. She smiled gently, as a baby does when it sees its mother tending its little cot; and continued her innocent, infantine gaze into his face, as if the sight gave her much unconscious pleasure. But by-and-by a different expression came into her sweet eyes; a look of memory and intelligence; her white flesh flushed the brightest rosy red, and with feeble motion she tried to hide her head in the pillow.

It required all Jem's self-control to do what he knew and felt to be necessary, to call Mrs. Sturgis, who was quietly dozing by the fireside; and that done, he felt almost obliged to leave the room to keep down the happy agitation which would gush out in every feature, every gesture, and every tone.

From that time forward, Mary's progress towards health was rapid.

There was every reason, but one, in favour of her speedy removal home. All Jem's duties lay in Manchester. It was his mother's dwelling-place, and there his plans for life had been to be worked out; plans, which the suspicion and imprisonment he had fallen into, had thrown for a time into a chaos, which his presence was required to arrange into form. For he might find, in spite of a jury's verdict, that too strong a taint was on his character for him ever to labour in Manchester again. He remembered the manner in which some one suspected of having been a convict was shunned by masters and men, when he had accidentally met with work in their foundry; the recollection smote him now, how he himself had thought it did not become an honest upright man to associate with one who had been a prisoner. He could not choose but think on that poor humble being, with his downcast conscious look; hunted out of the workshop, where he had sought to earn an honest livelihood, by the looks, and half-spoken words, and the black silence of repugnance (worse than words to bear), that met him on all sides.

Jem felt that his own character had been attainted; and that to many it might still appear suspicious. He knew that he could convince the world, by a future as blameless as his past had been, that he was innocent. But at the same time he saw that he must have patience, and nerve himself for some trials; and the sooner these were undergone, the sooner he was aware of the place he held in men's estimation, the better. He longed to have presented himself once more at the foundry; and then the reality would drive away the pictures that would (unbidden) come, of a shunned man, eyed askance by all, and driven forth to shape out some new career.

I said every reason "but one" inclined Jem to hasten Mary's return as soon as she was sufficiently convalescent. That one was the meeting which awaited her at home.

Turn it over as Jem would, he could not decide what was the best course to pursue. He could compel himself to any line of conduct that his reason and his sense of right told him to be desirable; but they did not tell him it was desirable to speak to Mary, in her tender state of mind and body, of her father. How much would be implied

by the mere mention of his name! Speak it as calmly, and as indifferently as he might, he could not avoid expressing some consciousness
of the terrible knowledge she possessed.

She, for her part, was softer and gentler than she had even been in
her gentlest mood; since her illness, her motions, her glances, her
voice were all tender in their languor. It seemed almost a trouble to
her to break the silence with the low sounds of her own sweet voice,
and her words fell sparingly on Jem's greedy, listening ear.

Her face was, however, so full of love and confidence, that Jem felt
no uneasiness at the state of silent abstraction into which she often
fell. If she did but love him, all would yet go right; and it was better
not to press for confidence on that one subject which must be
painful to both.

There came a fine, bright, balmy day. And Mary tottered once more
out into the open air, leaning on Jem's arm, and close to his beating
heart. And Mrs. Sturgis watched them from her door, with a blessing
on her lips, as they went slowly up the street.

They came in sight of the river. Mary shuddered.

"Oh Jem! take me home. Yon river seems all made of glittering,
heaving, dazzling metal, just as it did when I began to be ill."

Jem led her homewards. She dropped her head as searching for
something on the ground.

"Jem!" He was all attention. She paused for an instant. "When may
I go home? To Manchester, I mean. I am so weary of this place; and
I would fain be at home."

She spoke in a feeble voice; not at all impatiently, as the words
themselves would seem to intimate, but in a mournful way, as if
anticipating sorrow even in the very fulfilment of her wishes.

"Darling! we will go whenever you wish; whenever you feel strong
enough. I asked Job to tell Margaret to get all in readiness for you to
go there at first. She'll tend you and nurse you. You must not go
home. Job proffered for you to go there."

"Ah! but I must go home, Jem. I'll try and not fail now in what's
right. There are things we must not speak on" (lowering her voice),
"but you'll be really kind if you'll not speak against my going home.
Let us say no more about it, dear Jem. I must go home, and I must
go alone."

"Not alone, Mary!"

"Yes, alone! I cannot tell you why I ask it. And if you guess, I know
you well enough to be sure you'll understand why I ask you never to
speak on that again to me, till I begin. Promise, dear Jem, promise!"

He promised; to gratify that beseeching face, he promised. And
then he repented, and felt as if he had done ill. Then again he felt as
if she were the best judge, and knowing all (perhaps more than even
he did), might be forming plans which his interference would mar.

One thing was certain! it was a miserable thing to have this awful forbidden ground of discourse; to guess at each other's thoughts, when eyes were averted, and cheeks blanched, and words stood still, arrested in their flow by some casual allusion.

At last a day, fine enough for Mary to travel on, arrived. She had wished to go, but now her courage failed her. How could she have said she was weary of that quiet house, where even Ben Sturgis's grumblings only made a kind of harmonious bass in the concord between him and his wife, so thoroughly did they know each other with the knowledge of many years! How could she have longed to quit that little peaceful room where she had experienced such loving tendence! Even the very check bed-curtains became dear to her, under the idea of seeing them no more. If it was so with inanimate objects, if they had such power of exciting regret, what were her feelings with regard to the kind old couple, who had taken the stranger in, and cared for her, and nursed her, as though she had been a daughter? Each wilful sentence spoken in the half-unconscious irritation of feebleness came now with avenging self-reproach to her memory, as she hung about Mrs. Sturgis, with many tears, which served instead of words to express her gratitude and love.

Ben bustled about with the square bottle of Goldenwasser in one of his hands, and a small tumbler in the other; he went to Mary, Jem, and his wife in succession, pouring out a glass for each, and bidding them drink it to keep their spirits up; but as each severally refused, he drank it himself; and passed on to offer the same hospitality to another with the like refusal, and the like result.

When he had swallowed the last of the three draughts, he condescended to give his reasons for having done so.

"I cannot abide waste. What's poured out mun be drunk. That's my maxim." So saying he replaced the bottle in the cupboard.

It was he who, in a firm commanding voice, at last told Jem and Mary to be off, or they would be too late. Mrs. Sturgis had kept up till then; but as they left her house, she could no longer restrain her tears, and cried aloud in spite of her husband's upbraiding.

"Perhaps they'll be too late for the train!" exclaimed she, with a degree of hope, as the clock struck two.

"What! and come back again! No! no! that would never do. We've done our part, and cried our cry; it's no use going over the same ground again. I should ha' to give 'em more out of yon bottle when next parting time came, and them three glasses they ha' made a hole in the stuff, I can tell you. Time Jack was back from Hamburgh with some more."

When they reached Manchester, Mary looked very white, and the expression of her face was almost stern. She was in fact summoning up her resolution to meet her father if he were at home. Jem had never named his midnight glimpse of John Barton to human being; but Mary had a sort of presentiment, that wander where he would, he would seek his home at last. But in what mood she dreaded to think. For the knowledge of her father's capability of guilt seemed to have opened a dark gulf in his character, into the depths of which she trembled to look. At one moment she would fain have claimed protection against the life she must lead, for some time at least, alone with a murderer! She thought of his gloom, before his mind was haunted by the memory of so terrible a crime; his moody, irritable ways. She imagined the evenings as of old; she, toiling at some work, long after houses were shut, and folks abed; he, more savage than he had ever been before with the inward gnawing of his remorse. At such times she could have cried aloud with terror, at the scenes her fancy conjured up.

But her filial duty, nay, her love and gratitude for many deeds of kindness done to her as a little child, conquered all fear. She would endure all imaginable terrors, although of daily occurrence. And she would patiently bear all wayward violence of temper; more than patiently would she bear it—pitifully, as one who knew of some awful curse awaiting the blood-shedder. She would watch over him tenderly, as the Innocent should watch over the Guilty; awaiting the gracious seasons, wherein to pour oil and balm into the bitter wounds.

With the untroubled peace which the resolve to endure to the end gives, she approached the house that from habit she still called home, but which possessed the holiness of home no longer.

"Jem!" said she, as they stood at the entrance to the court, close by Job Legh's door, "you must go in there and wait half an hour. Not less. If in that time I don't come back, you go your ways to your mother. Give her my dear love. I will send by Margaret when I want to see you." She sighed heavily.

"Mary! Mary! I cannot leave you. You speak as coldly as if we were to be nought to each other. And my heart's bound up in you. I know why you bid me keep away, but——"

She put her hand on his arm, as he spoke in a loud agitated tone; she looked into his face with upbraiding love in her eyes, and then she said, while her lips quivered, and he felt her whole frame trembling:

"Dear Jem! I often could have told you more of love, if I had not once spoken out so free. Remember that time, Jem, if ever you think me cold. Then, the love that's in my heart would out in words; but now, though I'm silent on the pain I'm feeling in quitting you, the love is in my heart all the same. But this is not the time to speak on such things. If I do not do what I feel to be right now, I may blame myself all my life long! Jem, you promised——"

And so saying she left him. She went quicker than she would otherwise have passed over those few yards of ground, for fear he should still try to accompany her. Her hand was on the latch, and in a breath the door was opened.

There sat her father, still and motionless—not even turning his head to see who had entered; but perhaps he recognised the footstep—the trick of action.

He sat by the fire; the grate, I should say, for fire there was none. Some dull grey ashes, negligently left, long days ago, coldly choked up the bars. He had taken the accustomed seat from mere force of habit, which ruled his automaton body. For all energy, both physical and mental, seemed to have retreated inwards to some of the great citadels of life, there to do battle against the Destroyer, Conscience.

His hands were crossed, his fingers interlaced; usually a position implying some degree of resolution, or strength; but in him it was so faintly maintained, that it appeared more the result of chance; an attitude requiring some application of outward force to alter,—and a blow with a straw seemed as though it would be sufficient.

And as for his face, it was sunk and worn,—like a skull, with yet a suffering expression that skulls have not! Your heart would have ached to have seen the man, however hardly you might have judged his crime.

But crime and all was forgotten by his daughter, as she saw his abashed look, his smitten helplessness. All along she had felt it difficult (as I may have said before) to reconcile the two ideas, of her father and a blood-shedder. But now it was impossible. He was her father! her own dear father! and in his sufferings, whatever their cause, more dearly loved than ever before. His crime was a thing apart, never more to be considered by her.

And tenderly did she treat him, and fondly did she serve him in every way that heart could devise, or hand execute.

She had some money about her, the price of her strange services as a witness; and when the lingering dusk drew on she stole out to effect some purchases necessary for her father's comfort.

For how body and soul had been kept together, even as much as they were, during the days he had dwelt alone, no one can say. The house was bare as when Mary had left it, of coal, or of candle, of food, or of blessing in any shape.

She came quickly home; but as she passed Job Legh's door, she stopped. Doubtless Jem had long since gone; and doubtless, too, he had given Margaret some good reason for not intruding upon her friend for this night at least, otherwise Mary would have seen her before now.

But to-morrow,—would she not come in to-morrow? And who so quick as blind Margaret in noticing tones, and sighs, and even silence?

She did not give herself time for further thought, her desire to be once more with her father was too pressing; but she opened the door, before she well knew what to say.

"It's Mary Barton! I know her by her breathing! Grandfather, it's Mary Barton!"

Margaret's joy at meeting her, the open demonstration of her love, affected Mary much; she could not keep from crying, and sat down weak and agitated on the first chair she could find.

"Ay, ay, Mary! thou'rt looking a bit different to when I saw thee last. Thou'lt give Jem and me good characters for sick nurses, I trust. If all trades fail, I'll turn to that. Jem's place is for life, I reckon. Nay, never redden so, lass. You and he know each other's minds by this time!"

Margaret held her hand, and gently smiled into her face.

Job Legh took the candle up, and began a leisurely inspection.

"Thou hast getten a bit of pink in thy cheeks,—not much; but when last I see thee, thy lips were as white as a sheet. Thy nose is sharpish at th' end; thou'rt more like thy father than ever thou wert before. Lord! child, what's the matter? Art thou going to faint?"

For Mary had sickened at the mention of that name; yet she felt that now or never was the time to speak.

"Father's come home!" she said, "but he's very poorly; I never saw him as he is now before. I asked Jem not to come near him for fear it might fidget him."

She spoke hastily, and (to her own idea) in an unnatural manner. But they did not seem to notice it, nor to take the hint she had thrown out of company being unacceptable; for Job Legh directly put down some insect, which he was impaling on a corking-pin, and exclaimed,

"Thy father come home! Why, Jem never said a word of it! And ailing too! I'll go in, and cheer him with a bit of talk. I never knew any good come of delegating it."

"Oh, Job! father cannot stand—father is too ill. Don't come; not but that you're very kind and good; but to-night—indeed," said she, at last, in despair, seeing Job still persevere in putting away his things; "you must not come till I send or come for you. Father's in that strange way, I can't answer for it if he sees strangers. Please don't come. I'll come and tell you every day how he goes on. I must be off now to see after him. Dear Job! kind Job! don't be angry with me. If you knew all, you'd pity me."

For Job was muttering away in high dudgeon, and even Margaret's tone was altered as she wished Mary good night. Just then she could ill brook coldness from any one, and least of all bear the idea of being considered ungrateful by so kind and zealous a friend as Job had been; so she turned round suddenly, even when her hand was on the latch of the door, and ran back, and threw her arms about his neck, and kissed him first, and then Margaret. And then, the tears fast falling down her cheeks, but no word spoken, she hastily left the house, and went back to her home.

There was no change in her father's position, or in his spectral look. He had answered her questions (but few in number, for so many subjects were unapproachable) by monosyllables, and in a weak, high, childish voice; but he had not lifted his eyes; he could not meet his daughter's look. And she, when she spoke, or as she moved about, avoided letting her eyes rest upon him. She wished to be her usual self; but while every thing was done with a consciousness of purpose, she felt it was impossible.

In this manner things went on for some days. At night he feebly clambered up-stairs to bed; and during those long dark hours Mary heard those groans of agony which never escaped his lips by day, when they were compressed in silence over his inward woe.

Many a time she sat up listening, and wondering if it would ease his miserable heart if she went to him, and told him she knew all, and loved and pitied him more than words could tell.

By day the monotonous hours wore on in the same heavy, hushed manner as on that first dreary afternoon. He ate,—but without relish; and food seemed no longer to nourish him, for each morning his face had caught more of the ghastly foreshadowing of Death.

The neighbours kept strangely aloof. Of late years John Barton had had a repellant power about him, felt by all, except to the few who had either known him in his better and happier days, or those to whom he had given his sympathy and his confidence. People did not care to enter the doors of one whose very depth of thoughtfulness rendered him moody and stern. And now they contented themselves with a kind inquiry when they saw Mary in her goings-out or in her comings-in. With her oppressing knowledge, she imagined their reserved conduct stranger than it was in reality. She missed Job and Margaret too; who, in all former times of sorrow or anxiety since their acquaintance first began, had been ready with their sympathy.

But most of all she missed the delicious luxury she had lately enjoyed in having Jem's tender love at hand every hour of the day, to ward off every wind of heaven, and every disturbing thought.

She knew he was often hovering about the house; though the knowledge seemed to come more by intuition, than by any positive sight or sound for the first day or two. On the third day she met him at Job Legh's.

They received her with every effort of cordiality; but still there was a cobweb-veil of separation between them, to which Mary was morbidly acute; while in Jem's voice, and eyes, and manner, there was every evidence of most passionate, most admiring, and most trusting love. The trust was shown by his respectful silence on that one point of reserve on which she had interdicted conversation.

He left Job Legh's house when she did. They lingered on the step, he holding her hand between both of his, as loth to let her go; he questioned her as to when he should see her again.

"Mother does so want to see you," whispered he. "Can you come to see her to-morrow; or when?"

"I cannot tell," replied she softly. "Not yet. Wait awhile; perhaps only a little while. Dear Jem, I must go to him,—dearest Jem."

The next day, the fourth from Mary's return home, as she was sitting near the window, sadly dreaming over some work, she caught a glimpse of the last person she wished to see—of Sally Leadbitter!

She was evidently coming to their house; another moment, and she tapped at the door. John Barton gave an anxious, uneasy side-glance. Mary knew that if she delayed answering the knock, Sally would not scruple to enter; so as hastily as if the visit had been desired, she opened the door, and stood there with the latch in her hand, barring up all entrance, and as much as possible obstructing all curious glances into the interior.

"Well, Mary Barton! You're home at last! I heard you'd getten home; so I thought I'd just step over and hear the news."

She was bent on coming in, and saw Mary's preventive design. So she stood on tip-toe, looking over Mary's shoulders into the room where she suspected a lover to be lurking; but instead, she saw only the figure of the stern gloomy father she had always been in the habit of avoiding; and she dropped down again, content to carry on the conversation where Mary chose, and as Mary chose, in whispers.

"So the old governor is back again, eh? And what does he say to all your fine doings at Liverpool, and before?—you and I know where. You can't hide it now, Mary, for it's all in print."

Mary gave a low moan,—and then implored Sally to change the subject; for unpleasant as it always was, it was doubly unpleasant in the manner in which she was treating it. If they had been alone Mary would have borne it patiently,—or so she thought, but now she felt almost certain, her father was listening; there was a subdued breathing, a slight bracing-up of the listless attitude. But there was no arresting Sally's curiosity to hear all she could respecting the adventures Mary had experienced. She, in common with the rest of Miss Simmonds' young ladies, was almost jealous of the fame that Mary had obtained; to herself, such miserable notoriety.

"Nay! there's no use shunning talking it over. Why! it was in the *Guardian*,—and the *Courier*,[1]—and some one told Jane Hodgson it was even copied into a London paper. You've set up heroine on your own account, Mary Barton. How did you like standing witness? Ar'n't them lawyers impudent things? staring at one so. I'll be bound you wished you'd taken my offer, and borrowed my black watered scarf! Now didn't you, Mary? Speak truth!"

1. Both Manchester weekly newspapers.

"To tell truth, I never thought about it, then, Sally. How could I?" asked she, reproachfully.

"Oh—I forgot. You were all for that stupid James Wilson. Well! if I've ever the luck to go witness on a trial, see if I don't pick up a better beau than the prisoner. I'll aim at a lawyer's clerk, but I'll not take less than a turnkey."

Cast down as Mary was, she could hardly keep from smiling at the idea, so wildly incongruous with the scene she had really undergone, of looking out for admirers during a trial for murder.

"I'd no thought to be looking out for beaux, I can assure you, Sally. But don't let us talk any more about it; I can't bear to think on it. How is Miss Simmonds? and everybody?"

"Oh, very well; and by the way she gave me a bit of a message for you. You may come back to work if you'll behave yourself, she says. I told you she'd be glad to have you back, after all this piece of business, by way of tempting people to come to her shop. They'd come from Salford to have a peep at you, for six months at least."

"Don't talk so; I cannot come, I can never face Miss Simmonds again. And even if I could——," she stopped, and blushed.

"Ay! I know what you are thinking on. But that will not be this some time, as he's turned off from the foundry,—you'd better think twice afore refusing Miss Simmonds' offer."

"Turned off from the foundry? Jem?" cried Mary.

"To be sure! didn't you know it? Decent men were not going to work with a——no! I suppose I mustn't say it, seeing you went to such trouble to get up an *alibi;* not that I should think much the worse of a spirited young fellow for falling foul of a rival, —they always do at the theatre."

But Mary's thoughts were with Jem. How good he had been never to name his dismissal to her. How much he had had to endure for her sake!

"Tell me all about it," she gasped out.

"Why, you see, they've always swords quite handy at them plays," began Sally; but Mary, with an impatient shake of her head, interrupted,

"About Jem,—about Jem, I want to know."

"Oh! I don't pretend to know more than is in every one's mouth: he's turned away from the foundry, because folks don't think you've cleared him outright of the murder; though perhaps the jury were loth to hang him. Old Mr. Carson is savage against judge and jury, and lawyers and all, as I heard."

"I must go to him, I must go to him," repeated Mary, in a hurried manner.

"He'll tell you all I've said is true, and not a word of lie," replied Sally. "So I'll not give your answer to Miss Simmonds, but leave you to think twice about it. Good afternoon!"

Mary shut the door, and turned into the house.

Her father sat in the same attitude; the old unchanging attitude. Only his head was more bowed towards the ground.

She put on her bonnet to go to Ancoats; for see, and question, and comfort, and worship Jem, she must.

As she hung about her father for an instant before leaving him, he spoke—voluntarily spoke for the first time since her return; but his head was drooping so low she could not hear what he said, so she stooped down; and after a moment's pause, he repeated the words,

"Tell Jem Wilson to come here at eight o'clock to-night."

Could he have overheard her conversation with Sally Leadbitter? They had whispered low, she thought. Pondering on this, and many other things, she reached Ancoats.

Chapter XXXV.

> "Oh, had he lived,
> Replied Rusilla, never penitence
> Had equalled his! full well I know his heart,
> Vehement in all things. He would on himself
> Have wreaked such penance as had reached the height
> Of fleshly suffering,—yea, which being told,
> With its portentous rigour should have made
> The memory of his fault o'erpowered and lost,
> In shuddering pity and astonishment,
> Fade like a feeble horror."
>
> SOUTHEY'S 'RODERICK.'[2]

As MARY was turning into the street where the Wilsons lived, Jem overtook her. He came upon her suddenly, and she started. "You're going to see mother?" he asked tenderly, placing her arm within his, and slackening his pace.

"Yes, and you too. Oh, Jem, is it true? tell me."

She felt rightly that he would guess the meaning of her only half-expressed inquiry. He hesitated a moment before he answered her.

"Darling, it is; it's no use hiding it—if you mean that. I'm no longer to work at Duncombe's foundry. It's no time (to my mind) to have secrets from each other, though I did not name it yesterday, thinking you might fret. I shall soon get work again, never fear."

"But why did they turn you off, when the jury had said you were innocent?"

"It was not just to say turned off, though I don't think I could have well stayed on. A good number of the men managed to let out they should not like to work under me again; there were some few who

---

2. Robert Southey (1774–1843) *Roderick: The Last of the Goths* (1814), XV, lines 173–82.

knew me well enough to feel I could not have done it, but more were doubtful; and one spoke to young Mr. Duncombe, hinting at what they thought."

"Oh, Jem! what a shame!" said Mary, with mournful indignation.

"Nay, darling! I'm not for blaming them. Poor fellows like them have nought to stand upon and be proud of but their character, and it's fitting they should take care of that, and keep that free from soil and taint."

"But you,—what could they get but good from you? They might have known you by this time."

"So some do; the overlooker, I'm sure, would know I'm innocent. Indeed, he said as much to-day; and he said he had had some talk with old Mr. Duncombe, and they thought it might be better if I left Manchester for a bit; they'd recommend me to some other place."

But Mary could only shake her head in a mournful way, and repeat her words,

"They might have known thee better, Jem."

Jem pressed the little hand he held between his own work-hardened ones. After a minute or two, he asked,

"Mary, art thou much bound to Manchester? Would it grieve thee sore to quit the old smoke-jack?"[3]

"With thee?" she asked, in a quiet, glancing way.

"Ay, lass! Trust me, I'll never ask thee to leave Manchester while I'm in it. Because I have heard fine things of Canada; and our overlooker has a cousin in the foundry line there. Thou knowest where Canada is, Mary?"

"Not rightly—not now, at any rate;—but with thee, Jem," her voice sunk to a soft, low whisper, "anywhere——"

What was the use of a geographical description!

"But father!" said Mary, suddenly breaking that delicious silence with the one sharp discord in her present life.

She looked up at her lover's grave face; and then the message her father had sent flashed across her memory.

"Oh, Jem, did I tell you? Father sent word he wished to speak with you. I was to bid you come to him at eight to-night. What can he want, Jem?"

"I cannot tell," replied he. "At any rate I'll go. It's no use troubling ourselves to guess," he continued, after a pause for a few minutes, during which they slowly and silently paced up and down the by-street, into which he had led her when their conversation began. "Come and see mother, and then I'll take thee home, Mary. Thou wert all in a tremble when first I came up to thee; thou'rt not fit to be

---

3. An affectionate nickname for Manchester, a smoke-jack was an apparatus placed in a chimney for turning a roasting spit.

trusted home by thyself," said he, with fond exaggeration of her help-lessness.

Yet a little more lovers' loitering; a few more words, in themselves nothing—to you nothing—but to those two, what tender passionate language can I use to express the feelings which thrilled through that young man and maiden, as they listened to the syllables made dear and lovely through life by that hour's low-whispered talk.

It struck the half hour past seven.

"Come and speak to mother; she knows you're to be her daughter, Mary, darling."

So they went in. Jane Wilson was rather chafed at her son's delay in returning home, for as yet he had managed to keep her in igno-rance of his dismissal from the foundry: and it was her way to prepare some little pleasure, some little comfort for those she loved; and if they, unwittingly, did not appear at the proper time to enjoy her preparation, she worked herself up into a state of fretfulness which found vent in upbraidings as soon as ever the objects of her care appeared, thereby marring the peace which should ever be the atmo-sphere of a home, however humble; and causing a feeling almost amounting to loathing to arise at the sight of the "stalled ox,"[4] which, though an effect and proof of careful love, has been the cause of so much disturbance.

Mrs. Wilson had first sighed, and then grumbled to herself, over the increasing toughness of the potato-cakes she had made for her son's tea.

The door opened, and he came in; his face brightening into proud smiles, Mary Barton hanging on his arm, blushing and dimpling, with eyelids veiling the happy light of her eyes,— there was around the young couple a radiant atmosphere—a glory of happiness.

Could his mother mar it? Could she break into it with her Martha-like cares?[5] Only for one moment did she remember her sense of injury,—her wasted trouble,—and then, her whole woman's heart heaving with motherly love and sympathy, she opened her arms, and received Mary into them, as shedding tears of agitated joy, she mur-mured in her ear,

"Bless thee, Mary, bless thee! Only make him happy, and God bless thee for ever!"

It took some of Jem's self-command to separate those whom he so much loved, and who were beginning, for his sake, to love one another so dearly. But the time for his meeting John Barton drew on: and it was a long way to his house.

---

4. Proverbs 15:17. "Better is a dinner of herbs where love is, than a stalled ox and hatred therewith."
5. Luke 10:38–42. Martha complained that she had to do all the housework while Mary sat and listened to Jesus.

As they walked briskly thither, they hardly spoke; though many thoughts were in their minds.

The sun had not long set, but the first faint shade of twilight was over all; and when they opened the door, Jem could hardly perceive the objects within by the waning light of day, and the flickering fire-blaze.

But Mary saw all at a glance.

Her eye, accustomed to what was usual in the aspect of the room, saw instantly what was unusual,—saw, and understood it all.

Her father was standing behind his habitual chair; holding by the back of it as if for support. And opposite to him there stood Mr. Car-son; the dark outline of his stern figure looming large against the light of the fire in that little room.

Behind her father sat Job Legh, his head in his hands, and resting his elbow on the little family table,—listening evidently; but as evi-dently deeply affected by what he heard.

There seemed to be some pause in the conversation. Mary and Jem stood at the half-open door, not daring to stir; hardly to breathe.

"And have I heard you aright?" began Mr. Carson, with his deep quivering voice. "Man! have I heard you aright? Was it you, then, that killed my boy? my only son?"—(he said these last few words almost as if appealing for pity, and then he changed his tone to one more vehement and fierce.) "Don't dare to think that I shall be merciful, and spare you, because you have come forward to accuse yourself. I tell you I will not spare you the least pang the law can inflict,—you, who did not show pity on my boy, shall have none from me."

"I did not ask for any," said John Barton, in a low voice.

"Ask, or not ask, what care I? You shall be hanged—hanged—man!" said he, advancing his face, and repeating the word with slow grinding emphasis, as if to infuse some of the bitterness of his soul into it.

John Barton gasped; but not with fear. It was only that he felt it ter-rible to have inspired such hatred, as was concentrated into every word, every gesture of Mr. Carson's.

"As for being hanged, sir, I know it's all right and proper. I dare say it's bad enough; but I tell you what, sir," speaking with an outburst, "if you'd hanged me the day after I'd done the deed, I would have gone down on my knees and blessed you. Death! Lord, what is it to Life? To such a Life as I've been leading this fortnight past. Life at best is no great thing; but such a Life as I have dragged through since that night," he shuddered at the thought. "Why, sir, I've been on the point of killing myself this many a time to get away from my own thoughts. I didn't! and I'll tell you why. I didn't know but that I should be more haunted than ever with the recollection of my sin. Oh! God above only can tell the agony with which I've repented me of it, and part perhaps because I feared He would think I were impatient of the misery He sent as punishment— far, far worse misery than any hanging, sir." He ceased from excess of emotion.

Then he began again.

"Sin' that day (it may be very wicked, sir, but it's the truth) I've kept thinking and thinking if I were but in that world where they say God is, He would, maybe, teach me right from wrong, even if it were with many stripes. I've been sore puzzled here. I would go through hell-fire if I could but get free from sin at last, it's such an awful thing. As for hanging, that's just nought at all."

His exhaustion compelled him to sit down. Mary rushed to him. It seemed as if till then he had been unaware of her presence.

"Ay, ay, wench!" said he, feebly, "is it thee? Where's Jem Wilson?"

Jem came forward. John Barton spoke again, with many a break and gasping pause,

"Lad! thou hast borne a deal for me. It's the meanest thing I ever did to leave thee to bear the brunt. Thou, who wert as innocent of any knowledge of it as the babe unborn. I'll not bless thee for it. Blessing from such as me would not bring thee any good. Thou'lt love Mary, though she is my child."

He ceased, and there was a pause for a few seconds.

Then Mr. Carson turned to go. When his hand was on the latch of the door, he hesitated for an instant.

"You can have no doubt for what purpose I go. Straight to the police-office, to send men to take care of you, wretched man, and your accomplice. To-morrow morning your tale shall be repeated to those who can commit you to gaol, and before long you shall have the opportunity of trying how desirable hanging is."

"Oh, sir!" said Mary, springing forward, and catching hold of Mr. Carson's arm, "my father is dying. Look at him, sir. If you want Death for Death, you have it. Don't take him away from me these last hours. He must go alone through Death, but let me be with him as long as I can. Oh, sir! if you have any mercy in you, leave him here to die."

John himself stood up, stiff and rigid, and replied,

"Mary, wench! I owe him summut. I will go die, where, and as he wishes me. Thou hast said true, I am standing side by side with Death; and it matters little where I spend the bit of time left of Life. That time I must pass wrestling with my soul for a character to take into the other world. I'll go where you see fit, sir. He's innocent," faintly indicating Jem, as he fell back in his chair.

"Never fear! They cannot touch him," said Job Legh, in a low voice.

But as Mr. Carson was on the point of leaving the house with no sign of relenting about him, he was again stopped by John Barton, who had risen once more from his chair, and stood supporting himself on Jem, while he spoke.

"Sir, one word! My hairs are grey with suffering, and yours with years——"

"And have I had no suffering?" asked Mr. Carson, as if appealing for sympathy, even to the murderer of his child.

And the murderer of his child answered to the appeal, and groaned in spirit over the anguish he had caused.

"Have I had no inward suffering to blanch these hairs? Have not I toiled and struggled even to these years with hopes in my heart that all centered in my boy? I did not speak of them, but were they not there? I seemed hard and cold; and so I might be to others, but not to him!—who shall ever imagine the love I bore to him? Even he never dreamed how my heart leapt up at the sound of his footstep, and how precious he was to his poor old father. And he is gone—killed—out of the hearing of all loving words—out of my sight for ever. He was my sunshine, and now it is night! Oh, my God! comfort me, comfort me!" cried the old man, aloud.

The eyes of John Barton grew dim with tears. Rich and poor, masters and men, were then brothers in the deep suffering of the heart; for was not this the very anguish he had felt for little Tom, in years so long gone by, that they seemed like another life!

The mourner before him was no longer the employer; a being of another race, eternally placed in antagonistic attitude; going through the world glittering like gold, with a stony heart within, which knew no sorrow but through the accidents of Trade; no longer the enemy, the oppressor, but a very poor and desolate old man.

The sympathy for suffering, formerly so prevalent a feeling with him, again filled John Barton's heart, and almost impelled him to speak (as best he could) some earnest tender words to the stern man, shaking in his agony.

But who was he, that he should utter sympathy or consolation? The cause of all this woe.

Oh, blasting thought! Oh, miserable remembrance! He had forfeited all right to bind up his brother's wounds.

Stunned by the thought, he sank upon the seat, almost crushed with the knowledge of the consequences of his own action; for he had no more imagined to himself the blighted home, and the miserable parents, than does the soldier, who discharges his musket, picture to himself the desolation of the wife, and the pitiful cries of the helpless little ones, who are in an instant to be made widowed and fatherless.

To intimidate a class of men, known only to those below them as desirous to obtain the greatest quantity of work for the lowest wages,—at most to remove an overbearing partner from an obnoxious firm, who stood in the way of those who struggled as well as they were able to obtain their rights,—this was the light in which John Barton had viewed his deed; and even so viewing it, after the excitement had passed away, the Avenger, the sure Avenger, had found him out.

But now he knew that he had killed a man, and a brother,— now he knew that no good thing could come out of this evil, even to the sufferers whose cause he had so blindly espoused.

He lay across the table, broken-hearted. Every fresh quivering sob of Mr. Carson's stabbed him to his soul.

He felt execrated by all; and as if he could never lay bare the perverted reasonings which had made the performance of undoubted sin appear a duty. The longing to plead some faint excuse grew stronger and stronger. He feebly raised his head, and looking at Job Legh, he whispered out,

"I did not know what I was doing, Job Legh; God knows I didn't! Oh, sir!" said he, wildly, almost throwing himself at Mr. Carson's feet, "say you forgive me the anguish I now see I have caused you. I care not for pain, or death, you know I don't; but oh, man! forgive me the trespass I have done!"

"Forgive us our trespasses as we forgive them that trespass against us,"[6] said Job, solemnly and low, as if in prayer: as if the words were suggested by those John Barton had used.

Mr. Carson took his hands away from his face. I would rather see death than the ghastly gloom which darkened that countenance.

"Let my trespasses be unforgiven, so that I may have vengeance for my son's murder."

There are blasphemous actions as well as blasphemous words: all unloving, cruel deeds, are acted blasphemy.

Mr. Carson left the house. And John Barton lay on the ground as one dead.

They lifted him up, and almost hoping that that deep trance might be to him the end of all earthly things, they bore him to his bed.

For a time they listened with divided attention to his faint breathings; for in each hasty hurried step that echoed in the street outside, they thought they heard the approach of the officers of justice.

When Mr. Carson left the house he was dizzy with agitation; the hot blood went careering through his frame. He could not see the deep blue of the night-heavens for the fierce pulses which throbbed in his head. And partly to steady and calm himself, he leaned against a railing, and looked up into those calm majestic depths with all their thousand stars.

And by-and-by his own voice returned upon him, as if the last words he had spoken were being uttered through all that infinite space; but in their echoes there was a tone of unutterable sorrow.

6. From "The Lord's Prayer" in the Anglican liturgy. See also: Genesis 50:17, I Samuel 25:28, Matthew 6:14, and Luke 17:3–4.

"Let my trespasses be unforgiven, so that I may have vengeance for my son's murder."

He tried to shake off the spiritual impression made by this imagination. He was feverish and ill,—and no wonder.

So he turned to go homewards; not, as he had threatened, to the police-office. After all (he told himself), that would do in the morning. No fear of the man's escaping, unless he escaped to the Grave.

So he tried to banish the phantom voices and shapes which came unbidden to his brain, and to recal his balance of mind by walking calmly and slowly, and noticing everything which struck his senses.

It was a warm soft evening in spring, and there were many persons in the streets. Among others a nurse with a little girl in her charge, conveying her home from some children's gaiety; a dance most likely, for the lovely little creature was daintily decked out in soft, snowy muslin; and her fairy feet tripped along by her nurse's side as if to the measure of some tune she had lately kept time to.

Suddenly up behind her there came a rough, rude errand-boy, nine or ten years of age; a giant he looked by the fairy-child, as she fluttered along. I don't know how it was, but in some awkward way he knocked the poor little girl down upon the hard pavement as he brushed rudely past, not much caring whom he hurt, so that he got along.

The child arose, sobbing with pain; and not without cause, for blood was dropping down from the face, but a minute before so fair and bright—dropping down on the pretty frock, making those scarlet marks so terrible to little children.

The nurse, a powerful woman, had seized the boy, just as Mr. Carson (who had seen the whole transaction) came up.

"You naughty little rascal! I'll give you to a policeman, that I will! Do you see how you've hurt the little girl? Do you?" accompanying every sentence with a violent jerk of passionate anger.

The lad looked hard and defying; but withal terrified at the threat of the policeman, those ogres of our streets to all unlucky urchins. The nurse saw it, and began to drag him along, with a view of making what she called "a wholesome impression."

His terror increased, and with it his irritation; when the little sweet face, choking away its sobs, pulled down nurse's head, and said,

"Please, dear nurse, I'm not much hurt; it was very silly to cry, you know. He did not mean to do it. *He did not know what he was doing*, did you, little boy? Nurse won't call a policeman, so don't be frightened." And she put up her little mouth to be kissed by her injurer, just as she had been taught to do at home to "make peace."

"That lad will mind, and be more gentle for the time to come, I'll be bound, thanks to that little lady," said a passer-by, half to himself, and half to Mr. Carson, whom he had observed to notice the scene.

The latter took no apparent heed of the remark, but passed on. But the child's pleading reminded him of the low, broken voice he had so lately heard, penitently and humbly urging the same extenuation of his great guilt.

"I did not know what I was doing."

He had some association with those words; he had heard, or read of that plea somewhere before. Where was it?

"Could it be——?"

He would look when he got home. So when he entered his house he went straight and silently up-stairs to his library, and took down the great large handsome Bible, all grand and golden, with its leaves adhering together from the bookbinder's press, so little had it been used.

On the first page (which fell open to Mr. Carson's view) were written the names of his children, and his own.

"Henry John, son of the above John, and Elizabeth Carson.
                    Born, Sept. 29th, 1815."

To make the entry complete, his death should now be added. But the page became hidden by the gathering mist of tears.

Thought upon thought, and recollection upon recollection came crowding in, from the remembrance of the proud day when he had purchased the costly book, in order to write down the birth of the little babe of a day old.

He laid his head down on the open page, and let the tears fall slowly on the spotless leaves.

His son's murderer was discovered; had confessed his guilt; and yet (strange to say) he could not hate him with the vehemence of hatred he had felt, when he had imagined him a young man, full of lusty life, defying all laws, human and divine. In spite of his desire to retain the revengeful feeling he considered as a duty to his dead son, something of pity would steal in for the poor, wasted skeleton of a man, the smitten creature, who had told him of his sin, and implored his pardon that night.

In the days of his childhood and youth, Mr. Carson had been accustomed to poverty; but it was honest, decent poverty; not the grinding squalid misery he had remarked in every part of John Barton's house, and which contrasted strangely with the pompous sumptuousness of the room in which he now sate. Unaccustomed wonder filled his mind at the reflection of the different lots of the brethren of mankind.

Then he roused himself from his reverie, and turned to the object of his search—the Gospel, where he half expected to find the tender pleading: "They know not what they do."[7]

7. Luke 23:34.

It was murk midnight by this time, and the house was still and quiet. There was nothing to interrupt the old man in his unwonted study.

Years ago, the Gospel had been his task-book in learning to read. So many years ago, that he had become familiar with the events before he could comprehend the Spirit that made the Life.

He fell to the narrative now afresh, with all the interest of a little child. He began at the beginning, and read on almost greedily, understanding for the first time the full meaning of the story. He came to the end; the awful End. And there were the haunting words of pleading.

He shut the book, and thought deeply.

All night long, the Archangel combated with the Demon.[8]

All night long, others watched by the bed of Death. John Barton had revived to fitful intelligence. He spoke at times with even something of his former energy; and in the racy Lancashire dialect he had always used when speaking freely.

"You see I've so often been hankering after the right way; and it's a hard one for a poor man to find. At least it's been so to me. No one learned me, and no one told me. When I was a little chap they taught me to read, and then they ne'er gave no books; only I heard say the Bible was a good book. So when I grew thoughtful, and puzzled, I took to it. But you'd never believe black was black, or night was night, when you saw all about you acting as if black was white, and night was day. It's not much I can say for myself in t'other world. God forgive me; but I can say this, I would fain have gone after the Bible rules if I'd seen folk credit it; they all spoke up for it, and went and did clean contrary. In those days I would ha' gone about wi' my Bible, like a little child, my finger in th' place, and asking the meaning of this or that text, and no one told me. Then I took out two or three texts as clear as glass, and I tried to do what they bid me do. But I don't know how it was, masters and men, all alike cared no more for minding those texts, than I did for th' Lord Mayor of London; so I grew to think it must be a sham put upon poor ignorant folk, women, and such like.

"It was not long I tried to live Gospel-wise, but it was liker heaven than any other bit of earth has been. I'd old Alice to strengthen me; but every one else said, 'Stand up for thy rights, or thou'lt never get 'em;' and wife and children never spoke, but their helplessness cried aloud, and I was driven to do as others did—and then Tom died. You know all about that—I'm getting scant o' breath, and blind-like."

Then again he spoke, after some minutes of hushed silence.

"All along it came natural to love folk, though now I am what I am. I think one time I could e'en have loved the masters if they'd ha' let-

8. Jude 1:9.

ten me; that was in my Gospel-days, afore my child died o' hunger. I was tore in two oftentimes, between my sorrow for poor suffering folk, and my trying to love them as caused their sufferings (to my mind).

"At last I gave it up in despair, trying to make folks' actions square wi' th' Bible; and I thought I'd no longer labour at following th' Bible mysel'. I've said all this afore, maybe. But from that time I've dropped down, down—down."

After that he only spoke in broken sentences.

"I did not think he'd been such an old man,—Oh! that he had but forgiven me,"—and then came earnest, passionate, broken words of prayer.

Job Legh had gone home like one struck down with the unexpected shock. Mary and Jem together waited the approach of death; but as the final struggle drew on, and morning dawned, Jem suggested some alleviation to the gasping breath, to purchase which he left the house in search of a druggist's shop, which should be open at that early hour.

During his absence, Barton grew worse; he had fallen across the bed, and his breathing seemed almost stopped; in vain did Mary strive to raise him, her sorrow and exhaustion had rendered her too weak.

So, on hearing some one enter the house-place below, she cried out for Jem to come to her assistance.

A step, which was not Jem's, came up the stairs.

Mr. Carson stood in the door-way. In one instant he comprehended the case.

He raised up the powerless frame; and the departing soul looked out of the eyes with gratitude. He held the dying man propped in his arms. John Barton folded his hands, as if in prayer.

"Pray for us," said Mary, sinking on her knees, and forgetting in that solemn hour all that had divided her father and Mr. Carson.

No other words would suggest themselves than some of those he had read only a few hours before:

"God be merciful to us sinners.[9]—Forgive us our trespasses as we forgive them that trespass against us."

And when the words were said, John Barton lay a corpse in Mr. Carson's arms.

So ended the tragedy of a poor man's life.

Mary knew nothing more for many minutes. When she recovered consciousness, she found herself supported by Jem on the "settle" in the house-place. Job and Mr. Carson were there, talking together lowly and solemnly. Then Mr. Carson bade farewell and left the house; and Job said aloud, but as if speaking to himself,

"God has heard that man's prayer. He has comforted him."

9. Luke 18:13.

Chapter XXXVI.

"The first dark day of nothingness,
The last of danger and distress."

BYRON.[1]

Although Mary had hardly been conscious of her thoughts, and it had been more like a secret instinct informing her soul, than the result of any process of reasoning, she had felt for some time (ever since her return from Liverpool, in fact), that for her father there was but one thing to be desired and anticipated, and that was death!

She had seen that Conscience had given the mortal wound to his earthly frame; she did not dare to question of the infinite mercy of God, what the Future Life would be to him.

Though at first desolate and stunned by the blow which had fallen on herself, she was resigned and submissive as soon as she recovered strength enough to ponder and consider a little; and you may be sure that no tenderness or love was wanting on Jem's part, and no consideration and sympathy on that of Job and Margaret to soothe and comfort the girl who now stood alone in the world as far as blood-relations were concerned.

She did not ask or care to know what arrangements they were making in whispered tones with regard to the funeral. She put herself into their hands with the trust of a little child; glad to be undisturbed in the reveries and remembrances which filled her eyes with tears, and caused them to fall quietly down her pale cheeks.

It was the longest day she had ever known in her life; every charge and every occupation was taken away from her: but perhaps the length of quiet time thus afforded was really good, although its duration weighed upon her; for by this means she contemplated her situation in every light, and fully understood that the morning's event had left her an orphan; and thus she was spared the pangs caused to us by the occurrence of death in the evening, just before we should naturally, in the usual course of events, lie down to slumber. For in such case, worn out by anxiety, and it may be by much watching, our very excess of grief rocks itself to sleep, before we have had time to realise its cause; and we waken, with a start of agony like a fresh stab, to the consciousness of the one awful vacancy, which shall never, while the world endures, be filled again.

The day brought its burden of duty to Mrs. Wilson. She felt bound by regard, as well as by etiquette, to go and see her future daughter-in-law. And by an old association of ideas (perhaps of death with churchyards, and churches with Sunday), she thought it necessary to

1. From Lord Byron's (1788–1824) *The Giaour* (1813), lines 70–71.

put on her best, and latterly unused clothes, the airing of which on a little clothes-horse before the fire seemed to give her a not unpleasing occupation.

When Jem returned home late in the evening succeeding John Barton's death, weary and oppressed with the occurrences and excitements of the day, he found his mother busy about her mourning, and much inclined to talk. Although he longed for quiet, he could not avoid sitting down and answering her questions.

"Well, Jem! he's gone at last, is he?"

"Yes. How did you hear, mother?"

"Oh, Job came over here, and told me, on his way to the undertaker's. Did he make a fine end?"

It struck Jem that she had not heard of the confession which had been made by John Barton on his death-bed; he remembered Job Legh's discretion, and he determined that if it could be avoided his mother should never hear of it. Many of the difficulties to be anticipated in preserving the secret would be obviated, if he could induce his mother to fall into the plan he had named to Mary of emigrating to Canada. The reasons which rendered this secrecy desirable related to the domestic happiness he hoped for. With his mother's irritable temper he could hardly expect that all allusion to the crime of John Barton would be for ever restrained from passing her lips, and he knew the deep trial which such references would be to Mary. Accordingly he resolved as soon as possible in the morning to go to Job, and beseech his silence; he trusted that secrecy in that quarter, even if the knowledge had been extended to Margaret, might be easily secured.

But what would be Mr. Carson's course? Were there any means by which he might be persuaded to spare John Barton's memory?

He was roused up from this train of thought by his mother's more irritated tone of voice.

"Jem!" she was saying, "thou mightst just as well never be at a death-bed again, if thou cannot bring off more news about it; here have I been by mysel all day (except when oud Job came in), but thinks I, when Jem comes he'll be sure to be good company, seeing he was in the house at the very time of the death; and here thou art, without a word to throw at a dog, much less thy mother: it's no use thy going to a death-bed if thou cannot carry away any of the sayings!"

"He did not make any, mother," replied Jem.

"Well to be sure! So fond as he used to be of holding forth, to miss such a fine opportunity that will never come again! Did he die easy?

"He was very restless all night long," said Jem, reluctantly returning to the thoughts of that time.

"And in course thou plucked the pillow away? Thou didst not! Well! with thy bringing up, and thy learning, thou mightst have known that were the only help in such a case. There were pigeons' feathers in the pillow, depend on't. To think of two grown-up folk like you and Mary, not knowing death could never come easy to a person lying on a pillow with pigeons' feathers in!"

Jem was glad to escape from all this talking, to the solitude and quiet of his own room, where he could lie and think uninterruptedly of what had happened and remained to be done.

The first thing was to seek an interview with Mr. Duncombe, his former master. Accordingly, early the next morning Jem set off on his walk to the works, where for so many years his days had been spent; where for so long a time his thoughts had been thought, his hopes and fears experienced. It was not a cheering feeling to remember that henceforward he was to be severed from all these familiar places; nor were his spirits enlivened by the evident feelings of the majority of those who had been his fellow-workmen. As he stood in the entrance to the foundry, awaiting Mr. Duncombe's leisure, many of those employed in the works passed him on their return from breakfast; and, with one or two exceptions, without any acknowledgment of former acquaintance beyond a distant nod at the utmost.

"It is hard," said Jem to himself, with a bitter and indignant feeling rising in his throat, "that let a man's life have been what it may, folk are so ready to credit the first word against him. I could live it down if I stayed in England; but then what would not Mary have to bear? Sooner or later the truth would out; and then she would be a show to folk for many a day as John Barton's daughter. Well! God does not judge as hardly as man, that's one comfort for all of us!"

Mr. Duncombe did not believe in Jem's guilt, in spite of the silence in which he again this day heard the imputation of it; but he agreed that under the circumstances it was better he should leave the country.

"We have been written to by government, as I think I told you before, to recommend an intelligent man, well acquainted with mechanics, as instrument maker to the Agricultural College they are establishing at Toronto, in Canada. It is a comfortable appointment,—house,—land,—and a good per-centage on the instruments made. I will show you the particulars if I can lay my hand on the letter, which I believe I must have left at home."

"Thank you, sir. No need for seeing the letter to say I'll accept it. I must leave Manchester; and I'd as lief quit England at once when I'm about it."

"Of course government give you your passage; indeed I believe an allowance would be made for a family if you had one; but you are not a married man, I believe?"

"No, sir, but——" Jem hung back from a confession with the awkwardness of a girl.

"But——" said Mr. Duncombe, smiling, "you would like to be a married man before you go, I suppose; eh, Wilson?"

"If you please, sir. And there's my mother, too. I hope she'll go with us. But I can pay her passage; no need to trouble government."

"Nay, nay! I'll write to-day and recommend you; and say that you have a family of two. They'll never ask if the family goes upwards or downwards. I shall see you again before you sail, I hope, Wilson; though I believe they'll not allow you long to wait. Come to my house next time; you'll find it pleasanter, I dare say. These men are so wrong-headed. Keep up your heart!"

Jem felt that it was a relief to have this point settled; and that he need no longer weigh reasons for and against his emigration.

And with his path growing clearer and clearer before him the longer he contemplated it, he went to see Mary, and if he judged it fit, to tell her what he had decided upon. Margaret was sitting with her.

"Grandfather wants to see you!" said she, to Jem, on his entrance.

"And I want to see him," replied Jem, suddenly remembering his last night's determination to enjoin secrecy on Job Legh.

So he hardly stayed to kiss poor Mary's sweet woe-begone face, but tore himself away from his darling to go to the old man, who awaited him impatiently.

"I've gotten a note from Mr. Carson," exclaimed Job, the moment he saw Jem; "and man-alive, he wants to see thee and me! For sure, there's no more mischief up, is there?" said he, looking at Jem with an expression of wonder. But if any suspicion mingled for an instant with the thoughts that crossed Job's mind, it was immediately dispelled by Jem's honest, fearless, open countenance.

"I can't guess what he's wanting, poor old chap," answered he. "Maybe there's some point he's not yet satisfied on; maybe—but it's no use guessing; let's be off."

"It wouldn't be better for thee to be scarce a bit, would it, and leave me to go and find out what's up? He has, perhaps, gotten some crotchet into his head thou'rt an accomplice, and is laying a trap for thee."

"I'm not afeard!" said Jem; "I've done nought wrong, and know nought wrong, about yon poor dead lad; though I'll own I had evil thoughts once on a time. Folk can't mistake long if once they'll search into the truth. I'll go and give the old gentleman all the satisfaction in my power, now it can injure no one. I'd my reasons for wanting to see him besides, and it all falls in right enough for me."

Job was a little re-assured by Jem's boldness; but still, if the truth must be told, he wished the young man would follow his advice, and leave him to sound Mr. Carson's intentions.

Meanwhile Jane Wilson had donned her Sunday suit of black, and set off on her errand of condolence. She felt nervous and uneasy at the idea of the moral sayings and texts which she fancied were expected from visitors on occasions like the present; and prepared many a good set speech as she walked towards the house of mourning.

As she gently opened the door, Mary sitting idly by the fire, caught a glimpse of her,—of Jem's mother,—of the early friend of her dead parents,—of the kind minister to many a little want in days of childhood,—and rose and came and fell about her neck, with many a sob and moan, saying,

"Oh, he's gone—he's dead—all gone—all dead, and I am left alone!"

"Poor wench! poor, poor wench!" said Jane Wilson, tenderly kissing her. "Thou'rt not alone; so donnot take on so. I'll say nought of Him who's above, for thou knowest He is ever the orphan's friend; but think on Jem! nay, Mary, dear, think on me! I'm but a frabbit woman at times, but I've a heart within me through all my temper, and thou shalt be as a daughter henceforward,—as mine own ewe-lamb. Jem shall not love thee better in his way, than I will in mine; and thou'lt bear with my turns, Mary, knowing that in my soul God sees the love that shall ever be thine, if thou'lt take me for thy mother, and speak no more of being alone."

Mrs. Wilson was weeping herself long before she had ended this speech, which was so different to all she had planned to say, and from all the formal piety she had laid in store for the visit; for this was heart's piety, and needed no garnish of texts to make it true religion, pure and undefiled.

They sat together on the same chair, their arms encircling each other; they wept for the same dead; they had the same hope, and trust, and overflowing love in the living.

From that time forward, hardly a passing cloud dimmed the happy confidence of their intercourse; even by Jem would his mother's temper sooner be irritated than by Mary; before the latter she repressed her occasional nervous ill-humour till the habit of indulging it was perceptibly decreased.

Years afterwards in conversation with Jem, he was startled by a chance expression which dropped from his mother's lips; it implied a knowledge of John Barton's crime. It was many a long day since they had seen any Manchester people who could have revealed the secret (if indeed it was known in Manchester, against which Jem had guarded in every possible way). And he was led to inquire first as to the extent, and then as to the source of her knowledge. It was Mary herself who had told all.

For on the morning to which this chapter principally relates, as Mary sat weeping, and as Mrs. Wilson comforted her by every tenderest word and caress, she revealed, to the dismayed and astonished

Jane, the sting of her deep sorrow; the crime which stained her dead father's memory.

She was quite unconscious that Jem had kept it secret from his mother; she had imagined it bruited abroad as the suspicion against her lover had been; so word after word (dropped from her lips in the supposition that Mrs. Wilson knew all) had told the tale, and revealed the cause of her deep anguish; deeper than is ever caused by Death alone.

On large occasions like the present, Mrs. Wilson's innate generosity came out. Her weak and ailing frame imparted its irritation to her conduct in small things, and daily trifles; but she had deep and noble sympathy with great sorrows, and even at the time that Mary spoke she allowed no expression of surprise or horror to escape her lips. She gave way to no curiosity as to the untold details; she was as secret and trustworthy as her son himself; and if in years to come her anger was occasionally excited against Mary, and she, on rare occasions, yielded to illtemper against her daughter-in-law, she would upbraid her for extravagance, or stinginess, or over-dressing, or under-dressing, or too much mirth, or too much gloom, but never, never in her most uncontrolled moments, did she allude to any one of the circumstances relating to Mary's flirtation with Harry Carson, or his murderer; and always when she spoke of John Barton, named him with the respect due to his conduct before the last, miserable, guilty month of his life.

Therefore it came like a blow to Jem, when, after years had passed away, he gathered his mother's knowledge of the whole affair. From the day when he learnt (not without remorse) what hidden depths of self-restraint she had in her soul, his manner to her, always tender and respectful, became reverential; and it was more than ever a loving strife between him and Mary which should most contribute towards the happiness of the declining years of their mother.

But I am speaking of the events which have occurred only lately, while I have yet many things to tell you that happened six or seven years ago.

Chapter XXXVII.

> "The rich man dines, while the poor man pines,
>   And eats his heart away;
> 'They teach us lies,' he sternly cries,
>   'Would *brothers* do as they?'"
>
>   'The Dream.'[2]

Mr. Carson stood at one of the breathing-moments of life. The object of the toils, the fears, and the wishes of his past years, was suddenly

---

2. Source unknown.

hidden from his sight,—vanished into the deep mystery which circumscribes existence. Nay, even the vengeance which he had cherished, taken away from before his eyes, as by the hand of God.

Events like these would have startled the most thoughtless into reflection, much more such a man as Mr. Carson, whose mind, if not enlarged, was energetic; indeed, whose very energy, having been hitherto the cause of the employment of his powers in only one direction, had prevented him from becoming largely and philosophically comprehensive in his views.

But now the foundations of his past life were razed to the ground, and the place they had once occupied was sown with salt, to be rebuilt no more for ever. It was like the change from this Life to that other hidden one, when so many of the motives which have actuated all our earthly existence, will have become more fleeting than the shadows of a dream. With a wrench of his soul from the past, so much of which was as nothing, and worse than nothing to him now, Mr. Carson took some hours, after he had witnessed the death of his son's murderer, to consider his situation.

But suddenly, while he was deliberating, and searching for motives which should be effective to compel him to exertion and action once more; while he contemplated the desire after riches, social distinction, a name among the merchant-princes amidst whom he moved, and saw these false substances fade away into the shadows they truly are, and one by one disappear into the grave of his son,—suddenly, I say, the thought arose within him that more yet remained to be learned about the circumstances and feelings which had prompted John Barton's crime; and when once this mournful curiosity was excited, it seemed to gather strength in every moment that its gratification was delayed. Accordingly he sent a message to summon Job Legh and Jem Wilson, from whom he promised himself some elucidation of what was as yet unexplained; while he himself set forth to call on Mr. Bridgenorth, whom he knew to have been Jem's attorney, with a glimmering suspicion intruding on his mind, which he strove to repel, that Jem might have had some share in his son's death.

He had returned before his summoned visitors arrived; and had time enough to recur to the evening on which John Barton had made his confession. He remembered with mortification how he had forgotten his proud reserve, and his habitual concealment of his feelings, and had laid bare his agony of grief in the presence of these two men who were coming to see him by his desire; and he entrenched himself behind stiff barriers of self-control, through which he hoped no appearance of emotion would force its way in the conversation he anticipated.

Nevertheless, when the servant announced that two men were there by appointment to speak to him, and he had desired that they might be shown into the library where he sat, any watcher might have perceived by the trembling hands, and shaking head, not only how much he was aged by the occurrences of the last few weeks, but also how much he was agitated at the thought of the impending interview.

But he so far succeeded in commanding himself at first, as to appear to Jem Wilson and Job Legh one of the hardest and most haughty men they had ever spoken to, and to forfeit all the interest which he had previously excited in their minds by his unreserved display of deep and genuine feeling.

When he had desired them to be seated, he shaded his face with his hand for an instant before speaking.

"I have been calling on Mr. Bridgenorth this morning," said he, at last; "as I expected, he can give me but little satisfaction on some points respecting the occurrence on the 18th of last month, which I desire to have cleared up. Perhaps you two can tell me what I want to know. As intimate friends of Barton's you probably know, or can conjecture a good deal. Have no scruple as to speaking the truth. What you say in this room shall never be named again by me. Besides, you are aware that the law allows no one to be tried twice for the same offence."

He stopped for a minute, for the mere act of speaking was fatiguing to him after the excitement of the last few days.

Job Legh took the opportunity of speaking.

"I'm not going to be affronted either for myself or Jem at what you've just now been saying about the truth. You don't know us, and there's an end on't; only it's as well for folk to think others good and true until they're proved contrary. Ask what you like, sir, I'll answer for it we'll either tell truth or hold our tongues."

"I beg your pardon," said Mr. Carson, slightly bowing his head. "What I wished to know was," referring to a slip of paper he held in his hand, and shaking so much he could hardly adjust his glasses to his eyes, "whether you, Wilson, can explain how Barton came possessed of your gun. I believe you refused this explanation to Mr. Bridgenorth."

"I did, sir! If I had said what I knew then, I saw it would criminate Barton, and so I refused telling aught. To you, sir, now I will tell everything and anything; only it is but little. The gun was my father's before it was mine, and long ago he and John Barton had a fancy for shooting at the gallery; and they used always to take this gun, and brag that though it was old-fashioned it was sure."

Jem saw with self-upbraiding pain how Mr. Carson winced at these last words, but at each irrepressible and involuntary evidence of feeling, the hearts of the two men warmed towards him. Jem went on speaking.

"One day in the week—I think it was on the Wednesday,—yes, it was—it was on St. Patrick's day,[3] I met John just coming out of our house, as I were going to my dinner. Mother was out, and he'd found no one in. He said he'd come to borrow the old gun, and that he'd have made bold, and taken it, but it was not to be seen. Mother was afraid of it, so after father's death (for while he were alive, she seemed to think he could manage it) I had carried it to my own room. I went up and fetched it for John, who stood outside the door all the time."

"What did he say he wanted it for?" asked Mr. Carson, hastily.

"I don't think he spoke when I gave it him. At first he muttered something about the shooting gallery, and I never doubted but that it was for practice there, as I knew he had done years before."

Mr. Carson had strung up his frame to an attitude of upright attention while Jem was speaking; now the tension relaxed, and he sank back in his chair, weak and powerless.

He rose up again, however, as Jem went on, anxious to give every particular which could satisfy the bereaved father.

"I never knew for what he wanted the gun till I was taken up,—I do not know yet why he wanted it. No one would have had me get out of the scrape by implicating an old friend,—my father's old friend, and the father of the girl I loved. So I refused to tell Mr. Bridgenorth aught about it, and would not have named it now to any one but you."

Jem's face became very red at the allusion he made to Mary, but his honest, fearless eyes had met Mr. Carson's penetrating gaze unflinchingly, and had carried conviction of his innocence and truthfulness; Mr. Carson felt certain that he had heard all that Jem could tell. Accordingly he turned to Job Legh.

"You were in the room the whole time while Barton was speaking to me, I think?"

"Yes, sir," answered Job.

"You'll excuse my asking plain and direct questions; the information I am gaining is really a relief to my mind, I don't know how; but it is,—will you tell me if you had any idea of Barton's guilt in this matter before?"

"None whatever, so help me God!" said Job, solemnly. "To tell truth (and axing your forgiveness, Jem), I had never got quite shut of the notion that Jem here had done it. At times I was as clear of his innocence as I was of my own; and whenever I took to reasoning about it, I saw he could not have been the man that did it. Still I never thought of Barton."

"And yet by his confession he must have been absent at the time," said Mr. Carson, referring to his slip of paper.

"Ay, and for many a day after,—I can't rightly say how long. But still, you see, one's often blind to many a thing that lies right under

3. March 17.

one's nose, till it's pointed out. And till I heard what John Barton had to say yon night, I could not have seen what reason he had for doing it; while in the case of Jem, any one who looked at Mary Barton might have seen a cause for jealousy clear enough."

"Then you believe that Barton had no knowledge of my son's unfortunate—," he looked at Jem, "of his attentions to Mary Barton. This young man, Wilson, had heard of them, you see."

"The person who told me said clearly she neither had, nor would tell Mary's father," interposed Jem. "I don't believe he'd ever heard of it; he weren't a man to keep still in such a matter, if he had."

"Besides," said Job, "the reason he gave on his death-bed, so to speak, was enough; 'specially to those who knew him."

"You mean his feelings regarding the treatment of the workmen by the masters; you think he acted from motives of revenge, in consequence of the part my son had taken in putting down the strike?"

"Well, sir," replied Job, "it's hard to say: John Barton was not a man to take counsel with people; nor did he make many words about his doings. So I can only judge from his way of thinking and talking in general, never having heard him breathe a syllable concerning this matter in particular. You see he were sadly put about to make great riches and great poverty square with Christ's Gospel"—Job paused, in order to try and express what was clear enough in his own mind, as to the effect produced on John Barton by the great and mocking contrasts presented by the varieties of human condition. Before he could find suitable words to explain his meaning, Mr. Carson spoke.

"You mean he was an Owenite;[4] all for equality and community of goods, and that kind of absurdity."

"No, no! John Barton was no fool. No need to tell him that were all men equal to-night, some would get the start by rising an hour earlier to-morrow. Nor yet did he care for goods, nor wealth; no man less, so that he could get daily bread for him and his; but what hurt him sore, and rankled in him as long as I knew him (and, sir, it rankles in many a poor man's heart far more than the want of any creature-comforts, and puts a sting into starvation itself), was that those who wore finer clothes, and eat better food, and had more money in their pockets, kept him at arm's length, and cared not whether his heart was sorry or glad; whether he lived or died,— whether he was bound for heaven or hell. It seemed hard to him that a heap of gold should part him and his brother so far asunder. For he was a loving man before he grew mad with seeing such as he was slighted, as if Christ himself had not been poor. At one time, I've heard him say, he felt kindly towards every man, rich or poor, because he thought they were all men alike. But latterly he grew aggravated

4. A follower of the utopian socialist Robert Owen (1771–1858).

with the sorrows and suffering that he saw, and which he thought the masters might help if they would."

"That's the notion you've all of you got," said Mr. Carson. "Now, how in the world can we help it? We cannot regulate the demand for labour. No man or set of men can do it. It depends on events which God alone can control. When there is no market for our goods, we suffer just as much as you can do."

"Not as much, I'm sure, sir; though I'm not given to Political Economy,[5] I know that much. I'm wanting in learning, I'm aware; but I can use my eyes. I never see the masters getting thin and haggard for want of food; I hardly ever see them making much change in their way of living, though I don't doubt they've got to do it in bad times. But it's in things for show they cut short; while for such as me, it's in things for life we've to stint. For sure, sir, you'll own it's come to a hard pass when a man would give aught in the world for work to keep his children from starving, and can't get a bit, if he's ever so willing to labour. I'm not up to talking as John Barton would have done, but that's clear to me at any rate."

"My good man, just listen to me. Two men live in a solitude: one produces loaves of bread, the other coats,—or what you will. Now, would it not be hard if the bread-producer were forced to give bread for the coats, whether he wanted them or not, in order to furnish employment to the other: that is the simple form of the case; you've only to multiply the numbers. There will come times of great changes in the occupation of thousands, when improvements in manufactures and machinery are made. It's all nonsense talking,—it must be so!"

Job Legh pondered a few moments.

"It's true it was a sore time for the hand-loom weavers when power-looms came in: them new-fangled things make a man's life like a lottery; and yet I'll never misdoubt that power-looms, and railways, and all such-like inventions are the gifts of God. I have lived long enough, too, to see that it is a part of His plan to send suffering to bring out a higher good; but surely it's also a part of His plan that so much of the burden of the suffering as can be should be lightened by those whom it is His pleasure to make happy, and content in their own circumstances. Of course it would take a deal more thought and wisdom than me, or any other man has, to settle out of hand how this should be done. But I'm clear about this, when God gives a blessing to be enjoyed, He gives it with a duty to be done; and the duty of the happy is to help the suffering to bear their woe."

"Still facts have proved, and are daily proving, how much better it is for every man to be independent of help, and self-reliant," said Mr. Carson, thoughtfully.

5. Economic theory.

"You can never work facts as you would fixed quantities, and say, given two facts, and the product is so and so. God has given men feelings and passions which cannot be worked into the problem, because they are for ever changing and uncertain. God has also made some weak; not in any one way, but in all. One is weak in body, another in mind, another in steadiness of purpose, a fourth can't tell right from wrong, and so on; or if he can tell the right, he wants strength to hold by it. Now to my thinking, them that is strong in any of God's gifts is meant to help the weak,—be hanged to the facts! I ask your pardon, sir; I can't rightly explain the meaning that is in me. I'm like a tap as won't run, but keeps letting it out drop by drop, so that you've no notion of the force of what's within."

Job looked and felt very sorrowful at the want of power in his words, while the feeling within him was so strong and clear.

"What you say is very true, no doubt," replied Mr. Carson; "but how would you bring it to bear upon the masters' conduct,—on my particular case?" added he, gravely.

"I'm not learned enough to argue. Thoughts come into my head that I'm sure are as true as Gospel, though maybe they don't follow each other like the Q.E.D. of a Proposition.[6] The masters has it on their own conscience,—you have it on yours, sir, to answer for to God whether you've done, and are doing all in your power to lighten the evils that seem always to hang on the trades by which you make your fortunes. It's no business of mine, thank God. John Barton took the question in hand, and his answer to it was No! Then he grew bitter and angry, and mad; and in his madness he did a great sin, and wrought a great woe; and repented him with tears of blood, and will go through his penance humbly and meekly in t'other place, I'll be bound. I never seed such bitter repentance as his that last night."

There was a silence of many minutes. Mr. Carson had covered his face, and seemed utterly forgetful of their presence; and yet they did not like to disturb him by rising to leave the room.

At last he said, without meeting their sympathetic eyes,

"Thank you both for coming,—and for speaking candidly to me. I fear, Legh, neither you nor I have convinced each other, as to the power, or want of power in the masters, to remedy the evils the men complain of."

"I'm loth to vex you, sir, just now; but it was not the want of power I was talking on; what we all feel sharpest is the want of inclination to try and help the evils which come like blights at times over the manufacturing places, while we see the masters can stop work and not suffer. If we saw the masters try for our sakes to find a remedy,— even if they were long about it,—even if they could find no help, and

6. Quod erat demonstrandum (Latin for "which was to be demonstrated").

at the end of all could only say, 'Poor fellows, our hearts are sore for ye; we've done all we could, and can't find a cure,'—we'd bear up like men through bad times. No one knows till they have tried, what power of bearing lies in them, if once they believe that men are caring for their sorrows and will help if they can. If fellow-creatures can give nought but tears and brave words, we take our trials straight from God, and we know enough of His love to put ourselves blind into His hands. You say, our talk has done no good. I say it has. I see the view you take of things from the place where you stand. I can remember that, when the time comes for judging you; I sha'n't think any longer, does he act right on my views of a thing, but does he act right on his own. It has done me good in that way. I'm an old man, and may never see you again; but I'll pray for you, and think on you and your trials, both of your great wealth, and of your son's cruel death, many and many a day to come; and I'll ask God to bless both to you now and for evermore. Amen. Farewell!"

Jem had maintained a manly and dignified reserve ever since he had made his open statement of all he knew. Now both the men rose, and bowed low, looking at Mr. Carson with the deep human interest they could not fail to take in one who had endured and forgiven a deep injury; and who struggled hard, as it was evident he did, to bear up like a man under his affliction.

He bowed low in return to them. Then he suddenly came forward and shook them by the hand; and thus, without a word more, they parted.

There are stages in the contemplation and endurance of great sorrow, which endow men with the same earnestness and clearness of thought that in some of old took the form of Prophecy. To those who have large capability of loving and suffering, united with great power of firm endurance, there comes a time in their woe, when they are lifted out of the contemplation of their individual case into a searching inquiry into the nature of their calamity, and the remedy (if remedy there be) which may prevent its recurrence to others as well as to themselves.

Hence the beautiful, noble efforts which are from time to time brought to light, as being continuously made by those who have once hung on the cross of agony, in order that others may not suffer as they have done; one of the grandest ends which sorrow can accomplish; the sufferer wrestling with God's messenger until a blessing is left behind, not for one alone but for generations.

It took time before the stern nature of Mr. Carson was compelled to the recognition of this secret of comfort, and that same sternness prevented his reaping any benefit in public estimation from the actions he performed; for the character is more easily changed than the habits and manners originally formed by that character, and to his dying day Mr. Carson was considered hard and cold by those who only casually saw him, or superficially knew him. But those who were admitted into his confidence were aware, that the wish that lay nearest to his heart was that none might suffer from the cause from which he had suffered; that a perfect understanding, and complete confidence and love, might exist between masters and men; that the truth might be recognised that the interests of one were the interests of all, and, as such, required the consideration and deliberation of all; that hence it was most desirable to have educated workers, capable of judging, not mere machines of ignorant men; and to have them bound to their employers by the ties of respect and affection, not by mere money bargains alone; in short, to acknowledge the Spirit of Christ as the regulating law between both parties.

Many of the improvements now in practice in the system of employment in Manchester, owe their origin to short earnest sentences spoken by Mr. Carson. Many and many yet to be carried into execution, take their birth from that stern, thoughtful mind, which submitted to be taught by suffering.

Chapter XXXVIII.

"Touch us gently, gentle Time!
    We've not proud or soaring wings,
Our ambition, our content,
    Lies in simple things;
Humble voyagers are we
O'er life's dim unsounded sea;
    Touch us gently, gentle Time!"
                    BARRY CORNWALL.[7]

Not many days after John Barton's funeral was over, all was arranged respecting Jem's appointment at Toronto; and the time was fixed for his sailing. It was to take place almost immediately: yet much remained to be done; many domestic preparations were to be made; and one great obstacle, anticipated by both Jem and Mary, to be removed. This was the opposition they expected from Mrs. Wilson, to whom the plan had never yet been named.

They were most anxious that their home should continue ever to be hers, yet they feared that her dislike to a new country might be an insuperable objection to this. At last Jem took advantage of an evening of unusual placidity, as he sat alone with his mother just before going to bed, to broach the subject; and to his surprise she acceded willingly to his proposition of her accompanying himself and his wife.

---

7. From Barry Cornwall's (pseudonym for Bryan Waller Proctor [1787–1874]), "A Petition to Time" (1832).

"To be sure 'Merrica is a long way to flit to; beyond London a good bit I reckon; and quite in foreign parts; but I've never had no opinion of England, ever since they could be such fools as to take up a quiet chap like thee, and clap thee in prison. Where you go, I'll go. Perhaps in them Indian countries they'll know a well-behaved lad when they see him; ne'er speak a word more, lad, I'll go."

Their path became daily more smooth and easy; the present was clear and practicable, the future was hopeful; they had leisure of mind enough to turn to the past.

"Jem!" said Mary to him, one evening as they sat in the twilight, talking together in low happy voices till Margaret should come to keep Mary company through the night, "Jem! you've never yet told me how you came to know about my naughty ways with poor young Mr. Carson." She blushed for shame at the remembrance of her folly, and hid her head on his shoulder while he made answer.

"Darling, I'm almost loth to tell you; your aunt Esther told me."

"Ah, I remember! but how did she know? I was so put about that night I did not think of asking her. Where did you see her? I've forgotten where she lives."

Mary said all this in so open and innocent a manner, that Jem felt sure she knew not the truth respecting Esther, and he half hesitated to tell her. At length he replied,

"Where did you see Esther lately? When? Tell me, love, for you've never named it before, and I can't make it out."

"Oh! it was that horrible night, which is like a dream." And she told him of Esther's midnight visit, concluding with, "We must go and see her before we leave, though I don't rightly know where to find her."

"Dearest Mary——"

"What, Jem!" exclaimed she, alarmed by his hesitation.

"Your poor aunt Esther has no home:—she's one of them miserable creatures that walk the streets." And he in his turn told of his encounter with Esther, with so many details that Mary was forced to be convinced, although her heart rebelled against the belief.

"Jem, lad!" said she, vehemently, "we must find her out,—we must hunt her up!" she rose as if she was going on the search there and then.

"What could we do, darling?" asked he, fondly restraining her.

"Do! Why! what could we *not* do, if we could but find her? She's none so happy in her ways, think ye, but what she'd turn from them, if any one would lend her a helping hand. Don't hold me, Jem; this is just the time for such as her to be out, and who knows but what I might find her close at hand."

"Stay, Mary, for a minute; I'll go out now and search for her if you wish, though it's but a wild chase. You must not go. It would be better to ask the police to-morrow. But if I should find her, how can I make her come with me? Once before she refused, and said she could not break off her drinking ways, come what might."

"You never will persuade her if you fear and doubt," said Mary, in tears. "Hope yourself, and trust to the good that must be in her. Speak to that,—she has it in her yet,—oh, bring her home, and we will love her so, we'll make her good."

"Yes!" said Jem, catching Mary's sanguine spirit; "she shall go to America with us; and we'll help her to get rid of her sins. I'll go now, my precious darling, and if I can't find her, it's but trying the police to-morrow. Take care of your own sweet self, Mary," said he, fondly kissing her before he went out.

It was not to be. Jem wandered far and wide that night, but never met Esther. The next day he applied to the police; and at last they recognised under his description of her, a woman known to them under the name of the "Butterfly," from the gaiety of her dress a year or two ago. By their help he traced out one of her haunts, a low lodging-house behind Peter Street. He and his companion, a kind-hearted policeman, were admitted, suspiciously enough, by the land-lady, who ushered them into a large garret where twenty or thirty people of all ages and both sexes lay and dozed away the day, choos-ing the evening and night for their trades of beggary, thieving, or pros-titution.

"I know the Butterfly was here," said she, looking round. "She came in, the night before last, and said she had not a penny to get a place for shelter; and that if she was far away in the country she could steal aside and die in a copse, or a clough,* like the wild animals; but here the police would let no one alone in the streets, and she wanted a spot to die in, in peace. It's a queer sort of peace we have here, but that night the room was uncommon empty, and I'm not a hard-hearted woman (I wish I were, I could ha' made a good thing out of it afore this if I were harder), so I sent her up,—but she's not here now, I think."

"Was she very bad?" asked Jem.

"Ay! nought but skin and bone, with a cough to tear her in two."

They made some inquiries, and found that in the restlessness of approaching death, she had longed to be once more in the open air, and had gone forth,—where, no one seemed to be able to tell.

Leaving many messages for her, and directions that he was to be sent for if either the policeman or the landlady obtained any clue to her whereabouts, Jem bent his steps towards Mary's house; for he had not seen her all that long day of search. He told her of his pro-ceedings and want of success; and both were saddened at the recital, and sat silent for some time.

After awhile they began talking over their plans. In a day or two,

---

*   A.S. "Clough," a cleft of a rock. [WG]

Mary was to give up house, and go and live for a week or so with Job Legh, until the time of her marriage, which would take place immediately before sailing; they talked themselves back into silence and delicious reverie. Mary sat by Jem, his arm round her waist, her head on his shoulder; and thought over the scenes which had passed in that home she was so soon to leave for ever.

Suddenly she felt Jem start, and started too without knowing why; she tried to see his countenance, but the shades of evening had deepened so much she could read no expression there. It was turned to the window; she looked and saw a white face pressed against the panes on the outside, gazing intently into the dusky chamber.

While they watched, as if fascinated by the appearance, and unable to think or stir, a film came over the bright, feverish, glittering eyes outside, and the form sank down to the ground without a struggle of instinctive resistance.

"It is Esther!" exclaimed they, both at once. They rushed outside; and, fallen into what appeared simply a heap of white or light-coloured clothes, fainting or dead, lay the poor crushed Butterfly— the once innocent Esther.

She had come (as a wounded deer drags its heavy limbs once more to the green coolness of the lair in which it was born, there to die) to see the place familiar to her innocence, yet once again before her death. Whether she was indeed alive or dead, they knew not now.

Job came in with Margaret, for it was bedtime. He said Esther's pulse beat a little yet. They carried her up-stairs and laid her on Mary's bed, not daring to undress her, lest any motion should frighten the trembling life away; but it was all in vain.

Towards midnight, she opened wide her eyes and looked around on the once familiar room: Job Legh knelt by the bed, praying aloud and fervently for her, but he stopped as he saw her roused look. She sat up in bed with a sudden convulsive motion.

"Has it been a dream, then?" asked she, wildly. Then with a habit, which came like instinct even in that awful dying hour, her hand sought for a locket which hung concealed in her bosom, and, finding that, she knew all was true which had befallen her since last she lay an innocent girl on that bed.

She fell back, and spoke word never more. She held the locket containing her child's hair still in her hand, and once or twice she kissed it with a long soft kiss. She cried feebly and sadly as long as she had any strength to cry, and then she died.

They laid her in one grave with John Barton. And there they lie without name, or initial, or date. Only this verse is inscribed upon the stone which covers the remains of these two wanderers.

Psalm ciii. v. 9.—"For he will not always chide, neither will he keep his anger for ever."

I see a long low wooden house, with room enough and to spare. The old primeval trees are felled and gone for many a mile around; one alone remains to overshadow the gable-end of the cottage. There is a garden around the dwelling, and far beyond that stretches an orchard. The glory of an Indian summer is over all, making the heart leap at the sight of its gorgeous beauty.

At the door of the house, looking towards the town, stands Mary, watching the return of her husband from his daily work; and while she watches, she listens, smiling,

> "Clap hands, daddy comes,
> With his pocket full of plums,
> And a cake for Johnnie."

Then comes a crow of delight from Johnnie. Then his grandmother carries him to the door, and glories in seeing him resist his mother's blandishments to cling to her.

"English letters! 'Twas that made me so late!"

"Oh, Jem, Jem! don't hold them so tight! What do they say?"

"Why, some good news. Come, give a guess what it is."

"Oh, tell me! I cannot guess," said Mary.

"Then you give it up, do you? What do you say, mother?" Jane Wilson thought a moment.

"Will and Margaret are married?" asked she.

"Not exactly,—but very near. The old woman has twice the spirit of the young one. Come, Mary, give a guess!"

He covered his little boy's eyes with his hands for an instant, significantly, till the baby pushed them down, saying in his imperfect way,

"Tan't see."

"There now! Johnnie can see. Do you guess, Mary?"

"They've done something to Margaret to give her back her sight!" exclaimed she.

"They have. She has been couched,[8] and can see as well as ever. She and Will are to be married on the twenty-fifth of this month, and he's bringing her out here next voyage; and Job Legh talks of coming too,—not to see you, Mary,—nor you, mother,—nor you, my little hero" (kissing him), "but to try and pick up a few specimens of Canadian insects, Will says. All the compliment is to the earwigs, you see, mother!"

"Dear Job Legh!" said Mary, softly and seriously.

THE END

---

8. Technique for removing cataracts by displacing them below the line of vision.

CONTEXTS

JOHN GEOFFREY SHARPS

The Genesis of *Mary Barton*†

* * *

Reproduced below are a rough sketch for the novel and an outline of its proposed conclusion. A copy of the former occurs in the *Mary Barton* section of the second volume of the Shorter-Symington typescript, 'Correspondence, Articles & Notes Relating to Mrs. E. C. Gaskell. Transcripts' (lodged in the Gaskell Section, Brotherton Collection, Leeds University Library): whether or not the original is extant remains unknown; it may once have been in the possession of the Howitts[1] and, later, of Meta Gaskell.[2] The manuscript of the latter (almost certainly the author's holograph) forms part of the Forster Collection at the Victoria & Albert Museum: possibly it came into Forster's hands when, as 'a reader for Chapman & Hall, . . . he recommended'[3] the novel for publication. Whereas in many places the first edition is at odds with the rough sketch, divergencies from the outlined conclusion are minor and few; but, not unnaturally, much appears in the printed version of which there is no suggestion in either. As regards the intended ending, it will be recalled that Mrs. Gaskell was required to supply additional material when the presses were already at work.

GASKELL (MRS. E. C.)
COPY OF THE ROUGH SKETCH MADE
BEFORE BEGINNING TO WRITE

---

† From *Mrs. Gaskell's Observation and Invention: A Study of Her Non-Biographic Works* (Sussex: Linden Press, 1970), pp. 551–62.
1. This surmise is suggested by a letter from Mary Howitt to Mrs. Gaskell, an undated extract from which appears in Shorter and Symington, 'Correspondence, Articles & Notes Relating to Mrs. E. C. Gaskell. Transcripts', Vol. II, Section on *Mary Barton*. Mrs. Howitt there speaks of her husband and herself reading the novel; she enquires how much more remains to be written, yet in such terms as show her aware of the happy ending. On the other hand, one could argue that the Howitts did not have the rough sketch, but rather the MS of the proposed conclusion or even a brief note from the author about her intended outcome. [The Howitts were friends of Gaskell's and published her earliest writings in their *Howitt's Journal.—Editor*].
2. 'Miss Gaskell tells me that her mother thought out the scheme of the book [*Mary Barton*], and even the subjects of the chapters, before starting to write it, and that she kept to her original plan precisely.'—Sarah A. Tooley, 'The Centenary of Mrs. Gaskell', *The Cornhill Magazine*, N.S. XXIX (1910), 322. We may also note that among items offered as help with preparing the Knutsford Edition the Miss Gaskells 'named "a rough sketch of the plot of 'Mary Barton,' drawn out before a word of the book was written, but strangely adhered to in the writing"' ([Huxley] *The House of Smith Elder*, p. 206)—see too Wright, *Mrs. Gaskell*, pp. ix, 265–268.
3. Sanders, *Elizabeth Gaskell*, p. 18.

"MARY BARTON"[4]
"MARY BARTON"
First Chap.

Scene in G. H.—Spring Evening—Wilsons & Bartons—The Wilsons speak of Esther's disappearance—are joined by the Bartons, &c.

Second Chap.

4 years passed away. Changes. The strong Alice Wilson and healthy Thomas Barton dead—while the feeble and less healthy remain behind—No news yet of Esther.

Good times—How flourishing Wilson is—How he joins a Chartist Club at the instigation of Job Leigh—How he apprentices Mary to a dress-maker. How Widow Barton strives on to keep her delicate twins with the help of her son Thomas and succeeds.

How Thomas Barton in his way to his work always meets Mary, and what arises therefrom.

How Mr. Chadwick Junior on his way home to dinner always meets Mary and what arises therefrom.

A Father and daughter's talk over the fire; Past life—gone and dead. The old always homing to the past, the young looking to the future. Plans for a day at Dunham next Whitsun week.

The day at Dunham.

Rumours of Bad times—Bad times.

Bradshaw & Co. fail. Wilson dismissed.

Mrs. Barton's sorrows.

Wilson engaged at Chadwick & Co's Mill.

How Charterism from a theory becomes an action in bad times.

END OF VOL. I.

How Mary suffers from the bad times.

Margaret Clegg and Mary have mourning to make.

---

4. Although the general lay-out of the Brotherton typescript has been followed, exact reproduction has not been sought.

Death at the Bartons' Mary and Aunt Esther sit up by turns.

Mary's first love.

How in the midst of much sorrow, Mary is happy in her own individual world of love.

Poor Thomas Barton.

Thomas and Mary quarrel. His despair.

Mary's bliss. Her conscience-struck visit to poor Widow Barton. Aunt Esther.

Mary's downfall of heart. Mr. Chadwick's threat.

Fanny's first visit to Wilson—her tale—her warning regarding Mary.

Mary undeceived. Who was listening.

Trades Unions, and desperation.

Mr. Chadwick murdered.

VOL. III

The police on the scent.

Barton arrested.

Mary's revulsion of feeling. Goes to see Widow Barton. Accompanies her to prison.

Barton in prison.

Mary's determination to prove Barton's innocence.

Discovers the Murderer.

Fanny.

Agony.

Visits Widow Barton. Aunt Hester's childishness.

A sympathizing and advising friend, Job Leigh.

How she proves an alibi by Margaret Clegg's help.

Interview with Barton. *He* knew too.

Father's death of remorse—Widow Barton's.

Aunt Hester's death.

Marriage—Sail for America.

NOTES

G.H. is for Green Heys.

The names are different in the novel:—

> Wilson and Barton being interchanged there, and Jem substituted for Thomas—and Carson for Chadwick.

Notes on Divergencies between the Rough Sketch and the First Edition

It may be well to supplement the notes in the Brotherton typescript by summarizing some main points of difference between the sketch and the book. The following list does not claim to be exhaustive; nor are the numerous additions in the printed version noticed.

1. Many names are altered. For example:
   (i)   Wilsons and Bartons are interchanged;
   (ii) Chadwick becomes Carson;
   (iii) Job Leigh becomes Job Legh;
   (iv) Esther/Fanny is apparently the Esther of the novel;
   (v)   Margaret Clegg becomes Margaret Jennings.
2. The Wilsons (=Bartons) are not joined by the Bartons (=Wilsons) after they have spoken of Esther's disappearance.
3. There is no four-year gap between the first and second chapter.
4. The death of healthy Thomas Barton (=George Wilson) does not occur till quite late in the story, after that of his twins.
5. Job Leigh (=Legh) is not an active Chartist, only a reluctant Unionist; nor does he introduce Wilson (=Barton) to Chartism.
6. Strictly speaking, one would say that Mary apprenticed herself to a dress-maker.
7. Thomas Barton (=Jem Wilson) does not always meet Mary as he goes to work.
8. There is no father-daughter fireside talk about the past and the future.

9. The day at Dunham occurs in 'Era II' of *Libbie Marsh's Three Eras,* not in *Mary Barton*.

10. There is no failure of Bradshaw & Co.; Wilson (=Barton) once had to be turned off when work at Mr. Hunter's stopped (*Works,* I, 24).

11. Wilson (=Barton) is never engaged at Chadwick & Co.'s (=Carsons') Mill.

12. Mary and Aunt Esther (?=Aunt Alice Wilson) never sit up by turns.

13. There is no real threat by Mr. Chadwick (=Carson), senior or junior.

14. The suggestion in the sketch that perhaps the murderer of Chadwick (=Carson) listens when Mary is undeceived is not borne out by the novel.

15. It is not quite clear in the sketch whether it is Mr. Chadwick (=Carson) senior or his son who is murdered.

16. Mary does not accompany Mrs. Barton (=Wilson) to prison; indeed neither visits there.

17. The help given by Margaret Clegg (=Jennings) in proving the alibi is slight compared with that of Will, the sailor.

18. Widow Barton (=Wilson) does not die, but emigrates to America with her son and daughter-in-law.

19. The sequence of events set out in the sketch differs in several ways from that found in the book.

20. The novel came out in two, not three, volumes.
    [page 1]

Conclusion yet to be written.[5]

Mary had a brain fever, and knew not the/
end of the trial; how Will had proved an alibi,/
if not to the satisfaction of all, at any rate sufficiently/
to make the jury give Jem the benefit of the doubt/
how Will snapped his fingers at the lawyers, and/
how Ben Sturgis & the pilot proved that he *had*/
been summoned back from sea. For many days/
Mary knew nothing,—she was nursed by M^{rs}/
Sturgis, and by Jem; at least by Jem after he had/
taken his mother home; accompanied by Will/
who hastened to see Aunt Alice once more;—she,/
blessed with a veiled blessing, (with second childhood,)/
sang her canticle of departure, believing her-/
self to be once more in the happy happy realms/

5. This manuscript (a single sheet, folded to make four pages), almost certainly Mrs. Gaskell's holograph, is in the Forster Collection—F. MS. 215* (pressmark: F. 48. E. 23, No. 138)— at the Victoria & Albert Museum. At the top right-hand corner of the first page is written, in a different hand, '(Mrs Gaskell)'.

of childhood, once more dwelling in the lovely/
scenes where she had so often longed to be—un=/
changed, & in the old radiant hues—and death/
came to her as Evening comes to the wearied child//

   [page 2]
But leaving Will & Margaret plighting their faith/
   \<b> y [Alice's death bed, *deleted*] Alice's grave; leaving his mother/
   \<in> Margaret's care, Jem returned to Mary, and/
   \<w> hen her reason returned his was the first face she/
   \<s> aw.—They came back to Manchester as soon as/
   \<h> er strength would admit, with a heavy weight on/ their hearts,
(although no word on the subject had/
   \<p> assed between them,—) in regard to John Barton, about/
   \<w> hom they had heard nothing, & durst make no/
   \<e> nquiries. But when Mary opened the apparently/
   \<s> hut up house there was her father sitting motion=/
   \<le> ss by the cold grey ashes of his hearth. His appearance/
   \<a> ll anguish-stricken by remorse made Mary for-/
   \<ge> t every thing but her love towards him—she forgot/
   \<th> e crime in her endeavours to soothe,—But he was/
   \<s> tony,—speechless—Do you remember the bit/
in Fuller's Worthies   /
   \<> 'I have read of a bird which hath a face like, &/
yet will prey upon a man,—who coming to the/
water to drink, and finding there by reflection/
   \<h> e hath killed one like himself pineth away by/
degrees."[6] And do you also remember an exquisite//
   [page 3]
piece of Wither ending with   /

                  But this I know full well/
   My Father who above the Heavens doth dwell,/
   An eye upon his wandering child will cast/
  And he will bring me to [his *deleted*] ^my^ home at last./[7]
And [th *deleted*] such was the beginning & ending of poor John/
Barton's last scene. His sin had found him out. His/
temptation was suicide. Death seemed as if it w^{d}/
take him to the Father whose judgments are more/
merciful than those of men, & who would teach him/
the right way which he had so wandered from here./

6. The passage occurs in Thomas Fuller's sketch of Sir Edward Harwood (which appears under the heading of Soldiers, in the section on Lincolnshire) in his *History of the Worthies of England* (1662). Besides modifying the spelling and punctuation, Mrs. Gaskell apparently omitted 'that' ('by reflexion, that he had') from this quotation.
7. These lines by George Wither, here slightly misquoted, come from the 'Nec Careo' section of *Wither's Motto* (1621).

But he resisted that temptation, [though he longed to *deleted*]
^no he would not^/
[escape from his remorse. *deleted*] ^escape^ He had not heard
of Jem's/
arrest or trial till it was over, & then he had reached/
home he knew not how. But he told Mary nothing,/
but sank day by day, conscience-stricken. Still he/
saw a duty;—unknown to Mary or to Jem (who/
avoided coming to the house from delicacy,) he sent/
for [a po *deleted*] Mʳ Carson, and to him he told his guilt &/
exculpated Jem fully; he was then dying, & told/
Mʳ Carson how thankful he would have been to be/
hanged, how infinitely more awful was a life of remorse/
But Mʳ C. did not understand him, & dying as he wa <s> /
gave him in charge to the police that night. But un <able> //

[page 4]
like King Darius[8] to rest upon his bed, he went/
early the next morning to John Barton's house, and/
found the police, who had watched him through the/
night, taking him to prison in spite of Mary's entreaties/
He [by his *deleted*] ^with a^ last penitent cry to God for
pardon, died, &/
as the breath fled, the stern Mʳ Carson joined in the/
prayer, and, softened by the agony which ended in Death,/
forgave him.   /
Then Jem & Mary talked over things, & told each other/
about Esther, & Jem resolved to find her out. By the/
help of the police he tracked her to a lodging house/
where all the outcasts sleep that have a penny to pay/
for a roof. He went in, early one morning and/
found her on her miserable couch ^of straw^ among twenty/
other men women & children—dead;—with a little/
lock of a child's yellow hair clenched in her hand./
Then I suppose Will & Margaret were married/
only I dare say she was couched first[9],—but/
Jem & Mary, & his mother, weary & sick of Manches/
=ter, resolved to go to America, & so, sailing along the/
path of the setting sun, they fade from my sight,/
& darkness mantles over their future, & shrouds/
it from my vision.   //

Notes on Divergencies between the Proposed Conclusion and the Ending of the First Edition

8. Daniel 6.19.
9. Cf. [Aldofus William Ward, *The Works of Mrs. Gaskell*, 8 vols. (London: Smith, Elder & Co., 1906)], I, 458.

Below are listed the chief differences between the MS plan and the ending as printed; no account is taken of events found in the first edition but not mentioned in the manuscript.

1. Will and Margaret do not plight their troth by Alice's deathbed or grave.
2. Strictly speaking, one must say that the face of Mrs. Sturgis, not that of Jem, was the first seen by Mary on her recovery (*Works*, I, 404).
3. Mr. Carson did not give John Barton in charge to the police; nor, on his return the following morning, did he find them taking Barton to prison.
4. Jem did not find Esther dead in a lodging-house.

Letters

ELIZABETH GASKELL

From Letters[†]

EDWARD CHAPMAN

121, Upper Rumford St
Manchester. March 21. [1848]

Dear Sir,

When I had the pleasure of being introduced to you at the beginning of the year, I think you led me to understand that my work was to follow Miss Jewsbury's[1] in the publication of your Series. I am naturally a little anxious to know when you are going to press.

I can not help fancying that the tenor of my tale is such as to excite attention at the present time of struggle on the part of work people to obtain what they esteem their rights; on the other side it is very possible that people are now so much absorbed by public work as to have very little time or interest to bestow on works of fiction.

As you have the MS in your hands I am trusting to you to see that it is set up so as to make the right quantity. Perhaps you will favour this with an answer at your convenience.

Believe me to remain dear Sir

Yours truly
E. C. Gaskell

Mr Chapman
Strand
London

---

† From *The Letters of Mrs Gaskell*, ed. J. A. V. Chapple and Arthur Pollard, 1998, Manchester University Press, Manchester, UK.
1. *Half Sisters.*

EDWARD CHAPMAN

[?]Gale Cottage
Tuesday, July 10th [1848]

Dear Sir,

I would rather leave the decision regarding the time of publication to you; as your experience must lead you to judge better than I can do on the subject. What is the opinion of the gentleman to whom you once before referred as the Editor of the Series? Perhaps you will let me know what you fix upon.

I hardly know what you mean by an 'explanatory preface'. The only thing I should like to make clear is that it is no catchpenny run up since the events on the Continent have directed public attention to the consideration of the state of affairs between the Employers, & their work-people.

If you think the book requires such a preface I will try to concoct it; but at present, I have no idea what to say.

I remain, dear Sir

Yours truly
E. C. Gaskell.

EDWARD CHAPMAN

121, Upper Rumford St
Decr 5th 1848.

Dear Sir,

I wish you could know how *very* much I dislike writing this note; and yet we are really beginning to think you have forgotten that you have never completed your part of the agreement respecting M Barton. I do not know how it is selling of course, but I understood that it was to be paid for on publication, independently of the success, or otherwise, of the sale. Hitherto the whole affair of publication has been one of extreme annoyance to me, from the impertinent and unjustifiable curiosity of people, who have tried to force me either into an absolute denial, or an acknowledgement of what they must have seen the writer wished to keep concealed.

In looking over the book I see numerous errors regarding the part written in the Lancashire dialect; 'gotten' should always be 'getten'; &c.—In the midst of all my deep & great annoyance, Mr Carlyle's letter has been most valuable; and has given me almost the only\unmixed/pleasure I have yet received from the publication of MB.

I remain, Sir,

Yours truly
E. C. Gaskell

EDWARD CHAPMAN

Friday morning
Decr 7th 1848.

My dear Sir,

I acknowledge, with many thanks, the first half of the 100£, due to me for the MS of 'Mary Barton'. I am very much obliged to you for your note; and for the friendly and just manner in which you write about my annoyance respecting my name being known. I certainly did not expect that so much curiosity would be manifested; and I can scarcely yet understand how people can reconcile it to their consciences to try and discover what it is evident the writer wishes to conceal. I have been made very unhappy by my own self-reproaches for the deceit I have practised, and into which I have almost been forced by impertinent enquiry; and these last few days I have thought it better simply to acknowledge the truth, in order to put a stop to all these unpleasant manifestations of curiosity.* * *

I do indeed value Mr Carlyle's note, and for the precise reason you mention; it bears the stamp of honesty and truth; in the discriminate praise; and\shows that he/thinks me worthy of being told of my faults. I half thought of sending you a copy, but I don't know if you would care to see it. I have seen enough of the way in which authors in general *flummery* each other up with insincere and overdone praise to be disgusted with flattery for ever. Neither Mr Dickens nor Mrs Davenport have ever acknowledged their copies; but I sent them more to satisfy my own feelings, than to receive thanks.

EDWARD CHAPMAN

121, Upper Rumford St
Janry 1st [1849]

Dear Sir,

* * *Half the masters here are bitterly angry with me—half (and the best half) are buying it to give to their work-people's libraries. One party say it shall be well abused in the British Quarterly, the other say it shall be praised in the Westminster; I had no idea it would have proved such a fire brand; meanwhile no one seems to see my idea of a tragic poem; so I, in reality, mourn over my failure.—Mr Carlyle's letter remains my real true gain.

Yours very truly
E C Gaskell.

MISS LAMONT

121, Upper Rumford St,
Manchester—
Jan—5th [1849]

* * * On my return home from a visit of a few days near Rochdale I found your note my dear Miss Lamont. You can not think how it pleased me; I don't know what other people feel, but I am so glad when any body will take the kind trouble of *expressing* satisfaction at Mary B. I should like much to have a long talk with you about it, but there you are far away in Ireland. 'John Barton' was the original name, as being the central figure to my mind; indeed I had so long felt that the bewildered life of an ignorant thoughtful man of strong power of sympathy, dwelling in a town so full of striking contrasts as this is, was a tragic poem, that in writing he was [?]my 'hero'; and it was a London thought coming through the publisher that it must be called *Mary* B. So many people overlook John B or see him merely to misunderstand him, that if you were a stranger and had only said that one thing (that the book shd have been called *John* B) I should have had pleasure in feeling that my own idea was recognized; how much more am I pleased then when the whole letter comes from one whom I so much liked and admired in our few & far between glimpses as I did you. Some people here are very angry and say the book will do harm; and for a time I have been shaken and sorry; but I have such firm faith that the earnest expression of any one's feeling can only do good in the long run,—that God will cause the errors to be temporary[,] the truth to be eternal, that I try not to mind too much what people say either in blame or praise. I had a letter from Carlyle, and when I am over-filled with thoughts arising from this book, I put it all aside, (or *try* to put it aside,) and think of his last sentence—'May you live long to write good books, or *do silently good actions which in my sight is far more indispensable.*' * * *

MRS GREG[2]

[?Early 1849]

My dear Mrs Greg,

    May I write in the first person to you, as I have many things I should like to say to the writer of the remarks on 'Mary Barton' which Miss Mitchell has sent me, and which I conjecture were written by your husband? Those remarks and the note which accompanied have given me great and real pleasure. I have heard much about the disapproval which Mr Greg's family have felt with regard to 'M. B.,' and

---

2. An 'uncompleted draft' from a printed source.

have heard of it with so much regret that I am particularly glad that Mr Sam Greg does not participate in it. I regretted the disapprobation, not one whit on account of the testimony of such disapproval which I heard was to arise out of it,[3] but because I knew that such a feeling would be conscientiously and thoughtfully entertained by men who are acquainted by long experience with the life, a portion of which I had endeavoured to represent; and whose actions during a long course of years have proved that the interests of their workpeople are as dear to them as their own. Such disapproval, I was sure, would not be given if the writing which called it forth were merely a free expression of ideas; but it would be given if I had misrepresented, or so represented, a part as the whole, as that people at a distance should be misled and prejudiced against the masters, and that class be estranged from class.

I value the remarks exceedingly, because the writer has exactly entered into my own state of mind, and perceived the weakness of which I was conscious. The whole tale grew up in my mind as imperceptibly as a seed germinates in the earth, so I cannot trace back now why or how such a thing was written, or such a character or circumstance introduced. (There is one exception to this which I will name afterwards.) I can remember now that the prevailing thought in my mind at the time when the tale was silently forming itself and impressing me with the force of a reality, was the seeming injustice of the inequalities of fortune. Now, if they occasionally appeared unjust to the more fortunate, they must bewilder an ignorant man full of rude, illogical thought, and full also of sympathy for suffering which appealed to him through his senses. I fancied I saw how all this might lead to a course of action which might appear right for a time to the bewildered mind of such a one, but that this course of action, violating the eternal laws of God, would bring with it its own punishment of an avenging conscience far more difficult to bear than any worldly privation. Such thoughts I now believe, on looking back, to have been the origin of the book. 'John Barton' was the original title of the book. Round the character of John Barton all the others formed themselves; he was my hero, *the* person with whom all my sympathies went, with whom I tried to identify myself at the time, because I believed from personal observation that such men were not uncommon, and would well reward such sympathy and love as should throw light down upon their groping search after the causes of suffering, and the reason why suffering is sent, and what they can do to lighten it. Mr Greg has exactly described, and in clearer language than I could have used, the very treatment which I am convinced is needed to bring such bewildered thinkers round into an

3. W. R. Greg's review appeared in the *Edinburgh Review* (April 1849, 89, pp. 402–35).

acknowledgment of the universality of some kind of suffering, and the consequent necessity of its existence for some good end. If Mary Barton has no other result than the expression of the thoroughly just, wise, kind thoughts which Mr Greg has written down with regard to characters like John Barton, I am fully satisfied. There are many such whose lives are magic [?tragic][4] poems which cannot take formal language. The tale was formed, and the greater part of the first volume was written when I was obliged to lie down constantly on the sofa, and when I took refuge in the invention to exclude the memory of painful scenes which would force themselves upon my remembrance. It is no wonder then that the whole book seems to be written in the minor key; indeed, the very design seems to me to require this treatment. I acknowledge the fault of there being too heavy a shadow over the book; but I doubt if the story could have been deeply realized without these shadows. The cause of the fault must be looked for in the design; and yet the design was one worthy to be brought into consideration. Perhaps after all it may be true that I, in my state of feelings at that time, was not fitted to introduce the glimpses of light and happiness which might have relieved the gloom. And now I return to the part I named before, where I can trace and remember how unwillingly and from what force of outside pressure (which is, I am convinced, a wrong motive for writing and sure only to produce a failure) it was written. The tale was originally complete without the part which intervenes between John Barton's death and Esther's; about 3 pages, I fancy, including that conversation between Job Legh, and Mr Carson, and Jem Wilson. The MS. had been in the hands of the publisher above 14 months, and was nearly all printed when the publisher sent me word that it would fall short of the requisite number of pages, and that I must send up some more as soon as possible. I remonstrated over and over again—I even said I would rather relinquish some of the payment than interpolate anything;* * *

LADY KAY-SHUTTLEWORTH

Silverdale, near Lancaster
July 16. [?1850]

My dear Lady,
* * *I cannot think that you could for a moment imagine that I should be 'offended' by, or 'think you impertinent' for evincing such kind interest in the direction and object of any future writing of mine. Several people whose opinion I have very much respected have suggested the same subject as that which you did; but after a good deal of thought I feel that if it is to be done, it must be by someone else. I think so, for several reasons, which I will tell you if it will

4. Dr J. M. S. Tompkins has also independently suggested this emendation.

not weary you. In the first place whatever power there was in Mary
Barton was caused by my feeling strongly on the side which I took;
now as I don't feel as strongly (and as it is impossible I ever should,)
on the other side, the forced effort of writing on that side would
{be}\end in/a weak failure. I know, and have always owned, that I
have represented *but one* side of the question, and no one would
welcome more than I should, a true and earnest representation of
the other side. I believe what I have said in Mary Barton to be perfectly true, but by no means the whole truth; and I have always felt
deeply annoyed at anyone, or any set of people who chose to consider that I had manifested the whole truth; I do not think it is possible to do this in any *one* work of fiction. You say 'I think there are
good mill-owners; I think the factory system might be made a great
engine for good'; and in this no one can more earnestly and heartily
agree with you than I do. I can not imagine a nobler scope for a
thoughtful energetic man, desirous of doing good to his kind, than
that presented to his powers as the master of a factory. But I believe
that there is much to be discovered yet as to the right position and
mutual duties of employer, and employed; and the utmost I hoped
from Mary Barton has been that it would give a spur to inactive
thought, and languid conscience in this direction. (Am I tiring you?)
I think the best and most benevolent employers would say how difficult they, with all their experience, found it to unite theory and
practice. I am sure Mr Sam Greg would. How could I suggest or
even depict modes of proceeding, (the details of which I never saw,)
and which from some error, undetected even by anxious and conscientious witnesses, seems so often to result in disappointment? It
would require a wise man, practical and full of experience,\one/able
to calculate consequences, to choose out the best among the many
systems which are being tried by the benevolent mill-owners. If I, in
my ignorance, chose out one which appeared to me good, but which
was known to business men to be a failure, I should be doing an
injury instead of a service. For instance Mr Sam Greg's plans have
been accompanied with great want of success in a money point of
view. This has been a stinging grief to him, as he was most anxious
to show that his benevolent theories, which were so beautiful in
their origin, might be carried into effect with good and *just* practical
results of benefit to both master and man. He knew that he was
watched in all his proceedings by no friendly eyes, who would be
glad to set down failure in business to what they considered his
Utopian schemes.[5] I think he, or such as he, might almost be made
the hero of a fiction on the other side of the question[—]the trials

5. Greg's efforts at industrial welfare and his energetic proselytising caused a breakdown of
health and compelled his retirement.* * *.

of the conscientious rich man, in his dealings with the poor. And I should like some *man*, who had a man's correct knowledge, to write on this subject, and make the poor intelligent work-people understand the infinite anxiety as to right and wrongdoing which I believe that riches bring to many.

I acknowledge,—no one feels more keenly than I do, the great fault of the gloominess of M B. It is the fault of the choice of the subject; which yet I did not *choose*, but which was as it were impressed upon me. Some time or other I should like to show you some letters I have had on the subject, if you cared to see them; and are not already wearied by what I have now written. ⁂ ⁂ ⁂

THOMAS CARLYLE

To Mrs. Gaskell, November 8, 1848[†]

Dear *Madam*
(for I catch the *treble*
of that fine melodious
voice very well),—

We have read your Book here, my Wife first and then I; both of us with real pleasure. A beautiful, cheerfully pious, social, clear and observant character is everywhere recognisable in the writer, which surely is the welcomest sight any writer can shew us in his books; your field moreover is new, important, full of rich materials (which, as is usual, required a soul of some opulence to recognize them as rich): the result is a Book deserving to take its place far above the ordinary garbage of Novels,—a Book which every intelligent person may read with entertainment, and which it will do every one some good to read. I gratefully accept it as a real contribution (almost the first real one) towards developing a huge subject, which has lain *dumb* too long, and really ought to speak for itself, and tell us its meaning a little, if there be any voice in it at all! Speech, or Literature (which is, or should be, Select-Speech) could hardly find a more rational function, I think, at present.

You will probably give us other Books on this same matter; for I see you are still young; and *Mary Barton*, according to my auguries of its reception here, is likely to procure you sufficient invitation. May you do it well and ever better! Unless I mistake, you are capable of going still deeper into this subject, and of bringing up Portraits of Manchester Existence still more strikingly *real*,—which latter quality is

† From John Rylands Library English Manuscript 730. By permission of the John Rylands Library.

the grand value of them in the end.—Your writing is already very beautiful, soft, clear, and natural: only learn evermore (what perhaps you can, and what very few can under present conditions) to be *concise*; I mean not in words only, but in thought and conception; to reject the unessential more and more, and retain only the essential, at whatever cost of sacrifice:—this, well understood, is really the Law and the Prophets for a Writer! Very fit that a good Book, or any other product that is to endure, have the *water* carefully roasted out of it, in the first place. Jem Wilson, too, knows very well that one should *hit the nail on the head*, always; and having riveted it home, go to the next nail, *not* beating on the intermediate spaces,—if we *are* smiths! In short, brevity and clear veracity,—these two, which make properly but *one*, are "the soul of wit,"[1]—the essence of all good qualities in writing. On the side of "veracity", or devout earnestness of mind, I find you already strong; and that will tend well to help the other side of the matter if there be any defect there.

May you live long to write good Books,—and to do *silently* good actions, which I believe is very much more indispensable!—With kind respects and thanks.

Thomas Carlyle

MARIA EDGEWORTH

Letter to Miss Holland†

Edgeworthstown.
Dec^r*. 27th*, 1848.

My dear Miss Holland—

You delighted your father by reading to him Mary Barton and I have been delighted by hearing it read by my sister Harriet Butler— I am persuaded that you both of you and the *author* into the bargain would have been happy to have been of the party—

In the first place as I have said Author I must tell you that I mean author to stand for male or female just as the case may be—But I opine that it is a she—From the great abilities—and from the power of drawing *from* the life and *to* the life so as to give the impression and strong interest of reality I should have attributed the book to Miss Martineau—especially as the tale shews such intimate knowledge of manufacturing miseries and of all those small details which can be

---

1. *Hamlet*, 2.2. 90.
† From Ross D. Waller, "Letters Addressed to Mrs. Gaskell by Celebrated Contemporaries Now in the Possession of the John Rylands Library," *Bulletin of the John Rylands Library* 19, pp. 102–69, 1935. Reproduced by courtesy of the University Librarian and Director, The John Rylands University Library, The University of Manchester.

obtained only from personal observation and which can be selected so as to produce great effect, only by the union of quiet feeling with cool discriminating judgement.

But in the Preface the writer says that she is 'no political economist'—I do not think Miss Martineau would be guilty of such a gratuitous and useless falsehood. There fell my supposition that Miss Martineau did write this story. But she need not be effronted but would I think be gratified by having it attributed to her—

The description of the coming on of deafness and of the evils or sense of privation felt by the deaf struck me particularly as being worthy of Miss Martineau's personal narrative—the coming on of blindness too is most beautifully described!—

In truth there is no bodily or mental evil to which flesh is heir which this author cannot describe most feelingly—The evils consequent upon over manufacturing or over population or both conjoined and acting as cause and effect—the misery and the hateful passions engendered by the love of gain and the accumulation of riches, and the selfishness and want of thought and want of feeling in master manufacturers are most admirably described and the consequences produced on the inferior class of employed or unemployed workmen are most ably shewn in action—There is great discretion in the drawing the characters of the Carson family—in not exaggerating—Jem—is a delightful noble creature and not over colored. John Barton too is admirably kept up from 1st to last—and Mary herself is charming—from not being too perfect—The mother of Jem (Mrs. Wilson) is, we think, the *best* drawn character in the book—tho that is a bold word where there are so many incomparables—Sally is very well drawn with redeeming good nature in the midst of her vanity and selfishness—Here are no such faultless nor any such vicious monsters as the world ne'er saw—But all such as have been seen and are recognised by all who have thought and by all who can feel—all who can look inwardly at their own minds or outwardly at the world we live in—

The story is ingenious and interesting—The heroine is in a new and good difficulty between her guilty father and her innocent noble lover—It is a situation fit for the highest Greek Tragedy yet not unsuited to the humblest life of a poor tender girl—heroism, as well as, love in a cottage—Her declaration of her love before the whole court in the trial is charming though useless to the lover so much the better for the truth of the drawing of the passion and the character—

I am sorry that she and her lover emigrate—I think the poetic justice and moral of the story would have been better and as naturally made out by Jems *good character* standing against the prejudice suspicion or envy of his fellow workmen as I really believe it would have done—and it would more shew the effect of good conduct in workmen and inspire hope for the future better without its being improbable that the noble conduct of Jem should have made such impression on the rich man and the master manufacturers that they took the case of the workmen for his sake into consideration—This would have been the finest reward and w^d have left not only an agreeable but beneficial feeling on the mind—

Rousseau says Judge of a book by the impression left on your mind when you lay it down.

I am not sure that this is quite just—but it has sense and justice in it—

I would not leave the reader in Despair—Despair never produced Virtue or the *energy of Virtue*. There must be hope for *that*.

The fault of this book is that it leaves such a melancholy I almost feel hopeless impression. When the box of evils was opened Hope sh^d have been left sticking to the lid.

> It is all too true
> But what can we do
> What can be done—

It is in fact difficult to say—for we cannot make a new division and equal distribution of wealth without *revolution* and even if we could do this without revolution and injustice to the present possessors of what permanent avail c^d it be? Wealth must immediately and incessantly tend to reaccumulate unless the efforts of INDUSTRY and its wages are stopped and this stoppage c^d not increase human happiness. There must then be rich and poor—Laborer[s] and Masters. All that can be done is to prevent the labourers from being made slaves and to deter the masters from becoming tyrants—Such a powerful writer as the author of Mary Barton *could* tend to this beneficial purpose by his pathetic representations and appeals to the feelings of pity and remorse—But I doubt whether this has been effected by the present tale—*Emigration* is the only resource pointed out at the end of this work, and this is only an escape from the evils not a remedy nor any tendency to reparation or improvement.—

We are haunted by the spectres of misery which have been raised to our view and we cannot lay them—We are in a worse condition than the man who was haunted by him who came continually to the side of the bed crying.

> *'Give me back my golden leg.'*

The cry from these spectres is worse 'Give me a leg to stand upon! or I'll cut off both yours' and the only answer is

> 'I cannot give you legs without cutting off my own.'

—My dear Mary Holland if you are acquainted with the author of Mary Barton as I suspect you are please to tell him or her as the case may be, as much or as little of the foregoing sense or nonsense as you see fit—or as can do any good—For the past work no use criticism but for the future there may be use—Such a writer cannot but write again and cannot but be candid and will *rejudge* the criticism and the book and profit by the rejudgement—at all events.

—I should add that I *feel* that there are too many deaths in the book—Death is an evil common to all and not a peculiar moral punishment and the mere contemplation of the difference between the death bed *hour* of the bad and the good is not according to my view a sufficient motive for the survivors—to make it advisable for a good moral writer to have recourse to this source of pathos.—hacknied too and worn to nought.

I may as well empty my mind of all the objections I *can* make that the author may the more believe in the perfect sincerity of my admiration—I have not given half the praise I could and that I did give as I heard the Work read—But upon reflexion a word or two more of blame occur—

I think or rather I *feel*—that not only there are too many deaths but too many living creatures in this book—The readers sympathy is too much divided—cannot flit as fast as called upon from one to another without being weakened. The more forcible the calls and the objects of pity the more the feelings are harassed and in danger of being exhausted

—I think that some of the miserables might be left out—For instance *Esther* who is no good and does no good to Mary or to anybody else—nor to the story—she might be and may be in every town in the Empire as well as at Manchester. Her faults are not the results of manufacturing wrongs from masters or evils of men—The circumstance of the husband in his rage pulling down the nail on wh[h] her bonnet hung is admirable and should not upon any account be omitted—I have heard it wished that the character of *Alice* should be expunged. But this is not my wish or feeling on the contrary this character does not increase the sum of painful or despairing feeling—But adds to the hopeful and salutary—because in spite of all external misfortunes she is happy through life and happy in death from her internal resources of benevolence and energetic virtue.

And I can believe in the existence and operation of such virtue—not too good for everyday life—though I never had the luck to meet with like—

Now I have done—and I only *hope* that I may not have added to the deaths by tiring you to death. I pray you to tell me who wrote Mary Barton and I will add no more—But all well here and *there* meaning at Clewer Windsor where Rosa and Willy still are and Mariquita[?] better.

I am with kindest wishes of this season and all seasons for your father and you: my dear Mary Holland,

Yours affectionately,
Maria Edgeworth.

SAMUEL BAMFORD

To the Authoress of "Mary Barton"[†]

Blakeley. Mar. 9th, 1849.

Dear Madam,

I finished reading Mary Barton last night, my feelings having become so interested in the narrative that I could not lay the book down until I had read to the end.

You have drawn a fearfully true picture: a mournfully beautiful one also have you placed on the tables of the drawing rooms of the great, and good it must there effect; good for themselves, and good also I hope for the poor of every occupation.

You are a genius, of no ordinary rank; I care not what the critics say, nor will I flatter you, if I know it, but truth, such as it appears to me will I dare to express, with whomsoever I may differ about it. It seems to me that you have begun a great work and I do hope you will not be discouraged from going on with it. You have opened and adventured into a noble apartment of a fine old dwelling house and on one of the English oaken pannels [*sic*] you have worked a picture from which the eyes cannot be averted nor the hearts best feelings withdrawn. A sorrowfully beautiful production it is, few being able to contemplate it with tearless eyes—I could not, I know.

Go on dear Madam, and fill all the other panels with the production of your strong but correct imagination, and the effusions of your right noble womanly heart, much remains yet to be done, and may God give you life and courage to finish what you have begun. Sorrow, it seems, has revealed to yourself and the world, the secret of your powerful mind, and the force and truth of your benign feeling. A noble gift have you discovered; a blessed, humanizing thing is sorrow. Let us be thankful for our afflictions, for, 'whomsoever HE chasteneth, those he loveth.'

Some errors may certainly be detected in the details of your work, but the wonder is that they are so few in number and so trifling in effect. The dialect I think might, have been given better, and some few incidents set forth with greater effect, but in describing the dwellings of the poor, their manners, their kindliness to each other, their feelings towards their superiors in wealth and station their faults, their literary tastes, and their scientific pursuits, as old Job

† From Ross D. Waller, "Letters Addressed to Mrs. Gaskell by Celebrated Contemporaries Now in the Possession of the John Rylands Library," *Bulletin of the John Rylands Library* 19, pp. 102–69, 1935. Reproduced by courtesy of the University Librarian and Director, The John Rylands University Library, The University of Manchester.

Legh for example, you have been very faithful; of John Bartons, I have known hundreds, his very self in all things except his fatal crime, whilst of his daughter Mary, who has ever seen a group of our Lancashire factory girls or dress makers either, and could not have counted Mary? Nor is Jem Wilson, and I [am] proud to say it, a solitary character in the young fellows of our working population, noble as he is, but my heart fills as I write, and I cannot go on.

Dear Madam, Give us some more of your true and touching pictures, and meantime believe me to be your obliged, Humble, and most respectful Servant.

Saml. Bamford

Contemporary Reviews

HENRY FOTHERGILL CHORLEY

Athenaeum (October 21, 1848)[†]

MARY BARTON. A TALE OF MANCHESTER LIFE.

2 VOLS. CHAPMAN & HALL.

How far it may be kind, wise, or right to make Fiction the vehicle for a plain and matter-of-fact exposition of social evils, is a question of limitations which will not be unanimously settled in our time. The theory and practice of "Agitation" are, as all the world knows, adjusted by a sliding scale, on which "Choleric word" and "Flat Blasphemy" indicate every conceivable degree of heat and excitement, according to conscience, convenience, or chances of success—as may be. But we have met with few pictures of life among the working classes at once so forcible and so fair as 'Mary Barton.' The truth of it is terrible. The writer is superior to melo-dramatic seductions, and has described misery, temptation, distress and shame as they really exist. Only twice has he (?) had recourse to the worn-out machinery of the novelist,—and then he has used it with a master's hand. But he is excellent in the anatomy of feelings and motives, in the display of character, in the lifelike and simple use of dialogue:— and the result is, a painful interest very rare in our experience.

The events of the tale are of the commonest quality. John Barton is a factory operative, with a delicate and pretty daughter who has longings for fine-lady-ism. Her mother's death has been hastened by anxieties concerning a sister—a coarser Effie Deans; and this calamity is the first of many which sour the widower. Mary, being admitted as a milliner's workwoman, becomes the object of pursuit to a rich manufacturer's son; and her head is turned for a passing moment by his flatteries, to the point of making her reject the love of a young engine-maker, Jem Wilson, who has courted her honestly and long. For this fit of coquetry she is doomed to suffer deeply. Meanwhile, her

† From *Athenaeum*, October 21, 1848, p. 1050.

father's fortunes are sorely darkened by bad times. He becomes sullen—savage—and listens to the worst counsels of the wildest agitators. From the collision of so many elements of disturbance crime is pretty sure to be struck out. But here we leave the plot of the story; since its nature must be guessed by the experienced, while fresher readers would not thank us for forestalling interest. The accessory characters are touched with the fidelity of a Daguerreotype. Wilson's irritable exacting mother—her true woman's heart setting her fractiousness to rights—placid, religious Alice—the shameless milliner's apprentice Sally—and the poor castaway Esther have seldom been surpassed. Many tears have been wept over *Nancy Sykes* in 'Oliver Twist,'—but there is nothing in the tragedy of her life and death in deep, dreary sadness surpassing the scene where the outcast visits her niece at midnight; counterfeiting respectability, swallowing down hunger, and concealing her own cravings for commiseration and help in order that she may rescue her sister's child from her own fearful lot. For power, delicacy and nature it is a masterpiece.

The author of 'Mary Barton,' however, is not of necessity confined to distress in Art. He has a power over what is quaint and whimsical, no less than over the deepest emotions of pity and terror.

MANCHESTER LITERARY TIMES

From Unsigned Review (October 28, 1848)[†]

MARY BARTON. *A TALE OF MANCHESTER LIFE.*

2 VOLS. CHAPMAN and HALL.

* * * *"Mary Barton, a Tale of Manchester Life,"* is a work of no ordinary talent in reference to the general characteristics of a novel, whilst its truthful pictures of the humbler classes of society among which we live is an evidence of much higher capacity on the part of the author. Who she or he may be we are quite ignorant,—we rather feel inclined to consider the writer new to the world of literature, were it not that we have evidence to bring against this opinion, in the style and practice of writing. There is no mock sentimentality, no false humanity, no utopian theories blazoned forth; the subject entered upon is well understood—the people familiar in all their habits of social life—and here and there touches of the finest and subtlest character, such as we might look for in the minute detail of Teniers or Hogarth. Everything is plain, simple, and truthful, both in its descriptive passages, and those of passion—its sunlight or its storm.

† From *Manchester Literary Times*, October 28, 1848, p. 290.

JOHN FORSTER

Examiner (November 4, 1848)[†]

MARY BARTON: A TALE OF MANCHESTER LIFE. TWO VOLS.

CHAPMAN AND HALL.

This is a story of unusual beauty and merit. It has a plain and powerful interest, a good and kind purpose, and a style which derives its charm from the writer's evident sincerity. Unquestionably the book is a woman's. If one of its casual remarks had not betrayed this (it would seem unintentionally), we might have known it from the delicate points of the portraiture where women and children are in question, from the minuteness of the domestic details, from certain gentle intimations of piety and pity perceptible throughout, and from the mixed diffidence and daring with which the question of employers and employed is treated in the course of it.

The "short and simple annals" of the poor supply the subject of the story, and these are dealt with honestly. When Mr Disraeli took a Chartist delegate for his hero, he gave him ancestors who had fought at Agincourt, and proved his lineal connection with one of the last abbots of the middle ages. John Barton, on the contrary, is very ordinary homespun stuff. There is nothing of what Mr Bayes calls elevating the imagination and bringing it off in an extraordinary way. There is no bragging, or tolling of things fantastical. The book is an ungilded and sorrowful picture of the life of the class of workpeople in such a town as Manchester, with which circumstances seem to have made the writer more than ordinarily familiar. She does not affect to offer any solution of a problem involving so much misery, but appears to think that good may be done by wholesome sympathy, and would seem to have written with this hope. Perhaps not unreasonably or unwisely. To treat the lives of our "dangerous classes" with the calm brevity of the Eastern chronicler, and be satisfied with the knowledge that they are born, are wretched, and die, is certainly no longer possible. It behoves everybody to know more of the matter, and fiction may be allowed to enter where philosophy cannot well find its way. We defy any one to read *Mary Barton* without a more thoughtful sense of what is due to the poor; without a stronger and healthier persuasion of the justice they have the right to claim, and the charity they have so many more reasons than the rest of the world to stand bitterly in need of. This is not

---

† From *Examiner*, November 4, 1848, pp. 708–9.

done in the least by contrasting class and class, for the faults of the poor are not spared any more than the thoughtlessness of the rich. The aim is rather to lessen the interval that separates them, and show with what advantage to both each might know more of the other.

We should convey a wrong impression if the reader supposed the book to be a political novel. It is not that. The internal passions and emotions are its materials of interest; that "dread strife" which the poet truly tells us to be equal, whether the shepherd's frock or the regal purple cover the heart that is agitated by it. It would indeed be difficult to say for whom the most tragic interest is inspired, for the wealthy father whose son is murdered, or for the poor maddened wretch whose crime makes wretched all his little world around him. There is a moral in the book which applies with equal force to all conditions; and its lighter sketches show the same catholic spirit of shrewd perception. The little girlish varieties which cost the heroine so dear; and, in the contrasted characters of Jane Wilson and Alice, the irritable exactions of temper which are bred by poverty as well as the humble religious patience which may alleviate and redeem it; are beautifully sketched. The author has a fund of quiet quaint humour, and pathos lying in its neighbourhood which the reader must be very stern to resist. Some of the tragic scenes are powerful in the extreme. We have rarely been more affected than by the evidence of Mary Barton at the trial of her lover, by the death of Esther, by the interview in which the poor gaudy outcast (a pitiable piece of truth which will force reflection on the most thoughtless) pretends to be what she is not that her services may not be rejected, and by the mill-owner's forgiveness of Barton.

These, and many similar passages in the tale, indicate power of a rare and unquestionable kind, and seem to promise us a new novelist who is likely to deserve and obtain popularity. Her fault is the occasional use of somewhat commonplace materials of effect, and the handling of questions now and then beyond her reach. Her power is with the sympathies, and if she carefully cultivates this she need not fear to have many competitors. She has a very right and keen perception of the motives which actuate ordinary life, as well as a knowledge of the higher and more out-of-the way regions of existence which is not vouchsafed to every "distressed novel-wright." Above all she seems to write according to her knowledge, fairly and without misgiving: her characters talk naturally, and in their native garb of speech; nor is she ashamed to let the homeliest truth have its own utterance. We shall say no more of the story, but proceed to give a few extracts which we may best detach, avoiding the principal interest. * * *

We shall be well pleased to hear again of the author of *Mary Barton*.

BRITISH QUARTERLY

From Unsigned Review (February 1849)[†]

*   *   *

It is a long time since there has existed, in the working men of Manchester, such a state of feeling as would have manifested itself in the tragical manner depicted in the work before us. Time has been, however, when murders were committed by members of trades'-unions, in order to terrify the masters into compliance. The murder of young Carson has a singular degree of resemblance to a diabolical act of the kind perpetrated in the beginning of the year 1831. A very determined and unreasonable strike was made by the spinners in some of the manufacturing districts of Lancashire at that time, to resist a reduction of wages that was proposed. Any one who will peruse the accounts of this strike (or, indeed, of almost any other which has taken place among the factory workers of Lancashire) will see that the author of 'Mary Barton' has given by no means a fair picture of the attitude which the two contending parties usually assume towards each other. In the instance in question, the masters invited the men to the fullest examination of the principles on which it was proposed to adjust the rate of wages, but through the mischievous efforts of the leaders of the strike, the men showed themselves by no means ready to accede to this proposal. Bloodier methods of securing their ends were resorted to. Mr. Thomas Ashton, of Pole Bank, near Gee Cross, was shot one evening in a lane leading from his father's house to the mill at Apethorn. Young Carson, also, is represented as shot in a lane close to his father's house. The amount of the reward offered by the family for the discovery of the murderer is the same in each case—£1000. It is curious, too, that in the actual, as well as the fictitious murder, the serene and composed aspect of the features of the unfortunate young man, when his corpse was laid out in one of the bedchambers, is remarked. It was hoped at first, likewise, that a piece of paper extracted from the wound, which had been used in loading the gun from which the fatal shot was fired, would afford some clue for the detection of the murderers. It does not appear, however, that Mr. Ashton's family had in any way provoked the especial hostility of the operatives; for his workmen had nothing to do with the strike, and were in full work at the time of the murder, and Mr. Ashton was held in great esteem as a kind and considerate employer—anything but the sort of millowner depicted in

[†] From *British Quarterly*, February, 1849, pp. 117–36.

'Mary Barton.' The murder of Mr. Ashton was speedily followed by no less than five other attempts at assassination, which happily proved abortive. These were directed, not only against employers, but against workmen who consented to take a lower rate of wages than the unionists demanded, or who would not take part in the strike. Whatever may be the faults or shortcomings of some employers, the most unscrupulous and cruel tyranny to which the operative classes in the manufacturing districts are exposed, proceeds from their own order. The author of 'Mary Barton' has touched slightly upon some of the atrocities to which the leaders of strikes have frequently resorted in order to prevent other workmen from taking the wages which they themselves refuse. Strikes, however, are much less in fashion than they used to be. The operatives are beginning to find that they do not pay, and in some branches of manufacture have come to the resolution that they will have nothing more to do with them. Where the unions are most active and resolute—as, for instance, in Sheffield—we are informed that they are rapidly annihilating the trade of the town, or driving it to other places. But our author shows some lack of acquaintance with the history of these movements in representing a strike, like that described in the tale, as taking place in a period of general destitution and want of employment. At the time to which the incidents of the tale are referred, the factory-workers were only too glad to get employment of any kind. Strikes take place when trade is prosperous, or else just at the point when wages begin to fall. The general turn-out of 1842 was quite a different sort of movement.

The chief excellence of 'Mary Barton' lies in the touching simplicity and force with which many of the cottage-scenes are depicted. These sketches are evidently drawn, at least in great part, from actual observation. Their graphic power is a good deal enhanced by the liberal use of the broad, though vigorous Lancashire dialect. The pathos of some of the scenes is hardly exceeded by anything that exists in our language.

The author has rather a hankering after death scenes. Besides the murder, there are no fewer than eight deaths introduced in the course of the tale, including a couple of unfortunate little twins, who might just as well have been left out. In the love portion of the story, there is a great deal that indicates the delicate touch of a female hand, and confirms the rumour which attributes the authorship of 'Mary Barton' to a lady resident in Manchester, whom it would, perhaps, be indecorous to name, as she has preferred publishing her work anonymously.

As we have before intimated, the chief objection which we have to bring against the work is, not that it represents anything to which an actual counterpart may not be found, but that it gives a one-sided picture. The working people introduced into the tale give, we fear, rather a flattering picture of the character and habits of the factory population of Manchester generally, though their prototypes may, undoubtedly, be found in considerable numbers. But, on the other hand, it amounts to a positive and very gross injustice, that, in a tale professing to give, and already, in many quarters, regarded as giving, an average picture of Manchester life, the only millowners introduced are Barton's old employer, who is represented very much in the character of a dishonest bankrupt, and the two Carsons—arrogant, selfish, unfeeling men, with no care for anything but their own aggrandizement. More than one modern writer of fiction, even among those who hold the foremost rank, need to be admonished, that to exhibit a caricature, which they cannot but know that the majority of their readers will accept as a portrait, is nothing less than an act of dishonesty, unless it be the result of sheer ignorance: there are cases in which ignorance treads hard upon the heels of wilful misrepresentation. To ascribe to the employers, as a body, 'a want of 'inclination to try and help the evils which come like blights at times 'over the manufacturing places, while the masters can stop work and 'not suffer,' (vol. ii. p. 301,) as the whole tenour of the work does, savours very little even of common justice. What the writer would have them do, we know not. What has been done, has been, to strive, with an energy, perhaps, never witnessed before, to secure fair play for the industry of the operative classes. It would be but a cruel kindness which went beyond this, and neutralized in any degree their own energy and self-reliance. The worst enemy with which the factory population have to contend is their own improvidence. The most ordinary foresight and caution would enable them to meet a temporary cessation of employment without more difficulty than a careful tradesman finds in providing against a few weeks of slack business, or an occasional bad debt. As it is, they usually spend all that they get as fast as it is earned; and in Manchester, the poorest and most desolate homes are usually those of men who get the highest wages; and the stoppage of a mill for a few weeks will often reduce to abject poverty hundreds of families, who, for a year or two, have had nearly constant employment, and have earned from two to three pounds, or even more, per week. As an instance of what may be done by those who exercise more prudence than the generality of their fellow-operatives, we may mention, that one of the men shot at by the turn-outs soon after the murder of Mr. Ashton, had just left a beer-house kept by a man and his wife, who, in five years, had saved sufficient to build five substantial houses, in one of which they themselves lived. And yet the husband was only a smith, and the wife had worked in a cotton factory at wages considerably lower than those to secure which the unionists thought assassination not too horrible a method. Only recently, we found that a number of work-men, in the employ of a friend of ours, who had formed a kind of provident association among themselves, had laid by above 100*l*. in less than three months.

The writer of 'Mary Barton' seems still under the influence of the very common misapprehensions entertained respecting the labori-ousness of occupation in the factories. The most absurd statements have, even of late, been put forth on this subject, especially by Lord Ashley and some other advocates of the Ten Hours' Bill; for which Act, by the way, the operatives are anything but thankful. Those of them who were in favour of it were under the delusion that they could get twelve hours' wages for ten hours' work, in which, of course, they have found themselves egregiously mistaken. The fact is, that the labour in a cotton-mill, especially for the women and young people, is extremely light. The readers of Mr. D'Israeli's 'Sybil' have probably puffed forth a great deal of sentimental air, in the shape of sighs and ejaculations of pity, at the idea of the man with the long stick tapping at the windows of the poor factory girls, to awaken them to their day's toil. One would not think, to see them at their tasks, or as they return home, that they were worn out with fatigue. There are, perhaps, few employments in which female industry can be employed where the labour is so slight; compared with the drudgery of dress-makers' apprentices it is mere play; nor is there anything about it, more than other departments of female industry, which has a neces-sary tendency to unfit young women for the discharge of domestic duties. The evils complained of in this respect belonged rather to the time when young people, from their childhood, spent almost their whole time in factories. Young women in Manchester commonly pre-fer factory work even to domestic service. Some, who had worked in factories from childhood, have told us, in answer to our inquiries, that they were perfectly happy and contented with their employment. As for legislation on the subject, it has sometimes occurred to us, that it would be a serviceable regulation if no member of parliament were allowed to vote on any question connected with factory labour until he had inspected a cotton-mill.

In a colloquy between John Barton and some other workpeople, (i. p. 133,) several of them are represented as crying out against machinery, and attributing the greater part of their distresses to it. That such ideas are very rare among the operatives is shown by the fact, that such a vast amount of machinery has for so long a time lain quite at their mercy, without the occurrence of anything to show a general suspicion on their part that it has an injurious effect upon their interests; and that, too, in spite of the efforts of various agitators to urge them to acts of violence. Even during the riots of 1842, when the mills were entirely in the power of the rioters, the abstinence of the latter from any such outrages was remarkable. Indeed, it is evident to all but the most blinded opponents of the whole system, that a perpetual influx would not keep taking place into the manufacturing districts, were it not that almost every fresh improvement gives an increased stimulus to industry in one form or other. It is perfectly true, that, by improvements in machinery, women, and even children, can do what formerly required the strength of a grown man; but it is quite inaccurate to speak of this as though the labour of men were *supplanted* by that of women and children. It is only turned into somewhat different channels, though, of course, it happens just at first that a few men may be left temporarily without employment in consequence of the change.

Lord Ashley stated some time ago, that 'factory employment 'injured the eyes, and caused lamentable accidents, of which the 'house had now records, and even these minor accidents, as they 'were called—the loss of fingers and hands—almost all occurred during the last hour of the evening, when the people were so blind, tired, 'and sleepy, that they almost became reckless of danger.' It looks like 'a quotation from this, when the writer of 'Mary Barton' makes John Barton learn, while in the infirmary, that 'by far th' greater part o' th' 'accidents as comed in happened in th' last two hours of work, when 'folk getten tired and careless.' (i. p. 128.) It is a sort of superstition, not very uncommon, that a large proportion of the unfortunate creatures employed in factories get killed, or crushed, or maimed by the machinery. Some pains were taken to enlighten the members of the legislature, and refute Lord Ashley's assertions. The following quotation is from the Report of the Central Committee of the Association of Millowners and Manufacturers for the year 1844.

'Out of 412 millowners making returns, 167 reported the following accidents as having occurred within an average period of 20½ years—viz., 72 occasioning death, 168 loss of limb, and 13 not specified. One hundred and ninety-six millowners reported that no accident involving loss of life or limb had occurred in their factories in an average period of 13½ years.

'The proportion of accidents, therefore, appears to have been about one death per annum in 104 mills, and one loss of limb in 41 mills. From 49 of the mills, no returns were made with respect to accidents.

'It appeared that 412 mills employed 116,281 persons, being an average of 282 in each mill; therefore, in 104 mills, employing 29,328 persons, only one fatal accident in a year occurs; and in 41 mills, employing 11,562 persons, only one accident occasioning loss of limb occurs in the same period. The committee venture to assert, that so favourable a result as to accidents, probably cannot be obtained from any other industrial occupation in this country.

'From the return by the coroners in the factory districts, it appeared that, out of upwards of 858 accidents occasioning loss of life, only 29 (3 2-5ths per cent.) have been occasioned by factory machinery, while 79 have been caused by carts, &c., and 85 occurred in coal-pits.'

*   *   *

PROSPECTIVE REVIEW

From Unsigned Review (February 1849)[†]

*   *   *

The immense concentration of population in our Northern seats of manufacturing industry, with the modes of thought and the conflict of tendencies generated by it—has become the great social feature of our age— the feature that will mark out and individualise its physiognomy through all coming time. A phenomenon so vast and startling—so ominous of good or of ill to future generations— demands a literature, at once for its interpretation and its guidance; and such a literature it will undoubtedly have, either freely developed out of itself, or brought to it by the loving sympathy of others.

The beautifully told Tale—the Poem in prose—of Mary Barton would on this account alone have excited attention and found a ready hearing. Its great and rapidly won reputation is due to its extraordinary merit. It represents the ideas and passions of a particular class, or rather of a certain portion of a particular class, during a crisis of strong local excitement, when the supposed interests of masters and men were brought into direct collision. With the license conceded to art for the sake of making a deeper impression on the imagination, the authoress has chosen an *exceptional* instead of the *normal* condition of social feeling, as the subject of her fiction. And this must be borne in mind, when its moral tendency is spoken of. From this point of view it should be judged.

*   *   *

Such is a brief outline of the story. The interest of which it is susceptible, must be obvious. To fulfil its demands and make the most of its opportunities, was a severe test of genius. It is high praise to say, that the authoress has reached the height of her argument, and that the treatment equals the design. The conception of the whole is compact and forcible. The incidents are so happily arranged, and flow so

†   From *Prospective Review* 17, February 1849, pp. 36–57.

easily and naturally out of each other with the progress of the narrative, that we could almost suspect a long-practised pen; and if this be indeed a first production, it is a surprising work. The style is full of life and colour, betraying a quick observant eye. It grasps its objects with remarkable steadiness and precision, does not dwell too long on any one, but throws in just enough of individual traits to realise it distinctly to the imagination.—We have thought the conclusions of the chapters particularly excellent. There is never any wearisome winding up, but attention is roused by a smart stroke or two, a question perhaps or significant hint, which leaves a pungent relish on the reader's mind, and makes him long for the next. As for the northern *patois* which is liberally introduced into the dialogue, we are not ourselves sufficiently masters of it, to say how far it may be taken as a correct representation of the language of the people; but the copious sprinkling of it on every page, is to our feelings very agreeable, as giving a peculiar raciness to the speech of shrewd and earnest men, and diffusing a warm local hue, without vulgarity or obscurity, over the whole narrative. It is only giving to the operatives of Lancashire, the same kind of picturesque individuality, which Scott in his immortal tales has conferred on the peasantry of Scotland.

Our authoress seizes with singular felicity the salient points of character and manners, and paints them distinctly to the very eye. Take the opening chapter. The description of the sauntering groups of holiday idlers—the dress and bearing of the girls, and the rude gallantry exchanged between them and the lads, with the married couples quietly trailing along their toddling little ones— will strike every inhabitant of Manchester with its vivid truthfulness. Then, the tea-party at Barton's at the conclusion of the afternoon's stroll—the arrangement and furniture of the house—the luxuries which cover the table, the self-forgetting heartiness with which the hospitality is dispensed, and the bright blazing fire filling the little room with its ruddy cheerful glow—are a complete and most admirable piece of Dutch painting, which for the accuracy of its details respecting the habits and economy of the poor might almost be studied by a collector of social statistics.

The characters in this Tale have great variety and contrast, are finely discriminated, and sustained with a vigilant consistency.— Barton himself, we have heard, is a draught from the life. Jem is a noble fellow, brave and enduring, and full of gentle feeling—the true hero of the story. Old Job Legh with his odd volumes of books and his entomological rarities is a fine specimen of a form of character not uncommon among the workmen of Lancashire, quiet, studious, contemplative—a philosopher of nature's making—amidst the din of manufactures and the many distractions of poverty, serenely finding his happiness in silent thought and the observation of God's works.

Mary's impulsiveness and lively fancy are set off by the plain sense and steady principle of her friend Margaret. Will Wilson is an honest kind-hearted sailor of the ordinary stamp. Old Sturgis has a more strongly-marked individuality, but somewhat inclining to caricature. Poor Esther's story throws a deeper shade into the dark background of the picture, and stands out in sad relief against the womanly purity which sheds over it a sweet and holy glow. Perhaps the most beautiful creation in the whole book is Alice. Her unconscious goodness, her faith in God never forsaking her, her unselfish devotion to the service of others, her gratitude for the smallest mercies, the childlike innocence and simplicity of her spirit, and the still and quiet happiness that floats round her whole being, like the fresh and pure air of her native hills—are truly delightful. But for the earlier conception of Jenny Deans (though cast in quite another mould), it would have been difficult to believe, that simple goodness in so humble a garb could be made so interesting and so beautiful. One such example drawn in these living colours, teaches us more than many sermons.

The passages which would probably most strike the general reader—the fire at Carson's factory, the pursuit of the ship containing the witness, and the scene at Jem Wilson's trial—are not those which we should ourselves select as the clearest proofs of genius. They are powerfully wrought and excite a thrilling interest; but the interest is of that kind and composed of those elements which we meet with in all novels, and which a clever imitator, void of all originality, might work up with tolerable effect. They are founded on the love of strong excitement, the least pure and exalted of all the resources of art. We turn with far greater delight and deeper admiration to the soft and quiet touches of natural pathos and the incidental revelations of character with which the tale abounds. Here we trace real genius, and own the presence of a beautiful and highly-gifted mind, full of sensibility—familiar with man's heart—giving out its sympathies in rich unconscious overflow wherever human joy or human sorrow come before it. It is in this by-play of the general action, where nothing great is thought of, and no effect is contemplated, that the workings of true genius betray themselves most unequivocally.

*   *   *

The fountains of mirth and sadness spring up side by side, and sometimes mingle their waters in their passage through the soul. Mary Barton is rich in humour as well as in pathos. The mermaid scene between Will Wilson and Job Legh is exceedingly comic. There are passages where the humour and the pathos are intermixed, and pass into each other. This power of rapid transition is no common gift. We might select as an example, John Barton's account of his deputation to London; and perhaps still better, Job Legh's description of his visit to the same place, to attend the death-bed of his only child and her husband, and of his return with the baby accompanied by the husband's father. The perplexities of the two old men about their infant charge, their trouble with it at night, their ludicrous expedients to keep it quiet, the sharp contrast of their characters and their altercations—are described with exquisite humour, and yet blended with such touches of natural feeling, such strains of sadness coming unbidden from the full heart, as render this whole narrative one of the most remarkable in the book, for the display it affords of the varied powers of the writer.

* * *

We have thought these few extracts would say more for Mary Barton, than any lengthened criticism. They will justify the high admiration that we feel and that we sincerely and heartily express—for the genius and sensibility —the true spirit of humanity—revealed in the book.—We would notice in passing an occasional peculiarity in the writer's treatment of her subject, which marks strong individuality, and implies great wealth of resources and ready command over all the springs of interest, but which, unless watched by a severe taste, may become mannerism:—we allude to her evident fondness for a sharp contrast of feelings—a bringing of two opposite states of mind into immediate collision—as if to show how near together lie the sources of joy and sorrow, of good and evil, in the human soul,—and producing in the representation of action a similar effect to that of antithesis or *concetto* in style. We have observed three remarkable instances of this.—Mary returning home with a heart full of sorrow and fear, having just heard of young Carson's murder, and distracted by her own unhappy relations with Jem, meets a little starving Italian boy, and at first absorbed by her own feelings, treats with indifference his piteous entreaties for a bit of bread,—till she bethinks herself, and fetches her only crust to give him, and feels softened and comforted by the return of her natural tenderness. This is sweetly and simply told.— Conceived in the same spirit, but with contrast more strongly brought out, is an incident in John Barton's dark history. As he quits his home moody and stern for Glasgow, with the consciousness of crime heavy on his soul, just after the short and passionate farewell to his daughter, which we have already quoted—he meets in the streets, now dusky with the shades of evening, a poor little child that has lost its way and is crying bitterly for its mother. His half-extinguished tenderness revives within him;—the sympathies of home come back; he takes the little wanderer by the hand; deposits it safely with its parents; and then gloomily pursues his destined way.—A third instance is, where the elder Carson, intent on vengeance, and determined never to forgive the murderer of his son, is reminded of the beauty of another feeling, on seeing a little sportive girl who has been rudely knocked down by a heedless passer by, though much hurt, exhibit no resentment, but entreat that the offender may be pardoned and let go.—It is evident that the same feeling,—the same general conception,—is at the bottom of all these incidents. The last of them is to our taste the least pleasing and the worst executed. There is something far-fetched and calculated in the effect aimed at, with more of an evident tendency to mannerism.

Mary Barton is so strong in genuine excellence, that it can well bear a faithful criticism. Some few blemishes have struck us in its conception and execution, which we shall not hesitate to mention.—We confess, then, that the worst thing in the whole Tale seems to us the character of its heroine, or rather the unnatural combination of the two elements that go to make up her character. Take away the extraneous addition, and leave us the genuine Mary Barton, the simple-hearted and faithful mistress of Jem,—such as we can suppose the first pure conception presented itself to the mind of the author—and nothing can be imagined more lovely and engaging. But to this is prefixed—whether from the supposed necessities of the plot or from a gratuitous love of contrast—a character of quite another hue, which is out of harmony with it; and the discrepancy between the two involves consequences in the development of the story, which form the chief drawback on its general impression of naturalness and probability. We refer of course to Mary's flirtations with Mr. Carson, and her strange ignorance of the real state of her feelings towards Jem.

* * *

A similar inconsistency, though of a slighter kind, is discernible in the character of John Barton, from the attempted union of incompatible elements. To extenuate his wild and erring career and reconcile it with the general nobleness and benevolence of his spirit, the blame is thrown on his want of education and his ignorance of the distinction between right and wrong. It is clear, however, that he knew enough to save him from his criminal courses, if he would have listened to reason and conscience, instead of passion. He had read the Bible and tasted—sufficiently to feel its divine power—the blessedness of following its precepts. He is described moreover as of strong and active intellect, capable of thoughtful action and fitted to command and guide his fellow-men. Taking the course he did, he must have sinned against the clear light of his better nature. We doubt whether a spirit capable of deliberately committing the crime imputed to him, could co-exist with the other qualities of John Barton's character. At least, we do not find, upon inquiry, that the men who are prominent in such social warfare as he took a leading part in, are distinguished for the humanity, the self-sacrifice and general uprightness of life with which he is represented as endowed. If the outlines of the portraiture are indeed drawn from reality, we suspect that lights and shades have been largely thrown in by the imagination of the writer.

A graver charge has been brought against the book, which must not be passed over—that it is one-sided and unfair, and places the relation of the whole class of masters to their workpeople in a false and invidious light.—We have already remarked, that the writer has taken an exceptional form of social condition as the theme of her fiction, and attempted to express the feelings which such a crisis called forth in large masses of the population. If such feelings actually existed, and they have been truthfully represented, the story has satisfied its conditions as a work of art. It only aims at the embodiment of a great social fact. How far the sufferings endured were caused or aggravated by past or present misconduct, or were capable of alleviation by foreign aid to the extent which the sufferers themselves believed possible, may be considered as a question rather falling within the province of the social economist than capable of satisfactory treatment in the pages of a novel. Still a novel exhibits results; and it may be asked, whether those which are so vividly presented in Mary Barton, leave as a whole upon the mind, an impression that is correspondent with justice and truth. A strong feeling exists in many quarters, that they do not, and that a person unacquainted with Manchester would derive from the book a very erroneous idea of the amount of benevolence ever in full operation there, and of the actual relations subsisting between a vast majority of the employed and their masters.

Any one reading the book with attention, will find in the story itself some correctives of this unfavourable impression. Barton's early improvidence and that of his parents are clearly admitted, so that when he is thrown out of work by the state of the times, he has not a shilling in the world to fall back upon. This fact should have been more strongly dwelt upon, when his embittered feelings on witnessing the ravages of want in his family are so forcibly described. It ought also to have been more distinctly noticed, that it was the possession of these very qualities of foresight and thought wanting in himself, which caused the disparities of wealth and comfort that he viewed with such alienation and hate. Barton himself confesses on his deathbed, that he has mistaken the course of justice: and the sober admissions of old Job Legh, who represents the wisdom of the working-class, effectually repel the wild pretensions of Socialism, and throw the responsibility of the social elevation of the poor on their own efforts and thoughtfulness—if only (*for that is the point on which he insists, and which constitutes the true moral of the Tale*) they can meet with consideration and sympathy and fraternal recognition from those who are already the possessors of wealth. The softening of the elder Carson's mind, and the more earnest devotion of his thoughts in his latter years to the improvement and happiness of the workpeople, though introduced as a collateral incident towards the close of the story, is evidently intended to intimate, that a more benevolent and enlightened spirit at the present time generally regulates the intercourse of the employers and the employed. John Barton's dying in the arms of Mr. Carson, who puts up a prayer at Mary's request, "God be merciful to us, sinners,"—is a kind of poetical justice to heal the strife of the contending parties represented by the two men, which sheds a spirit of peace on the concluding scenes of the mournful Tale. The fault seems to be, that these corrective touches are not brought out with sufficient strength. They are there, but the careless or prejudiced reader will probably overlook them. It is rather a defect in the execution than an omission in the general design. The picture wants keeping. The dark shades are laid in too deep and thick; the redeeming lights are too faint and few.

* * *

We have expressed our opinion freely about Mary Barton. The openness of our censure, where we have thought it deserved, may be taken as an earnest of the sincerity of our praise. It is a charming book; after every deduction, rich in wisdom and truth. It shows us, what a deep poetry may be lying hid under the outward meanness and triviality of humble life; what strong and pure affections, what heroism and disinterestedness, what high faith in God and immortality under all the sorrow and trial of a hard world, may be nursed in the homes of poor and unpolished men. We rise from its pages with a deeper interest in all our fellow-beings; with a firmer trust in their great and glorious destiny; and with a strengthened desire to co-operate with its gifted authoress and with all of kindred spirit, in every effort to ennoble and bless them.

CHARLES KINGSLEY

Fraser's Magazine (April 1849)†

* * *

Here we had intended to end our review; but since writing the above a book has come into our hands, known already, we hope, to many,

† From Fraser's Magazine 39, April 1849, pp. 428–32.

as it is now in its third edition: but lest any human being, whose eyes these pages may reach, should remain ignorant of the book and its contents, we notice it here. Had we wit and wisdom enough, we would placard its sheets on every wall, and have them read aloud from every pulpit, till a nation, calling itself Christian, began to act upon the awful facts contained in it, not in the present peddling and desultory manner, but with an united energy of shame and repentance proportionate to the hugeness of the evil. For we must hope—we dare not but hope for the honour of humanity, that in spite of blue-books and commissions, in spite of newspaper horrors and parliamentary speeches, Manchester riots and the 10th of April, the mass of the higher orders cannot yet be aware of what a workman's home is like in the manufacturing districts. The book to which we allude is *Mary Barton, a Tale of Manchester Life*—Manchester life in England in the nineteenth century. Not of Indian cholera famines, or Piedmontese persecutions, or Peruvian tortures, or old Norman Conquest butcheries, or any of those horrors which distance of place and time makes us quiet, easy-going folks, fancy impossible in civilised, Christian, nineteenth-century England; but of the life-in-death—life worse than many deaths, which now besets thousands, and tens of thousands of our own countrymen.

We might praise the 'talent' of the book; we might, and justly, attribute to it higher artistic excellency, than we have done even to the novel we last mentioned; but the matter puts the manner out of sight. The facts—the facts are all in all; for they are facts. As a single instance of corroboration, if any were needed, a Manchester clergyman has just assured us, that his own eyes have seen the miseries there described (as he asserts, without the least exaggeration) not merely in the years in which the scene of the book is laid—1839–41, but now, in these very last years of 1847–9, when people on Turkey carpets, with their three meat meals a-day, are wondering, forsooth, why working men turn Chartists and Communists.

Do they want to know why? Then let them read *Mary Barton*. Do they want to know why poor men, kind and sympathising as women to each other, learn to hate law and order, Queen, Lords and Commons, country-party, and corn-law leaguer, all alike—to hate the rich, in short? Then let them read *Mary Barton*. Do they want to know what can madden brave, honest, industrious North-country hearts, into self-imposed suicidal strikes, into conspiracy, vitriol-throwing, and midnight murder? Then let them read *Mary Barton*. Do they want to know what drives men to gin and opium, that they may drink and forget their sorrow, though it be in madness? Let them read *Mary Barton*. Do they want to get a detailed insight into the whole 'science of starving,'—'clemming,' as the poor Manchester men call it? Why people 'clem,' and how much they can 'clem' on; what people look like

while they are 'clemming' to death, and what they look like after they
are 'clemmed' to death and in what sort of places they lie while they
are 'clemming,' and who looks after them, and who — oh, shame
unspeakable! — do not look after them while they are 'clemming;'
and what they feel while they are 'clemming;' and what they feel while
they see their wives and their little ones 'clemming' to death round
them; and what they feel, and must feel, unless they are more or less
than men, after all are 'clemmed;' and gone, and buried safe out of
sight, never to hunger, and wail, and pine, and pray for death any
more for ever? Let them read *Mary Barton*. Lastly, if they want to
know why men learn to hate the Church and the Gospel, why they
turn sceptics, Atheists, blasphemers, and cry out in the blackness of
despair and doubt, 'Let us curse God and die,' let them read *Mary
Barton*. God knows it is a book, Christian and righteous as it is, to try
one's faith in God to the uttermost; to tempt one to believe that this
world is, after all, nothing but a huge pitiless machine, with the devil and misrule, tyranny and humbug, the only lords thereof, if we did
not believe that its true Lord was even now 'coming out of His place
to judge the world righteously, to help the fatherless and poor unto
their right, that the man of the world be no more exalted against
them.'

* * *

W. R. GREG

Edinburgh Review (April 1849)[†]

* * *

The literary merit of the work is in some respects of a very high order.
Its interest is intense: often painfully so; indeed it is here, we think,
that the charm of the book and the triumph of the author will chiefly
be found. Its pictures and reflections are, however, also full of those
touches of nature which 'make the whole world kin:' and its dialogues
are managed with a degree of ease and naturalness rarely attained
even by the most experienced writers of fiction. We believe that they
approach very nearly, both in tone and style, to the conversations
actually carried on in the dingy cottages of Lancashire. The authoress
— for 'Mary Barton' is understood to be, and indeed very palpably is,
the production of a lady — must not be confounded with those writ-

---

† From *Edinburgh Review*, April 1849, pp. 402–35.

ers who engage with a particular subject, because it presents a vein which they imagine may be successfully worked — get up the needful information, and then prepare a story as a solicitor might prepare a case. She has evidently lived much among the people she describes, made herself intimate at their firesides, and feels a sincere, though sometimes too exclusive and undiscriminating, sympathy with them. In short, her work has been clearly a 'labour of love,' and has been written with a most earnest and benevolent purpose. We can conscientiously pronounce it to be a production of great excellence, and of still greater promise.

But it must also be regarded in a more serious point of view. It comes before us professing to be a faithful picture of a little known, though most energetic and important class of the community; and it has the noble ambition of doing real good by creating sympathy, by diffusing information, and removing prejudices. To its pretensions in these respects, we regret that we cannot extend an unqualified approbation. With all the truthfulness displayed in the delineation of individual scenes, the general impression left by the book, on those who read it as mere passive recipients, will be imperfect, partial, and erroneous. Notwithstanding the good sense and good feeling with which it abounds, it is calculated, we fear, in many places, to mislead the minds and confirm and exasperate the prejudices, of the general public on the one hand, and of the factory operatives on the other. Were 'Mary Barton' to be only read by Manchester men and master manufacturers, it could scarcely fail to be serviceable; because they might profit by its suggestions, and would at once detect its mistakes. But considering the extraordinary delusions of many throughout the south of England respecting the great employers of labour in the north and west; as well as the ignorance and misconception of their true interests and position, which are still too common among the artisans of many of our large towns, — the effect of the work, if taken without some corrective might, in these quarters, be mischievous in the extreme. And this must be our apology for pointing out, in some detail, both the false philosophy and the inaccurate descriptions which detract so seriously from the value of these most interesting volumes.

*   *   *

But we are putting off the unpleasant part of our duty. There are representations made — at least impressions left — by the book before us which we have signalised as inaccurate and full of harm. Some of these we must proceed to notice: and first among them, the exaggeration of describing an animosity against masters and employers as the common quality and characteristic of the operative population. The narrative imports that the angry and vindictive feelings by which the soul of John Barton is absorbed, are constant and pervading.

* * *

It is presumptuous perhaps to pronounce decidedly upon a point on which opinions will vary; — the experience of every man of course depending on the local and personal circumstances in which he has been thrown. But both our own observation, and the confirming views of others whose acquaintance with artisan life has been even more extensive and intimate than our own, enable us to speak with some confidence. It is unquestionably and unfortunately true that sentiments of animosity of this description do exist in a considerable degree, and in a degree which varies with the times. All that we contend for is, that they are exceptional, not general — local, limited, and transient, — and certainly not entertained by the working population at large. As a picture of an individual, — that is, of the feelings of this or that person, — John Barton is unhappily true to the life; as the type of a class, though a small one, he may be allowed to pass muster: but to bring him forward as a fair representative of the artisans and factory operatives of Manchester and similar towns generally, is a libel alike upon them and upon the objects of their alleged hatred. Much, no doubt, has been done, and is still being done, by those emissaries of ill-will who live upon the passions they excite, to create and foster bad feeling between classes so intimately bound together as the manufacturing capitalist and the manufacturing labourer. Much has been done, too, both by senators and journalists, through slanders protected by privilege of parliament, and propagated by that mighty press against whose injuries there is no defence, towards spreading among the more distant public the belief that this bad feeling does exist to a perilous extent. Notwithstanding which, however, we rejoice to know that the feeling is becoming every year rarer and less acrimonious; that it is more and more exclusively confined to the irregular, dissolute, and discontented *ex*-workmen who form the acting staff of trades' unions and delegations; and more and more exclusively directed against those employers — daily becoming fewer — who look upon the operatives they employ in the mingled light of coadjutors and antagonists — with whom their only concern is to drive as hard a bargain as they can; and that it is fast giving way before the increasing conviction of a common interest, and the humanising influence of faithful services rendered, on the one hand, and just treatment, willing aid, and benevolent kindness on the other.

There is, too, it seems to us, a double error, both an artistic error and an error of fact, in representing a man of Barton's intelligence and habits of reflection and discussion, to be so ignorant of the first principles of commercial and economic science as he is here described. Probably this arises from the writer's acknowledged unacquaintance with social and political economy herself, and from her ignorance how far the rudiments of these sciences have been mastered by the more thoughtful and the better educated artisans of our large towns. But indeed the lights and shades are thrown too strongly on every thing relating to John Barton. The effect may have thus been made more startling: but, we think, at the expense of probability. It is not that he has, more or less, two natures. That is common to us all. Our objection is, that his conduct is radically inconsistent with his qualities and character. He is not only an intelligent man, but a steady and skilful workman; and so confident in his own capacity always procuring for him certain employment, that he never, when in receipt of the highest wages (i. 33.), lays by a farthing for a time of sickness at home or stagnation of trade. Meanwhile, whenever these periods come, he is found cursing his masters instead of his own improvidence; spending his time and money on trades' unions, when both his child and himself are unsupplied with the barest necessaries of life; and wasting (as so many operatives do), in subscriptions for such objects, funds which, duly husbanded, would have saved his only son (whose loss, we are told, has warped his temper) from an early grave. Yet neither to the authoress, nor to the supposed subject of her delineation, is it at any time intimated as occurring that, if ever there was a clear case in which a man had to thank himself for most of his sorrows and misfortunes, John Barton's was that case. On the contrary, he is painted as utterly unconscious, even to the last, of his own improvidence and of its sinister influence on his condition. Instead of drawing from his privations those lessons of warning and remorse which, to an intellect like his, must have been as patent as the day, they are merely made to heap up fresh fuel for that funeral pile to which his senseless and vindictive passion is at last to set fire.

* * *

It was only the more necessary to inform them (as numerous stoppages of wealthy firms might indeed readily bring home to their conviction) that their masters *do* suffer, and suffer most painfully, from those reverses and stagnation of trade which they imagine to fall solely on themselves; to picture, however cursorily, the position of those employers who, on such occasions, have seen the accumulations of years of patient and honest industry suddenly swept away, and who, at an advanced period of life, have had to set to work to reconstruct the shattered fabric of their fortunes — and of those who, compromised more deeply still, find the prospects of their children blighted, their objects defeated, and their occupation gone. It is not true that such periods as 1842, when the scene of the narrative is laid, pass lightly over any of the great employers of manufacturing labour. Their sufferings are not the less severe because the worst part of them are of a kind into which their dependents cannot at once enter. And the simple reason — the explanation which lies upon the surface — why they do not suffer as severely and as *obviously* as the operatives is, that *they*, in the days of prosperity, had laid by a portion of their earnings, and that the operatives had not; and that, therefore, when profits ceased and losses took their place — a change which long precedes the reduction of wages or the cessation of employment — they could subsist out of their previous savings, while the improvident operatives had no savings to fall back upon. How came it never to occur to the authoress, or to her hero, that had Mr. Carson (who is represented as having raised himself from the operative class) thought as little of saving as John Barton, who so envied and so wronged him, their condition and their sufferings, when the period of distress arrived, would have been precisely equal? It was, in truth, because the one had been prudent and foreseeing, and the other confident and careless — because the one had busied himself about his work, while the other had busied himself about unions and politics, that their positions, when the evil day came, which came alike to both, were so strangely contrasted.[1]

The forgetfulness — or the delusion, whichever it be—which we have here noted, is unhappily so common, and it discloses so much of the secret both of the present and the future condition of the manufacturing population, that we must dwell upon it for a few moments longer. People at a distance are not aware, either to what an extent the actual wealth of the master manufacturers is the result of patient savings from very moderate *average* profits, nor (which is our immediate point) of the extent to which saving is within the power of the factory operatives. In the first place, it should be known that, in spite of all we hear of fluctuations and stagnation of trade, this class suffers less perhaps than any other from variations of employment. There are two reasons for this: one is, that their employers, being

1. We admit readily, however, and should always bear in mind, that the sufferings of the operative, even when occasioned by what may be called the total ruin of the master, are, while they last, greatly more intense than the master's. There is no instance, we suppose, of a bankrupt master being reduced to the squalid cellar life of the Davenports, or even to breaking stones on the highways, or to the asylum of the workhouse. Unless he has been fraudulent as well as unfortunate or imprudent, his connexions, or even his creditors, interpose to save him from these dreadful extremities; and it would be equally heartless and absurd to deny that *these* are beyond measure worse, and more trying both to our moral and our physical nature, than a mere descent from wealth to poverty, from the luxuries and vanities of life to its scantiest comforts, cares, and privations. There is this approach, however, to a compensation in the case of the operative, that his trials, though more bitter and overwhelming for the time, are generally shorter. The enterprising manufacturer, who loses in one desolating season the wealth accumulated by the patient and anxious labour of many preceding years, can seldom hope to regain either the fortune or the position he has lost; and he generally passes the remainder of his life a broken-spirited and unprosperous man — while as soon as employment returns, the operative is as well off, and too often as imprudent, as ever; and though the thoughtful and sensitive among them may be occasionally depressed or irritated by anticipating the probable recurrence of such terrible visitations, it is certainly true that a far larger proportion of them soon recover their natural cheerfulness, than is the case with the unfortunate among their employers.

generally wealthy, are able to carry on their business through any *ordinary* periods of depression, without curtailing or suspending production; in other words, they can afford to hold stocks. The other reason is, that the fixed capital employed is generally so large, and the consequent loss when it stands idle so enormous, that mills are never allowed to stop if it is *possible* to keep them going. A large manufacturer, according to the evidence of the factory inspectors, cannot stop his factory without a dead loss of from 4000*l*. or 5000*l*. a year. Profits, therefore, cease long before either wages or employment are affected; and it is only after a long continuance of unprofitable trade, that either are reduced. Operatives generally are now, indeed, aware of this fact; and, therefore, when their employer closes his mill, they know well what an amount of pecuniary pressure such a step indicates, and they feel that he must be truly a fellow-sufferer. In the winter of 1847–48, when, owing to the failure in the American cotton crop, a greater number of mills ceased working or reduced their hours of work, than had ever previously been the case, so well was this understood, that scarcely one angry murmur or reproach was heard, though the sufferings of the people were severe beyond all former example.

But not only is the employment of the factory population generally constant and regular, their wages also have long been, and doubtless will soon again be, comparatively very high. The wages of men in most such establishments, vary from 10*s*. to 40*s*., and those of girls and women from 7*s*. to 15*s*. a week. And, as from the nature of the work, in which even children can be made serviceable, several individuals of the same family are generally employed, the earnings of a family will very frequently reach 100*l*. a year — and by no means unfrequently, when the father is an overlooker or a spinner, 150*l*. or 170*l*. — a sum on which families in a much higher rank contrive to live in decency and comfort. Saving then, out of such earnings, is obviously not only practicable but easy. Unhappily it is rare: for not only is much wasted at the ale-house (though less now than formerly); not only is much squandered in subscriptions to trades' unions and *strikes*; but among the more highly paid operatives, spinners especially, gambling both by betting and at cards is carried on to a deplorable extent.[2] Much also is lost by bad housewifery; and we do not scruple to affirm that, were it possible (and who shall say that it is not?) to transport among these people, those thrifty habits, that household management, that shrewd, sober, steady conduct, characteristic of the Scotch peasantry, and which are so well depicted in

---

2. We have now lying before us some particulars, showing the prevalence of this vice, in one single factory. One man had lost 7*l*., another 3*l*., another 2*l*. 10*s*. in a single night at cards. In the same mill the losses incurred on one occasion, in the betting on a foot-race, by the hands in one department only, exceeded 12*l*.

Somerville's 'Autobiography of a Working Man;' not merely comfort, but wealth and independence, would speedily become the rule instead of the exception among our Manchester artisans. Even as it is, we are cognisant of many cases where hundreds — in some instances thousands — of pounds have been laid by, for future calls, by factory workmen. Indeed, whenever you find one of this class too sensible or too religious to frequent the ale-house, too shrewd or too peaceable to subscribe to clubs or turn-outs, and wise enough to spend his money efficiently, or to marry a wife who can; you are almost sure to learn that he has some independent property — often deposited in his master's hands, oftener still laid out in the purchase of cottages or railway shares. Many of them become in time managers of mills, and, ultimately, proprietors and master manufacturers.

As a confirmation of this statement, and as a contrast to the unnatural blindness and self-delusion of John Barton, we will give a picture drawn from the life by one thoroughly acquainted with the operative classes in the northern end, at least, of the island. It is an account of the actual progress upwards of a young mechanic, given by Mr. Robert Chambers.

'Englishmen have much to be thankful for, inasmuch as there is probably no country on the face of the globe where sober, industrious, young mechanics and labourers can so soon raise themselves to ease, comparative independence, and comfort, as in England. Many instances in real life might be given in proof thereof. Yet our present purpose may be best answered by presenting the case of one, who, having lost his father and mother in childhood, has been indebted to the kind-hearted for the school learning he has acquired. During his apprenticeship he gained little beyond habits of industry. In the seven years of his apprenticeship, his master fell from a respectable station to one of abject poverty; owing to his taking the one glass, then the two, three, four, and onwards, till by steps almost imperceptible, his business and family were neglected, whilst he joined his associates at the ale-house. But let us not dwell on this sad picture. On completing his twenty-first year, our orphan boy engaged in a situation where he received 15s. per week wages; eight shillings of which he appropriated to food and lodgings, and two shillings to clothing, and a few books, to rub up his school-day learning. Warned by the example of his late master, he shunned the ale-house, and his steady conduct soon gained him the confidence of his employer, who, at the end of his first year, raised his wages to twenty-one shillings per week. At the end of the second year he found himself possessed of 40l.; five shillings per week had been regularly deposited in the bank for savings during the first year, which amounted to 13l.; and in the second year eleven shillings per week, which was 28l. 12s. more. We need not follow him step by step in his steady but onward course. He has now been nineteen years in his present situation; for the last ten he has been the foreman, with a salary of thirty shillings per week. Twelve years ago he married a virtuous young woman, and he has now six fine children. The house he lives in is his own; a good garden is attached to it, and a fruitful and lovely spot it is; it serves as an excellent training ground for his children, whose very amusements in it are turned to good account. The mother brought no fortune with her, except herself. She had indeed lived as servant some years in a respectable family, where she had high wages; but all she could spare was devoted to the support of an infirm mother, who on her marriage was received into her husband's house, where the evening of her life is rendered happy. How is it, you ask, that a man of forty years of age, who has had nothing to depend upon but his own labour — who has a wife and six children and an infirm mother-in-law to support — can have bought a piece of ground, built a house upon it, and can have it well furnished, and, after all, has upwards of 200*l.* out on interest? for he has been a servant all along, and is a servant still. Well, let us see if we can find out how it is. In the first place, and which after all is the main point, he spends nothing at the ale-house. The money which too many worse than waste there, he saves. At the age of twenty-three we find he had in the bank of savings 40*l.*

At the age of 24 he has	-	-	-	£70
" 25 "	-	-	-	-	102
" 26 "	-	-	-	-	135
" 27 "	-	-	-	-	170
" 28 "	-	-	-	-	206

He now marries, and expends on furniture 40*l.*, reducing the amount at interest to 166*l.*, but his wages are now advanced to 25*s.* per week; his saving of 5*s.* per week and interest in one year amount to 21*l.*, added to 166*l.*, makes 187*l.* when twenty-nine years of age.

'At thirty years of age he has 210*l.*; wages now 30*s.* per week; saves 10*s.* and interest; he has 237*l.* at thirty-one years of age; at thirty-two he has 286*l.*; buys a plot of ground for 100*l.*, expends 150*l.* in building his dwelling-house, so that he reduces his money at interest to 36*l.*, saves his 10*s.* per week and interest on 36*l.* — 27*l.* 16*s.*, makes 63*l.* 16*s.* at the age of thirty-three.

At 34 he has	-	-	-	-	£93
— 35 he has	-	-	-	-	125
— 36 he has	-	-	-	-	155
— 37 he has	-	-	-	-	181
— 38 he has	-	-	-	-	207

He now expends the interest, and saves only 10*s.* per week.

| At 39 he has | - | - | - | - | - | 233 |
| — 40 he has | - | - | - | - | - | 250 |

in addition to his house and garden.'

It is with many such facts as these fresh in our recollection, and with the knowledge that such facts might easily become characteristic of a whole class, — instead of remaining that of isolated individuals, — that we feel most vividly the injurious tendency of a tale like 'Mary Barton,' where these facts are wholly ignored, and the salutary conclusions to be drawn from them neglected or suppressed.

*   *   *

The plain truth cannot be too boldly spoken, nor too frequently repeated: the working classes, and they only, can raise their own condition; to themselves alone must they look for their elevation in the social scale; their own intellect and their own virtues must work out their salvation; their fate and their future are in their own hands, — and in theirs alone.

*   *   *

ELIZABETH GASKELL

Libbie Marsh's Three Eras.

ERA I.

VALENTINE'S DAY.

Last November but one, there was a flitting in our neighbourhood; hardly a flitting, after all, for it was only a single person changing her place of abode from one lodging to another; and instead of a cartload of drawers and baskets, dressers and beds, with old king clock at the top of all, it was only one large wooden chest to be carried after the girl, who moved slowly and heavily along the streets, listless and depressed, more from the state of her mind than of her body. It was Libbie Marsh, who had been obliged to quit her room in Dean Street, because the acquaintances whom she had been living with were leaving Manchester. She tried to think herself fortunate in having met with lodgings rather more out of the town, and with those who were known to be respectable; she did indeed try to be contented, but, in spite of her reason, the old feeling of desolation came over her, as she was now about to be thrown again entirely among strangers.

No. 2. —— Court, Albemarle Street, was reached at last, and the pace, slow as it was, slackened as she drew near the spot where she was to be left by the man who carried her box, for, trivial as her acquaintance with him was, he was not quite a stranger, as everyone else was, peering out of their open doors, and satisfying themselves it was only "Dixon's new lodger."

Dixon's house was the last on the left-hand side of the court. A high dead brick wall connected it with its opposite neighbour. All the dwellings were of the same monotonous pattern, and one side of the court looked at its exact likeness opposite, as if it were seeing itself in a looking-glass.

Dixon's house was shut up, and the key left next door; but the woman in whose charge it was left knew that Libbie was expected, and came forward to say a few explanatory words, to unlock the door, and stir the dull grey ashes that were lazily burning in the grate; and then she returned to her own house, leaving poor Libbie standing alone with the great big chest in the middle of the house-place floor, with no one to say a word to (even a common-place remark would have been better than this dull silence), that could help her to repel the fast-coming tears.

Dixon and his wife, and their eldest girl, worked in factories, and were absent all day from the house: the youngest child, also a little girl, was boarded out on the week-days at the neighbour's, where the door-key was deposited, but although busy making dirt-pies at the entrance to the court when Libbie came in, she was too young to care much about her parents' new lodger. Libbie knew that she was to sleep with the elder girl in the front bedroom, but, as you may fancy, it seemed a liberty even to go upstairs to take off her things, when no one was at home to marshal the way up the ladderlike steps. So she could only take off her bonnet and sit down, and gaze at the now blazing fire, and think sadly on the past, and on the lonely creature she was in this wide world—father and mother gone, her little brother long since dead—he would have been more than nineteen had he been alive, but she only thought of him as the darling baby; her only friends (to call friends) living far away at their new house; her employers, kind enough people in their way, but too rapidly twirling round on this bustling earth to have leisure to think of the little work-woman, excepting when they wanted gowns turned, carpets mended, or household linen darned; and hardly even the natural though hidden hope of a young girl's heart, to cheer her on with the bright visions of a home of her own at some future day, where, loving and beloved, she might fulfil a woman's dearest duties.

For Libbie was very plain, as she had known so long that the consciousness of it had ceased to mortify her. You can hardly live in Manchester without having some idea of your personal appearance: the factory lads and lasses take good care of that; and if you meet them at the hours when they are pouring out of the mills, you are sure to

hear a good number of truths, some of them combined with such a
spirit of impudent fun that you can scarcely keep from laughing, even
at the joke against yourself. Libbie had often and often been greeted
by such questions as—"How long is it since you were a beauty?"
"What would you take a day to stand in the fields to scare away the
birds?" &c., for her to linger under any impression as to her looks.

While she was thus musing, and quietly crying, under the pictures
her fancy had conjured up, the Dixons came dropping in, and surprised her with her wet cheeks and quivering lips.

She almost wished to have the stillness again that had so oppressed
her an hour ago, they talked and laughed so loudly and so much, and
bustled about so noisily over everything they did. Dixon took hold of
one iron handle of her box, and helped her to bump it up-stairs, while
his daughter Anne followed to see the unpacking, and what sort of
clothes "little sewing body had gotten." Mrs. Dixon rattled out her
tea-things, and put the kettle on, fetched home her youngest child,
which added to the commotion. Then she called Anne downstairs,
and sent her for this thing and that: eggs to put to the cream, it was
so thin; ham, to give a relish to the bread-and-butter; some new
bread, hot, if she could get it. Libbie heard all these orders, given at
full pitch of Mrs. Dixon's voice, and wondered at their extravagance,
so different from the habits of the place where she had last lodged.
But they were fine spinners, in the receipt of good wages; and confined all day in an atmosphere ranging from seventy-five to eighty
degrees. They had lost all natural, healthy appetite for simple food,
and, having no higher tastes, found their greatest enjoyment in their
luxurious meals.

When tea was ready, Libbie was called downstairs, with a rough
but hearty invitation, to share their meal; she sat mutely at the corner of the tea-table, while they went on with their own conversation
about people and things she knew nothing about, till at length she
ventured to ask for a candle, to go and finish her unpacking before
bedtime, as she had to go out sewing for several succeeding days. But
once in the comparative peace of her bedroom, her energy failed her,
and she contented herself with locking her Noah's ark of a chest, and
put out her candle, and went to sit by the window, and gaze out at the
bright heavens; for ever and ever "the blue sky, that bends over all,"
sheds down a feeling of sympathy with the sorrowful at the solemn
hours when the ceaseless stars are seen to pace its depths.

By and by her eye fell down to gazing at the corresponding window
to her own on the opposite side of the court. It was lighted, but the
blind was drawn down: upon the blind she saw, first unconsciously,
the constant weary motion of a little spectral shadow, a child's hand
and arm—no more; long, thin fingers hanging down from the wrist,
while the arm moved up and down, as if keeping time to the heavy

pulses of dull pain. She could not help hoping that sleep would soon come to still that incessant, feeble motion: and now and then it did cease, as if the little creature had dropped into a slumber from very weariness; but presently the arm jerked up with the fingers clenched, as if with a sudden start of agony. When Anne came up to bed, Libbie was still sitting, watching the shadow, and she directly asked to whom it belonged.

"It will be Margaret Hall's lad. Last summer, when it was so hot, there was no biding with the window shut at night, and theirs was open too: and many's the time he has waked me with his moans; they say he's been better sin' cold weather came."

"Is he always in bed? Whatten ails him?" asked Libbie.

"Summat's amiss wi' his backbone, folks say; he's better and worse, like. He's a nice little chap enough, and his mother's not that bad either; only my mother and her had words, so now we don't speak."

Libbie went on watching, and when she next spoke, to ask who and what his mother was, Anne Dixon was fast asleep.

Time passed away, and as usual unveiled the hidden things. Libbie found out that Margaret Hall was a widow, who earned her living as a washerwoman; that the little suffering lad was her only child, her dearly beloved. That while she scolded pretty nearly everybody else, "till her name was up" in the neighbourhood for a termagant, to him she was evidently most tender and gentle. He lay alone on his little bed, near the window, through the day, while she was away toiling for a livelihood. But when Libbie had plain sewing to do at her lodgings, instead of going out to sew, she used to watch from her bedroom window for the time when the shadows opposite, by their mute gestures, told that the mother had returned to bend over her child, to smooth his pillow, to alter his position, to get him his nightly cup of tea. And often in the night Libbie could not help rising gently from bed, to see if the little arm was waving up and down, as was his accustomed habit when sleepless from pain.

Libbie had a good deal of sewing to do at home that winter, and whenever it was not so cold as to benumb her fingers, she took it upstairs, in order to watch the little lad in her few odd moments of pause. On his better days he could sit up enough to peep out of his window, and she found he liked to look at her. Presently she ventured to nod to him across the court; and his faint smile, and ready nod back again, showed that this gave him pleasure. I think she would have been encouraged by this smile to have proceeded to a speaking acquaintance, if it had not been for his terrible mother, to whom it seemed to be irritation enough to know that Libbie was a lodger at the Dixons' for her to talk at her whenever they encountered each other, and to live evidently in wait for some good opportunity of abuse.

With her constant interest in him, Libbie soon discovered his great want of an object on which to occupy his thoughts, and which might distract his attention, when alone through the long day, from the pain he endured. He was very fond of flowers. It was November when she had first removed to her lodgings, but it had been very mild weather, and a few flowers yet lingered in the gardens, which the country people gathered into nosegays, and brought on market-days into Manchester. His mother had brought him a bunch of Michaelmas daisies the very day Libbie had become a neighbour, and she watched their history. He put them first in an old teapot, of which the spout was broken off and the lid lost; and he daily replenished the teapot from the jug of water his mother left near him to quench his feverish thirst. By and by, one or two of the constellation of lilac stars faded, and then the time he had hitherto spent in admiring, almost caress-ing them, was devoted to cutting off those flowers whose decay marred the beauty of the nosegay. It took him half the morning, with his feeble, languid motions, and his cumbrous old scissors, to trim up his diminished darlings. Then at last he seemed to think he had bet-ter preserve the few that remained by drying them; so they were care-fully put between the leaves of the old Bible; and then, whenever a better day came, when he had strength enough to lift the ponderous book, he used to open the pages to look at his flower friends. In win-ter he could have no more living flowers to tend.

Libbie thought and thought, till at last an idea flashed upon her mind, that often made a happy smile steal over her face as she stitched away, and that cheered her through the solitary winter—for solitary it continued to be, though the Dixons were very good sort of people, never pressed her for payment, if she had had but little work to do that week; never grudged her a share of their extravagant meals, which were far more luxurious than she could have met with any-where else, for her previously agreed payment in case of working at home; and they would fain have taught her to drink rum in her tea, assuring her that she should have it for nothing and welcome. But they were too touchy, too prosperous, too much absorbed in them-selves, to take off Libbie's feeling of solitariness; not half as much as the little face by day, and the shadow by night, of him with whom she had never yet exchanged a word.

Her idea was this: her mother came from the east of England, where, as perhaps you know, they have the pretty custom of sending presents on St. Valentine's day, with the donor's name unknown, and, of course, the mystery constitutes half the enjoyment. The fourteenth of February was Libbie's birthday too, and many a year, in the happy days of old, had her mother delighted to surprise her with some little gift, of which she more than half-guessed the giver, although each Valentine's day the manner of its arrival was varied. Since then the fourteenth of February had been the dreariest of all the year, because the most haunted by memory of departed happiness. But now, this year, if she could not have the old gladness of heart herself, she would try and brighten the life of another. She would save, and she would screw, but she would buy a canary and a cage for that poor little laddie opposite, who wore out his monotonous life with so few pleasures and so much pain.

I doubt I may not tell you here of the anxieties and the fears, of the hopes and the self-sacrifices—all, perhaps, small in the tangible effect as the widow's mite, yet not the less marked by the viewless angels who go about continually among us—which varied Libbie's life before she accomplished her purpose. It is enough to say it was accomplished. The very day before the fourteenth she found time to go with her half-guinea to a barber's who lived near Albemarle Street, and who was famous for his stock of singing-birds. There are enthusiasts about all sorts of things, both good and bad, and many of the weavers in Manchester know and care more about birds than any one would easily credit. Stubborn, silent, reserved men on many things, you have only to touch on the subject of birds to light up their faces with brightness. They will tell you who won the prizes at the last canary show, where the prize birds may be seen, and give you all the details of those funny, but pretty and interesting mimicries of great people's cattle shows. Among these amateurs, Emanuel Morris, the barber, was an oracle.

He took Libbie into his little back room, used for private shaving of modest men, who did not care to be exhibited in the front shop decked out in the full glories of lather; and which was hung round with birds in rude wicker cages, with the exception of those who had won prizes, and were consequently honoured with gilt-wire prisons. The longer and thinner the body of the bird was, the more admiration it received, as far as external beauty went; and when, in addition to this, the colour was deep and clear, and its notes strong and varied, the more did Emanuel dwell upon its perfections. But these were all prize birds; and, on inquiry, Libbie heard, with some little sinking at heart, that their price ran from one to two guineas.

"I'm not over-particular as to shape and colour," said she, "I should like a good singer, that's all!"

She dropped a little in Emanuel's estimation. However, he showed her his good singers, but all were above Libbie's means.

"After all, I don't think I care so much about the singing very loud; it's but a noise after all, and sometimes noise fidgets folks."

"They must be nesh folks as is put out with the singing o' birds," replied Emanuel, rather affronted.

"It's for one who is poorly," said Libbie, deprecatingly.

"Well," said he, as if considering the matter, "folk that are cranky

often take more to them as shows 'em love than to them as is clever
and gifted. Happen yo'd rather have this'n," opening a cage-door, and
calling to a dull-coloured bird, sitting moped up in a corner, "Here—
Jupiter, Jupiter!"

The bird smoothed its feathers in an instant, and, uttering a little
note of delight, flew to Emanuel, putting his beak to his lips, as if
kissing him, and then, perching on his head, it began a gurgling war-
ble of pleasure, not by any means so varied or so clear as the song of
the others, but which pleased Libbie more; for she was always one to
find out she liked the gooseberries that were accessible, better than
the grapes that were beyond her reach. The price, too, was just right,
so she gladly took possession of the cage, and hid it under her cloak,
preparatory to carrying it home. Emanuel meanwhile was giving her
directions as to its food, with all the minuteness of one loving his subject.

"Will it soon get to know any one?" asked she.

"Give him two days only, and you and he'll be as thick as him and
me are now. You've only to open his door, and call him, and he'll follow you round the room; but he'll first kiss you, and then perch on
your head. He only wants larning, which I have no time to give him,
to do many another accomplishment."

"What's his name? I did not rightly catch it."

"Jupiter—it's not common; but the town's o'errun with Bobbies
and Dickies, and as my birds are thought a bit out o' the way, I like to
have better names for 'em, so I just picked a few out o' my lad's school
books. It's just as ready, when you're used to it, to say Jupiter as
Dicky."

"I could bring my tongue round to Peter better; would he answer
to Peter?" asked Libbie, now on the point of departing.

"Happen he might; but I think he'd come readier to the three syllables."

On Valentine's day, Jupiter's cage was decked round with ivy leaves,
making quite a pretty wreath on the wicker work; and to one of them
was pinned a slip of paper, with these words, written in Libbie's best
round hand:—

"From your faithful Valentine. Please take notice his name is
Peter, and he'll come if you call him, after a bit."

But little work did Libbie do that afternoon, she was so engaged in
watching for the messenger who was to bear her present to her little
valentine, and run away as soon as he had delivered up the canary,
and explained to whom it was sent.

At last he came; then there was a pause before the woman of the
house was at liberty to take it upstairs. Then Libbie saw the little face
flush up into a bright colour, the feeble hands tremble with delighted
eagerness, the head bent down to try and make out the writing

(beyond his power, poor lad, to read), the rapturous turning round of the cage in order to see the canary in every point of view, head, tail, wings, and feet; an intention in which Jupiter, in his uneasiness at being again among strangers, did not second, for he hopped round so as continually to present a full front to the boy. It was a source of never-wearying delight to the little fellow, till daylight closed in; he evidently forgot to wonder who had sent it him, in his gladness at his possession of such a treasure; and when the shadow of his mother darkened on the blind, and the bird had been exhibited, Libbie saw her do what, with all her tenderness, seemed rarely to have entered into her thoughts—she bent down and kissed her boy, in a mother's sympathy with the joy of her child.

The canary was placed for the night between the little bed and window; and when Libbie rose once, to take her accustomed peep, she saw the little arm put fondly round the cage, as if embracing his new treasure even in his sleep. How Jupiter slept this first night is quite another thing.

So ended the first day in Libbie's three eras in last year.

ERA II.

WHITSUNTIDE.

The brightest, fullest daylight poured down into No. 2 —— Court, Albemarle Street, and the heat, even at the early hour of five, as at the noontide on the June days of many years past.

The court seemed alive, and merry with voices and laughter. The bedroom windows were open wide, and had been so all night, on account of the heat; and every now and then you might see a head and a pair of shoulders, simply encased in shirt sleeves, popped out, and you might hear the inquiry passed from one to the other:

"Well, Jack, and where art thee bound for?"

"Dunham?"

"Why, what an old-fashioned chap thou be'st. Thy grandad afore thee went to Dunham: but thou wert always a slow coach. I'm off to Alderley, me and my missis."

"Ay, that's because there's only thee and thy missis. Wait till thou hast gotten four childer, like me, and thou'lt be glad enough to take 'em to Dunham, oud-fashioned way, for fourpence apiece."

"I'd still go to Alderley; I'd not be bothered with my children; they should keep house at home."

A pair of hands, the person to whom they belonged invisible, boxed his ears on this last speech, in a very spirited though playful manner, and the neighbours all laughed at the surprised look of the speaker, at this assault from an unseen foe. The man who had been holding conversation with him cried out:

"Sarved him right, Mrs. Slater; he knows nought about it yet: but when he gets them he'll be as loth to leave the babbies at home on a Whitsuntide as any on us. We shall live to see him in Dunham Park yet, wi' twins in his arms, and another pair on 'em clutching at daddy's coat tails, let alone your share of youngsters, missis."

At this moment our friend Libbie appeared at her window, and Mrs. Slater, who had taken her discomfited husband's place, called out:

"Elizabeth Marsh, where are Dixons and you bound to?"

"Dixons are not up yet; he said last night he'd take his holiday out in lying in bed. I'm going to the old-fashioned place, Dunham."

"Thou art never going by thyself, moping!"

"No; I'm going with Margaret Hall and her lad," replied Libbie, hastily withdrawing from the window, in order to avoid hearing any remarks on the associates she had chosen for her day of pleasure— the scold of the neighbourhood, and her sickly, ailing child!

But Jupiter might have been a dove, and his ivy leaves an olive branch, for the peace he had brought, the happiness he had caused, to three individuals at least. For of course it could not long be a mystery who had sent little Frank Hall his valentine; nor could his mother long entertain her hard manner towards one who had given her child a new pleasure. She was shy, and she was proud, and for some time she struggled against the natural desire of manifesting her gratitude; but one evening, when Libbie was returning home, with a bundle of work half as large as herself, as she dragged herself along through the heated streets, she was overtaken by Margaret Hall, her burden gently pulled from her, and her way home shortened, and her weary spirits soothed and cheered, by the outpourings of Margaret's heart; for the barrier of reserve once broken down, she had much to say, to thank her for days of amusement and happy employment for her lad, to speak of his gratitude, to tell of her hopes and fears—the hopes and fears that made up the dates of her life. From that time, Libbie lost her awe of the termagant in interest for the mother, whose all was ventured in so frail a bark. From this time, Libbie was a fast friend with both mother and son, planning mitigations for the sorrowful days of the latter as eagerly as poor Margaret Hall, and with far more success. His life had flickered up under the charm and excitement of the last few months. He even seemed strong enough to undertake the journey to Dunham, which Libbie had arranged as a Whitsuntide treat, and for which she and his mother had been hoarding up for several weeks. The canal boat left Knott-mill at six, and it was now past five; so Libbie let herself out very gently, and went across to her friends. She knocked at the door of their lodging-room, and, without waiting for an answer, entered.

Franky's face was flushed, and he was trembling with excitement—partly with pleasure, but partly with some eager wish not yet granted.

"He wants sore to take Peter with him," said his mother to Libbie, as if referring the matter to her. The boy looked imploringly at her.

"He would like it, I know; for one thing, he'd miss me sadly, and chirrup for me all day long, he'd be so lonely. I could not be half so happy a-thinking on him, left alone here by himself. Then, Libbie, he's just like a Christian, so fond of flowers and green leaves, and them sort of things. He chirrups to me so when mother brings me a pennyworth of wall-flowers to put round his cage. He would talk if he could, you know; but I can tell what he means quite as one as if he spoke. Do let Peter go, Libbie; I'll carry him in my own arms."

So Jupiter was allowed to be of the party. Now Libbie had overcome the great difficulty of conveying Franky to the boat, by offering to "slay" for a coach, and the shouts and exclamations of the neighbours told them that their conveyance awaited them at the bottom of the court. His mother carried Franky, light in weight, though heavy in helplessness, and he would hold the cage, believing that he was redeeming his pledge, that Peter should be a trouble to no one. Libbie proceeded to arrange the bundle containing their dinner, as a support in the corner of the coach. The neighbours came out with many blunt speeches, and more kindly wishes, and one or two of them would have relieved Margaret of her burden, if she would have allowed it. The presence of that little cripple fellow seemed to obliterate all the angry feelings which had existed between his mother and her neighbours, and which had formed the politics of that little court for many a day.

And now they were fairly off! Franky bit his lips in attempted endurance of the pain the motion caused him; he winced and shrank, until they were fairly on a macadamised thoroughfare, when he closed his eyes, and seemed desirous of a few minutes' rest. Libbie fell very shy, and very much afraid of being seen by her employers, "set up in a coach!" and so she hid herself in a corner, and made herself as small as possible; while Mrs. Hall had exactly the opposite feeling, and was delighted to stand up, stretching out of the window, and nodding to pretty nearly every one they met or passed on the footpaths; and they were not a few, for the streets were quite gay, even at that early hour, with parties going to this or that railway station, or to the boats which crowded the canals on this bright holiday week; and almost every one they met seemed to enter into Mrs. Hall's exhilaration of feeling, and had a smile or nod in return. At last she plumped down by Libbie, and exclaimed, "I never was in a coach but once afore, and that was when I was a-going to be married. It's like heaven; and all done over with such beautiful gimp, too!" continued she, admiring the lining of the vehicle. Jupiter did not enjoy it so much.

As if the holiday time, the lovely weather, and the "sweet hour of prime" had a genial influence, as no doubt they have, everybody's heart seemed softened towards poor Franky. The driver lifted him out with the tenderness of strength, and bore him carefully down to the boat; the people then made way, and gave him the best seat in their power—or rather I should call it a couch, for they saw he was weary, and insisted on his lying down—an attitude he would have been ashamed to assume without the protection of his mother and Libbie, who now appeared, bearing their baskets and carrying Peter.

Away the boat went, to make room for others, for every conveyance, both by land and water, is in requisition in Whitsun-week, to give the hard-worked crowds the opportunity of enjoying the charms of the country. Even every standing-place in the canal packets was occupied, and as they glided along, the banks were lined with people, who seemed to find it object enough to watch the boats go by, packed close and full with happy beings brimming with anticipations of a day's pleasure. The country through which they passed is as uninteresting as can well be imagined; but still it is the country; and the screams of delight from the children, and the low laughs of pleasure from the parents, at every blossoming tree that trailed its wreath against some cottage wall, or at the tufts of late primroses which lingered in the cool depths of grass along the canal banks; the thorough relish of everything, as if dreading to let the least circumstance of this happy day pass over without its due appreciation, made the time seem all too short, although it took two hours to arrive at a place only eight miles from Manchester. Even Franky, with all his impatience to see Dunham woods (which I think he confused with London, believing both to be paved with gold), enjoyed the easy motion of the boat so much, floating along, while pictures moved before him, that he regretted when the time came for landing among the soft, green meadows, that came sloping down to the dancing water's brim. His fellow-passengers carried him to the park, and refused all payment, although his mother had laid by sixpence on purpose, as a recompense for this service.

"Oh, Libbie, how beautiful! Oh, mother, mother; is the whole world out of Manchester as beautiful as this? I did not know trees were like this! Such green homes for birds! Look, Peter! would not you like to be there, up among those boughs? But I can't let you go, you know, because you're my little bird-brother, and I should be quite lost without you."

They spread a shawl upon the fine mossy turf, at the root of a beech-tree, which made a sort of natural couch, and there they laid him, and bade him rest, in spite of the delight which made him believe himself capable of any exertion. Where he lay—always holding Jupiter's cage, and often talking to him as to a playfellow—he was on the verge of a green area, shut in by magnificent trees, in all the glory of their early foliage, before the summer heats had deepened their verdure into one rich, monotonous tint. And hither came party after party; old men and maidens, young men and children—whole families trooped along after the guiding fathers, who bore the youngest in their arms, or astride upon their backs, while they turned round occasionally to the wives, with whom they shared some fond local remembrance. For years has Dunham Park been the favourite resort of the Manchester work-people; for more years than I can tell; probably ever since "the Duke," by his canals, opened out the system of cheap travelling. Its scenery, too, which presents such a complete contrast to the whirl and turmoil of Manchester; so thoroughly woodland, with its ancestral trees (here and there lightning blanched); its "verdurous walls;" its grassy walks leading far away into some glade, where you start at the rabbit rustling among the last year's fern, and where the wood-pigeon's call seems the only fitting and accordant sound. Depend upon it, this complete sylvan repose, this accessible quiet, this lapping the soul in green images of the country, forms the most complete contrast to a town's-person, and consequently has over such the greatest power of charm.

Presently Libbie found out she was very hungry. Now they were but provided with dinner, which was, of course, to be eaten as near twelve o'clock as might be; and Margaret Hall, in her prudence, asked a working-man near to tell her what o'clock it was.

"Nay," said he, "I'll ne'er look at clock or watch to-day. I'll not spoil my pleasure by finding out how fast it's going away. If thou'rt hungry, eat. I make my own dinner-hour, and I have eaten mine an hour ago."

So they had their veal pies, and then found out it was only about half-past ten o'clock; by so many pleasurable events had that morning been marked. But such was their buoyancy of spirits, that they only enjoyed their mistake, and joined in the general laugh against the man who had eaten his dinner somewhere about nine. He laughed most heartily of all, till, suddenly stopping, he said:

"I must not go on at this rate; laughing gives one such an appetite."

"Oh! if that's all," said a merry-looking man, lying at full length, and brushing the fresh scent out of the grass, while two or three little children tumbled over him, and crept about him, as kittens or puppies frolic with their parents, "if that's all, we'll have a subscription of eatables for them improvident folk as have eaten their dinner for their breakfast. Here's a sausage pasty and a handful of nuts for my share. Bring round a hat, Bob, and see what the company will give."

Bob carried out the joke, much to little Franky's amusement; and no one was so churlish as to refuse, although the contributions varied from a peppermint drop up to a veal pie and a sausage pasty.

"It's a thriving trade," said Bob, as he emptied his hatful of provisions on the grass by Libbie's side. "Besides, it's tiptop, too to live on the public. Hark! what is that?"

The laughter and the chat were suddenly hushed, and mothers told their little ones to listen—as, far away in the distance, now sinking and falling, now swelling and clear, came a ringing peal of children's voices, blended together in one of those psalm tunes which we are all of us familiar with, and which bring to mind the old, old days, when we, as wondering children, were first led to worship "Our Father" by those beloved ones who have since gone to the more perfect worship. Holy was that distant choral praise, even to the most thoughtless; and when it, in fact, was ended, in the instant's pause, during which the ear awaits the repetition of the air, they caught the noontide hum and buzz of the myriads of insects who danced away their lives in the glorious day; they heard the swaying of the mighty woods in the soft but resistless breeze, and then again once more burst forth the merry jests and the shouts of childhood; and again the elder ones resumed their happy talk, as they lay or sat "under the greenwood tree." Fresh parties came dropping in; some laden with wild flowers—almost with branches of hawthorn, indeed; while one or two had made prizes of the earliest dog-roses, and had cast away campion, stitchwort, ragged robin, all to keep the lady of the hedges from being obscured or hidden by the community.

One after another drew near to Franky, and looked on with interest as he lay sorting the flowers given to him. Happy parents stood by, with their household bands around them, in health and comeliness, and felt the sad prophecy of those shrivelled limbs, those wasted fingers, those lamp-like eyes, with their bright, dark lustre. His mother was too eagerly watching his happiness to read the meaning of those grave looks, but Libbie saw them and understood them; and a chill shudder went through her, even on that day, as she thought on the future.

"Ay! I thought we should give you a start!"

A start they did give, with their terrible slap on Libbie's back, as she sat idly grouping flowers, and following out her sorrowful thoughts. It was the Dixons. Instead of keeping their holiday by lying in bed, they and their children had roused themselves, and had come by the omnibus to the nearest point. For an instant the meeting was an awkward one, on account of the feud between Margaret Hall and Mrs. Dixon, but there was no long resisting of kindly mother Natures's soothings, at that holiday time, and in that lonely tranquil spot; or if they could have been unheeded, the sight of Franky would have awed every angry feeling into rest, so changed was he since the Dixons had last seen him; and since he had been the Puck or Robin Goodfellow of the neighbourhood, whose marbles were always rolling under other people's feet, and whose top-strings were always hanging in nooses to catch the unwary. Yes, he, the feeble, mild, almost girlish-looking lad, had once been a merry, happy rogue, and as such often cuffed by Mrs. Dixon, the very Mrs. Dixon who now stood gazing with the tears in her eyes. Could she, in sight of him, the changed, the fading, keep up a quarrel with his mother?

"How long hast thou been here?" asked Dixon.

"Welly on for all day," answered Libbie.

"Hast never been to see the deer, or the king and queen oaks? Lord, how stupid."

His wife pinched his arm, to remind him of Franky's helpless condition, which of course tethered the otherwise willing feet. But Dixon had a remedy. He called Bob, and one or two others, and each taking a corner of the strong plaid shawl, they slung Franky as in a hammock, and thus carried him merrily along, down the wood paths, over the smooth, grassy turf, while the glimmering shine and shadow fell on his upturned face. The women walked behind, talking, loitering along, always in sight of the hammock; now picking up some green treasure from the ground, now catching at the low hanging branches of the horse-chestnut. The soul grew much on this day, and in these woods, and all unconsciously, as souls do grow. They followed Franky's hammock-bearers up a grassy knoll, on the top of which stood a group of pine trees, whose stems looked like dark red gold in the sunbeams. They had taken Franky there to show him Manchester, far away in the blue plain, against which the woodland foreground cut with a soft clear line. Far, far away in the distance on that flat plain, you might see the motionless cloud of smoke hanging over a great town, and that was Manchester—ugly, smoky Manchester; dear, busy, earnest, noble-working Manchester; where their children had been born, and where, perhaps, some lay buried; where their homes were, and where God had cast their lives, and told them to work out their destiny.

"Hurrah! for oud smoke jack!" cried Bob, putting Franky softly down on the grass, before he whirled his hat round, preparatory to a shout. "Hurrah! hurrah!" from all the men. "There's the rim of my hat lying like a quoit yonder," observed Bob quietly, as he replaced his brimless hat on his head with the gravity of a judge.

"Here's the Sunday-school children a-coming to sit on this shady side, and have their buns and milk. Hark! they're singing the infant-school grace."

They sat close at hand, so that Franky could hear the words they sang, in rings of children, making, in their gay summer prints, newly donned for that week, garlands of little faces, all happy and bright upon that green hill-side. One little "Dot" of a girl came shyly behind Franky, whom she had long been watching, and threw her half-bun at his side, and then ran away and hid herself, in very shame at the boldness of her own sweet impulse. She kept peeping from her screen at

Franky all the time; and he meanwhile was almost too much pleased and happy to eat; the world was so beautiful, and men, women, and children all so tender and kind; so softened, in fact, by the beauty of this earth, so unconsciously touched by the spirit of love, which was the Creator of this lovely earth. But the day drew to an end; the heat declined; the birds once more began their warblings; the fresh scents again hung about plant, and tree, and grass, betokening the fragrant presence of the reviving dew, and—the boat time was near. As they trod the meadow-path once more, they were joined by many a party they had encountered during the day, all abounding in happiness, all full of the day's adventures. Long-cherished quarrels had been forgotten, new friendships formed. Fresh tastes and higher delights had been imparted that day. We have all of us our look, now and then, called up by some noble or loving thought (our highest on earth), which will be our likeness in heaven. I can catch the glance on many a face, the glancing light of the cloud of glory from heaven, "which is our home." That look was present on many a hard-worked, wrinkled countenance, as they turned backwards to catch a longing, lingering look at Dunham woods, fast deepening into blackness of night, but whose memory was to haunt, in greenness and freshness, many a loom, and workshop, and factory, with images of peace and beauty.

That night, as Libbie lay awake, revolving the incidents of the day, she caught Franky's voice through the open windows. Instead of the frequent moan of pain, he was trying to recall the burden of one of the children's hymns—

> Here we suffer grief and pain,
> Here we meet to part again;
> In Heaven we part no more.
> Oh! that will be joyful, &c.

She recalled his question, the whispered question, to her, in the happiest part of the day. He asked Libbie, "Is Dunham like heaven? the people here are as kind as angels, and I don't want heaven to be more beautiful than this place. If you and mother would but die with me, I should like to die, and live always there!" She had checked him, for she feared he was impious; but now the young child's craving for some definite idea of the land to which his inner wisdom told him he was hastening, had nothing in it wrong, or even sorrowful, for—

In Heaven we part no more.

ERA III.

MICHAELMAS.

The church clocks had struck three; the crowds of gentlemen returning to business, after their early dinners, had disappeared within offices and warehouses; the streets were clear and quiet, and ladies were venturing to sally forth for their afternoon shoppings and their afternoon calls.

Slowly, slowly, along the streets, elbowed by life at every turn, a little funeral wound its quiet way. Four men bore along a child's coffin; two women with bowed heads followed meekly.

I need not tell you whose coffin it was, or who were those two mourners. All was now over with little Frank Hall: his romps, his games, his sickening, his suffering, his death. All was now over, but the Resurrection and the Life.

His mother walked as in a stupor. Could it be that he was dead? If he had been less an object of her thoughts, less of a motive for her labours, she could sooner have realised it. As it was, she followed his poor, cast-off, worn-out body as if she were borne along by some oppressive dream. If he were really dead, how could she be still alive?

Libbie's mind was far less stunned, and consequently far more active, than Margaret Hall's. Visions, as in a phantasmagoria, came rapidly passing before her—recollections of the time (which seemed now so long ago) when the shadow of the feebly-waving arm first caught her attention; of the bright, strangely-isolated day at Dunham Park, where the world had seemed so full of enjoyment, and beauty, and life; of the long-continued heat, through which poor Franky had panted away his strength in the little close room, where there was no escaping the hot rays of the afternoon sun; of the long nights when his mother and she had watched by his side, as he moaned continually, whether awake or asleep; of the fevered moaning slumber of exhaustion; of the pitiful little self-upbraidings for his own impatience of suffering, only impatient in his own eyes, most true and holy patience in the sight of others; and then the fading away of life, the loss of power, the increased unconsciousness, the lovely look of angelic peace, which followed the dark shadow on the countenance, where was he?—what was he now?

And so they laid him in his grave, and heard the solemn funeral words; but far off in the distance, as if not addressed to them.

Margaret Hall bent over the grave to catch one last glance—she had not spoken, nor sobbed, nor done aught but shiver now and then, since the morning; but now her weight bore more heavily on Libbie's arm, and without sigh or sound she fell an unconscious heap on the piled-up gravel. They helped Libbie to bring her round; but long after her half-opened eyes and altered breathings showed that her senses were restored, she lay, speechless and motionless, without attempting to rise from her strange bed, as if the earth contained nothing worth even that trifling exertion.

At last Libbie and she left that holy, consecrated spot, and bent their steps back to the only place more consecrated still—where he had rendered up his spirit; and where memories of him haunted each common, rude piece of furniture that their eyes fell upon. As the woman of the house opened the door, she pulled Libbie on one side, and said:

"Anne Dixon has been across to see you; she wants to have a word with you."

"I cannot go now," replied Libbie, as she pushed hastily along, in order to enter the room (*his* room) at the same time with the child-less mother: for, as she had anticipated, the sight of that empty spot, the glance at the uncurtained open window, letting in the fresh air, and the broad, rejoicing light of day, where all had so long been darkened and subdued, unlocked the waters of the fountain, and long and shrill were the cries for her boy that the poor woman uttered.

"Oh! dear Mrs. Hall," said Libbie, herself drenched in tears, "do not take on so badly; I'm sure it would grieve *him* sore if he were alive, and you know he is—Bible tells us so; and maybe he's here watching how we go on without him, and hoping we don't fret over much."

Mrs. Hall's sobs grew worse and more hysterical.

"Oh! listen," said Libbie, once more struggling against her own increasing agitation, "listen! there's Peter chirping as he always does when he's put about, frightened like; and you know he that's gone could never abide to hear the canary chirp in that shrill way."

Margaret Hall did check herself, and curb her expressions of agony, in order not to frighten the little creature he had loved; and as her outward grief subsided, Libbie took up the large old Bible, which fell open at the never-failing comfort of the fourteenth chapter of St. John's Gospel.

How often these large family Bibles do open at that chapter! as if, unused in more joyous and prosperous times, the soul went home to its words of loving sympathy when weary and sorrowful, just as the little child seeks the tender comfort of its mother in all its griefs and cares.

And Margaret put back her wet, ruffled, grey hair from her heated, tear-stained, woeful face, and listened with such earnest eyes, trying to form some idea of the "Father's house" where her boy had gone to dwell.

They were interrupted by a low tap at the door. Libbie went. "Anne Dixon has watched you home, and wants to have a word with you," said the woman of the house, in a whisper. Libbie went back and closed the book, with a word of explanation to Margaret Hall, and then ran downstairs to learn the reason of Anne's anxiety to see her.

"Oh, Libbie!" she burst out with, and then, checking herself with the remembrance of Libbie's last solemn duty, "how's Margaret Hall? But, of course, poor thing, she'll fret a bit at first; she'll be some time coming round, mother says, seeing it's as well that poor lad is taken; for he'd always ha' been a cripple, and a trouble to her—he was a fine lad once, too."

She had come full of another and a different subject; but the sight of Libbie's sad, weeping face, and the quiet, subdued tone of her manner, made her feel it awkward to begin on any other theme than the one which filled her companion's mind. To her last speech Libbie answered sorrowfully:

"No doubt, Anne, it's ordered for the best; but oh! don't call him, don't think he could ever ha' been, a trouble to his mother, though he were a cripple. She loved him all the more for each thing she had to do for him—I am sure I did." Libbie cried a little behind her apron. Anne Dixon felt still more awkward in introducing the discordant subject.

"Well! 'flesh is grass,' Bible says;" and, having fulfilled the etiquette of quoting a text, if possible, if not of making a moral observation on the fleeting nature of earthly things, she thought she was at liberty to pass on to her real errand.

"You must not go on moping yourself, Libbie Marsh. What I wanted special for to see you this afternoon, was to tell you, you must come to my wedding to-morrow. Nanny Dawson has fallen sick, and there's none as I should like to have bridesmaid in her place as well as you."

"To-morrow! Oh, I cannot!—indeed I cannot!"

"Why not?"

Libbie did not answer, and Anne Dixon grew impatient.

"Surely, in the name o' goodness, you're never going to baulk yourself of a day's pleasure for the sake of yon little cripple that's dead and gone!"

"No—it's not baulking myself of—don't be angry, Anne Dixon, with him, please; but I don't think it would be a pleasure to me—I don't feel as if I could enjoy it; thank you all the same. But I did love that little lad very dearly—I did," sobbing a little, "and I can't forget him and make merry so soon."

"Well—I never!" exclaimed Anne, almost angrily.

"Indeed, Anne, I feel your kindness, and you and Bob have my best wishes—that's what you have; but even if I went, I should be thinking all day of him, and of his poor, poor mother, and they say it's bad to think very much on them that's dead, at a wedding."

"Nonsense," said Anne, "I'll take the risk of the ill-luck. After all, what is marrying? Just a spree, Bob says. He often says he does not think I shall make him a good wife, for I know nought about house matters, wi' working in a factory; but he says he'd rather be uneasy wi' me than easy wi' anybody else. There's love for you! And I tell him I'd rather have him tipsy than any one else sober."

"Oh! Anne Dixon, hush! you don't know yet what it is to have a drunken husband. I have seen something of it: father used to get fuddled, and, in the long run, it killed mother, let alone—oh! Anne, God above only knows what the wife of a drunken man has to bear. Don't tell," said she, lowering her voice, "but father killed our little baby in one of his bouts; mother never looked up again, nor father either, for that matter, only his was in a different way. Mother will have gotten to little Jemmie now, and they'll be so happy together—and perhaps Franky too. Oh!" said she, recovering herself from her train of thought, "never say aught lightly of the wife's lot whose husband is given to drink!"

"Dear, what a preachment! I tell you what, Libbie, you're as born an old maid as ever I saw. You'll never be married to either drunken or sober."

Libbie's face went rather red, but without losing its meek expression.

"I know that as well as you can tell me; and more reason, therefore, as God has seen fit to keep me out of woman's natural work, I should try and find work for myself. I mean," seeing Anne Dixon's puzzled look, "that, as I know I'm never likely to have a home of my own, or a husband that would look to me to make all straight, or children to watch over or care for, all which I take to be woman's natural work, I must not lose time in fretting and fidgetting after marriage, but just look about me for somewhat else to do. I can see many a one misses it in this. They will hanker after what is ne'er likely to be theirs, instead of facing it out, and settling down to be old maids; and, as old maids, just looking round for the odd jobs God leaves in the world for such as old maids to do. There's plenty of such work, and there's the blessing of God on them as does it." Libbie was almost out of breath at this outpouring of what had long been her inner thoughts.

"That's all very true, I make no doubt, for them as is to be old maids: but as I'm not, please God to-morrow comes, you might have spared your breath to cool your porridge. What I want to know is, whether you'll be bridesmaid to-morrow or not? Come, now do; it will do you good, after all your working, and watching and slaving yourself for that poor Franky Hall."

"It was one of my odd jobs," said Libbie, smiling, though her eyes were brimming over with tears; "but, dear Anne," said she, recovering itself, "I could not do it to-morrow, indeed I could not."

"And I can't wait," said Anne Dixon, almost sulkily, "Bob and I put it off from to-day because of the funeral, and Bob had set his heart on its being on Michaelmas-day; and mother says the goose won't keep beyond to-morrow. Do come; father finds eatables, and Bob finds drink, and we shall be so jolly! and after we've been to church, we're to walk round the town in pairs, white satin ribbon in our bonnets, and refreshments at any public-house we like, Bob says. And after dinner there's to be a dance. Don't be a fool; you can do no good by staying. Margaret Hall will have to go out washing, I'll be bound."

"Yes, she must go to Mrs. Wilkinson's, and, for that matter, I must go working too. Mrs. Williams has been after me to make her girl's winter things ready; only I could not leave Franky, he clung so to me."

"Then you won't be bridesmaid! is that your last word?"

"It is; you must not be angry with me, Anne Dixon," said Libbie, deprecatingly.

But Anne was gone without a reply.

With a heavy heart Libbie mounted the little staircase, for she felt how ungracious her refusal of Anne's kindness must appear to one who understood so little the feelings which rendered her acceptance of it a moral impossibility.

On opening the door she saw Margaret Hall, with the Bible open on the table before her. For she had puzzled out the place where Libbie was reading, and, with her finger under the line, was spelling out the words of consolation, piecing the syllables together aloud, with the earnest anxiety of comprehension with which a child first learns to read. So Libbie took the stool by her side, before she was aware that any one had entered the room.

"What did she want you for?" asked Margaret. "But I can guess; she wanted you to be at th' wedding that is to come off this week, they say. Ay, they'll marry, and laugh, and dance, all as one as if my boy was alive," said she, bitterly. "Well, he was neither kith nor kin of yours, so I maun try and be thankful for what you have done for him, and not wonder at your forgetting him afore he's well settled in his grave."

"I never can forget him, and I'm not going to the wedding," said Libbie, quietly, for she understood the mother's jealousy of her dead child's claims.

"I must go work at Mrs. Williams' to-morrow," she said, in explanation, for she was unwilling to boast of her tender, fond regret, which had been her principal motive for declining Anne's invitation.

"And I mun go washing, just as if nothing had happened," sighed forth Mrs. Hall, "and I mun come home at night, and find his place empty, and all still where I used to be sure of hearing his voice ere ever I got up the stair: no one will ever call me mother again." She fell crying pitifully, and Libbie could not speak for her own emotion for some time. But during this silence she put the keystone in the arch of thoughts she had been building up for many days; and when Margaret was again calm in her sorrow, Libbie said: "Mrs. Hall, I should like—would you like me to come for to live here altogether?"

Margaret Hall looked up with a sudden light in her countenance, which encouraged Libbie to go on.

"I could sleep with you, and pay half, you know; and we should be together in the evenings; and her as was home first would watch for the other, and" (dropping her voice) "we could talk of him at night, you know."

She was going on, but Mrs. Hall interrupted her.

"Oh, Libbie Marsh! and can you really think of coming to live wi' me. I should like it above—but no! it must not be; you've no notion what a creature I am at times; more like a mad one when I'm in a rage, and I cannot keep it down. I seem to get out of bed wrong side in the morning, and I must have my passion out with the first person I meet. Why, Libbie," said she, with a doleful look of agony on her face, "I even used to fly out on him, poor sick lad as he was, and you may judge how little you can keep it down frae that. No, you must not come. I must live alone now," sinking her voice into the low tones of despair.

But Libbie's resolution was brave and strong. "I'm not afraid," said she, smiling; "I know you better than you know yourself, Mrs. Hall. I've seen you try of late to keep it down, when you've been boiling over, and I think you'll go on a-doing so. And, at any rate, when you've had your fit out you're very kind, and I can forget if you've been a bit put out. But I'll try not to put you out. Do let me come: I think *he* would like us to keep together. I'll do my very best to make you comfortable."

"It's me! it's me as will be making your life miserable with my temper; or else, God knows, how my heart clings to you. You and me is folk alone in the world, for we both loved one who is dead and who had none else to love him. If you will live with me, Libbie, I'll try as I never did afore to be gentle and quiet-tempered. Oh! will you try me, Libbie Marsh?" So out of the little grave there sprang a hope and a resolution, which made life an object to each of the two.

When Elizabeth Marsh returned home the next evening from her day's labours, Anne (Dixon no longer) crossed over, all in her bridal finery, to endeavour to induce her to join the dance going on in her father's house.

"Dear Anne, this is good of you, a-thinking of me to-night," said Libbie, kissing her, "and though I cannot come—I've promised Mrs. Hall to be with her—I shall think on you, and I trust you'll be happy. I have got a little needle-case I have looked out for you; stay, here it is—I wish it were more—only——"

"Only, I know what. You've been a-spending all your money in nice things for poor Franky. Thou'rt a real good un, Libbie, and I'll keep your needle-book to my dying day, that I will." Seeing Anne in such a friendly mood, emboldened Libbie to tell her of her change of place; of her intention of lodging henceforward with Margaret Hall.

"Thou never will! Why, father and mother are as fond of thee as can be; they'll lower thy rent if that's what it is—and thou know'st they never grudge thee bit or drop. And Margaret Hall, of all folk, to lodge wi'! She's such a Tartar! Sooner than not have a quarrel, she'd fight right hand against left. Thou'lt have no peace of thy life. What on earth can make you think of such a thing, Libbie Marsh?"

"She'll be so lonely without me," pleaded Libbie. "I'm sure I could make her happier, even if she did scold me a bit now and then, than she'd be a-living alone; and I'm not afraid of her; and I mean to do my best not to vex her: and it will ease her heart, maybe, to talk to me at times about Franky. I shall often see your father and mother, and I shall always thank them for their kindness to me. But they have you and little Mary, and poor Mrs. Hall has no one."

Anne could only repeat, "Well, I never!" and hurry off to tell the news at home.

But Libbie was right. Margaret Hall is a different woman to the scold of the neighbourhood she once was; touched and softened by the two purifying angels, Sorrow and Love. And it is beautiful to see her affection, her reverence for Libbie Marsh. Her dead mother could hardly have cared for her more tenderly than does the hard-hearted washerwoman, not long ago so fierce and unwomanly. Libbie, herself, has such peace shining on her countenance as almost makes it beautiful, as she tenders the services of a daughter to Franky's mother, no longer the desolate lonely orphan, a stranger on the earth.

Do you ever read the moral, concluding sentence of a story? I never do, but I once (in the year 1811, I think) heard of a deaf old lady, living by herself, who did; and as she may have left some descendants with the same amiable peculiarity, I will put in, for their benefit, what I believe to be the secret of Libbie's peace of mind, the real reason why she no longer feels oppressed at her own loneliness in the world—

She has a purpose in life; and that purpose is a holy one.

FRIEDRICH ENGELS

Results of Industrialisation†

* * *

If one individual inflicts a bodily injury upon another which leads to the death of the person attacked we call it manslaughter; on the other hand, if the attacker knows beforehand that the blow will be fatal we

---

† [Engels's rather bald title for this chapter consisted of the single word 'Resultate'.] From *The Condition of the Working Class in England in 1844*, trans. and ed. W. O. Henderson and W. H. Chaloner (Stanford, Calif.: Stanford University Press). Notes have been edited.

call it murder. Murder has also been committed if society[1] places hundreds of workers in such a position that they inevitably come to premature and unnatural ends. Their death is as violent as if they had been stabbed or shot. Murder has been committed if thousands of workers have been deprived of the necessities of life or if they have been forced into a situation in which it is impossible for them to survive. Murder has been committed if the workers have been forced by the strong arm of the law to go on living under such conditions until death inevitably releases them. Murder has been committed if society knows perfectly well that thousands of workers cannot avoid being sacrificed so long as these conditions are allowed to continue. Murder of this sort is just as culpable as the murder committed by an individual. But if society murders a worker it is a treacherous stab in the back against which the worker cannot defend himself. At first sight it does not appear to be murder at all, because responsibility for the death of the victim cannot be pinned on any individual assailant. Everyone is responsible and yet no one is responsible, because it appears as if the victim has died from natural causes. If a worker dies no one places the responsibility for his death on society, though some would realise that society has failed to take steps to prevent the victim from dying. But it is murder all the same. I shall now have to prove that, every day and every hour, English society commits what the English workers' press rightly denounces as social murder. I shall now have to prove that English society has created for the workers an environment in which they cannot remain healthy or enjoy a normal expectation of life. I shall have to prove that English society gradually undermines the health of the workers and so brings them to an early grave. Moreover I shall also have to prove that English society *is fully aware* how dangerous is this environment to the health and life of the workers, and yet takes no action to reform the situation. I shall have proved my point if I can produce evidence concerning the deaths of workers from such unimpeachable sources as official documents, Parliamentary papers and Government reports. Evidence of this kind proves conclusively that society is aware of the fact that its policy results not in manslaughter but in murder.

It is self-evident that a social class which lives under the conditions that we have described and is so poorly supplied with the most indispensable necessities of existence can enjoy neither good health nor a

---

1. Here and elsewhere I speak of society as a responsible entity which has its rights and duties. But by 'society' I do not mean the whole population, but only that social class which at this moment actually wields political and social authority. It is this class which is responsible for the position of those members of society who are excluded from exercising any political or social authority. In England, as in other civilised countries, this position as the ruling class is held by the middle classes. As this book is being written for German readers there is no need for me to approve the proposition that society as a whole, and in particular the middle classes—which wield social power—have the duty of at least protecting the lives of all individual citizens and must take measures to prevent anybody from starving. If I were writing for the English middle classes I would have to explain this in greater detail.

normal expectation of life. Let us, however, review once more the various factors which have a detrimental effect upon the state of health of the English workers. The concentration of the population in great cities has, in itself, an extremely deleterious influence. The air of London is neither so pure nor so rich in oxygen as that of the countryside; two and a half million pairs of lungs and two hundred and fifty thousand coal fires concentrated in an area of three to four geographical square miles[2] use up an immense amount of oxygen, which can only be replaced with difficulty since the layout of English towns impedes ventilation. The carbon dioxide gas produced by people breathing and fires burning fails to rise from the streets because of its specific gravity and is not dispersed by the winds which blow over the rooftops. The inhabitants of the towns do not take in sufficient oxygen when they breathe and this leads to mental torpor and low physical vitality. Consequently the dwellers in great towns suffer from chronic ailments to a greater extent than country people who breathe a purer atmosphere.

On the other hand the town dweller is less exposed to acute attacks of inflammatory disorders. If life in the great towns is unhealthy, how much worse must it be for those who live in the unwholesome atmosphere of the working-class quarters where, as we have already seen, everything combines to pollute the air. In the country no harm may come from having a dung heap near a house, because it is more exposed to the fresh air. In the middle of a big town, on the other hand, it is quite a different matter to have dung heaps in alleys and courts in built up areas where there is no ventilation. Decaying animal and vegetable refuse produces gases which are injurious to health and if these gases are not blown away they pollute the atmosphere. The filth and the stagnant pools in the working class quarters of the great cities have the most deleterious effects upon the health of the inhabitants because they engender just those gases which give rise to disease. The same effect follows from the miasma exuded by foul streams. But that is not the whole story by any means. The way in which the vast mass of the poor are treated by modern society is truly scandalous. They are herded into great cities where they breathe a fouler air than in the countryside which they have left. They are housed in the worst ventilated districts of the towns; they are deprived of all means of keeping clean. They are deprived of water because this is only brought to their houses if someone is prepared to defray the cost of laying the pipes. River water is so dirty as to be useless for cleansing purposes. The poor are forced to throw into the streets all their sweepings, garbage, dirty water, and frequently even disgusting filth and excrement. The poor are deprived of all proper means of refuse disposal and so they are forced to pollute

2. The German geographical mile is 7.42 kilometres or 4.64 English miles.

the very districts they inhabit. And this is by no means all. There is no end to the sufferings which are heaped on the heads of the poor. It is notorious that general overcrowding is a characteristic feature of the great towns, but in the working-class quarters people are packed together in an exceptionally small area. Not satisfied with permitting the pollution of the air in the streets, society crams as many as a dozen workers into a single room, so that at night the air becomes so foul that they are nearly suffocated. The workers have to live in damp dwellings. When they live in cellars the water seeps through the floor and when they live in attics the rain comes through the roof. The workers' houses are so badly built that the foul air cannot escape from them. The workers have to wear poor and ragged garments and they have to eat food which is bad, indigestible and adulterated. Their mental state is threatened by being subjected alternately to extremes of hope and fear. They are goaded like wild beasts and never have a chance of enjoying a quiet life. They are deprived of all pleasures except sexual indulgence and intoxicating liquors. Every day they have to work until they are physically and mentally exhausted. This forces them to excessive indulgence in the only two pleasures remaining to them. If the workers manage to survive this sort of treatment it is only to fall victims to starvation when a slump occurs and they are deprived of the little that they once had.

* * *

Insecurity is even more demoralising than poverty. English wage-earners live from hand to mouth, and this is the distinguishing mark of their proletarian status. The lower ranks of the German peasantry are largely filled with men who are also poor, and often suffer want, but they are less subject to that sort of distress which is due solely to chance. They do at least enjoy some measure of security. But the proletarian is in quite a different position. He possesses nothing but his two hands and he consumes to-day what he earned yesterday. His future is at the mercy of chance. He has not the slightest guarantee that his skill will in future enable him to earn even the bare necessities of life. Every commercial crisis, every whim of his master, can throw him out of work. He is placed in the most revolting and inhuman position imaginable. A slave is at least assured of his daily bread by the self-interest of his master, while the serf at any rate has a piece of land on the produce of which he can live. Slaves and serfs are both guaranteed a basic minimum existence. The proletarian on the other hand is thrown wholly upon his own resources, and yet at the same time is placed in such a position that he cannot be sure that he can always use those resources to gain a livelihood for himself and his family. Everything that the factory worker can do to try and improve his position vanishes like a drop in the bucket in face of the flood of chance occurrences to which he is exposed and over which he has not the slightest control. He is the passive sufferer from every possible combination of mishaps, and can regard himself as fortunate if he keeps his head above water even for a short time. And it is self-evident that the character of the worker and his way of life should be moulded by this state of affairs. He may fight for survival in this whirlpool; he may try to maintain his dignity as a human being. This he can do only by fighting the middle classes,[3] who exploit him so ruthlessly and then condemn him to a fate which drives him to live in a way unworthy of a human being. On the other hand, the worker may give up the struggle to improve his position, as being of no avail, and seek only to snatch what profit he can from any circumstances favourable to himself which may present themselves. It is useless for him to try and save, because he can never put aside any more money than will keep him going for a few weeks, and if he falls out of work he is usually unemployed for far more than a few weeks. He has no opportunity of acquiring any property, and if he could do so, he would cease to be a worker and someone else would take his place in the working classes. * * * There can be no doubt that in England the social war is already being waged. Everyone looks after his own interests and fights only for himself against all comers. Whether in doing so he injures those who are his declared enemies is simply a matter of selfish calculation as to whether such action would be to his advantage or not. It no longer occurs to anybody to come to a friendly understanding with his neighbours. All differences of opinion are settled by threats, by invoking the courts, or even by taking the law into one's own hands. In short, everyone sees in his neighbour a rival to be elbowed aside, or at best a victim to be exploited for his own ends. The criminal statistics prove that this social war is being waged more vigorously, more passionately and with greater bitterness every year. Social strife is gradually developing into combat between two great opposing camps—the middle classes and the proletariat. No one need be surprised at the existence either of the social war of all against all or of the struggle between the workers and the bourgeoisie. These conflicts are no more than the logical consequence of the fundamental principle upon which free competition is based. It is, however, somewhat surprising that the bourgeoisie should remain so complacent and placid in the face of the thunderclouds which are gathering overhead and grow daily more threatening. How can the middle classes read about these things in the newspapers every day without showing some anxiety as to the consequences? Do they not see that the individual crimes of which they read will one day

---

3. We shall see later how the struggle of the English working classes against the middle classes has been legalised by the right to form free associations.

culminate in universal revolution? It would, of course, be too much to expect from the middle classes any sign of indignation at the state of affairs which gives rise to this threat of social upheaval. For, after all, this is the bourgeoisie, and as such is naturally blind to the facts of the situation and to the consequences which will follow from this state of affairs. It is indeed astonishing that ingrained prejudices and preconceived ideas should afflict a social class to such an extent that this blindness might well be called a form of madness. Meanwhile national affairs take their course, whether the middle classes realise what is happening or not, and one fine day the property-holding class will be overwhelmed by events far beyond their comprehension and quite outside their expectations.

LEON M. FAUCHER

From Manchester in 1844: Its Present Condition and Future Prospects[†]

The wide-spread physical and moral degradation of the labouring classes, which is such a lamentable feature, not only in Manchester, but in all the great manufacturing towns, is a fact which engages in an especial manner, the anxious solicitude of benevolent minds in England. They feel that it is a reproach upon the public conscience, and that in a country like England, where evils of such magnitude are permitted to exist, the men who have the direction of public affairs, cannot escape from all responsibility. Whatever may be the form of its political institutions, whether aristocratic or democratic, it governs itself, and belongs entirely to itself. Its destinies are not in the hands of any foreign power; and no artificial influences constrain or limit public opinion. The middle classes, which the natural progress of society has elevated to political power, exercise that power freely; and they are accountable to Providence, as well as to the world, not only for the evil which they have not prevented, but for the good which they have not effected.

This wide-spread misery is moreover a reproach to the self-love of the nation. It aspires to a renown for wealth, power, and morality; and yet, beholds itself marked out by the nations of Europe, as a subject of reproach on the one hand, and an object of pity on the other. It gratuitously assumes superiority over every other people. It vaunts itself as a model for surrounding nations, when it cannot govern itself. The world, dazzled by the *prestige* of its brilliant mil-

---

[†] From *Manchester in 1844; Its Present Condition and Future Prospects* (London: Simpkin, Marshall, 1844), pp. 85–90. One of the author's footnotes has been deleted.

itary and naval successes, has for a long time taken it at its word; but the tales of misery which continually resound in its parliament, have at length dissolved the charm. There is not now a child in Europe, who does not know that, side by side of its colossal grandeur, there exists misery of equal magnitude; and history has only to recount the details of it, and to probe the ulcers which eat into the vitals of the colossus.

England at length, perceives that its future prospects are menaced. A people so profoundly attached to the development of the Material, should place Physical health and strength in the first rank of the elements essential to its power, and should take the alarm as soon as ever the influence of intemperance and privations, combined with excess of labour, undermines the constitution of its labourers. Talk with the English, and you will find that they attribute their military achievements much less to any superiority of tactics, than to the physical strength of their soldiers, which enables them to maintain their position a longer time. Read the parliamentary documents, and you will see with what care they endeavour to prove that the English labourer is superior in strength to the labourer of every other nation; and that this superiority is the real foundation of its pre-eminence.

The English profess to be an athletic people. With the same attention which Rome paid to the games of the circus, and to the combats of its gladiators, England has organized itself for a struggle with the whole civilized world, which it defies alike in the acquisition of territory, and in the monopoly of industry. How then, must it tremble at the bare idea of a diminution in the efficacy of the instruments with which it fights its battles, and produces its wealth?

When the evils connected with its industry were first brought to light, efforts were made to divert public attention from the subject; and, in some quarters, the existence of these evils was denied. Mr. Baines, in his researches, (otherwise full of interest,) undertook to establish, that manufacturing labour was not more injurious to the health than any other sort of labour. Dr. Ure followed in the same track, and represented manufactures as the Arcadia of civilization, and as the palladium of the labourer. But when the recent census of the population had shown the frightful mortality of the manufacturing districts, and also the increase of crime, it was no longer possible to maintain the delusion. Then came the discussion as to the cause of this newly-discovered disorder. Whilst the landed proprietors accused industry itself as the cause, and saw in the crowded workshops so many germs of death, the industrial aristocracy betook themselves to the laws, and to the state of society. Shortly after, however, they quitted the defensive, and sought to prove, that the rural population was inferior to that of the manufacturing; but, in casting so horrible a light upon the subject, they have only proved that the evil exists upon both sides.[1]

Are the disorders which manifest themselves in the large centres of industry, a necessary consequence of the manufacturing system? Are we to consider them as accidental features, or as a regular phenomenon of production? Is it not possible to spin and weave cotton, wool, or silk, in large quantities, and at a cheap rate, by the powerful aid of machinery, without conjuring up at the same time, those frightful consequences which now result from it, and which are the destruction of the family tie, slavery, premature decay, and demoralization of children; drunkenness of the men, prostitution of the women, and an universal decay of morality? Or, are not these the inevitable sufferings which always accompany the birth of a new era in social progress?

Certainly, if industrial wealth could only be obtained by the sacrifice of every thing which constitutes the strength of a people, it would be a hundred times better to renounce it altogether; for it would be to sacrifice for a morsel of bread, the essential attribute of humanity, and, (as a Latin poet has said,) for the sake of life, to let the principle of life perish.

1. [That the manufacturing districts are superior to the agricultural, (so far as the general condition of the labourer is concerned,) is incontestably proved by the constant immigration into the towns from the country. This immigration is perfectly voluntary on the part of the peasantry; and, whatever writers on the subject may say, it is at least clear that the towns are preferred, as offering greater facilities for subsistence than the country. The censuses clearly prove that the agricultural districts do not increase in so great a proportion as the manufacturing. The number of *families* in Great Britain, employed in agriculture, was, in 1811, 35·2 per cent. of the whole population; in 1821, 33·2 per cent.; and in 1831, only 28·2 per cent. Those employed in trades formed in 1811, 44·4 per cent.; in 1821, 45·9; and in 1831, 42 per cent. In the last census, that of 1841, the numbers represent *individuals actually engaged* in the occupation under which they are classed, and the result for Great Britain and the Channel Islands, is 7·64 per cent. for agriculturalists, and 29·21 for trades and manufactures. The remainder, including females and children, form 63·13 per cent. But if this evidence be insufficient, the fact of nearly all the manufacturing towns having increased in a far greater ratio than the general increase of population by births, ought to suffice to set this question at rest. To this, however, it has been objected, that in the manufacturing districts, early and improvident marriages prevail to an extent which will sufficiently account for the extraordinary increase of population. To show how destitute of truth this assertion is, we may state that, from the Registrar-General's reports, it appears, that for the year ending June, 1840, in the manufacturing counties of Lancashire and Cheshire, 17,565 couples were married, of whom 10 per cent. only were under twenty-one years of age. For the same year, in the ten agricultural counties of Hertfordshire, Buckinghamshire, Oxfordshire, Northamptonshire, Huntingdonshire, Bedfordshire, Cambridgeshire, Essex, Suffolk, and Norfolk, the total number of couples married, was 14,675, *of whom 28½ per cent. were under twenty-one years of age*. This proves that early marriages must be looked for rather in the agricultural districts. The large proportion of juvenile population in the manufacturing districts, is likewise often alleged; but this assertion is equally destitute of proof. On the contrary, the Census Commissioners for 1841, state, "It will be seen, that in Lancashire, where the large manufactories are supposed to include so large a juvenile population, the numbers between fifteen and twenty years of age, (viz. in every 10,000 of population, 1047 males, and 1055 females,) are little above the average of England, and as nearly as possible, the same as in Huntingdon, (1038 males, and 1002 females,) whereas, in Manchester, the proportion of the numbers between those ages, nearly coincides with the average of all England, 1004 males, 989 females."]

"Et propter vitam vivendi perdere causas."

If Industry, whilst it raised the wages of the labourer, tended, as a necessary result, to corrupt and enervate them, the *Standard* would have had some reason, when it exclaimed, "England would be as great and powerful, and all useful Englishmen would be as rich as they are, though one ruin should engulph all the manufacturing towns and districts in Great Britain."

But I cannot believe that Providence has given to mankind such maleficent institutions. It is not possible that the progress of the industrial arts can have for a necessary result, the degradation of the human race. When the mind of man attains, by repeated efforts of genius, to those grand combinations of steam-power and machinery; when it becomes, in a manner, Lord of the elements, it is impossible that such discoveries can add to his weakness. Down to the present day, all the great *facts* achieved by a progressive civilization, have increased the happiness as well as intelligence of mankind. It is the destiny of the world which we inhabit, and this destiny will assuredly be fulfilled. At the same time, there are for nations, and for the institutions of a country, periods of transition, which are marked by a large amount of suffering. The manufacturing system in England and elsewhere, is in this period of trial. The rapidity of its growth; the magnitude of its proportions; every thing connected with it, even the energy which it displayed, ere it established itself, and which was so necessary in penetrating the ranks of a feudal state of society, all prove that it is far from a state of maturity. The newly-developed powers, both human and mechanical, have to find their equilibrium. Manufactures, animated by a competition without bounds, are like the soldiers who sprung up from the dragon's teeth, sown by Cadmus, and who slaughtered one another as quickly as they sprung up. Industry is evidently in a state of anarchy; but it will, sooner or later, make a better use of its liberty.

ANONYMOUS

The Mutual Dependence of Men in a Social State[†]

The saying, 'one man soweth and another reapeth,' has been applicable to the condition of mankind in all ages, and will doubtless continue to be so to the end of time. It is too true in a sense which we

† From *Christian Teacher* 6.26 (1844) 436.

cannot but lament, and, if it were possible, would gladly put an end to,—when we see a large part of every community toiling on from day to day, and from year to year, without any adequate compensation; while the fruits of their industry are enjoyed by others, who seem as if they were born not to minister, but to be ministered unto, and to live in the possession of luxuries provided for them by the ill-requited labour of those around them.

But this principle, which appears so little agreeable in some of its aspects, is nevertheless intimately connected with the social nature of man, and with the attributes which more especially constitute his superiority to the brutes. It expresses universally his condition and circumstances as a member of society;—and the more so, in proportion as the relations he sustains to other members of it become more various and extensive, and as the constitution of the society itself partakes of the general improvement of the human mind. It is true in every condition of life (and a most wise and excellent provision it is, contributing to our essential welfare both here and hereafter), that it is scarcely possible for any man to live altogether to himself,—to labour for his own benefit alone,—to sow in such a manner that no other human being shall reap the harvest. It is true, not merely of *beneficial* labours, but also of the mischievous and abusive employment of our talents. So variously are we connected in this world,—in the relations of domestic life,—as neighbours, friends, companions, and in many other ways, by which our fellow-creatures are more or less interested in the consequences of our conduct, that no one can confine those consequences entirely to his own home, still less to his own person. If they are good, others must share them with him,—if bad, the evil effects of his vice or folly of necessity extend to those around him:—"we must suffer or rejoice together, for we are every one members one of another."

*   *   *

DION BOUCICAULT

The Long Strike: A Drama in Four Acts†

DRAMATIS PERSONÆ.—THE LONG STRIKE.

As originally played at the Lyceum Theater, London.

NOAH LEAROYD ....*Leader of the Strike.*
JEM STARKEE ....*Foreman of Engineers.*

† (New York: Samuel French, no date).

RICHARD READLEY ⎫ MR. ARMITAGE, MR. ASPINWALL, MR. BROOKE, ⎭	................*Manufacturers.*
MONEYPENNY, ⎫ MR. SPURRIER, ⎬ MR. WIGLEY, ⎭	..................*Solicitors.*
CRANKSHAW	*A Policeman.*
JOHNNY REILLY	*An Irish Sailor.*
CAPTAIN WOLF	*Capt. of "Eliza and Mary."*
TELEGRAPH OPERATOR	
GENTLEMAN FROM LONDON	
JAOK O'BOBS, ⎫ JOHN O'DIOK, ⎬ TOM O'BILLS, ⎭ OLD SHARROCK,	.................*Strikers.*
SIR JOHN FAIRFIELD	*Presiding Judge.*
COURT CRIER	
POLICEMAN, &C.	
JANE LEAROYD	
BETSEY	
MAGGIE, ⎫ SUSAN, ⎭	.......................*Operators.*

ACT I.

SCENE I.—*Parlor of Seven Star Inn. Box scene. Practical door,* R. 3 E.; *practical window,* R. 2 E.; *set fireplace,* L. 2 E.; *grate, etc.; rug on floor; baise down; mantlepiece and looking glass; ornaments; clock on mantel; sideboard with decanters, glasses, cigars, etc., against flat: long table,* L. C.; *8 chairs set same as 1st scene, 3rd act, "School for Scandal;" one arm-chair at head of table, elevated; writing materials and books on table; office settee,* R. 2 E., *by window;* WAITER *discovered at sideboard;* ARMITAGE *discovered head of table;* BROOKE, R. H. *corner table;* ASPINWALL, L. H., *second chair;* READLEY *at table;* CRANKSHAW *discovered at door,* R. 3 E.; *noise outside; voices outside at rise; music.*

Armitage Have you dispersed the crowd?

Crankshaw No, sir, the people are very orderly but they will not move on.

Readley The street below is impassable; the mob increases.

Arm Very well. [*Exit* CRANKSHAW. ARMITAGE, *rising.*] Gentlemen, we have to deal with a most perilous crisis. The workingmen of Manchester have now maintained the longest stike on record. The claims I advanced some weeks ago, were, I confess, extravagant, but I hear that moderate counsels have lately prevailed amongst them. Let us hope the moment has arrived when, by manual concession,—

Read I, for one, will concede nothing. The longer this strike is maintained, the more salutary will be the lesson. Their suffering, wantonly self-inflicted, will remain a tradition amongst singular combination.

Brooke I agree with Mr. Readley. Concession, to these people, is encouragement.

Aspinwall If this demand be just, it may be provoking to find it widely prevented, but our dignity should not stand in the way of our honesty.

Enter Crankshaw, r. 3 e.

Crank The deputation of the working committee is below, gentlemen.

Arm How is it composed? D'ye know the men?

Crank Yes, sir—there's Noah Learoyd—

Arm The crazy enthusiast? I am sorry he is amongst them—well?

Crank James Starkee, John O'Dick and Old Sharrock.

Read These are the ringleaders.

Arm So much the better—show them in.

[*Exit* Crankshaw, r. 3 e.

Read It seems, gentlemen, we are divided in our policy—our party is for firm measures, the other for conciliation. We who are resolute will hold aloof from this interview, leaving the negotiations for peace in your hands.

Enter Crankshaw, r. 3 e. *and is about to admit the delegates; is stopped by* Readley *saying*

One moment, officer. [Crankshaw *closes door—delegates still outside*.] If terms be proposed to you which are acceptable, we consent to adhere to your resolution; but if, on the other hand, terms are offered by these men which you reject, then you pledge yourselves to follow in your wake and support the measures we resolve to adopt.

[*Omnes, except* Armitage, *signifying consent by saying "agreed, very good."* Readley, Brooke *and one* Gentleman *retire to fireplace*.]

Arm [*To* Crankshaw.] You may admit the deputation.

[Crankshaw *opens door*.

Enter Noah Learoyd, John O'Dick *and* Old Sharrock, r. 3 e.

Arm Well, my men, which of you is spokesman?

Noah I am.

Arm You come as delegates from the discontented workmen?

Noah We come from the men of Manchester, and we come to a Manchester man. Thou wer'st a working man once thyself, John Armitage, and to thee—

Arm We don't want a speech—expose your griefs. What are they?

Noah No one knows but Him above, who looks down on our alleys and lanes. He's keeping a reckonin', and when you get up there He'll show it up to ye.

Delegation Hear, hear!

Arm My good men, we shall be glad to redress your wrongs if you will but state them.

Read Aye, and state them humbly.

Noah Aye, as workingmen should—I know how you look upon the workingmen, Dick Readley—they are at home in three places—the mill, the felon's dock and the grave.

Arm Noah Learoyd, the people have chosen you unwisely to represent them. This is no place for such language.

Noah That's so; I know it; I am wrong; I have no right to speak so here. It's only once a week you rich folks go to hear the truth, and I am not licensed to tell it ye. No offense, but there on that bit o' paper is writ the people's prayer. It's not so big as the Magna Charta, but, small as it is, a million of men do take their stand upon it.

Arm This, then, contains your ultimatum?

Noah What's that?

Arm I mean is it all the concession the people are prepared to make?

Noah Aye, aye, you may call it the last word to a proud heart, to an empty bully.

Arm [*After reading paper.*] I hope you have some other proposal more moderate than this?

Aspin [*Reading paper.*] You ask too much.

Noah If I thought there was one word there that was not right, I'd cut the hand off that wrote it, and that's my own. I'd starve, man, before I'd ask it, and if I tried to let a lie out on it I'd choke.

Arm Please to retire while we take your terms into consideration. We are very desirous to adjust our unhappy differences.

Noah You are, John Armitage, but some here ain't.

Read If you mean me, my man, you are right—if I had my way with you I would not listen to a word until you had learned submission.

Noah Aye, condemn and execute us first and then hear what we've to say.   [*Exit* NOAH, O'DICK *and* OLD SHARROCK, R. 3 E.

Read Those ruffians are always ready with some vulgar retort.

                         [*Crosses c. and joins* BROOKE *and party up stage.*

Aspin It is impossible to meet those demands.

                  [READLEY *and party laugh after reading paper in undertone.*

Arm The city is in a fever—we should not expect cool judgment from a distempered body.   [READLEY *and party repeat bus. as before.*

Aspin But we may interpose moderation in their counsel. Readley is inclined to go too far.

Read [*Advancing to* L. H. *corner.*] Well, gentlemen, I presume you

reject this precious document, and if so, you resign yourselves to support
our measures.   [*Omnes, except* ARMITAGE, *exclaim yes, yes.*

Arm Then you must permit me to vacate the chair if I must submit. I
decline to be the leader of an action I can not approve.
                                        [*Rises and stands by chair.*

Brooke Gentlemen, I propose that Richard Readley do take the chair.
Omnes Aye, Readley, Readley.
                                [READLEY *bows; goes up and takes chair.*

Read Gentlemen, I shall endorse, on this paper, and in a few words, the
proposal (we are agreed to) I think, to make to these misguided fellows.
Should our terms be rejected, we bind ourselves to a general lockout. When
they find there is no hope of coercing us they will come to their senses.

Arm Or lose them altogether.

[*The paper on which* READLEY *has written he hands to* GENTLEMAN *on* B.
    and it is passed around table and to ARMITAGE *by fireplace.*]

Read You may admit those men. [*To* CRANKSHAW, *who opens door
and admits* NOAH *and others.*] We have considered your proposal.

—*Noah* I know ye have and I know what'll come of it. I am sorry to see
thee in the chair, Richard Readley.

Readley You have set down your terms; they are not quite such as we
can entertain, so we have embodied our views and you will find them
endorsed on your own paper.

Arm [*Aside to* READLEY, *handing paper.*] This is a most serious step.

Read I accept the responsibility.

[READLEY *hands paper to* NOAH *who reads and consults delegates in an
undertone.*]

Noah Do you mean this? It ain't no joke? Is this the stone you gave us
when we asked for bread?

Read We are resolved to abate no jot of those conditions. You have
formed a league to coerce your employers; beware, or the masters may
combine against you. The few mills now open will then be closed and
there will follow a general lockout.
                                        [*Striking table with hand.*

Noah This is thy writing, too?

Read Aye, in reply to yours. It is well that you should learn that there
are those here as firm as you are stubborn.

Noah Do you not know that this will harden the hearts of the men?
Iron as they are, they will become steel.

Read Return to work then and open the mills.

Noah and Delegates Give us our rights.

Read Further discussion is useless.

Noah Come, lads, we have no further business here.

[GENTLEMEN *are in earnest conversation, and* NOAH *and* DELEGATES *are
about to exit as*

SCENE CLOSES.

SCENE II.—*First groove. Old Millgate Lane; a view of mills in distance.*

Enter JANE LEAROYD, L. 1 E., *looking around as if expecting some one; throws back hood she wears over head.*

Enter JEM STARKEE, L. 1 E.

Jem Why, Jane, why are you loitering here? This is a lone place for a girl like you; I'll see you home; there's rough folk abroad tonight.

Jane Nay, I'm not afraid, Jem.

Jem But I am, and bodily scared for your sake. This ain't the first time you've chosen this way home in the dark, and if you ain't afraid it's because you had some one with you.

Jane You have spied on me, Jem Starkee. What right have you to watch my doings?

Jem What right? Oh, can you ask me? I have the right to love you, Jane.

Jane Who gave it to you?

Jem You did. What has my life been but one long service of love to you? You saw it plain enough and you never told me to go my ways.

Jane I—I—looked on you as a friend, Jem, as a brother.

Jem No you didn't; you know better; and not long ago you grew to love me a bit, until—

Jane Until what?

Jem Until Richard Readley, your master, took to meeting you nightly in the lane on your way home from the mill, until he filled your ears with lies and your heart with vanity.

Jane I don't know what rights I have given you, but I've given no man the right to insult me. You said I never told you to go your ways—I do so now—I don't care for ye—I never did—there, [*Crosses to* R. 1 E.] you have no excuse now to play the spy upon me.

[*Exit,* R. 1 E.

Jem I don't care for ye, and I never did! Was it Jane who spoke? Was it my girl? She told me to go my ways! Where shall I go where she is not? Ah! yonder is Readley; I knew why she was loitering here. I knew it all over me. [*Looks off,* R. 1 E.] He crosses the lane—they speak—oh, Jane!—Jane!—but what is she to me? She never cared for me—I must not watch them—she turns back wi' him—they come—his eyes on hers, her breath mixin' wi' his'n. [*Crosses to* L. II.] They come, and I must go my ways—I must go my ways.   [*Exit,* L. 1 E.

Enter READLEY *and* JANE, *his arm around her waist.*

Jem You must not stop me, sir. Indeed, I must go home.

Read Your home must not be a hovel, Jane; those bright eyes must not grow dim over night work; those delicate hands were never made for labor.

Jane Pray let me go.

Read Not until you whisper you would rather stay. Give me some little word to nurse until we meet again.

Jane What shall I say?

Read Say that you will meet me to-morrow night in the lane, behind my house.

Jane Hush! Some one is stirring yonder—see!

Read It is a policeman.

Jane Nay not him. There is the gloom sittin' on yonder block o' stone. Good night, sir, I must be gone.

Read How you tremble.

Jane Good night.   [*Exit*, R. 1 E.

Read She loves me. I must not chide her fears; they are the proof of her innocence and of the power of her passion for me, but to-morrow night I will put her heart to the test.

JEM STARKEE *enters during speech and walks to c. as* READLEY *turns.*

Jem May I speak a word to you, sir?

Ready Certainly—who are you?

Jem Jem—Jem Starkee, sir—foreman of the engineers at Aspinwalls.

Read Well, what do you want with me? Make haste—I'm hurried, so come to the point.

Jem I will, sir. I think you are keeping company wi' a young woman called Jane Learoyd?

Read [*Aside.*] Who the deuce is this? Some low admirer of hers—a rival? It's rather degrading to be mixed up with such cattle.

Jem Well?

Read I was thinking—let me see—Jane—you mean the daughter of old Norah Learoyd—a little blue eyed hussey?

Jem She's a good girl, sir, tho' may be a little set up wi' her beauty, but she's her father's only child and—

Read What's all this to me? Have you stopped me here to tell me the girl is pretty? I know it. Good night.

Jem Stop, sir, I'll tell you in plain words what I've got to say. Jane Learoyd loves ye. I ha' known her long enough to feel sure she'll make a noble wife for any man, be he who he may. Do you mean to marry the girl?

Read Are you her brother?

Jem I mean to stand by her like one. If you mean rightly, you won't think the worse of me for what I'm saying, but if not, for your own sake, as well as for hers, let her alone and never speak to her more.

Read Has she authorized you to take this step?

Jem I want no authority to do what's right.

Read You are neither her father or her brother, and you have no right to interfere.

Jem Neither father nor brother could love her as I ha' done. Aye, as I love her still. If love gives any claims, then no one can come up to my right. Do you mean fair by Jane or not?

Read Confound you, man, stand back.

Jem Not until you have answered me.

Read Then I'll make you.

[*Strikes* JEM, *who seizes him; struggle. Music.*

Enter CRANKSHAW, L. 1 E., *who separates them.*

Crank I saw the assault, sir; shall I take the man into custody?

Read No, I struck him first—let him go. But don't think this sort of bullying will serve your end or help the girl. I shall not forget you, my man.

Jem I'll take care ye sha'n't. Dare to injure my girl and I'll find ye where no policeman can step in to serve ye. Heaven shall judge between us two.

[*Exit* READLEY, R. 1 E.

Crank Take care, my lad, there's no woman in the world worth what you will bring upon yourself, if you don't mind.

Jem D'ye think I'll stand by and have him injure my girl? No, no, I'll—

Crank Come, come—move on, move on now!

[CRANKSHAW *forces him off*, L. 1 E.

WHISTLE SCENE.

SCENE III.—NOAH'S *dwelling; box scene in four; plain rustic chamber; practical door,* L. 3 E. ; *practical,* R. *flat; set staircase,* L. C., *against flat, ascending to a practical door to open up stage—real lock on door; set platform behind door,* L. C. ; *flat interior backing cut window, flat,* L. 3 E. ; *table and two chairs,* C.; GENTLEMEN *from London,* JACK O'BOBS, TOM O'BILLS, MAGGIE, SUSAN, *and two small children, and all the mill hands discovered at change.* CLERK *seated at table upon which is a bag of money, ledger, writing materials and lighted candles; crowd gathers round table; murmurs by crowd.*

Gentleman from London [*Taking stage* L. *of* C., *back to audience, reading list.*] Susan Olland—two h'infants and von 'usband, h'operatives h'on the strike—one shilling and three pence for the man, h'eight pence for the woman, and three pence a 'ead for h'each h'infant—total, two an' three pence ha' penny.

Maggie [*As* SUSAN *is about to take money.*] Stop! Her man be dead. Thou hast no right to draw for he, lass?

Gent Dead?

Tom Aye, he be as dead as a door post.

Gent For shame, Mrs. Olland, 'ow could you h'impose h'on the "London Central Strike Fund?"

Susan Oh, sir, my babies are clemming.

Gent Clemming! What does she mean?

Jack Starving, sir—that's all.

Gent Retire, Mrs. Olland, babies h'ain't on the list. [*Reads.*] Jack O'Bobs!

Jack That's me   [*Goes to table.*

Gent Full growed h'operative—one and three pence.

                         CLERK *hands money to* JACK.

Jack [*Turns to* SUSAN.] Here, lass, take it. I can clem better than thee and thy childer.

              [*Gives money to* SUSAN. *Crowd murmurs approvingly.*

Tom That's right, Jack, thou art a good lad, and as long as I have a shilling, we'll share it together.

Omnes Aye! Aye!

Tom But here comes the delegates.

Omnes Aye! the delegates! The delegates!

        Enter NOAH, SHARROCK, STALEY *and* O'DICK.

Noah [*Making way through crowd stands by table.*] We came from the masters.

Omnes Well—well?

Noah [*Hands paper to* CLERK, *who hands it to* GENTLEMAN *from London.*] There, man, read it out, for I've not the heart to do it.

Gent [*Reads.*] "The masters give you twenty-four hours to return to work. [*Murmurs.*] After that time every mill will be closed against you. [*Murmurs.*] No further communications will be received. Signed for the Masters' League, Richard Readley."

Noah [*Loud murmurs.*] They're right, lads, they're right. For when a man has said his last word the time has come to strike the first blow.

Omnes Aye, aye!

Gent The Central Fund h'is h'opposed to h'any violence, unless the blows is constitootional, and—   [*Murmurs.*

Noah Silence, lads, the gentleman from London is going to speak. Well—well—what does London advise Manchester to do?

Gent Be h'ordley, h'igitate, and the Central Fund, which have supported the strike, will continue to discharge its dooties.

Noah You mean that it will enable us to starve by inches, and by so doing, it will continue to support us in the strike. Go tell Lunnin' that we've looked death in the face long enough—long enough not to be afeard of it now, and if it's got to come, we may as well fetch it in striking for our rights.

Gent Really, this here talk is getting beyond the h'object of the fund—I withdraw.   [*Takes money from table.*

Noah Go then, men, for I'll argue wi' my tongue no more, but wi' my hands.

Omnes Aye! Aye!

Gent Go! It's all very well to say go, but look at this money. How shall I carry it through the famishing crowd outside?

Noah [*Looking round.*] Come here, Maggie. Go wi' this man, and, as you walk along, tell them ye meet that he's carrying the poor man's money. Go wi' that lass, man, and ye'll meet wi' no harm. [*Exit* GENTLE-MAN, *followed by* CLERK *and* MAGGIE, D. F. R. C.] Home wi' ye lads and leave me wi' the delegates. I've brought ye to this pass and I'll die but I'll see ye righted.

Jack Come, lads, we'll go to Readley's mill and give the glaziers a job, and woe betide his carcass if he shows his nose in Manchester.

[*Exit omnes except* NOAH, SHAMICLE, STALEY *and* O'DICK, D. F.

Omnes Aye! to Readley's! To Readley's.

Noah To-night we must fix on what we've to do and where the first blow shall fall.   [*Exeunt in room,* L. 3 E.

Enter JANE, D. R. F.

Jane The streets are full of angry men. The night will not pass wi' out some outrage. As I hurried home I heard the name of Readley in their mouths, coupled with such threats that made my very heart stand still with terror.   [*Knock at* D. F.

Enter JEM STARKEE, D. F

Jem Jane, I've come to ax your pardon.

Jane Say no more about it, Jem, I'm sorry I spoke unkindly to thee, lad, but I was vexed sorely.

Jem Thank ye, Jane, I mun say no more about it. I've said too much or I've said too little; don't stop me, for I mun have it out this night.

Jane Well?

Jem Since we were boy and girl, I have loved thee above father, mother and all. I dare na speak to you, for I had no way of keeping a wife then, but oh! I lived in fright some one else should take ye from me afore I'd made a home for ye.

Jane I knew it! I knew it!

Jem But now I have a home to offer thee. It ain't a rich one, may be, but if a loving heart and a strong right arm can shield ye from sorrow and want, mine shall do it. I—I—can't speak as I would like to, nor as you deserve; nay, love won't let itself be put in words, but won't ye help me out a bit?

Jane [*Placing her hand in his.*] Jem, I won't deceive ye—I can not be your wife.

Jem Not be—I—I—I—can not swallow these words.

Jane I did love you once.

Jem Aye, aye.

Jane And may be I would a had ye then but that time went by and then I came to look upon ye as a brother.

Jem But would not that other time may be coom again? I'd wait, Jane; I'd weary out. Just say the word, won't ye? No! no! don't answer—don't!

I see what's a comin'! Oh, think a while and try to—to—oh! if you only knew how I love ye!

Jane I do!—I do! but don't ask me, Jem!

Jem D'ye mean it, Jane? Is it once for all? You are silent, and this is the end on it. It is the end of my life, then, for it's the end of all that's worth living for. My bitter curse on him that took ye from me. The time will soon coom when he and I will square this thing. I feel it in me, and after we meet again there will be one of us less to trouble ye. Good-by, Jane, I won't cross ye again. If ye hear of me as a drunkard you may say I drove him to that, or if, may be, I stand in a felon's dock as a murderer, or thief, when all are speaking ill of me don't you blame me, for you will make me what I shall become. [*Turns and goes to door.*] You won't even say you will try and like me, will ye? Oh! will ye, Jane?

Jane [*Crosses to him.*] Nay, Jem, don't leave me in anger. I'm not worth one of them big tears in your eyes; if I was, I'd ha' loved ye as you deserve. But I—I—can't—I can't and I'm too honest to gi' ye a heart wi' another man in it.

[*Music hurried. Murmurs outside in distance gradually increasing.*

Enter READLEY, *breathlessly,* D. F., *without hat. Closes door.*

Read Jane!

Jane Readley!

Read Save me! The infuriated mob beset me! I tore myself from a hundred murderers and fled here!

Jane My father is in yon room.

Read Your father? and [*Sees* JEM.] he here? I am lost! [*Murmurs outside.*] Hark! They are coming to kill me!

Jane No! In there—quick!

[*Points to staircase. Exit* READLEY *up staircase and through* D. L. F.

Jane Oh, Jem! [*Music.*

Enter JACK O'BOBS, *followed by* TOM O'BILLS, SUSAN *and* MAGGIE, *and all mill hands,* D. R. F., *shouting—where is he? where is he? Enter* NOAH *and* DELEGATES *same time,* L. 2 E.

Jack Where is he?

Noah Who d'ye seek?

Jack Readley.

Noah What? Readley in my house?

Jack I could not ha' been mistaken. Did no one coom in here but now?

Jane Yes, Jem Starkee came in, and there he is.

Jack So he be; but did no one coom in since?

Jane How could they unless we seed them?

Noah Speak out, Jem Starkee—did ye see the man?

Jem [*Catching* JANE's *eye.*] No!

Jack He sped down the lane and he can't get from it, so we are safe to find him.

[*Exit* JACK, D. F., *followed by crowd shouting. Exit* NOAH, SHARROCK, STALEY *and* O'DICKS, *into room* L. 3 E.]

Read [*Appears at door above.*] Are they gone?

Jane Nay, they beset the lane. They will be back here anon or my father will find you and cast you out amongst them, and they'll tear thee limb for limb.

Read Oh, save me, Jane!

Jane I couldn't, but Jem can do it if he will.

Read He loves you and will do anything you ask him.

Jane [*To* JEM.] You coom here. You asked me but now to marry you and I said I'd never be your wife; well, now I say—save his life and take mine.

Jem Can you ask me to do this, and will he let you? Ah, now I feel you will never love—never—your life for his'n. No, Jane, I will not take thy heart wi' another man in it. Good-by, my darling, it's all over wi' me now. [*To* READLEY.] I'll save thy life for her sake. Stand by, sir, while I lead the crowd away—I'll coom back for ye when the lane is clear. [*Exit* D. F.

Read May I trust him?

Jane Aye, till they kill him—then thou must take care of thyself. Hark! I hear my father stirring—in wi' thee—quick! [*Exit* READLEY *up stairs.*] Oh, why did he let me gi' myself away and never said a word.

Enter NOAH *and the* THREE DELEGATES, L. 3 E.

Noah Go, lass, speed thee cross the lane to thy sister's house and spend the night there; I have business wi' these men alone—work to do—and do not need thee—get thee gone, lass.

Jane [*Aside, as she takes up shawl.*] Do they know that he is there? There's a wild, red mischief in their eyes, and they're fain to tremble and look pale at what they're goin' to do.

[*Goes up staircase; locks door and takes key.*

Noah What are you doing there, lass?

Jane Locking my bedroom door. [*Exit* D. F. *Music pp.*

Noah Now we are alone, lads. [*After locking door,* D. F.] Are we all agreed?

Omnes We are.

Noah Then, to night, let them feel our vengeance. Each night a mill shall be burned to the ground. The first may look like accident, but they shall soon find by the chimneys standing how long Manchester will last.

[*During above speech* READLEY *appears at window in flat* R. *of door, up staircase.*]

Read [*Aside.*] A plot to destroy the city.

Noah Let Readley be the first to feel it.

Omnes Aye, let him have it!

Read [*Aside.*] Villains! what do I hear?

Noah Mark me—I tear this bit o' paper into four. [*Music pp.*]   On one I put a cross. [*Business of same.*] Now gi' me your hat. [SHARROCK *gets hat from rail in flat* R.] I throw in the four lots. Now let each man draw and go his way alone. Him as draws the cross shall be the people's executioner. None shall know which one of us is elected—so he will have no accomplice. Now, James Staley, you begin. [STALEY *draws slip of paper and goes off slowly,* D. F.; O'DICK *and* SHARROCK *do same;* NOAH *draws last lot, goes slowly to window,* L. 3 E., *looks at it—pause.*] I knew it.

[*Exit* L. 2 E.

Enter JANE, D. F., *goes up staircase and unlocks door.* READLEY *appears.*

Jane Quick—make haste!

Enter JEM, D. F., *as* READLEY *descends.*

Jem Come—nay, do not doubt me—for her sake, I save your life.

JANE *on staircase,* JEM *at door,* READLEY *back to audience.*

CURTAIN.

ACT II.

SCENE 1.—*Same as last scene first Act.* JANE *discovered laying table for tea; goes to* D. F.; *looks out; returns.*

Jane He let me give myself away and never said a word. Oh! how it galls me to think on't. And Jem wouldn't have me either. I never liked as well as when so—"I'll save his life for your sake," said he, "but I'm too proud to take your heart wi' another man in it." [*Bell strikes five o'clock.*] Hark! There goes five o'clock and all day I've sat here waiting for thee, lad. I can't bear this any longer—I'll write to him and ask him to come to me. [*Writes*] "Dear Jem—come and see me. Jane." That will do.   [*Knock,* D. F.] Ah! there he is.   [*Crushes paper in hand and throws on floor.*]   I— I—won't seem glad to see him.   [*Knock,* D. F.]   I won't ask him to come in either. Past five o'clock—why wasn't he here before? There he is.

Enter JOHNNY REILLY *with bundle and stick,* D. F.

Ah! what's there? Why, Johnny Reilly, is it thee, lad?

John I've come to say good-by, Jane; my ship sails from Mersey to-morrow.

Jane You have come here twice a week for the last three months to say the same thing.

John It is your fault, Jane, that I couldn't get away.

Jane Don't be foolish, Johnny, I told you not to think of me, it's only wasting good love that many another girl would be grateful for.

John I knew that and I'm not going to court ye any more—never mind me—it's Jem I want to talk to ye about. Jem and me have been sweet on you this many a while—bout of us was bad about you—one worse than the other—but especially Jem. Ah! a pair of honester hearts a girl never had to her back. Many a night we've spent the night talking over you and swapping minds about ye.

Jane Pulled me to pieces, you mean?

John No we didn't; if we had I'd 'a' wept a bit.

Jane I'm sorry if I've given you any pain.

John I've got a cargo of it aboard and I'd not part wi' an ounce of it for all the pleasure in the world. But never mind me, it's Jem I'm here about. Oh, Jane dear, what did you say or do to him last night?

Jane I was cruel and scarce knew what I said.

John Then I'll tell you. You broke his heart—that's all you did. You know we lodge together? Well, all night long I heard him walkin' the deck of his room until I couldn't stand it, and then I opened his door. He turned and looked at me. What's the matter wi' you? says I. He never spoke, but I saw that his eyes were white, his lips turned dim and death was all over his face. On the table before him I found that.
                    [*Draws pistol from his pocket and places on table.*
Jane Oh!

John And beside it I found that, and [*Places powder-flask, bullets, etc. on table.*] oh, Jane! when I saw them things my heart turned over inside me.

Jane As mine does now.

John Never mind if it comes the right side up and turns that side to him.

Jane Had I awakened this morning and learned what I had done—

John That's what I said to Jem. Do you want to leave Jane a widow at her time o' life? Won't she feel that t'was herself that murdered you? And if you bring that shame upon the girl I love, I'm your enemy to your dying day says I, and a heap more, for I passed the night between him and his sorrow, and what a night it was. I never knew how much he loved you—but I know it now—and sure I'm going away for his sake, because, d'ye see. Jem and I went shares in you and I want to give my share to Jem.

Jane Did he not tell you what I had done?

John How could he without speakin' against you. But I know it was mighty bad because he never said a word.

Jane Oh! what shall I do?

John Put them things away and never let on I told you this, and begged you to be kind to him. His love is as proud as that gunpowder, and would take fire more easy. But oh, Jane! do let your heart soften to him—do dear, and then if—if—you marry him some day when I'm gone, and you are happy together—you can give him back them things and tell him what I have done for his sake and yours. Good-by. I've nothing to give you for a keepsake except my heart, and small blame to you for leaving that behind, because it won't follow me anyhow.

Jane Oh! if you could, indeed, leave it with me, if I could place it here in my breast instead of the frightful, vain, worthless thing that shames me. I—I—do not deserve that two such men should go to waste upon me.   [*Exit into room up staircase.*

John She's gone. I have seen the last of her. Let me take one more good look at the place that holds her—good luck to it. The place I'm going to leave her in when I am far away.

Enter CRANKSHAW, D. E.

Crank Good morning! Johnny Reilly, ain't it? Now, Noah Learoyd wouldn't be at home, would he?

John D'ye want him?

Crank Not particularly—I can wait a bit. Hello, what's here?

John Sugar toys.

Crank Firearms. Yours I suppose?

John No. Jem Starkee's.

Crank Bad companions for a hasty man.

John That's why I took them out of his hands and brought them here.

Crank To show this girl what she might drive him to, eh?

John He is in sore trouble, but sure, blowing a man's brains out h'is a poor way of giving ease to his mind.

Crank Hello, has it come to this?

John If I had not been nigh hand last night Jane would have had one sweet missing this morning—but that's what she's going to have to-morrow, anyway, for I am off to join my ship at last.

Crank I'm glad to hear it, for you were wasting your time and money on Jane Learoyd. Why, lad, she's no better than a—

John [*Dropping bundle.*] Don't say it! Don't tack a bad word to my girl's name! I won't stand by and let any man hurt a letter of it! Look in my eye twice before you speak once.

Crank Well, well, good-by.

John Good-by.   [*Takes up bundle and exits,* D. F.

Crank I must warn Mr. Readley. If he don't mind, this girl will cost him more than he reckons to pay. [*Picks up* JANE's *letter.*] Humph! "Dear Jem—come and see me. Jane." So she begins to fear she may push the poor lad too far and now she will fill his heart with sweet lies and when his back is turned be off with t'other one.   [*Throws letter on table.*

Enter NOAH, D. F.

Noah Crankshaw!

Crank Don't be scared, I come here as a friend not as an officer. I am ordered to help you to escape.

Noah Escape?

Crank Aye, you and your mates met here last night. There was a witness to that meeting you little suspected. He saw and heard all that passed and made his desposition before the magistrate this morning.

Noah It's a lie!

Crank Don't deny it—your plot to burn the mills one by one are sworn to. Your three accomplices are already in custody and if you are not in jail beside them on a capital charge, you owe it to your daughter, who saved young Readley's life.

Noah Saved his life! What do you mean?

Crank When he was hunted by the mob, he found shelter here.

Noah No! no, man! Not here!

Crank Yes—I tell you—she had him in her room yonder.

Noah There, there?

Crank And there he overheard your doings and saw you draw the lots.

Noah She—she did this! She, my child!

Crank That is the only thing in your favor. Don't you see he can't with any grace, bring against you what he discovered whilst she was saving his life.

Noah So I am allowed to creep away whilst they are in prison suffering for my doings?

Crank Readley will take care of you, for he is Jane's sweetheart.

Noah My Jane—his—

Crank Don't be hard upon him. He has been an admirer of hers for a long time. You may thank his love for her that you are safe. He will find the money for you to escape at once. Jane is to meet him to-night when all will be arranged. There's a letter he gave me for the girl. [*Puts letter on table.*] Take my advice, Noah, I've known you a good many years and I'd be sorry to find you in my hands, where you will be if you don't quit Manchester at once, and for the girl's sake, take her wi' ye or she'll get into more trouble. Good evening.   [*Exit,* D. F.

Noah [*Sinks into chair.*] My child—my flesh and blood—his paramour? It was for this, then, she locked him in! 'Twas for this that she betrayed the cause we have starved for—we have prayed for! They are in prison asking one another, where is Noah Learoyd? There—don't you see him—skulking behind his daughter?—livin' on her shame? She is to meet Readley to-night! [*Rises—sees pistol on table.*] Ah! what's this? [*Takes up pistol.*] Their fate hangs on Readley's breath. No breath of his shall ever testify against them. [*Loads pistol. Music p.*] Now, dinna ye see why free? 'Tis to scotch the snake, lads—to scotch the snake.

[*He loads pistol, using the letter* JANE *has written to* JEM STARKEE
for wadding.
[*Music continued till change.*

SCENE II.—*Whiting Street. Plain English,* 1.

Enter JEM STARKEE, *followed by* JACK O'BOBS, TOM O'BILLS, SUSAN
MAGGIE, *and all the mill hands murmuring,* R. 1 E.

Jem My lads, I dinna hold wi' ye.

Tom They have sent our delegates to prison for talkin' our part—
standin' oop for the people.

Jack Our men have been thrown into prison, and for what? Why, for
standing up for the workin'man's rights. Well, we'll tear it down stick and
stones but we'll have them out. Aye, that we will.

Omnes Aye, that we will—give us our men!

Tom We have right wi' us, lads—now let us show 'em we have might
on our side as well.

Omnes Aye, aye!

Jem Stop, lads. Why, what are thee going to do? See thee, lads, there
have been many a strike in Manchester—men have starved, and women
and babies have gi' 'em up and died, but no blood has stained our cause—
no act can be recorded against us that makes the honest workmen turn
back with shame. If the masters be wrong don't let us be on the other
side—two wrongs don't make a right.

Tom What right have they to be ridin' in their carriages while we ha'
not bread to eat?

Omnes Aye, aye!

Tom Why do they waste what we want?

Jem What right have you to be walkin' about in health and strength
when so many lie sick abed? Why don't ye gie a coat to a beggar and share
your bed wi' the tramp?

Tom Because I ain't got a coat, and I've got a wife.

Omnes Ha! ha! ha!

Jem Well said, Tom—get thee home, then—and there, lads, there's all
I have to share among ye—fill your mouths with something better than
wild words—[*Gives money.*] get thee home, and good night.

[Music. All exit, shouting, R. 1 E.

Jem Poor lads, how bright their sorrow seems beside mine.

Enter JOHNNY REILLY, L. 1 E.

Jem Oh, Johnny, but I've waited sorely for thee, lad. Thou hast seen
her?

John Aye, I've seen her—I've said good-by.

Jem And did she sorrow any at parting wi' ye?

John For my sake she did, not for her own. I didn't mane to hurt ye,
but I couldn't help it.

Jem Just what she said to me. Johnny, lad, I've made up my mind I can
not stop here; I'm going wi' thee.

John Wi' me?

Jem Aye, wherever your ship is bound—anywhere—it don't matter.

John Are you going to desert the girl only because she does not love you? Are you going to leave her in trouble and want, wid a bad man in her head and a devil stirring in her pocket.

Jem What can I do?

John Stand by her like a man—work for her if she wants it and see that the blackguard she loves treats her well. That's what one of us must stop to do, and you must be the one.

Jem Oh, Johnny, thou art more worthy of her than I am.

John May be that's why I've so little chance, bad luck to me.

Jem I'll remain then.

John Good-by then.

Jem Nay, we munna part so, I'll go wi' thee as far as the station and see the last of thee.

John Thank ye, Jem, I'm not going to Liverpool by rail.

Jem How then?

John You see I've been idling about Jane for the last five months until I spent every shillin' of my pay; then, bit by bit, I sold everything I had, till devil a thing I have but what I stand up in.

Jem Nay, I can gi' thee a trifle I have at home.

John Never fear, Jem, I've a shipmate keeps the "Load of Hay" public house, t'other side of Prescote. That's not four and twenty miles from here and it is a fine night for a walk. I'll reach his place by six in the morning. There I'll find all I want and welcome, so good-by and bless thee, Jem.

Jem Nay, then I'll walk wi' ye as far as Fox Hill; it'll lightenin' the road a bit.

John And we'll talk of her?   [*Exit*, R. I E.

Enter JANE, *with letter,* L. I E.

Jane Who brought this letter? How came it where I found it? [*Reads.*] "My dearest Jane—Meet me to-night in Fuller's Lane, at the gate behind my house I must see you! Richard Readley." Yes, I will go and meet him for the last time. I'll be honest with him. I dreamed that I loved him and I have just awoke to find there is nothing real or true in it, and then I'll go to Jem and ax his pardon—I'll be honest wi' him too, and let my heart out to him. Then, if he will ha' me—if–eh!—don't I know he will—I'm foolin' with myself.   [*Exit* R. I E. *Music.*

Enter NOAH LEAROYD, *stealthily, with pistol,* L. I E., *following* JANE.

Noah She is going to meet wi' young Readley now!   [*Exit,* L. I E.

CHANGE SCENE.

SCENE. III.—*Fuller's Lane, with* READLEY'S *house and garden; entire stage; set house, with garden wall in front,* L. 2 E., *running to 3rd entrance behind wall; some real fir-tree raised so as to show over wall. Running obliquely from* R. 2 E. *to* L. 4 E., *is a low stone wall about 2 feet high, behind which is placed real fir-trees to represent hedge; near the upper end of hedge a passageway through; a view of the mills at back illuminated; time, night; lights down; lime light,* R. 2 E., *for moon; practical gate in garden wall.*

Enter CRANKSHAW *from behind house,* L. U. E., *with bulls-eye lantern.*
Enter TOM O'BILLS, *singing,* L. U. E.

Tom This is a fine night.   [*To* CRANKSHAW.]   Will you give me a light for my pipe? These are hard times! What o'clock is it?
Crank [*Gives light.*] Never you mind. Move on, move on.

[*Exit* TOM, *singing,* R. 1 E.

READLEY *appears at garden gate.*

Read Is that you, Crankshaw?
Crank All is right, sir.
Read Has she come?
Crank Here she is coming up the lane.

[*Looks off* L. U. E. *Exits,* L. U. E.

Read Now this little coy beauty must surrender at discretion. She can scarcely escape the toils she has woven for herself.

Enter JANE, L. U. E.

My dear little torment, how shall I thank you for this delightful interview?
Jane Don't speak to me like that, if you please, Mr. Readley, I can't hear such words from you any more.
Read Come, don't be a little fool, Jane.
Jane No sir, I will not be if I can help it, for I have been very foolish, or worse, may be, and that's what I've come to tell you, sir. When first you showed a fancy for me I was vain enough to think that I deserved to be a lady. I believe I did not rightly know my own mind, but now I do know it, and I do not wish to keep company with you any more. I humbly beg your pardon, sir, if I led you to think too much of me.
Read Jane, you are in jest.
Jane I have been wrong, very wrong, to lead you to think I liked you, but, indeed, sir, I am in earnest when I say that to-night is the last time I will ever speak to you.
Read And what has made this change? Have I done anything to offend you?
Jane No, I can't lay any blame on you, Mr. Readley, it is all my fault, and, as I said before, I beg your pardon, if I have done any wrong by you, and now, sir, if you please, good night.
Read But I don't please.   [*Catches her.*]   You shan't go till you tell me how I have vexed you.

Jane Oh, let me go! you can not change my mind! Oh, sir, why do you hold me? Oh, do let me go!

Read Not till you tell me what is the matter with you.

Jane [*Facing him.*] Well, if you will know why I won't have anything more to do with you, it is that I can not love you.

Read Not love me?

Jane No. I have tried and I really can not.

Read You little coquette, and when did you find that out?

Jane Last night when I found I loved another man—the honest lad that had courted me ever sin' I was a child, and whom I was vain enough to leave for you.

Read And you discovered all this since last night?

Jane I felt there was something wrong the matter wi' me, and I find that it—I can never be you wife.

Read My wife?

Jane Your wife. I am sorry I ever led you to think I would be.

Read Ha! ha! ha! My wife! My dear girl, I never comtemplated imposing matrimony upon you.

Jane What? You did not mean—to make me—to marry me? Oh! I am obliged to you for lettin' me know that! That's a great relief! When I thought you loved me I did feel sorry and humbly begged your pardon. That was before I knew what you are. Now I owe you naught.

Read Aye, but you do though—you owe me your father's life.

Jane What do you mean?

Read Last night, while hidden in your chamber, I heard your father, and those with him, plan to commit a felony. This morning I denounced his accomplices—they are now in prison. Him alone I spared for your sake.

Jane No, no—not for my sake only, but for your own. 'Twas I who placed you there—'twas I, then, who betrayed him and these men.

Read If I appear, as I am bound to do, to-morrow morning, before the magistrates, no influence of mine—no power can save him.

Jane And no power can hinder my father from taking his place beside them if he ain't done it already—ye dunna know him. Oh, sir, canna ye do something to spare me this? It's my father's life, his blood may be, that I have to answer for. Oh! what ha' I done? What ha' I done?

Read Yes, I can do something—I can abandon the prosecution—but to do so, I must leave Manchester to-night so that when I am called to-morrow I shall be missing.

Jane Aye, aye!

Read And you must be missing with me.

Jane I do not understand you.

Read Jane, dearest, I can not part with you. Tell me you were but joking when you said you found you could not love me. You have fostered a passion which you will not, can not trifle with.

Jane Stop! I understand you now. Speak plain, man. It is a bargain you offer me. You want me to sell myself against my father's life.

Read 'Tis you who drive me to this base extremity. If I am desperate with a passionate love, blame your own beauty with which you tempted me.

Jane Oh! what are ye man, that puts a child in such a straight?

Read I am what you have made me. Fortune has given this power over your inclination and I love you too deeply not to use it.

Jane In the toils! I am in the toils! I must be my father's murderer or this man's—no! no! you will have pity on me! I bad rather die! I would— I would—I saved your life! Spare mine! oh! hear me!

Read [*Embracing her and drawing her up stage.*] No, dearest, not a word.

[*A shot is fired through the hedge,* R. H.; READLEY *utters a cry, throws up arms, reels back and falls,* L. C.]

Jane [*Screaming.*] Help! help! help!   [*Falls fainting,* R. H.

Enter CRANKSHAW.

Crank That sounded like the report of firearms. What's here? [*Throws light from lantern on* READLEY.] Ah! sure enough—sure enough!

[POLICEMAN *outside springs rattle.*
Enter POLICEMAN *hastily, through hedge. Enter* BROOKE, *and* ASPINWALL, *and mill hands,* L. U. E. *and* R. 1 E.; *Servants from house with lighted candles.*

Brooke What's the matter?

Crank Only a murder, that's all.

Omnes Murder!

Aspin Who has done this?

Crank Perhaps that girl can tell us when she comes to. Go and fetch a shutter or a leaf of your dining table, and one of ye run for doctor. I'm afraid it's no use—come, be handy. [*To crowd pressing on.* Come now, move on now. There [*To* POLICE.] keep the crowd off the ground. Bill, keep the crowd back.   [*Music.*

CURTAIN.

ACT III.

SCENE I.—*Fuller's Lane. Readley's house same as in Act 2nd, Scene 3rd*

ARMITAGE *near gate;* CRANKSHAW *examining ground with bulls-eye lantern;* BROOKE *near house;* POLICEMAN. *All discovered at rise. Music.*

Arm Can you find no trace? Eh?

Crank No, sir, I am inclined to believe the girl knows more about it than she chooses to confess.

Arm Her story seemed to be a truthful but reserved confession. However, when she has recovered sufficiently she will able to explain the circumstances more clearly.

Brooke Here she is.

Enter JANE, L. U. E., *behind house.*

Arm Come here, my girl, and do not be afraid.

Brooke We do not connect you in any manner with this dreadful crime, and it is but right to inform you that you are not compelled to answer any questions we may ask you.

Jane Thank you, sir—I don't see why I should fear answering anything about it.

Brooke Where did you stand when the fatal shot was fired?

Jane There; and he, as it might be, beside me. He was moving toward the gate.

Crank There was no one in sight? No one near you while you and Mr. Readley were talking?

Jane No one. It came all of a sudden.

Arm From which side?

Jane [*Points back.*] I couldn't tell. Somewhere behind me.

Arm The position of the wound agrees with that supposition, but if the assassin stood there you must have seen him.

Jane But I did not, indeed, sir; I only saw a flash and heard the shot.

Crank I have it, Bill, we have been on the wrong scent searching the lane—the girl was right—the shot was fired through the hedge—our man was in the field—come this way.

[*Exit* CRANKSHAW, *followed by* POLICEMAN, *over stile.*

Arm You have exhibited so much candor and proper feeling throughout this painful affair that I may venture to ask you another question. Do you entertain any suspicions as to the person who committed this deed?

Jane No, sir; Mr. Readley had many enemies.

Crank [*Outside.*] Here we have it.

Arm They have some clue.

Crank [*Outside.*] Stay there, Bill, while I go on t'other side.

Enter CRANKSHAW *over stile.*

We have discovered the nest, sir. There it is, plain enough. We can trace the mould of a man from where he lay among the long grass in the ditch close against the hedge. Come, Jane, you and I know who it was that lay on the watch?

Brooke The girl says she has no suspicions.

Crank Hain't she? Well, I have—

Enter 2ND POLICEMAN, R. 1 E.

—and I sent this officer to make sure. Well, have you been to his house?

2nd Policeman Yes, and he hasn't been home all night.

Crank I thought not. All right, gentlemen, we have spotted the man we want.

Jane Not him! Not him! Why, he saved Mr. Readley's life two days ago!

Arm Who?

Jane James Starkee.

Crank I never said it was he.

Brooke Who is this fellow?

Crank I never said 'twas he. He's the girl's sweetheart. I'm main sorry for thee, Jane.

Jane I wouldna', I canna' believe it, for I ha' seen them together, and Jem would not hurt a hair of his head.

Crank Wouldn't he? I saw them together t'other night at Millgate, where I interfered. Jem swore he'd find Mr. Readley somewhere when no policeman should get between, and it seems that he has kept his word.

1st Police [*Outside.*] Hello, over there.

Crank Well, what now?

1st Police [*Outside.*] There is something in the hedge there, something bright.

Crank Something bright? I don't see it.

1st Police [*Outside.*] Move to your right.

Crank I see it now.   [*Draws pistol from hedge.*]   Oh! I think I've seen this article before.

Brooke A pistol—evidently the one the deed was committed with.

Crank I say, Jane, it ain't the first time you seed this weapon, eh? [*Holds up pistol.*]   You have some suspicions now? There, lass, it is only natural you should like to shield him. This is Jem Starkee's pistol, sir, I've reason to know it. 'Tis plain he dodged the girl, and she led him here.

Enter 1ST POLICE, *over stile.*

1st Police I found this bit o' paper yonder.

[*Hands small piece of black and half burned paper to* CRANKSHAW.

Crank 'Tis the wadding of the pistol—see, it is blackened—[*Smells paper.*] and with gunpowder, and half burned away.

Arm [*Taking paper and examining it by* CRANKSHAW's *lantern.*] Ah! 'tis part of a letter. [*Reads.*] "Dear Jem—Come and see me." The signature is wanting.

Jane [*Hiding face.*] It is mine—'twas I wrote it—but he, Jem, never received it—never!

Arm Then how came it here?

Jane I do not know.

Arm The evidence is all sufficient.

Brooke Immediate steps should be taken to secure this man—he' no doubt hiding away and may escape.

Arm This girl had better be detained until the inquest is over.

Crank I'd rather let her go, if you please, sir.

Jane Oh! do not keep me! Do not keep me!

Arm Very well, I presume that you know where to find her when her evidence is required.

Crank All right, sir. [JANE *exits*, L. U. E. *To* POLICEMAN.] Follow her, Bill, and when she lights on Jem Starkee, pop the word to the station; I shall be ready with warrant by that time. You see, gentlemen, she is the bait with which we must catch our man.

[*Exit.* POLICEMAN *and* BROOKE *go up stage as scene is closed in.*

SCENE II.—*Millgate Lane—same as Scene 2nd, Act 1st.*

Enter JACK O'BOBS, L. 1 E., *meeting* MAGGIE *and three* FEMALE OPERATIVES *who enter*, R. 1 E. *Music p. at change.*

Maggie Well, lad, is it thee? Is it thee?

Jack Aye, lass, all the town is astir wi' it.

Maggie I see thee, lad. I don't mind throwin' a brick through a pane o' glass or distroyin' a man's jacket in a nob stick, but when it comes to shootin' or stabin', I don't hand wi' thee. For my part, I be going back to work, whether I get paid or not.

Omnes So be I—so be I!   [*Exit omnes but* JACK, R. 1 E.

Enter TOM O'BILLS *and four* MALE OPERATIVES, L. 1 E.; *crosses to*
R. 1 E.

Jack Where be thee going, lads?

Tom We be going back to work. The strike be at an end, and we be main glad of it. Come, lads, let's to work.

[*Exit all but* JACK, R. 1 E.

Enter JEM STARKEE, L. 1 E., *looking off.*

Jem Why, what has come to Manchester since I left it last night. The folks look scared and hold down their heads as if ashamed like. [*Turns and sees* JACK.] What be the matter, Jack?

Enter GENTLEMAN *from London, with carpet-bag*, R. 1 E.

Jack The strike be at an end. The people are going back to work by thousands, just to show they have no hands in this business.

Jem What business?

Jack Why, Mr. Readley's murder.

Jem What?

Jack Don't you know that Readley was shot last night in Fuller's Lane? I thought you'd a known it. Why, all the city is talking about it. She is in custody.

Jem She? Who?

Jack Jane Learoyd!

Jem She—Jane killed him?

Jack Nay, but him and she was there together in the lane last night, courting, they say, when the shot was fired. The policeman found young Readley dead and Jane by his side in a faint.

Jem Where do you hear of this?

Jack Everywhere—there be a grand crowd now all about Noah's door. I jist coom from there but I could not get in, but the folk outside told me the old man was found, this morning, lying stark on his face across his own doorstep, and when he coom to they could'na sense him but he sat up crazy like. See—here he be. [*Music p.*

Enter NOAH, R. 1 E., *followed by* MAGGIE, SUSAN *and other female operatives.*

Susan Come, come, Noah—go home, man.

Jem Stand back, there. Noah, man, is it true? Where is Jane?

Noah [*Crazed.*] Jane—Jane—in Fuller's Lane wi' young Readley.

Jem Don't you know me, Noah? Jem—Jem Starkee?

Jack He sees ye, but his brain is blind; his lassie's shame has broke the old man's heart.

Omnes Aye, aye—that's it.

Jem Leave me wi' him—I'll take care of him.

Omnes Poor man—heaven help him.

[*Exit all bul* STARKEE *and* NOAH, R. 1 E.

Jem Poor shattered vessel. And has she brought ye to this? Oh, Jane, Jane! but thou art fatal to all who love ye!

Enter JANE, *breathless*, L. 1 E.

Jane Jem, I've found thee at last—lose no time to escape.

Jem Escape?

Jane Already the warrant is out against thee.

Jem What for?

Jane They say 'twas thee that killed young Readley.

Jem They lie that say it. I was far away from your guilty meeting.

Jane Thank heaven he suspects me, for now I am sure he was not there. Had'st thou been there, Jem, thou had'st known I have no cause to blush for what I saw or did. Father, thou knowest well thy life was in Readley's power.

Noah [*Crazed.*] Hide in my house in her room, where she locked him in.

Jem [*Crosses to* NOAH.] Look there, Jane, over-much sorrow has crazed the old man. He is spared the sense of the shame.

Jane Father! father! speak to me! look at me! I am thy child, dear!

Noah Yes, in Fuller's Lane—there—there they are together. Come, I'll show a spot where we can hide. There they are—see—see my child—his paramour?

Jane Ah! he accuses me! No—I have been foolish but not guilty. Indeed, indeed, father, I have not. I am helpless, for I can not prove what passed between us in the lane. None but that guilty wretch who committed this crime can testify that I am innocent. Oh! heaven grant that he may be brought to justice!

Noah Hush—quiet—they are together—they'll hear ye.

Jane Father, father!

Noah Come, we'll hide in the hedge by the ditch.

Jane [*Recoiling.*] Oh!

Noah Plan to commit a felony—denounced his comrades—they are in prison—him I spared for father's sake.

Jane Merciful heavens!

Noah It's a bargin ye offer—speak plain! Sell myself against my father's life?

Jane My words—my words to Readley in the lane!

Noah What a man are ye—put a child in such a straight.

[*Imitates firing pistol.*

Jane 'Twas he! 'Twas he! There—he killed him!

Jem He killed him and for thy sake!

Jane Oh! Jem, Jem! He is guilty!

Jem But thou art innocent! [*Embraces* JANE.

Enter CRANKSHAW, R. 1 E., *with* POLICEMAN, *who carries handcuffs.*

Crank This is a bad business, lad.

Jem Yes.

Crank [*Crosses* L. H.] It is fortunate that you were not hereabouts.

Jem Aye! I was a good mile from the place when it happened.

Crank At home, eh? Sound asleep in bed?

Jem No. I was wi' a friend journeying to Liverpool. I never left him till after midnight.

Crank That's lucky for you. Of course, he can prove all that when the time comes.

Jem What time?

Crank Your trial for the murder of Mr. Readley. You are my prisoner.

[*Signs* POLICEMAN, *who handcuffs* JEM.

Jane Father, see, they take him to prison.

Jem What does thee mean? Hold thy peace, Jane.

Jane No, I canna see it! I will not not stand by! Hold ye hands—I know who did the deed! Oh! Jem, Jem! I canna see them take thee! Father, father! speak! Tell them he is not guilty! You know he did not kill young Readley!

Noah Done it? Well, it was—

[JANE *places her hand across his mouth.*

Jane No, no—come away.   [*Forces* NOAH *off*, R. 1 E.

Crank There, lad, I'll throw my handkerchief over the irons, and nobody need know our business. There, come along.

Jem Thanks, thanks.

[*Exeunt* L. 1 E. CRANKSHAW, POLICEMAN *and* JEM.

CHANGE SCENE.

SCENE III.—MONEYPENNY's *library in 3 box scene; doors* R. *and* L. 2 E.; *table and arm chair,* O., *three other chairs flat; writing materials and newspaper.*

Enter MONEYPENNY *in overcoat, hat and comforter, with umbrella and lawyer's bag,* L. 2 E. *Takes off coat, etc., places them on chair against flat, looks at watch.*

Money Halfpast eight. No more business to-day. I've been in court since nine o'clock this morning. Betsey, Betsey! you may close the office!

[*Sits at table.*

Enter BETSEY, R. 2 E., *with kerosene lamp lighted, with shade. Places it on table.*

Betsey If you please, sir, there's been a young person here three times to see you. I believe she's hanging about the streets still.

Money I can't see any young person at this hour. Tell her to call at nine to-morrow morning. [*Bell rings at prompt.*] Ah! that is your young person, I suppose? [*Exit* BETSEY.] Why don't they pass a ten-hour bill, for lawyers' clients have no conscience. How many of mine, I wonder, would take six-and-eight to be rung up from a comfortable nap.

Enter BETSEY, R. 2. E.

Money Well?

Betsey I told her what you said, sir—that she should call to-morrow morning.

Money That satisfied her, I suppose?

Betsey No, sir, she is still sitting on the doorstep.

Money I can't help it. Let her come in office hours. Well, well, what did she say?

Betsey She made no reply but, too late, too late. I left her sitting there hard enough.

Money If this is to go on I might as well put up a night-bell like a doctor, or a bullseye blood shot wide open all night to show I never close mine. No, I have earned a quiet evening, and I mean to have it. Get me a nice cup of tea.

Betsey Yes, sir.   [*Exit*, R. 1 E.

Money Now I dismiss the cares of the world without. I'll not think of anybody's business but give myself up to enjoyment. That girl has gone away—of course she has; what fools women are now. What earthly satisfaction could be derived from sitting down upon a cold doorstep to cry? not that it matters to me if she were to stop there all night. Fancy my going out in the morning and finding her there still. Pooh, nonsense; what's in the paper to-night? [*Takes up paper and reads.*] "Latest from America." What did she mean by too late? If I had said it was too late there would have been some sense in it. [*Reads.*] "Negotiations for peace. Fall in the rate of discount." I wonder if that girl is out there still? What's the use of her stopping out there? Betsey!

Enter BETSEY, R. 2 E.

Just see if that girl is gone, will you?

   Betsey Yes, sir.   [*Exit*, R. 2 E.

   Money I wager she is there. It is some one who is in a scrape and got no money to pay costs; send a girl to cry to old Moneypenny. That's it. On one occasion I refused to take costs from a fellow whom I thought hardly used and I gave him a trifle for charity. Well, what was his gratitude? The ruffian went and published it all over Manchester, and, within a week, I had every vagabond at my door expecting advice gratis and a sovereign.

Enter BETSEY, R. 2 E.

   Betsey No, sir—I looked out the door and there she is.

   Money Did you tell her I would not see her?

   Betsey Of course I did.

   Money Very well, then show her up and I'll tell her myself.

   Betsey [*Aside.*] I thought it would come to that.   [*Exit*, R. 2 E.

   Money I must put an end to this sort of thing or my life will be rendered intolerable. I won't listen to a word she has to say—no, not a word.

Enter BETSEY, R. 2 E., *showing in* JANE.

   Betsey Here she is, sir.   [*Exit*, R. 2 E.

   Money Well, what do you want? Is this a time of night to come crying round a respectable doorstep?

   Jane I beg your pardon, sir.

   Money Of course you do—I should think you did.

   Jane He told me to come to you, and I've been waiting here since two o'clock.

   Money He? who's he? But don't tell me some vagabond in a scrape. I really can not enter into business. Don't speak. [*Pause.*] What's your name?

   Jane Jane Learoyd.

   Money Now, this rascal is your husband or your lover, eh?

   Jane [*Crying.*] Yes, sir.

   Money What is it? Robbery? larceny?—

   Jane No, sir—murder.

Money [*Dropping paper.*] Lord bless us! Murder, eh?

Jane He is accused of killing Mr. Readley, and the evidence is very strong against him.

Money Strong?—it's conclusive! I know the evidence in the hands of the police. I never heard a clearer case.

Jane [*Crying.*] Clear or not, sir, Jem Starkee is as innocent as you are.

Money He doubtless made you believe it, but his jury will not be composed of his sweethearts, and they will scarcely take his own word for it.

Jane I did not take his word for it, I took the word of him as did the deed.

Money You know him?

Jane [*Crying.*] He is my father.

Money [*Rising.*] Good heavens! no!

Jane [*Crying.*] I've come here to ask you to help a poor lad and an honest girl out of their sad trouble. I can't tell you half the truth for to tell you rightly you must know the whole.

Money Your father killed him?

Jane [*Crying.*] And none can prove that but one person, and that is—

Money Yourself.

Jane [*Crying.*] Yes, sir.

Money He refuses to confess?

Jane No, sir, he is out of his mind. He was so, I believe, when he committed the deed. I gathered from his ravings enough to satisfy me that it was he who fired the shot. But oh, sir! how can I accuse him? Yet, how can I let poor Jem die?

Money Then how can your lover be exculpated? The circumstantial evidence is strong against him.

Jane [*Crying.*] Jem was far away from the place when the deed was done. He was at Eccles, on the Liverpool road, in company with Johnny Reilly, a sailor.

Money Where is this man?

Jane By this time he is in Liverpool. His ship was to sail to-day.

Money To-day? But, my dear girl, do you know that your lover's life hangs on a single hour? If that man has left England, and we can not obtain him as witness, I would not give sixpence for this lad's chance of escaping the gallows. Why didn't you come before?

Jane I have been waiting for seven hours at your door, sir.

Money Seven hours, at my door? That damned Betsey wouldn't let her in. What is the name of the ship?

Jane [*Sobbing.*] The name? Stay, he did tell me but I forgot, I am so bewildered. It was the Susan and—no—the Mary—it was two womens' names.

Money Two women? egad, that's a bad omen. [*Takes paper—reads.*] "Shipping cleared: The James Dunbar, for Valparaiso; Red Rover, for Sydney; the Stonewall, for New York; the Eliza and Mary—

Jane That's it.

Money Aye, but too late. My poor girl, the vessel has left the Mersey, and, by this time, must be out to sea.

Jane [*Crying.*] Oh! Then ain't there no hope?

Money There is none.

Jane [*Crying.*] My poor lad—my poor lad—what can I do for thee?

Money How can I tell? There, don't cry. [*Wipes his eye.*] Damn it, don't cry! I hate to see a woman cry—I don't allow it!

Jane I ax your pardon, sir. I thank you for being so kind.

Money What's the use of being kind? Will that save the vagabond's life? No! Very well, what do you bring me such a case for, depriving me of my peace of mind? Stop! I said there was no hope, eh? There is one. That sailor must be brought back, if it is not too late. I never thought of that.

Jane [*Crying.*] Oh, sir, what is it? Can I do aught?

Money Hold your tongue. No—nothing—yes—that will do. But it will cost money, and mind, I won't advance a penny—mind, not one penny.

Jane Oh, sir, I thought of that—I have money—here it is. [*Takes silver coin and two tickets from her pocket and places them on table.*] There, sir, there is fourteen-and-ninepence.

Money What are these? [*Takes up tickets.*] Pawnbroker's tickets?

Jane [*Picks up tickets quickly.*] Oh, sir, I ax your pardon—I didn't mean them.

Money So you've been pawning your little things to raise this money to save him?

Jane [*Crying.*] Yes, sir—ain't it enough? Oh, ain't it enough? Please, here's my shawl, it will fetch four-and-threepence more, sir. Oh, sir, won't it do? Won't it do?

Money Take up your money! Take it up this instant! How dare you insult me by offering me money? Give me my coat and hat—there's not a moment to lose.

Jane [*Eagerly.*] Yes, sir.   [*Gets coat and comforter.*

Money Help me on with it. This is how I dismiss the cares of the world without, and give myself up to enjoyment. Give me my comforter.

Jane [*Puts comforter around his neck.*] Are we going to Liverpool, sir?

Money Hold your tongue—you're a fool.

Jane Yes, sir.

Money Now don't rely on this hope! Don't rely on it! Don't dare to rely on it! It ain't the size of a pea! I'm going to telegraph to the heads to see if the vessel can be communicated with, and if so, we may recall the witness.

Jane Heaven bless you, sir, for taking a poor girl's troubles to your heart.

Money I don't take them to any such place—don't deceive yourself—this is all professional—my actions are purely in a professional way, without any feeling whatever—you understand? Without any feeling whatever. I am a poor man and I can not afford to indulge in any such damned nonsense. Don't cry—if you cry I'll throw up the case.

Enter BETSEY *with waiter on which is the cup of tea and muffin.*

Betsey Here's the tea, sir.

Money [*Crosses to table.*] The tea? Ah! nice and hot, too—a nice muffin. See what I'm sacrificing for you. I'm going in the cold air on an empty stomach.

Betsey Your surely not going out again, sir?

Money [*Taking hat and umbrella.*] Yes, I am. [*To* JANE.] Take my arm, now—don't cry. I've promised a quiet evening, and egad, I think I'm going to have it. [*Exit with* JANE, L. 1 E. BETSEY *at table.*

CURTAIN.

ACT IV.

SCENE I.—*Telegraph office in 3; box scene; circular counter; real apparatus; tormenter doors used only; painted window* C. *of* F.; *curtain painted on window to appear rolled up; letters on window to read backward—"Telegraph Office—Messages sent to all parts of the United Kingdoms." Chair at* R. *end of counter; gas-lights with shade's over operatives desk, (lighted); high stools behind counter for operatives; writing materials on counter and different desks; two small desks on counter with blank despatches and writing materials; two kerosene lamps by desks and desk and counter telegraph operatives working as curtain rises.* SLACK, TWO OPERATIVES *and* ONE MESSAGE BOY *discovered.* GENTLEMAN *passing on and off.*

Slack [*At center—to* GENT.] Fourteen words? What's the address? Lake Street, Chicago, United States? Twenty pounds, sir.

[GENT *passes money and exits,* L. 1 E.

Enter BROOKE, L. 1 E.

Brooke Is the line working through to Clitheroe?

Slack No, sir—nothing but the main lines open. The side line closes in the evening at nine o'clock, some of them as early as seven.

Brooke Are you aware, sir, that much inconvenience may result to the public by this early closing?

Slack The telegraph is a private enterprise, and maintained for profit. The business coming in after nine o'clock would not pay, except on the main lines.

Brooke Are you sure that Clitheroe is not working through.

Slack To satisfy you, sir, I can signal and see. Mr. Russel, just signal Blackburn and ask if Clitheroe is through. If you will wait for a few moments we will get an answer.

1st Operator I say, Tom, there's a big fire going on in Glasgow, they can't get it under.

2nd Operator Answer from Blackburn—Clitheroe gone.

Brooke Thank you, sir—good evening.   [*Exit*, L. 1 E.

Slack Good evening, sir. [*To* BOY.] Take this despatch to Portland Terrace, Oxford Square, one shiling to pay.

[*Exit* BOY, L. 1 E. OPERATIVES *quit work and turn out gas over desk;*
prepare to go home.]

Slack [*To* 1ST OPERATIVE.] Mr. Russel, be sure to return at eleven o'clock to relieve me. [*Exit* OPERATIVES, R. 1 E.] Miller, Miller. Where is that imp, Miller? Oh! here he is, asleep under the counter. Come, get up, Miller. [BOY *rises, rubbing his eyes.*] Take them despatches to the newspaper offices, and then you may go home. [*Exit* BOY, *yawning as if half asleep.*] Poor boy, he's run so much today he must be sadly tired.

[*Takes up newspaper; stands behind counter*, L. C.

Enter MONEYPENNY *and* JANE, L. 1 E.

Money Here we are. Now let me attend to this. Now, you sit here. [*Places* JANE *in chair*, R. C. *To* SLACK.] This young person wishes to send a telegram to the signal station at the north of the Mersey.

Slack Too late, sir, by half an hour, but if you will leave your message I will send it the first thing in the morning.

Jane Too late? Oh, sir, do try—do!

Money Hold your tongue. Surely there must be some means of communicating in cases of extreme emergency.

Slack Let me see. You can reach Liverpool by rail at Midnight. There you can hire a boat, and if the tide serves you might reach the cars by two o'clock in the morning.

Money But this process will take four, perhaps six hours, and, in the meantime, the ship may have sailed.

Slack I'm very sorry, sir, but I assure you that the office at the heads is closed.

Jane Oh, sir, try! Can't you try to open it.

Money Will you keep quiet? This, sir, is a matter of life and death. If we fail to transmit a message to that vessel a man's life will be sacrificed as surely as we stand here.

Slack I am as powerless as yourselves to avert the calamity, but to satisfy you I will summon the heads, yet I assure you it is not of the slightest use.

Jane Oh, thank you, sir.

Slack I have two messages for ships expected to arrive, and I signaled the heads some half hour since and could get no answer.

Jane Oh, sir, what shall we do? What shall we do?

Money If you cry and get me nervous I shall go home. Sit quiet.

Slack [*Having worked apparatus.*] There, sir, you see the wires are dumb. [JANE *falls on knees.*] I am truly sorry, sir, but if you were to give me one thousand pounds I could not make them speak.

Money Of course you can't. Thank you, it is not your fault, but this poor girl, sir—this poor girl—it is her sweetheart that will be tried for murder—that wire was the thread on which the lad's life was suspended and it fails her. It is hard, sir. I am a lawyer, and used to hard cases, but this does appear to me a cruel one. Come, Jane.

Jane Oh! let me pray—let me pray!

Money Heaven help you, my poor girl, for we can do no more. [*To* SLACK.] You see, sir, this being assize time, his trial will come off at once. I fear it will go hard with him. [JANE's *head falls against chair.*] Why, what is the matter, Jane?

Jane I am faint, sir. I feel very cold.

Slack [*Having come from behind counter, stands* L.] Can I assist you, sir?

Money She is swooning, sir. Oh, dear—what shall I do. Jane! Jane!
                                        [*Instrument at back begins to tap.*

Slak Hark, sir! hark! There's a signal! Stop a bit! [*Runs behind counter.*] By some accident the station at the head is alive.

Money Jane, Jane! do you hear? The line is open—the wire is working!

Jane [*Still on knees, hands clasped.*] Heaven has heard my prayer.

Slack Now then, sir, for your message.

Money [*To* JANE.] Stop there. [*To* SLACK.] Ask them has the Barque Eliza and Mary left the Mersey. [*Pause*—JANE *sobs.*] Hush—keep quiet!

Slack [*Who has sent message as directed by* MONEYPENNY—*receives reply.*] Barque Eliza and Mary inside the bar waiting for a tide.

Money Hurrah! hurrah!

Slack What next?

Money Can you communicate with the Barque? If so, how?

Slack [*As before.*] Yes—by pilot boat.

Money Despatch it at once, with message from Jane Learoyd to John Reilly, sailor—"Come back; give evidence required in favor of James Starkee, accused of murder; case now on. Signed, Jane Learoyd."

Slack [*As before.*] I don't think the boat will take the message unless you are acquainted with some one there who will pay expenses.

Money [*Takes out pocket-book.*] There, there's twenty pounds—say you have it—say you have any amount. Damn me, I'll see this thing through.

Slack [*Sending message.*] I have twenty pounds in my hands to pay expenses. [*Pause.*] One moment, sir, here comes the answer. *Pilot boat gone.*

[*During the latter part of the dialogue* JANE *listens breathlessly. Crosses to* MONEYPENNY *and kisses his hands as*

SCENE CLOSES.

SCENE II.—*The after cabin of the ship "Eliza and Mary;" window in flat,*
L. H., *representing the cabin window of ship; lively music, as scene*
opens

Enter JOHN REILLY, L. H.

John [*Looking through window.*] Good-by, Ould England, it will be
many a day before we meet again, and when that day comes it may be I'll
be dead and buried in a foreign land. Tramp, tramp, I hear the men at
the capstan—the anchor is coming up, and, when it leaves the bottom,
my heart quits hould of the world forever entirely—good-by, Jane. [*Voice*
outside, R. 1 E., "vast heavin!"] Vast heavin? What's the matter? Something foul on deck, or maybe there's too heavy a sea?

Enter CAPTAIN WOLF *with spyglass in his hand,* L. 1 E.

Capt What's amiss? Go up and order the pilot to find out what's wrong
and why he told the men to vast heavin.

John Aye, aye, sir. [*Exit,* L. 1 E.

Capt The old fool must be dreaming. [*Goes to window and looks*
through spyglass.] Hello, yonder is some lights, though, and they appear
to be signaling to some vessel, but it can't be the Eliza and Mary they
want, yet it looks like our number. The fellow is right, and is—

John He says, sir, that a pilot boat is making for this ship, here away
on the lee quarter.

Capt [*Still at window.*] I see her—she is burning a blue light now—
some message from our owners—they'll toss it on board—so tell them to
heave on.

John I ax pardon, but I know this bar right well, an with such a sea on
as we have to night, if we leave go the bottom, we'll have to run for it, we
can't dodge about on these narrow quarters to stop for visitors.

Capt Well, damn you impudence! Do you want to teach me navigation?

Voices outside, R. 1 E. Pilot boat, ahoy!

Voices outside Aye, aye!

Capt There's the pilot boat.

Voices outside Stand by for a message from the shore.

Capt I thought so—they'll throw it aboard. Go fetch it. [*Exit* REILLY,
L. 1 E.] Some last instructions from a consignee I suspect [*Goes to win-*
dow and looks out.] Here she comes. Look out! port your helm, you lub-
bers, or you'll be aboard of us! Well done—steady—what is he after now?
I declare, he is lying under our lee.

Enter REILLY *with despatch,* L. 1 E.

John 'Tis a despatch, sir.

Capt [*Takes despatch and reads.*] What's this? Jane Learoyd, Manchester, to John Reilly, sailor, on board Barque "Eliza and Mary."

John To me? To me—from Jane?

Capt Well, by thunder, the service is come to a fine fix when a ship's to heave to for a beggarly sailor to receive a message from his sweetheart.

John 'Tis a mistake.

Capt [*Reads.*] Come back; give evidence required in favor of James Starkee, accused of murder; case now on. Jane Learoyd.

John Jem accused of—oh, murther! who did the murther?

Capt I am very sorry for Jem, whoever he is, as my ship is short of hands I can't spare you.

John But, Captain, darlint, sure, don't you see he has murthered somebody, and she wants me to swear he hasn't?

Capt [*Calling off,* L. 1 E.] Heave away there—in two minutes I'll have the anchor apeak, and in half an hour I shall be clear of the bar.

John I—I'll go back in the pilot boat when she leaves the ship outside.

Capt Out of this craft you don't budge.—If this fellow's life is in danger so is every man's life in danger on board this ship, if we go to sea short handed. Remember, you have signed articles with me and aboard this ship you stop. [*Exil* I. 1 E.

John [*Pause; snaps fingers.*] That for my articles. Jane has called me back, and back I'll go. Sure, didn't she write me a letter by telegraph? Now if I had a telegraph to go back on. There goes the anchor. [*Runs to window.*] We're moving. Where's the pilot boat? I see her. Murther, but there's a devil of a sea on—but I've got the tide on my favor. Jane, darlin', I'll come to you.

[*Music p., hurried; business ad lib; goes to window, throws out coat and hat, takes stage to foot lights, runs up, springs though window, disappears.*]

CHANGE SCENE.

SCENE III.—*See all ready behind for court scene. The crown side. Entire depth of stage,* U.C.; *opposite 4th* E. *is an elevated platform with desk in front for presiding judge and two associates, over which is built a canopy, on top of which are the arms of Great Britian; immediately in front of presiding judge, are seated a few associate judges, side by side; long table,* C., *strewn with books, papers, lawyer's brief, writing materials, etc., etc. On extreme* R., *running from first to third entrance obliquely, a railing, behind which, numerous spectators stand; prisoner's dock,* R. H.; *witness stand,* L. C.; *railing on* L., *running obliquely from 2nd to 4th entrance, behind which are seated twelve jurors; entire scene backed by arch, through which is seen a platform elevated about 4½ fc.t, running across from* R. *to* L. *crowded with spectators; eight or ten chairs around table,* C; SIR JOHN FAIRFIELD, *presiding judge and two associates;* JUDGES *dressed in red gowns, ermine capes and white bags; four associate judges in black gowns and white wigs;* SPURRIER, WIGLEY *and*

others; BARRISTERS *dressed the same; all discovered as scene opens.*
JAMES STARKEE *in prisoner's dock,* R. C.; CRANKSHAW *in witness stand;*
SPURRIER L. II. *of table;* WIGLEY R. H. *of table;* MONEY-PENNY L. II. *corner of table;* BARRISTERS *seated at table examining papers;* SPECTATORS,
JURORS, BAILIFF, *etc.* CRIER R. 1 E. *with staff of office; murmurs by
crowd as scene opens.*

Crier Silence in the Court.

Spurrier [*To* CRANKSHAW.] Did you not hear the prisoner say he would
do for Mr. Readley?

Crank Yes, sir; his words were—I'll find you where no policeman can
step in between us.

Spur Do you know a sailor named John Reilly?

Crank I do.

Spur Where did you see him last?

Crank On the day of the murder at Learoyd's. He showed me a pistol
which he said he had taken from the prisoner.

Spur Did he tell you he had taken it from him?

Crank Yes; he said he was afraid Jem Starkee was minded to kill Mr.
Readley.

Jem Johnny never said that.

Spur Silence, prisoner!

Crank I so understood him.

Spur May it please your lordship and gentlemen of the jury, that closes
the case for the crown.   [*Sits.*

Wigley [*Rising.*] At what time did you see the pistol at Noah Learoyd's?

Crank Between seven and eight in the evening.

Wig Don't you know that the prisoner left Manchester about that
time, with a sailor named John Reilly, for Liverpool?

Crank I have heard so.

Judge Is this man Reilly here?

Wig No, my lord, we have used every means to secure his presence,
but to no purpose. Very well, you may stand down.   [CRANKSHAW
retires up stage] Call Jane Learoyd.

Crier Jane Learoyd, come into Court.   [*Murmurs.*

Enter JANE, R. 1 E., *followed by* NOAH. MONEYPENNY *grasps* JANE's *hand
as she ascends witness-box.*

Noah [R. C.] No offense—I come to speak for the people. I only come
for our rights—I've got them writ down on this bit o' paper.

Judge Who is this man? Officer, preserve order.

Money It is the father of the witness, my lord; he is a little crazy.

Judge He must keep quiet or be removed from the Court.
                                    [CRIER *forces* NOAH *in chair,* R. C.

Wig So your name is Jane Learoyd?

Jane Yes, sir.

Wig On the day previous to this fatal occurrence, did not Mr. Readley escape from the hands of the mob and seek refuge in your house?

Jane He did.

Wig Was not the prisoner there at the time?

Jane He was.

Wig Did not the prisoner point out to the mob where they might find him?

Jane No; he helped me to hide him and afterwards helped Mr. Readley to escape.

Wig Helped to hide Mr. Readley and afterwards helped him to escape, and by so doing ran a risk of violence from the hands of the excited populace?

Jane I feared for him.

Wig That is, he risked his own life to save that of the deceased, for whose murder he is now accused?

Jane It is true, sir.

Wig Did not John Reilly tell you he had the pistol from the prisoner because he had threatened Mr. Readley?

Jane No, sir; he said he was afraid Jem was agoin' to take his own life with it.

Wig Out of love for you, I suppose?

Jane Yes, sir.   [WIGLEY *sits.*

Spur [*Rising.*] The prisoner is a sweetheart of yours, eh?

Jane Yes, sir.

Spur And Mr. Readley was another admirer?

Jane He said so, sir.

Spur [*To* CRIER.] Hand the paper to the witness. [CRIER *hands paper to* JANE.] Is that your hand writing?

Jane Yes, sir.

Spur Read it.

Jane [*Reads.*] Dear Jem—come and see me.

Spur Did you not write it to the prisoner?

Jane I wrote it, but never sent it.

Spur You said the prisoner was about to do himself a mischief. Now, was that out of jealousy?

Jane I can not tell.

Spur On your oath, girl—on your oath—did you not drive the prisoner to despair by your heartless conduct?

Jane Yes, I did.

Spur Now, of your two lovers, which do you prefer?   [*Sits.*

Jane You—you ax me which I like best? Well, sirs, I'll answer ye's as I did poor Mr. Readley, in the lane. I have been giddy and vain, for you see, sir, mother died when I was bare thirteen, afore I well knew right from wrong—ah, sir, a mother is a pitiful loss to a girl—so, when my master showed a liking for me, I put aside for him the lad who courted me ever since I was a child, but I had scarce been cruel when my heart smote me back and rose up against me, and then I knew—I knew—

Jem Oh, Jane!

Jane —I knew I loved but one, and that one I have brought to shame this day, and maybe to death. Forgive me, Jem, forgive me!

Jem Forgive thee, lass? Thy words have taken away sorrow and my sufferings. Bless thee—bless thee! [*Murmurs.*

Crier Silence in the Court.

Judge [*To* JURY.] Gentlemen, you have heard the evidence. The prisoner and the deceased were rivals. It has been shown that an altercation with violence had occurred between them. The same night the prisoner buys the pistol produced. The girl, having rejected his favors, grants Mr. Readley an assignation. Here we have the motive followed by facts in consistent sequence—nothing is denied. The defense is, the prisoner could not have committed this crime, for he was, at the moment, near Eccles, in company with a sailor man named John Reilly. It is for you to weigh the facts, giving the prisoner full benefits of your doubts if you have any.

Foreman [*After consulting* JURY *rises.*] My lord, we have none.

[*Murmurs.*

Judge Officer, preserve order.

Money [*To* WIGLEY.] The absence of Reilly is fatal—the man will be hung. [JURY *still consulting.*

Jane [*To* MONEYPENNY.] Why do they speak together?

Money Maybe to recommend him to mercy.

Crier Silence in the Court!

Judge There, how say you—guilty, or not guilty? [*Murmurs.*

Crier Silence in the Court, for the gentlemen of the jury to declare their verdict!

Johnny [*Outside,* R. 1 E.] Let me in; don't stop me, I say.

[*Commotion outside.*

Jane 'Tis he—'tis Johnny! [REILLY *rushes in,* R. 1 E.

John Where is he? am I too late? [*Presses* JEM's *hand.*] Here I am; long life to ye; never fear. [*Murmurs.*

Crier Silence in the Court!

Judge Who is this man?

Wigley My lord, this is the missing witness. This, my lord, is John Reilly.

Judge Let him get in the box.

John I will, sir. [*Tries to climb in prisoner's box; is stopped by* CRIER. All right; anywhere you like. [CRIER *conducts him to witness-stand, and motions him to hold up his right hand.*

Reilly Never fear, Jane; I'll swear him off

Wigley Did you walk to Liverpool?

John Every mile of the way.

Wigley Where were you at nine o'clock?

John At Fox Hill.

Wigley At nine o'clock he was at Fox Hill, my lord. Were you alone?

John No; Jem Starkee, there, was wid me.

Wigley That you swear?

John Och, man alive, what has brought me back from aboard my ship? Did n't the Captain want to kape me afther I got Jane's letter to come back? But I took to the wather, and was picked up by the pilot boat, that put me ashore at Southport. On regards of the winds being contrary, I made across to the railroad, where I found they would n't take me, bekase I had no money, until I found a stoker who knew Jane, and he took me to Wiggan, and from there I ran all the way here. Do ye think I've done all that to tell a lie?

Judge 'Tis for you, gentlemen, to consider what weight is to be attached to the evidence.

Foreman Not Guilty! [JEM STARKEE *descends from dock.* JANE *rushes into his arms.* MONEYPENNY *turns and grasps* REILLY *by the hand. Loud shouts by the crowd. Lively music.*

CURTAIN.

Illustrations

Mary and her father.
Randolph Caldecott, illustrator; E. Evans, engraver.
Frontispiece from Elizabeth Gaskell, *Mary Barton and Other Tales* (London: Smith & Elder, 1881).

" 'Child, we must be all to one another, now she is gone.' "
Chris Hammond, illustrator. Elizabeth Gaskell, *Cranford* and *Mary Barton*
(London: Gresham, 1899).

" 'You won't even say you'll try and like me; will you, Mary?" '
Chris Hammond, illustrator. Elizabeth Gaskell, *Cranford* and *Mary Barton*
(London: Gresham, 1899).

"Ben bustled about with the square bottle of Golden Wasser in one of his hands and a small tumbler in the other."
Chris Hammond, illustrator. Elizabeth Gaskell, *Cranford* and *Mary Barton* (London: Gresham, 1899).

"The door opened and in bounded Amy."
Ivor Symes, illustrator. Elizabeth Gaskell, *Mary Barton*
(London & Glasgow: Collins' Clear-type Press, no date,
c. 1905).

"An old-fashioned saying about a pair of gloves came into Jem's mind."
Ivor Symes, illustrator. Elizabeth Gaskell, *Mary Barton*
(London & Glasgow: Collins' Clear-type Press, no date, c. 1905).

" 'It's Jem Wilson and his father.' "
Ivor Symes, illustrator. Elizabeth Gaskell, *Mary Barton*
(London & Glasgow: Collins' Clear-type Press, no date, c. 1905).

"An instant afterwards he lay stretched in the muddy road."
Ivor Symes, illustrator. Elizabeth Gaskell, *Mary Barton*
(London & Glasgow: Collins' Clear-type Press, no date, c. 1905).

"'O lad, hunger is nothing—nothing!'"
Ivor Symes, illustrator. Elizabeth Gaskell, *Mary Barton*
(London & Glasgow: Collins' Clear-type Press, no date, c. 1905).

" 'What do you want?' she asked wearily."
Ivor Symes, illustrator. Elizabeth Gaskell, *Mary Barton*
(London & Glasgow: Collins' Clear-type Press, no date, c. 1905).

"'O Jem! Take me home.'"
Ivor Symes, illustrator. Elizabeth Gaskell, *Mary Barton*
(London & Glasgow: Collins' Clear-type Press, no date, c. 1905).

"'Oh, Mother! Mother, are you really dead?'"
Illustration. Elizabeth Gaskell, *Mary Barton*
(London & Felling-on-Tyne: Walter Scott, no date, c. 1900).

Mary Barton
Frontispiece. C. M. Relyea, illustrator. Elizabeth Gaskell, *Mary Barton*.
English Comedie Humaine Home Library (New York: Century, 1907).

" 'I'm come to say good-bye.' "
C. M. Relyea, illustrator. Elizabeth Gaskell, *Mary Barton*.
English Comedie Humaine Home Library (New York: Century, 1907).

"There sat her father still and motionless."
C. M. Relyea, illustrator. Elizabeth Gaskell, *Mary Barton*.
English Comedie Humaine Home Library (New York: Century, 1907).

CRITICISM

KATHLEEN TILLOTSON

["The Gentle Humanities of Earth"]†

More is contributed to the unity of the novel by what is indicated in its sub-title—'a tale of Manchester life'. It is the diversity and density of Manchester life, and the figure of John Barton rising craglike above it, that is built up before our eyes in the slow-moving expository opening chapters. They needed to be slow, because of the novelty of the material; they needed also to be reassuring.[1] The author had to enlist the reader's sympathy for her hero; she could not abruptly introduce him as a Trades Union man, a Chartist, an advocate and perpetrator of violence; and it would indeed be foreign to her purpose, which is not to demand approval or condemnation, but interest and understanding. With instinctive craftiness, she does not at once demand sympathy for hardship, but gently engages the reader's participation in a simple family outing to Greenheys Fields and a north-country high tea in a basement kitchen.[2] The contrasts are so far unsensational; but there is light and shade—the back-to-back houses with their open drains, the firelit glow of the interior and the clever contrivances of small-scale housekeeping; the ripples of domestic gossip meeting sudden conversational rocks, and making us aware of such past events as little Tom's death and Esther's disappearance. John Barton's outburst, rooted in its context in the first chapter, gives out the theme and forecasts his relation to it:

> 'Thou never could abide the gentlefolk', said Wilson, half amused at his friend's vehemence.
> 'And what good have they ever done me that I should like them?' asked Barton, the latent fire lighting up his eye. . . . 'Don't think to come over me with the old tale, that the rich know nothing of the trials of the poor. I say, if they don't know, they ought to know. We are their slaves as long as we can work; we pile up their fortunes with the sweat of our brows; and yet we are to live as separate as if we were in two worlds. . . . [3]

---

† From *Novels of the Eighteen-Forties* (Oxford: Oxford University Press, 1956), pp. 214–23. By permission of Edmund Tillotson.
1. 'Our readers need not be alarmed at the prospect of penetrating the recesses of Manchester. The king's daughter, washing the linen of the Phæacian palace, is scarcely more unsuggestive of anything like vulgarity, than are these descriptions' (*North British Review*, August 1951, p. 426).
2. Ch. ii; 'A Manchester tea-party' is the title in the collected edition.
3. Ch. i.

Precarious present happiness, shadowed by past and future, is the 'note' of the opening chapters. But, though precarious, it yet recurs and persists, not for all characters, but as an uncovenanted hope; throughout the tribulations of the narrative, we are kept aware of another world than Manchester, another world than the two worlds of rich and poor. Its light falls on Greenheys Fields, on the recollected Cumberland childhood of old Alice (a fully substantiated 'poor Susan'),[4] on a chance-met child's face in the street, the blind girl's singing, Job Legh's absorption in his collection of insects, Mary's desperate courage at the trial, her face haunting an onlooker like 'some wild sad melody, heard in childhood'. Its broader radiance is perhaps best seen in a passage which may at first sight seem an excrescence, an interlude; in the chapter later called 'Barton's London experiences'.[5] John Barton has returned from London, and tells Mary, Job, and Margaret the story of the Chartists' march through the West End with their petition, in ironic juxtaposition to the carriage procession for the Queen's drawing-room. The actual rejection of the petition is too bad to be spoken of:

> 'I canna tell of our down-casting just as a piece of London news. As long as I live, our rejection that day will bide in my heart; and as long as I live I shall curse them as so cruelly refused to hear us; but I'll not speak of it no more.'
>
> So, daunted in their inquiries, they sat silent for a few minutes.

The social point has been made (the description of the march is full of bitter detail) and there a propagandist might stop. But equally a part of Mrs. Gaskell's world view are 'the gentle humanities of earth'. From them springs the transition:

> Old Job, however, felt that someone must speak, else all the good they had done in dispelling John Barton's gloom was lost. So after a while he thought of a subject, neither sufficiently dissonant from the last to jar on the full heart, nor too much the same to cherish the continuance of the gloomy train of thought.
>
> 'Did you ever hear tell,' said he to Mary, 'that I were in London once?'

There follows the story of how many years ago he planned a Whitsuntide visit to his married daughter in London, only to hear from her father-in-law that both she and her husband were stricken with fever. The two men had gone to London together, to find daughter and son dead, leaving a young infant; then he tells at length, in garrulous yet reticent Lancashire style, of their journey north with the child, and all their

---

4. William Wordsworth's "The Reverie of Poor Susan." [*Editor*].
5. Ch. ix.

bewildered expedients. Falling into that context, this narrative, with its basis of hardship, the implicit tenderness of the two men's purpose, and the comic awkwardness of the situation, is more than a temporary relief to gloom. There is no simple contrast; Job Legh's experience shares the common ground of poverty with John Barton's grievances, but its unembittered tone supplies an unconscious corrective, a suggestion of values beyond the frustrations of political action. And because it is something past and safely lived through, it stands for hope.

That funeral cost a mint o' money, but Jennings and I wished to do th' thing decent. Then we'd the stout little babby to bring home. We'd not overmuch money left; but it were fine weather, and we thought we'd take th' coach to Brummagem, and walk on. It were a bright May morning when I last saw London town, looking back from a big hill a mile or two off. And in that big mass o' a place I were leaving my blessed child asleep—in her last sleep. Well, God's will be done! She's gotten to Heaven afore me; but I shall get there at last, please God, though it's a long while first.

The babby had been fed afore we set out, and th' coach moving kept it asleep, bless its little heart. But when th' coach stopped for dinner it were awake, and crying for its pobbies. So we asked for some bread and milk, and Jennings took it first for to feed it; but it made its mouth like a square, and let it run out at each o' the four corners. 'Shake it, Jennings', says I; 'that's the way they make water run through a funnel, when it's o'er full; and a child's mouth is broad end of the funnel, and th' gullet th' narrow one.' So he shook it, but it only cried th' more. 'Let me have it', says I, thinking he were an awkward oud chap. But it were just as bad wi' me. . . . Well, poor babby cried without stopping to take breath, fra' that time till we got to Brummagem for the night [a chambermaid feeds and quiets the child]. It looked so quiet and smiling, like, as it lay in her arms, that we thought 'twould be no trouble to have it wi' us. I says 'See, Jennings, how women folk do quieten babbies; it's just as I said.' He looked grave; he were always thoughtful-looking, though I never heard him say anything very deep. At last says he—'Young woman! have you gotten a spare nightcap? . . . Th' babby seems to have taken a mind to yo', and may be in th' dark it might take me for yo if I'd getten your nightcap on. . . .' Such a night as we had on it! Babby began to scream o' th' oud fashion, and we took it turn and turn about to sit up and rock it. My heart were very sore for the little one, as it groped about wi' its mouth; but for a' that I could scarce keep fra' smiling at th' thought of us two oud chaps, th' one wi' a woman's nightcap on, sitting on our hinder ends for half the night, hushabying a babby as wouldn't be hushabied.

They tramp through another day and night, and next day are helped by a cottage woman who has lost her own child.

> 'Last look I had o' that woman she were quietly wiping her eyes wi' the corner of her apron, as she went about her husband's breakfast. But I shall know her in heaven.'

He stopped to think of that long-ago May morning, when he had carried his grand-daughter under the distant hedgerows and beneath the flowering sycamores.

> 'There's nought more to say, wench,' said he to Margaret, as she begged him to go on. 'That night we reached Manchester, and I'd found out that Jennings would be glad enough to give up babby to me, so I took her home at once, and a blessing she's been to me.'

The return to the present, to the grown granddaughter, and John Barton with his daughter asleep at his knee, is unstressed; no moral is drawn; it is the reader, rather than John Barton, who is effectively reminded of 'the gentle humanities'. In the next chapter, the present closes over him; its opening words are 'Despair settled down like a heavy cloud'. As a Chartist delegate and Trades Union man, he can find no work; his rooms are stripped to buy food:

> He would bear it all, he said to himself. And he did bear it, but not meekly; that was too much to expect.[6]

The ninth chapter points the significance of Job Legh, who is more than a minor character; he is the point of rest in the narrative, and in the theme, the embodiment of 'the gentle humanities of earth' and of the practical possibilities of the Christian ethic. Almost inactive in events until then, it is thus appropriate that it should be he who appeals for Mr. Carson's forgiveness, he who presses home the social and spiritual lesson after John Barton's death: 'I'm clear about this, when God gives a blessing to be enjoyed, He gives it with a duty to be done; and the duty of the happy is to help the suffering to bear their woe.'

A novelist of narrower purpose might have didactically emphasized the difference between Job Legh and John Barton. But Mrs. Gaskell holds the balance fairly between John Barton's bitter protest and Job Legh's acceptance of his lot; resignation to the power of the masters and to the divine will are not confused. The lesson that Job Legh presses home is that of John Barton's terrible act, without which Mr. Carson's eyes could not have been opened, and for which the masters must share the responsibility. Even by Job, John Barton's failure as a Christian is almost extenuated:

6. Ch. x.

'You see he were sadly put about to make great riches and great poverty square with Christ's Gospel. . . . For he was a loving man before he grew mad with seeing such as he was slighted, as if Christ himself had not been poor',[7]

whereas Mr. Carson's failure provokes the severest of the author's rare comments:

Oh! Orestes! you would have made a very tolerable Christian of the nineteenth century![8]

She makes no equivalent condemnation of the murder; and Job's summing up emphasizes the chain of cause and effect:

'The masters has it on their own conscience,—you have it on yours, sir, to answer for to God whether you've done, and are doing all in your power to lighten the evils, that seem always to hang on the trades by which you make your fortunes. . . . John Barton took the question in hand, and his answer to it was NO! Then he grew bitter and angry, and mad; and in his madness he did a great sin, and wrought a great woe; and repented him with tears as of blood, and will go through his penance humbly and meekly in t'other place, I'll be bound. . . .'[9]

§5

These two men, John Barton and Job Legh, may perhaps stand not only for different yet related aspects of 'Manchester life', different responses to life's hardships, but for the defiant courage and persistent loving-kindness that are seen now colliding, now cooperating, in all Mrs. Gaskell's novels. Courage to give utterance to unfamiliar points of view—that of the workman driven to violence; of the stern self-made factory-owner; of the seduced girl and the parson who protects her;[1] but always with the purpose, unconscious perhaps, of promoting sympathy, not sharpening antagonisms; between regions, classes, sexes, generations; on the quiet assumption that to know is to understand, to forgive, and even to respect.

Not even George Eliot shows such reverence for average human nature as Mrs. Gaskell; and this is evident from her earliest work. It helped to teach her the art which her later novels perfected; helped to guide her instinctive tact in avoiding the overemphases of sentimentality and sensationalism, even in situations that tempt towards them. For she accepts, and not ruefully, the ordinariness of people

---

7. Ch. xxxvii.
8. Ch. xviii.
9. Ch. xxxvii.
1. A reference to Gaskell's 1853 novel *Ruth*. [*Editor*].

and the dailiness of life. Already in her first novel the minor characters (such as the boy Charley, Mrs. Wilson, Sally Leadbitter) are solid
and distinct; each character, however small, has its scale of moral values, and its social medium; all are closely associated with the domestic detail of their surroundings. (Her explicit descriptions are mainly
of what people use or make themselves at home in.) This unheight-
ened truthfulness establishes confidence, so that we are ready to
accept her 'big scenes'—the chase down the Mersey, the murder trial;
like the bank failure in *Cranford*, they seem simply emergencies
which must occasionally arise in ordinary life and which test character. And more: this almost pedestrian truthfulness is already accompanied by something spacious: her common flowers of human nature
are rooted in earth, but over them arches 'the divine blue of the
summer sky'.[2]

It would be better then to remove from *Mary Barton* the old tag of
'novel with a purpose', implying social, extra-artistic purpose. It was
indeed, more perhaps than any other of the time, a novel with a social
effect; but Mrs. Gaskell wrote, then as always, not with her eye on the
effect, but as one possessed with and drenched in her subject:

> I *can* not (it is not *will* not) write at all if I ever think of my
> readers, and what impression I am making on them. 'If they
> don't like me, they must lump me', to use a Lancashire proverb.
> It is from no despising my readers. I am sure I don't do that, but
> if I ever let the thought or consciousness of them come
> between me and my subject I *could* not write at all.[3]

RAYMOND WILLIAMS

[Structure of Feeling in *Mary Barton*]†

Mary Barton, particularly in its early chapters, is the most moving
response in literature to the industrial suffering of the 1840s. The
really impressive thing about the book is the intensity of the effort
to record, in its own terms, the feel of everyday life in the working-
class homes. The method, in part, is that of documentary record, as
may be seen in such details as the carefully annotated reproduction
of dialect, the carefully included details of food prices in the account
of the tea-party, the itemized description of the furniture of the Bar-

---

2. Henry James, speaking not of this quality but of the completeness of the world in *Wives
   and Daughters* (review, 1866; [Henry James], *Notes and Reviews* [Cambridge: Dunster
   House Press], 1921, p. 154).
3. [Jane Whitehill, ed.], *Letters of Mrs. Gaskell to Charles Eliot Norton* ([London: Oxford UP],
   1932), p. 20 (letter of 1858).
† From *Culture and Society 1780–1950* by Raymond Williams, published by Chatto and
   Windus. Reprinted by permission of The Random House Group Ltd.

tons' living-room, and the writing-out of the ballad (again annotated) of *The Oldham Weaver*. The interest of this record is considerable, but the method has, nevertheless, a slightly distancing effect. Mrs Gaskell could hardly help coming to this life as an observer, a reporter, and we are always to some extent conscious of this. But there is genuine imaginative re-creation in her accounts of the walk in Green Heys Fields, and of tea at the Bartons' house, and again, notably, in the chapter *Poverty and Death* where John Barton and his friend find the starving family in the cellar. For so convincing a creation of the characteristic feelings and responses of families of this kind (matters more determining than the material details on which the reporter is apt to concentrate) the English novel had to wait, indeed, for the early writing of D. H. Lawrence. If Mrs Gaskell never quite manages the sense of full participation which would finally authenticate this, she yet brings to these scenes an intuitive recognition of feelings which has its own sufficient conviction. The chapter *Old Alice's History* brilliantly dramatizes the situation of that early generation brought from the villages and the countryside to the streets and cellars of the industrial, vividly embodies that other kind of response to an urban industrial environment: the devoted, lifelong study of living creatures—a piece of amateur scientific work, and at the same time an instinct for living creatures which hardens, by its very contrast with its environment, into a kind of crankiness. In the factory workers walking out in spring into Green Heys Fields; in Alice Wilson, remembering in her cellar the ling-gathering for besoms in the native village that she will never again see; in Job Legh, intent on his impaled insects—these early chapters embody the characteristic response of a generation to the new and crushing experience of industrialism. The other early chapters movingly embody the continuity and development of the sympathy and cooperative instinct which were already establishing a main working-class tradition.

The structure of feeling from which *Mary Barton* begins is, then, a combination of sympathetic observation and of a largely successful attempt at imaginative identification. If it had continued in this way, it might have been a great novel of its kind. But the emphasis of the method changes, and there are several reasons for this. One reason can be studied in a curious aspect of the history of the writing of the book. It was originally to be called *John Barton*. As Mrs Gaskell wrote later:

> Round the character of John Barton all the others formed themselves; he was my hero, *the* person with whom all my sympathies went.[1]

1. A. B. Hopkins, *Elizabeth Gaskell: Her Life and Work* (1952), p. 77.

And she added:

> The character, and some of the speeches, are exactly a poor
> man I know.[2]

The change of emphasis which the book subsequently underwent,
and the consequent change of title to *Mary Barton*, seem to have
been made at the instance of her publishers, Chapman and Hall. The
details of this matter are still obscure, but we must evidently allow
something for this external influence on the shape of the novel. Certainly the John Barton of the later parts of the book is a very shadowy
figure. In committing the murder, he seems to put himself not only
beyond the range of Mrs Gaskell's sympathy (which is understandable), but, more essentially, beyond the range of her powers. The
agony of conscience is there, as a thing told and sketched, but, as the
crisis of 'my hero; *the* person with whom all my sympathies went', it
is weak and almost incidental. This is because the novel as published
is centred on the daughter—her indecision between Jem Wilson and
'her gay lover, Harry Carson'; her agony in Wilson's trial; her pursuit
and last-minute rescue of the vital witness; the realization of her love
for Wilson: all this, the familiar and orthodox plot of the Victorian
novel of sentiment, but of little lasting interest. And it now seems
incredible that the novel should ever have been planned in any other
way. If Mrs Gaskell had written 'round the character of Mary Barton
all the others formed themselves', she would have confirmed our
actual impression of the finished book.

Something must be allowed for the influence of her publishers, but
John Barton must always have been cast as the murderer, with the
intention perhaps of showing an essentially good man driven to an
appalling crime by loss, suffering and despair. One can still see the elements of this in the novel as we have it, but there was evidently a point,
in its writing, at which the flow of sympathy with which she began was
arrested, and then, by the change of emphasis which the change of title
records, diverted to the less compromising figure of the daughter. The
point would be less important if it were not characteristic of the structure of feeling within which she was working. It is not only that she
recoils from the violence of the murder, to the extent of being unable
even to enter it as the experience of the man conceived as her hero. It
is also that, as compared with the carefully representative character of
the early chapters, the murder itself is exceptional. It is true that in
1831 a Thomas Ashton, of Pole Bank, Werneth, was murdered under
somewhat similar circumstances, and that the Ashton family appear to
have taken the murder of Carson as referring to this. Mrs Gaskell, dis-
claiming the reference in a letter to them, turned up some similar inci-

2. Ibid.

dents in Glasgow at about the same time. But in fact, taking the period as a whole, the response of political assassination is so uncharacteristic as to be an obvious distortion. The few recorded cases only emphasize this. Even when one adds the cases of intimidation, and the occasional vitriol-throwing during the deliberate breaking of strikes, it remains true, and was at the time a subject of surprised comment by foreign observers, that the characteristic response of the English working people, even in times of grave suffering, was not one of personal violence. Mrs Gaskell was under no obligation to write a representative novel; she might legitimately have taken a special case. But the tone elsewhere is deliberately representative, and she is even, as she says, modelling John Barton on 'a poor man I know'. The real explanation, surely, is that John Barton, a political murderer appointed by a trade union, is a dramatization of the *fear of violence* which was widespread among the upper and middle classes at the time, and which penetrated, as an arresting and controlling factor, even into the deep imaginative sympathy of a Mrs Gaskell. This fear that the working people might take matters into their own hands was widespread and characteristic, and the murder of Harry Carson is an imaginative working-out of this fear, and of reactions to it, rather than any kind of observed and considered experience.

The point is made clearer when it is remembered that Mrs Gaskell planned the murder herself, and chose, for the murderer, 'my hero, *the* person with whom all my sympathies went'. In this respect the act of violence, a sudden aggression against a man contemptuous of the sufferings of the poor, looks very much like a projection, with which, in the end, she was unable to come to terms. The imaginative choice of the act of murder and then the imaginative recoil from it have the effect of ruining the necessary integration of feeling in the whole theme. The diversion to Mary Barton, even allowing for the publishers' influence, must in fact have been welcome.

Few persons felt more deeply than Elizabeth Gaskell the sufferings of the industrial poor. As a minister's wife in Manchester, she actually saw this, and did not, like many other novelists, merely know it by report or occasional visit. Her response to the suffering is deep and genuine, but pity cannot stand alone in such a structure of feeling. It is joined, in *Mary Barton*, by the confusing violence and fear of violence, and is supported, finally, by a kind of writing-off, when the misery of the actual situation can no longer be endured. John Barton dies penitent, and the elder Carson repents of his vengeance and turns, as the sympathetic observer wanted the employers to turn, to efforts at improvement and mutual understanding. This was the characteristic humanitarian conclusion, and it must certainly be respected. But it was not enough, we notice, for the persons with whom Mrs Gaskell's sympathies were engaged. Mary Barton, Jem

Wilson, Mrs Wilson, Margaret, Will, Job Legh—all the objects of her
real sympathy—end the book far removed from the situation which
she had set out to examine. All are going to Canada; there could be
no more devastating conclusion. A solution within the actual situation might be hoped for, but the solution with which the heart went
was a cancelling of the actual difficulties and the removal of the persons pitied to the uncompromised New World.

RICHARD D. ALTICK

Dion Boucicault Stages *Mary Barton*†

At a London dinner party given in 1866 by the dramatist and actor
Dion Boucicault, the guests debated whether "the literary element in
a drama was rather an impediment than an assistance to popular success." Boucicault at once proposed to settle the question by writing
three new plays: "one a society drama, relying primarily on its literary treatment; the second a domestic drama, and the third a sensation drama. The pieces," he told his friends, "shall be produced at the
same time, and I guarantee that the success of each shall be in the
inverse ratio of its merits."[1] To anyone but Boucicault, this would
have seemed a large order, but he dispatched it with the casual ease
that made him the most prolific workman in the Victorian theatre.
The three plays—*Hunted Down* (the society drama), *The Long Strike*
(the domestic drama), and *Flying Scud* (the sensation piece)—were
duly produced in the autumn of the same year, and the results,
Boucicault wrote, were precisely what he had foretold. *Flying Scud*
was the most successful of the three.

Or so Boucicault maintained twenty-three years later. But the so-
called "domestic" member of the trio, *The Long Strike,* which actually had as high a voltage of sensationalism as *Flying Scud,* was at
least as successful. Whatever its strictly literary merits, of its theatrical effectiveness there was never any doubt. Charles Fechter, the producer, in addition to having his friend Charles Dickens on hand,
according to custom, at important rehearsals, sent him Boucicault's
script for criticism, and Dickens hastened to reassure the author on
one or two points of which he was doubtful. The dialogue, he wrote,
was "exactly what is wanted"; and the lack of a specific comic element
was not to be regretted, since the role of the Irish sailor, Johnny

† From *Nineteenth-Century Fiction,* 14.2 (1959): 129–41. One of the author's footnotes has
   been deleted. Richard D. Altick, author of *The Scholar Adventurers* and *The English Common Reader,* is professor of English, Ohio State University.
1. Boucicault, "Leaves from a Dramatist's Diary," *North American Review,* CXLIX (1889), 234.

Reilly, provided adequate contrast to the other main parts. "The play," Dickens continued, "is done with a master's hand. Its closeness and movement are quite surprising. Its construction is admirable. I have the strongest belief in its making a great success."[2] The London production, which opened at the Royal Lyceum on September 15, 1866, with Boucicault himself in the role of Johnny Reilly and his wife as the heroine, Jane Learoyd, was a hit. The electrifying "telegraph scene" immediately became a classic of Victorian melodrama and was responsible in large part for the play's remaining in the popular repertory for at least two decades. Produced in New York six weeks later, *The Long Strike* was revived on the American stage time after time.[3] Its American success was due not only to the telegraph scene, which sometimes was performed separately on variety bills, but to J. H. Stoddart's popularity in the character part of the lawyer, Moneypenny, which he played over two hundred times.

Like virtually all of Boucicault's plays (and according to at least one stage historian,[4] he had a hand in over four hundred), *The Long Strike* was adapted from an already existing work. * * *

The inspiration for *The Long Strike* was Mrs. Gaskell's *Mary Barton,* published eighteen years earlier.[5] To compare Boucicault's dramatic version with the novel offers an instructive glimpse of the ways of the Victorian stage-adapter. And more: it shows how the same materials had different values for the novelist and the playwright, and therefore were treated by them in different ways; and by observing what Boucicault took over from Mrs. Gaskell and what he rejected, it is possible to see the novel with freshly perceptive eyes—the eyes not of the literary critic but of the shrewd practical dramatist. What, then, appealed to Boucicault in *Mary Barton,* and how did he transform a novel of social criticism into a highly successful stage melodrama?

Boucicault threw overboard the first ten chapters, or about one-third of the novel. In Mrs. Gaskell's version, the essential story thenceforward is this:

> Mary Barton, a Manchester milliner's girl, rejects the proposal of marriage made her by Jem Wilson, an ambitious factory mechanic and inventor. Having done so, however, she realizes she prefers him to her other suitor, Harry Carson, son of a wealthy millowner. She therefore decides to break with Carson and wait for Jem to ask her again. Several days later she

2. *Letters* ([London], Nonesuch edition, [1938]), III, 482–483.
3. See, for example, the record of performances in New York City alone, 1866–1892, in George C. D. Odell, *Annals of the New York Stage,* VIII–XV.
4. Laurence Hutton, *Plays and Players* (New York, 1875), p. 208.
5. In various playbills that have been preserved, *The Long Strike* is said to be "based on *Mary Barton* and *Lizzie Leigh.*" So far as I can see, the only thing Mrs. Gaskell's story *Lizzie Leigh* and *The Long Strike* have in common is their Manchester setting.

meets Carson in the street and tells him she has changed her mind. He counters by offering her the marriage which, it develops, he had not provided for in his original plans for her. She turns him down, but he persists.

Jem confronts Carson and demands what his true intentions are toward Mary: "Do you mean fair by Mary, or not?" Carson strikes Jem with his cane, Jem knocks him down, and a policeman intervenes. But Carson will not prosecute Jem, who, in the policeman's presence, breathes dire threats against him, "if you dare to injure her in the least."

Meanwhile a strike is in progress. The workmen and millowners meet, and the latter's final offer, a raise of a shilling a week, is refused. In retaliation, the owners decide on a lockout. That evening the workers meet in a public house; Mary's father, John Barton, a Chartist and union leader, makes a speech enumerating the workers' grievances, and a "deadly plan" is agreed upon. Lots are drawn for the role of assassin. His identity is not divulged.

Two days later Will Wilson, a relative of Jem, bids farewell to Mary, as he is about to rejoin his ship at Liverpool. Following this, John Barton, restless and haggard, says goodbye to Mary; supposedly he is on his way to Glasgow, to try to win other unions' support for the strike. The same night, Harry Carson is brought home dead—shot in the street by an unknown assailant—and his father vows revenge. Jem Wilson is arrested on the strength of his scuffle with Carson and his mother's identification, to a disguised detective, of the gun found at the murder scene.

Mary Barton's Aunt Esther happens upon another clue at the scene: the scrap of paper that had been used for gun wadding. It is the corner of a valentine that Jem had sent Mary, on which she had copied some lines of Samuel Bamford's poetry and which she had subsequently given to her father. Shown this paper, Mary realizes that her father must be the murderer. At the risk of exposing John Barton's guilt, she sets out at once to find an alibi for Jem and recalls that he had said he was going to walk with Will Wilson to Liverpool. The problem is, Can Will, who alone can prove Jem's whereabouts at the time of the murder, be located before he sails?

Mary finds Will's lodgings in Liverpool, but he has sailed that morning. His landlady's son takes her to the waterfront, and they hire a boat to overtake Will's ship. The captain refuses to stop, but Will, on deck, overhears the exchange between the captain and the pursuers, and promises to return. Now the question becomes, Will he manage to get back in time? Mary collapses and is cared for by her boatman and his wife.

At the trial, all the circumstantial evidence is against Jem.

On the stand Mary publicly protests her single-minded devotion to him. Just in the nick of time, Will arrives in the courtroom with the crucial alibi. Mary is borne, "stiff and convulsed," out of court. The jury acquits Jem.

In the remaining six chapters, Mary recovers from her critical illness to be reunited with Jem. John Barton confesses the murder to Harry Carson's father, who determines to send the police, but who, after spending the whole night over his Bible, returns to Barton's rooms to forgive him just as Barton dies. Mary and Jem marry and emigrate to Canada.

Now, what did Boucicault do with all this? The plot of the play as first performed in 1866 runs as follows:

The strikers turn down the employers' offer and are thereupon locked out of the factories (Act I, scene I). Richard Radley (= a combination of the two Carsons of the novel) is the most adamant of the masters, prevailing over the more moderate faction. (Act I, scene 2) Jem Starkie (= Jem Wilson) and Jane Learoyd (= Mary Barton) meet; and, impulsively, she tells him she never cared for him. She then meets Radley, and, while Jem overhears them, makes an appointment with him for the following night. There is a violent encounter between Jem and Radley, broken up by a policeman (Crankshaw) (Act I, scene 3). The millhands meet at Noah Learoyd's (= John Barton's) house, with a London organizer present; aroused, they go out to break windows at Radley's mill. Jem and Jane talk; she turns down his plea to marry him, because her heart belongs to Radley. Radley bursts in, having been attacked by the workingmen's mob outside. Jane hides him in another room, and Jem, out of love for her, goes to decoy the crowd away. Noah and the union delegates return, to plan a series of nightly factory-burnings, beginning with Radley's. They draw lots and Noah gets the first assignment. Jem having returned to report the coast is clear, Jane spirits Radley out of the house.

The next day Johnny Reilly (=Will Wilson) comes to say goodbye to Jane, with whom he too is in love (Act II, scene I). He produces a pistol and bullets which he found on the table before his roommate, Jem Starkie, the night before; Jem, he says, was bent on suicide. Crankshaw the policeman enters, looking for Noah. He sees the gun, which he learns from Johnny is Jem's, and a note Jane had written, but then thrown on the floor, asking Jem to come to see her. Crankshaw tells Noah that Radley has informed the magistrates of the workers' arson plot, which he overheard while hiding in this house, but that Radley will not press charges against Noah since it was his daughter who saved him from the mob. Crankshaw advises Noah to leave town; his confederates are in jail. He further tells

Noah of the impending interview between Jane and Radley. Noah, stunned, sees Jem's pistol before him and determines to kill Radley so that he cannot testify against the other workers. He takes for wadding Jane's note to Jem (Act II, scene 2). Jem dissuades the millhands from mobbing the jail to rescue their delegates. Johnny Reilly appears, to urge Jem to stand by Jane and "see that the blackguard she loves treats her well." Jem decides to walk part way to Liverpool with Johnny, and they leave. Jane enters on her way to her tryst with Radley. She has realized she loves Jem, not Radley, and will tell Radley so (Act II, scene 3). Jane meets Radley ("Now this coy little beauty must surrender at discretion. She can scarcely escape the toils she has woven for herself"). She tells him she cannot marry him. (Radley: "Ha ha ha! My wife! My dear girl, I never contemplated imposing matrimony upon you.") He will make a bargain with her: if she will leave the city with him, he will not denounce Noah before the magistrates. She pleads with him; he embraces her and draws her upstage; a shot rings out. He falls. The police take charge.

The police find the damning evidence (Act III, scene I)— Jem's gun, the wadding; and Crankshaw recalls Jem's altercation with Radley. Jem returns to Manchester (Act III, scene 2) to find that the workers, shocked by the murder, have ended the strike. Noah has gone mad; his ravings, which show that he witnessed the meeting between Jane and Radley, prove to Jane and Jem that he was the murderer. Crankshaw enters and arrests Jem, and Noah is only just prevented from blurting out his guilt in the presence of the policeman (Act III, scene 3). After some suspenseful minutes (will or will not the lawyer Moneypenny, who has had a hard day at the office, agree to see Jane, who has been outside his door for seven hours?), Jane is admitted and tells him the situation. Jem's only hope is in Johnny's alibi—but Johnny's ship has sailed. Suddenly Moneypenny (a man of brusque exterior and heart of gold) remembers the telegraph. Exeunt in great excitement.

Evening at the telegraph office (Act IV, scene I). Jane and Moneypenny arrive. There is no hope. Only the main lines are open; those to less important points, including the signal station at the mouth of the Mersey, are closed for the night. Jane faints. Then, inexplicably, the Morse instrument begins to tick, announcing that the line to the signal station is open after all! Johnny's ship is reported to be inside the bar, awaiting the tide. The message is sent, to be relayed by pilot boat (Act IV, scene 2). The scene is the cabin of the ship; the anchor is being weighed. The pilot boat arrives with the message, but the captain will not allow Johnny to return. Johnny jumps through the porthole and swims toward the pilot boat (Act IV, scene 3). The

trial, *Crown* v. *Jem Starkie,* is ending. In the witness box Jane
tells of her love for Jem. The judge charges the jury, which consults without even leaving the room. The verdict of guilty is
about to be rendered when Johnny bursts in, climbs first into
the prisoner's dock (comic relief), and then gives the all-
important evidence. Quick, tumultuous end.[6]

In analyzing the nature of Boucicault's changes as he made a popular novel into a stage success, one is perhaps first struck by the way
in which he dispensed with all characters not essential to the main
plot. In the novel Esther, sister of John Barton's dead wife, is,
unknown to her brother-in-law and niece, a fallen woman, and Mrs.
Gaskell allots to her a full Victorian measure of retribution; but
Boucicault did not need her. Jem Wilson's possessive mother and his
Aunt Alice, a kindly washerwoman who dies at some length in the
novel, were similarly omitted, as were the important characters of
Margaret Legh, a blind ballad singer, and her grandfather Job, a
workingman-naturalist. Nor was there room for Sally Leadbitter,
Mary Barton's co-worker in the milliner's shop, an amoral and
scheming go-between for Mary and Carson. By way of economy, also,
Boucicault merged the Carsons, father and son, into the single character of Richard Radley, who thereby had to bear the double villainy
of being a labor-oppressing millowner and a would-be seducer. The
effect of all this, of course, was to eliminate the variety of emotional
values which Mrs. Gaskell, as a novelist, could afford, but which
Boucicault, intent only upon theatrical effectiveness, could not. The
pity and horror embodied in the furtive person of Esther, whose
ruin—could Mary Barton only know—serves as an awful warning of
what happens to ambitious girls who believe men's promises; the
lesson conveyed by wise Job Legh, that workingmen have warm
human feelings and are even capable of avocations like botanizing;
the character contrasts supplied by Jem's complaining mother and
his more agreeable aunt—these and other themes, by which Mrs.
Gaskell widened the range of her novel's interest and effect, had to
be sacrificed.

In the same fashion, several major episodes in the novel were omitted from the play, not counting the pathetic deaths of numerous
working-class infants and adults. (No Victorian social novel would
have been complete without these, but Mrs. Gaskell's peculiar pre-

---

6. In the 1869 revision, * * * Johnny Reilly's troubles are only beginning when he dives overboard and swims to the pilot boat. Arriving in Liverpool, he has no money to ride on the
passenger train to Manchester, where the trial is taking place. Providentially he encounters a friend, an engine-driver who detaches the engine from his goods train and takes
Johnny aboard for a totally unscheduled run to Manchester. This episode of course has no
warrant in the novel. But in one way the 1869 version is closer to the novel than the earlier one: it restores John Barton's (Noah Learoyd's) deathbed confession, and Radley, who
turns out to have been only wounded by his bullet, forgives him:

occupation with death, which once led Dickens to "wish to Heaven her people would keep a little firmer on their legs," rendered them rather more numerous than was necessary.) The fire at Carson's mill early in the novel, from which Jem rescues his father, and John Barton's trip to London to join the Chartist procession of 1839 were cut out, since they have no bearing on the plot. And whereas Mrs. Gaskell took several chapters to tie up her loose threads after Jem's acquittal, Boucicault brought the story to an abrupt close at that point; he did not even indicate what happens to Noah, the true murderer, who appears, with unbalanced mind, early in the courtroom scene but who is given no chance for confession and/or forgiveness. All that matters is that Jem is acquitted and united with Jane.

Indeed, Boucicault's treatment of Noah (the novel's John Barton) is typical of the way in which the Victorian popular playwright used characters chiefly as the means of advancing the plot and as participants in exciting episodes. Mrs. Gaskell originally intended to name the novel after John Barton rather than after his daughter, because the theme of the book—the injustices of the industrial system—is most notably exemplified in the tragic deterioration of his character and body. It is his fate, not his daughter's, that illustrates the point Mrs. Gaskell wanted to make. But Boucicault would have none of this. Instead of showing Barton's gradual degeneration, under the stress of cruel events, from intelligent, embittered working-class leader to shattered old man, as Mrs. Gaskell did, Boucicault transformed him suddenly (Act III, scene 2) and without any attempt to make this personal catastrophe believable or significant. The long speeches and detailed descriptions lavished upon John Barton in the novel had no counterpart in the play; he became simply an agent of the plot, which now centered in his daughter. And Mary was herself simplified in the course of transfer from novel to stage. As portrayed by Mrs. Gaskell, much of her interest resides in the strength and poignancy of her ambivalent feelings toward Jem (a member of her own class, and therefore, according to the logic governing such matters in Victorian fiction, the man she should marry) and Carson (whose attentions flatter her Cinderella-like yearnings for leisure and luxury). While the bare circumstance of Mary's conflict was retained in the play, Boucicault, by failing to explain her encouragement of Carson in terms of a poor girl's natural desire for a fuller life, reduced a serious moral issue to hardly more than a frivolous dilemma on the part of a light-witted girl.[7]

The subordination of John Barton to his daughter was part of

7. In one respect, however, Boucicault added to, rather than simplified, Mrs. Gaskell's characterization. For the sake of making his own acting role more appealing, he portrayed Johnny Reilly as being in love with Jane but cheerfully renouncing his suit in favor of Jem. In the novel his counterpart, Will Wilson, loves, and eventually marries, Margaret Legh.

Boucicault's total reorientation of the novel as he adapted it for the theatre. Mrs. Gaskell's purpose was only secondarily to tell an interesting and, on occasion, exciting story. Her dominant concern was to convey her message of social protest, and at many points in the novel the action stops while the characters, or sometimes the novelist herself, discuss the relationships between employers and workers and the pros and cons of industrialism generally. As in many other Victorian novels of ideas, in *Mary Barton* the thesis and the story get in each other's way. Boucicault, who had no social conscience to speak of, and who knew that his audiences, if they had any, left it at the door as they entered the theatre, threw out the didactic content of the novel without a qualm. (In an earlier, even more successful play, *The Octoroon* [1859], he had succeeded in treating the incendiary question of slavery so neutrally that neither side took offense.) In *The Long Strike*, the antagonism between millowners and workmen serves only as a convenient trigger for the plot. Admittedly, sympathy for the strikers is generated in the first act by the stubbornness of the employers, but as soon as the Jane-Jem-Radley triangle is established, with the ensuing murder, the strikers go back to work and we hear no more about such dull sociological subjects. *The Long Strike* could not possibly be viewed as a *pièce à thèse;* it is melodrama, pure and simple.[8]

Obviously it was the melodramatic character of Mrs. Gaskell's plot, at least in the latter two-thirds of the novel, which induced Boucicault to borrow it. And it is here that it is most instructive to watch the stage-adapter at work. The most striking change was in the new way the murder of Radley was brought about. In the novel, the murder is the simple, direct outcome of the striking workers' decision. John Barton is delegated to kill young Carson for the sake of injuring his employer-father; Barton does not even know that Mary and Carson have been meeting, and Mary in fact has no connection with the murder. Boucicault, however, arranged for the murder in a way which, though more complicated and roundabout, is theatrically far more effective. He began with an original invention, the hiding of the mob-endangered Radley in Noah's house. This allowed Radley to gain a moral advantage over Jane as a consequence of his overhearing the workers' conspiracy. At the same time, it made the role of Jem Starkie more sympathetic, giving him the opportunity for self-sacrifice by magnanimously protecting his hated rival for Jane's love. The murder itself is not the result of a workers' plot; the conspiracy

8. To assist this dissociation of the play from "controversial" issues, as well as simply to make it more timely, Boucicault moved the story from 1839–1842 to the very recent past, in fact the year prior to the play's first performance. In Moneypenny's newspaper the "latest from America" is "Negotiations for peace. Fall in the rate of discount." And Mrs. Gaskell's symbolic use of a bit of Samuel Bamford's proletarian verse for gun wadding was too much for Boucicault; he substituted a mere one-sentence note from Jane to Jem.

Radley overhears involves only arson. Hence the motivation of the murder becomes more complex: Noah kills Radley strictly on his own initiative, first, because he has learned that Radley is responsible for throwing the other delegates into jail on conspiracy charges, and second, because he has also discovered that Radley is attempting to seduce Jane. Thus the love-plot is tied directly with the murder, whereas in the novel it has only an incidental connection.

Judged by the standards set by her more practiced contemporaries in the field of popular fiction and by the expectations of their readers, Mrs. Gaskell, in fact, regrettably neglected the dramatic potentialities of the murder. Avoiding an actual description of it, she allowed the reader to know of it only indirectly, through the extended scene at the Carsons' when Harry's body is brought home and his father dedicates himself to revenge.[9] Boucicault not only showed the murder onstage, as the climax to Act II, but managed it so that it comes as the logical conclusion to the interwoven events already shown. And not only is Jane's prior involvement with Radley one of the reasons for the shooting; she is on the verge of being assaulted by him at the moment he is killed. Furthermore, for the sake of tighter construction, Boucicault reversed a bit of chronology in the novel. In Mrs. Gaskell's version, Mary Barton turns down Harry Carson some time before the murder (chap. xi), and it is after she has done so that the altercation occurs between Jem and Carson (chap. xv). In the play, the tussle comes first (Act I, scene 2), and the crucial interview in which Jane turns down Radley (Act II, scene 3) ends in the murder itself. The gain in dramatic effectiveness and the close meshing of events is obvious. Where Mrs. Gaskell was leisurely, discursive, and loose in her contrivance of events (as, of course, contemporary fictional practice allowed her to be), Boucicault was taut and economical.

The other major alteration of the plot was dictated equally by stage necessity and by Boucicault's celebrated, and profitable, fondness for using mechanical devices onstage, not merely for atmosphere but as an actual means of resolving the plot. In *The Octoroon,* for example, the *machina ex machina* had been a camera—a great novelty at the time—which, unprompted by human hands, snapped a picture of a crime. In the novel, Mrs. Gaskell's heroine wanders from place to place in Liverpool, in desperate search of Will Wilson and his vital alibi, and eventually puts out in a boat. Easy as these movements would be to portray in a film, they were not adaptable to the restricted facilities of the Victorian theatre; the difficulties were too great even for so resourceful a stage mechanic as Boucicault. He replaced Mary Barton's various

9. This scene, by which Mrs. Gaskell evokes considerable sympathy for the Carsons—hath not capitalists also deep domestic affections?—was omitted by Boucicault as irrelevant to his purposes. It was enough to portray Radley (the novel's Harry Carson) as a villainous seducer.

working-class helpers (the son of Will Wilson's land-lady, and the boat-man Sturgis and his wife) with a single, very different, agent, the lawyer Moneypenny, whom he developed into a rich character part. And instead of using an old-fashioned boat, he exploited the wonder of modern instantaneous communication by having the crucial contact with the sailor made vicariously, through the suspenseful clicking of the telegraph machine while the human characters stand in silent awe. However absurd it may strike the modern taste, the telegraph scene illustrates, better than anything else in the play, the difference between Mrs. Gaskell's plodding use of narrative and Boucicault's unerring sense of effects proper to gas-lit melodrama.

To be sure, the balance is not always in Boucicault's favor. Mrs. Gaskell achieved an ironic point by having Jem's own mother inno-cently add to the evidence against him by identifying the murderer's gun as his. But because Boucicault dispensed with Mrs. Wilson, he thus—somewhat clumsily—had to have the policeman Crankshaw see the gun and learn from Johnny Reilly whose it is before the mur-der is committed, and then find it at the scene immediately after-ward. In the novel, too, Aunt Esther is responsible for finding the telltale gun wadding and returning it to Mary, who immediately rec-ognizes it as proof of her father's guilt. The part of Esther, however, was lost in the transfer of *Mary Barton* to the stage, and so Boucicault had again to rely on policemen (whose business it is, after all) to find this bit of evidence. And he dropped completely, for the very good rea-son that he could not present it satisfactorily on the stage, the little episode in the novel in which Harry Carson, during the negotiations with the strikers, idly draws a caricature of the men—"lank, ragged, dispirited, and famine-stricken"—and captions it with Falstaff's uncomplimentary remarks about the soldiers under his command. One of the men surreptitiously retrieves it from the fireplace where Carson has thrown it, and by subsequently exhibiting it to his fellow strikers he intensifies their animosity toward their unfeeling employ-ers. Such strokes are within the power of the novelist but frequently not that of the playwright.

Mrs. Gaskell's weakness in this, her first novel, lay only partly in the slackness of her narrative; it is also apparent in her handling of pivotal scenes, especially those laid outside the home. Simply as a woman, she was less at liberty to realize the full dramatic effects of certain situa-tions than Dickens, Reade, or Collins would have been. She was lim-ited, furthermore, by her own temperament, which most naturally led her in the direction of the placid, rural *Cranford,* and by her position as the wife of a Unitarian minister in a thoroughly respectable middle-class provincial society. It may well be that, at the outset of her career, she felt inhibitions and obligations to decorum which later disappeared as she entered the ranks of the professional novelists. In the author of

Mary Barton, in any event, one senses a certain feminine uneasiness in the face of melodramatic situations that Dickens would have embraced with gusto. In addition to passing up the murder scene entirely, Mrs. Gaskell omitted to take advantage of the possibilities inherent in that dependable old standby, the courtroom scene. The writing of that scene (chap. xxxii) is so wordy that most of the dramatic tension is dissipated. Admittedly, we are given generous patches of dialogue in the examinations of Mrs. Wilson and Mary Barton; but the very climax of the scene, the sort of moment every melodramatic craftsman lives for—the arrival of Will Wilson not a second too soon—is deplorably botched. Mrs. Gaskell's sudden abandonment of dialogue and reversion to her custom of pedestrian description, just as Will bursts into the room, is perhaps the most serious defect of the passage, but others will occur to everyone who reads it. It is one of the most leaden courtroom scenes in literature. Boucicault, of course, as a dramatist required to tell his story only through brisk dialogue, slashed through Mrs. Gaskell's thick paragraphs and reduced the episode to its bare essentials of speech and action. One feels nevertheless that this, the concluding scene of the play, is unduly skimped. As has already been noted, Boucicault made no effort to provide a coda, especially by way of accounting for Noah Learoyd. Within three minutes after Johnny Reilly's entrance into the courtroom, the foreman of the jury cries "Not guilty!" Jem and Jane embrace, Moneypenny shakes Johnny's hand, the crowd cheers, and the curtain falls. But Boucicault may well have felt that in this play, the courtroom scene was a little anticlimactic. The peak of dramatic suspense undoubtedly had been reached in the telegraph scene, and so the courtroom sequence, while not to be wasted, did not require the same amplitude of treatment as it would have if it had not been overshadowed by what preceded it.

In Boucicault's adaptation, unlike the original, there is no leisureliness of pace. Mrs. Gaskell had a story to tell, but, as an early Victorian novelist, she was in no hurry to get it over with. Her numerous domestic scenes—for example, Mary's visit to Mrs. Wilson after Jem is arrested (chap. xxii)—were indispensable to her purpose of portraying the life of the Manchester working-class, but they slowed down the narrative. Since, in this case, Boucicault was not interested in the pathetic value of such scenes (as is shown too by his cavalier omission of various characters who figure in them), he cut them completely and devoted himself to the main business, which was to provide his audience with an unbroken series of exciting episodes. By raising his curtain on the bitter interview between the millowners and the workers' delegation, he provided the play from the very outset with an atmosphere of tension—something Mrs. Gaskell spent many chapters slowly developing. (It is significant that to achieve this effect, Boucicault showed the owners and strikers meeting before he passed to the scuffle between Jem and Radley—another reversal of Mrs. Gaskell's chronology.)

Mrs. Gaskell attempted a great deal more than Boucicault did. She tried simultaneously to portray a certain way of life, to paint a variety of characters in some depth, to convey a social message, and to tell a melodramatic story. As a novice in the art of fiction, she was betrayed by the contemporary convention that virtually required a novel about the working class to have a melodramatic plot. While *Mary Barton* is less deficient in some respects than in others, it suffers most from its author's lack of dramatic sense. The handling of plot and episode is its weakest point. Boucicault, however, perceived the potentialities of the very element in *Mary Barton* which Mrs. Gaskell was least equipped to manage. He seized upon the story alone, improved it, and made it the substance of an acting play, thus restoring it to the medium to which, one feels, it was best suited in the first place. In doing so, he sacrificed nearly all of Mrs. Gaskell's other concerns, such as social commentary and depth of characterization. He was interested only in broad effects; his characters were two-dimensional, his plotting devised with the single purpose of exciting the audience, at whatever cost to probability, his "realism" confined to the externals of setting and accessory. But these are the inherent limitations of Victorian melodrama, and within them Boucicault exhibited the craftsman's sure touch. *The Long Strike* is much more satisfying as a demonstration of the special art of the sensational play than *Mary Barton* is as an example of serious fiction.

GRAHAM HANDLEY

Mrs. Gaskell's Reading: Some Notes on Echoes and Epigraphs in *Mary Barton*†

* * *

There are, however several other interesting sequences which show when an author or authors were running in Mrs. Gaskell's mind, and perhaps the most fascinating of these is the one which looks back verbally and imaginatively to *The Ancient Mariner,* so that John Barton becomes subtly linked with the Mariner in the mind of a reader who knows Coleridge's poem. Perhaps it is as well to remember that, although Mrs. Gaskell's echoes here may be a subconscious reflex, her own conception of John Barton was central to the novel:

† From *Durham University Journal* 28 (1967): 134–36. Reprinted by permission of Graham Handley.

> Round the character of John Barton all the others formed them-
> selves; he was my hero, *the* person with whom all my sympathies
> went, with whom I tried to identify myself at the time . . . [1]

Now just as there is an overwhelming swing of sympathy towards the
Mariner as his terrible isolation is felt by the reader, so there is unmit-
igated compassion for John Barton at the end of Mrs. Gaskell's novel.
The Mariner and John Barton are murderers, and although John Barton dies his message is the same as the Mariner's:

> He prayeth best, who loveth best,
> All things both great and small;
> For the dear God who loveth us
> He made and loveth all.[2]

The Mariner is compelled to live on, whereas John Barton dies regretting that he has forsaken the Christian love which he once had:

> All along it came natural to love folk, though now I am what I
> am. I think one time I could e'en have loved the masters if
> they'd ha' letten me; that was in my Gospel days, afore my child
> died o' hunger. I was tore in two oftentimes, between my sor-
> row for poor suffering folk, and my trying to love them as
> caused their sufferings (to my mind).[3]

At the end of the poem and the novel there is this degree of similar-
ity; Mr. Carson, like the Wedding Guest, cannot choose but hear
John Barton's tale, and he is a poignantly sadder and wiser man as he
holds the body of his son's murderer in his arms.

The epigraph to Chapter XIX is from 'The Pains of Sleep', though
Mrs. Gaskell does not give the reference.

> Deeds to be hid which were not hid,
> Which, all confused, I could not know,
> Whether I suffered or I did
> For all seemed guilt, remorse, or woe.[4]

It is in this chapter that Mary learns of Harry Carson's murder and
Jem is arrested on suspicion. The tone of the poem is certainly present here in the novel: 'Mary felt as though the haunting horror were
a nightmare, a fearful dream, from which awakening would relieve
her'[5], Mrs. Wilson 'falls into another doze, feverish, dream-haunted,
and unrefreshing', while later her 'sleep was next interrupted . . . like

---

1. Quoted by A. W. Ward (letter from Mrs. Gaskell to Mrs. Greg) in the 1906 Knutsford edition of *Mary Barton* [Editor].
2. *The Ancient Mariner* (*The Poems of Coleridge*, with an introduction by Ernest Hartley
Coleridge, John Lane, N.D.) lines 614–18).
3. *Mary Barton*, pp. 320–21 (all page numbers to *Mary Barton* refer to this Norton Critical
Edition.)
4. *The Pains of Sleep*, lines 27–30.
5. *Mary Barton*, p. 193.

a recurring nightmare'.[6] There is, of course, a strong connection between this poem and *The Ancient Mariner,* but perhaps even more significant are certain lines in it which approximate to John Barton's state of mind before the murder (and even Mr. Carson's after it):

> Thirst of revenge, the powerless will
> Still baffled, and yet burning still!
> Desire with loathing strangely mixed
> On wild or hateful objects fixed.[7]

Mrs. Gaskell is able to absorb Coleridge's mood, and obviously its strange, mystical, fearful tension, the keen awareness of the evil within, is an area of the consciousness she wished to explore in *Mary Barton*.

At first the echoes of *The Ancient Mariner* are the commonplaces of imagery, perhaps even the platitudes of all time. Mary, we are told, 'reddened like a rose'; 'The old Hebrew prophetic words fell like dew on Mary's heart'; 'Deep sank those words into Mary's heart'.[8] Esther's return (in a chapter containing an epigraph in verse called 'Street Walks') contains a re-iterative irony in an overt reference to the Mariner. When Esther speaks to Jem of Mary we are told:

> The spell of her name was as potent as that of the Mariner's glittering eye. He listened like a three-year-child.[9]

This comes after the chapter called 'A Traveller's Tales' (perhaps the introduction of Will Wilson into the story set Mrs. Gaskell's mind working on *The Ancient Mariner*), and Esther most certainly has a tale to tell—which she subsequently does—a tale as harrowing and bitter as the Mariner's in its conscious acknowledgement of sin. Later Mary feels 'as if a sudden spring of sisterly love had gushed up in her heart'[1], and this would appear to be a direct echo of

> A spring of love gushed from my heart,
> And I blessed them unaware:[2]

After the epigraph from 'The Pains of Sleep' the echoes of *The Ancient Mariner* in the text are much thicker. The first is particularly significant in its associative suggestion:

> And then Heaven blessed her unaware, and she sank from wandering, unconnected thought and thence to sleep, . . . and once more the dead were alive again in that happy world of dreams.[3]

---

6. *Mary Barton*, pp. 195 and 196.
7. *The Pains of Sleep*, lines 21–24.
8. *Mary Barton*, pp. 75, 89 and 122.
9. *Mary Barton*, p. 141.
1. *Mary Barton*, p. 169.
2. *The Ancient Mariner*, lines 285–6.
3. *Mary Barton*, pp. 203–204.

There is little need for me to refer to the opening phrase here, but there is a strong and insistent parallel with the Mariner's situation at a certain stage in the poem. That 'the dead were alive again' is his fervent wish; 'wandering, unconnected thought' is his frequent state. Shortly afterwards we are told of Mary 'Was she not lonely enough to welcome the spirits of the dead'[4], an approximation to the Mariner's inner feelings in his isolation. Coleridge continues to be present in Mrs. Gaskell's mind, and his mystical-religious imaginative predilections, exemplified in a related poem, leads her to *Christabel*. Thus Esther feels 'as if some holy spell would prevent her (even as the unholy Lady Geraldine was prevented in the abode of Christabel) from crossing the threshold of that home of her early innocence'.[5] Here the omniscient author intrudes, for Esther is the victim snared by natural rather than supernatural sin.

It is when Mary goes to Liverpool, and follows the *John Cropper* in the pilot-boat, that the verbal reminiscences of Coleridge recur forcefully, and in these verbal images there is sometimes the deeper association of atmosphere and mood. Below is a loosely connected passage which runs over several pages:

> When the wind, which had hitherto been against them, stopped, and the clouds began to gather over the sky, shutting out the sun, and casting a chilly gloom over everything . . . The boat gave a bound forward at every pull of the oars. The water was glassy and motionless, reflecting tint by tint of the Indian-ink sky above. Mary shivered, and her heart sank within her . . . the same wind now bore their little craft along with easy rapid motion . . . the ship began to plunge and heave, as if she were a living creature impatient to be off . . . Mary sat down looking like one who prays in the death agony. For her eyes were turned up to that heaven where mercy dwelleth . . . She arose and followed him with the unquestioning docility of a child.[6]

Finally, there is the reference at the trial of Jem Wilson to the 'awful tranquillity of the life-and-death court', at least a half echo of the 'Nightmare Life-in-Death was she of the poem. Readers of the latter will undoubtedly recognize that the sequence quoted above has its equivalents in the poem, for example

> But in a minute she gan stir,
> With a short uneasy motion[7]

and

4. *Mary Barton*, p. 204.
5. *Mary Barton*, p. 208.
6. *Mary Barton*, pp. 256–61.
7. "The Ancient Mariner," lines 354–5.

> The harbour-bay was clear as glass
> So smoothly was it strewn[8]

and

> Then like a pawing horse let go
> She made a sudden bound[9]

and

> Forthwith this frame of mine was wrenched
> With a woeful agony.[1]

Barton is certainly mindful of the 'curse in a dead man's eye', but the impressive and moving quality of Mrs. Gaskell's writing, a pervasive sympathetic tension, is heightened by her conscious and perhaps sub-conscious derivations from Coleridge. The message of the Mariner is that of love for one's fellow creatures; the theme of Mrs. Gaskell is movingly the same. The legacy of sin is penance, but it is a penance which knits suffering with reconciliation, so that the sinner moves from isolation to participation in life. Admittedly the Mariner only enjoys 'the goodly company' from time to time, but his transfixing of the Wedding Guest is profoundly for good. Esther comes home to die, having shown a great and self-sacrificing love to Mary, and John, as I have said, tells his terrible tale to Mr. Carson. The effect of these echoes is to deepen the imaginative experience of the reader; the texture of the novel is all the richer for their inclusion.

JOHN LUCAS

[Carson's Murder and the Inadequacy of Hope in *Mary Barton*][†]

* * *

Mrs. Gaskell finds the muddle every bit as overwhelming as do Barton and Wilson. Like them she wants to make sense of it, but unlike them she finds the way to understanding made out of liberalism generously tinged with Christianity. In itself this is not remarkable; it was the way many took. But *Mary Barton* is a remarkable novel because it so powerfully suggests the guilt at which all liberalism must even-

---

8. "The Ancient Mariner," lines 472–3.
9. "The Ancient Mariner," lines 389–90.
1. "The Ancient Mariner," lines 578–9.
† From *Tradition and Tolerance in Nineteenth-Century Fiction*, ed. David Howard, John Lucas, and John Goode. © 1966 Taylor and Francis. Reproduced by permission of Taylor and Francis Books UK.

tually connive, and which therefore requires Mrs. Gaskell to put it behind her with a resoluteness for which few liberals would feel the need: that the happy *may* be the selfish; that her religion *may* be for the masters only; that caring for individual freedom *may* mean caring for the freedom of a relatively few individuals: it is from the shocked recognition of such possibilities that Mrs. Gaskell finally turns away. So it is that trying as honestly as she can to present the denseness and bewildering complexity of the industrial experience, and for that very reason finding it bearable only as it can be accounted for, she produces moments in the novel where interpretation usurps and contradicts imaginative exploration, and the 'truths' of liberalism become the novel's lies. Most troublingly this is the case with the murder of the manufacturer Carson's son, and what stems from it.

There can be little doubt that Mrs. Gaskell always intended the murder to happen, even though it would be bound to put great strain upon her claim that Barton was '*the* person with whom all my sympathies went'. And undoubtedly she does her best to make it seem fitting. In particular, she makes the victim the son of a bullying manufacturer and the would-be seducer of Mary; and the *Westminster Review* critic spotted the implications of this: '[Carson's morals] are only of, and for, a class . . . a beauty in humble life might—without any blot on his class-character, detriment to his station, or remorse to his conscience—be made to serve the purpose of his mere animal indulgence . . . Class-morality naturally made him thoughtless of the feelings of those not of his rank . . .' So in having Barton kill him Mrs. Gaskell closes the circle of moral retribution with a neatness that recalls Carlyle's grim pleasure in pointing out that the widow of the Glasgow slums 'proves her sisterhood; her typhus-fever kills them: they actually were her brothers, though denying it'. Indeed, so positively does Mrs. Gaskell appear to accept the proof of brotherhood that she has the elder Carson forgive his son's murderer and plan to become a more considerate employer.

So far so good. But, as Raymond Williams has quite rightly noticed, the trouble with the murder is that it is so unrepresentative an act for a novel whose focus is predominantly representative; it is altogether too exceptional. And in addition it seems an excessively crude way of dramatising class conflict. Where I disagree with Williams is in his explanation of why Mrs. Gaskell falls back on the murder: 'The real explanation, surely, is that John Barton, a political murderer appointed by a trade union, is a dramatisation of the *fear of violence* which was widespread among the upper and middle classes at the time, and which penetrated, as an arresting and controlling factor, even into the deep imaginative sympathy of a Mrs. Gaskell' (Williams' italics). I think not. True, as we have seen in *Sybil* and

Alton Locke,[1] fear of such violence was widespread, and it may even be the case that Mrs. Gaskell was partly conditioned by it when she came to deal with the murder; but that is not the central reason for the violence. It seems to me that she finds the murder necessary, because by means of it she can *simplify* a complexity which has become too terrific for her to accept consciously. Her mind shuts out the awareness of a muddle so colossal that it defeats the explanations of her social creeds, and so she attempts to impose order by turning to murder, where a neat pattern can realise itself: class antagonism producing a violence from which springs reconciliation. It is far too simple, principally because the antagonism is *reduced* to a matter of individual violence, so that though the pattern itself is intendedly representative it is fashioned out of quite arbitrary material.

Mrs. Gaskell may, however, have been additionally persuaded to adopt it, since it has the apparent advantage of disposing of Barton. I put the matter callously, and that is as it should be, for there *is* something callous in her attempt to write him off. The word seems an odd one to use about her, but her treatment of her hero justifies it. For Williams, 'she recoils from the violence of murder, to the extent of being unable even to enter it as the experience of the man conceived as her hero'. Again, this seems to me not the whole truth. It is not so much that Mrs. Gaskell is unable to enter the experience as that she sees she does not need to; Barton's act means that she need no longer take him seriously. More and more he has been leading her to an understanding of the limitations of her consciously held beliefs, but now she can stand back and judge him, as she had earlier when she noted that 'his thoughts were touched by sin'. As soon as Barton commits murder he becomes at best an object of pity; and that phrase fairly suggests the position of superiority to which Mrs. Gaskell retreats. She can now take up an attitude to Barton.

Mrs. Gaskell, then, profits from the murder in two ways, though at the cost of damaging all that is best in her novel. Because of Barton's act she can simplify the issues *Mary Barton* has been exploring, and she can also dismiss from serious attention its disturbing centre. I do not say that this latter gain had always been intended, in fact I am certain that the murder must have come as a tremendous relief to her, since it offered the way out of her problem with Barton, his so awkwardly leading her to the exposure of false hopes she dare not abandon. It is these which are meant to be realised by the consequences of the murder. Carson's forgiveness and vow of reform seem to represent a triumph for the best hopes of liberalism. Mrs. Tillotson, seizing on the detail of Barton's dying in Carson's arms, says: 'And this

---

1. 1 *Sybil, or The Two Nations* (1845) by Benjamin Disraeli. *Alton Locke* (1849) by Charles Kingsley. [*Editor*].

points to the book's true theme: not this or that feature of industrial society is being criticised, but its whole principle, excluding any human contact between masters and men; and the hope of better-ment lies not in this or that reform, but in the persistence, against all odds, of humanheartedness'. But this is a grotesquely inadequate hope in terms of the novel itself. For one thing, even if Carson's reform is genuine it is a purely individual matter, whereas one side of Mrs. Gaskell certainly hopes it will emerge as a general recommen-dation. For another, it *is* only one side of her, and the shallower, inter-pretive side, at that. The side which is truer to the novel knows that such a resolution is impossible, and indeed at the very end of *Mary Barton* all the main characters are sent off to Canada to make a fresh start, and so are given a purely fortuitous, and individual, release from a context which had been shown to be so inescapable. As Williams remarks, there is at this point 'a kind of writing-off, when the misery of the actual situation can no longer be endured'. Human heartedness indeed! If only the matter were *that* simple, Mrs. Gaskell's liberalism need not have been in conflict with all that is finest in her novel.

JOHN LUCAS

[Why We Need *Mary Barton*]†

* * *How remarkable it seems, that the young, ardent Rhinelander and the mild-mannered liberal lady should have so much in common. And what a tribute to her powers. Yet there are important distinctions. Mrs Gaskell doesn't in the end offer precisely the same account and diagnosis as Engels [in *The Condition of the Working Class*], even though Steven Marcus thinks that she does. 'What Mrs Gaskell does have to say in large measure and at almost every critical juncture con-firms what Engels had said before her.'[1] It won't do, and not simply because she sees more. No, the fact is that she understands things that he didn't, knows about matters of which he's inevitably ignorant, and therefore implicitly challenges his position. We do not need to take seriously that when she is at her weakest she goes against Engels (and in doing so unintentionally reveals the rightness of his analysis of bourgeois attempts at self-justification). But we do need to take very seriously the fact that her account of the condition of the working class in Manchester can be at odds with him at precisely those moments where she is at her strongest.

By way of trying to pin down some important distinctions between

† From *The Literature of Change: Studies in the Nineteenth-Century Provincial Novel* (Sus-sex: Harvester Press, 1980). By permission of John Lucas
1. Steven Marcus, *Engels, Manchester and the Working Class* (New York: Random House, 1974).

the two, and of suggesting why Engels's account is insufficient, let me begin with him on London. He observes a London crowd, jostling and thronging footpaths, and he remarks:

> The brutal indifference, the unfeeling isolation of each in his private interest becomes the more repellant and offensive, the more these individuals are crowded together, within a limited space. And, however much one may be aware that this is the isolation of the individual, this narrow self-seeking is the fundamental principle of our society everywhere, it is nowhere so shamelessly barefaced, so self-conscious as just here in the crowding of the great city. The dissolution of mankind into monads of which each one has a separate principle and a separate purpose, the world of atoms, is here carried out to its utmost extreme [p. 58].[2]

Marcus at least sees that this passage is strikingly inadequate. As he admits, the confusion is not so much in the object 'as in the observing eye and mind . . . it is an incapacity to differentiate, to discover articulated structures in—or impose them upon—the materials of existence'. And Marcus instances a parallel example in *Nicholas Nickleby*, where 'objects are contiguously related, but the contiguity is precisely the term of their disrelatedness as well'.[3] In short, Engels's atomistic view of the city is inadequate because external, too little aware of structures of relationship in the experience avowedly being studied or explored. In a word, he doesn't know enough.

Now when he gets to Manchester, he more or less repeats what he had said about London, though with a slight, and I think undeveloped (perhaps unperceived?), difference. 'The great towns are chiefly inhabited by working-people . . . these workers have no property whatsoever of their own and live wholly upon wages, which usually go from hand to mouth. Society, composed wholly of atoms, does not trouble itself about them . . .' (p. 106). The important shift is of course that Engels has now set up an opposition between workers and society, whereas in the case of London society was the whole. Why the change? The reason must be that Engels wants to insist that the working class in Manchester has its own consciousness, which by its very nature must be anti-atomistic, which is entirely new, and which depends absolutely on these people being *workers in the city*. It is out of the combination of worker and city that the new consciousness springs, for it creates the energy of violent hatred. Or so Engels insists. And Marcus agrees with him. There are no other articulated structures of experience, or none that can be regarded as relevant to the creation and growth of working-class consciousness. Here is Marcus both paraphrasing Engels and endorsing his view:

2. Engels, Friedrich. *The Condition of the Working Class in England in 1844*. (Institute of Marxism—Leninism of Moscow. London: Panther Press, no date).
3. Marcus, *Engels*, pp. 145–53.

[The workers' settlements] embody a division of labour on an unprecedented mass social scale, and are immense industrial barracks or encampments. They are at this moment in their history almost purely functional or skeletal communities and have not yet provided themselves with such visible structures as make manifest these extra-economic institutions and activities through which communities of men are also ordinarily regarded as maintaining themselves, their ancestors and their children. They and their work represent a new, frightening and highly developed order of human existence. Yet what is most striking about this complexity is its inexpungeable, contradictory uniformity—uniformity of life, of style, even of colour. This uniformity is part of the experience of murderous, quasi-military discipline that generations of working men have had to undergo. . . . [4]

Reading that and the passages in Engels's work which it relates to, and recognizing how near it is to the unsatisfactory externality of Dickens's presentation of Coketown–'It contained several large streets all very like one another, and many small streets still more like one another, inhabited by people equally like one another'[5]–I return with a sense of unease and suspicion to Engels's claim that he knows Manchester 'as intimately as my own native town, more intimately than most of its residents know it'.

For at the very least one is forced to regard the claim as extraordinarily daring when one thinks that Engels had no naturally acquired knowledge of the place's history, and did not even know where the majority of its inhabitants had come from, and what that might mean. In the new towns Engels remarks, 'The centralization of property has reached the highest point; here the morals and customs of the good old times are most completely obliterated; here it has gone so far that the name Merry Old England conveys no meaning, for Old England itself is unknown to memory and to the tales of our grandfathers' (p. 56). Not so. The people coming in off the land brought their customs with them, and they survive all right, in no matter how modified a form. Folk song blends into industrial ballad, field sports into street games, fairs continue in new surroundings and become important festive–and potentially revolutionary—occasions, family ties remain for all the terrific strains they have to undergo. Are these things trivial, of no account in the development of working-class consciousness? I do not think so. And there is nothing trivial in Engels's

4. Marcus, *Engels*, p. 168. Engels remarks that the conditions in the towns amount to warfare and this war grows from year to year, as the criminal tables show, more violent, passionate, irreconcilable. The enemies are dividing gradually into two main camps—the bourgeoisie on the one hand, the workers on the other (p. 162).
5. From *Hard Times* (1854) by Charles Dickens. [*Editor*].

mistaken claim: 'The English working-man is no Englishman nowa-days. . . . English nationality is annihilated in the working man' (p. 239). As the Irish poor who lived in little Ireland, one of the worst slum areas in Manchester, had every reason to know, nationality could assert itself in decidedly ugly if partly understandable ways (ways which are brought out in Mrs Gaskell's *North and South*). In 1851 Queen Victoria visited Manchester and was able to report:

> The streets were immensely full . . . and the cheering and enthusiasm most gratifying. The order and good behaviour of the people, who were not placed behind barriers, were the most complete we have seen in our many progressions through cap-itals and cities. . . . Everyone says that in no other town could one depend so entirely upon the quiet and orderly behaviour of the people as in Manchester. You had only to tell them what ought to be done, and it was sure to be carried out.

And this, it should be noted, although the Queen recognized that it was 'a painfully unhealthy-looking population'.[6]

* * *Now companionship is an important feature of both Mrs Gaskell's Manchester novels and to some extent her recognition of its possibility depends on her awareness of different kinds of living con-ditions among working-class people, which she knows to be impor-tant, yet which Engels doesn't see at all or, if he does, takes to be of no account. The result is that Mrs Gaskell can present evidence of structures of experience, ways of living, adaptations and changes that are importantly present in the creation of working-class conscious-ness, though they are set quite apart from the shop floor. This is in no way to deny that Mrs Gaskell shares Engels's perception of the energy of hatred that has much to do with the creation of that con-sciousness. It should cause no surprise, Engels insists, if the workers 'can maintain their consciousness of manhood only by cherishing the most glowing hatred, the most unbroken rebellion against the bour-geoisie in power' (p. 144). When John Barton returns from the for-lorn presentation of the 1842 charter, he tells Job Legh: 'It's not to be forgotten, or forgiven either, by me or many another. . . . As long as I live, our rejection that day will abide in my heart; and as long as I live I shall curse them as so cruelly refused to hear us . . .' (ch. 9). And we learn much earlier that after the death of his son Barton builds 'hoards of vengeance in his heart against the employers'.

Mrs Gaskell indeed presents Barton as very much a man of hatred, and quite clearly feels nervous enough about the probability of our finding him both credible and sympathetic to warn us that his heart is touched with 'sin'. Engels would approve of John Barton, right

---

6. Quoted in Asa Briggs, *Victorian Cities*. New York: Harper & Row, 1965, p. 109.

enough; but there is more to the man than hatred. For Mrs Gaskell doesn't think that hatred and vengeance make the sum total of working-class consciousness. Engels does. It is only *there* that the working class is anti-atomistic, becomes more than merely a congregation of monads. Or rather, for all the few attempts he makes to go beyond that—for example, quoting and agreeing with Canon Parkinson that 'only the poor give to the poor'—he does not seem to me to have succeeded in all that he avowedly set out to do. 'I wanted', he says, 'to see into your own homes, to observe you in your every-day life, to chat with you on your conditions and grievances, to witness your struggles against the social and political power of your oppressors. I have done so.' He has done many of those things, yes; and done them magnificently. Nevertheless some things remain undone or insufficiently done. Or perhaps it is rather that Engels simply didn't understand all that he experienced—and as a result assumed that he was experiencing something else. To be specific. At the end of his long and harrowing account of working-class living conditions, Engels sums up:

> We must admit that 350,000 working people of Manchester and its environs live, almost all of them, in wretched, damp filthy cottages, that the streets which surround them are usually in the most miserable and filthy conditions, laid out without the slightest reference to ventilation, with reference solely to the profit secured by the contractor. In a word, we must confess that in the working-man's dwellings of Manchester, no cleanliness, no convenience, and consequently no comfortable family life is possible; that in such dwellings only a physically degenerate race, robbed of all humanity, degraded, reduced morally and physically to bestiality, could feel comfortable and at home [p. 96].

We may be impressed by the rhetoric, we can hardly fail to be moved and appalled by the detail which Engels has so insistently thrust at us. Yet at the same time we are bound to feel that Engels's standards are those of the rich Rhinelander, and that as such he is hardly likely to make important distinctions between, shall we say, the Barton and Wilson households, or the Davenport and Alice Wilson cellars.[7] Yet the distinctions are important, and Mrs Gaskell knows how to make them. Alice Wilson's cellar is called 'humble', but the word isn't a polite evasion. Its floor 'was bricked; and scrupulously clean, although so damp that it seemed as if the last washing would never dry up'. Mrs Gaskell isn't suggesting that Alice Wilson should have to

7. It is worth comparing Engels on Manchester with Orwell on working-class people who want, among other things, 'a bath once a day'. That has much more to do with Orwell's own middle-class hatred of smells and dirt than with working-class desires. See *Looking Back on the Spanish War* [in *Homage to Catalonia* (Harmondsworth: Penguin Books, 1966)].

live in such conditions. But the fact is that Alice does achieve some degree of cleanliness, convenience and hence comfortable family life. And of course one of her strengths is that she can still recall her earlier days in rural surroundings, has a sense of continuity in human assertiveness which Engels would want to deny her.

*   *   *

But it is not merely in the comparatively exceptional figures of Alice and Job Legh that we discover something that is missing from Engels's account of the growth of working-class consciousness. How odd, for example, that he should say nothing about the grimness, acidity, sadness and sometimes consoling wit and warmth of work songs. How odd that he should think every pub is a gin palace. How odd that he has nothing to say about entertainment: about cheap 'blood-tub' theatres, musical events, clubs, halls even; or about the possibilities of railway excursions. Reach has a fascinating section on Manchester pub and club entertainments, and he mentions the social function of the railway. By the end of *Mary Barton* Margaret Legh, Job's blind granddaughter, has started on a career of club singing and the novel as a whole takes in the experiences of work songs,[8] of family teas, visits, marriages, exchanges of hospitality, kinship. And Mrs Gaskell's story, *Libbie Marsh's Three Eras* (1847), mentions railway excursions, boat trips on the canals, picnics. None of which has any part to play in Engels's account of Manchester.

To say this is not to decry the importance of the *Condition of the Working Class*. It remains a masterpiece of observation and fierce anger; and its account of how Manchester developed, of the strategies implicit in the creation of high streets, shops, suburbs etc., is formidably intelligent and thoroughly convincing. And as I have shown, in many ways Mrs Gaskell endorses Engels's study of working-class life in the town. But her understanding of the growth of working-class consciousness inevitably goes wider and deeper than his. (Not that she would put her understanding in the terms I have used). Of course he was right to emphasize the terrible degradation of many working-class lives, the squalor, misery, and human insufficiency that often typified life in Manchester and which made hundreds of thousands of human beings helpless victims of a system which they could do very little about. But not to recognize that some discriminations are necessary, not to see that there are structures of experience which are positive and not merely created out of negativeness or enmity—however excusable such failures of vision may be, they finally limit Engels's 'intimate' knowledge of Manchester. That is why we need *Mary Barton*.

8. Some indication of Mrs Gaskell's knowledge of working-class literature can be found in an article by Michael D. Wheeler, 'The Writer as Reader in *Mary Barton*', *Durham University Journal* (December 1974).

ROSEMARIE BODENHEIMER

Private Grief and Public Acts in *Mary Barton*†

Mary Barton is a novel about responding to the grief of loss or disappointment. Its pages are filled with domestic disaster; the sheer accumulation of one misfortune after another is the organizing principle of
the first half of the narrative. The story begins with Mrs. Barton's grief
about the disappearance of her sister, and the Barton-Wilson tea party
that is organized to help comfort her ends with the social awkwardness
of her returning tears. The contrasting characterizations of immediate
responses to deaths in the family—John Barton's stunned and silent
dignity, Jane Wilson's garrulous hysteria, Jem Wilson's quiet stance
when his little brothers die—elicit much of the best writing in the
novel. The pretentious Ogden funeral, for which Margaret Legh
strains her eyes to stitch mourning gowns, is set against the simple feeling of the Davenport pauper's burial. And the novel's middle-class centerpiece, the Carson family portrait, is taken at the moment when each
member reacts characteristically to the news of Harry Carson's murder. When we hear, in the little Canadian epilogue, that Margaret Legh
has regained her sight, the news comes with a sense of violated tone,
for it is the only piece of simple "good tidings" in the book.[1]

If steadily widening and worsening doses of bad news and hard
times form the main substance of the narrative, the question of what
to do about them is at its core, the source of the novel's deepest
energy, and division. *Mary Barton*, itself a response to devastating
personal grief, was its author's first assumption of a public voice,
raised on behalf of other private grieving voices. The careers of both
major characters, John and Mary Barton, are shaped in some image
of their creator's: both father and daughter, out of their personal woe,
fare forth on journeys that render them momentarily public figures,
voices raised in middle-class forums of judgment in the name of
working-class victims of social or legal injustice. Yet the narrative pre-
sentations of those actions and the other responses to misfortune

† From *Dickens Studies Annual* 9 (1981). Copyright © 1981, AMS Press, Inc. Used with permission.
1. The almost unrelenting atmosphere of grief that pervades *Mary Barton* can be related to
the fact that Gaskell undertook the novel, at her husband's suggestion, to help take her
mind from the death of her infant son in 1845. See Winifred Gerin, *Elizabeth Gaskell: A
Biography* (Oxford: Clarendon Press 1976), pp. 74–75. Gaskell herself acknowledged the
source of the "heavy shadow" over the book in a letter to Mrs. Greg: "The tale was formed,
and the greater part of the first volume was written when I was obliged to lie down constantly on the sofa, and when I took refuge in the invention to exclude the memory of painful
scenes which would force themselves on my remembrance." *The Letters of Mrs. Gaskell*, ed.
J. A. V. Chapple and Arthur Pollard (Cambridge, Mass.: Harvard University Press, 1967),
p. 74.

that are explored are riddled with ambivalence, shifts of class perspective, and frustrating revisions of moral terminology. Meanwhile,
an astonishing and hitherto unemphasized proportion of the novel is
devoted to the depiction of domestic scenes: family life, neighborly
help, and the apparently irrelevant small talk that humanizes private
and daily life.

What, then, are the real animating divisions, the structures of conflict that shape the movement of this narrative? *Mary Barton* has
always been seen as a "split" novel. Its well-deserved status as the best
of the industrial novels to come out of the 1840s[2] has led almost all
of Gaskell's critics to notice the problematical split between her sympathy for the poor and her occasional retreats to middle-class liberal
platitude.[3] Moreover, the novel has conventionally been seen to fall
into two unequally serious parts: the "tragic" story of John Barton's
vision of social injustice, with its consequent action and suffering,
and the "conventionally romantic" story of his daughter Mary's love
triangle, with her exciting mission to save her working-class lover
from conviction for a crime committed by her father against her
would-be seducer. It has been assumed almost universally that these
plots are only circumstantially connected, that the important contribution of the novel is the portrait of John Barton, and that the story
of Mary relies directly on romantic patterns and is designed to entertain the reading public.[4]

In the face of such readings, I want to argue for an essential consistency in the novel's internal conflicts, and for the ways that its
troubling issues cut across both plots, and even shape the fluctuations of the narrative voice. The issues might best be posed, at the
outset, in the form of two questions: Should the response to misfortune or injustice be active or passive?; and, What is the relation
between public actions and domestic virtues? These questions are
knotty ones, ones that remain unresolved; and they pertain not only
to Gaskell's uneven presentation of social problems, but also to her

2. Raymond Williams, who made the "industrial novels" into a recognized group in literary
history, calls *Mary Barton* "the most moving response in literature to the industrial suffering of the 1840s." *Culture and Society 1780–1950* (London: Chatto & Windus, 1958; rpr.
New York: Harper & Row, 1966), p. 87.
3. Almost every critic of *Mary Barton* notices how the narrative commentary retreats to
middle-class judgments of Barton's radicalism. The best, most thorough and sympathetic
analyses of the inconsistencies of Gaskell's political position may be found in Margaret
Ganz, *Elizabeth Gaskell: The Artist in Conflict* (New York: Twayne, 1969) pp. 55–66; and
John Lucas, "Mrs. Gaskell and Brotherhood," in *Tradition and Tolerance in Nineteenth-
Century Fiction*, ed. David Howard, John Lucas, and John Goode (New York: Barnes and
Noble, 1967), pp. 161–174.
4. Most Gaskell critics follow Williams's lead in calling Mary's part "the familiar and ortho-
dox plot of the Victorian novel of sentiment" p. 89). See, for example, Ganz, p. 69; W. A.
Craik, *Elizabeth Gaskell and the English Provincial Novel* (London: Methuen, 1975), pp.
5 and 31; and Lucas, p. 162. Coral Lansbury's discussion in *Elizabeth Gaskell: The Novel
of Social Crisis* (New York: Barnes and Noble, 1975), is an exception that emphasizes
Mary's central role and her strength of character.

wavering performance as a narrator in this first of her public appearances. They are also responsible, however, for what I would call the genuine seriousness of the novel: its concrete account of the dignity, and the historical integrity, of working-class family life.

Of all the important nineteenth-century novelists, Gaskell is the one whose themes most consistently emerge implicitly, from juxtaposition without explicit narrative direction, and in apparently artless repetition, without the glue of narrative metaphor. *Mary Barton* works like this, but *Mary Barton* is also, noticeably, an apprentice novel. Because its technical discontinuities are significantly related to its political ones, I begin with some attention to the important virtues and failures of Gaskell's first sustained piece of narrative.

Technical difficulties are most prominent in the first half, which juggles multiple story-lines and covers a period of several years. Here the transitions from dramatized scene to narrative summary are awkward and abrupt. Many chapters seem at first to be collections of disparate material, giving us what would seem to be thematically unimportant scenes, while crucial movements of mind are left to be generally accounted for in narrative summary. It is surprising, for example, to discover how rarely John Barton appears as an actor in dramatized scenes, and how often he is "one of those" men about whom we get, in several installments, an historical account centering on the failure of Chartism and the growth of trade unionism. Although the narrator tells us feelingly of Barton's increasing depression and its causes, there is little sense of an inevitable dramatic set of choices determined by defined complexities in his character. A similar failure to develop character can be seen in other cases as well; many scenes offer new introductions to a character's dominant traits, rather then developments of previously demonstrated conflicts.

Such apparent weaknesses of direction suggest that we must look at the content of the dramatized scenes for the material that most engaged Gaskell's novelistic skills. These prove to be predominantly scenes of familial or neighborly mutual help, grief-sharing, storytelling, or opinion-giving; they are the activities that provide the novel's true tone and texture. Next to them some of the "plot actions", like Barton's and Jem's interviews with the prostitute Esther, or Jem's confrontation with his rival Harry Carson, stick out as contrivances of a different kind. "It's the poor, and the poor only, as does such things for the poor." Barton says in the first chapter;[5] and Gaskell's series of domestic tableaux show just how well, how graciously, how sensitively, how courageously and good-humouredly, the poor do such things.

5. *Mary Barton,* ed. Angus Easson, Oxford English Novels, (London: Oxford University Press, 1973), chapter 1. Subsequent quotations will be indicated by chapter number in the text.

While she often has been praised for her inventories of domestic interiors,[6] Gaskell may be even better at noting details of manners in close quarters: how the Wilsons pretend not to hear the Bartons' negotiations about buying food for their tea-party; how Margaret Legh can tell from the sounds in the apartment below, when it would be appropriate to knock at Alice Wilson's door. In a similar way, whole scenes that may appear to be distractions insist quietly upon the resources indigenous to working-class culture. Story-telling, for example, is an important source of entertainment and hospitality in *Mary Barton*, and the skill of the tellers forms part of our sense that Gaskell's working-class world is full of hidden talent. Margaret's kitchen comedy of the scorpion loose in the house, Will Wilson's tall tales, Barton's account of London folk, Job Legh's story of Margaret's birth, even Jane Wilson's story about the first time she cooked potatoes for her new husband, amuse or move their audiences as fully as do the verses that Gaskell writes into her text. While the narrator makes no summary comment about her subjects' ability and inclination to transform their own painful experience into art, her decision to give us so many instances constitutes just such a point, and effectively identifies the storyteller herself with the activities of her fictional working-class characters.

Gaskell's most persuasive holds upon her readers' sympathies come from the recording of such family talents, dignities, and traditions; and there is a wide gap between the particular accounts of daily life and the more general attempts at social explanation and apology undertaken in some of the narrative summaries. The gap results both from the awkward melding of scene and summary, and from an unacknowledged shift in narrative role, from domestic observer to social historian. The uneasiness of the fit between the domestic and the political activities of the narrative is audible in the sometimes disconcerting shifts of language and tone in the storytelling voice.

While Gaskell assumes an unusually direct stance in relation to the "you" she often addresses, she is not always certain about who the "you" is, or what it might be assumed to believe. Characterized most generally, the narrative is astonishingly informal; it sounds like the spoken voice of a habitual story-teller, perhaps improvising out loud to her children about the hearth.[7] To take a short "clip" from the account of Mary's apprenticeship:

> Besides, trust a girl of sixteen for knowing well if she is pretty; concerning her plainness she may be ignorant. So with this

6. See especially Angus Easson, *Elizabeth Gaskell* (London: Routledge and Kegan Paul, 1979), pp. 74–76.
7. Gaskell described her narrative stance in a letter to Eliza Fox (May 29, 1849): "I told the story according to a fancy of my own; to really SEE the scenes I tried to describe . . . and then to tell them as nearly as I could as if I were speaking to a friend over the fire on a winter's night and describing real occurences." *Letters*, p. 82.

consciousness she had early determined that her beauty should make her a lady; the rank she coveted the more for her father's abuse; the rank to which she firmly believed her lost Aunt Esther had arrived. Now, while a servant must often drudge and be dirty, must be known as her servant by all who visited at her master's house, a dressmaker's apprentice must (or so Mary thought) be always dressed with a certain regard to appearance; must never soil her hands, and need never redden or dirty her face with hard labour. Before my telling you so truly what folly Mary felt or thought injures her without redemption in your opinion, think what are the silly fancies of sixteen years of age in every class, and under all circumstances. The end of all the thoughts of father and daughter was, as I said before, Mary was to be a dressmaker; and her ambition prompted her unwilling father to apply at all the first establishments, to know on what terms of painstaking and zeal his daughter might be admitted into ever so humble a workwoman's situation. But high premiums were asked at all; poor man! he might have known that without giving up a day's work to ascertain the fact. (Ch. 3)

This charming mixture of neighborly gossip, social irony, general psychologizing, and spontaneous exclamation is typical of the almost "unwritten" quality of the narrative throughout. The "you" seems to be a friendly audience which may have a tendency to jump too quickly to negative judgments; and the job of the story-teller is to get this audience to sympathize with even the more dangerous fantasies of her characters, and to share the concrete considerations that her practical intelligence notices—Barton's sacrifice of a day's work for nothing is a strong touch.

When it comes to the passages in which Gaskell feels compelled to present Barton as a piece of social history, however, her sympathetic imagination can turn defensive. It is as though her "you" then becomes a public audience, better-informed and more articulate than she is; and when that audience enters her head, she bows to the teachings of its liberal-economic members. Her disturbing leaps to middle-class platitudes have been well-discussed elsewhere, and her unwillingness to challenge such dicta has been variously described.[8] What seems especially interesting about those leaps is, however, a matter of language: when Gaskell turns to placate her middle-class audience, she sounds like a novelist who has dropped momentarily into sociologese. There is simply no continuity of imagination

---

8. See Ganz, pp. 55–66, and Lucas, pp. 161–174. For the remarkable view that Gaskell deliberately lets her characters speak for themselves, while presenting the narrative stance as a strategic sop to her middle-class readers, see Lansbury, pp. 9, 25. Lansbury's analysis is a compelling view of the effect, but Gaskell seems to be so consistently double-visioned in every aspect of the novel that I cannot accept a description of effect as an accurate account of intent.

between her concrete presentation of the visible evidence affecting John Barton and sentences like ". . . what I wish to impress is what the workman thinks and feels. True, that with childlike improvidence, good times will often dissipate his grumbling, and make him forget all prudence and foresight" (Ch. 3). That generic "him," the workman as a species of child, is the creation of social essayists and religious moralists; and when Gaskell turns to such talk, she herself sounds like a child reciting its lessons. The defensiveness suggests, I think, her fear of drawing social conclusions from the evidence she records, and some distrust of her own powers of generalization that leads her to shy away—at least in this first novel—from extending a position for public judgment.

Gaskell's finest imaginative energy is directed toward the project of uncovering hidden histories; of taking us into minds, and cellars, through descriptions that quite consciously defy the middle-class instinct to categorize and distance. There is a palpable narrative identification with the "hidden power" (Ch. 4) of Margaret Legh's voice singing working-class ballads; and with the Chartist belief that "their misery had still to be revealed in all its depths, and then some remedy would be found" (Ch. 8). And Gaskell's primary technique of "discovery" is to get us to see her characters in the context of their whole lives, with family histories, pet stories, favorite objects, and generational continuities. By creating a set of interlocking families, she succeeds in avoiding the contemporary rhetorical tendencies to create images of an ahistorical, rootless mass, on the one hand, and dispossessed middle-class "working-class heroes," on the other. Yet this apparently unrhetorical and domestic activity exists in a perpetual state of tension with the essay-like social commentary. And the dichotomizing impulse that creates those uneven levels of diction in the narrative voice may also be found in the structures that organize Gaskell's invention of characters, families, and plot actions.

The Barton and Wilson families are carefully distinguished in ways that focus the conflict between active social thought and passive domestic response, and the differences are grounded in the social histories of the families. John Barton is the son of Manchester manufacturing folk; even that simple fact gives an immediate historical depth of tradition to the town that figures so often as a visual symbol in contemporary accounts of industrial culture. George Wilson and his sister Alice have, by contrast, come to Manchester from an impoverished rural family; George has successfully found work and fathered a son who has risen to foundry work, and who becomes responsible for a technical invention. But if Jem Wilson is a technological as well as a moral hero, he nonetheless shares the indifference to class politics, and the lack of intellectual curiosity, that characterizes his countrybred family. Preoccupied with his love for Mary, Jem is immune to John Barton's attempt to involve him in the "short hours" issue. His inability to listen to talk that actually draws conclusions from social observation is like his father's; George Wilson's part in his dialogues with Barton is to take the personal line, or one sympathetic to the masters' accounts of themselves. Gaskell suggests, both in this pair of characters and through incidental narrative comments, that town life breeds admirably independent intelligences while rural life is conducive to mental passivity. Mrs. Barton, for example, has "somewhat of the deficiency of sense in her countenance, which is likewise characteristic of the rural inhabitants in comparison with the natives of the manufacturing towns" (Ch. 1).

The richest episode in the Barton-Wilson contrast is the finely organized sixth chapter, in which the two men nurse and feed the family of the dying Davenport. It is one of the few chapters in the novel that juxtaposes scenes of rich and poor for ironic effect: we see the brilliantly lighted shops in the London Road, "within five minutes' walk" of the Davenport's cellar; and we hear the Carson servants and children discuss the high prices of salmon and hothouse flowers while Wilson quietly sickens from hunger in their kitchen. But the two men, both heroically generous in domestic action, bring very different minds to these contrasts, as each goes forth on an errand for medical help. Barton "felt the contrast between the well-filled, well-lighted shops and the dim gloomy cellar, and it made him moody that such contrasts should exist." His bitterness is dutifully chastised by the same voice that calls our attention to the contrast; it is said to be caused by Barton's ignorance of the hearts of the passers-by in the streets, and his quite natural thoughts are condemned in religious terms: "the thoughts of his heart were touched by sin, by bitter hatred of the happy, whom he, for the time, confounded with the selfish." Although the narrator here seems to align herself with the "Methodee" sentiments of Davenport, "that we mun bear patiently whate'er he sends," her intelligent distinction between the happy and the selfish softens her judgment; and she goes on to dramatize, in the Carson section, more and more actual reasons for bitterness. In that section, however, Wilson becomes the witness; and this narrative choice increases the discomfiting ironies in the portrayal even as it mutes the possibility of drawing inferences from it.

Wilson brings to the factory owner's house an essentially feudal spirit. He is tempted to stop and admire the pictures and gilding, "but then he thought it would not be respectful." Let into the comfortable kitchen, he amuses himself by guessing at the nature and use of the familiar utensils hanging about, as though he had not just come from a painfully different place. Surrounded by odors of cooking food, he starves in silence, and it is only a piece of good luck, the cook's second thoughts, that sends him away with a handful of bread and meat.

As he emerges with an inadequate out-patient's order and a casually bestowed five shillings, Wilson's conclusions are muddy, to say the least: "Wilson left the house, not knowing whether to be pleased or grieved. It was long to Monday, but they had all spoken kindly to him, and who could tell if they might not remember this, and do something before Monday." These are clearly naive and child-like responses; as alternatives to Barton's "sinful thoughts" they are hardly acceptable. Yet it seems that Gaskell can fully dramatize the contrast between rich and poor only in the presence of a political innocent: *we* get the point, but Wilson retains a sort of unfallen virtue which is the legacy of his rural origin, while the narrator remains free not to draw conclusions.

This troubled contrast between Wilson and Barton[9] represents an impasse that is related to Gaskell's position as a narrator. Wilson is incapable of generalization or intellectual connection; he is a good character because he functions generously in family and neighborly spheres. Barton's ability to connect renders him dangerous, even sinful; his self-consciousness is that of the fallen man, the creature of industry. When Gaskell demurs at Barton's intelligence, she is simultaneously retreating from her own: she allows neither her narrator nor her character to challenge the authority that describes the world in middle-class terms. Yet at the same time as she fears the arrogance of critical generalization, Gaskell dramatizes, with admiration, the superior powers of intelligence that would inevitably reach for it.

In the portrait of old Alice Wilson, Gaskell's mixed feelings about domestic tranquillity—and rural ignorance—are stabilized through the creation of a recognizably literary figure. If her brother is naive, Alice is regressive: she has made a seamless transition from childhood to old-maidenhood. Her history brings the pastoral world into the novel, but not as an alternative to Manchester life: there is no pastoral sentimentality even in the presentation of Alice's unfulfilled longing to return to her childhood home, as there is no trace of retreatist rural nostalgia in the novel.[1] Rather, Gaskell pays homage to Alice's "prelapsarian" virtue by imagining her as a genre character, a "tale from humble life."[2]

---

9. Ganz identifies a related thematic opposition of resignation and rebellion, primarily in terms of the contrast between Barton and Alice Wilson (pp. 66–67). David Smith, who reads Mary Barton as a straightforward plea for Christian resignation, seems to take certain narrative statements as more definitive moral postures than others. See "*Mary Barton* and *Hard Times*: Their Social Insights," *MOSAIC*, 2(1971–1972), 97–112.

1. To see Alice Wilson's yearning for the country as a rural-industrial contrast is to oversimplify. See, for example, Arthur Pollard, *Mrs. Gaskell: Novelist and Biographer* (Cambridge, Mass.: Harvard University Press, 1966), pp. 44–45. Lansbury gives a fine account of all the ways that Gaskell works against stereotypical town-country and pastoral-industrial contrasts, especially through the treatment of Old Alice (pp. 25–28 and 33–35).

2. Old Alice may well be a holdover figure from the rural tale that Gaskell first intended to write. (See her "Perface" to *Mary Barton*); and that she might have seen as a prose version of the "sketches among the poor, *rather* in the manner of Crabbe" that she and William Gaskell had discussed earlier. She describes this unfulfilled plan, quoting a passage from "The Cumberland Begger," in a letter to Mary Howitt of August 8, 1838. *Letters*, p. 33.

The rocky terrain of Alice's childhood, the heather-gathering children, and the fatalism suggest above all a Wordsworthian figure—a version of an idiot boy, perhaps, or one of those who tell tales of loss with bleak pleasure. And Alice's function in the moral terrain of the novel is akin to that of Wordsworth's Cumberland Beggar: she is there to be revered and cared for, despite her social blunders and in the midst of other woes; for she is a precious link with the past, a test of the virtue of others. A good deal of narrative attention is paid, for example, to the arrangements for nursing Alice during the period when Mary's plot is at its most frantic. Alice is there to provide the domestic grounding, the reality of slow mortality, against which the fast-moving excitement of Mary's brief adventure is deliberately set. Mary passes the moral test when she pays emotional attention to the dying old woman as well as to her falsely accused lover. The case of Old Alice thus treats and rejects the pastoral "solution," but at the same time it brings up an alternative locus for virtue and stability in the idea of family life and domestic affection.

The family is the novel's base of activity as well as its source of consolation; and the successful "heroic" actions are essentially domestic ones. This point might best be made, as Gaskell makes it, through the juxtaposition of the two London stories in Chapter Nine: Barton's experiences as a participant in the Chartist march and petition, and Job Legh's moving account of his rescue of the infant Margaret after the deaths of her parents. Job's journey, a private family rescue mission, is a success; John's public and political one, a failure. Job's story is full of anonymous people who help the men in their comic and pathetic attempts to feed the infant; Barton's of pretentious coachmen and insulting policemen. It is not that Job's story is "better" than Barton's—as a satirist, John has good eyes and ears—but that he tells it in order to move his audience's minds away from Barton's deep sense of political failure, as a consolatory tale of domestic affection. It is possible to save lives in *Mary Barton*: Jem saves his father from the fire at Carson's mill; Job saves his granddaughter; Mary saves Jem, the man she wants to marry. The implicit pattern is an apolitical one, suggesting that one is responsible to the lives of family members, to save or to grieve. Such displacements of attention from political issues to individual acts are basic impulses in the novel, as, indeed they prove to be in most fictions about industrial stress. But Gaskell's version of the shift is bound in a special way to the subject of family integrity.

All of the major threats in the novel are rendered in terms of their potential to destroy family life. Factory work for women, a subject discussed at several points, is just such a threat. Esther's gradual spin out of the family orbit leads to a life on the streets, while Barton's fear of that sexual availability leads him to insist that Mary avoid factory

work. After the death of Mrs. Barton, the Barton household is composed of two workers—not quite a family; in the absence of that bal-
last, John begins to swerve toward the union, Mary toward her
flirtation with Harry Carson. Turning to the structures of those two
main stories, it is especially interesting to observe how consistently
Gaskell denies the outer world its full reality by treating such "lapses"
from domesticity as the stuff of melodrama and romance.

John Barton comes most fully alive as a particular, internally realized character in the scene describing his reactions and memories at
the moment of his wife's death (Ch. 3). It is the single situation in
which Gaskell's concrete imaginative energy flows into his character,
unimpeded by the ideas that disturb her when she speaks of Barton
as a political example. For the rest, Barton's "domination" of the
novel's first half may be as much due to the problematical character
of the narrative presentation as to his centrality as a character. His
story appears in only ten of the first eighteen chapters, after which
he disappears from the narrative until the end; and he does rather
little on stage. After the opening chapters, he helps the Davenports,
leaves and returns from London, rejects his sister-in-law, and turns
the anger of his union colleagues from the scabs to the masters. This
last scene, done up in the gas-lit melodramatic style conventional in
the depiction of unions,[3] is the only one in which we see Barton in a
public situation, despite the fact that we hear of his leadership in the
movement.

The absence of other public scenes is important, for it is one of the
ways that Gaskell blurs Barton's status as a political personage. Most
of the time he is present as a sitting, brooding household presence,
often registered through the worried consciousness of Mary. The
union's impact on the Barton household is described through Mary's
nightmare images: "Strange faces of pale men, with dark glaring eyes,
peered into the inner darkness, and seemed desirous to ascertain if
her father were at home. Or a hand and arm (the body hidden) was
put within the door, and beckoned him away" (Ch. 10). This is
remarkably effective writing, despite the immediate conventional
melodrama of "dark glaring eyes"; those truncated pieces of bodies
are dangerous because they intrude insidiously into the safe space of
home, threatening to beckon the father away both physically and psychologically. The dehumanization of the union suggested by those
images is extended in the depiction of its effect on Barton: he
becomes more isolated as he becomes more involved, as though a
union could not provide the companionship that it might naturally

3. Patrick Brantlinger has shown how the images of unionization prevalent among middle
class writers developed from reports of the Glasgow cotton spinner's strikes and violence
in 1837. See "The Case Against Trade Unions in Early Victorian Fiction," *Victorian Studies*, 13(1969), pp. 37–52.

foster. I am not interested in these matters primarily for the sake of berating Gaskell yet again for her failure to transcend the stereotypes she had absorbed from her own culture, but because of the way the union is placed in relation to the kinds of communal activity that *can* be imagined and dramatized in this novel: the nuclear or extended family and the neighborhood.

Even Barton's political animus is reducible to family sentiment, for it is grounded in his personal desire to revenge the death of his only son. The description of that moment of conversion reveals some of Gaskell's most frightened political leaps:

> Hungry himself, almost to an animal pitch of ravenousness, but with the bodily pain swallowed up in anxiety for his little sinking lad, he stood at one of the shop windows where all edible luxuries are displayed; haunches of vension, Stilton cheeses, moulds of jelly—all appetising sights to the common passer-by. And out of this shop came Mrs. Hunter! She crossed to her carriage, followed by the shop-man loaded with purchases for a party. The door was quickly slammed to, and she drove away; and Barton returned home with a bitter spirit of wrath in his heart, to see his only boy a corpse!
>
> You can fancy, now, the hoards of vengeance in his heart against the employers. For there are never wanting those who, either in speech or in print, find it in their interest to cherish such feelings in the working classes; who know how and when to rouse the dangerous power at their command; and who use their knowledge with unrelenting purpose to either party. (Ch. 3)

Those exclamation points, creating melodrama as in a child's story, are the first clue to what is wrong here: the scene is less realized than insisted upon. And the second paragraph transforms Barton—now again a representative of the distant mass—into someone with strong feelings, but incapable of commanding a political intelligence. His feelings become mindless stores of gun-powder in the arsenals of "outside agitators." And yet the ostensible point of this passage is to make us sympathetic with Barton's union activities through engaging us with the power of his domestic grief. Barton's reality lies in those feelings; what happens to them is abstract, someone else's responsibility. The evil of unions lies, it is implied, in the fact that they extend impulses of feeling into the inappropriate sphere of political action. And that analysis is borne out by the events that precede and explain the murder.

Gaskell's strength in this part of the book lies in her depiction of tempers wearing down under the stress of loss and poverty: Jane Wilson's temper provides a domestic parallel with Barton's in the development of the theme. Barton's first act of violence is a domestic one: he strikes Mary, then quickly repents and apologizes. His second mistake, also set up in parallel with his political behavior, is to reject Esther, whom he blames for his wife's death; again the pattern of action followed by repentance prefigures the end of the story. The decision to kill Harry Carson, set off by the casual cruelty of his caricature, is depicted as a "last straw" move, an attempt to maintain some vestige of manhood under unendurable circumstances. During the union meeting that follows the failure of the negotiation with the masters, Barton demonstrates his humanity by arguing against violence to scabs, and then defends himself against an accusation of cowardice by redirecting the men's violence at the masters. The necessity to do something is made palpable, but it is represented as a form of action necessary to relieve feelings, not as a strategic decision in a political program.

The crime itself is often said to be the act that places Barton beyond our political sympathies.[4] It does have the effect of dealing the final blow to the image of unionization, turning the union into a criminal bond. But in fact it seems to me that the murder works to strengthen our personal sympathies, both toward the murderer and his victim's family. Through killing Harry, Barton creates in the elder Carson a master who is capable of becoming a "brother" in suffering: the reconciliation of Barton and Carson depends on their shared, or parallel, griefs at the loss of an only son. The murder is "successful" in the sense that it is responsible for both Barton's redemption and Carson's; and their similarities of character—revenging and then relenting—effect the temperamental brotherhood that would seem to overleap the social gap. Thus when the possibility of sharing information with workers emerges as a shadow of a solution at the end, we are apt to feel that the industrial relation is really a severed family tie that ought to be repaired rather than a radical change in the nature of industrial social arrangements.[5]

The peculiarity of the murder's function in the plot does not end with the social reconciliation that it engenders. John Barton "ought" to be murdering Harry Carson because Carson has sexual designs upon his daughter; and Barton's sensitivity to that issue has been carefully created through his antipathy to factory work for women. But the plot is divided in such a way that he does not know the sexual sins of his victim; this knowledge, and its attendant anger, is left for Jem Wilson, who has the interview with Esther that John Barton refuses. Thus Barton and the falsely accused Jem become split

---

4. See Raymond Williams, pp. 89 and 90. John Lucas amends Williams's analysis in an interesting way, asserting that the murder plot simplifies the political situation enough so that a moral pattern can be made from "a muddle so colossal that it defeats the explanations of her social creeds" (p. 173).
5. I have described Gaskell's very different embrace of social change in *North and South* in "*North and South*: A Permanent State of Change," *Nineteenth-Century Fiction*, 34 (1979), 281–301.

doubles in the murder plot. Jem provides the public cover for John's political murder; the cover is a personal and sexual revenge story, not an industrial one.

This splitting does some other work to soften the novel's analysis of the middle-class and its institutions. First and most simply, the false accusation plot deflects our judgment of John Barton as a criminal, turning our "legal" interest to the wish to have Jem legally absolved. The outcome of the trial allows "justice to be done" by the legal machinery in a way that upholds the character of the assizes and shows working-class characters winning a court case against an employer, at the same time as it retains our sympathy for the actual murderer. For we are absorbed into the imaginations of Jem and Mary, each going to the brink in an attempt to keep the guilty one from suspicion; Barton's presence in their anguish keeps him firmly within the circle of our assent. Thus the difficult opposition of justice and legality—which has haunted John Barton—is happily reconciled in two ways at once. Mary's faith in the law as an impartial instrument of justice is upheld when her production of an "alibi" for Jem proves successful. At the same time a combination of natural and divine justice governs the repentance and end of John Barton, beyond the system of law. While the law—demonstrably an instrument of the middle class— retains its technical authority, the higher law prevails as well.

The plot provides a similar muffling of the connection between industrial and sexual exploitation.[6] Harry Carson is a seducer; but Mary is not his employee, and he has no direct economic hold over her. He remains a threat only so long as Mary is willing to entertain the idea of a class romance. Neither Jem nor John is a Carson employee; again the personal and economic connections are of the loosest kind. Even Esther, an example of "the seduced and abandoned," has been betrayed not by a factory owner but by that traditional literary seducer, an army officer. And, because the stories of sexual harassment and economic exploitation are split between Harry Carson and his father, on the one hand, John and Jem on the other, we are not required by the novel's structure to put them back together into a systematic analysis of industrial oppression.

The intertwinings of the two main plots are thus arranged to defuse political issues, but these reflections must also suggest the interdependence of the stories. The structure of Mary's experience has a good deal in common with that of her father. Neither Barton is

6. I take issue here with Ivan Melada's argument in *The Captain of Industry in English Fiction 1821–1871* (Albuquerque: University of New Mexico Press, 1970), pp. 73–86. Melada calls *Mary Barton* "the novel that consistently criticizes the employer according to assumptions about factory owners common among the working classes . . ." (p. 86). Melada identifies these with a set of accusations made by radical factions against the self-serving legal system, sexual exploitation of women factory workers, and the arrogant pride of class.

resigned; both are pulled away from domestic activities by imaginations of a better life. John is beckoned forth by the ghostly hands of the union; Mary is temporarily drawn toward a chimera depicted with equal unreality, the dream of a middle-class marriage. Both father and daughter go out of Manchester on missions to save their people by telling the truth in a public forum. Mary, focused on a single and personal situation within a legal context, is allowed to be successful. Her story offers a vision of action immersed in loyalty to domestic ties that serves as an antidote and a release of the tensions established in her father's.

Mary's story is often written off as a conventional romance: a young girl chooses between the rich, handsome, dangerous fantasy prince and her true working-class childhood love. This view requires some important amendments. First, Gaskell is almost completely uninterested in the relationship between Mary and Harry Carson. She dramatizes it once, in their final interview; and Mary fends him off during every dialogue we hear between her and the go-between Sally Leadbitter. It is Sally who interests Gaskell, because Sally wants to make Mary into the kind of romantic heroine that Gaskell has been made responsible for in some critical accounts. Secondly, the real issue of heroism in Mary's life lies not in her choice of lovers, but in the question of whether or how to act, once she has recognized her love for Jem. When the murder plot allows her to act, she becomes, though only briefly and ambiguously, a heroine of stature.[7] Two pairs of friends and lovers press on either side of Mary's character, organizing the opposition of domestic tranquillity and romance: Sally Leadbitter and Harry Carson on the false romantic side; Margaret Legh and Jem Wilson on the other.

Mary's flirtation with Carson is introduced with an almost incredible casualness, subordinated to a description of Mary's growing confidential friendship with Margaret Legh (Ch. 5). This nearly parenthetical treatment is in keeping with the general portrayal of Carson: he is important primarily because he is a secret that divides Mary from her loyal, familial friends. Carson is minimally realized, and even Mary is said to know that she is in love, not with him, but with the possibility of wealth and status that her reading of cheap romances has taught her to covet. That by-the-way introduction is also consistent with the most painful results of the public revelation of Mary's relationship with Carson: Margaret's withdrawal at the discovery of her friend's deception, and the tongue-lashing Mary gets from her future mother-in-law.

---

7. Mary's character and plot are given some positive critical attention by W. A. Craik, who also emphasizes Mary's public acting (pp. 35–38), and by Lansbury, who stresses her independence and activity, though without notice to the parts of the narrative that pull Mary in more passive and conventional directions (pp. 23, 29–30, and 31).

Margaret and Sally are Mary's good and bad angels; each, in her way, is devoted to art. Margaret makes a gold mine of her blindness by becoming a professional singer of working-class ballads; this, of course, is the proper use of art, to transmute the grief of living into song that moves the hearts of its listeners. Sally wants to create in life the kind of spurious escapist romance celebrated in the novels that form the staple of discussion at Miss Simmons' millinery workroom. Gaskell's diction about Sally is directly reminiscent of Jane Austen:

> She had just talent enough to corrupt others. Her very good nature was an evil influence. They could not hate one who was so kind; they could not avoid one who was so willing to shield them from scrapes by any exertion of her own; whose ready fingers would at any time make up for their deficiencies, and whose still more convenient tongue would at any time invent for them. (Ch. 8)

Playing Isabella Thorpe to Mary's Catherine Morland,[8] Sally's vulgar imagination thrills to the plot that she sustains between Mary and Carson, with no thought for the implications of the seduction she knows to be its only possible fulfillment. The witty, markedly literary, self-consciousness in the treatment of Sally is sustained throughout the novel, making it very clear that Gaskell is offering, by way of contrast, a very different kind of woman's heroism.

Sally's inability "to become a heroine on her own account" (Ch. 8) renders her eager to play a supporting role even when Mary bows out of the Carson fantasy. When Mary becomes a public character, about to set off for the Liverpool Assizes, Sally's value as a source of sheer comic relief is proven in a witty scene. Memorizing Mary's clothes and looks like a fashion reporter, Sally prepares herself to be "a Gazette Extraordinary the next morning at the work-room" (Ch. 25), and she urges Mary to return there after the trial so that her status as heroine will help pick up trade. Once Mary has returned, Sally's mixture of failure, admiration, and envy are expressed in the line "You've set up heroine on your own account, Mary Barton" (Ch. 34). By this time Mary has indeed been set up as heroine, on Gaskell's account—in ways that show her creator in yet another struggle with Victorian conventions.

The positive portrait of Mary has two distinct parts that co-exist rather uncomfortably, corresponding to the opposition of domestic passivity and political action in the John Barton sections. As a heroine of the domestic life celebrated in so much of the narrative, Mary is shown as the impulsive comforter of Jem in trouble, daughter solicitous of her father, neighborly nurse of old Alice Wilson, and maker of the resolve to abstain from telling Jem of her love—even after

8. Reference to Jane Austen's *Northanger Abbey* (1817). [*Editor*].

refusing his proposal—in the name of shrinking from "unmaidenly action" (Ch. 15). As a heroine of rescue, on the other hand, Mary persuades Job and Margaret to support her, travels alone to Liverpool, chases the steamer on which Will Wilson is about to sail away, survives being lost in a strange place, and testifies in a public courtroom to those feelings which would have been "unmaidenly" to reveal in private to her lover. These two portraits are clearly not compatible, and Gaskell does her best to blur the more active one by presenting Mary in a state of near-collapse and then delirious illness during her stay in Liverpool. Still, at the moment she is brought into being, that heroine of rescue touches some of her author's fiercest feelings on the question of action and resignation.

Mary's decision to wait in womanly passivity for Jem to return to his courtship is apparently supported in the narrative: the good angel Margaret counsels patience, and Gaskell gives us a little chapter (Ch. 12) devoted explicitly to the theme of waiting and reward, in which old Alice's desire for Will Wilson's return is set next to Mary's own ordeal of waiting. Yet the action during this period is designed so that Mary misses every opportunity of seeing Jem, even in those sickroom scenes which provide the primary settings for their familial courtship throughout the novel. This Victorian modesty strains against the energy of Mary's character, and the tension produces a small narrative explosion when it comes time for Mary to act.

After Mary deduces that her father is the murderer of Carson (Ch. 22), she discovers "a little spring of comfort" in "the desert of misery": "And that was the necessity for exertion on her part which this discovery enforced." With that, Gaskell goes off into the novel's most personal aside: "Oh! I do think that the necessity for exertion, for some kind of action (bodily or mentally) in time of distress, is a most infinite blessing, although the first efforts at such seasons are painful," she exclaims; and she goes on to have a little fit of anger at those who counsel against grief in situations where no help can be given. This highly charged state of feeling extends into the few sentences that do the work of transforming Mary into an active heroine:

> But with the call upon her exertions, and her various qualities of judgment and discretion, came the answering consciousness of innate power to meet the emergency . . . And you must remember, too, that never was so young a girl so friendless, or so penniless, as Mary was at this time. But the lion accompanied Una through the wilderness and the danger; and so will a high, resolved purpose of right-doing ever guard and accompany the helpless.

> But Mary re-entered her home . . . with . . . a still clearer conviction of how much rested upon her unassisted and friendless

self, alone with her terrible knowledge, in the hard, cold, populous world. (Ch. 22)

Two images come into play simultaneously: Mary as the noble quester, full of internal strength, and a vision of the larger world as wilderness, vast and threatening. The combination of admiration for Mary's courage and fear of the public arena is intensified by the exaggerated, melodramatic account of Mary's isolation. When Mary's excitement grows into a vision of herself as heroine, that isolation remains part of the picture: "She longed to do all herself; to be his liberator, his deliverer; to win him life, though she might never regain his lost love by her own exertions" (Ch. 23). This vision of chivalric rescue carries a dynamic force that merges Mary's romantic imagination with her moral one. Yet one must recall the word "enforced" which accompanies the initial discovery of the need for action: Mary is released into an active, responsible, and independent role only because there is an "emergency."

Even before the emergency is over, the determined actor with her "terrible knowledge" is on the verge of dissolving into something very like a heroine of sensibility. During the trial scene itself, Gaskell falls into some disturbingly romantic and pictorial language about Mary:

> The mellow sunlight streamed down that high window on her head, and fell on the rich treasure of her golden hair, stuffed away in masses under her little bonnet-cap. . . . I was not there myself; but one who was, told me that her look, and indeed her whole face, was more like the well-known engraving from Guido's picture of "Beatrice Cenci" than anything else he could give me an idea of. He added, that her countenance haunted him, like the remembrance of some wild sad melody heard in childhood; that it would perpetually recur with its mute imploring agony. (Ch. 32)

This is a shocking break in the normal narrative relationship with Mary and with her beauty; the objectification of the heroine, from a cultured male middle-class point of view, seems symptomatic of Gaskell's distress at having gotten her heroine into so public a fix. Gaskell apparently needs to pretend that she did not place Mary on the witness stand without some factual precedent that has already made Mary into a well-known legendary figure—and, in fact, into a piece of art.

The oddness of this withdrawal from Mary's own experience in the courtroom may be related to the class confrontation of the trial scene itself. Mary is on display before the middle-class world, for the first and only time; and once again, as Gaskell imagines such an audience, she begins to talk its language, as though Mary's power to move the middle-class world lay only in her ability to push those conventional buttons of sentiment that suddenly intrude upon the prose. Or, perhaps, Mary's moment of public soulbearing raises the spectre of female immodesty; lest she become material for Sally's "Gazette Extraordinary," she is transfixed in a more respectable art form. In any case, it immediately becomes possible to measure the difference between this kind of pictorial ballad-making and the success with which Gaskell takes us into the world of the poor when the middle class isn't looking.

The passage is also, however, a prelude to the more general withdrawal of narrative assent to the daring part of Mary's character. Illness purges her, as it does many a middle-class heroine, of all but the most angelic and domestic impulses. Thereafter the predominant images are of Mary's clinging to Jem on the one hand, and protecting her broken father, "as the Innocent should watch over the Guilty" (Ch. 34) on the other. What remains to be resolved returns us to the world of domestic romance that encloses the courtship of Jem and Mary: Mary and her future mother-in-law must struggle for the possession of Jem's affection; Mary, now fully domesticated, must be received into the family, the relation cemented by the shared secret knowledge of John Barton's crime.

A merger of the Bartons and the Wilsons, repairing the decimation of the original families, is the proper resolution in a novel that locates its virtues so firmly in family solidarity and tradition. The domestic management of grief might even be said to triumph in the private extralegal reconciliation of Barton and Carson, which allows Barton's crime to remain forever buried in the family closet. Thus the primacy of the family finally overcomes the impulse to action in the larger world, allowing Gaskell to dissolve the disturbing aspects of Barton's radicalism and Mary's romantic energy in the brew of familial sympathy. The ending puts Barton in Carson's arms; Mary in Jem's; and Gaskell goes on to apply the liberal-economist's pet panacea, voluntary emigration.

To center the novel in this way is, finally, to see its political movements in their proper context. It is easy enough, by focusing on the plot resolutions, to group *Mary Barton* with other industrial novels that portray social injustices while showing working-class political initiative as manipulated action or animal violence. But *Mary Barton* asks its questions of life in rather different ways. Starting and ending always with the personal grief, the novel is only secondarily about politics as such. Politics figures rather like romance, as a form of "bodily or mental action" that might alleviate or muffle the pain of domestic grief and suffering that is represented as the fundamental matter of experience. The public realm appears as a threatening place of resort in the desperation of poverty or injustice. This world, run by the middle-class, may fortuitously remedy a specific injustice, as in the release of Jem, but it is not likely to answer to generalized social accusations. The proper forum for grief is, rather, the familial and neighborly world. And because Gaskell realizes this world so fully and warmly, she offers an image of her subjects that is at once more conservative and more human than the aggregated urban masses or disintegrating industrial families of Disraeli or Dickens. Her society of the poor is so full of its own dictions and traditions, and so various in its own right, that the middle class voices we hear at the Carsons' or before the Liverpool Assizes seem genuine intrusions from another linguistic universe.

At the same time, the centrifugal pull out of the domestic orbit is one of the powerful forces at work in the text, in ways that link the characters with Gaskell's own dilemmas of authorship. So many episodes are devoted to the anatomy of grief that it is nearly impossible to forget that *Mary Barton* was part of Gaskell's grieving process; but it is equally touching to watch the assertions and withdrawals which attend upon her first appearance as a public storyteller. The character of John Barton is based on the same troubled relationship between direct social apprehension and general theory that Gaskell's own narrative reveals. Barton arrives at his radical social conclusions about the gulf between classes out of a battered and embittered spirit. Seeing what he sees, Gaskell's ameliorating narrator leaps in the opposite direction, toward middle-class liberal formulae. If Barton is mimicking his union agitators, Gaskell is, no less, imitating her liberal theorists; and what the book most movingly demonstrates is exactly that conceptual impasse, in narrator and character alike.

In Mary's burst of heroism Gaskell imagined an even more direct image of her own situation. For writing *Mary Barton* was her kind of "bodily or mental action in time of distress," and it leads, like Mary's journey, out of the domestic world and into a public one where one's deepest feelings are put on display for a curious crowd. "I am almost frightened at my own action in writing it," Gaskell wrote to Mary Ewart late in 1848;[9] and Mary's story is shaped by that divided and quickly repentant sense of public assertiveness for women. But despite its fits and starts, its bows to imagined audiences, and its retreats to political and feminine stereotypes, the concrete substance of Elizabeth Gaskell's narrative remains, like Mary's truthful testimony, a genuine mission of rescue.

9. *Letters*, p. 67.

CATHERINE GALLAGHER

[Causality versus Conscience: The Problem of Form in *Mary Barton*]†

* * *

Gaskell's use of contrasting narrative forms is one of the most interesting and overlooked features of *Mary Barton*. In a sense, the first
half of the novel is about the dangers inherent in various conventional
ways of organizing reality. The two most obviously false and destructive conventional perspectives on the novel's action are the sentimen-
tally romantic and the farcical. The narrator herself never adopts
these modes; rather, they enter the narrative as the distorted literary
viewpoints of a few characters. Esther and young Mary hold the sentimental perspective; Sally Leadbitter and Harry Carson hold the
complementary viewpoint of farce. Gaskell is careful to point out that
the sentimental perspective originates in literature; Mary's "foolish,
unworldly ideas" come not only from her Aunt Esther's talk about
"making a lady" of her, but also from "the romances which Miss Simmonds' young ladies were in the habit of recommending to each
other." And although the narrator excuses both Esther and Mary on
the grounds of their youth, she indicates that their conventional literary delusions are truly pernicious. Esther's elopement ruins her and
apparently also contributes to the death of Mary's mother, and Mary's
desire to marry a gentleman brings her and almost all of the other
characters in the book "bitter woe" (p. 41).[1]

   The complement to these sentimental notions, the convention that
they play into and that makes them dangerous, is farce. Both Sally
Leadbitter and Harry Carson see their lives and the lives of others as
farce. Sally becomes a *farceuse* because she cannot be a sentimental
heroine. Being "but a plain, red-haired, freckled, girl," she tries to
make up for her lack of beauty "by a kind of witty boldness, which
gave her, what her betters would have called piquancy" (p. 82). Sally
is a working-class version of the witty female rogue: "Considerations
of modesty or propriety never checked her utterance of a good thing"
(p. 82). Her vision is entirely comic; it excludes any serious thought
about the consequences of Mary's flirtation with young Carson at the
same time that it denies the very possibility that Mary's romantic fantasies might be sincerely held: "Sally Leadbitter laughed in her sleeve

† From *The Industrial Reformation of English Fiction: Social Discourse and Narrative Form 1832–1867* (Chicago: University of Chicago Press, 1985), pp. 68–73, 74–78, 80–82, 83–84. By permission of the University of Chicago Press.
1. All page numbers for *Mary Barton* refer to this Norton Critical Edition.

at them both, and wondered how it would all end,—whether Mary
would gain her point of marriage, with her sly affectation of believing such to be Mr. Carson's intention in courting her" (p. 120). Harry
Carson, of course, shares this farcical perspective on Mary's actions.
Both he and Sally imagine her to be a character in their own farcical
world—a "sweet little coquette" (p. 121), "a darling little rascal" (p.
121) with an "ambitious heart" (p. 122). For Sally and Harry Carson,
this characterization gives a conventional authorization, indeed a
conventional imperative, to Mary's seduction.

Moreover, Mary's is not the only reality that the farcical perspective distorts: everything that enters Sally's or young Carson's purview
becomes comic material. Sally is always "ready to recount the events
of the day, to turn them into ridicule, and to mimic, with admirable
fidelity, any person gifted with an absurdity who had fallen under her
keen eye" (p. 82). The ability to mimic "with admirable fidelity" is also
a talent, indeed a fatal talent, of Harry Carson. Young Carson's farcical vision leads him to caricature not only Mary, but the whole of the
working class as well, and as Gaskell points out, these comic carica-
tures both mask and perpetuate working-class suffering. In her exposition of the dangers inherent in farcical distortions, the author
brings together the sexual and social themes of the novel: both Mary
and the delegation of striking workers are victimized by Harry Carson's conventional blindness.

If working-class women are seducible "little rascals" for Harry Carson, working-class men are clowns. Young Carson exhibits his blindness to the human reality of working-class men on several occasions
(for instance, in his treatment of Mr. Wilson, in his interview with
Jem, and in his obstinate behavior at the negotiating table), but the
conventional attitude that motivates his behavior is most clearly
expressed in the action that precipitates his murder. He is killed for
making a joke, for attempting to transform a workers' delegation into
a troop of Shakespearean clowns:

> Mr. Harry Carson had taken out his silver pencil, and had
> drawn an admirable caricature of them—lank, ragged, dispir-
> ited, and famine-stricken. Underneath he wrote a hasty quota-
> tion from the fat knight's well-known speech in Henry IV. He
> passed it to one of his neighbours, who acknowledged the like-
> ness instantly, and by him it was set round to others, who all
> smiled and nodded their heads. (p. 163)

The caricature, tossed away by Carson but retrieved by a curious member of the workers' delegation, so enrages John Barton that he con-
spires with the ridiculed workers to kill the caricaturist. It is significant
that the fatal joke is as much Shakespeare's as it is Carson's: that fact
emphasizes the unreal, literary nature of Carson's perception. It also

stresses how deeply entrenched the farcical distortion of working-class life is in English culture. Carson's destructive use of Shakespeare reminds Gaskell's readers that although they have the best precedents for laughing at rags and tatters, they must now free themselves from the conventional association between "low" characters and comedy.

But the whole incident raises another question: what new associations should replace the old? It is quite clear that Gaskell intends to expose the dangerous falseness of both sentimental romance and farce; but the ground of her exposition, the narrative mode that she adopted because she believed that it did reflect working-class reality, is difficult to identify. Most literary practices calling themselves realistic rely on contrasts with other, presumably false and outdated narrative perspectives.[2] In *Mary Barton* Gaskell purposely sets up false conventions for contrast, thereby calling attention to her own narrative method as the "true" perspective. The problem is that she then has trouble fixing on any one narrative mode; the ground of the contrast continually shifts in the first half of the book while the author searches for a mode of realism adequate to her subject matter. Thus, in her attempt to juxtapose reality and these false conventions, Gaskell employs several alternative narrative modes: tragedy, melodrama, domestic fiction, and finally religious homily.

The most obvious realistic contrast to both the sentimentality of Esther and Mary and the farce of Sally Leadbitter and Harry Carson is the tragedy of John Barton. Barton is the most active and outspoken adversary of both of these false conventions. It is from his perspective that we first see Esther's romantic folly; the story of the girl's elopement is completely contained within John Barton's gloomy interpretation of it: "bad's come over her, one way or another" (p. 13), he tells his friend Wilson. And his interpretation, of course, immediately undercuts all the story's romance. Moreover, his version of Esther's story makes it merely a part of a larger social tragedy. It includes the girl's social determinism: factory work, he is convinced, led to Esther's downfall by making her recklessly independent and giving her the means to buy finery. As Barton tells Esther's story, he reveals his perspective on the relationship between the classes, a perspective that is itself tragic and productive of tragedy. He opposes Esther's romantic dreams not only because they are dangerous, but also because he hates the class she wishes to join. Barton's is a completely polarized view of social reality: only rich and poor seem to exist, and the rich are the constant oppressors of the poor. The ubiquitous slavery metaphor makes its appearance here, attesting to Barton's radicalism, his polarized social vision, and the determinism that informs his thinking:

2. As Harry Levin has pointed out in *The Gates of Horn: A Study of Five French Realists* (New York, 1966), p. 19, "the movement of realism, technically considered, is an endeavor to emancipate literature from the sway of conventions."

> "We are their slaves as long as we can work; we pile up their for-
> tunes with the sweat of our brows; and yet we are to live as sep-
> arate as if we were in two worlds; ay, as separate as Dives and
> Lazarus, with a great gulf betwixt us: but I know who was best
> off then," and he wound up his speech with a low chuckle that
> had no mirth in it. (p. 12)

Even this closing reference to heavenly justice is a gloomy prophecy
of revenge, not a joyful anticipation of saintly rewards.

Barton's tragic perspective, therefore, contrasts sharply with Esther's
and, later, with Mary's romantic fantasies. Moreover, his interpretation
is corroborated by the plot itself; he is correct to note that Esther's
romantic dreamworld is really a disguised stage for tragedy. Barton's
relationship to the farcical viewpoint is similar: again he opposes it
energetically, and again in his opposition he speaks the truth. In
fact, in the most decisive moment of his own tragedy, Barton contrasts Harry Carson's caricature, his fixed, farcical representation,
with the tragic reality that lies behind the conventionally ludicrous
appearance:

> "it makes my heart burn within me, to see that folk can make a
> jest of earnest men; of chaps, who comed to ask for a bit o' fire
> for th' old granny, as shivers in the cold; for a bit o' bedding, and
> some warm clothing to the poor wife as lies in labour on th'
> damp flags; and for victuals for the childer, whose little voices
> are getting too faint and weak to cry aloud wi' hunger." (p. 166)

Through Barton's eyes we see behind the cartoon images of the
ragged men to the suffering of thousands of helpless people. The
delegates caricatured by Harry Carson are tragic; they are compelled to strike by their noblest characteristics: their sympathy with
and sense of responsibility to their hungry dependents. But Carson's Shakespearean joke attempts to freeze the imagination at the
level of appearances, where the workmen become a troop of clowns.
In Falstaff's speech, alluded to but not quoted, they are "good
enough to toss; food for powder, food for powder; they'll fill a pit as
well as better. Tush, man, mortal men, mortal men."[3] Such dehumanization obscures the tragedy, making it perfectly appropriate
that the story's central tragic action should be the destruction of
this *farceur*, the murder of Harry Carson. Thus farce, the mask of
tragedy, becomes its stuff, just as Falstaff's callous speech trails off

---

3. It is Stephen Gill who suggests in footnote 58 of the Penguin edition of *Mary Barton*
[Stephen Gill, ed. Harmondsworth: Penguin Books, 1970] that this is the quotation, from
Henry IV, Part 1, 4.3, to which Gaskell alludes. However, my colleague Paul Alpers suggests informally that, although these are his most famous lines in the scene, Falstaff has a
much longer speech that yields lines possibly more appropriate to Carson's purpose, such
as "ragged as Lazarus in the painted cloth" and "a hundred and fifty tattered prodigals lately
come from swine-keeping."

into a sad and even leveling refrain: "Tush, man, mortal men, mortal men."

Tragedy, then, is the immediate realistic ground against which both romance and farce are contrasted. But the narrative method of this novel cannot be called tragic. As we will see, tragedy is forced to compete with other realistic forms in the book's first half, and in the last half it is present only as a suppressed reality. By examining the part of the story that Gaskell specifically intended as tragic—John Barton's own story—we can see why the author continually shifted to other modes of narration. For John Barton's tragedy is self-contradictory. Because she draws both on traditional ideas of heroic character and on determinist, Owenite ideas of character formation, the author encounters a paradox as she attempts to trace a continuous line of tragic development.

The causality Gaskell attempts to trace follows a traditional tragic pattern; it is the result of the interaction between the character's heroic qualities and external circumstances. As Gaskell told a correspondent after the book's publication, her original intention was to show the operations of inner and outer causes in the destiny of a Manchester weaver:

> I can remember now that the prevailing thought in my mind at the time . . . was the seeming injustice of the inequalities of fortune. Now, if they occasionally appeared unjust to the more fortunate, they must bewilder an ignorant man full of rude, illogical thought, and full also of sympathy for suffering which appealed to him through his senses. I fancied I saw how all this might lead to a course of action which might appear right for a time to the bewildered mind of such a one.[4]

This was, she said, her original "design": the very qualities that made Barton a hero, his thoughtfulness and sympathy, were to combine with external circumstances to produce a tragic action.

This tragic design is certainly apparent in John Barton's story. We are often reminded by both Barton's speeches and the narrator's characterizations of him that his love for his family and his sympathy for the suffering poor cause his hatred of the rich. His unselfishness is emphasized repeatedly; he feels angry not on his own behalf, but on behalf of those who are weaker and poorer. The need to stress Barton's heroic unselfishness determines many of the plot's details; it is significant, for example, that he is not one of the workers caricatured by Harry Carson. His rude thoughtfulness, his desire to understand the suffering he sees, is a second admirable trait contributing to his downfall. Barton is the only character who consistently seeks causes for the world's

---

4. [J. A. V. Chapple and Arthur Pollard, eds.], *Letters of Mrs. Gaskell* [(Manchester: Manchester UP, 1966)], p. 74.

phenomena, but his analyses are marred by his ignorance, by the fact that his understanding is circumscribed by his limited experience.

Gaskell carefully shows how these qualities of mind are impressed with a tragic stamp by external circumstances, by what comes to Barton "through his senses." The links in the tragic chain are clearly identified and labeled: his parents' poverty, his son's death, his wife's death, the trade depression and the consequent suffering of neighbors, his trip to London, his hunger, his opium addiction. Each of these incidents or circumstances is noted by the narrator as yet another cause of Barton's bitterness. The account of his wife's death, for example, concludes with the gloss: "One of the good influences over John Barton's life had departed that night. One of the ties which bound him down to the gentle humanities of earth was loosened, and henceforward the neighbors all remarked he was a changed man" (p. 23). The story of his son's illness and death also ends with emphasis on its consequences: "You can fancy, now, the hoards of vengeance in his heart against the employers" (p. 25).

Even the narrator's disavowals of Barton's ideas and feelings are intended to contribute to his story's tragedy. Remarks such as "I know that this is not really the case [that the workers alone suffer from trade depressions]; and I know what is the truth in such matters: but what I wish to impress is what the workman feels and thinks" (p. 24) may seem annoying intrusions to twentieth-century readers, but they were designed to keep the nineteenth-century readers' own opinions from interfering with their ability to follow Barton's tragedy. The disavowals are there to prevent the reader from becoming distracted by the issue of whether or not Barton's ideas are objectively true; Barton, we are told in these asides, reached the wrong conclusions, but the circumstances of his life did not allow him to reach any other.

* * *

Consequently, a tension developed in her portrayal of John Barton, a tension between his social determinism and his tragic heroism. This tension increases as his crisis approaches until it finally emerges as an observable contradiction when the narrator directly confronts the political model of freedom Barton has come to advocate. His radical ambition to become a shaper of society, to cast off the role of a passive creature, acts as a magnet that draws both poles of the author's ambivalence about freedom toward one paradoxical center. The paradox is most clearly visible in the narrator's very last expository attempt to explain the causality of John Barton's story:

> No education had given him wisdom; and without wisdom, even love, with all its effects, too often works but harm. He acted to the best of his judgment but it was a widely-erring judgement.

The actions of the uneducated seem to me typified in those of Frankenstein, that monster of many human qualities, ungifted with a soul, a knowledge of the difference between good and evil.

The people rise up to life; they irritate us, they terrify us, and we become their enemies. Then, in the sorrowful moment of our triumphant power, their eyes gaze on us with a mute reproach. Why have we made them what they are; a powerful monster, yet without the inner means for peace and happiness?

John Barton became a Chartist, a Communist, all that is commonly called wild and visionary. Ay! but being visionary is something. It shows a soul, a being not altogether sensual; a creature who looks forward for others, if not for himself. (p. 150)

All the elements of the tragedy are present in these metaphoric exchanges. Barton represents the uneducated, who are collected into the image of Frankenstein's tragically determined, larger-than-life monster. Then the monster, defeated and gazing at us, shrinks back to the dimensions of John Barton, the unselfish visionary. But these smooth metaphoric transitions do not quite cover the passage's central paradox: the "actions of the uneducated" grow out of their soullessness, their incapacity to make moral choices. Barton became a "Chartist, a Communist," a visionary in consequence of this soullessness. But the metaphor is too harsh, too denigrating to the hero, and the narrator pulls back and reverses herself: "But being visionary is something. It shows a soul." Suddenly John Barton's rebellious actions, instead of showing him to be a creature "ungifted with a soul," become the proof that he has a soul, the emblem of his humanity and his moral freedom. His heroism is saved, but only at the expense of the causality implied by the Frankenstein metaphor, a causality that traces Barton's crime to "us."

We can argue, therefore, that the paradoxical nature of Gaskell's tragic vision forces her to abandon it in the novel's second half. Even in the first half of the book, though, the narrator never confines her own view to this tragic dynamic, dangerous as it was to the very idea of moral freedom. Instead, she juxtaposes three "realistic" narrative modes in the book's early chapters: tragedy, melodrama, and a working-class domestic tale. The presence, indeed the competition, of the melodrama and the domestic tale allows two things. First, the author is able to avoid her tragic responsibilities, which are too contradictory to fulfill successfully; these other modes distract attention from and obscure the problematic causality of John Barton's story. Second, the presence of the melodrama, in particular, allows Gaskell to extend her critical exploration of conventional ways of interpreting reality.

Gaskell's use of melodrama is skillful: she first invites us into a melodramatic narrative, sets up melodramatic expectations, and then reveals that melodrama is a mere conventional distortion, a genre inappropriate to modern reality. Critics have claimed that *Mary Barton* becomes melodramatic with the murder of Harry Carson,[5] but this formulation is backwards. The first half of the book is much more seriously melodramatic than the second because in the first half there is a melodrama just offstage, in the wings, as it were, which threatens to take over the drama entirely. Indeed, the reader cannot initially tell whether the early chapters are part of a melodrama or of some other kind of narrative. They contain many melodramatic characteristics.[6] We view Esther's elopement not only from Barton's tragic perspective, but also through the unarticulated, excessive grief of her sister Mary, young Mary's mother. Her grief is so excessive that it kills her, suddenly and surprisingly. It is the kind of parabolical death that abounded in nineteenth-century melodramas, and it leads into young Mary's potential melodrama—the threat of her seduction by the rakish Harry Carson. The narrator, in true melodramatic manner, continually suspends any resolution of Mary's fate and makes dark prognostications about it: "Mary hoped to meet him every day in her walks, blushed when she heard his name, and tried to think of him as her future husband, and above all, tried to think of herself as his future wife. Alas! poor Mary! Bitter woe did thy weakness work thee" (pp. 40–41). The wholly conventional language here ("Alas! poor Mary!") leads us to expect, mistakenly, that Mary's "bitter woe" will also be of the conventional melodramatic kind.

Although romance and farce finally do turn into tragedy in *Mary Barton*, they threaten repeatedly in the first half to turn into melodrama. Mary's renunciation of Harry Carson, her abandonment of romance, brings the melodrama even closer; for it is after his rejection that Harry Carson becomes truly villainous, indeed a potential rapist: "From blandishments he had even gone to threats—threats that whether she would or not she should be his" (p. 154). It is only after she has awakened from her romantic dream that Mary is in danger of

5. Patrick Brantlinger, in "Bluebooks, the Social Organism, and the Victorian Novel," *Criticism* 13 (1972):328–44, contrasts the detailed evocation of working-class life with the "melodrama of the murder plot," and Stephen Gill ("Introduction") also contrasts the realistic sketches of the first half with the conventional "romantic" sensationalism of the second half (p. 22).

6. My paradigm of melodrama is based primarily on the discussions by Peter Brooks in *The Melodramatic Imagination: Balzac, Henry James, Melodrama, and the Mode of Excess* (New Haven, 1976), pp. 11–20, and by R.B. Heilman, *Tragedy and Melodrama* (Seattle, 1968), passim. Brooks stresses that melodramas portray uncompromising struggles between good and evil. Their mode of action is excessive and parabolical. Heilman discusses the affective difference between tragedy and melodrama, arguing that the former, by portraying an irresolvable internal conflict, produces a complex emotional response, while the latter, by portraying a heroic fight against an external evil force, produces a simpler, self-righteous emotional reaction in the audience.

becoming a true melodramatic heroine: an innocent girl sexually per-
secuted by a villain. Indeed, Mary registers the change linguistically. As
soon as she understands her true position she declares: "if I had loved
you before, I don't think I should have loved you now you have told me
you meant to ruin me; for that's the plain English of not meaning to
marry me till just this minute. . . . Now I scorn you, sir, for plotting to
ruin a poor girl" (p. 123). This is not "plain English," the language
Mary usually speaks. It is popular stage English,[7] and it temporarily
throws a melodramatic light across Mary's features. Harry Carson's
murder, instead of beginning the novel's melodrama, effectively termi-
nates it. In fact, as we will see, in the second half of the book melodrama joins romance and farce as an overtly discredited convention.

In the first half, however, Mary's potential melodrama competes
for our attention with her father's tragedy. Through the melodramatic
mode of presentation, our concern is solicited for Mary in a way that
it never is for John. Indeed, Gaskell so arranges her narrative that we
end up looking for the catastrophic event in the wrong plot. The
melodrama of Mary's story, therefore, makes us inattentive to the
threatening nature of John's career. The careful tracing of his decline
does not have the interest of Mary's melodrama because we are not
expecting John's story to culminate in some disastrous event. Our
sense of impending catastrophe, which is essential to a tragic narrative, is misplaced in *Mary Barton*. It is attached not only to the wrong
plot but also to the wrong set of narrative conventions. We mistakenly expect a melodramatic catastrophe, one arising from a simple
confrontation between good and evil, but we are given a tragic catastrophe, a complexly and carefully motivated revenge murder, the outcome of an inner as well as an outer struggle. The presence of the
melodrama in the book's first half, therefore, prevents us from clearly
seeing John Barton's decline as the successive complications of a
tragedy, and his story, with its unresolved contradictions, tends to
fade into the background.

In the book's second half, most of the characters repeat our mistake. They continue to interpret the plot according to a preconceived
melodramatic pattern, assuming that Jem killed Harry Carson. It
then becomes Mary's job to discredit their conventional assumptions.
To save Jem is to disprove the melodramatic interpretation of the
murder. Melodrama is, therefore, explicitly consigned to the category
of false conventions. It is associated with other kinds of sensation-
seeking, and Sally Leadbitter is its most determined spokeswoman.
Because her cliché-ridden mind is only able to perceive situations in
terms of popular stage conventions, after Carson's murder she moves
with ease from a farcical to a melodramatic interpretation of the plot.

7. Kathleen Tillotson, *Novels of the Eighteen-Forties* (London, 1956), p. 214.

She holds to her melodramatic version of the story even after Jem's acquittal. In explaining why Jem was dismissed from his job, she reveals the source of her opinions: "Decent men were not going to work with a—no! I suppose I musn't say it, seeing you went to such trouble to get up an *alibi*; not that I should think much the worse of a spirited young fellow for falling foul of a rival,—they always do *at the theatre*" (p. 310) latter emphasis added). Mary, who is concerned for Jem, gasps, "Tell me all about it," and Sally continues, "Why, you see, they've always swords quite handy at them plays" (p. 310).

At this point in the story, Sally's melodramatic viewpoint is relatively harmless—the basis of a joke. But the same viewpoint predominates among the spectators at Jem's trial, almost costing him his life. It is Mary's hard task to disabuse the court of the notion that Jem was a "young fellow" who had "fallen foul of a rival." However, the courtroom, like Sally Leadbitter, seems receptive only to melodrama; even Mary's struggle to save Jem must be rendered melodramatically before it can be admitted: "The barrister, who defended Jem, took new heart when he was put in possession of these striking points to be adduced . . . because he saw the opportunities for a display of forensic eloquence which were presented by the facts; 'a gallant tar brought back from the pathless ocean by a girl's noble daring'" (p. 286). This bit of parody points up the difference between the narrative we have just read and the same facts couched in melodramatic language.

Far from being melodramatic, therefore, the last half of the book takes melodrama as its specific point of contrast. The fact that we ourselves formerly shared the melodramatic assumption, however, allows us to understand what a natural reading of the events it is and how difficult it will be to overcome. Because Mary must overthrow the assumptions not only of the other characters, but also of one of the major narrative conventions of the book's first half, we feel that her task is almost overwhelming. The drama of Mary's plight, therefore, is heightened by the narrative reversal, and the reader's interest in Mary's story intensifies.

By discrediting melodrama however, the later chapters raise the question of realistic narrative form even more insistently than do the earlier chapters. For the narrator's reversed attitude toward melodrama broadens her criticism of the conventional, a criticism that depends on a contrastingly realistic narrative ground. Again, the obvious candidate for such a ground is tragedy; the tragic interpretation of the murder is, after all, the truth that the melodramatic interpretation hides. But the tragic reality is precisely what all the actions of the book's second half are designed to conceal. The very causality that the narrator meticulously traced through the first half is hidden in the second. The events of the second half are more than an escape, an avoidance, of the tragic problem; they represent the problem's deliberate suppression.

In the second half of the book, Mary knows the truth, but she refuses to probe it, to ascertain its meaning. Instead, all her energies go into suppressing both public knowledge of her father's crime and her own consciousness of it. The "why" of the crime, the very substance of the tragedy is not even a subject for speculation in the later chapters: "[Mary] felt it was of no use to conjecture his motives. His actions had become so wild and irregular of late, that she could not reason upon them" (pp. 214–215). In the chapters that are largely confined to Mary's consciousness, therefore, those that take place between the murder and Mary's return to Manchester after the trial, the narrator imposes a moratorium on reasoning about John Barton's life, on thinking about tragic causation. Mary's truth-concealing action takes the place of reason; finding an alibi substitutes for seeking the truth. Tragedy is still present as a narrative ground, but is increasingly shadowy; like melodrama, it is a genre Mary struggles against inhabiting. Thus, at precisely the moment when a stable, realistic narrative form is most needed, tragedy becomes unavailable and another genre emerges into prominence as Mary's special domain. Restricted almost entirely to Mary's viewpoint, the narrative becomes a working-class domestic tale that formally authorizes the suppression of tragic causality.

*   *   *

Mary's existence is "ordinary," but it is also seriously threatened by the emergency she faces. A flawed social order has allowed melodrama and tragedy to break into Mary's world, and she must reestablish its domestic boundaries. Her task involves travel, public notoriety, and extraordinary events of all kinds, but these are necessary to combat melodrama, suppress tragedy, and save what little remains of her family. Mary's homelessness in the later chapters is symptomatic of the social evils the author is trying to illustrate. Mary's struggle to remain a domestic heroine is itself a social criticism with an ideal image of family life at its center. The domestic keynote of these later chapters sounds again and again: in Mary's relationship to Mrs. Wilson; in the minute but emotionally constrained accounts of Mary's tentative and fearful actions and reactions; in the descriptions of the lives and homes she encounters in Liverpool; and in the idyllic, domestic dreamworld that old Alice inhabits throughout the book's second half. Alice's reverie is both a vision of her own past and of Mary's future; Alice imagines the domestic world Mary's actions are retrieving.

For most of the book's second half, then, the domestic tale predominates and suppresses the tragedy, although the two genres are complexly interrelated throughout the novel. Barton's tragedy is itself fundamentally domestic. The loss of his son is the most decisive blow against him. Domestic also is the tragic reality behind the clownish appearance of the workers' delegation, the barren rooms and the sickly wives and children that *Mary Barton* tries to expose. The book was inspired by scenes of blighted domestic life in the working class,[8] and John Barton's narrative sketches the disastrous course that such suffering might initiate.

Although reality is always domestic in *Mary Barton*, it is by no means always tragic. Tragedy may grow out of working-class domestic life, but it ultimately excludes that life. For the most part, *Mary Barton* is a domestic tale, not a domestic tragedy, and the two genres present mutually exclusive kinds of reality in this novel.[9] Barton's tragic career, we are repeatedly told, increasingly takes him away from home; furthermore, most of the working-class characters, drawn in the domestic mode, are uninterested in Barton's talk about social injustice. In fact, the book's first dialogue, between Barton and Wilson, typifies the interaction between the hero and most of the working-class characters. Barton rails on for half a page against the "gentlefolk," but Wilson cuts him short: "Well, neighbour, . . . all that may be very true, but what I want to know now is about Esther" (p. 13). This kind of exchange is repeated on other occasions with Jem Wilson and with Job Leigh; the other men all express the assumptions that are built into Gaskell's domestic convention: being too aware of social injustice only distracts one from the principal realities of family and home; conversely, home and family can protect one from the tragedy that attends class conflict.

His respondents never try to refute Barton's social analyses in these exchanges. Rather, the other men quietly recur to their private preoccupations. Thus, after John Barton tells the sad story of his London journey and concludes that "as long as I live I shall curse them as so cruelly refused to hear us" (p. 92), Job Leigh tells his own London story, which includes his daughter's death and his retrieval of his granddaughter Margaret.[1] The narrator confides that Job chose the domestic subject matter because it was "neither sufficiently dissonant from the last to jar on the full heart, nor too much the same to cherish the continuance of the gloomy train of thought" (p. 92). The domestic tale suppresses the tragedy not by explicitly denying it, but rather by eluding its causality. John Barton's tragedy, as we have

---

8. The often-repeated story is that Gaskell was inspired to write *Mary Barton* while on a mission of mercy to a poor family during the depression of the early 1840s: "She was trying hard to speak comfort, and to allay those bitter feelings against the rich which were so common with the poor, when the head of the family took hold of her arm, and grasping it tightly said, with tears in his eyes, 'Ay, ma'am, but have ye ever seen a child clemmed to death.'" The story is from M. Hompes, "Mrs. E. C. Gaskell," *Gentleman's Magazine* 55 (1895): 124.

9. For a discussion of the various narrative modes in *Mary Barton* as deviations from a dominant domestic mode, see Rosemarie Bodenheimer, "Private Grief and Public Acts in *Mary Barton*," *Dickens Studies Annual: Essays on Victorian Fiction* 9 (New York, 1981): 195–216.

1. Tillotson, *Novels of the Eighteen-Forties*, pp. 215–21, contains an excellent discussion of the two London stories.

seen, is primarily concerned with cause and effect, with showing how and why the hero became "a Chartist, a Communist, all that is commonly called wild and visionary." Gaskell's domestic tales, on the other hand, aim at showing how to circumvent tragic cause-and-effect logic by simply acting, doing one's immediate duty, without stopping to ponder all of the consequences.

* * *

The concluding chapters of *Mary Barton* return us to the story of John; Mary continues in the domestic mode, specifically refusing to think about causes. Indeed, where her father's story should be, there is nothing but a blank in Mary's mind: "He was her father! her own dear father! and in his sufferings, whatever their cause, more dearly loved than ever before. His crime was a thing apart, never more to be considered by her" (p. 306). The narrator, however, cannot so easily refuse to consider the causes of John Barton's suffering. Having returned to the subject, she must try to conclude it, but she faces the same bind she encountered earlier: she must indict society as the source of Barton's crime and still grant Barton his free will. Whereas her strategy in the Liverpool chapters was to suppress John Barton's story, her strategy in the concluding chapters is to tell different versions of the story. Since she has declared herself free from the necessity to "disentangle the real motives," she allows herself the luxury of presenting an "involved set" of interpretations without really striving after consistency. Thus the recapitulations contain elements of both social determinism and voluntarism. Finally, however, salvation comes in this novel not through retelling John Barton's story, but through making it irrelevant. All John Barton's and the narrator's explanations are for naught; his story is redeemed through the intervention of another story that makes all talk of causality superfluous.

The issues tangled in the summaries of Barton's life and crime (whether he is fully responsible or not, free or determined) are never finally sorted out. We must accept this "involved set" of accounts, but we are also reassured that ultimately it does not matter how we interpret Barton's story. For the novel we have been reading is finally resolved by the introduction of a different book, the Bible. The narrator finds relief from the multiple reinterpretations of John Barton's story by superimposing the ending as well as the meaning of the Gospel onto her novel, and the meaning of the Gospel is that we need not choose among the several versions of John Barton's story.

While John Barton is recounting his failure to live "Gospel-wise," Henry J. Carson recreates himself (in both senses of the phrase) through the other story: "He fell to the narrative now, afresh, with all the interest of a little child. He began at the beginning, and read on almost greedily, understanding for the first time the full meaning of the story" (p. 320). The "full meaning" of the story turns out to be that John Barton should be forgiven, no matter what the sources or consequences of his crime. Henry Carson comes to forgive John Barton not because he has been told the hero's own story, but because Barton's words "I did not know what I was doing" (p. 319) referred him to the Gospel story.[2] Forgiveness is mandated by the other narrative, and all versions of John Barton's life thus become irrelevant to the novel's concluding and redeeming action: Carson's forgiveness, which is a foretaste of the Christian spirit that the narrator assures us will allow Carson to effect industrial social change.

Thus the conclusion of John Barton's story points to narrative as an instrument of God's Providence without having to sort out the tangle of its own narrative threads. In the few episodes that remain, the characters settle in Canada, and the domestic tale is finally protected by distance from the tragedy caused by industrial vicissitudes. But the final episodes fail to settle the question that the novel repeatedly raises: the question of an appropriate narrative form. It is not surprising that, in Gaskell's words, no one "saw" her "idea of a tragic poem," for the tragedy is even more obscured by antagonistic interpretations at the end of the novel than in the early chapters. We must therefore agree with the author's judgment that she failed to express perfectly her tragic intentions. But we must also remember that her tragic purpose contained its own contradiction, which had definite historical roots in the Unitarianism of the 1840s and in certain features of the tradition of industrial social criticism that Gaskell inherited. We should also remember that her failure is the foundation of the book's formal significance, for its very generic eclecticism points toward the formal self-consciousness of later British realism.

PATSY STONEMAN

[The Feminization of Working-Class Men in *Mary Barton*][†]

A MANCHESTER LOVE STORY (WORKING TITLE FOR *MB*; *L* 23)[1]

Most critical accounts of *Mary Barton* begin with the *a priori* assumption that it falls into a clear category of fiction—the 'industrial' or

---

2. For a discussion of a possible source for this scene in the work of Caroline Bowles, see Michael D. Wheeler, "The Writer as Reader in *Mary Barton*," *Durham University Journal* 67 (1974): 92–106.

† Reprinted from *Elizabeth Gaskell*, 2nd ed. (Manchester: Manchester University Press, 2006), with the permission of the publisher and author.

1. L refers to *The Letters of Mrs. Gaskell*. J. A. V. Chapple and Arthur Pollard, eds. Manchester: Manchester UP, 1966. The abbreviation is used throughout this essay.

'social-problem' novel—which defines both its proper subject-matter—class relations—and its proper orientation—political and economic. The 'faults' which most critics identify stem from this assumption. Firstly they deplore the presence of 'extraneous factors' such as the love story and the murder plot (e.g. Lucas, 1966: 162; 173–4), and secondly they regret Elizabeth Gaskell's inadequate political grasp, taking her disclaimer, that she knows 'nothing of Political Economy' (*MB*: p. 6)[2] as a naive acknowledgement of unfitness for the task she has undertaken. Yet her father's *Blackwood's* articles on 'The Political Economist' (Stevenson, 1824–25) make it plain that the term 'economist' then meant 'only those who felt that the market mechanism was the best guide to economic development' (Fetter: 90). Like her father, Elizabeth Gaskell dissociated herself from 'political economy' because she believed that humane ethical attitudes, rather than blind market forces, should govern social relationships (see also Hopkins, 1931: 60).

Mary Barton develops a contrast between two ethical systems, that of the working class, based on caring and co-operation, and that of the middle class, based on ownership, authority and the law. The dichotomy is similar to the conventional gender-role division, and Elizabeth Gaskell has been criticised (e.g. Lucas, 1966: 174) for trying evade the question of class-struggle with an inappropriate domestic ethic. She had, however, some justification for presenting the working class as observing a 'female ethic'. Like Wordsworth, she observed that one product of extreme poverty is mutual aid (*L* 12), and historians confirm that 'the workers . . . made thousands of tiny sacrifices daily in automatic response to the promptings of common humanity' (Cazamian: 71). The result was a 'feminisation' of working-class men who performed from necessity the roles of child-care, sick-nursing and housekeeping; Angela Davies identifies the same effect in American slave families (Davis: 18). Although these same men, in *Mary Barton*, take part in strikes, assaults and murders, Elizabeth Gaskell presents this aggressive action as an enforced and psychologically damaging expression of essentially nurturing motives. The single-minded masculinity of bourgeois men, on the other hand, finds appropriate articulation in their aggressive use of the forces of law and order. Rather than evading the question of class-struggle, therefore, *Mary Barton* offers a *critique* of confrontational politics. Since aggression is the language of authority, the concept of class-struggle as necessarily aggressive appears not as the will of the people, but as a masculine, middle-class imposition.

Marxist critics like John Lucas see the love story and the murder plot as extraneous to *Mary Barton* because they see class confrontation as

---

2. All page numbers for *Mary Barton* refer to this Norton Critical Edition.

the only valid focus for the 'industrial theme'. Materialist feminists such as Nancy Chodorow, however, emphasise that individuals of both classes acquire the values which perpetuate or challenge capitalism through childhood socialisation, in which the status of the father is crucial. Although class struggle is most clearly seen in public confrontations, the family is the mechanism which reproduces class attitudes, and parent-child relationships, as worked out in the 'extraneous' sections of this novel, demonstrate how the personal becomes the political. If we approach the novel through the ethics of the family, therefore, we do not detract from its value as an exploration of class-relations, but instead of seeing it as an 'industrial novel' flawed by political naivety and superfluous sub-plots, we can see it as an attempt to understand the interaction of class and gender. In particular, its opposed class-based images of fatherhood prompt us to re-think the political concept of 'paternalism'.

Mary Barton begins with a chapter which stresses the nurturing role of working-class fathers. The rural family scene suggests the 'elementary feelings' of Wordsworth's 'low and rustic life' (Wordsworth: 245), feelings which are shown to persist in the urban environment of the ham-and-egg tea. Eli Zaretsky confirms that 'proletarianisation' put a new emphasis on the family. Because the family 'was the only space that proletarians "owned"' it became the focus for personal fulfilment and the basis for social attitudes. 'The . . . Victorian ideology of the family as the repository of "human values" converged with the tradition of romantic revolt' (Zaretsky: 61). In Chapter 1, John Barton is shown partly as nurturing father, and partly as political activist, as if mediating in his person the Latin meaning of 'proletarian'—'he who has no wealth but his children'—and its meaning in capitalism—'he who has no wealth but his labour' (O'Brien: 177). In every speech of his, throughout the book, which shows class antagonism, there is also mention of starving children. ' "If my child lies dying (as poor Tom lay, with his white wan lips quivering, for want of better food than I could give him), does the rich man bring the wine or broth that might save his life?" ' (*MB*: p. 12; also 61, 77, 80, 90–91, 166, 175).

Barton has learned his nurturing role from his mother, and identifies with her:

> when he was a little child, [he] had seen his mother hide her daily morsel to share it among her children, and . . . he, being the eldest, had told the noble lie, that 'he was not hungry, could not eat a bit more', in order to imitate his mother's bravery, and still the sharp wail of the younger infants. (p. 102)

Men who define themselves primarily in relation to the family at subsistence level partake of its 'female ethic', based on the survival of infants, which extends itself beyond the family in neighbourly help like that to the Davenports. 'Male morality', on the other hand, stresses transcendence of mere survival, and the middle-class father, Carson, is 'proud' of his son and daughter for being accomplished, well-dressed and well-mannered (*MB*: p. 63)—features which distinguish them from common humanity. The novel explicitly criticises Carson for not extending the same sort of paternal care to his workers that they show for one another (e.g. p. 333), and modern critics see this 'paternalism' as a weakness in Elizabeth Gaskell's political vision, confirming a relationship of inequality between the classes. The 'paternalism' practised by her working-class characters, however, is not only nurturing rather than authoritative, it is functional rather than innate. It can be temporary and *ad hoc*; John Barton feeds Mrs Davenport like a baby when she is sick, but later she becomes a nurse to old Alice. More importantly, it revolves with successive generations. Working-class 'parents' educate their children to take responsibility. Alice Wilson makes sure Will knows what a seafaring life is like, but then lets him go; when Margaret goes blind, her grandfather watches her down the street, and, seeing that she can manage, lets her go (*MB*: p. 176). Moreover, they accept what Noddings calls the 'commitment of the cared-for to turn about and act as one-caring . . .' (Noddings: 95). In the course of the novel old Alice changes from foster-mother to foster-child, and calls young Mary 'mother' (*MB*: p. 190); Jane Wilson calls her son Jem 'mammy' (p. 236); John Barton becomes 'childish' and is cared for by his daughter (p. 308). This pattern gives a new meaning to 'paternalism'. The middle-class concept of fatherhood, separated from motherhood and based on 'innate' authority, is indeed a cheat as a paradigm for class-relations because the working class cannot acquire in turn the authority of the 'father' and 'grow up' into a class of owners. The caring, temporary, and functional notion of fatherhood which Gaskell presents as characteristic of the working-class, on the other hand, easily passes into the principle of co-operation.

If *any* kind of parent-child paradigm seems offensive applied to adults, we should remember that proletarianisation was a new phenomenon. Elizabeth Gaskell's urban workers are the first or second generation of their kind. The codes of conduct evolved in a land-based environment are inappropriate to urban capitalism. The inadequacy of the workers to their new situation is rendered in all the social writings of the period in terms of inarticulacy and unsteadiness—characteristics of children (*infant* = unable to speak; cf Beer, G, in Barker, 1978). But Gaskell also sees that the manufacturers have in a sense *created* this class of people, and have therefore a functional responsibility towards them. In Chapter 15, explaining the growth of class-antagonism, Elizabeth Gaskell uses the image of Frankenstein and his monster (making the common mistake of giving the monster his creator's name):

> The actions of the uneducated seem to be typified in those of Frankenstein, that monster of many human qualities, ungifted with a soul . . .
>
> The people rise up to life; they irritate us, they terrify us, and we become their enemies. Then, in the sorrowful moment of our triumphant power, their eyes gaze on us with mute reproach. Why have we made them what they are; a powerful monster, yet without the inner means for peace and happiness? (p. 150)

This image has only been noticed with embarrassment by critics of *Mary Barton* (e.g. Ganz: 64), but feminist critics have seen the social significance of Mary Shelley's novel itself. Ellen Moers, for instance, sees it as a 'fantasy of the newborn as at once monstrous agent of destruction and piteous victim of parental abandonment' (Moers: 97). Mary Daly says that 'Mary Shelley . . . unmasks the mentality of the technological "parent"' (Daly: 70). Both claim that although the technocratic 'father' can *create* a 'child', he cannot nurture it. Frankenstein attempts to control his monster by physical restraint and by rules, which are ineffective, just as 'magistrates, and prisons, and severe punishments' (*MB*: p. 153) fail to restrain the Manchester strikers. Constraint by law alone is absurd, as if parents should 'make domestic rules for the pretty behaviour of children without caring to know that those children had been kept for days without food' (p. 77). In a domestic economy of 'separate spheres' primary child-care is the province of the mother, but the Frankenstein model of the economy attempts to dispense with the maternal function. The monster is deprived, above all, of socialisation, and is left to educate himself, obsessed with questions of origin, identity and purpose—' "Who was I? What was I? Whence did I come? What was my destination?"' (Shelley: 170). In the same way Barton is obsessed with 'the problems and mysteries of life . . . bewildered and lost, unhappy and suffering' (*MB*: p. 150).

Articulacy is the goal of the 'infant'. The monster confronts his maker with his speech on Mont Blanc; Barton takes the Chartist petition to Parliament. Speech promises participation in the symbolic order * * *; it is a claim to be heard and replied to, accepted as 'adult' by the 'father'. Parental refusal of dialogue closes that path; the monster then 'learns' refusal, antagonism. The 'father' creates, instead of a son, an adversary. ' "I ought to be thy Adam, but I am rather the fallen angel, whom thou drivest from joy for no misdeed"', says the monster (Shelley: 142). Chapter 15 of *Mary Barton* makes it plain that the workers, as they move from the 'female ethic' of the family to the 'male morality' of the public world, 'learn' silence and resistance from the masters. At the end of the novel, John Barton, now repenting of the murder of Harry Carson, feels 'as if he could never lay bare the perverted reasonings which had made the performance of undoubted sin appear a duty' (*MB*: p. 317). But the ethic of revenge is part of the dominant ideology which Barton invokes in Ch.1 when he cites the parable of Lazarus and Dives, gaining satisfaction from the punitive chasm set between them by Abraham/God. This invocation of revenge, or what Noddings calls 'the judgemental love of the harsh father' (Noddings: 98), puts Barton on a level with Carson, who says '"Let my trespasses be unforgiven, so that I may have vengeance for my son's murder"' (*MB*: p. 317). The 'murder plot' which critics see as an 'irrelevance' to the 'industrial theme' (e.g. Gill: 22), is necessary to show that the avenging force which appears 'lawless' in the hands of the workers is in fact the ethic of the dominant ideology, supported by church and law. The masters must refuse dialogue with the workers (*MB*: p. 160) because to engage in speech with them would be to accept them as 'adults' and thus legitimise their access to the dominant 'language' of vengeance.

In *Mary Barton*, the agents of the law prevent not crime but unauthorised speech; John Barton is struck by a London policeman when going to present the petition (p. 91); Esther is arrested ('a clear case of disorderly vagrancy' (p. 112) when she tries to speak to John Barton, and a policeman threatens Jem when he tries to speak to Harry Carson (p. 159). After the murder, the police become nakedly the agents of revenge. Carson treats the superintendent as a personal servant and is prepared to buy 'justice' (p. 185). The phrase 'brought to justice' (p. 187) comes to have an ironic ring, and Gaskell emphasises the revenge motive:

> True, his vengeance was sanctioned by law, but was it the less revenge?
> Are ye worshippers of Christ? or of Alecto? [one of the furies]
> Oh! Orestes! you would have made a very tolerable Christian of the nineteenth century! (p. 188)

The mechanism of the law is implicated in Carson's 'craving thirst for blood. He would have fain been policeman, magistrate, accusing speaker, all; but most of all, the judge, rising with full sentence of death on his lips' (p. 194). Whereas William Gaskell uses the words 'vengeful and unjust' as equivalents (* * *), the trial scene shows that the law equates vengeance with justice. Carson is likened to a 'beast of prey' fearing that 'his victim [would be] taken from his hungry jaws' (p. 287), 'would slip through the fangs of justice' (p. 288). Mrs Wilson feels that 'the judge were some wild animal trying to rend thee from me' (p. 296). The narrative also exposes the adversarial system of law itself, in which lawyers are paid, not to discover the truth, but to attack one another (pp. 286–287).

And all the time Carson is 'a noble-looking old man . . . so stern and inflexible, with such classical features' like 'some of the busts of Jupiter' (p. 277). Patriarchal power, symbolised by the 'father of the gods' and sanctioned by the institutions of law and order, is exposed as the primitive antagonism of wild animals.

The working-class 'female ethic' is endangered not only by the 'male morality' of adversarial justice, but also by the middle-class concept of ornamental femininity. John Barton's hostility to Esther in Ch.1 seems unreasonable when all he has against her is that she is ' "fond of thinking herself" ' a lady, and is fond of dress (p. 10). Yet his sketch of the ' "do-nothing lady, worrying shopmen all morning, and screeching at her pianny all afternoon, and going to bed without having done a good turn to any one of God's creatures but herself" ' (p. 12), shows the incompatibility between decorative ladyhood and the useful, caring habits of the working class.

The cash-nexus economy forces men 'who have no wealth but their labour' into an antagonistic stance towards employers; for women the situation is complicated by the fact that not only their work, but their bodies, have a cash value. Middle-class women play the marriage market; working-class women can take a risk—they may land a husband, as Mrs Carson did (p. 107), they may end up a cheap bargain, as Mary nearly does (p. 120), or as spoiled goods, like Esther (p. 112). What John Barton hates in all three categories is the fact that women are changed from useful, caring people into commodities incapable of doing anyone 'a good turn'. Reacting against the middle-class ideology of the 'pleasing female', he rightly focusses on dress. Ironically, he objects to factory work for Mary because the good wages would give her spare cash to spend on clothes (p. 11), and so she ends up working for a dressmaker, 'where the chief talk was of fashions, and dress, and . . . love and lovers' (p. 88)—the very ideology he wishes to avoid. Most critics see Mary's attention to dress and her ambition to marry Harry Carson as personal, moral failings, as 'vanity' and 'frivolity' (e.g. Ganz: 70; Bergmann: 30, 109). But ideologically they represent a switch from the ethic of caring and co-operation to that of the commodity market. At the trial, Mr Carson sees Mary as 'the fatal Helen' (p. 280), a phrase which combines the concept of woman as a piece of disputed property, with the ethic of adversarial 'justice'—the dispute over Helen was settled by the Trojan war.

John Barton's encounter with Esther in Chapter 10 comes in the context of his growing hatred of the 'do-nothing' class which she seems to have joined, a class whose antagonism has changed him from 'Adam' to 'the fallen angel' (Shelley, Frankenstein: 142), and they meet in the 'darkness visible' of Milton's hell (MB: p. 110; Paradise Lost I 63). Gilbert and Gubar note that Frankenstein, 'one of the key Romantic "readings" of *Paradise Lost* . . . is most especially the story of hell' (Gilbert and Gubar: 221). Barton and Esther are here both 'fallen' from the 'Eden of innocence' (*MB*: p. 208), the 'elementary feelings' of 'low and rustic life', into the divisive ideology of separate spheres. Both might have said, with Anne Finch, ' "How are we fal'n, fal'n by mistaken rules" ' (quoted Gilbert and Gubar: 219); Esther has become a sexual commodity, and John an avenger, 'a sort of accusing angel' (*MB*: p. 208). It is appropriate, therefore, that for the only time in the novel he behaves like a middleclass man, and asserts superiority over a woman. Esther is left sobbing, ' "He would not listen to me . . . " ' (p. 112), a poignant echo of John's own earlier words, ' "we mun speak to our God to hear us, for man will not hearken . . . " ' (p. 89).

Esther's attempts at speech, however, follow, rather than precede, her 'fall', and are born of a 'monomaniacal' compulsion like the Ancient Mariner's, to tell her ghastly tale with its moral of love (158). When she tries to speak to Jem in Chapter 14, he initially shrugs her off, in a gesture that becomes a *leit-motif* for the novel (p. 141; cf. 91, 111, 157). But the 'spell' of Mary's name 'was as potent as that of the mariner's glittering eye. "He listened like a three-year child" ' (p. 141). Jem is thus the wedding-guest, who may learn the 'moral' without himself having to suffer the purgatorial journey.

When Esther visits Mary in Chapter 21, she feels 'as if some holy spell would prevent her (even as the unholy Lady Geraldine was prevented, in the abode of Christabel) from crossing the threshold of that home of her early innocence' (p. 208). Christabel's 'holy' mother and the usurping Geraldine in Coleridge's poem function as ideological 'doubles' like the double Lucy in *The Poor Clare*. * * * In *Mary Barton* also, the physical likeness of the fallen Esther and her virtuous sister seems ironically to point their moral divergence. Unexpectedly, however, no 'holy spell' prevents Esther from speaking to Mary. In a remarkable apotheosis at the end of Chapter 20 (recalling the moon/mother scene in Ch.27 of *Jane Eyre*, which Elizabeth Gaskell had not yet read (*L* 25a)), Esther functions as the agent of divine/maternal influence.

> There, against the moonlight, stood a form, so closely resembling her dead mother, that Mary never doubted the identity, but exclaim[ed] (as if she were a terrified child, secure of safety when near the protecting care of its parent):
> 'Oh! mother! mother! you are come at last?' (p. 204)

As so often in Elizabeth Gaskell's work, the parental impulse is more important than parental identity. In the moment of crisis, Esther functions as a mother for Mary, and the madonna/magdalen double is united.

Esther's maternal message, the fruit of her 'fallen' experience, is the opposite of the gentlewoman's 'duty', to 'suffer and be still'. By bringing Mary the valentine/gun wadding, she raises her from the posture of prostrate suffering (p. 202) to 'the necessity for exertion' (p. 215).

Mary's whole story is a chiasmic change from being the silent object of others' contemplation to a speaking subject unconscious of her appearance. In the early chapters her concern even with other people who are to appear in public is with their clothes (p. 76, 85). Absorbed in the gossip of the dress-shop, she doesn't hear of the failure of the petition (p. 88), and when her father and Job Legh discuss it, she falls asleep. The over-pretty description of her 'sleeping as soundly as any infant' (p. 99), presents her as a 'picture' and as a baby. By the time of the trial, however, she shrugs off Sally, who wants to know what she will wear (p. 241), and appears with 'the rich treasure of her golden hair [. . .] stuffed away in masses under her little bonnet-cap' (p. 281). On the other hand, her determination to speak brings 'dignity, self-reliance, and purpose' (p. 228); 'she began to take confidence, and to have faith in her own powers' (p. 237).

Ironically, although Esther and Jem, and indirectly her father, are all concerned to 'save' Mary from Harry Carson, she does not need 'saving' and deals with him competently herself on the basis of the ethics learned in her childhood (138; cf Noddings: 1). Her real test comes with her discovery that her father is a murderer, which casts doubt not only on his personal worth, but on the system of values which he represented. The act 'seemed to separate him into two persons,—one, the father who had dandled her on his knee, and loved her all her life long; the other, the assassin, the cause of all her trouble and woe' (346). Like Esther in the 'darkness visible', John has become a 'phantom likeness of John Barton—himself, yet not himself' (p. 300).

The effect on Mary is to make her doubt her own identity and values. Chapter 19 is prefaced with a quotation from Coleridge's 'The Pains of Sleep', stressing moral confusion: 'I could not know,/ Whether I suffered or I did,/ For all seemed guilt, remorse, or woe' (p. 188); and in Chapter 20 she asks, 'Was it not she who had led him to the pit into which he had fallen?' (p. 203). The valentine/gun-wadding symbolises the involution of innocence with guilt. John Barton's act of murder is motivated by love as 'innocent' as Samuel Bamford's verses, 'God help the poor', or Jem's message of love for Mary, both of which are inscribed on the valentine which 'innocently' facilitates the fatal shot. Yet the 'guilty' act must somehow be separated from the 'innocent' motive. Like Elizabeth Gaskell's ghost stories, John Barton's phantom 'double' is best seen in terms of conflicting ideologies. * * * Ideologies do not provide motives (such as parental love) but they provide the means by which these primary impulses can 'speak'. John Barton, having failed to speak 'openly, clearly, as appealing to reasonable men' (p. 160), 'falls' into the middle-class 'language' of violence. Mary's sense of her father's 'fall' is suggested by the quotation at the head of Chapter 22, from Keats's *Hyperion*, where Thea approaches the old god Saturn, king of the Titans, defeated in his war with Jupiter. Bereft of paternal guidance, she has a 'conviction of how much rested upon her unas- sisted and friendless self, alone with her terrible knowledge' (p. 216). In order to act and speak, she draws 'a black veil . . . over her father's past, present and future life' (p. 232) and focusses her mind on Jem, the 'wedding-guest' who has inherited both Esther's 'moral' and the lessons of the unfallen fathers of Chapter 1. In this way, she is able to speak from an alternative ethic to the adversar- ial system. Although the legal summons requires her ' "to bear wit- ness again[st] Jem Wilson" ' (p. 224), she finds a way 'to bear witness to the truth'; to prove Jem innocent without accusing anyone; to seek remedy rather than revenge; in Carol Gilligan's terms, she favours 'that resolution in which no one is hurt' (Gilligan: 515). The novel thus suggests that in the class war, also, it is unnecessary to accuse. Everyone has an 'innocent motive'; what is in question is whether the motives will 'speak' in the mode of remedial, or adversarial, justice.

Mary's clarity on behalf of Jem is undermined by the moral chaos behind the 'veil' hiding her father's fall. Since it is through the father that adults acquire access to language, the father's 'fall' threatens the child with inarticulacy. As soon as the immediate object of finding Will is achieved, Mary finds that she has no secure ethical base; 'her very words seemed not her own, and beyond her power of control' (*MB*: p. 259). Her moral danger is indicated when, at the trial, she is likened to Beatrice Cenci (p. 281), who turned her father's violent methods against himself. Unlike Beatrice, Mary uses her brief pub- lic power not to kill her father but to affirm her love for Jem, but Jem's safety cannot validate her father's crime. Exhausted by the effort of distinguishing truth and silence from falsehood (p. 284), unable either to accept or reject her 'double' father, she refuses conscious- ness. In delirium, 'sight and hearing were no longer channels of information to that poor distracted brain' (p. 290).

The *impasse* is resolved by a process which reads like a curious pre- vision of Chodorow's psychoanalytic insight that social change must begin with the imprinting on infantile minds of maternal care from men. * * * Mary, her mind reduced by trauma to 'the tender state of a lately-born infant's' (*MB*: p. 301), recognises Jem 'as a baby does when it sees its mother tending its little cot' (p. 301). In this strange parody of a mother—child dyad, Mary's avenging father is an 'awful forbidden ground of discourse' (p. 304) until, strengthened by Jem's 'maternal' care, she is able to see not his 'savage . . . wayward violence' (p. 305) but his 'smitten helplessness' (p. 306). Assuming adult responsibility, Mary now becomes mother to her own father, who speaks 'in a weak, high, childish voice' (p. 308). Chapters 33–6 pass in a dizzying permutation of mother/child relationships. Even the patriarchal Carson is prompted to re-read the Bible in the spirit of a 'little child' (p. 320); and his support of the dying Barton is like that of the madonna in Michelangelo's *Pietà* (p. 321). The novel thus urgently seeks to redress what Noddings identifies as a major lack in our culture;

> ethics has been discussed largely in the language of the father: in principles and propositions. . . . The mother's voice has been silent. . . . the memory of caring and being cared for, which I shall argue form the foundation of ethical response, have not received attention except as outcomes of ethical behaviour. (Noddings: 1)

It is ironic, therefore, that the parental theme has been invisible to critics of *Mary Barton*, who understandably find its message somewhat thin—'grotesquely inadequate' according to Lucas (Lucas, 1966: 174), while Stephen Gill complains that 'the diagram at the end of Barton dying in Carson's arms appears to say something about conflict and brotherhood, when in fact it has grown out of a progressive simplification of the issues with which the novel confronted us at its outset' (Gill: 27; cf Ganz: 80). The novel may not say much about brotherhood, but it says a great deal about fatherhood.

If we read *Mary Barton* as a novel about fatherhood—a relationship rather than a person—we can to some extent escape the debate about who is the central character. We should also be able to see, however, why Elizabeth Gaskell conceived John Barton as her 'tragic . . . "hero"' (*L* 39). As a working-class father, male proponent of a 'female ethic', he suffers in his person that disjunction of private and public values which was the nineteenth century's most traumatic schism. As father to his family, he is his mother's son—feeding the children comes first. As a 'child' in the public world, however, he encounters only the patriarch Carson, who doesn't '"pretend to know the names"' of his workers (*MB*: p. 64). The 'piteous victim of parental abandonment' (Moers: 97), he receives neither help nor instruction; '"no one learned me, and no one told me"' (*MB*: p. 320). In the context of an aggressive individualism whose motto is '"'Stand up for thy rights'"', the official altruism of the New Testament seems '"a sham put upon . . . women"', yet it still comes '"natural to love folk"'. Barton's attempts at self-education founder in this ideological rift between a language in which 'father' = 'love' and one in which 'father' = 'law', a rift which tears him '"in two"' (p. 321). Sanity and the social contract alike depend on shared meanings; '"you'd never believe black was black . . . when you saw all about you acting as if black was white"' (p. 320). The incomprehensibly double meaning of fatherhood reduces him progressively to silence (p. 89, 105), 'incipient madness' (p. 150) and a ghoulish 'double' existence (p. 300).

As a critique of fatherhood, *Mary Barton* needs its 'irrelevant' sub-plots. The 'murder plot' demonstrates how the dominant ideology sanctions vengeance, not succour, as the expression of paternal 'care', and the 'romance plot' offers Jem as the worker/father of the future, when workers will be 'educated . . . , not mere machines of ignorant men' (*MB*: p. 335). Jem the inventor is the real source of technological progress, 'The Modern Prometheus' instead of 'Frankenstein's monster', but he is also a 'family man', whose marriage is contracted in an ambience almost absurdly maternal, with everyone acting as mother to everyone else, and whose little son greets him at the end with 'a crow of delight' (p. 339). Yet the family grouping at the end curiously effaces Mary. Under necessity, she reasoned, spoke and acted in the public world, protecting her father and rescuing Jem, but her role ends with this enablement of her menfolk. Jem, his roots nourished by the 'female ethic', blossoms in the world of technology, but Mary's life is as private as her mother's.

Mary Barton thus embodies an irony. Born of its author's grief as a mother at the death of her infant son (*L* 25a), and of her care as a woman for the sufferings of her neighbours, its impulse is profoundly maternal. Yet its most notable absence is Mary's mother, whose 'female ethic' is the standard from which John and Esther fall, but whose domestic field of action is too small for the crusading message Elizabeth Gaskell wishes to spread. The 'mother's voice' speaks in the public world only through men – not only the male characters of the novel, but also the male writers whose 'language' defines its parametres.

The domestic ending, which irritates socialists and feminists alike, is generally read as a peculiarly feminine lapse – a case of 'Mrs Gaskell' naively or carelessly reverting from radical politics to cosy romance. Yet it is more likely to derive from the masculine tradition of Romantic revolt which she uses to 'authorise' her radical text. For the novel is densely haunted by literary 'fathers': her own father's essays on political economy; her husband's lectures on 'The Poets and Poetry of Humble Life'; Wordsworth's reverence for the poor who are '"the fathers . . . Of . . . small blessings"' (*L* 12); the New Testament which promises maternal care from the suffering son of a loving father; the People's Charter in which women are invisible; Carlyle, who on the title-page addresses the novelist as 'worthy brother'; the Romantic poets of the chapter-mottoes – Goethe, Coleridge, Burns, Crabbe, Keats, Southey, Shelley, Byron; *Franken-stein*, another woman's text with a notably absent mother, haunted by Godwin, Shelley and Byron (cf Rubinstein, 1976); and ulti-mately, though there is no explicit reference, Rousseau, whose influ-ence permeated the Romantic movement and early Utopian socialism. Rousseau's strength is his wish to 'bring to public life sym-pathy, love, affection and the supportive solidarity of family rela-tionships'. His now notorious weakness is to exclude women. His ideal is a Brotherhood of man working for the public good, while women 'choose' to fertilise 'its enigmatic roots in the private realm' (O'Brien: 96–7).

This is the programme which indirectly determines the ending of *Mary Barton*. Its political naivety is thus not that of female incompe-tence but of the male-stream tradition of pre-Marxist revolt. But as a dutiful daughter of Romanticism, Elizabeth Gaskell unwittingly betrays her maternal text, entrusting her female ethic to a Brother-hood defined by its difference from women.

Only in this first novel, in fact, does she put faith in an ideal father. From *North and South* she confronts the fact that men of all classes are governed, in the public sphere, by a masculine code which pre-cludes 'feminine' tenderness.

REFERENCES

BARKER, Francis *et al.* (eds), 1978. *The Sociology of Literature: 1848* (University of Essex).

BERGMANN, Helena, 1979. *Between Obedience and Freedom: Women's Role in the Mid-Nineteenth Century Industrial Novel* (Acta Universitatis Gothenburgensis, Goteborg, Swe-den).

CAZAMIAN, Louis, 1973. *The Social Novel in England 1830–1850*, trans. Martin Fido (Routledge and Kegan Paul, London and Boston; first published 1903).

DALY, Mary, 1979. *Gyn/Ecology: The Metaethics of Radical Feminism* (Women's Press, Lon-don; Beacon Press, Boston, 1978).

DAVIS, Angela, 1982. *Women, Race and Class* (Women's Press, London; Random House, New York, 1981).

FETTER, F.W., 1960. 'The Economic Articles in Blackwood's Edinburgh Magazine, and their Authors, 1817–1853', *Scottish Journal of Political Economy*, 7, 85–107.

GANZ, Margaret, 1969. *Elizabeth Gaskell: the Artist in Conflict* (Twayne Publishers Inc., New York).

GILBERT, Sandra, and GUBAR, Susan, 1979. *The Madwoman in the Attic: The Woman Writer and the Nineteenth-Century Literary Imagination* (Yale University Press, New Haven and London).

GILL, Stephen, 1982. 'Introduction', Elizabeth Gaskell, *Mary Barton* (Penguin, Har-mondsworth).

GILLIGAN, Carol, 1977. 'In A Different Voice: Women's Conceptions of Self and Morality', *Harvard Educational Review* 47, 481–517.

HOPKINS, Annette B., 1931. 'Liberalism in the Social Teachings of Mrs Gaskell', *Social Ser-vice Review* 5, 57–73, (Chicago).

LUCAS, John, 1966. 'Mrs Gaskell and Brotherhood', in *Tradition and Tolerance in Nineteenth-Century Fiction*, ed. David Howard *et al.* (Routledge and Kegan Paul, Lon-don).

MOERS, Ellen, 1978. *Literary Women* (Women's Press, London).

NODDINGS, Nel, 1984. *Caring: A Feminine Approach to Ethics and Moral Education* (Cal-ifornia University Press, Berkeley, Los Angeles and London).

O'BRIEN, Mary, 1981. *The Politics of Reproduction* (Routledge and Kegan Paul, Boston, London and Henley).

RUBINSTEIN, Marc A., 1976. '"My Accursed Origin": The Search for the Mother in Frankenstein', *Studies in Romanticism* 15, 165–94.

SHELLEY, Mary, 1985. *Frankenstein*, ed. Maurice Hindle (Penguin, Harmondsworth; first published 1818).

STEVENSON, William, 1824–25. 'The Political Economist', *Blackwood's Edinburgh Magazine*, 15(88), 522–31; 15(89), 643–55; 16(90), 34–45; 16(91), 202–14, 17(97), 207–20.

WORDSWORTH, William, 1963. *The Lyrical Ballads*, ed. R.L. Brett and A.R. Jones (Methuen, London; first published 1798).

ZARETSKY, Eli, 1976. *Capitalism, the Family and Personal Life* (Pluto Press, London; first published in Socialist Revolution (Calif.), January–June, 1973).

HILARY M. SCHOR

[Maternal Authority in *Mary Barton*]†

* * *

At this point I want to return to *Mary Barton* to interrogate further the connections between the politics of discourse, anxiety about authorship, and the faith in maternal power. If the structure of *Mary Barton* has seemed to readers somewhat jumbled, blurring genres and moving between one narratorial tone and another, I want to argue that its mixture actually signals an intense examination of what made for both fictional and political authority in the England of the Chartists. What this examination suggests further is that the heroine's plot and the possibility of a maternal language are at the heart of the novel's critique of authority.

In the strangest scene in *Mary Barton*, the original Mary Barton (the heroine's mother, dead since the novel's second chapter) returns to comfort her grieving daughter. Mary has returned to her father's empty house after Jem's arrest for the murder of her rich lover, and lies dreaming on the floor, delirious, remembering "those days when she hid her face on her mother's pitying, loving bosom, and heard tender words of comfort," "those days when she had felt as if her mother's love was too mighty not to last for ever," "those days when hunger had been to her . . . something to be thought about, and mourned over;—when Jem and she had played together," the days "when her father was a cheery-hearted man," "when mother was alive, and *he* was not a murderer" (p. 203).[1] As Mary re-creates this past—which is pre-narrative, re-creating a moment just before the novel's tense first chapter—there "came a strange forgetfulness of

---

† From "'I Have Tried to Write Truthfully': Authority and Authorship in *Mary Barton*," in *Scheherezade in the Marketplace: Elizabeth Gaskell and the Victorian Novel* (Oxford: Oxford University Press, 1992), pp. 29–37. By permission of Oxford University Press.

1. Page numbers for *Mary Barton* refer to this Norton Critical Edition.

the present, in thoughts of long-past times," more specifically in the thought of a maternal love ("too mighty not to last for ever," in the words of Gaskell's *Diary*) that connects food, paternal love, romantic love, even undoes the death of Harry Carson. Mary falls asleep, and dreams "of the happy times of long ago, and her mother came to her, and kissed her as she lay, and once more the dead were alive in that happy world of dreams" (pp. 203–204). But then, in a truly uncanny scene, the dead come alive, for Mary awakens to hear a voice outside telling her to open the door, a voice with "the accents of her mother's voice; the very south-country pronunciation, that Mary so well remembered; and which she had sometimes tried to imitate when alone, with the fond mimicry of affection." And when Mary goes to the door she sees

> a form, so closely resembling her dead mother, that Mary never doubted the identity, but exclaiming (as if she were a terrified child, secure of safety when near the protecting care of its parent,)—
>
> "Oh, mother! mother! you are come at last!" She threw herself, or rather fell into the trembling arms, of her long lost, unrecognized, Aunt Esther. (p. 204)

It *couldn't*, of course, be Mary's dead mother at the door, but Gaskell moves so successfully between realism and gothic that we would not be surprised if it were; we are completely inside Mary's thoughts here, in some haunted half-world. The reader has not been told that Aunt Esther is coming to see Mary at this point; the suspense that has been built up is maintained until the last moment, as is the close attention to Mary's nervous state and her fear. But the scene—and the confusion and desire it creates in us as well as Mary—also works thematically: the novel argues that what we all want, like Mary, is security, the "safety when near the protecting care of the parent."

The confusion of Mary's aunt with her mother suggests some of what is at work here: Aunt Esther, whose quest for love and riches first inspired Mary's romance with Harry Carson, is the novel's chief outcast, left in the exile reserved for those who abandon their families. But in this scene she is not only the prostitute, a lonely, haunted alcoholic, but an amateur detective, a would-be mother, and a narratorial surrogate—she is there, in large part, because she has already been working as a narrator. It is she who warned Jem that Mary loves Harry Carson; through this warning, Jem came to quarrel with Carson, striking the blow witnessed by the policeman who will later accuse Jem of Carson's murder. Further, it was Esther who found the evidence pointing to John; by giving the paper to Mary she prevents John's discovery and inspires Mary to act to save Jem. She seems both to read and watch over the plot: as the novel's "street-walker," moving about at the mercy of the weather and the police, she is also herself a conduit for information.[2] She follows Mary and overhears her conversation with Carson; she follows Jem to warn him to protect Mary; she returns to the scene of the crime and hunts for the evidence she turns over to Mary, the evidence that brings her to the dark house, in her double capacity as maternal presence and narrating surveyor.

The relation between narration and knowledge is evident throughout the novel, and Esther is far from the only surveyor: the police, overseers, interfering friends abound in *Mary Barton*, much as they do in Gaskell's correspondence when she accuses friends of fixing suspicion on her and accusing her of authorship. The police, as the most visible representatives of the state, seem to be around only to arrest the poor: they catch Esther when she falls after Barton pushes her and, assuming that she is drunk, trot her off to jail on charges of vagrancy; when Harry Carson swings at Jem, and Jem hits him in return, the policeman who has been observing them since the beginning of their conversation offers to "take [Jem] to the lock-ups for assault." The police do, sympathetically, help Jem and Mary find Esther at the end of the novel, but more typical of their activity is the eager young detective who dresses himself as a worker and traps Jane Wilson into identifying the murder weapon as her son's gun. But these policemen, it is important to note, are also novelists in training: the police feel a

> pleasure in unravelling a mystery, in catching at the gossamer clue which will guide to certainty. . . . Their senses are ever and always on the qui-vive, and they enjoy the collecting and collating evidence, and the life of adventure they experience; a continual unwinding of Jack Sheppard romances, always interesting to the vulgar and uneducated mind, to which the outward signs and tokens of crimes are ever exciting. (pp. 193–194)

Here, the novel seems to make explicit the connection between the detective, the prostitute, and the novelist, the "romancer" always on the "qui-vive," "collecting and collating evidence"—like Esther, both observing and altering the evidence as she finds it. This is the

---

2. Prostitution, as Judith Walkowitz suggests in *Prostitution and Victorian Society: Women, Class and the State* (Cambridge: Cambridge University Press, 1980), provided the central imagery of contagion associated with the "Great Unwashed": "Pollution became the governing metaphor for the perils of social intercourse between the 'Two Nations'" (p. 4). Aunt Esther's role in the novel as "connection" echoes what Walkowitz claims for the Victorian prostitute: "Literally and figuratively, the prostitute was the conduit of infection to respectable society. She was nonetheless an object of class guilt as well as fear, a powerful symbol of sexual and economic exploitation under industrial capitalism." Here, the "conduit" is narrative, much as Peter Brooks suggests in his chapter "The Mark of the Beast: Prostitution, Serialization and Narrative," in *Reading for the Plot* (New York: Knopf, 1984).

insidious watchfulness Gaskell's early letters suggest, fiction becoming surveillance, narration (and "excitement") linked to criminal acts.[3]

But through describing Esther's experience of "supervision" and her desire for another, more beneficent observation of "signs and tokens," *Mary Barton* leads its readers to a different view of both official and narrative surveillance: one of affection rather than curiosity, one not of the "romancer" but of the narrating "mother." When Esther goes to prison for vagrancy and drunkenness, just at the moment when she wants to be free to save Mary, her experience is one of "shrinking," of "hopelessness," of total surveillance. She becomes doubly a "character," for she "received a good character in the governor's books: she had picked her daily quantity of oakum, had never deserved the extra punishment of the tread-mill, and had been civil and decorous in her language." Gaskell echoes the language of the prison warden to undermine it, criticizing the severity of the prison and commending Esther's superiority to her surroundings. But the shift suggests the degree of Esther's own identification of her "character" with the "civil and decorous" language of the prison, and suggests further that this is the *only* world in which she receives a "good character" in the "books." The nature of this comfort in the world of limitations is suggested in the next sentence, which describes her release, for when she is out of prison, "the door closed behind her with a ponderous clang, and in her desolation she felt *as if shut out of home*—from the only shelter she could meet with, houseless and pennyless as she was, on that dreary day" (emphasis added).

Here again, the mother's absence is felt, for to be shut out of home is the worst fate in this novel: home may be variously cold, dark, or cheerless, but it is home. Even Mary, in the depths of her troubles, "instinctively chose the shortest cut to that home . . . the hiding place of four walls where she might vent her agony, unseen and unnoticed by the keen, unkind world without." Esther's leaving "home" begins the novel: she haunts that old home in scene after scene, not-

---

3. See Walkowitz generally on surveillance: on the collaboration between police and streetwalkers, and on the difficulty of naming, limiting, and proving the act of prostitution. She stresses that traditionally British prostitution resisted the model of "continental" prostitution, "where the regulation system fostered police corruption, women's dependence on pimps, and on organized brothel systems." English prostitutes tended to live with two or three other women in dwellings that resembled "low class lodging houses," and in other ways maintained a "'quiet' truce with the police" (p. 24). But with the new emphasis on "humanitarian reform and on greater efficiency," came increased bureaucracy and regulation (p. 74). *Mary Barton* reflects that new concern, and the intensified scrutiny that came with it. The discussion that follows, of Aunt Esther and the role of surveillance in connecting the two halves of the novel, focuses not just on sexual politics but on narrative self-consciousness: the two plots are unified by both thematic and formal concerns. My treatment of narrative surveillance obviously owes much to D. A. Miller's crucial "Discipline in Different Voices: Bureaucracy, Police, Family, and *Bleak House*" (*Representations* 1 [February 1983]: 1), though I would resist seeing a novel like *Mary Barton* as imposing quite so fierce a discipline as he suggests Victorian fiction must. In *Mary Barton*, one might argue, the struggle to "maintain" discipline is so evident as to put discipline more firmly in question.

ing "in her wild night wanderings . . . the haunts and habits of many a one who little thought of a watcher in the poor forsaken woman," who takes a "double interest" in "the ways and companionships of those with whom she had been acquainted in the days which, when present, she had considered hardly-worked and monotonous, but which now in retrospection seemed so happy and unclouded." It is only her return to those places where she is a "watcher," an exile from home and yet its guardian, that gives her a purpose when she is "turned out" from prison, so that she "did not feel her desolation of freedom as she would otherwise have done."

Esther, like all victims in the novel, has no real "home"—the penniless and homeless need authority to give them identity, because there is no loving "watcher" for them. Freedom here seems to be nothing more than desolation—the desolation of the unloved and unwatched over, the desolation Mary finds at home "where no welcome, no love, no *sympathising tears* awaited her" (emphasis added). What this view of homeless desolation does is create a *need* for both watchful love and for loving watchfulness—and it is Gaskell here who is the prime watcher, her narrative authority offering an identity to these characters she declared were so "real" to her in writing that parting with them was like parting with friends. The novel becomes a kind of haven, a closed-in place where nothing lacks meaning.

But that haven must be recast as a different kind of home, unlike the domestic authority we have traced in Gaskell's letters, or the fictional and political certainties that have enclosed John and Mary Barton. The scene with which we began suggests some of what is at stake in the novel: that by bringing back the dead mother, creating a different kind of fiction (blurring genres and moving between melodrama and psychological realism), by drawing on her own need to believe in persistent "traces" of love, Gaskell suggests a way back to both sympathizing tears and sympathizing fiction.

The dead mother is the key to much of this recasting of authority—and of fiction. The parent previously in this novel has been the angry father; if God is the father, the Bible told John Barton, we must bear what he sends us, and the critique of the cold, indifferent father extends beyond the home into the marketplace. What brings grace for Mary is a mother who will take her back to a time when she was not hungry rather than tell her to bear her hunger more cheerfully now, who might offer a way out of patriarchal authority. Mother love offers a similar model of care to Esther, who says that Mary is like her own child; to Mrs Wilson, who tells the orphaned Mary that she shall be her own "ewe-lamb"; to the dying Alice Wilson, who talks once more to her dead but forgiving mother. Maternal wisdom suggests a way of watching over that protects, nurtures, binds, connects—that restores what has been lost.

That is to say, this "watching over" is a narrative impulse, which in turn will revision authority. Maternal authority, unlike supervision, is an authority that can *name* its charges. Its opposite is embodied in Mr Carson, who, when Wilson goes to his home to ask for a medical order for the dying Davenport, does not "know the name" of this man. Wilson reminds him he "worked in your factory better nor three year." "Very likely," says Carson, "I don't pretend to know the names of those I employ: that I leave to the overlooker" (p. 64). The overlooker—like Carson—does, indeed, manage to overlook: to overlook breaks in machinery like the one that cripples Jane Wilson, or those injuries that even the doctors at the hospital where Barton once stayed know come late in the day when the workers are tired. "Overlooking," barely listening, judging harshly are all forms of missed connections and failed love in the novel—real "overlooking," in the sense that Gaskell means to reinstate here, is the watching out of sympathetic love, the provenance of mothers—or here, of mothers turned novelists. Reinstating the authority of the mother also places Gaskell as (maternal) author at the center of her text, and makes the mother the perfect novelistic authority. If mother love is to redeem the world, who better to write novels than Gaskell herself? Just as Mary assumes her dominant role in the second half of the novel in part by taking on the authority of the *dead* Mary Barton, so the providence behind the fiction becomes female, a different kind of authorship.

At this point, my argument might be seen as overlapping with recent feminist theory, which argues that it is through the mother—and specifically, through the mother's body—that we get the kind of textual disruption I am arguing Gaskell invokes here. For such critics, maternal language, as Mary Jacobus explains it, has the power to disrupt phallogocentric authority: the "discourse of maternity," the "archaic language of the pre-oedipal . . . rhythms, melodies, and bodily movements" "precede[s] and prepare[s] the way for the language of signification."[4] Though the paternal, "symbolic dimension of language works to repress the semiotic . . . the maternal nonetheless persists in oral and instinctual aspects of language which punctuate, evade or disrupt the symbolic order—in prosody, intonation, puns, verbal slips, even silences." Such a criticism, rooted in a psychoanalytic view of language, argues, in Julia Kristeva's words, that language separates itself from the body through the mother's body; "the woman-subject" is a "thoroughfare, a threshold where 'nature' confronts 'culture.' "[5]

4. Mary Jacobus, "*Dora* and the Pregnant Madonna," in *Reading Woman* (New York: Columbia University Press, 1986), pp. 145, 148. For a further discussion of these issues, see Margaret Homans, *Bearing the Word: Language and Female Experience in Nineteenth-Century Women's Writing* (Chicago: University of Chicago Press, 1986), especially pp. 29–32.
5. Julia Kristeva, "Motherhood According to Giovanni Bellini," in *Desire in Language: A Semiotic Approach to Literature and Art* (New York: Columbia University Press, 1980), p. 238.

One could read the scenes of maternal visitation in *Mary Barton* in such a way, as Mary's mother's "ghost" invokes the *sounds* of memory, speaking the soft dialect Mary recognizes. The scene's disruption of genre, its gothic use of the mother's haunting return, might be seen as disrupting the symbolic order, as does the repetition of the maternal figure in the text. The mother blurs into her darker self, the prostitute Mary almost became, or, most movingly, as in the hallucination Aunt Esther recounts, her own daughter, her mother, and her sister (Mary's mother) walk around and around her bed as she lies in prison. In this Burne-Jones–like duplication of some eternal (familiar) woman, endlessly repeating herself in Esther's nightmares, endlessly authoring and erasing herself, we see what Kristeva recounts: the mother who "by giving birth . . . enters into contact with her mother; she becomes, she is, her own mother; they are the same continuity differentiating itself"[6]—that is, the mother / daughter who is *both* Mary Bartons, and neither.

But I want to historicize this psychoanalytic move, to ask again what particular power the "semiotic" might have in this novel's political economy—to argue, in fact, that the nightmare / vision of maternal presence has a more powerful (and specifically political) authority. Elizabeth Gaskell imagined a maternal authority that would make of England a home; that would cure the condition of England; that would feed the hungry workers; that would redeem the lost children. More than a maternal, slippery language (the "fond mimicry of affection") Gaskell describes something like a maternal plot: an alternate structure of power, an alternate family, an alternate England. In the new world, families "will go up as well as down," so that Mary and Jem can bring Mrs Wilson with them to Canada, instead of a child; in the new world, as Mrs Wilson somewhat comically but hopefully announces, "Perhaps in them Indian countries they'll know a well-behaved lad when they see him"; in the new world, Mary will be restored as "a ewe lamb" to a new mother. In this new world, there is more than maternal "continuity differentiating itself"; there is a potentially new order.

We can ask, of course, how far the "authority" of these dead mothers extends. To make only the most obvious point, the end of the novel finds Aunt Esther dead ("she held the locket containing her child's hair still in her hand, and once or twice she kissed it with a long soft kiss"), finds Mary Barton transformed into Mary Wilson, and the voice of her dead mother presumably silenced. Judith Newton has noted that female authority too often takes the form of "influence" instead of "ability"; as she quotes Sarah Ellis's *The Wives of England*, to have influence, "all that has been expected to be enjoyed from the indulgence of selfishness,

6. Ibid., p. 239.

must then of necessity be left out of our calculations, with all that ministers to the pride of superiority, all that gratifies the love of power, all
that *converts the woman into the heroine* (emphasis added)."[7] Only in
Mary's efforts to save Jem from hanging do we find female action
directly embraced by the text; later, when Mary wants to perform the
same redemptive work for Aunt Esther, "vehemently" rising "as if she
was going on the search there and then," Jem "fondly restrain[s] her,"
ending the progress of "the woman into the heroine." But the other conversion, of woman into mother, remains, and maternal activity, as it can
be learned and imitated, is at the novel's heart. The scene where Job
Legh carries his dead daughter's child from London, wearing a woman's
nightcap to try to calm the baby's screams, suggests that it is as mothers that we will love, teach, travel best.

But even if one allows it to be a real power, with a wider sphere
than that of "influence," matriarchal authority creates a second problem: what does wielding this power do to those around you? If the
problem with the patriarchal power of the masters is that it turns
workers into animals to be guided and governed, matriarchal power
in the novel seems to make the workers infants. The recipients of
maternal wisdom move back, almost beyond language, to what Tennyson described as a state of "no language but a cry." (In *Mary Barton*, once you get the mother back in the world, you can't talk to her.)
In Gaskell's mind, all her characters are like "terrified children," only
"secure of safety when near the protecting care" of the mother, and
they attain moral goodness only when they become "protecting."

On the text's conscious level, that protection is Christ's, the "friend
of the orphan," but on its deepest level, it is the care of the mother.
The messianic overtones of Mary's "you are come at last!" are echoed
in the "they know not what they do" of Mr Carson's final revelation,
and its implicit message (be like Christ, be like a mother) is brought
out in a series of scenes with children. When John Barton leaves
home to assassinate Carson, he stops long enough to help a small
child; in the scene before Mary's mother's "return," Mary has been
stopped in her panicked run by a little Italian boy who utters "in his
pretty broken English," the words "Hungry! so hungry!" Mary races
past him, only to think better of her impatience, and returns to where
"the little hopeless stranger had sunk down . . . in loneliness and
starvation, and was raining down tears as he spoke in some foreign
tongue, with low cries for the distant 'Mamma mia!'" (p. 202). The
most important scene of conversion in the novel, Mr Carson's, is also
prepared for by an encounter with a child. After he has left the home
of John Barton, still unwilling to forgive the worker who claims not

7. Judith Lowder Newton, *Women, Power and Subversion: Social Strategies in British Fiction,
1778–1860* (Athens: University of Georgia Press, 1981), p. 5.

to have known what he was doing, Carson sees a rough young boy run headlong into a beautiful, well-dressed girl and knock her down. The girl's governess pounces on the boy, only to have the angelic young girl forgive him, exclaiming that he didn't know what he was doing; this message haunts Carson till he goes home, takes down the family Bible and reads the Gospels. Then he comes to "the end: the awful End. And there were the haunting words of pleading" (p. 320). Only after witnessing the young child's forgiveness toward her enemy on account of his essential ignorance can Carson absorb the message of this explicitly Christian novel, picking up the text he and John Barton share and have both "puzzled over." But for this to happen, for Carson to be moved to compassion for Barton, Barton must become like that child and be forgiven for not knowing what he is doing. For Carson to be Christ-as-mother, Barton's autonomy (his most articulate demands, the wickedness of the masters) must be denied.

The problem with mothering, then, is that it requires children: the more they are like the Italian boy, uttering brokenly, "Hungry! so hungry" the better. People are returned to that world where desire and demand become one; they have a language to ask for only the simplest needs to be fulfilled. The workers themselves become, in the words of one of Barton's visitors before his trip to London, people who have "been clemmed long enough, and [who] donnot see whatten good they'n been doing, if they can't give what we're all crying for sin' the day we were born" (p. 78). However moving this plea is, and it is in some ways the perfect summary of the blighted lives of the workers, it is also reductive, compared to the strongest arguments for dignity Barton makes in the course of the novel. There is a difference, which Gaskell never addresses, between Barton's reasoned arguments for work, for reform, for individual autonomy, and the crying of starving children, to which this statement reduces the Charter—there was more at stake, somehow, before.

However much we might prefer the sympathizing mother to the angry father, and whatever the creation of maternal narratives allowed Gaskell to do, the mother's return does not seem to solve all the problems the novel set out to answer. The difficulty Gaskell faces as she nears the end of her novel is to avoid setting up yet another structure of authority that will silence people like John and Mary Barton as effectively as did the structure she set out to criticize. As John Barton's voice gets swallowed up by the discourse around him, be it Job Legh's or Carson's, so the potential for transforming the language of authority seems to disappear as well. Gaskell appears to have trouble imagining a world without authority, in England at least, and this may be why she moves the novel to Canada for its final chapter. It may also be why she tells us so little of life in Canada, that mythic place where class relationships will no longer exist. If happy marriages could not take place in the world of Manchester but had to occur in the new world, perhaps free, unlegislated space can exist only there as well. And perhaps that space exists only outside the novel; to impose any narration may be to freeze it into something supervised and "over-looked." It may, further, reduce the narrative to one of expertise, of "political economy," rather than "truth." Gaskell's novel does not promise a solution; it promises, rather, a changed heart.

If the move to Canada is not a solution, Gaskell's vision of mater-nal narrative presence, along with her questioning of narrative authority in general, does present solutions of a different kind. If the world cannot be transformed absolutely, our ways of seeing and describing it can—and as the novel's critique of received languages suggests, to write the story differently may be to write a different story. *Mary Barton* contains within it the story of Gaskell's learning to speak, a rewriting of stories of female heroism and female author-ship played out in a world of spectacle and silencing in which Gaskell finds for herself a language "expressing her wants" that is more than just "a cry," and for her heroine, a chance to speak openly, choose her life, and overcome some of the plots that have been written for her.

DEBORAH EPSTEIN NORD

[Class Antagonism and the Sexual Plot in *Mary Barton*][†]

*   *   *

In his seminal work on the industrial novel in *Culture and Society*, Raymond Williams credits *Mary Barton* with offering "the most mov-ing response in literature to the industrial suffering of the 1840s" and then goes on to make the critical point that has had the greatest influ-ence on subsequent readings of the novel: after the early chapters, in which the narrative focuses on the agonies of the working man John Barton (the center of Gaskell's original plans for the novel), the "flow of sympathy" is redirected in the text to the "less compromising fig-ure" of Mary. Furthermore, the murder of Harry Carson by John Bar-ton irrevocably cripples the reader's identification with the working man and serves to dramatize the "fear of violence . . . widespread among the upper and middle classes."[1] Unable to sustain real sym-pathy for a man whose rage against "the masters" leads him to trade

---

† From *Walking the Victorian Streets: Women, Representation, and the City*. Copyright © 1995 by Cornell University. Used by permission of the publisher, Cornell University Press.
1. Raymond Williams, *Culture and Society, 1780–1950* (Harmondsworth: Penguin, 1961), p. 102.

unionism, Chartism, and beyond, Williams suggests, Gaskell lets her class identification overwhelm her initial intentions, and she uses the murder—an unrepresentative action—to drive a wedge between herself and John Barton. But Williams's next comment on the murder complicates this reading: this "act of violence, a sudden aggression against a man contemptuous of the sufferings of the poor, looks very much like a projection, with which, in the end, [Gaskell] was unable to come to terms."[2] The murder, then, places Gaskell imaginatively in two conflicting positions: as fearful middle-class victim of working-class violence and as enraged perpetrator of that violence. Gaskell did indeed see herself and her novel as mediators between these two positions or visions, and she understood her task as one of translation. Just as her husband, because of his knowledge of etymology, was able to provide glosses for the Lancashire dialect in the text, so Gaskell believed herself particularly well placed to explain to her own class the sensibility and grievances of the Lancashire workers.[3]

Another version of the novel's origins—this one related by Gaskell to a journalist—suggests why she may have felt this way. The impulse to write *Mary Barton* came to her not on the street but in a laborer's cottage, she claimed, while she was trying to calm the anger of a hungry and bitter father. The man grabbed her arm and challenged her tearfully, "Ay, ma'am, but have ye ever seen a child clemmed to death?"[4] Although the anecdote ends there, with the clear implication that Gaskell had no retort and would take upon herself the amplification and dramatization of this query in fiction, we can imagine a slightly different, albeit unstated, conclusion. Gaskell's ten-month-old son had not starved to death, but her experience of loss and profound grieving—she wrote to a friend that this "wound will never heal on earth," that it had changed her beyond what anyone could imagine—corresponded in some way to the agony of this man.[5] Because she had seen her child die, she could write from both inside and outside his despair, expressing it as her own and rendering it coherent to readers of her own class. Indeed, she uses the death of a son as the primary healing link between Barton, the murderer, and Carson, the mill owner and father of his victim.[6]

2. Ibid., p. 102.
3. William Gaskell's notes on Lancashire dialect do not simply translate the words but very often locate them in passages from classic English works such as *Piers Plowman* and *The Canterbury Tales* in order to suggest their legitimacy. His wife's novel appears to share the same impulse and the same method.
4. John Geoffrey Sharps, *Mrs. Gaskell's Observation and Invention: A Study of Her Non-Biographic Works* (Fontwell, Sussex: Linden Press, 1970), p. 56. If readers of Gaskell's novels retain just one word of Lancashire dialect, it is bound to be "clemmed," which means starved.
5. *The Letters of Mrs. Gaskell*, ed. J. A. V. Chapple and Arthur Pollard (Manchester: Manchester University Press, 1966), pp. 56–57.
6. See Sharps, *Mrs. Gaskell's Observation and Invention*, p. 70, for his discussion of three incidents in the novel in which central characters' encounters with unknown children in the street interrupt their self-absorption.

Engels argued in *The Condition of the Working Class* that separation and invisibility were the geographic and social principles that governed relations between the proletariat and the bourgeoisie of Manchester. The town was unique in Engels's experience in "the systematic way in which the working classes have been barred from the main streets" and the "tender susceptibilities of the eyes and nerves of the middle classes" were thereby protected (p. 56).[7] A middle-class man might live in Manchester for years, he claimed, and travel daily to and from work in the center of town without ever seeing a slum or a slum dweller. For Gaskell, given her experience of the streets and the laborer's cottage as well as her Christian commitment to reconciliation, the primary principle that defines relations between classes in *Mary Barton* is not, of course, separation but connection.[8] The novel also makes clear, however, that connection itself can be invisible to a callous and uneducated middle class, and that a second, more insidious principle—contrast—can supplant it in the minds of the aggrieved working class.

Although Gaskell's aim is to replace the structure of contrast between rich and poor with a structure of encounters (like her own) and connection, her narrative gives powerful emotional weight to the poor's perception of inequality and painful difference which in John Barton's case becomes a "monomania" (p. 149).[9] As his son lies at home dying of scarlet fever and malnutrition, an out-of-work John Barton stands before a shop window filled with "haunches of venison, Stilton cheeses, moulds of jelly," and watches in amazement as his former master's wife emerges from the shop loaded down with delicacies. The narrator turns the screw of ironic contrast once more: "And Barton returned home with a bitter spirit of wrath in his heart, to see his only boy a corpse!" (p. 25).

---

7. In relation to Engels's observations on the separation of classes in Manchester, Marcus quotes from John Stuart Mill's essay "Civilization": "One of the effects of civilization (not to say one of the ingredients in it) is, that the spectacle, and even the very idea of pain, is kept more and more out of the sight of those classes who enjoy in their fullness the benefits of civilization" (*Marcus, Engels, Manchester and the Working Class*, 1974). Gaskell emphasizes the tormenting visibility of these "benefits" to those who are in pain.

8. The precise nature and extent of Gaskell's personal observation of the poor in their homes, rather than on the streets, is difficult to establish. Sharps records that she was one of the first volunteer visitors for the Manchester and Salford District Provident Society (*Mrs. Gaskell's Observation and Invention*, pp. 56–57), and we know too that she was active in prison philanthropy and in teaching girls' Sunday school. See "A Manchester Correspondent" [Mat Hompes], "Mrs. Gaskell and Her Social Work among the Poor," *Inquirer and Christian Life* (London), October 8, 1910, p. 656. R. K. Webb, however, suggests that Gaskell's "immediate experience of the poor" has been exaggerated, and that "much of what she wrote to enlighten her ignorant and unfeeling audience she had to learn from reading." R. K. Webb, "The Gaskells as Unitarians," in *Dickens and Other Victorians: Essays in Honour of Philip Collins* (London: Macmillan, 1988), p. 159. I suspect that Webb is correct here; but Gaskell's sympathetic evocation of the lives of industrial workers nonetheless surpasses in power and verisimilitude those of other industrial novelists, for, whether she spent much time in workers' homes or not, she did indeed live in their midst.

9. Page numbers for *Mary Barton* refer to this Norton Critical Edition.

Well-filled and brightly lit shop windows figure in a second, more extended use of contrast in the novel, when Barton and George Wilson, after visiting the fever-racked Davenports in their damp, dark, fetid cellar dwelling, attempt to buy medicine and obtain an infirmary order from Davenport's employer. As Barton searches for a druggist, the narrative insists on the difference between the middle-class reader's delighted and nostalgic response to the phantasmagoria of the gaslit streets and Barton's angry awareness that they merely provide a painful contrast to the Davenports' gloomy cellar (p. 58). Similarly, when Wilson enters the kitchen of Davenport's employer, Mr. Carson, the narrative exploits the contrast between the worker's typhus-ridden dwelling and the master's kitchen, where smells of coffee brewing and steaks broiling fill the air and comfort the soul. What the middle-class reader might take for granted, Gaskell repeatedly underlines, the poor have never known; and when the starving witness the bounty of the well fed, they feel betrayal and anger.

Gaskell's own anger about the contrasts she so skillfully evokes—and to which Williams seems to allude when he writes of her "projection"—seeps into the text even as she tries to enlighten her readers in a measured and nonpartisan way. Her efforts at being evenhanded are often disrupted by both the sense of injustice she feels on behalf of the poor and her anxiety over seeming to accuse the rich. In the novel's preface her prose gets twisted out of shape by defensiveness and denial. She observes straightforwardly that working people are sore and irritable toward the rich, but she then introduces the language of equivocation: "whether" their grievances are "well-founded or no" is not for her to judge; the workers' sense of "injustice and unkindness" is a "belief"; the belief might be erroneous; and, finally, since she knows nothing of "Political Economy or theories of trade," it is only by accident that her views match those of theorists and other systematic critics (pp. 5–6). These disavowals are in turn undercut by parenthetical phrases that legitimate the workers' rage, such as reminders that the fortunes amassed by the rich were in fact produced by the poor.

A similar kind of equivocation characterizes the description of the depression of 1839–41 which prefaces a discussion of John Barton's Chartist activity. Here Gaskell oscillates between blaming her Christian readers for their indifference to suffering and excusing them by reason of their ignorance (pp. 76–77). She manipulates her readers' arrogance, pride, and guilt and, in so doing, tries to camouflage and control the sense of injustice she feels on behalf of the poor. Ostensibly she wants to explain the resentment that fueled Chartism without justifying it, but her own declaration of the guilty ignorance or callousness of the middle class establishes a justification nonetheless.

The murder of Harry Carson, then, constitutes a gesture that gives full vent to Gaskell's anger and seemingly closes her off from an identification with the deed. But the murder is not simply an act of vengeance against a man who is, as Williams observes, contemptuous of the sufferings of the poor. It is also an act of aggression against the man who threatens the chastity and future of Mary Barton. Thus, the "projection" of which Williams speaks expresses an overdetermined need to punish Carson for his crimes against worker and woman alike. The murderer is, of course, Mary's father, who, although he does not know of her secret relationship with Carson, is anxious about her chastity. In addition, Carson's arrogant indifference to Mary's well-being—an analogue of his extreme harshness toward the striking workers—functions as an important element in the novel by making it difficult for the reader to feel his murder as a loss or even as an unequivocal moral wrong. The narrative uses his caricatured upper-class lecherousness to mitigate, almost to cancel out, the horror of the crime against him. Here, as elsewhere, the novel conflates the story of threatened female virtue with that of the oppression of the poor. The murder is often identified by critics, however, as the turning point after which the novel's focus shifts from John Barton's working-class plot to the romantic plot involving his daughter.[1] As I hope to show, Gaskell's rewriting of the sexual plot is at all points inseparable from the plot of class antagonism and is in a real sense both the starting point and the dominant preoccupation of her text.

The novel opens on the scene of a group of factory girls walking in Green Heys Fields and soon thereafter enters into the debate about the liabilities of factory work for women which we have seen in the commentaries of Faucher and Engels. The "merry and loud-talking" girls, clad in inventively arranged shawls, introduce the novel's implicit concern with the dangers and delights of woman's public role (p. 8). Although John Barton will, in a matter of pages, articulate the view that factory work corrupts women and is in all likelihood the cause of his sister-in-law Esther's sexual fall and disappearance, we have before us in these opening pages an image of young women unremarkable in every respect save "an acuteness and intelligence of countenance" (p. 9). Although no one character in the novel fully

---

1. Raymond Williams is, I have said, foremost among those critics who have described this narrative shift. Catherine Gallagher treats the narrative inconsistencies in *Mary Barton* at some length in *The Industrial Reformation of English Fiction, 1832–1867* (Chicago: University of Chicago Press, 1985), chap. 3. Only after the murder, she argues, does Gaskell achieve "a kind of generic consistency by retreating into the domestic mentality of her heroine"; but this involves a "suppression of the tragic narrative" which seems to separate the novel into "mutually exclusive stories" (p. 67). Rosemarie Bodenheimer, in her excellent essay "Private Grief and Public Acts in *Mary Barton*," in *Dickens Studies Annual*, vol. 9 (New York: AMS Press, 1981), p. 207, argues that the plot of the novel "muffles" the connection between the stories of industrial and sexual exploitation, so that the two stories are split and never reconnected.

articulates the argument against Barton's position, the narrative itself—beginning with its opening portrait of the energetic, healthy, and intelligent-looking factory girls—continually undercuts the connection he makes between women's factory work and their sexual corruption.[2] Barton, who would prefer that Mary take up domestic service or dressmaking—occupations associated with a more private, less exposed setting—remains ignorant of the circumstances under which Mary finds employment. When Barton tries to find a job for Mary as a dressmaker he fails, not realizing that if she had accompanied him, her beauty would have won her a position as a "showwoman" (p. 26). Ultimately, of course, Mary finds herself a job as an apprentice on her own. But far from sheltering Mary from exposure, the dressmaker's shop "in a respectable little street" provides the setting for her introduction to Harry Carson, who notices her while waiting for his sisters to make purchases (p. 73). Neither was the factory responsible for Esther's seduction into an illicit relationship: her lover, an army officer, had no connection to the world of industrial manufacture.

For John Barton it is the economic independence, the money to spend on finery, and the late hours that make factory work so dangerous to women's virtue. Mary's and Esther's experiences with men, however, have little or nothing to do with their work. This point is underscored by Esther's conviction that dressmaking—"a bad life for a girl"—puts Mary in danger by forcing her to return home late at night and subjecting her to such tedium that she will search after "any novelty that makes a little change" (p. 144). The street does expose women to danger, Gaskell suggests, but it is the desire to escape work rather than the work itself that imperils them. Before her disappearance Esther talks seductively to Mary of becoming a lady, and Mary, too, in a subtle form of rebellion against her father's detestation of "gentlefolk," aspires to marry out of her class. Gaskell endorses the apparently traditional notion that hard work is the safe and moral course to good fortune, but she insists that this precept should apply to working-class women as well as men. We need only think of fictional heroines from Richardson's Pamela to Brontë's Jane Eyre to Disraeli's Sybil to appreciate the cultural power of the competing idea of marriage as the route to upward mobility for "women of the people."

The novel's challenge to the myth that work, and especially factory work, corrupts women complements its undermining of a number of myths surrounding the figure of the fallen woman. Esther's narrative in chapter 14 contests the notion that sheer depravity determines the

2. Critics have often assumed that Gaskell essentially endorsed John Barton's position on factory work for women. See, for example, Aina Rubenius, *The Woman Question in Mrs. Gaskell's Life and Work* (Uppsala: Lundequistka Bokhanden, 1950), pp. 147–48.

prostitute's life; it is rather economic necessity that drives those decisions that appear sinful to the respectable world. Esther ran off with her officer for love rather than for vanity's sake, and she took to the streets only when, abandoned, impoverished, and unable to make a go of her shop in Chester, she had no other way to provide for her small daughter, by now starving and deathly ill.[3] By playing the card of the dying child, Gaskell reclaims Esther from her status as pariah and situates her within the framework of parental devotion and bereavement that weaves classes together in the novel and binds John Barton and the elder Carson to the author herself.[4]

Although the novel represents Esther as beyond redemption— she is treated as a leper, addicted to drink, allied with an urban underworld of beggars, thieves, and whores—it also suggests that hers is a role created by society, not decreed by nature or by some higher morality. The novel accomplishes this in the remarkable and chilling scene of Esther's visit to Mary after the murder of Harry Carson. Wishing to place in her niece's hands the incriminating evidence she had found at the scene of the murder and yet hoping to spare her the knowledge that her aunt is "a prostitute; an outcast," Esther disguises herself as a respectable laborer's wife.[5] Reversing the usual downward trajectory associated with the theme of the pawnshop, Esther goes to a shop where she is well known and trades her gaudy streetwalker's clothes for "a black silk bonnet, a printed gown, a plaid shawl . . . the appropriate garb of that happy class to which she could never, never more belong" (p. 208). The disguise of respectability requires not merely clothing, however, but the "manners and character . . . of a mechanic's wife" (pp. 208–209); and Esther plays the part so convincingly that she leaves the Barton home disappointed that she has not elicited from Mary the sympathy for her desperate situation she had silently craved. This scene raises the possibility that even "character" can be adopted, put on and taken off, played like a part, and that a woman like Esther is no more definable by the prostitute's finery that first announces her profession to John Barton than she is by the costume of a laborer's wife.

3. Amanda Anderson, in *Tainted Souls and Painted Faces* (Ithaca: Cornell University Press, 1993), remarks that Esther's seduction by her army officer has "a distinctly literary flavor" (p. 118), unlike Mary's near-seduction by a manufacturer's son. Although Esther's narrative does have the "literary" character Anderson detects, the moment when Esther goes out on the streets to prostitute herself has a crucial economic dimension.
4. Esther is closely associated with her brother-in-law John Barton, who had shunned her after she became a prostitute. They both end up outcasts or "wanderers," buried in the same grave (*Mary Barton*, p. 338).
5. See Hilary Schor's discussion of this scene, in which she treats Esther's appearance at Mary's door as the ghostly return of Mary's mother and also considers Esther's role as a "narratorial surrogate" (*Scheherezade in the Marketplace* [(New York: Oxford UP, 1992)], p. 30). Amanda Anderson reads Esther's disguise as a means of protecting Mary from contamination (*Tainted Souls and Painted Faces*, p. 123).

The scene also breaks the imagined circuit of influence into which some feared that Mary would be drawn by her aunt. Her father frets over the potential threat of Esther's legacy, worries about the foolish desire for wealth that Mary has in common with her aunt, and even, after Esther has gone, about the "very bodily likeness" between the two women which to him signals the possibility of "a similar likeness in their fate" (p. 113). Here the idea of an inherited taint affecting the female line, so crucial to Dickens's vision in *Dombey and Son* and *Bleak House*, is offered and then decisively rejected. Just as John Barton mistakenly believes that the factory itself would have a corrupting effect on his daughter, so too does he assign moral meaning to her physical resemblance to her aunt. But Esther's influence on Mary has not been indelible; and although the niece also attracts the attention of a man above her in station, she escapes sexual danger. She will, in fact, end as a mechanic's wife, the very role that Esther chooses for her disguise. For this one moment at least, the two women's identities are suggestively interchangeable.

The connection between Barton's fear for his daughter's chastity and his murder of Harry Carson, the man who threatens that chastity, is one of the elements in the novel that fuses the plot of class antagonism with the sexual plot. Barton does not, of course, know of the relationship between Mary and the mill owner's son, but his intense psychic involvement from the very beginning of the narrative with the possibility of Mary's sexual fall suggests that his motives for murder are complex, multiple, and buried. And just as the picking of lots among the union men is meant to obscure and minimize the importance of the murderer's identity, so does the motive for murder float freely among many who know the victim. Jem, the prime suspect, knows about Mary's liaison with Carson, for Esther resorted to confiding in Jem about the danger to Mary's chastity when John Barton refused to listen. Barton is thus a surrogate both for Jem, the man who stands in for Barton in people's suspicions, and for his fellow workers.[6]

Moreover, the text underscores the parallel between Carson's treatment of Mary and his treatment of the striking workers. When Jem approaches Carson to try to reason with him about Mary, Carson treats him with disdain and mocks him as a meddling negotiator in their affairs: "Neither Mary nor I called you in as a mediator," he sneers (p. 158). Jem's "mediation" having failed, the interview ends in violence, with Carson striking the first blow and Jem's assault on the suddenly supine Carson—like Barton's fatal attack—elided from the text.[7] In the

---

6. Rosemarie Bodenheimer refers to Jem and John Barton as "split doubles" in the murder plot ("Private Grief and Public Acts," p. 207).
7. "The young man raised his slight cane, and smote the artizan across the face with a stinging stroke. An instant afterwards he lay stretched in the muddy road, Jem standing over him, panting with rage" (*Mary Barton*, p. 158).

chapter that follows Carson reveals himself to be unyielding and punitive toward the strikers: he is identified as an extremist, "the head and
voice of the violent party among the masters" (p. 162). He proposes
that all communication between masters and union be suspended, that
scabs be hired, and that no workers be employed in the future unless
they swear independence from any trade union. Before the chapter
ends, the aggrieved strikers, as if in direct and commensurate response
to the kind of oath Carson wishes to extract from them, swear their
own oath to murder him. They use for lots pieces of paper torn from a
caricature of themselves—"lank, ragged, dispirited, and famine-
stricken"—which Carson had sketched earlier that day (p. 163). The
upper-class rake and the mocking oppressor of the poor are joined in
Harry Carson.

Although I would not disagree entirely with the critical view that
after the murder the joint plot of industrial strife and sexual danger is sundered, I would describe this change in the narrative differently. As I have suggested, the novel concerns itself from the
very first with the public role of women, especially but not exclusively Mary's role. After the murder, however, Mary is transformed
from the passive subject of discussions of her sexual virtue and
proper role to the active agent of her own fate. The efforts of those
around her in the early part of the novel to keep her out of the public eye, to tie her safely to private domestic space, are totally
defeated in the second half. Her ascendancy in the story marks an
awakening of consciousness and purpose that reproduces the
workers' earlier mobilization. Like them, she must go beyond even
the public sphere of work and engage in the wider world of politics
and law.[8] To the extent that she is the workers' double—that they
are parallel victims of Carson's callousness and arrogance—she
serves to vindicate them as she exonerates Jem and herself. The
actual murderer, John Barton, never does come to trial, and the
elder Carson's desire for revenge is severely criticized in the novel.
As a result, the hearing in Liverpool takes the place of a public
judgment of Barton and dispels the need to punish the perpetrator
of an act whose criminality is represented with equivocation.[9]
Mary succeeds, after all, not only in establishing Jem's innocence
but also in protecting her father's guilt.

8. Rosemarie Bodenheimer's reading of the novel here, as elsewhere, is very close to mine.
   She writes: "In Mary's burst of heroism Gaskell imagined an even more direct image [than
   John Barton] of her own situation. For writing *Mary Barton* was her kind of 'bodily or mental action in time of distress,' and it leads, like Mary's journey, out of the domestic world
   and into a public one where one's deepest feelings are put on display for a curious crowd"
   ("Private Grief and Public Acts," p. 214).
9. Commenting on Mr. Carson's passion for revenge, the narrator declares, "Oh! Orestes! you
   would have made a very tolerable Christian of the nineteenth century!" (*Mary Barton*,
   p. 188). Although the text evinces sympathy for Carson's loss, at no point does it sanction
   his desire to avenge his son's murder.

Mary's entry into public life is inaugurated dramatically by the novel experience of travel: she journeys to Liverpool on her first train ride and then searches for Will Wilson's ship at the Liverpool docks by going on a boat, also for the first time. The train ride places her definitively in a world cut off from the limitations and protection of home and also offers her the chance to understand her home as the city of Manchester itself. Facing backwards as the train leaves for Liverpool, Mary looks "towards the factory-chimneys, and the cloud of smoke which hovers over Manchester" (p. 246) and feels the new sensation of homesickness (Gaskell uses the German *Heimweh*). These sights, which the narrator concedes are unpleasant to most, evoke in Mary a yearning for the place she has never left before. Leaving gives her an identity in the wider world, and yet it gives her a civic identity too by tying her in a wholly new way to the city itself. The solitary train ride also, of course, exposes her to public scrutiny, and as she visits the docks and finally enters the courtroom, her vulnerability deepens. In the rowboat, alone with two "rough, hard-looking men," Mary is subjected to the curses and insults of sailors and captains, who assume that her pursuit of Will to supply an alibi for Jem masks some illicit purpose (p. 255). Even the wife of the old boatman who befriends Mary and takes her to his home wonders if she can actually be as virtuous as she seems. The woman muses, "Perhaps thou'rt a bad one; I almost misdoubt thee, thou'rt so pretty" (p. 272). It is in the courtroom, however, that Mary is most traumatically read and misread by a crowd that has, after all, gathered to hear her "heart's secrets" (p. 281).

Mary's extraordinary exertions on Jem's behalf, and her father's, culminate in the hearing on the Carson murder and in her testimony under the scrutiny of hundreds of onlookers. As in the riot scene in *North and South*, to which this is a companion piece, the heroine claims for herself a public role in order to bear witness to what is just, and in so doing struggles painfully with the sexually charged image she unwillingly creates. Her very appearance and the stories that have circulated about her place in a romantic triangle that has ended in murder mark her in the eyes of "the hundreds [who] were looking at her" as a woman sullied by sexual scandal (p. 281). To Mr. Carson she is "the fatal Helen" (p. 280); to an acquaintance of the narrator who was present that day, she resembles nothing so much as an engraving of Beatrice Cenci, the Renaissance heroine whose portrait, as we saw in chapter 4, had so captured the imagination of the diarist Anna Jameson.[1] It is the essential innocence and "mute imploring agony" of the young woman that this allusion to Beatrice Cenci is

1. The notes to the Penguin edition of *Mary Barton* indicate that an engraving of a portrait of Beatrice Cenci in the Barberini Gallery in Rome appeared with an article on her in vol. 12 of *Bentley's Miscellany* (1847).

intended to evoke; but the image also calls up the stain of incest, the crime of parricide, and the heroic force of the victim who rises to accuse the powerful. Beatrice Cenci is, then, a woman whose heroism is inseparable from taint, and Gaskell's choice of this allusion implies a far more extreme and dramatic level of scandal and guilt than Mary's case would seem to suggest. Also striking in this passage is the degree of distance the narrator puts between herself and this image of Mary: "I was not there myself; but one who was, told me . . ." (p. 281). As the narrative moves outside Mary to describe the spectator's point of view, the narrator begins to disclaim the description. It is as if the objectification of Mary that automatically associates her with sin must be put in someone else's mouth, and yet it must also be included in the narrative because of its powerful ability to shape the condition and consciousness of the public woman.

The eager young barrister who questions Mary gives voice to the prurient curiosity of the spectators as he asks her which man—Jem Wilson or Harry Carson—had been her "favoured lover" (p. 281). Already implicitly accused of transgression, Mary feels compelled to explain her misguided interest in Carson in terms of moral ignorance, a result of having lost her mother when a girl.[2] She admits to foolishness, giddiness, and vanity, and she "confesses" twice to loving Jem Wilson. Not on trial for any crime, not guilty of any sexual sin, she must nevertheless make her confession. At this moment Mary's acceptance of sin and her consciousness of her *father's* guilt merge, reminding us again of the complex meaning of the murder as retribution for Carson's analogous crimes against worker and woman. The authentic accomplishment of Mary's presence at the hearing, the successful clearing of Jem's name, is eclipsed by the trauma of personal exposure and the overwhelming tension of knowing and suppressing her father's story. Devastated by assuming her father's guilt and by being cast as a scandalous woman— as Helen or Beatrice Cenci—by the gawking crowd, Mary collapses in convulsions. As if her subjective self had been crushed by this assault, she is reduced to a delirious, disintegrated consciousness.

The narrative of woman's public identity that began with the factory girls in Green Heys Field comes to a strange close in what can only be described as the rebirth of Mary Barton following her collapse in Liverpool. After a prolonged delirium Mary awakens, her mind "in the tender state of a lately-born infant's" (p. 301). Upon first opening her eyes she sees Jem, who has been watching by her bedside throughout her illness: "She smiled gently, as a baby does when it sees its mother tending its little cot; and continued her innocent, infantine gaze into his face as if the sight gave her much unconscious pleasure" (pp.

2. In *Ruth* Gaskell makes the same connection between the loss of motherly guidance and moral ignorance.

301–302). After the trauma of public exposure Mary is thus reborn into innocence, purged of whatever intimations of sin had clung to her in the role of scandalous woman. Jem's maternal presence hovers over and protects her, a replacement for the mother whose absence Mary had blamed for her inability to make moral discriminations. This rebirth is stamped with the author's pained ambivalence toward women's experience beyond the domestic sphere. Although the value of public testimony is affirmed in the narrative, the dangers of exposure require the restorative of a radical cleansing. Even Mary's breakdown and revival are not quite sufficient to banish all remnants of the taint, and so, in a strange displacement, the task falls to Jem. No one in Manchester will employ the once suspect mechanic. "Too strong a taint was on his character," Jem fears, "for him ever to labour [there] again" (p. 302). Although a court has declared him innocent, he, like Mary, stands indelibly accused and seems still to carry the burden of John Barton's guilt. Jem even understands why the men shun him, for they have only their name and character on which to rely and so must "keep that free from soil and taint" (p. 312). Indistinguishable from the convicts and prostitutes who emigrate to the colonies at the conclusion of other nineteenth-century narratives, Jem and Mary must also leave England to make a life for themselves. It is as if once she had left home to take her place in the world, Mary could never quite go back.

JOSEPHINE M. GUY

[Morality and Economics in *Mary Barton*]†

* * *

A detailed attention to what I earlier termed the 'micro-economic analysis' of *Mary Barton* reveals that actions in the novel are nearly always motivated by financial expediency: this is obvious in the first half of the novel where the disintegration of working-class family life and of individual morality (particularly in John Barton and Esther) is traced directly to the pressures of poverty. Indeed it is precisely this gesture towards a social explanation of working-class violence and moral degradation which many critics have commended in the novel. By contrast, little attention has been given to the fact that money is just as central to the more melodramatic events in the second half of the novel. For example, the suspense surrounding the arrest of Jem, the search for Jem's alibi and the ensuing trial scenes

† From *The Victorian Social-Problem Novel: The Market, the Individual and Communal Life* (Basingstoke, U.K.: MacMillan, 1996), pp. 141, 152–61. Reprinted by permission of Josephine M. Guy.

all depend crucially upon financial transactions which are documented with Gaskell's customary precision. Initially it is Carson's great wealth which permits him to put up a reward that leads to Jem's sudden arrest; the amount of money, described as 'a temptation' for the police, is set at a 'thousand pounds' rather than the superintendent's suggestion of the 'munificent' sum of 'three, or five hundred pounds'. Carson believes that he can buy justice; he can afford the 'attorneys skilled in criminal practice' and the 'barristers coming from the Northern Circuit' who, he believes, will ensure a 'speedy conviction, a speedy execution'. By contrast, the case for the defence is constantly threatened by the absence of money: poverty nearly prevents Mary from travelling to Liverpool (she has to rely on a sovereign lent to her by Margaret); and when she does arrive, lack of money again nearly thwarts her attempt to contact Will (she is unable to pay the full fare for the boat trip). Once the court proceedings are under way, money continues to be central in the creation of dramatic tension. The effort expended on contacting Will and his dramatic entrance into the courtroom seem doomed when the prosecution casts doubt on his evidence by suggesting that he had been paid for his story by 'good coin of her majesty's realm'. Will's indignant reply echoes a theme central to the first half of the book: that the possession of money corrupts the wealthy far more than its absence corrupts the poor.

> Will you tell the judge and jury how much money you've been paid for your impudence towards one, who has told God's blessed truth, and who would scorn to tell a lie, or blackguard any one, for the biggest fee as ever a lawyer got for doing dirty work. Will you tell, sir?—But I'm ready, my lord judge, to take my oath as many times as your lordship or the jury would like, to testify to things having happened just as I said.[1] (p. 287)

It is fitting that the evidence in question concerns Will's inability to afford a 'three-and-sixpence' train-fare to Liverpool. Possessing only a 'jingling . . . few coppers', he had been forced to walk, and Jem's agreement to accompany him as far as Parkside provides the all-important alibi. On this evidence the jury eventually acquits Jem, but there is little sense of victory. On the contrary, the verdict is described as 'unsatisfactory', the jurors 'neither being convinced of his innocence, nor yet quite willing to believe him guilty'. The resulting ambiguity taints Jem's reputation and eventually forces him to leave England. At this point the story is far from endorsing the values of melodrama and romance; there is no simple triumph of right over wrong, of Christian virtue over financial expediency. Rather the

---

1. Page numbers for the quotation and all subsequent page numbers for *Mary Barton* refer to this Norton Critical Edition.

opposite: the attention given to the economics of every situation is a forcible reminder of how vulnerable morality is to money. One incident in particular provides a poignant illustration of the inevitable interconnection between morality and the market. When Mary returns home after the trial she is shocked to encounter her father 'still and motionless' beside the cold fire-grate in their former home. Mary's earlier revulsion at his crime is immediately overcome by compassion for his 'smitten helplessness'. The strength of blood-ties— 'He was her father! her own dear father!'—is a typical melodramatic trope, and Mary's emotional response to her father's plight is entirely appropriate to the genre: 'Tenderly did she treat him, and fondly did she serve him in every way that heart could devise or hand execute.' However, this generalised expression of compassion immediately finds its expression in economic terms: 'comfort' for John Barton turns out to be material as well as spiritual. It involves some 'purchases', those necessary to furnish a house which 'was bare as when Mary had left it, of coal, or of candle, of food, or of blessing in any shape'. Ironically, Mary is only able to afford these commodities because 'she had some money about her, the price of her strange services as a witness'. Here, as everywhere in *Mary Barton*, conventional expressions of piety (a daughter's dutiful love for her father) are registered in terms of their economic cost.

The most sustained example of this interpenetration of the moral and the economic is provided in the early chapters of the novel, in the detailed descriptions of working-class culture. The main way in which we are introduced to that culture is through witnessing working-class meals, either within families or, more often, by small celebrations which accompany meetings between families. The purchase, preparation and consumption of food are not just to sustain life; they are also important social rituals. And it is through these rituals that the working classes enact their sense of community: compassion and benevolence are typically demonstrated through giving and receiving food. Our very first introduction to urban working-class culture is via the preparation of a meal by the Bartons for their friends the Wilsons. A succession of meals at various homes—at Alice's cellar, at the Leghs', at the Davenports'—follows, and in each case the nature of the specific meals is an index both of the moral character of the giver and of the strength of community between giver and receiver. In this respect the failure of the Carsons even to think of offering George Wilson any sustenance when he visits them is indicative not only of the absence of community between the two classes, but also of the Carsons' own moral inadequacies. They feel no sense of unease in consuming an elaborate breakfast while Wilson stands in front of them faint with hunger. Eventually it is the cook, a servant in fact, who 'thinks' to offer Wilson some 'meat and bread' just as he is leaving. The stark contrast between the selfishness of the rich and the generosity of the poor (the scene at the Carson home is immediately followed by a visit to the Davenports) is biblical in tone; it enacts the distinction between 'Dives and Lazarus' alluded to earlier. It is significant, though, that the biblical reference comes from Barton, not from the narrator; Gaskell's understanding of the relationship between money and morality is, as I have suggested, more subtle than the simple opposition to which Barton refers.

The first working-class meal which we witness is prefaced by 'a long whispering, and chinking of money' as the Bartons consult to see if they can afford to be hospitable. Similarly their guests, although 'too polite to attend' to this consultation, are themselves only too aware that accepting the meal will incur costs when the favour has to be returned. The reader is then given a shopping list which details the cost of the bread, eggs, ham, milk, tea and rum needed to turn alimentation into a communal event. Later in the novel, when the money for provisions runs out, the sense of community becomes fragile and threatened. In homes where there is no work and no wages there are 'desperate fathers . . . bitter-tongued mothers . . . reckless children'; in 'trial and distress', the narrative continues, 'the very closest bonds of nature were snapped'. In the very same passage the reader is also reminded (in biblical terms) that the same circumstances produced 'Faith such as the rich can never imagine on earth; there was "Love strong as death"; and self-denial, among rude, coarse men'. Certainly these qualities are exhibited by working-class characters in the novel, but significantly they are most consistent in those who are *not* subject to 'trial and distress'—that is, those who are not totally impoverished. Margaret Legh, for example, the moral paragon of the novel, never falls into absolute penury; her blindness, although preventing her from earning a living by sewing, allows her a more profitable career in singing. Moreover she and her father have substantial savings—a 'mint . . . laid by in an old teapot'. Described as a 'hoard', this 'mint' contains enough money to pay the fees for Jem Wilson's lawyer.

Jem, another moral paragon, is also financially secure. He works in a foundry and not in a mill, and as a result is protected from the cyclical poverty experienced by Barton. Moreover, the success of his 'invention' provides an income of 'twenty pound a year' for his mother and aunt, enough money for 'the best o' schooling, and . . . bellyfulls o' food'. Even when Jem is eventually forced out of his job, a good reference from his previous employer ensures he finds profitable work in Canada. In contrast to all this are the finances of the Barton household. Extreme poverty leads both father and daughter to exhibit some of that 'desperation, recklessness and bitter-tongued speech' associated with times of 'trial and distress'. Barton becomes violent, first towards his daughter and later (and more dramatically) towards Carson; in response Mary is sullen and resentful, emotions which in turn contribute to her incautious flirtation with Harry Carson. Parent and child also become estranged from each other and the family breaks down. Mary is forced to seek friendship and moral guidance from outside her own home. Importantly she turns to Margaret and Job Legh; neither are directly involved in the strike, and consequently their home is one of the few still able to *afford* hospitality and community. We are forcefully reminded that sustaining Christian virtues of morality, community and benevolence, whether in a Manchester cellar or in a Liverpool courtroom, requires money. Put crudely, Christian brotherhood appears to have a price; morality paradoxically turns out to be vulnerable to exactly the realm of action—that of the economic—which it is supposed to transcend. In formal terms, it is in the carefully contrived *interaction* between the novel's realism and its melodrama—between matters of 'fact' and a concern with 'human nature'—that we glimpse Gaskell's self-consciousness about the weakness of moral critiques of political economy.

There are two related suggestions which Gaskell puts forward to suggest how economic conditions might be improved sufficiently to permit morality (and therefore charity to others) to flourish. Very early in the novel the narrator comments that one of the problems for the working classes was the huge discrepancy between 'the amount of the earnings . . . and the price of their food'; all too often the gap was unbridgeable and resulted in 'disease and death'. Much of the first half of the novel is devoted to demonstrating the truth of this insight. The cost of living, as I have already noted, is an obsessive preoccupation with Gaskell and it leads to a compulsive description of financial transactions in which the precise cost of the goods is detailed with laborious care. Why do we need this information, and why do we need it in such abundance? One obvious reason is related to Gaskell's interest in the relationship between price and value.

About a third of the way through the novel there is a long story-within-a-story. Job Legh relates the poignantly comic tale of his attempt with his daughter's father-in-law, Jennings, to convey their orphan grand-daughter back to Manchester. The tale makes much of the traditional literary oppositions between town and country, London and the provinces, rich and poor, inn and home; it is also full of examples of native wit and warmth, and seems intended to illustrate the strength of community among the Manchester working classes. There are two related moments in the tale when all these values crystallise; the first occurs when Legh and Jennings come to pay for their meal at an inn in 'Brummagen' (as we might expect, mealtimes, for the men and the baby, are a focal point of the tale). The shocking price is 'half-a-crown apiece' (for food which they had hardly tasted) together with 'a shilling for th'bread and milk as were possetted all over the baby's clothes'. Legh and Jennings vainly protest against this injustice: 'We spoke up again it; but every body said it were the rule, so what could two poor oud chaps like us do again it?' Next morning they leave Brummagem (as 'black a place as Manchester, without looking so much like home') in disgust, and penury forces them to walk all day and through the night before early the following morning, and close to Manchester, they finally stop for refreshment at a cottage. They are invited in to a 'cheery, clean' room, and given a hearty breakfast while the baby is looked after by a womanly hand. When it comes to paying for these generous services, Legh is momentarily embarrassed:

> 'So giving Jennings a sharp nudge . . . I says, "Missis, what's to pay?" pulling out my money wi' a jingle that she might na guess we were all bare o'cash. So she looks at her husband, who said ne'er a word, but were listening wi'all his ears nevertheless; and when she saw he would na say, she said, hesitating, as if pulled two ways, by her fear o'him, "Should you think sixpence over much?" It were so different to public-house reckoning'.[2]

The price is low because the wife had recently lost her own baby and enjoyed the company, particularly that of the child. At the inn the price of food had been determined wholly by profit, and was rigidly fixed—it was 'the rule' to pay 'half-a-crown'. In the cottage, however, price is negotiable, and is defined in part by moral feeling. A similar contrast between what might be called a 'moral' value and a purely 'economic' price occurs during the haggling over the cost of the boat-trip to contact Will. Initially, the boatmen demand 'thirty shillings' for the fare, but this is subsequently reduced to 'a sovereign', then 'fourteen shillings and ninepence plus a shawl', until finally the fare accepted is the plain 'fourteen and ninepence'. They arrive back at the quayside and as Mary alights one of the boatmen apologises for the rough way in which she had initially been treated, commenting that the haggling over money 'were only for to try you,—some folks say they've no more blunt, when all the while they've getten a mint'. In these incidents Gaskell seems to suggest that financial transactions should be infused with moral value: that there is both an honest price and a dishonest or exploitative price. The second kind of price is one determined solely by market values: it is, in the language of economics, the highest price which the market will bear. The former, by contrast, results from the divorce of value from market conditions; it is a negotiation between individuals based on what a particular individual can reasonably *afford* to pay. Like Dickens,

2. *MB*, p. 98

Gaskell is attempting to replace the selfish, profit-seeking model of humanity (derived from the market and assumed by political economy) with the notion that individuals should be motivated by moral feeling and community spirit. Where Gaskell differs from Dickens, though, is in her insistence that such moral individuals can still be *economic* agents. Indeed it is a moral model of humanity which in her view defines the proper or 'ideal' economic agent—someone whose decisions about cost, value and price are made not on the basis of private interest, but rather in terms of how individual financial needs relate to those of the community. Such ideas are very similar to John Ruskin's strident attack on political economy in *Unto this Last* (1860). On publication, Ruskin's arguments were ridiculed, not least because in the eyes of 'professional' economists the notion of an 'honest' price wholly failed to recognise the complexity of the relationship between cost and value. Indeed it is perhaps not an accident that the most sustained argument in the nineteenth century for 'honest' pricing is to found in another work of fiction—William Morris's Utopian novel, *News from Nowhere* (1890).

Gaskell's second suggestion concerns the idea of a subsistence wage. In *Mary Barton* it is significant that we know much more about the price of a loaf of bread and a couple of eggs than we do about the price of cold partridge and broiled steaks. The difference in treatment is partly explained by the emotive contrast between wealth and poverty; for the working class, partridges will always be beyond their means, so for them their actual cost is wholly irrelevant. When the price of upper-middle-class living is occasionally mentioned, such as Harry Carson's 'half-a-crown' for a bunch of lilies of the valley, it is only as an index of the huge disparity between rich and poor: the same amount of money would buy many meals for the starving Barton. But as I suggested earlier, Gaskell does not confine her energy simply to exhibiting the vulgar contrast between middle-class wealth and working-class poverty. On the contrary, one consequence of her energetic detailing of working-class lives is to focus attention on the more subtle topic of the relative nature of poverty *within* a class. What we see in Gaskell's detailed portrait of an urban working-class community is a hierarchy of working-class incomes which in turn permit the possibility of morality and benevolence. Rather than address the vexed question of the distribution of wealth, Gaskell opts for the safer topic of defining a 'subsistence' wage. Here we can see the thematic importance of the apparently causal reference to the 'twenty pound' a year which Jem judges to be sufficient to provide for his mother and aunt. It is the amount of money below which it is unreasonable to expect an individual to live and to remain fully human—to act, that is, as a moral agent.

To the modern reader this strategy will of course seem like an evasion of political responsibility. But we need to recognise that Gaskell did
not have a real alternative in the sense that there was no coherent economic theory which she could draw upon to theorise a new concept of
wealth distribution. Socialist explanations of value were simply not
available to her (nor perhaps would they have been of much practical
help on the issue). By contrast, though, the whole issue of subsistence
would have been a familiar one. Since Ricardo's formulation of the
notorious 'iron law of wages', subsistence, or minimal income, had
become central to political economy's understanding of wealth distribution. The law, which drew upon Malthus's views about population,
stated that labour had a natural price, one which permitted the worker
to survive, but which at the same time, through the threat of starvation,
prevented the working population as a whole from increasing or
decreasing. In practice the law could be used to justify poverty as an
unfortunate but necessary consequence of a market economy; certainly
it denied the need for government intervention to control wages. In
focusing on subsistence rather than on the equality of wealth, Gaskell
is clearly only working within the conceptual paradigms established by
political economy. Where she was challenging, however, was in her
expanded definition of what subsistence involved. In *Mary Barton* subsistence means not simply staying alive (feeding oneself and one's family) but being part of a human community. In other words, the notion
of subsistence ceases to be solely an economic issue (as political economists had assumed), and becomes instead a moral and political one.

In economic terms, Gaskell's attention to 'honest' pricing and subsistence wages seems naïve in the extreme. Certainly such proposals
could not in any way resolve the fundamental macroeconomic problem of the gap between wages and prices. The failure, though, is
understandable given a mid-nineteenth-century frame of reference.
What is commendable is Gaskell's willingness in *Mary Barton* to
address such problems in the first place—her willingness, that is, to
use the resources of fiction (the interplay of realism and melodrama)
to see them *as problems*. Certainly Gaskell does not engage directly
with the 'theory' or laws of political economy. Instead she follows her
father's example and focuses on details—on discovering those awkward facts and *all* their circumstances. That evidence is then used to
expose the complacency of political economy. Like Dickens, Gaskell
suggests that the heart of the problem is the model of humanity with
which political economists work; unlike Dickens, though, she goes
on to argue that morality and economics (moral agency and economic agency), far from being mutually opposed, *must* be reconciled,
for the first requires the second. In the end, Gaskell is of course
unable to fix the right relationship between the moral and the economic. But such failure is a measure not of confusion or timidity, but

rather of courage. In *Mary Barton*, Gaskell refuses to opt for the simple answer, for those Christian platitudes of which modern critics have too glibly accused her.

DEIRDRE D'ALBERTIS

[The Streetwalker and Urban Observations in *Mary Barton*]†

*   *   *

Gaskell introduces the idea of the prostitute and social worker as "secret sharers" by downplaying the observational powers of her protagonist. *Mary Barton* is a novel with a disappointing heroine: incurious, unself-aware, prevented from any meaningful involvement in political thought or action in a "Condition-of-England" novel. Gaskell intended originally to focus the narrative on the tragedy of Mary's father, John Barton, a radical Chartist and assassin. Yet as Catherine Gallagher points out, in the battle of generic conventions underway in this text, domestic fiction (and by extension, the domestic heroine) emerges triumphant.[1] And this is a traditional domesticity: the dramatic interest of the novel springs from various assaults on Mary's purity and her own and others' heroic efforts to expunge from her consciousness any taint of guilty sexual or political knowledge.[2] The price of this protection, which enables Mary to function ethically and socially as an insulated middle-class subject, is the assumption of knowledge and experience, or "sin," by another woman, her mysterious Aunt Esther, who serves as the girl's secret guardian throughout the story.

Mary Barton opens with the disappearance of Esther from the relatively stable domestic world of the Barton household. John Barton,

---

† From *Dissembling Fictions: Elizabeth Gaskell and the Victorian Social Text* (New York: St. Martin's Press, 1997), pp. 50–58. Reprinted by permission of Deirdre d'Albertis.
1. See Gallagher's discussion of genre and domesticity in industrial fiction, 77–87 [Catherine Gallagher, *The Industrial Reformation of English Fiction 1832–1867* (Chicago: U of Chicago P, 1985)]. Gallagher writes that it is the function of the domestic tale "not only to describe how the working class lives, but also to dictate how it should live." Ibid., 137. An influential discussion of the power of domestic narrative in nineteenth-century culture may be found in Nancy Armstrong's *Desire and Domestic Fiction: A Political History of the Novel* (New York: Oxford University Press, 1987). For a considered analysis of the conservative role of domestic heroines in social fiction, consult Ruth Bernard Yeazell's "Why Political Novels Have Heroines: *Sybil*, *Mary Barton*, and *Felix Holt*," *Novel* 18 (Winter 1985): 126–44.
2. Although she appears to enjoy some agency in the plot, Mary's courageous action in clearing Jem's name at his trial for murder is followed by a complete mental breakdown, leaving the young woman in a temporary infantile state. Before this extreme crisis, however, Mary is not in strong control of her consciousness: she faints or sleeps through several important events in the novel. Ultimately, her awareness of events around her is mostly limited by her own ignorance and lack of interest or observation.

prophesying her eventual ruin, has just reprimanded his strong-willed sister-in-law for "stopping out when honest women are in their beds," asserting "you'll be a street-walker, Esther."[3] The plot of the novel unfolds to fulfill this prediction, yet it is both Esther and John Barton who alienate themselves from the domestic sphere represented by Mary and her mother. Barton, radicalized through economic hardship and working-class politics, drifts into an underworld of secret societies, union agitation, and class warfare, forsaking home and family in pursuit of social justice. He acts not as an "honest man" but as a conspirator and assassin. Esther, on the other hand, estranged from a traditional sexual role through her economic independence and work in the factories, inadvertently relinquishes the protection of family and home when she becomes the mistress of a soldier. She loses her status as a "true woman" along with her "honor," degenerating into meretricious display and sexual self-abandonment.[4] The criminal and the prostitute, to quote Peter Brooks, here jointly emblematize the "deviant body" of Victorian culture, "the maximal, most daring social deviance" imaginable in nineteenth-century England.[5] The homology between John and Esther's fates is made utterly clear by the conclusion of *Mary Barton:* both die, physically broken and dehumanized, and find their final resting place in a common grave "without name, or initial, or date" (MB 338) to mark their passing.

Barton and Esther, the most flamboyant characters in *Mary Barton,* flaunt their disaffection with the order of things—he rejects a system of political representation that recognizes workers only in the form of caricature, while she rebels against a standard of feminine conduct that rewards only self-abnegation. Consequently, the two are driven underground: leading subterranean existences, they become silent and thoroughly ineffectual watchers of a society they can neither destroy nor support. The bitter knowledge each possesses proves utterly devastating to the possessor. Mary Barton's ignorance is valorized by the novel, but it can only be protected by the heroine's removal from the England that produced her father and her aunt. Even so, the dangerous wisdom these outcasts import into the rep-

3. Elizabeth Gaskell, *Mary Barton: A Tale of Manchester Life,* ed. Edgar Wright (Oxford: Oxford University Press, 1987). Page number (11) is in this Norton Critical Edition. All further references are to this text and will be noted parenthetically.
4. Recently, Hilary Schor, Elsie B. Michie, and Amanda Anderson have directed much needed attention to the role of the streetwalker in Gaskell's novel, for Esther's story graphically embodies the anxieties attendant upon women's entry into urban public space. See Schor, *Scheherezade in the Marketplace* [(New York: Oxford UP, 1992)], Michie, *Outside the Pale* [(Ithaca, N.Y.: Cornell UP, 1993)] and Anderson, *Tainted Souls and Painted Faces* [(Ithaca, N.Y.: Cornell UP, 1993)]. Margaret Homans was one of the first critics to focus primarily on the character of Esther in her study *Bearing the Word: Language and Female Experience in Nineteenth-Century Women's Writing* (Chicago: University of Chicago Press, 1986).
5. Peter Brooks, *Reading for the Plot: Design and Intention in Narrative* (New York: Vintage Books, 1984), 158.

resented frame of the novel cannot be so easily dispelled. Esther's role, in particular, is to provide a contrasting definition against which Gaskell strives to describe the female philanthropist's activities as a watcher and intermediary.

The prostitute is unequivocally marked as a sinner for Gaskell—more than unwomanly, less than human—and described as one of the "obscene things of night" (MB   206). The streetwalker seemingly breeds only infection and contamination: "Hers is the leper-sin, and all stand aloof dreading to be counted unclean" (MB 140). By nature shut out of the domestic space of the family dwelling (in the final stages of consumption, Esther lingers outside the windows of the Barton home, gazing in wistfully upon Mary and her fiancé, Jem Wilson), the prostitute's only alternative to the inhospitable streets are the carceral "homes" of the workhouse or prison. Perpetually subject to charges of "disorderly vagrancy," the hapless streetwalker temporarily shelters in entries and on doorsteps, liminal zones of residential buildings, until driven by hunger or cold to return to the streets. She explains to the uncomprehending Jem: "Do you think one sunk so low as I am has a home? Decent, good people have homes. We have none. No; if you want me, come at night, and look at the corners of the streets about here. The colder, the bleaker, the more stormy the night, the more certain you will be to find me" (MB 146).

Despite her misery and her bitterness, Esther refuses Jem's pleas to return to the domestic haven she has left behind: "I tell you, I cannot. I could not lead a virtuous life if I would" (MB 145). Gaskell was well acquainted with the low success rate of reclamation campaigns for prostitutes; only a small percentage of the women she visited in prisons were actually "reformed" through placement in group homes or emigration.[6] Social patronage of "fallen women," like designs for model low-income housing or hostels for young female factory workers, was entirely dependent upon the willing cooperation of those being helped. Writing to Samuel A. Steinthal with regard to one such housing scheme, Gaskell expressed reservations:

> It requires that the factory girls themselves should be conscious of wants of a high kind . . . *before* they consent to enter the place where these advantages are offered, but where [other] certain liberties and licenses are denied them, [of] lib-

6. Pinchbeck discusses the popularity of emigration as an all-purpose solution to social problems, such as the surplus supply of women in the general population of England and the disturbing prevalence of independent young working women in major urban areas, 199–200. (Ivy Pinchbeck, *Women Workers and The Industrial Revolution 1750–1850* London: George Routledge & Sons, Ltd., 1930.) Gaskell corresponded frequently on the subject of girls she tried to help to emigrate or to enter group homes. For instance, see Elizabeth Gaskell to Grace Schwabe [19 June? 1853], *The Letters of Mrs. Gaskell*, ed J. A. V. Chapple and Arthur Pollard (Cambridge, MA: Harvard University Press, 1967), 235–38. All further references to the letters will be noted parenthetically within the text by page number.

> erties & licenses . . . which they [recognize the] set above the
> higher privileges offered to them in a "home". . . . They leave
> home (in general) because some home regulation is distasteful
> to them. . . . the other causes for such a step would unfit them
> for being inmates of a "Home." (*Letters* 806)

Gaskell tacitly acknowledges the dilemma facing such women
between the economic hardship and physical dangers of street life on
the one hand and the oppressiveness of disciplinary regimes, whether
in the family or an institutional "home," on the other. Esther's fear of
the lock-up (she suffers hallucinations and other withdrawal symptoms for a month in the New Bailey jail) mirrors the terror of a family like the impoverished Davenports, who are threatened with
internment in a Poor Law Union workhouse. Neither "home" is
designed to attract new inmates.

In other words, independence, no matter how high the cost, was
preferable to the illusory comforts of this sort of "home." Victorian
prostitutes often preferred the discomfort and risks of streetwalking
to the uncertain prospect of entering a protected house or brothel.
Streetwalkers retained greater freedom in contracting for rooms with
lodging-house keepers, according to historian Judith Walkowitz, than
they could in an organized establishment such as those inhabited by
"dress-lodgers."[7] Being outside these oppressive "houses" afforded
the streetwalker some fraction of self-determination in pursuing her
livelihood. With passage of the Contagious Diseases Acts of 1864 and
1866, establishment of venereal disease "lock-hospitals," and esca-
lating debate over "the criminalization of all street-soliciting," the
streetwalker's distrust of institutions and her reliance on collective
action with fellow sex-trade workers was confirmed, as was her sense
of identity as an outcast from both her own class and society in general.[8]

Esther's plight, like that of many Victorian streetwalkers,
resonated—however distantly—with middle-class women who abandoned the safe (if cloying) confines of private domesticity writ small
for the uncertainty of public domesticity writ large. Gaskell clearly
was of two minds when it came to weighing the benefits and the dis-
advantages of quitting one for the other. "To be shut out of home is
the worst fate in this novel," declares Hilary Schor; it "may be variously cold, dark, or cheerless, but it is home."[9] Yet to be an outcast or
"disorderly vagrant" is to enjoy a paradoxical freedom of movement

7. Judith R. Walkowitz, *Prostitution and Victorian Society: Women, Class, and the State* (Cambridge: Cambridge University Press, 1980). For more on the plight of the dress-lodger, see
   Mariana Valverde, "The Love of Finery: Fashion and the Fallen Woman in Nineteenth-
   Century Social Discourse," *Victorian Studies* 32 (Winter 1989): 169–88.
8. Valverde links the "dress lodger" explicitly to the history of the Contagious Diseases Acts.
   Valverde, 175–80.
9. Schor, 31–32.

in the urban landscape. In a dark parody of Walter Benjamin's *fla-neur*,[1] Gaskell's streetwalker is a detached observer of city life, inter-ested in protecting only one other dweller there—her niece—from the degradations she herself endures. Esther's "fallen" status allows her to go anywhere, to observe anything, as if she were invisible or immune to the restrictions ordinarily placed upon her sex. Acting as private investigator, Esther provides the clues and information that establish Barton's guilt and guard Mary's innocence. The narrator remarks that "in her wild night wanderings, she had noted the haunts and habits of many a one who little thought of a watcher in the poor forsaken woman" (MB 140). Although Esther is denied entrance (except through subterfuge) into any but the lowest dwelling, she is acutely aware of the doings of her former friends and neighbors.

Gaskell's cautionary tale, while designed ostensibly to warn, thus informed her female readers of the intricate social mapping of Man-chester's city streets. The streetwalker, much like the middle-class district visitor Gaskell later wrote about and herself became, enjoyed unparalleled access to the social geography of the city, seeing and hearing every aspect of urban life in her nightly perambulations, no matter how forbidden or dangerous. The prostitute was able to accomplish most of the things middle-class social workers did, in terms of observing and noting the habits of the poor, yet she moved through this terrain with a claim to special knowledge unrivaled by visitors from outside the slums.

Gaskell's streetwalker struggles to do more than passively observe in her role as invisible "watcher"; she actively attempts to intervene in the respectable world that has rejected her as "fallen." Moreover, Esther acts to influence events in the novel, first by soliciting the assistance of Barton in saving Mary's honor, and later, bent on the same mission, in apprehending Jem Wilson on a lonely street corner. Esther is shown performing a traditional "feminine" task—practicing moral suasion over men in the manner prescribed by domestic ideologues—in a striking inversion of her anti-domestic role in soci-ety. Although Esther uses her painfully won power of mobility to serve the very sphere of society that has disowned her, her special form of "solicitation" is possible only in the streets: she perversely reinvents feminine influence to encompass seduction, culpability, and carnal experience, all ostensibly beyond the domestic sphere.

Unfortunately, Esther's unique perspective, while unfettered by domestic conventions, is nearly impossible to communicate or to enforce. John Barton's response to her street-corner pleas is to fling her "trembling, sinking, fainting from him" and to stride away with-

---

1. Walter Benjamin, *Charles Baudelaire: A Lyric Poet in the Era of High Capitalism*, trans. Harry Zohn (London: New Left Books, 1973).

out heeding her words (MB p. 111). If Gaskell uses the streetwalker's Cassandra-like quandary to explore the failures of feminine advocacy, her narrator resists the urge to move through urban space as Esther does. Despite her perpetual disclaimers with regard to her own authority, Gaskell's narratorial perspective is more extensive and varied than that of the streetwalker/observer. Able to draw back at a distance from her subject, Gaskell's narrator alternates between intensive examination of individual actions—detailed scrutiny of particular people and places—and a more comprehensive gaze seemingly capable of taking in the mass of working-class humanity and explaining it to Victorian readers in universal terms. Drawn to identify with the pathos of Esther's impotent testimonials, Gaskell ultimately resists the temptation to merge the prostitute's point of view with that of the clearly vulnerable narrator, preserving the latter's power of superordinate vision at the expense of such an identification.

From her initial dramatic presentation of the fire at Carson's mill, complete with heroic rescues, before an eager audience of breathless, sympathetic workers, to her description of the benighted Chartist march through the thickly populated avenues of London, Gaskell's narrator—through her all-encompassing perspective—possesses the power to rise above city streets and represent them as the only public forum accessible to the working classes in this novel. As such, Gaskell exploits the theatrical potential of her crowd scenes, orchestrating them to assert her own theories about the "mob" so feared by the middle classes: "The people rise up to life; they irritate us, they terrify us, and we become their enemies. Then, in the sorrowful moment of our triumphant power, their eyes gaze on us with mute reproach. Why have we made them what they are; a powerful monster, yet without the inner means for peace and happiness?" (MB 150). Gaskell flatters her middle-class readers by granting them "triumphant power," while expecting them to feel and to answer the workers' "mute reproach." "The actions of the uneducated seem to me typified," the narrator explicitly declares, "in those of Frankenstein, that monster of many human qualities, ungifted with a soul" (MB 150). Confounding the creator with his creature, Gaskell speaks directly here (literally as "me") to the "masters" on behalf of their erring "men."[2] Shuttling back and forth between the particular and the general—from John Barton, "a Chartist, a Communist," to the maddened mob, "all that is commonly called wild and visionary" (MB 150)—Gaskell's narrator is torn between two modes of observation or perception.

2. For cogent readings of the "monster" and "the masses," see Franco Moretti, *Signs Taken for Wonders* (London: Verso, 1983), and Warren Montag, "'The Workshop of Filthy Creation': A Marxist Reading of *Frankenstein*," in *Mary Shelley: Frankenstein* (Case Studies in Contemporary Criticism), ed. Johanna M. Smith (Boston: Bedford Books, 1992).

As stage manager of all these crowd scenes, Gaskell confirms Asa Briggs's observation that Manchester was the mid-Victorian urban "theatre of contrasts" par excellence.[3] *Mary Barton* is carefully structured around a series of contrasts or theatrical moments: quasi-allegorical encounters punctuate the text at crucial plot junctures. Street life furnishes Gaskell's characters (and readers) with lessons in charity, tolerance, and even political economy. Set-piece passages such as the journey of John Barton and Wilson through the most squalid courts and alleyways of Manchester to the cellar slum-dwelling of the destitute Davenport family, have encouraged critics to assert Gaskell's own disgust with the urban environment she recreated in her novels. Enid Duthie's critique of the "claustrophobic world" of the workers assumes that such an alien place could only feel "naturally uncongenial" to Gaskell; the contrast "between the Davenports' miserable cellar and lighted, well-filled shops" nearby, rather than an unrelenting catalogue of filth and despair, suggests Angus Easson, makes the urban setting of Manchester ideally suited to Gaskell's didactic purposes as a novelist.[4]

If the image of Frankenstein's monster establishes one means of representing the massing of people in the public realm, Gaskell also employs the countertechnique of isolating individual characters in surreal street encounters that emphasize the author's moral design in the novel.[5] En route to his clandestine task as political executioner, Barton stumbles upon a lost boy, whom he guides home to a grateful Irish family. The encounter stimulates memories of Barton's own dead son and excites in him sensations of pity, yet it fails to prevent him from carrying out his murderous resolve against the masters. Likewise, when Mary encounters a starving Italian child in "the busy, desolate, crowded street" (MB 201), she rouses herself only momentarily from her personal cares to share what little food she has with the urchin. The act of charity briefly diverts her "from the thought of her own grief," but Mary's good deed seems futile, leaving her despair essentially untouched.

These momentary encounters suggest that personal charity is unmotivated save by impulse and unrelated to any real social change. Yet Gaskell uses them to prepare the reader for a third street scene. Carson, the vengeful millowner intent on punishing his son's murderer and the class that produced such a man, witnesses an act of

---

3. [Asa] Briggs [Victorian Cities (New York: Harper & Row, 1965)], 94.
4. Enid Duthie, *The Themes of Elizabeth Gaskell* (London: Macmillan, 1980), 66, 67; and Angus Easson, *Elizabeth Gaskell* (London: Routledge & Kegan Paul, 1979), 50.
5. For a thorough discussion of the biblical resonance of these scenes, see Deborah Denenholz Morse, "Stitching Repentance, Sewing Rebellion: Seamstresses and Fallen Women in Elizabeth Gaskell's Fiction," in *Keeping the Victorian House,* ed. Vanessa D. Dickerson (New York: Garland Publishing, 1995), 27–73. This volume is an excellent introduction to Victorian representations of women's work and domestic space.

unintentional violence in the roadway. A "rough, rude errand-boy" accidentally tramples a middle-class girl, whose outraged nurse collars and berates the boy, threatening to summon the police. Carson observes the struggle, amazed to see the injured "fairy-child" urge her nurse to release the boy: "He did not mean to do it. *He did not know what he was doing*" (MB 318). The incident proves deeply affecting for Carson, who remembers these words in conjunction with John Barton's crime and eventually overcomes his bitterness to forgive his son's murderer.

Gaskell uses these allegorical moments to construct a moral framework for the narrative that is marked specifically as transcendent. That is, by offering her readers otherworldly interpretive strategies through the medium of allegory, Gaskell situates her narrator on a plane higher than the localized and experiential one occupied by the streetwalker. In the third encounter, the reader is trained to interpret the urban landscape as a form of morality play directed by a persuasive, gently didactic narrator. Asa Briggs has characterized the industrial fiction writers of the 1840s and 1850s as "social explorers."[6] Gaskell takes on the responsibility of an urban "explorer" when she translates her findings into a discourse legible to middle-class readers. Yet she also aspired to a truly universal readership. Intelligent people of every class consulted Gaskell's novel as a guide or hand-book, a veritable social map of the new urban culture in Manchester; "*Mary Barton* was read by the cotton operatives also—they clubbed together to buy it—" Asa Briggs notes, "because it helped them to realize 'the heights as well as the depths' of their nature."[7] Nothing less than an emissary to the rest of England, Gaskell represented "an acute and sympathetic outsider" who strove to interpret what was new and dangerous and thrilling about "Cottonopolis" to her readers.[8]

Gaskell's allegory of the streets was structured to teach middle-class readers, particularly Londoners, how to "read" northern industrial life. *Mary Barton* also aspired to translate the experience of urban poverty into a humanistic language that would reflect working-class life through the lens of middle-class morality back to the workers it purported to represent. In addition, it was meant to speak to potential female intermediaries of class conflict who might learn from the novel's example how to avoid the pitfalls of over-involvement, impotent observation, and personal loss of reputation

6. Briggs, 97. Sheila Smith writes that "in *Mary Barton* an observant stranger leads the enquiring reader into Manchester life" and uses the incidents that take place in London and Liverpool to distinguish "between the kinds of Victorian cities." Sheila Smith, *The Other Nation: The Poor in English Novels of the 1840's and 1850's* (Oxford: Clarendon Press, 1980), 84.
7. Briggs, 98.
8. Martha Vicinus, "Literary Voices of an Industrial Town: Manchester, 1810–70," in *The Victorian City: Images and Realities*, vol. 2, ed. H. J. Dyos and Michael Wolff (London: Routledge & Kegan Paul, 1973), 748.

suffered by the streetwalker as a "body double" for the female philanthropist.

The chief problem the narrator of *Mary Barton* has with persuasion
is that it is obviously linked to sexual experience, not social exploration, through the most "acute and sympathetic outsider" in the
novel, the prostitute Esther, known colloquially as "the Butterfly." (For
all her flitting from street corner to street corner, Esther as "Butterfly" is never simply a "bearer of the word," to recall Margaret
Homans's influential work on domestic realism). There is too much
continuity between Esther's powers and the prerogative assumed by
the narrator of *Mary Barton*. In offering to guide readers through the
labyrinth of working-class Manchester, for example, Gaskell's narrator speaks as urgently to her audience as Esther does to the male
characters in *Mary Barton*. Critics have reacted with much the same
mixture of confusion and dismay to Gaskell's imploring narrator as
Jem and Barton do to Esther's hysterical appeals.[9] Stephen Gill, for
instance, complains about "bewildering shifts of voice where Mrs.
Gaskell interpolates a comment or addresses her audience direct."[1]
Gaskell, like Esther, seeks in her address to persuade a disinterested
auditor, and both work to guide the auditor's sympathies into new
channels. Thus the writer inevitably courts being discounted as a
"false" or fallen woman, literally incapable—as Esther is said to be—
of conveying truth to others. Indeed, Gaskell comes close to taking on
the role of outcast in allying herself with this most common form of
female public appearance, at moments seeming to erase distinctions
between a woman who walks the streets—Esther's "wild night
wanderings"—and one who traverses them under the cover of urban
social work. Both the night visitor, Mrs. Wightman, and the prostitute
can be accused of "stopping out," in John Barton's words, "when honest women are in their beds." Rather than accept the rhetorical conflation of "criminal, prostitute, mother," however, as Hilary Schor asks
us to do in understanding the woman novelist's problematic authority
in mid-Victorian England, it is crucial to recognize the separation the
novel itself enforces between women who walk the streets for money
and women who walk the streets for the sake of charitable causes.[2]

---

9. See, for instance, the unsigned review of *Mary Barton* published in *The British Quarterly
Review* (1 February 1849): 117–36. For a comprehensive overview of critical reaction to
Gaskell's first novel see Easson, ed., 14–24.
1. Stephen Gill, introduction to *Mary Barton: A Tale of Manchester Life*, by Elizabeth Gaskell
(Harmondsworth, Middlesex: Penguin Books, 1970), 23.
2. Schor, 44. Mary Poovey observes that certain key passages in *Mary Barton* "resemble the
sympathetic identification that Gaskell advocates as an alternative to government interference in the social domain. So extreme is this identification, however, that Gaskell (or
the narrator?) momentarily becomes a character in her novel. Instead of enforcing rules,
as any form of administration must do, this identification undermines the conventions necessary to both the reader's trust in the novelist and the fictive nature of the novelistic
world." Mary Poovey, *Making A Social Body: British Cultural Formation, 1830–1864* (Chicago: University of Chicago Press, 1995), 152–53.

Esther's presence, no matter how powerful, is rendered insignificant by her failure to interact with others in the proper manner, place, or time (she is incapable, for instance, of entering a court of law, working instead for justice in the dark byways of the city). So too, the language Esther speaks and the literary discourse she mobilizes in the novel is strictly limited. "Gaskell isolates melodrama and romance as the specific genres of prostitution and fallenness," observes Amanda Anderson: "Esther is a ghost from another genre."[3] Regarding the prostitute as a peculiarly "literary" figure, Anderson proposes that Esther's primary role is "to allegorize literary reformism."[4] Gaskell feared that the seductions of reading could come to substitute for the proper, active exercise of sympathy through charity. She thus approaches prostitution as a melodramatic construct, a form of romance representing only one of several competing genres in *Mary Barton*. As a genre, melodrama reinforces and rewards quietism in its audience.[5] But Gaskell employs sympathy to rouse her readers to action. The narrator therefore positions herself not with the prostitute Esther, the suffering subject of melodrama, but with the ambulatory observer capable of standing outside, deciphering and transmitting "the wild romances" of working-class lives as a call to reform the world that produces such tales (MB 58). Gaskell wrote in 1859 to her sister-in-law, Nancy Robson, "I don't call the use of words *action*: unless there is some definite, distinct, practical *course of action* logically proposed by those words" (*Letters* 530). Her experiments in genre underscore a fine gradation between words that lead to action and words that do not; clearly she preferred those that ended in deeds, even if she undercut her own stated purpose as a writer by creating conflicted, hybrid plots composed in equal parts of reportage-like realism and melodrama.

Using two separate but closely linked forms of solicitation, Gaskell aligns Esther's powers of observation with melodrama while she identifies her narrator's with social investigation.[6] We might plausibly ask why Gaskell chose to combine two such incompatible modes of representation or address. Does not the dilution of industrial fiction with melodramatic excess, which is never given a chance to succeed in the novel, weaken her call to action, her charge to potential female philanthropists? Esther may fleetingly take on the trappings of respectability, but she will never be able to disguise, disavow, or expiate her "crimes." *Mary Barton* forcefully reinstates a system of difference among women by endorsing the narrator's beseeching

---

3. Anderson, 110, 116.
4. Ibid., 120.
5. Martha Vicinus, " 'Helpless and Unfriended': Nineteenth-Century Domestic Melodrama," *New Literary History* 13 (Autumn 1981): 127–43.
6. See Mary Poovey, "Anatomical Realism and Social Investigation in Early Nineteenth-Century Manchester," *differences* 5, no. 3 (1993): 1–30.

anonymity and compassionate objectivity as the true stance of social realism while purging the narrative of a melodramatic strain of feminine power and persuasion represented by the streetwalker. Esther dies a wretched death at the end of the novel, in plain sight, as it were, of domestic bliss. * * * This system of difference among women was often organized through an aggressive campaign against masculine intervention in philanthropy. Esther's form of observation is brought down by her polluting contact with the world of men. So too, melodrama appears to be a representational mode Gaskell may have associated with victimized women pleading their causes before powerful men. As much as she disapproved of this form of suasion, however, Gaskell was not about to drop it from her representational repertoire. Instead, she incorporated melodramatic appeals into the larger structure of *Mary Barton*. Gaskell both needed Esther and needed to dispense with her. It was this local use of "melodramatic tactics,"[7] the introduction and eventual disposal of the "Butterfly's" story, I would contend, that enabled women such as Mrs. Wightman to walk through city streets at night without fear, confident in their new identity as female social workers. Mapping urban space through the twinned perspectives of an all-too-experienced Esther and a self-doubting neophyte of a narrator, as well as the formal fusion of melodrama and social realism, Gaskell began her literary career with a voice and a perspective that was bound to be equivocal.

* * *

SUSAN ZLOTNICK

The Curse of Leisure: Unemployment in *Mary Barton*[†]

In a letter sent to Lady Janet Kay-Shuttleworth during the summer of 1850, Elizabeth Gaskell once again found herself defending a novel she believed had been universally misunderstood: "I can not imagine a nobler scope for a thoughtful energetic man, desirous of doing good to his kind, than that presented to his powers as master of a factory. But I believe that there is much to be discovered yet as to the right position and mutual duties of employer and employed;

---

7. This term is borrowed from Elaine Hadley's *Melodramatic Tactics: Theatricalized Dissent in the English Marketplace, 1800–1885* (Stanford, CA: Stanford University Press, 1995).
† From *Women, Writing, and the Industrial Revolution*, pp. 76–87. © 1998 The Johns Hopkins University Press. Reprinted by permission of The Johns Hopkins University Press.

and the utmost I hoped from Mary Barton has been that it would give a spur to inactive thought, and languid conscience a direction" (*Letters* 119).[1] On the surface, the dual objectives of this letter—a defense of both the industrial system and a text Raymond Williams has called "the most moving response in literature to the industrial suffering of the 1840s" (*Culture and Society* 87)[2]—seem at odds. Yet Gaskell defuses the tension she creates, and the resolution she ventures for these apparently contradictory impulses lies in her defense of the novel as a "spur to inactive thought." Throughout the writing of *Mary Barton*, Gaskell's chief enemy was inactivity, whether it was the moral laziness of the British public, seemingly indifferent to the tragedies of men like John Barton, or the destructive, indulgent, and idle speculations Gaskell herself engaged in after the death of her infant son, and to which *Mary Barton*, begun at the urging of her husband, was the remedial measure. So it is only fitting that a novel born out of Gaskell's own personal and political desire for action should be a text about the perils of inactivity. In *Mary Barton*, Gaskell writes a novel about unemployment, and in this way she meets the demands made by her dual objectives: she exposes to the public the pitiable circumstances under which Manchester's workers live without condemning the factory system as an inherent and unalterable evil. Gaskell saves Victorian industrialism by shifting the focus of her novel from the dangers of factory work to the dangers of being out of work: *Mary Barton* does not so much address the "crushing experience of industrialism" (Williams, *Culture and Society* 88) as it does the crushing experience of unemployment.

Or to be more precise, *Mary Barton* is a response to the crushing effects of the boom/bust cycle endemic to infant industrialism. For as Gaskell informs us in her preface, it was the "strange alternations between work and want" and the "lottery-like nature" (p. 5)[3] of working-class existence that first aroused her sympathies for the mill hands. In *Capital*,[4] Marx provides a brief summary of the "ebbs and flows" of those years, and it is a daunting chronicle of instability:

> White slave trade; 1835, great prosperity, simultaneous starvation of the hand-loom weavers; 1836, great prosperity; 1837 and 1838, depression and crisis; 1839, revival; 1840, great depression, riots, the military called out to intervene; 1841 and 1842, frightful suffering among the factory workers; 1842, the manufacturers lock their hands out of the factories in order to enforce the repeal of the Corn Laws. Workers stream in their thousands

1. J. A. V. Chapple and Arthur Pollard, eds., *The Letters of Mrs. Gaskell* (Manchester: Manchester UP, 1966). [*Editor*].
2. Raymond Williams, *Culture and Society 1780–1950* (New York: Harper & Row, 1958). [Editor].
3. Page numbers for *Mary Barton* refer to this Norton Critical Edition.
4. Karl Marx, *Capital*, vol. 1, trans. Ben Fowkes (New York: Vintage, 1977). [*Editor*].

into the towns of Lancashire and Yorkshire, are driven back by
the military, and their leaders brought to trial at Lancaster; 1842,
great misery; 1844, revival; 1845, great prosperity; 1846, continued improvement at first, then reaction. (583)

Gaskell reproduces the fitful nature of the early industrial economy,
with its periodic lurches from good times to hard times. When things
are bad, they are very bad indeed, so that during the economic
slumps, the workers "only wanted a Dante to record their sufferings"
(76). Indeed, all the horrors Gaskell details, from the needless death
of John Barton's son to the pathetic end of the cellar-dwelling Ben
Davenport, come about during trade depressions and directly result
from them. Significantly, the sole mill to surface in this tale of life in
the nineteenth century's premier mill town makes a brief appearance
when a blaze reduces it to a pile of ruins and thereby throws the mill
hands out of work. In this telling detail we can read Gaskell's insistence that the mill's determining influence on the lives of her characters rests in its ability to provide employment. Thus the mill
becomes visible—as a significant fact of Manchester life—only at the
moment that it ceases to function.

Gaskell's Manchester is the urban equivalent of Dr. Jekyll and Mr.
Hyde. It is only by recognizing the duality of life in Manchester, its
"lottery-like nature," that one can understand how Gaskell could produce a novel that has been praised by such an astute critic as
Williams as capturing both "the characteristic response of a generation to the new and crushing experience of industrialization" and the
"development of the sympathy and cooperative instinct which were
already establishing a main working-class tradition" (*Culture and
Society* 88). Somewhat paradoxically, Williams applauds Gaskell's
text for revealing the factory system as hostile to working-class life,
yet hospitable to working-class culture: for how can the experience
of industrialization be inimical to human life when it is capable at the
same time of sustaining strong family and community bonds as well
as a sophisticated intellectual culture, all the apparatus and institutions of urban proletariat life that Gaskell records? Gaskell understands, however, that the emerging working-class culture depends on
the high wages the mill workers earn combined with the stimulations
of urban life. Indeed, when one juxtaposes Gaskell's Manchester with
"The Great Towns" section of Engels's *Condition of the Working
Class,* one might forget that the two accounts claim to represent the
same city at the same historical moment. Engels sees nothing but
squalor and shame, a populace completely crushed by its surroundings: "We must confess that in the working-men's dwellings of Manchester, no cleanliness, no convenience, and consequently no
comfortable family life is possible; that in such dwellings only a

physically degenerate race, robbed of all humanity, degraded, reduced morally and physically to bestiality, could feel comfortable at home" (96). But the Bartons, who are neither physically degenerate nor bestial, feel quite comfortable in their Manchester home, which Gaskell evokes precisely and lovingly as her novelistic eye for detail lingers over the material solidity of a household overflowing with furniture, crockery, and tea-trays. When work is plentiful, the factory workers enjoy high wages, live in relative comfort, and have the time, energy, and spare shillings for leisure pursuits, like Job Legh's amateur entomology. In *Mary Barton,* the significant accomplishments of the Manchester working class come about because of—not in spite of—the burgeoning factory system.[5]

Gaskell remains as invested in defending the industrial system as in condemning its local evils, and nowhere does this defense emerge more strikingly than in the play between past and present she keeps before the reader: the industrial present may be far from ideal, but the rural past is decidedly worse. An out-of-work mill hand who dies of starvation and disease in a damp cellar refuses to seek public assistance because, as his wife says, "my master is Buckinghamshire born; and he's feared the town would send him back to his parish" (59). Apparently, starving in a Manchester cellar with the hope that good times will soon return is preferable to the poverty of one's native village, where destitution and the workhouse are the only two options. Indeed, testifying to the sad logic of the man's decision are the memories of Alice Wilson, the Manchester washerwoman who retains strong links with the preindustrial past. Although Alice bathes the recollections of her country childhood in a nostalgic glow, Gaskell approaches them with an ironic detachment that gently but deftly subverts the old woman's fondness for the past. As Coral Lansbury reminds us, "The landscape Alice describes so rapturously is a barren waste. The Wilson farm was a shaded hillside, stone covered and eroded, where heather flourished but not crops or cattle. . . . It is a scene of bleak poverty, but in memory it can become a lost paradise" (34)[6]. Gaskell frames the intermittent sufferings of the workers not against a backdrop of pastoral contentment but against one of rural deprivation, so that the dying mill worker's refusal to return to Buckinghamshire and Alice's childhood of poverty serve to situate the lives of the factory operatives in a broadly progressive vision of rising working-class standards.

5. In *The Literature of Change,* John Lucas sympathetically compares Gaskell's treatment of Manchester to Engels's, and he concludes that Gaskell, who spent all her adult life there, understood certain aspects of working-class culture and domestic life that eluded the German-born Engels.
6. Lansbury, Coral. *Elizabeth Gaskell, The Novel of Social Crisis.* (New York: Barnes & Noble, 1975.)

Gaskell also carefully frames the feast-or-famine existence of Manchester's industrial operatives against the living and working conditions of those employed in nonindustrial occupations, so that the true image of impoverishment can be found in Alice Wilson, a single woman who supports herself as a domestic servant and washerwoman. By juxtaposing the tea party thrown by the Bartons against one hosted by Alice, Gaskell neatly contrasts the Bartons' material prosperity with the material poverty endured by old Alice. No wonder Alice marvels at the "aspect of comfort" (18) she finds at the Barton tea party when, as a counter to the bounty of their table, she can barely afford the requisite bread, butter, and tea for her guests:

> Half an ounce of tea and a quarter of a pound of butter went far to absorb her morning's wages; but this was an unusual occasion. In general, she used herb-tea for herself, when at home, unless some thoughtful mistress made a present of tea-leaves from her more abundant household. The two chairs drawn out for visitors, and duly swept and dusted; an old board arranged with some skill upon two old candle-boxes set on end (rather rickety, to be sure, but she knew the seat of old, and when to sit lightly; indeed the whole affair was more for apparent dignity of position than for any real ease); a little, very little round table, put just before the fire, which by this time was blazing merrily; her unlacquered, ancient, third-hand tea-tray arranged with a black tea-pot, two cups with a red and white pattern, and one with the old friendly willow pattern, and saucers, not to match. (29)

Through sheer accretion of detail, from the scant meal to the pathos of the unmatched china, Gaskell sketches a scene of poverty; and no matter how clean Alice's cellar dwelling may be, or how exhaustingly cheerful Alice is, it remains a portrait of economic distress. Nor does Gaskell try to argue that the social stability of Alice's life amply compensates for her poverty since, as a servant, Alice is as subject to frequent bouts of unemployment as Manchester's mill workers. Moreover, the occasional gift of tea-leaves only highlights her quasi-feudal dependence of the random kindnesses of her employers.

By deploying Manchester's seesawing economy as the organizing principle behind her representation of industrial life, Gaskell can defend the present from the nostalgic incursions of the past. But just as important, given Gaskell's larger design, Manchester's "strange alternations between work and want" permit her to raise the woman question without causing a radical disjunction between the text's industrial material and its feminist explorations because in *Mary Barton* both women and workers struggle against a common foe: unemployment. Feminist critics in recent years have refused to read Mary's plot as a distraction from the genuine and lasting interest generated by Gaskell's investigation of the condition of England through John Barton's narrative. On the contrary, they have insisted on the thematic connections between the father's industrial plot and the daughter's love plot because to ignore these connections is to reduce the novel's scope from an examination of industrialism's impact on men and women to its impact on men alone.[7]

If one does not recognize that the same economic and political issues inform and unite both father's and daughter's plot, one risks reproducing the sentimental reading of the heroine's plot that Gaskell disavows. In her nuanced interpretation of *Mary Barton* in *The Industrial Reformation of English Fiction*, Catherine Gallagher identifies a crazy quilt of narrative forms—melodrama, tragedy, domestic realism—that bespeak Gaskell's self-aware inability to represent working-class life adequately. Gallagher places particular emphasis on the dangers of melodrama, which can conceal the truth of class hatred behind a screen of romance by transforming political issues into personal matters. This concealment occurs most notably when Mary's relationship with Carson enters the public sphere after his murder as tragic tale of romantic jealousy: the murder becomes "some dispute about a factory girl" (*Mary Barton* 247), and in the eyes of the dead man's father, Mary is "the fatal Helen, the cause of all" (280), even though the reader knows that the genuine "cause of all" is the murderous alienation between the men and the masters, not the murderous resentment of a spurned lover. To read Mary's story melodramatically is to ignore Gaskell's warnings about the distortions of melodrama.

In particular, *Mary Barton* focuses on the way melodrama misrepresents women's lives by erasing their role within a political economy. The novel may, as Gallagher argues, hesitate to assign causality in John Barton's plot, but the text reinfuses economic causality into the

---

7. The Marxist critics who first rehabilitated the critical reputation of *Mary Barton* did so at the expense of Mary's plot. Writing in *Culture and Society* [(New York: Harper & Row, 1958)], Raymond Williams found Mary's story "of little lasting interest," nothing but the "familiar and orthodox plot of the Victorian novel of sentiment" (89); and in "Mrs. Gaskell and Brotherhood," *Tradition and Tolerance in Nineteenth-Century Fiction*, (New York: Barnes & Noble, 1967)] John Lucas declared Mary's love story extraneous to the novel. In recent years, feminists have abandoned this position. [Catherine] Gallagher's *Industrial Reformation* [*The Industrial Reformation of English Fiction 1832–1867* (Chicago: U of Chicago P, 1985)] and Hilary Schor's *Scheherezade in the Marketplace* [(New York: Oxford UP, 1992)] argue for a connection between the love plot and the industrial plot, identifying the problems that both women and workers have with language and representation, while Nancy Armstrong's *Desire and Domestic Fiction* [(New York: Oxford UP, 1987)] and Ruth Bernard Yeazell's "Why Political Novels Have Heroines" ["*Sybil*, *Mary Barton*, and *Felix Holt*," *Novel* 18 (1985), pp. 126–44] contend that the romance plot is used to deflect or displace the anxieties raised in the political plot. At the other end of the spectrum from either the Marxist or the feminist approaches is Felicia Bonaparte's *The Gypsy-Bachelor of Manchester* [*The Life of Elizabeth Gaskell's Demon* (Charlottesville: UP of Virginia, 1992)], which wrongheadedly depoliticizes Gaskell, arguing that she "had no genuine interest in social, economic, and political questions" (135). For an excellent overview of Gaskell criticism, see Schor's "Elizabeth Gaskell: A Critical History and a Critical Revision."

women's stories by directly and uninhibitedly ascribing economic motives to the female characters' actions. For through Mary's entanglement with Harry Carson, Gaskell reveals that romance is the business of Victorian heroines. From the first, Gaskell makes clear that Mary regards her wealthy lover with the shrewd, appraising eye of a woman who understands the socioeconomic realities of the world. Lucre as much as love is a motivating force behind Mary's dangerous liaison with Carson, a fact the narrator openly admits: "Mary was ambitious, and did not favour Mr Carson the less because he was rich and a gentleman. . . . Mary dwelt upon and enjoyed the idea of some day becoming a lady" (73). Unlike Jem Wilson, her future husband, who by dint of hard work and talent fashions himself into that particular Victorian hero, the self-made man, and equally unlike Margaret Jennings, her best friend, who carves out a career as a singer, Mary possesses only one option—marriage—if she wants to fulfill her ambition and rise into the middle classes. So while Jem exploits his mechanical skills and Margaret her musical ability, Mary takes advantage of her special talents when she makes the rational economic choice that "her beauty should make her a lady" (26). Mary's flirtation with Harry Carson is not the act of a simple-minded girl but the conscious decision of an ambitious young woman pursuing one of the few avenues for advancement open to working-class women.

By unveiling the economic truths behind Mary's romantic cover story, Gaskell invites us to resituate the stories of the novel's other women, like Mrs. Carson and Aunt Esther, in an economic context as well. In the first half of the novel, Mary remains delicately poised between two possible futures: on the one side stands Mrs. Carson, the former factory girl who married well and is now luxuriously installed in the Carson villa, while on her other side stands the tragic counterpart to Mrs. Carson's success story, the novel's other ex-factory girl, Mary's Aunt Esther, now a prostitute. But as far apart as the suburban matron and the fallen woman may seem, Gaskell brings them together as two sides of the same coin: the triumphant and the failed capitalist. Simply, Esther is a speculator who went bust. Her elopement with an officer who subsequently abandoned her is a speculation on her capital (her beauty) that did not pay off. "As [Mary] is loving now, so did I love once, one above me far" (142), Esther tells Jem, but the comparison—knowing what we do about Mary's economic interest in Carson—nearly collapses under the weight of irony. Like her niece, Esther expected her beauty to be the making of her, and while she claims to have followed her army officer out of love, she also admits that "he promised me marriage" (142), and marriage to an army officer would have been her passport to gentility.

Moreover, through Esther, Gaskell exposes the ultimately deadly consequences of scripting one's life melodramatically. While Gaskell endows Esther with economic motives for her affairs of the heart, Esther revises her economic history into a self-defeating melodramatic narrative. So when Esther tells Jem the story of her life, she casts it as a tragic tale of how she risked all for love: "He was so handsome, so kind! Well, the regiment was ordered to Chester (did I tell you he was an officer?), and he could not bear to part from me, nor I from him, so he took me with him" (142). Esther's use of sentiment conceals the cold economic facts of her fall, for in Esther's rewriting of her life's story the economics of the elopement gets suppressed, and her lover's social class is derogated to a parenthetical inclusion: the most important element in Esther's history (her social ambition) is subordinated to the least (romance). Like the ragged finery that earns her the nickname "Butterfly," Esther's melodramatic narrative is a bad fit and full of holes because it prevents her from grasping the economic factors at work in her life, and thus it bars her from taking any remedial action. Instead of displaying anger at the officer who seduced and abandoned her, Esther turns her tale of abuse at the hands of an upper-class man into a story of her own moral lapse and wallows in guilt, self-pity, and alcohol, rejecting Jem Wilson's offer of redemption on the grounds that she needs drink to anesthetize herself against her fall into prostitution, to which she was driven by poverty and the cries of her dying child. In contrast, John Barton responds to the death of his son under similar dire circumstances by blaming the masters and channeling his anger into political activism. Although Gaskell ultimately recoils from Barton when his activism turns violent, she nevertheless acknowledges that his Chartist activities ennoble him, as she must in a book that is so heavily invested in the importance of action. So even if Gaskell has reservations about (male) working-class activism, she nevertheless attacks female inaction throughout the text and identifies melodrama, a dominant mode of narrating women's lives, as one source of female inertia.[8]

Mary Barton evidences as much interest in women's work—and the lack of it—as it does for the poor "care-worn men" (5) Gaskell regularly met on the streets of Manchester. For the "strange alternations between work and want" that Gaskell identifies as the central feature of Manchester life plays itself out in a modified form across class and gender lines, in both the idleness of wealthy ladies and the unemploy-

8. Amanda Anderson takes up the problem of Esther in her rich discussion of the relationship between aesthetic form and social reform in *Mary Barton*. But while Anderson reads Esther as a character out of melodrama who dramatizes the "limits of sympathizing with a literary representation" (122), my reading of Esther focuses on the way "real" people deploy cultural narratives to give meaning to their lives. The dangers of the melodramatic narrative for women like Esther is not only that it will produce a hopeless response in readers but that it limits the agency of the subject.

ment of poor men. Gaskell spins out a series of dialectical oppositions—between action and inaction, independence and dependence, proletariat and bourgeoisie—through which she organizes her exploration of women's work and women's want of work. Active and independent, Mary Barton becomes Gaskell's representative working woman, and it is her virtues, set off against the inactivity and dependency of middle-class women, that *Mary Barton* tries to uphold.

By paralleling the idleness of middle-class women with the unemployment of working-class men, Gaskell allows the emotional power of her analogy to affirm what explicitly goes unsaid: for both men and women, "leisure was a curse" (53). Out of boredom, Mrs. Carson turns hypochondriacal, a mental state the narrator insists could be remedied "if she might have taken the work of one of her own housemaids for a week; made beds, rubbed tables, shaken carpets" (178). Not surprisingly, presiding over a brood of somnambulant daughters who sleep through breakfast and yawn over tea does not provide enough stimulation. On the whole, the women in the Carson family bear an uncanny resemblance to John Barton's description of a "do-nothing lady, worrying shopmen all morning, and screeching at her pianny all afternoon, and going to bed without having done a good turn to any one of God's creatures but herself" (12). One might be willing to dismiss Barton's rancorous characterization of the middle-class woman as originating in his venomous hatred of the master class, but the novel confirms Barton's view. In *Mary Barton*, a lady is a woman who does nothing, so that when Mary daydreams of becoming a lady, she fittingly pictures herself "doing all the elegant nothings appertaining to ladyhood" (73).

Much to Mary's advantage, Gaskell contrasts the slugabeds of the Carson household with the bustling Mary, and although Mary's exertions may disqualify her for ladyhood, they do transform her into a heroine. In the dark days after Carson's murder, Mary's "mind unconsciously sought after some course or action in which she might engage. Any thing, any thing, rather than leisure for reflection" (232). This decision to take action not only preserves her sanity but it also saves the day, for if she had not discovered an alibi or pursued the *John Cropper* after it had set sail, Jem Wilson would surely have been convicted for a murder he did not commit. Although critics have been quick to dismiss Mary's adventurous rescue on the Mersey as a melodramatic set scene, it underscores the saving power of activity: in this particular case, Mary's leisure would certainly have been a curse because it would have cost Jem his life.

Unfortunately, Gaskell's inability to disentangle her incipient feminism from certain class-bound notions of femininity ultimately destabilizes the text: for the novelist's defense of Mary's sexual innocence will eventually undermine her excoriation of middle-class idleness. As a working woman, Mary was subject to the intense eroticization all working-class women underwent: Mary's prostitute aunt is not only the skeleton in the Barton family closet but the skeleton lurking in every working woman's closet.[9] In order to lift Mary above the sexual suspicions her working-class status might raise, Gaskell insists on the innate femininity of all women and posits (to take a liberty with Burns) that "a woman's a woman for a' that." Yet an irresolvable contradiction emerges out of Gaskell's championing of both middle-class femininity and woman's work. For the qualities that Gaskell most admires in Mary are those that stand in starkest contrast to Victorian notions of femininity. Mary's working-class virtues of self-reliance and assertiveness align her most dangerously with her prostitute aunt, the former factory girl whose fall John Barton attributes to an independent spirit derived from an independent income. Caught in an ideological bind and unable to imagine a possible third alternative for her heroine between the deadly inertia of the Carson women and the spiritual death of prostitution—between sleepwalking and streetwalking—Gaskell will in the end be forced to condemn Mary to the bourgeois idleness that the novel ostensibly rejects.

In spite of the high value Gaskell places on action, Mary's heroic acts come into direct conflict with her maidenly modesty, which requires passivity, inactivity, and uselessness. Quite appropriately, maidenly modesty begins exerting an influence on Mary's life immediately after she realizes she loves Jem Wilson, whose marriage proposal she has just rejected. At the moment she fulfills her destiny as a Victorian heroine by falling in love, she lapses into inertia: "Maidenly modesty (and true love is ever modest) seemed to oppose every plan she could think of, for showing Jem how much she repented her decision against him, and how dearly she had now discovered that she loved him. She came to the unusual wisdom of resolving to do nothing, but try and be patient, and improve circumstances as they might turn up. . . . she would try and do right, and have womanly patience, until he saw her changed and repentant mind in her natural actions" (118). Mary's decision to do nothing appears as "unusual wisdom" indeed in a book that usually counsels action. Moreover, in her case the decision proves to be a particularly unwise one because had Mary resolved on taking some course of action, like running after Jem, it might have circumvented his arrest for Carson's murder. By adopting maidenly modesty and its attendant virtue of patience, Mary moves precipitously close to her father's definition of a lady as some-

9. Factory women in particular were assumed to possess few moral scruples. The promiscuity of the mill girl was such a common stereotype in Victorian England that one writer in the *Morning Chronicle* flatly declared that there was scarcely a thing as a "chaste factory girl" (qtd. in [John] Rule [*The Labouring Classes in Early Industrial England, 1750–1850* (London: Longman, 1986)], 199). Of course, Mary is a seamstress, but as the daughter and niece of factory workers, she is closely aligned with them and subject to the same stereotyping.

one who goes "to bed without having done a good turn to any one of God's creatures but herself."[1]

Independent female action of the sort that makes Mary a heroine proves incompatible with the values of Victorian femininity. Mary's final collapse into inertia occurs at the trial, and when she emerges after a long illness, it is as a childlike parody of her former self, a woman who looks into her fiancé's face with an "innocent, infantine gaze" (301). At the end of *Mary Barton*, Gaskell allows Victorian femininity to triumph over woman's work. The young woman who began the novel running errands for her mother and quickly graduated to running the Barton household is ultimately reduced to a state of infantile dependence. No wonder that when Jem tells her after the trial that "thou'rt not fit to be trusted home by thyself," he must do so "with fond exaggeration of her helplessness" (313). Only by exaggerating the helplessness of a woman who has just proven herself capable of saving his life can he possibly justify his "natural" role as Mary's protector. Like Jem, Gaskell too must exaggerate Mary's helplessness, even though it translates, in a different context, into the wasted lives of the Carson women.

Ironically, when Mary marries Jem she gets what she asks for—a life of "elegant nothings." Appointed "as instrument maker to the Agricultural College" in Toronto, a "comfortable appointment,—house,—land,—and a good percentage on the instruments made" (324), Jem may never become a wealthy industrialist like Mr. Carson. But the Wilson clan has evidently begun its climb into the respectable middle classes. Our last glimpse of Mary reveals her installed in the suburban paradise of the new world, patiently and passively waiting for her husband to return from work: Jem's old mother, long crippled by an industrial accident, now has "twice the spirit" of Mary (339). While Gaskell celebrates the active and useful lives led by Manchester's working-class women, she nevertheless dooms her heroine to life as a sleeping beauty in the Canadian wilderness, for in spirit if not in name, Mary becomes the second Mrs. Carson. Ensnared in an ideology that conflates independence and assertiveness with female sexuality, Gaskell resorts to conservative notions of femininity that enshrine dependence and inactivity in order to save her working-class heroine from the taint of immorality. But in the process, she destroys Mary because the values of work and the virtues of ladyhood are not reconcilable after all. Gaskell embraces what she had tried to repudiate and accepts for Mary the life of bourgeois "do-nothingism" in Canada that she had rejected

---

1. Maidenly modesty also rears its unattractive head in the romance of Margaret and Will Wilson. While walking home from Old Alice's funeral, Jem asks Margaret to keep Will occupied for a few minutes while Jem talks to his mother, but, "No! that Margaret could not do. That was expecting too great a sacrifice of bashful feeling" (296). Here again Gaskell calls attention to how "bashful feeling," which is just another way of saying "maidenly modesty," actively prevents women from making themselves useful.

in Manchester. In *Mary Barton* the brave new world looks remarkably like the old.[2]

JONATHAN H. GROSSMAN

[Trial, Alibi, and the Novel as Witness][†]

Readers of the novel will recall that after Mary Barton burns the paper evidence she realizes she must not only protect her father but also rescue her lover, Jem, who is wrongfully accused but will not incriminate her father. Recognizing that Jem "must have been somewhere else when the crime was committed; probably with some others, who might bear witness to the fact, if she only knew where to find them," she sets out to find out if "an *alibi* . . . might mean the deliverance she wished to accomplish" (217).[1]

In the text the word *alibi* always appears in italic type, as it customarily did throughout most of the nineteenth century, to indicate its status as a foreign, Latin word. Aligned with Mary, the reader may also begin to see this italicized *alibi* as extrinsic, suggesting the "elsewhere" not just of the accused but of the courtroom itself. For Mary her physical journey to the courtroom turns into a trip toward the courtroom as an alternate space of storytelling. The "alibi" is the real story that Mary strives to ensure is told in court, while for the reader the novel at this point becomes the story of reconstructing an alibi—a story about the makings of a forensic story. Later this alibi will barely materialize in the court scene. The reader is told merely that Jem's cousin Will Wilson "told the story you know so well" (286). In part its ghostly presence in court reflects that the fact that this alibi is, like all alibis, a kind of antistory, a story canceling another story. Also, however, as "the story you know so well," the alibi points us

---

2. One could argue that by sending her heroine off to the splendors of Canada's open spaces, Gaskell beats a pastoral retreat from the problems of industrialism. But the novel's conclusion does not represent a flight from industrialism, even though emigration was frequently proposed (and acted upon) as a solution to both male and female unemployment throughout the nineteenth century. Rather, the Canada Gaskell chooses for Jem and Mary resembles the Green Heys Fields of the novel's first chapter. She does not send them off to the frontier but to a suburb of Toronto, and thus Gaskell restores the happy times that existed at the novel's opening, when both the Bartons and the Wilsons were fully employed and living in relative prosperity. Moreover, even though Jem becomes an agricultural instrument maker, one assumes this is still essentially industrial work, since his experience is in industrial engineering. Presumably, he will help manufacture the farm machinery needed for the vast tracts of Canadian wilderness that were being transformed into arable land.

† From *The Art of Alibi: English Law Courts and the Novel*, pp. 118–29. © 2002 The Johns Hopkins University Press. Reprinted by permission of The Johns Hopkins University Press.

1. Page numbers for *Mary Barton* refer to this Norton Critical Edition.

straight back to the novel, like the fleeting echo of a novel listening to itself through the court.

In a larger sense this legal inflecting of her speech, in which the court acts like an echo-chamber, serves as one of the primary ways Gaskell fashions this novel. Unlike Dickens, who discovers the forum of his novel in part by depicting the forum of the court, Gaskell puts this relationship to work, drawing attention to the boundary between courtroom and novel. Her trial scene is certainly not merely about the suspense of awaiting a verdict; to the horror of some readers the chapter title proclaims: "THE TRIAL AND VERDICT—'NOT GUILTY!' "[2] Instead, it complicates the goal Gaskell has claimed in her preface of trying "to write truthfully" (6). "The truth, and the whole truth" (279) of the courtroom obviously represents a different means to truth than that of the novel, and, specifically for Gaskell, the depiction of a trial scene offers a parallel, but different, space of representation which productively throws into relief the formal and stylistic boundaries of her novel as verbal act and artifice.

The beginning of *Mary Barton*'s trial scene sets the stage. The narrator initially draws a straightforward comparison between the reader and the courtroom spectators: "The circumstances of the murder, the discovery of the body, the causes of suspicion against Jem, were as well known to most of the audience as they are to you, so there was some little buzz of conversation going on among the people" (277). But in this "little buzz of conversation," consisting of a series of anonymous quotations, the courtroom spectators can only shallowly speculate on the characters' physical appearances. The narrator then returns to voice and sympathize with the reader's actual disjunction from the court spectators: "Poor Jem! His raven hair . . . was that, too, to have its influence against him?" (278). As in Dickens's depiction of Fagin's trial in *Oliver Twist*, the narrator constructs the reader's perspective by contrasting it with that of the courtroom spectators' purely visual perspective. Unlike Dickens, however, Gaskell has first carefully pointed out the similarities between reader and spectator. This strange shift from defining the reader as essentially another courtroom spectator to defining the reader in opposition to the courtroom spectators emphasizes the differences between the two spaces of storytelling, exposing both the novel's and the court's limits. We are made aware of two interlocking views of the story. Gaskell can thereby point to what she sees as a truth that lies beyond the conventions structuring either of their generic limits—or, rather, she can harness these limits to express her meaning.

At the trial Mrs. Wilson's testimony concerns exactly this sort of limit, the problem of the courtroom's concept of the "whole truth." When

2. Chapter titles were added to the third edition. They were removed in the fifth edition [*Editor*].

she must incriminate her son by identifying his gun, she dramatically asks him, "What mun I say?" He replies, "Tell the truth, mother" (279). Mrs. Wilson concludes, however, by protesting the codes of representing "truth" in the courtroom: "'And now, sir, I've told you the truth, and the whole truth, as *he* bid me; but don't ye let what I've said go for to hang him; oh, my lord judge, take my word for it, he's as innocent as the child as has yet to be born. For sure, I, who am his mother, and have nursed him on my knee, . . . ought to know him better than yon pack of fellows' (indicating the jury . . .) 'who, I'll go bail, never saw him before this morning in all their born days'" (279).

Because the reader knows Jem is innocent, Mrs. Wilson's humorously accurate accusation that the jury "never saw him before this morning" carries some weight. By extension the reader must acknowledge her protest against the methods the court uses to arrive at the truth. Most obviously, Mrs. Wilson objects that she has been forced to articulate words invested with someone else's aim—"the whole truth, as *he* bid me; but don't ye let what I've said go for to hang him." Gaskell thus has Mrs. Wilson expose the seemingly passive, descriptive process of witnessing as consisting of speech acts, even as she calls attention to the distortions imposed by the question-and-answer truth-telling format of the court.[3] By then having Mrs. Wilson swear figuratively and tragicomically that "[she]'ll go bail" at the very moment she protests the court's rules, Gaskell further gently puts us in mind that those rules are filters for reality even outside the court and that truth does not just depend on context but carries its contexts with it.

Gaskell goes on to portray Will Wilson, the final witness, in opposition to Mrs. Wilson. Will understands the rules of the courtroom only too well. He cannot be stopped until he has assumed the role of a narrator in the court, meaning (for Gaskell) that he is "telling his tale in the witness-box, the legitimate place" (285). He replies to the lawyer's accusation that he is a paid witness by pointing more accurately to the lawyer as the one being paid to talk. Returning impudence for impudence, as Job, who also understands the unwritten rules of the court, has earlier advised Mary to do (225), Will clears Jem. In contrast to Mrs. Wilson, Will is able to use his words to good effect. Yet, although Will's words change the court's verdict, bearing out the power of testimonial evidence to effect material change, his testimony has been orchestrated by the love and work of Mary and only establishes the local facts.

Gaskell makes it clear that Will has merely conformed to the trial's procedures, a man manipulating the male-controlled space

---

3. See J. L. Austin, *How to Do Things with Words,* ed. J. O. Urmson and Marina Sbisà, 2d ed. (Cambridge: Harvard University Press, 1962). At issue here, as elsewhere in this section, are the distinctions, if not the terminology, that Austin makes in his theory of speech acts (for example, Mrs. Wilson's persuasive testimony might be called a "perlocutionary act").

of the court. He has used words to convey necessary facts. Mrs. Wilson has provided heartfelt caring. According to the novel, each alone is finally inadequate. Mary's confessional words of love for Jem, spoken aloud to the court but directed to Jem (who does not yet know she loves him), combine the two; she provides both a surprising truth in the court and the long-awaited revelation of the novel's romantic plot. Although Mary's testimony has little bearing on the verdict—as a lawyer says, her "evidence would not be much" (231)—it stands as the centerpiece of the trial scene and the novel, framed between these two depictions of different approaches to the court, both of which focus on the court's rules of storytelling.

Unlike either Mrs. Wilson or Will, Mary neither rejects nor adapts to the courtroom's rules. This independence is not surprising; her journey to the courtroom has been a willful self-construction as heroine. As her earlier dramatic boat ride suggests, she has literally and metaphorically fought her way against the tide. At the trial, her testimony, expected to be a mere public repetition of the known, of so-called reality, disrupts the conventional plotting of reality anticipated by her audience. The narrator explicitly warns us that this disruption is approaching: "Old Mr. Carson felt an additional beat at his heart at the thought of seeing the fatal Helen . . . for you see it was a fixed idea in the minds of all, that the handsome, bright, gay, rich young gentleman must have been beloved in preference to the serious, almost stern-looking smith, who had to toil for his daily bread" (280). The courtroom spectators here may have their individual perspectives, but these perspectives are all blinkered by formulaic assumptions ("the fatal Helen," "a fixed idea"). Gaskell presumably sees the same predicament in her own audience, and Mary's testimony can thus both model and make real the type of speech act which Gaskell envisions her novel to be for her audience.

Just as Gaskell situates her book vis-à-vis material evidence, gaining pressure and meaning from its prooflike presence, she here promotes a similar channeling of her novel through testimonial evidence. Mary Barton's legitimate establishment of herself (albeit reluctantly) as a heroine to the public at the trial represents, within the novel, what the novel is attempting to do for *its* public. In this respect Hilary Schor[4] quite rightly sees that Gaskell meaningfully places Mary in the role of narrator: Mary, like the author Gaskell, negotiates becoming a public figure and gives evidence for a differently plotted reality. In Schor's view, however, the court operates simply as a convenient mirror, the metaphoric equivalent of depicting a woman writing a novel. In reality the uneven parallels between the

4. Hilary Schor, *Scheherezade in the Marketplace* (New York: Oxford UP, 1992). [*Editor*].

courtroom and the storytelling of the novel enable Gaskell not only to reflect on herself as author but also to imbue her novel with a testimonial form, as serious and "real" as that which might be told in court.

Indeed, one way to understand the onset of Mary's delirium after her testimony is as a dramatization of the logical breakdown that occurs when Gaskell mixes together two different narrative epistemologies—the law court's and the novel's. The result is a crisis of narration. First, in an odd moment the narrator herself abdicates, declaring: "I was not there myself; but one who was, told me" (281). Immediately thereafter, as a reflection not of her weakness but, rather, of the heroic communicative power she has expended on the stand, Mary becomes delirious: "Mary never let go her clutched hold on the rails. She wanted them to steady her, in that heaving, whirling court. . . . [I]t was such pain, such weary pain in her head, to strive to attend to what was being said. They were all at sea, sailing away on billowy waves, and every one speaking at once, and no one heeding her father, who was calling on them to be silent, and listen to him" (284).

As Schor has noted, Mary's physical reaction in the courtroom recalls her earlier trip up the river to catch the sailing ship departing with Will Wilson; in the court she experiences a ship full of narrators steering in different directions on a linguistic ocean. Moreover, if the day before she was grimly heroic (enduring, for instance, a young boy's condescending wish to show off the town's stock exchange in the midst of her frenzied chase after Will's boat), now her story is blandly recast as a clichéd romance novel within the court: "A gallant tar brought back from the pathless ocean by a girl's noble daring" (286). The key to Mary's madness, and perhaps even the narrator's strange absence, may lie in this multilayered overlapping of novel with court: a certain wobbliness arises when those incompatible enframings of this story confront each other head on.

More important, however, what this way of seeing the central trial scene particularly brings out is how at this moment the novel and the trial overlap as storytelling forums that both hinge upon—and here come unhinged by—the suppression of another, truly absent narrator: John Barton, "her father, who was calling on them to be silent, and listen to him" (284). It is a central juncture. For both novel and law court their claims to truth telling turn out to be built on the suppression of John Barton's self-justification of the assassination he has committed.

I will come back to this crucial suppression in a moment, but for now we may observe that in the trial scene, the oppressive secret knowledge that her father has committed the murder and has a very different story to tell about it makes some sense of Mary's complicated, demented "repetition of the same words over and over again": "I must not go mad. I must not, indeed. They say people tell the truth when they're mad; but I don't. I was always a liar. I was, indeed; but I'm not mad. I must not go mad. I must not, indeed" (285). Presumably, Mary "must not go mad" in part simply because if she does she might accidentally reveal her father as the murderer. On another plane, however, Mary plunges us here into all-too-sane questions about the truth-telling properties of speech with which the trial has been concerned. Like the mad Caleb in the original ending of *Caleb Williams,* Mary has abandoned the parallel distinctions that suggest truth opposes lies as reason opposes madness. She points out that these binaries are easily and commonly reversed, aligning truth and madness: "They say people tell the truth when they're mad." Pursuing this logic, however, Mary strangely rejects the possibility that her madness will bring out the truth with the words *I don't* by declaring she "was always a liar." Her words are ambiguous but meaningful in the aftermath of her performance as the novel's narrator. One formulation, that she tells the truth by lying, recalls Gaskell's own project, her "truthful" documentarylike fiction making. The other, that truth telling requires a coherence and sanity that involve a lying, unfaithfulness to reality, touches on the axiom coiled within all realistic novels: not that they tell the truth by lying but that lying, that fiction making, is always a part of telling the truth.

In terms of the unfolding formal concerns about novelistic speech and evidence, testimonial and physical, Mary's mental whirl after her testimony in court thus represents something of an overheated climax. In terms of the plot, however, it tolls the downbeat after the novel's climax, signaling the beginning of the story's denouement. Mary's breakdown after her testimony in the trial marks her finish as the novel's active heroine. From then on she cedes control to the male characters. In fact, as portended by the anonymous male spectator at the trial who ostensibly informs the suddenly absent narrator of what happened, the novel's focus also shifts to its potential effect upon its audience of male industrial management, and Gaskell wraps up for them the question of class justice, still unaddressed by this trial after its official legal conclusion.

In a rather blunt manner the novel goes on to show a figurative conclusion to the trial by depicting how Mr. Carson, the factory owner, discovers and judges the truth about his son's murder. Focusing on Mr. Carson, the only developed middle-class character besides the narrator, the scene shifts to his mind as the real judge's chambers, with the novel becoming a kind of higher court of appeals. Where are those characters who represent the working class, Mary and John Barton? John Barton is soon dead, and as Raymond Williams correctly declares of the ending, "All are going to Canada; there could be no more devastating conclusion." Yet it is not, as Williams continues, that "a solution within the actual situation might be hoped for, but the solution with which the heart went was a cancelling of the actual difficulties and the removal of the persons pitied to the uncompromised New World."[5] This novel intentionally gives the reader some healing closure for its ground-down working-class heroes and their sad story but not for the situation in Manchester which produced it, where nothing is yet settled. This didactic novel does not offer solutions; it aspires to create (middle-class) readers who have formed a judgment based on the evidence of working-class oppression it presents.[6]

In a conspicuous step-by-step sequence Mr. Carson walks through the production of this judgment. After Jem's trial he implacably determines to begin legal proceedings against the dying John Barton, despite Barton's voluntary confession to him and tearful plea for forgiveness. Witnessing an incident of forgiveness between children of different classes in the street in which the police are pointedly avoided—"Nurse won't call a policeman, so don't be frightened" (318)—Mr. Carson returns home and rereads "the Gospel." The narrator then reports succinctly: "He shut the book, and thought deeply" (320). Having seen a model for behavior and been moved by his reading, Mr. Carson changes his mind and forgives John Barton, who dies in his arms. Gaskell thus presents Mr. Carson's verdict, and by extension her reader's, as dependent upon the observation of exemplary behavior and a shift from recognizing the meaning of a text to acting upon that meaning. She illustrates, with an almost religious tract-style clarity, the construction of sympathy for the working class which the earlier part of her book has presumably stirred in her reader. The process completes in a final tribunal scene that takes place, appropriately, in Mr. Carson's library. There he is turned from his cross-examination of Job and Jem, as they testify about John Barton and his difficulty with the masters, toward an empathetic judgment that extends his support to the workers as part of his own interest. Having modeled how reading can elicit sympathy (and, one might add, represented a physical book taking its effect), Gaskell fig-

---

5. Raymond Williams, *Culture and Society* [*1780–1950* (New York: Harper & Row, 1958)], 91.
6. Gaskell's attempt to sway her readers' judgment forms the subject of her novel's second epigraph, which extends the first epigraph's concerns with her novel's effect on its readers and her own act of authorship. This second epigraph—written in German and unfortunately mistranslated in every modern edition and everywhere misapprehended as a cryptic reference to the death of her baby—invokes the novel's goal of providing a spiritual ferrying for the masters and the workmen:

> Take only ferryman, take the fare,
> That I gladly three times offer.
> The two that came over with me,
> Were spiritual natures.
> (My trans.)

ures the power of testimonial words to transform social positions and material relations. One speech act leads to another, and improvements, we are told, are subsequently produced by the "short earnest sentences spoken by Mr. Carson" (335).

The narrator's earlier advice to the reader—"it is for you to judge" (26)—turns out to be, not surprisingly, disingenuous. Mr. Carson presents the judgment for which *Mary Barton* is striving to be evidence. But what is interesting about this ending as a pronounced extension and resolution of the legal trial is that at the close of the book we discover that even the seemingly incidental realistic depictions of working-class life of the beginning are to be connected to the story's central depiction of a law court, as if the court scene somehow quietly but meaningfully neighbors every event and detail told. During and after the climactic trial scene it becomes clear that the trial is not simply a scene in this novel; it is more like the scene *of* the novel, inflecting the entire speech act Gaskell wishes to perform by threading the novel back through the law courts. In purely formal terms a sustaining interplay between the novel and the law courts underlies Gaskell's construction of her novel such that—to borrow Michael McKeon's apposite description of dialectical relations— "'unity' and 'difference' are kept simultaneously before our eyes."[7] This novel is meaningfully like and unlike the law courts it depicts, as Gaskell specifically constitutes our reading in terms of evidence and testimony.

This formal structure, moreover, makes historical sense. For the novel thereby actively participates in the contemporary Chartist movement with which it is concerned. This connection may not be immediately obvious to readers today: Chartism, the world's first working-class movement, now most likely conjures up images of crowds, of organized marches on parliament like the one John Barton attends, and of massive signed petitions calling for the six-point political charter to be accepted, not of trials. But in the decade before this novel's publication the trials of Chartists garnered the same sort of electric attention as their meetings and protests. For *Mary Barton*'s contemporary readers the story's central trial would have registered directly with John Barton's Chartist and trade union politics.

When Gaskell addressed mistaken accusations from an upset family that she had fictionalized the story of an actual murder, she naturally and pointedly assumed precisely this context for her novel. Writing apologetically but firmly to the family that she "had heard of young Mr. Ashton's murder at the time when it took place; but . . . knew none of the details, nothing about the family, never read the trial," she adds: "It's [*sic*] occurrence, and that of one or two similar

7. McKeon, *Origins of the English Novel*, [*1600–1740* (Baltimore: Johns Hopkins UP, 1987)] 16.

cases at Glasgow at the time of a strike, were, I have no doubt, suggestive of the plot, as having shown me to what lengths the animosity of irritated workmen would go."[8] The Glasgow trials to which she refers were those of cotton spinners, whose trade union struck in the winter of 1836–37, amid widespread starvation. The trial of their strike leaders for the murder of a blackleg worker was a key early catalyst to the Chartist movement: the first trial seen as a national concern.

By 1848, when *Mary Barton* was published, the history and identity of Chartism would be indissociable from its legal trials. In 1839 a large number of court cases followed on the conviction of Joseph Rayner Stephens (a Lancashire preacher against the New Poor Law) which marked the onset of a judicial disciplining of the Chartist movement. As Dorothy Thompson recounts: "By the autumn of 1839 nearly all the leaders of Chartism were either in prison or on bail awaiting trial."[9] While Chartist protests produced leaders and resulted in trials, trials themselves generated protests and brought leaders into national focus. At the beginning of 1840 those deemed responsible for the Newport uprising were tried (sentenced to death, they were later transported). Shortly thereafter, trials of ordinary participants in the movement became ubiquitous. Thompson reports that in 1842 "more people were arrested and sentenced for offences concerned with speaking, agitating, rioting and demonstrating than in any other year [of the nineteenth century]."[1] This mass movement passed through the law courts. Asa Briggs computes that, "taking the years from 1839 to 1848 as a whole, more than 3,500 Chartists were tried (some of them more than once)."[2] This staggering number includes Chartism's leader, Feargus O'Connor, who dramatically defended himself in trials for seditious libel in 1840 (which he lost) and seditious conspiracy in 1843 (in which he prevailed).

Briggs comments: "For the authorities . . . the trials were more than instruments of repression: they opened a window on Chartism, enabling an assessment of the extent of the 'Chartist threat.' For the Chartists themselves, the trials provided an opportunity for self-justification."[3] It is precisely this two-way view through the law court which is denied in *Mary Barton*. John Barton is *not* legally tried for his political assassination. No wonder Mary deliriously imagines in court there is "no one heeding her father, who was calling on them

---

8. Gaskell to John Potter, 16 August 1852, *The Letters of Mrs. Gaskell*, ed. J. A. V. Chapple 8nd Arthur Pollard (Manchester: Manchester University Press, 1966), 196.
9. Dorothy Thompson, *The Chartists* (London: Temple Smith, 1984), 78.
1. Ibid., 295.
2. Asa Briggs, *Chartism* (Phoenix Mill, Eng.: Sutton, 1998), 75.
3. Ibid., 75.

to be silent, and listen to him." Instead, the novel steps in, as it were, to both provide a window on the working classes and render their testimony.

The false accusation that Jem has committed the murder removes John Barton's charged political trial back to the homes of those concerned, allowing specific, private individual relations to intervene in abstract class animosity, just as the trial itself explicitly brings ordinarily private relations into the public realm of which they are already part. Thus, Mr. Carson, the factory owner whose son has been murdered, enters sympathetically into the Chartist John Barton's personal experience and vice versa, making them "brothers in the deep suffering of the heart" (316). Master comforts workman in a deathbed reconciliation scene; end of novel. What Gaskell pointedly has not done is rehash another polarizing Chartist or trade union trial.

As a result, the novel may seem to provide a superficial, apolitical answer to the vivid economic distress it initially evokes. A deathbed reconciliation may appear a fanciful resolution to an otherwise unresolved, real-life class conflict. We know and understand that the problems plaguing the working class in Manchester are part of the industrialization of England. Some economic change to the contemporary laissez-faire capitalist system might help; in *Mary Barton* we seem to get, as Raymond Williams respectfully despairs, "the characteristic humanitarian conclusion": "Efforts at improvement and mutual understanding."[4]

This economically oriented view, however, misapprehends the politics of *Mary Barton* in its time. From the perspective of the Chartists, as Gareth Stedman Jones has argued, the causes of their distress were essentially *political,* not economic.[5] The Chartists overwhelmingly saw themselves as living at the end of a long history of governmental tyranny. From eighteenth-century Enclosures Acts depriving the poor of their livelihood to the aid afforded southern paupers to migrate to northern industry, they were at the mercy of a state that controlled the economy, not at the mercy of industrial economic forces whose power centers the state simply reflected. Moreover, since the 1832 reform act the middle class had direct political power. The working classes were now for the first time isolated in their official disenfranchisement. Their Charter and protests were thus directed, in a long-standing English radical tradition, against the ruling state. The Charter calls for reform of parliament and, most important, for the vote for the working classes.

4. Williams, *Culture and Society,* 91.
5. Gareth Stedman Jones, "The Language of Chartism," in *The Chartist Experience: Studies in Working-Class Radicalism and Culture, 1830–60,* ed. James Epstein and Dorothy Thompson (London: Macmillan, 1982), 3–58.

Yet, by the time Gaskell was writing *Mary Barton,* the possibility of changing government was clearly a lost cause. The petitioning of the House of Commons had failed signally: in 1839 the House voted 235 to 46 against cosidering the petition; in 1842 the vote was 287 to 49; and in 1848, the year of the novel's publication, its possibility was simply ridiculed. If Gaskell sought justice for the working classes, she would have to outflank purely legislative politics. Besides, Benjamin Disraeli had already expertly told the parliamentary-political story of trade unions and Chartism in *Sybil* (1845).[6]

Gaskell thus seized upon a different political side to the story: the judicial. Her novel does not sidestep John Barton's trial; it absorbs and redirects its political energies. By the end of the novel John Barton may not have publicly explained the political and social dimensions of his act, but the novel has in ways he never could. Moreover, by engaging an epistemology of witnessing throughout her story and placing the narrative arena of the court at its heart, Gaskell gains as a fundamental premise of her novel the notion that part of the political problem lies at the level of language and storytelling. The depicted trial centers a novel that, as Catherine Gallagher has shown, works hard to expose how "contrasting narrative forms" become "conventional ways of organizing reality," political ruts.[7]

At the same time, the novel's judicial framework, with its pervasive trope of witnessing and providing evidence, is of a piece with the Chartist agenda itself. Chartist leader Bronterre O'Brien opened an early discussion of petitions (in this case one concerning the 1834 Poor Law) as follows:

> I would recommend that instead of petitioning for a mere repeal of the Act, we should petition—
>
> "THAT THE POOR OF ENGLAND SHALL BE HEARD BY COUNCIL AT THE BAR OF THE HOUSE OF COMMONS, AGAINST THE LATE TYRANNICAL AND INHUMAN ENACTMENT, MISCALLED THE POOR-LAW AMENDMENT ACT."
>
> A petition of this sort, accompanied to the House by 200,000 people, and headed by all the popular leaders of good repute throughout the country, would be worth ten thousand petitions of the ordinary kind. Mr. Feargus O'Connor, who first suggested the idea to me, would make a capital counsel on the

---

6. The narrative structures patterning mid-Victorian social problem novels such as *Mary Barton* and *Sybil,* and the interrelations of these novels, are explained by Rosemarie Bodenheimer in *The Politics of Story in Victorian Social Fiction* (Ithaca: Cornell University Press, 1988).

7. Catherine Gallagher, *The Industrial Reformation of English Fiction: Social Discourse and Narrative Form, 1832–1867* (Chicago: University of Chicago Press, 1985), 68. Gallagher shifted discussion of the industrial novels from concerns with their ideological effectiveness and the reality of their depictions to historically oriented analyses of their structure and form.

occasion. Few are better acquainted with the feelings of the poor and with their legal rights as subjects.[8]

O'Brien asks not for majority votes and divisions but to testify and to prove his case.

We can hear the same epistemology of the law court undergirding *Mary Barton*'s political history: "So a petition was framed, and signed by thousands in the bright spring days of 1839, imploring Parliament to hear witnesses who could testify to the unparalleled destitution of the manufacturing districts" (78). Gaskell's novel's political edge lies in providing such testimony to the conditions of the working classes. Nor, as we have seen, does she present this evidence naively. Truth within this novel is understood as a constructed thing, not an a priori category. As Gaskell commented to Mary Ewart in 1848: "I wanted to represent the subject in the light in which some of the workmen certainly consider to be *true,* not that I dare to say it is the abstract absolute truth."[9] We must not be misled because the novel's witnesses to working-class struggles, including the narrator as well as the characters, appear ingenuous: Gaskell's presentation, if sometimes heavy-handed, is ultimately percipient. But this is not surprising: the realism of Victorian novels is as patently designed as the physical organization of the law courts.

AMY MAE KING

Taxonomical Cures: The Politics of Natural History and Herbalist Medicine in Elizabeth Gaskell's *Mary Barton*[†]

> In the factory workers walking out in spring into Green Heys Fields; in Alice Wilson, remembering in her cellar the ling-gatherings for besoms in the native village that she will never again see; in Job Legh, intent on his impaled insects—these early chapters embody the characteristic response of a generation to the new and crushing experience of industrialism.
>
> —Raymond Williams

8. *Bronterre's National Reformer, in Government, Law, Property, Religion, and Morals,* 4 February 1837. For readers in the United States it is important to keep in mind that the separation between judicial and legislative branches is historically much less clear in England, where the House of Lords is England's highest court.

9. Gaskell to Mary Ewart (late 1848), *Letters of Mrs. Gaskell,* [J. A. V. Chapple and Arthur Pollard, eds. (Manchester: Manchester UP, 1966) 67.

† Reprinted by permission from *Romantic Science: The Literary Forms of Natural History,* edited by Noah Heringman, the State University of New York Press, © 2003, State University of New York. All rights reserved. The epigraph to this chapter is from *Culture and Society 1780–1950* (London: Chatto and Windus, 1958), 88.

On the very night in Elizabeth Gaskell's 1848 *Mary Barton, A Tale of Manchester Life* that the eponymous heroine's mother will die in childbirth, Alice Wilson is invited to an impromptu supper at the Bartons' home; the younger Mary Barton runs to her cellar apartment and finds old Alice, like them just come in from a Sunday spent in Green Heys Fields just outside Manchester. Unlike the Wilsons and the Bartons, though, Alice has not been taking a social walk:

> she had been out all day in the fields, gathering wild herbs for drinks and medicine, for in addition to her invaluable qualities as a sick nurse and her worldly occupations as a washerwoman, she added a considerable knowledge of hedge and field simples; and on fine days, when no more profitable occupation offered itself, she used to ramble off into the lanes and meadows as far as her legs could carry her. This evening she had returned loaded with nettles, and her first object was to light a candle and see to hang them up in bunches in every available place in her cellar-room.[1]

Her nettles, intended as she tells Mary for "spring drink," are not the sentimental plucking of a Sunday walk; their stinging properties belie that, as does the more general description of her humble cellar room,

> oddly festooned with all manner of hedge-row, ditch, and field-plants which we are accustomed to call valueless, which have a powerful effect either for good or for evil, and are consequently much used among the poor. The room was strewed, hung, and darkened with these bunches, which emitted no fragrant odour in their process of drying. In one corner was a sort of broad hanging shelf . . . where some old hoards of Alice's were kept. (*MB* 17–18)

Alice Wilson's gatherings suggest an alternative medical practice, one whose exact relation to vernacularized medicine and natural history alike has remained beyond the reach of critical clarity. In our accounts of eighteenth- and nineteenth-century medicine, we have begun to recognize and describe alternative medical practices, including demotic or folk traditions as well as spheres such as quackery previously thought outside any traditional understanding of the history of medicine.[2] That this has yet to be registered in relation to Gaskell's

---

1. *Mary Barton, A Tale of Manchester Life,* ed. Macdonald Daly (New York: Penguin, 1996). Page number for this quotation (17) and all subsequent page numbers refer to this Norton Critical Edition, cited parenthetically in the text hereafter as *MB*.
2. See, for instance, Roy Porter, *Health for Sale: Quackery in England, 1660–1850* (Manchester: Manchester UP, 1989) and *In Sickness and in Health: The British Experience, 1650–1850* (London: Fourth Estate, 1989); Anne Digby, *Making a Medical Living: Doctors and Patients in the English Market for Medicine, 1720–1911* (Cambridge: Cambridge UP, 1994); G. Gisse, R. L. Numbers, and J. W. Leavitt, eds., *Medicine without Doctors* (New York: Science History Publications, 1977); W. F. Bynum and Roy Porter, eds., *Medical Fringe and Medical Orthodoxy, 1750–1850* (London: Croom Helm, 1987).

mid-century social fictions—no stranger, as the characters of Dr. Gibson and Roger Hamley of *Wives and Daughters* (1866) suggest, to the figure of the professional scientist or doctor—is evident in the failure to recognize Alice Wilson's vocation beyond that of her status as a washerwoman.[3] In our persistence in apprehending characters through an exaggerated emphasis on professional forms of scientific medicine, we not only risk misunderstanding the social placement of a single character but also the discourse through which Gaskell's novelistic representation of "social ills" is best achieved.[4] My purpose here is to sketch an account of the lingering vernacular medical tradition in the nineteenth century—specifically, the vernacular medicine of the herbalist—and to suggest two important facets of this tradition: its deep epistemological links with natural history and the importance of this medical epistemology to novelistic representations of social ills. In *Mary Barton*, the physical ills that Alice's herbalist medicine intends to cure are extended to the "remedies" for social ills by one important bridge: a cure for what I will call the "ills of perception" that the taxonomical basis of natural history implicitly suggests.

Insofar as *Mary Barton* has been understood as one of the industrial novel's chief prototypes, the choice to look to the epistemologies of natural history in order to account for the text's political energies may seem puzzling. It is perhaps less odd when one turns briefly to Gaskell's life, for her biography suggests that she was conversant with natural history topics and the emergent scientific questions of the early Victorian era. Jenny Uglow states that in 1830 Gaskell went to stay with her relative the Reverend William Turner, a pioneering figure in linking local society with larger scientific movements of the day. Just during her immediate stay in his home, he gave three lectures at the Society for the Promotion of Natural History and the Literarary and Philosophical Society: "The Vegetable Kingdom," "Mineralogy and Geology," and "Optics and Astronomy."[5] If Manchester had been a scientific backwater, during the 1820s and 1830s it inaugurated five separate scientific societies and even hosted the annual meeting of the British Association in 1842.

Two versions of amateur natural history are represented in *Mary Barton*: Job Legh's studies of botany and entomology place him

3. For an interesting account of the medical and scientific contexts in *Wives and Daughters*, see Deirdre D'Albertis, *Dissembling Fictions: Elizabeth Gaskell and the Victorian Social Text* (New York: St. Martin's, 1997).

4. Narratives of professionalization in the Victorian period are, in fact, often based on the development of the medical profession. As a result, literary–critical interest in Victorian medicine has emphasized the growth of its contemporary, professional contours—perhaps so much so that we have failed to recognize a medical scene in *Mary Barton* that lies outside that professional context. For excellent accounts about the discourse of medical professionalization, see Penelope Corfield, *Power and the Professions in Braitain, 1700–1850* (London: Routledge, 1995); Magali Sarfatti Larson, *The Rise of Professionalism: A Sociological Analysis* (Berkeley and Los Angeles: U of California P, 1977).

5. *Elizabeth Gaskell: A Habit of Stories* (Boston: Faber and Faber, 1993), 213.

squarely within the tradition of the nineteenth-century natural historian, while Alice Wilson's knowledge of medicinal plants evokes an older tradition of the village herbalist or wisewoman. Although *Mary Barton* most obviously is a sympathetic documentation of the sufferings of the industrial poor that Gaskell herself witnessed as the wife of a Manchester minister, it also turns to the occupations and pleasures of certain of those very same people:

> weavers, common hand-loom weavers, who throw the shuttle with unceasing sound, though Newton's "Principia" lies open on the loom . . . there are botanists among them, equally familiar with either the Linnaean or the Natural system, who know the name and habitat of every plant within a day's walk . . . there are entomologists, who may be seen with a rude looking net, ready to catch any winged insect. (*MB* 36–37)

Gaskell's attempt to capture a certain documentary reality—what Raymond Williams called her "intensity of effort to record, in its own terms, the feel of everyday life in the working-class homes"—included the realities of amateur natural history and vernacular medicine among the working-class industrial poor.[6] The elaborate references to working-class scientific pursuits gesture to one of the ways in which *Mary Barton*, although generically eclectic as Catherine Gallagher has shown, strives to be a documentary record of and argument for an enlightened proletariat.[7] The fact that the novel opens outside the city, in a space characterized by natural history collecting—the source of Alice's herbal medicine—and situates its working-class denizens amid narrative energies that verge on the taxonomic, suggests the importance of natural history to this industrial novel.

In *Mary Barton*, Gaskell invites her readers to see the rural not as a flight from contemporary urban–industrial reality but as a literal cure for its worse ills, the source of the very sort of medical and educational relief for which reform agitates.[8] Although Alice Wilson is nostalgic for the rural village she left as a child, her herbalist work, like the naturalist studies of Job Legh, is resolutely work for the present; her knowledge of herbal "simples" is rural in origin but urban in practice: she gathers nettles for "spring drink," and dries herbs and other plants, to revive the health of her neighbors and prepare for future illness. Gaskell's remedy for the social ills she depicts, like

---

6. Williams, *Culture and Society* [1780–1950 (New York: Harper & Row, 1958)], 87.
7. *The Industrial Reformation of English Fiction: Social Discourse and Narrative Form, 1832–1867* (Chicago: U of Chicago P, 1985).
8. As such I tend to disagree with those who see the opening scene of the novel as a nostalgic representation of what has been lost because of industrialization—what Coral Lansbury calls a "lost arcadia . . . a landscape of a lost world that can only be visited on holidays and in the dreams of nostalgia." Lansbury, *Elizabeth Gaskell: The Novel of Social Crisis* (New York: Harper and Row, 1975), 25.

Alice's remedies, is present-directed and firmly unnostalgic: it is not a position that urges a return to the country, a position underscored by the desperation of the replacement workers ("knob-sticks") who come from the outlying countryside.[9] The text's representation of herbalist medicine and the study of nature is not nostalgic but progressive, for they suggest a model for reform in a novel that has been described as dramatizing, but not offering remedies for, social ills.

However, the true importance of herbalist medicine to the text is not simply thematic but structural; the city's outer reaches not only contain the symbols of proposed reforms but also, more significantly to Gaskell's narrative purpose, suggest a reform of perception. That is, Gaskell uses the taxonomical logic of natural history to propose a more humane way of seeing the working class, not as another species or as types of a larger order but as individual specimens whose ills can be ameliorated. Gaskell's most sustained and coherent political call in *Mary Barton* is for the two classes to *see* each other and classify themselves as like species. Chartism, which is the novel's avowed politics, is invoked but not elaborated on, while the text oddly has sustained and detailed references to natural history. If natural history does not seem political, it also is in no way oppositional to the political energies of working-class movements; in fact, as Friedrich Engels wrote in his 1844 *Condition of the Working Class in England*, working-class institutes run by trade unions and socialists sponsored lectures, the most popular of which were on "economics and on scientific and aesthetic topics."[1] That natural history was a site of connection

---

9. Even when Alice becomes senile after her stroke, her mental retreat to the countryside is less a nostalgic evocation of a better time and place than a continuation of her practical approach to nature. For instance, one of the places her dementia returns her to is the fields she went to with her sister; the "heather and ling for besoms" that she recalls searching for is a reference to the folk knowledge she embodies, for heather and ling (similar broomlike plants) were gathered to make brooms, or "besoms." Neither are the scenes of her returned childhood hazy or romantic; they are specific in their evocation of the natural world: "the bees are turning homeward for th'last time, and we've a terrible long bit to go yet. See! Here's a linnet's nest in this gorse-bush. Th'hen bird is on it. Look at her bright eyes, she won't stir. . . . Won't mother be pleased with the bonny lot of heather we've got" (*MB* 190).

1. *Condition of the Working Class in England*, trans. W. O. Henderson and W. H. Chaloner (Stanford: Stanford UP, 1968), 272. Engels makes a distinction between the mechanics institutes, which he considers middle-class propaganda machines, and working-class institutes run by trade unions. He writes that "the middle-classes hope also that by fostering such studies they will stimulate the inventive powers of the workers to the eventual profit of the bourgeoisie" (271). He states that the socialists and trade unions do a far better job at educating workers, some of whom he admires for a very high degree of natural history learning: "I have sometimes come across workers, with their fustian jackets falling apart, who are better informed on geology, astronomy, and other matters, than many an educated member of the middle classes in Germany" (272). One way in which Gaskell's novel seems to conform to the distinction that Engels would draw between the Mechanics Institutes and educational programs sponsored by trade unions is the contrast between Jem Wilson's and Job Legh's learning. Jem makes an "invention for doing away wi' the crank, or somewhat. His master's bought it from him, and ta'en out a patent" (*MB* 126). In inventing a new industrial tool, Jem represents in no small measure the middle-class fantasy that Engels describes with such derision; his knowledge, that is, can be coopted by the bourgeoisie. Job Legh, on the other hand, pursues knowledge without any productive or economic value and, hence, more fully represents the kind of educational enlightenment that Engels valued.

between political and medical heterodoxy has also been well established: for instance, Isaiah Coffin, the leader in England of a working-class medical self-help movement centering on herbalism, called for the establishment of local botanical societies to provide working-class access to practical plant knowledge.[2] Moreover, the amateur natural historian Job Legh is not apolitical; aside from being John Barton's most faithful listener, he is a symbol of the kind of working-class enlightenment that reformers supported.

Whatever sympathy Gaskell brought to the documentation of everyday life for the industrial poor of the 1840s, she also brought a strong opinion about the source of their problems: a misperception on the part of the industrialists about the nature of the working class and the cause of their social ills. As such, Gaskell's challenge was to balance the representation of working-class suffering with her belief that poverty was not natural but a state engendered by industrial practices.[3] Through Alice Wilson's herbalist remedies and Job Legh's naturalist studies—two seemingly discordant, but nevertheless persistently evoked, practices in this industrial novel—*Mary Barton* ultimately suggests a cure for the "ills of perception" that inform the suffering and strife in the novel.

HERBAL MEDICINE IN *MARY BARTON*

Alice Wilson's herbal knowledge in *Mary Barton* points us toward the complex and long history of vernacular medicine in England. Clearly, Alice's knowledge does not stem from a professional, or perhaps even literate, tradition, but rather a tradition of proverbial lore. Poor enough that she drinks herbal rather than black tea and lives in a cellar, Alice may not have been literate and most likely would not have owned an herbal. Her knowledge is folk knowledge, popular, rural, and most likely eighteenth-century in origin and nature; Alice was raised in Cumberland, we are told, but emigrated to Manchester as a young woman. Her social position as a sick nurse and herbalist, as well as washerwoman, gestures back to a much older and, by and large, fading vernacular medical tradition in England. In early modern England, for instance, aside from medical professionals of various sorts, there were, as Roy Porter has shown, informal healers: people who "practiced healing without a view to reward, but out of motives of neighborliness, paternalism, good housekeeping, religion or simple self help. Every village had its 'nurses' and 'wise women'

2. J. F. C. Harrison, "Early Victorian Radicals and the Medical Fringe," *Medical Fringe and Medical Orthodoxy: 1750–1850*, eds. W. F. Bynum and Roy Porter (London: Croom Helm, 1987), 198–215.
3. Hilary Schor's work on *Mary Barton* makes a compelling case for the novel's success as political critique. See Schor, *Scheherezade in the Marketplace: Elizabeth Gaskell and the Victorian Novel* (New York: Oxford UP, 1992).

well versed in herb-lore and in secret brews and potions."[4] By the Georgian and early Victorian periods, with the increasing dominance of regular medicine, the tradition of the "wise woman" was fading, with Victorian collectors of folk medicine believing they were preserving a dying art.[5]

And yet it would be a mistake to create a simple opposition between a fading amateur tradition and a rising professionalized medicine; Alice's knowledge represents not simply a disappearing art of healing but an established tradition of vernacular medicine that had staying power throughout the eighteenth century and into the nineteenth. Although Alice's knowledge seems predominantly proverbial and oral, the printed record of that knowledge is retained in a fashion in the herbals that remain. The most influential early English herbal was the early Latin herbal of Apuleius Barbarus (or Pseudo-Apuleius); the chief source of botanical knowledge in Europe during the so-called Dark Ages, it was probably translated into Anglo-Saxon about A.D. 1000 and revived as a source with its mid-nineteenth century translation in the compilation known as *Leechdom's Wortcuning and Starcraft of Early England*. Other important English herbals, such as the *Grete Herball* (printed in 1526), *Bancke's Herball* (1525), Gerard's *Herball* (1633), and *Hortus Sanitatis* (1485), formalize folk knowledge; they picture the herb through a woodcut, describe the plant, list its popular and botanical names, and describe its "virtues"—that is, its medicinal uses. The healing virtues of an herb might stand alongside suggestions for how to poison a pest or flavor a soup.

The diffusion of medicine to the public had long taken two channels: word of mouth and printed books purveying medical advice. Thus, it is not entirely clear if Alice's herbal knowledge comes strictly from proverbial lore or if her knowledge stems in part from printed vernacular medical sources. That is, although her herbal knowledge has links to the practical advice of the medieval and early modern herbals, her self-help model also suggests a popular medical culture that thrived throughout the eighteenth century and into the nineteenth, despite the rise of professional and paraprofessional medicine among the middle classes beginning in the eighteenth century.[6] Like the residual Anglo-Saxon in John Barton's northern, working-class dialect, Alice's herbal knowledge is both ancient and thoroughly contemporary. That mixed status—a domain of medical knowledge that operated both within and without formal texts and remained viably modern for all of its long heritage—is attested by publication histories: John Culpeper's *Herbal* from the mid-seventeenth century on had

---

4. *Disease, Medicine, and Society in England, 1550–1860* (London: Macmillan, 1987), 21.
5. Ibid., 43–44.
6. See Mary Chamberlain and Ruth Richardson, "Life and Death," *Oral History: Journal of the Oral History Society* 11.1 (1983): 41; Porter, *Health for Sale*.

assumed "exemplary status as a household name," while William Buchan's *Domestic Medicine* (1769) was reprinted well into the nineteenth century.[7] Domestic manuals—medical lore books, such as Eliza Smith's *The Compleat Housewife* (1729), that contained an assortment of household hints, recipes, and medical cures—were another way in which medical knowledge accumulated.[8] Nevertheless, as Porter has shown, although much "lay therapeutic lore was put down on paper . . . it circulated and snowballed in many other ways."[9]

John Wesley's 1747 *Primitive Physic, or an Easy and Natural Method of Curing Most Diseases* played a large role in the diffusion of medical knowledge, particularly within his chosen audience, the working poor. Wesley knew that going to a doctor or buying prepared medicine was financially difficult, so his book offers traditional remedies for disease:

> a mean hand has made here some little attempt towards a plain and easy way of curing most diseases. . . . Who would not wish to have a Physician always in his house, and one that attends without fee or reward? . . . Is it enquired, but are there not books already, on every part of the art of medicine? . . . [T]hey are too dear for poor men to buy, and too hard for plain men to understand. . . . I have not seen one yet, either in our own or any other tongue, which contains only safe, and cheap, and easy medicines.[1]

Wesley's *Primitive Physic* went through many editions, inspiring a formal revival of interest in herbal medicine just prior to the era when it would be most endangered; as the historian Mary Chamberlain has claimed, Wesley's tract "enabled that tradition to continue when the social and practical supports had been destroyed by emigration from the villages to the city."[2] Herbalism, then, had roots in pre-industrial England, but it also, tellingly, had a nineteenth-century history that included the new medical cosmology known as medical botany. "Thomsonianism," after the American herbalist Samuel Thomson, or Coffinism, after Thomson's English follower Isaiah Coffin, rejected orthodox medicine in favor of natural herbal remedies; their following was primarily in the artisan and petit bourgeois social zones, but their rhetoric was populist and sympathetic to heterodox political movements such as the Owenites and Chartists. Alice's herbal knowledge, however, seems too proverbial—as the result of informal exchange networks—to be derived from these movements and might

---

7. See Roy Porter, "Introduction," *The Popularization of Medicine: 1650–1850*, ed. Roy Porter (London: Routledge, 1992), 2.

8. Philip Wilson, "Acquiring Surgical Know-How: Occupational and Lay Instruction in Early Eighteenth-Century London," *The Popularization of Medicine: 1650–1850*, 47–57.

9. *In Sickness and in Health*, 268.

1. *Primitive Physic: or an Easy and Natural Method of Curing Most Diseases*, ed. A. Wesley Hill (London: Epworth, 1960), 27–28.

2. Ibid., 32.

be traced with more accuracy back to her rural background. Notwith-standing Alice's folk-derived knowledge, the political tendencies of a newly publishable herbalism remain suggestive and well within the range of Gaskell's own social sphere.

Alice's herbalist remedies are part, therefore, of a more general community of medicine that would have included the informal and generally unremunerated work of midwifery and laying out; Alice may have performed each of these roles, as well as making medicines, despite nominally being employed as a washerwoman. George Wilson brags that "there's not a child ill within the street, but Alice goes to offer to sit up, and does sit up too, though may be she's to be at her work by six the next morning" (MB 13). Later, Alice's nephew strikes a similar note: "I used to be wakened by the neighbours knocking her up; this one was ill, and that body's child was restless; and for as tired as ever she might be, she would be up and dressed in a twinkling. . . . How pleased I used to be when she would take me into the fields with her to gather herbs . . . she knew such a deal about plants and birds, and their ways" (MB 172). Among the working classes, access to doc-tors was limited throughout the nineteenth century; folk medicine, as well as informal aids for childbirth and illness, filled the gap, as Alice's medicine and the several allusions to neighbors functioning as nurses suggest. When John Barton goes to the apothecary on behalf of the starving and fever-ridden Ben Davenport, he has to pawn his valuables; the prosperous-looking shop darkens Barton's mood, where he is given "sweet spirits of nitre," a medication Gaskell informs us is useless, but which Barton took with "comfortable faith . . . for men of his class believe that every description is equally efficacious" (MB 58). Engels had sharper criticism for plyers of patent medicines, calling them "charlatans" and their medicines "quack remedies."[3] In contrast, the nettles that Alice gathers, or the "meadow-sweet" that she sought out "to make tea for Jane's cough," are clearly medicinal references to plants; by contrast to her scathing criticism of the opium-dispensing apothecaries, the narrator never criticizes or condescends about Alice's simples.[4] Alice's medicines

3. Engels writes about the propensity of the working class to be swindled by medical charla-tans. He discusses the Manchester Infirmary, an institution that he praises but which in 1832 could only treat 22,000 patients, a number which could not nearly meet the needs of the population. However, the relationship between the Manchester that Elizabeth Gaskell saw and the Manchester of Engels's narrative is tenuous at best. Susan Zlotnick suggests that "one might forget that the two accounts claim to represent the same city at the same historical moment." Zlotnick, *Women, Writing, and the Industrial Revolution* (Baltimore: Johns Hopkins UP, 1998), 78.

4. Their utility is explicitly contrasted with the Carsons' discussion of plants, whose interest is strictly aesthetic. The youngest Carson daughter begs her father for a "new rose," a species that costs an astounding half-guinea; she calls it "one of her necessaries," and pout-ing, says that she does not consider dandelions and peonies flowers (MB 64). Tellingly, the flowers that she rejects in favor of the new hybrid rose are plants that can be used; dan-delion greens may be eaten, and the seeds of peonies induced labor, while its roots were thought to cure palsy and lunacy.

represent an alternative medical culture that reaches back into a preindustrial past to cure the ills that literally surround her. More crucially, perhaps, her medical practice comes out of the herbal tradition, which marries medical knowledge with classificatory botanical knowledge; it is a combination that points the way to the other body of naturalist knowledge in *Mary Barton*, Job Legh's natural history.

MANCHESTER'S NATURAL HISTORIAN

If Alice's herbalism reaches back to an early modern paradigm of naturalizing, *Mary Barton* presents us with a modern naturalist, Job Legh, whose natural history enthusiasm finds a vocabulary and structure in a slightly more contemporary source: the classificatory schemes of eighteenth- and nineteenth-century taxonomy. Nor is Job alone in these pursuits: we might recall the weavers who read Newton and know the Linnaean system, figures who evoke a working-class familiarity with natural history. Gaskell's narrative method—primarily that of the sympathetic observer, or documenter, of working-class life—is not unlike the method of natural history: both emphasize, to the point of bias, visuality because both privilege vision over the other senses as the mode for conveying description and characterization. It is a bias that gives sight, as Foucault demonstrates, an "almost exclusive privilege" in natural history classification, and makes it the dominant mode of representation in the novel form: the blind man can "perfectly well be a geometrician, but he cannot be a naturalist."[5]

The epistemological links between novel writing and the practice of natural history are concretized in the suggestive mapping of taxonomical language and situation onto the human sphere. In the passage that immediately follows the narrative revelation that John Barton had become "a Chartist, a Communist, all that is commonly called wild and visionary," we learn of his "rough Lancashire eloquence," his particular talent for "method and arrangement," and most important, the fact that "he was actuated by no selfish motives; that *his class, his order,* was what he stood by, not the rights of his own paltry self" (*MB* 151; emphasis added). His class, his order: these are words that separately have sociopolitical significations (as perhaps they are at first understood here) but which in combination also suggest the taxonomical organization of the natural world: kingdom, phylum, class, order, family, genus, species. *Mary Barton* opens with a scene that seems to situate humans within a similar taxonomical logic; walking in the fields outside the city, we learn that the land-

5. Michel Foucault, *The Order of Things: An Archeology of the Human Sciences* (New York: Vintage, 1994), 133.

scape is populated with types of people—specifically, toddlers, girls, boys, whispering lovers, husbands, and wives—all grouped by Gaskell into a totalizing mass: "the manufacturing population" (*MB* 8–9). As the narrative narrows its focus from the group to an individual, it focuses on what it calls "a thorough specimen of a Manchester man." A "specimen," then, of the order known as the manufacturing population, walking amid a new spring day, surrounded by specimens of nature that the narrative is just as eager to detail, such as the "young green leaves, which almost visibly fluttered into life" (*MB* 8).

Job Legh never appears in the novel without reference to his natural history avocation; repeatedly, his appearance brings with it a sustained discussion or at the very least a minor reference. In one instance, his speech is paired with this description—"for Job Legh directly put down some insect, which he was impaling on a cork-pin, and exclaimed"—while in another, we learn that he is absent from the house because he "has been out moss-hunting" (*MB* 307, 42). In another instance, Margaret explains why she continues to sew, despite the threat of blindness, by bringing up natural history: "grandfather takes a day here, and a day there, for botanising or going after insects, and he'll think little enough of four or five shilling for a shilling: dear grandfather! And I'm so loath to think he should be stinted of what gives him such pleasure" (*MB* 45). When Margaret goes on tour to sing, Job Legh shuts the house for—what else?— natural history: "her grandfather, too, had seen this to be a good time for going on his expeditions in search of specimens" (*MB* 125). In failing to write from Liverpool, Job is excused because "writing was to him little more than an auxiliary to natural history; a way of ticketing specimens" (*MB* 294). The novel, of course, ends with Job, who is contemplating coming to Canada not to see them, but to "pick up some specimens of Canadian insects . . . all the compliments . . . to the earwigs" (*MB* 339). This odd habit of tagging Job Legh's appearances in the text with references to natural history keeps natural history present to the reader; in light of the sustained quality of the references, the more extended discussions of natural history topics in the novel seem to be more than mere curiosities.

One such discussion, on the topic of a flying fish, introduces taxonomical language into the text: Job knows the flying fish is "the Exocetus, one of the Malacopterygii Abdominales" (*MB* 136). On two occasions the difference between vernacular and taxonomical language is discussed; on this occasion, Alice's nephew Will says, "you're one o' them folks as never knows beasts unless they're called out o' their names. Put 'em in Sunday clothes, and you know 'em, but in their work-a-day English you never know nought about 'em" (*MB* 136). When Mary meets Job for the first time, she is "bewildered" by the "strange language," the "technical names which Job Legh pattered

down on her ear" (*MB* 38). These overt references to Job's learned-
ness separate him from Alice Wilson, whose references to plants are
in an untutored vernacular. In both cases, however, these naturalists
do not represent a desire to return to a nostalgic past: the social ills
produced by the industrial context are not meant to be remedied by
a return to the country because Gaskell is unsentimental about rural
poverty.

The fact that Job Legh and Alice Wilson thrive amidst a generally
more bleak landscape is itself telling: Alice dies of old age, not of illness or starvation, and raises a foster son to robustness; in a time and
place where "very few strong, well-built, healthy people are to be
found among them," Will's physical health and beauty distinguish
him.[6] Job, perhaps more astoundingly, is happy and enlightened;
despite the absence of teeth, his eyes "gleamed with intelligence" as
he sits amid a room lined with "rude wooden frames of impaled
insects . . . [and] cabalistic books" (*MB* 38). Moreover, his education
enables a practical competence that enables Jem's defense; Mary,
who was overwhelmed by the word "alibi," thinks to consult Job
because he is "gifted with the knowledge of hard words, for to her, all
terms of law, or natural history, were alike many-syllabled mysteries"
(*MB* 217). Gaskell goes so far as to link Job's ability to secure a lawyer
with his knowledge of natural history; he knows a lawyer, a "Mr.
Cheshire, who's rather given over to th' insect line . . . he and I have
swopped specimens many's the time, when either of us had a duplicate" (*MB* 228).

Job's dedication to natural history is perhaps most evident in an
extended story about a scorpion. He acquires the scorpion by walking to Liverpool in order to inquire of sailors if they had accidentally
brought a specimen back from overseas. The story of the scorpion has
usually been read in relation to the passage in the chapter entitled
"Return of the Prodigal": "the people had thought the poverty of the
preceding years hard to bear, and had found its yoke heavy; but this
year added sorely to its weight. Former times had chastised them with
whips, but this chastised them with scorpions" (*MB* 102). Gaskell
here is deliberately echoing 1 Kings 12:11: "my father made your
yoke heavy, and I will add to your yoke: my father chastised you with
whips, but I will chastise you with scorpions." Elaine Jordan, in light
of the context of the story in 1 Kings, understands the story of the torpid scorpion as a parable of the present labor situation; the scorpion
is "apparently a random choice" except for its symbolic association
with the biblical passage.[7]

6. Engels, *Condition*, 118. The statistics that Engels cites are stark: 54 percent of the working poor's children did not survive.
7. "Spectres and Scorpions: Allusion and Confusion in *Mary Barton*," *Literature and History*
7 (1981): 59.

I would argue that even if the scorpion symbolically invokes rebellious slaves, it also is situated within a tale of natural history collection, and as such suggests intellectual curiosity and equality. In this way the scorpion may very well invoke the biblical context of slavery pushed too far, but it also is a symbol of enlightenment. Job acquires the scorpion by walking to Liverpool in order to possibly acquire a specimen from a place he could never afford to go; as such, it is an act of pure intellectual curiosity. In neglecting the context of this resonant image, we neglect his avocation—the very thing he performed outside the context of remunerated labor; in neglecting natural history as such in order to emphasize the image of the scorpion as a biblical image of punishment and rebellion, we neglect the potency of the image of the enlightened working class. Here, the biblical allusion and the natural history context work together to make a similar political point: together they advocate for moderation and enlightenment for the working classes.

CURES FOR PERCEPTUAL ILLS

What, then, might the implications of this natural history practice—as well as a similarly taxonomic herbalist medicine—be for an understanding of the social ills that my examples have heretofore seemingly skirted? Although Gaskell does not efface her knowledge of natural history in the way that she falsely disowns knowledge of "political economy" in the preface, the political implications of natural history are nevertheless never made explicit in the text. And yet natural history's methodological reliance on sight, and its emphasis on classification, perhaps suggest a more coherent basis for the novel's politics than John Barton's avowed, but incompletely realized, Chartism. Gaskell obliquely proposes that the deterioration of the relationship between what Engels would describe as "the industrial proletariat" and the "capitalists" is caused by a *perceptual* error: the class system that enforces such a wide economic divide between the working-class denizens of Manchester and their capitalist bosses threatens the correct perception that each man, regardless of social position, is of the same species.

Catherine Gallagher has noted that "all versions of John Barton's life thus become irrelevant to the novel's concluding and redeeming action: Carson's forgiveness, which is a foretaste of the Christian spirit that the narrator assures us will allow Carson to effect industrial social change."[8] Carson's forgiveness is Christian in its structure, but it is based in sympathetic identification achieved by a change in perception. As we will see, the penitence of John Barton is matched, at the novel's climactic meeting of the two, by Mr. Carson's renunciation

8. *Industrial Reformation*, 87.

of violence and commitment to remedying his workers' lot. A humanitarian's fantasy, perhaps, but also a serious challenge to the very social
distinctions that drive the social ills that the novel portrays. If
Gaskell's politics reside most comfortably in a kind of familiar humanitarianism, it is a humanitarianism not restricted to sympathy or pity
for the industrial poor; instead, Gaskell's humanitarianism more radically places the responsibility on the industrialist to reorder his cate-
gorization of his workers as less human than himself.

The fact that *Mary Barton* also contains an herbal medical tradition
is telling in light of the fact that it is a novel about social ills ending with
a projected "remedy." The social ills that are most clearly articulated in
the novel are environmental and domestic; following John Barton's
death, Jem talks with Mr. Carson about the working class's need to
know that a remedy was being sought; "remedy" is then repeated twice
to describe the amelioration of social suffering. Engels too uses the
image of disease to discuss the social situation of the working class in
England: "the social disorder from which England is suffering is running the same course as a disease which attacks human beings."[9]
Engels of course is unlike Gaskell in that he would hasten the disease
in order to promote socialist revolution, while Gaskell has perhaps
been justifiably accused of dramatizing the "fear of violence" among
the upper and middle classes at the time.[1] What, then, is Gaskell's proposed cure, and how is it linked to natural history and herbal medicine?
The herbalist tradition suggests a cure based in a self-reliant folk
knowledge, a cure that would put to use a knowledge that already
exists. The methodology of natural history requires that one visually
examine a species that one *sees* in order to make an analytical judgment. The remedy that is being proposed through the cognate fields of
herbalist medicine and natural history, then, is a combination of self-
reliance and change in perception between the different social classes.

In this light, one can see that the tragic arc of *Mary Barton* is structured around the loss and regaining of the perception of the other as
human. The violent explosion that leads to Harry Carson's murder is
incited by a caricature, the drawing that makes fun of the trade-union
men's appearance by likening them to Falstaff's clowns: he "had
drawn an admirable caricature of them—lank, ragged, dispirited, and
famine-stricken. Underneath he wrote a hasty quotation from the fat
knight's well-known speech in Henry IV" (*MB* 163).[2] That the men

9. *Condition*, 139.
1. Williams, *Culture and Society*, 90.
2. Gallagher points out that the younger Mr. Carson is killed for turning a "worker's delegation into . . . Shakespearean clowns." Gallagher's reading of Gaskell's use of Shakespeare
   with the caricature speaks to Gaskell's social critique of literature. She writes, "Carson's
   destructive use of Shakespeare reminds Gaskell's readers that although they have the best
   precedents for laughing at rags and tatters, they must now free themselves from the conventional association between 'low' characters and comedy" (*Industrial Reformation* 69–70).

cannot laugh in light of their hunger is unsurprising; it marks the end of sympathetic imagination on the part of the workers because they plot the murder on the back of the very piece of paper that had caricatured their hunger. The workers' shift in sympathetic imagination occurs when the caricature tangibly reveals the owners' perception that the working-class men are of a different order, a different species of man. Of course, the reader had been privy to this already; the owners call them brutes and animals, and most damagingly nonhuman: "I for one won't yield one farthing to the cruel brutes; they're more like wild beasts than human beings'" (*MB* 161). Their lack of sympathetic identification, however, is literalized in the caricature; their failure to correctly perceive them as human proves to be the final indignity. In not empathizing with their starvation and caricaturing their plight, the owners upset the fragile sympathy upon which the civil relationship between the two classes of men had been based.[3] The caricature turns violent what had been a linguistic tendency toward the breakdown in sympathetic imagination; that is, the linguistic tendency, dramatized in the novel's first pages, to divide the world into "employers and employed": "the differences between the employers and employed . . . [are] an eternal subject for agitation in the manufacturing districts, which, however it may be lulled for a time, is sure to break forth again with fresh violence at any depression of trade" (*MB* 23).

The industrialists' failure is a failure of perception and classification; their breach is in misclassifying their workers as brutes, hence setting in motion the cycle of violence that the novel then depicts. Job Legh's natural history avocation is thus not only a detail about working-class life but a structural model for reform: it offers a cure for the ills of perception. In seeing the affinity between the working-class man and himself, the industrialist rights the wrongs of misclassification that had set in motion the violence. Of course, with that perceptual change comes a return of sympathetic imagination—for the elder Carson, the incitement to sympathy occurs in the house of John Barton, where he has been summoned to hear the man's confession. In thinking about it in his study afterward, it is the visual impact of the distraught man's poverty that elicits his empathy:

> In the days of his childhood and youth, Mr. Carson had been accustomed to poverty; but it was honest, decent poverty; not the grinding squalid misery he had remarked in every part of

---

3. Raymond Williams writes about sympathetic imagination, but he does so in relation to the writing act rather than within the bounds of the plot. That is, his reading of *Mary Barton* discusses Gaskell's sympathetic imagination and the threat made to it by the "fear of violence"; Williams acknowledges her "flow of sympathy" and evaluates the novel as a "largely successful attempt at imaginative identification," but suggests that the fear of violence explains her dramatization of the murder (*Culture and Society* 90–91).

John Barton's house, and which contrasted strangely with the
pompous sumptuousness of the room in which he now sat.
Unaccustomed wonder filled his mind at the reflection of the
different lots of the brethren of mankind. (*MB* 319)

The promise of a confession to his son's murder had brought Carson to the Barton's house, a face-to-face confrontation with the
poverty the trade unions had described but which he had been
unable to perceive before literally *seeing* it here. The return of
a Christianized, humanitarian vocabulary—the "brethren of
mankind"—marks the return of sympathy, a sympathy that had begun
at Barton's but which he had initially rejected in order to pursue
vengeance. Barton's confession revolves around a similar transfor-
mation, what the text calls the return of "sympathy for suffering, formerly so prevalent a feeling with him, again filled John Barton's
heart." The change in perception is articulated by the narrative,
which sees the return of sympathy as the cessation of false difference: "the mourner before him was no longer the employer, a being
of another race, eternally placed in an antagonistic attitude . . . no
longer the enemy, the oppressor, but a very poor and desolate old
man" (*MB* 316). Although the scene climaxes with a reference to the
Old Testament—"forgive us our trespasses"—it is the mutual shift in
perception that gets the two men to the religious proverb. The linguistic tendency that reveals the threat to perception is overcome; in
not seeing him as a "being of another race" but as a "man," Barton
initiates the political cure that Gaskell is implicitly advocating; in seeing him anew, "no longer the employer . . . the enemy . . . the oppressor," Barton's perception is reformed, which in turn models the
reform required for the cure of social ills.

Could the nettles that Alice had gathered on that spring Sunday
have been intended to aid in the approaching childbirth of John Barton's wife, with its possible, even probable, complications? Pliny, a
source for English herbals, suggests nettle juice for "prolapsus of the
uterus," a specific uterine complaint that the English herbalist tradition both picks up on and broadens. The breadth of "virtues" in
plants, however, is so great as to defy simple analogical connections
between medical and literary text. In many ways, Pliny's recording of
folk wisdom about nettles registers the irony of Mrs. Barton's death
more completely than the suggestive connection between female illness and nettles; he records that in the spring nettles are eaten with
the "devout belief that it will keep diseases away throughout the
whole year."[4] That we can trace John Barton's despair, and subsequent radical political thoughts and actions, to the death of his wife

4. Plinius Secundus, C., *Natural History, Vol. VI*, trans. W.H.S. Jones (Cambridge: Harvard
   UP, 1938), 229, 315.

is all the more suggestive about the import of herbal medicine and natural history to the politics of *Mary Barton*. If the irony of Alice's nettles arriving too late is less present to us than the arrival of a doctor only after Mrs. Barton's death, it is only because we have forgotten the prevalence of nineteenth-century herbalist medicine for the working classes. In the persistent evocation of natural history and herbal medicine, the techniques of reformist realism are broadened. Gaskell, in a sense, proposes a taxonomical cure: a way of *seeing* the working class, not as brutes, or just as "the manufacturing population," but as individuals whose ills should be ameliorated.

LIAM CORLEY

The Imperial Addiction of *Mary Barton*[†]

> Here was a panacea—a [pharmakon nepenthez] for all human woes: here was the secret of happiness, about which philosophers had disputed for so many ages, at once discovered . . .
>
> Thomas de Quincey

During the early Victorian period, a slow and at first imperceptible euphoria spread within Great Britain's public sphere, a delirium resulting from and contributing to a burgeoning national addiction to the sociopolitical and economic privileges of empire. A growing belief in Great Britain's imperial destiny was reflected and injected dose by dose through a variety of unlikely literary, political, and ephemeral texts. Elizabeth Gaskell made a purgative contribution to this project of national discovery in her 1848 novel of working class suffering, *Mary Barton*. It is common enough to assert that Elizabeth Gaskell insists through the substance of her narrative that the material conditions and individual integrity of members of Manchester's working class must be considered important elements in any rendering of the English social body and economic well-being. However, *Mary Barton* presents not only a challenge to the domestic, economic and political ideas of her contemporaries, it also contains a critique of the imperial addictions and assumptions which increasingly characterized early Victorian descriptions of economic and political normalcy.

Elizabeth Gaskell sets *Mary Barton* during one of the worst periods of economic depression in Manchester in order to depict the suffering that had heretofore gone unmarked by much of the country. The cotton economy of Lancashire experienced seemingly unpredictable

† From *Gaskell Society Journal*. 17 (2003): 1–11. By permission of the Gaskell Society and the author.

cycles of boom and bust throughout the middle of the nineteenth century which caused immense suffering among the workers in the cotton manufacturing industry.[1] The main action of the novel occurs between 1839 and 1842, a period in which a downturn in global trade contributed to widespread unemployment and partial employment among the Manchester working class. As both a contribution to and a formulation of the 'condition of England' question, *Mary Barton* has been evaluated primarily as a description of a local problem: what should be done about the poverty and degradation of the operatives in Manchester? Or more broadly, how should middle-class England understand its Christian responsibilities to the labouring classes?[2] In most cases, the insular focus of criticism on *Mary Barton* contributes to a 'domestication' of Gaskell's challenge to developing 'theories of trade' (*MB*, p. 6)[3] by causing readers to overlook the significant internal evidence which implicates *Mary Barton* in the construction of a global hegemony—the complex of attitudes in which the 'condition of England' could only be considered as the 'condition of England in the world'.[4] Gaskell's attempt to construe the ways in which the working class was enmeshed in the construction of Britain's overseas hegemony leads to a contradictory resolution which both interrogates and relies upon assumptions about English colonial power.

Elizabeth Gaskell begins her story of industrial Manchester after its dependence on foreign trade for both raw materials and markets is well established. Manchester's cotton production far exceeded the demand of domestic English consumers. Gaskell represents this reliance of British mercantile interests on foreign markets amenable to monopoly and control by describing the commission that precipitates the worker's strike as coming from 'a new foreign market' (*MB*, p. 151). The potential instability of this foreign demand causes the manufacturers to assert their control over the means of production by offering lower wages to the already desperate operatives. The industrialists are able to enforce their contract despite the violent protests of the workers, and this continuing economic violence con-

---

1. Steven Marcus, *Engels, Manchester, and the Working Class* (New York: Random House, 1974), p. 11.
2. See, for instance, Monica C. Fryckstedt's discussion of the similarities between *Mary Barton* and the Unitarian 'Reports of the Ministry to the Poor' in *Elizabeth Gaskell's Mary Barton and Ruth: A Challenge to Christian England* (Stockholm: Uppsala, 1982), pp. 90–97. See also Hilary M. Schor, *Scheherezade in the Marketplace: Elizabeth Gaskell and the Victorian Novel* (New York: Oxford UP, 1992), pp. 21–28. Deirdre d'Albertis discusses *Mary Barton*'s contribution to debates about women as charity workers in *Dissembling Fictions: Elizabeth Gaskell and the Victorian Social Text* (New York: St. Martin's, 1997), pp. 58–64.
3. Page numbers for *Mary Barton* refer to this Norton Critical Edition.
4. For more on why we should not accept at face value Gaskell's claim that she knows nothing of 'Political Economy, or the theories of trade', see Mary Lenard, *Preaching Pity: Dickens, Gaskell, and Sentimentalism in Victorian Culture* (New York: Peter Lang Press, 1999), pp. 115–16.

stitutes the masters' power to control foreign demand. Despite the emphasis of the action on domestic factors, the industrialists' goal remains the assurance of foreign demand, and the narrator insists that 'in the long run the interests of the workmen would have been thereby benefited' (*MB*, p. 151). While Gaskell spends most of her narrative depicting the negative effects of low wages and partial or unemployment, here she subordinates her concern for working class suffering to the imperative of guaranteeing foreign demand.

Gaskell also relies on the economic opportunities of empire for the successful resolution of the marriage plot which unites Mary Barton and Jem Wilson and relocates them to Canada. Coral Lansbury argues that Gaskell's choice to have the young couple emigrate indicates that 'Gaskell could see no resolution to the industrial conflict . . . Emigration was always an admission of failure at the same time as it held out the promise of a better life.[5] While this may accurately reflect Gaskell's pessimism about the prospects for Manchester, it also reveals that to be an English failure is still to hold a position of privilege in the world. Jem Wilson receives a lucrative colonial position in a Canadian agricultural college: 'a comfortable appointment,—house,—land,—and a good percentage on the instruments made' (*MB*, p. 324). By utilizing extant assumptions about the power of the English to control wealth abroad for a successful resolution of her plot, Gaskell constructs a vision of domestic social harmony that is necessarily underwritten by the forcible extension and maintenance of empire. This association of domestic harmony and overseas empire extends even to seemingly minor details in the story. When Mary takes refuge with the Sturgises after her pursuit of Will and the *John Cropper*, Mrs. Sturgis leads her 'into a little room redolent of the sea and foreign lands', in which there is 'a small bed for one son, bound for China' (*MB*, p. 273). After the trial, this will serve as Mary's sick bed, and she will rave and recuperate in a space created by the absence of a sailor 'bound for China'.

Job Legh's fascination with foreign creatures expresses another aspect of domestic trends which served to normalize among the British their nation's imperial relation to a world increasingly denominated as 'colonial'. Legh's interest in taxonomic control over creatures from foreign lands is facilitated by Britain's mercantile power, a relation given expression in the person of Will, the sailor. Legh's interest in foreign insects and animals causes him to be 'deep in conversation with the young sailor, trying to extract from him any circumstances connected with the natural history of the different countries he had visited' (*MB*, p. 133). Job and Will's amusing debate about Mermaidicus and Exocetus exemplifies the clash between taxonomic and

5. Coral Lansbury, *Elizabeth Gaskell* (Boston: Twayne, 1984), p. 22.

romantic notions of travel, and Will's complaint that some folks 'never knows beasts unless they're called out o' their names' reflects the same sensibility which led Gaskell to write her challenge to 'theories of trade' in 'work-a-day-English' rather than theoretical 'Sunday clothes' (*MB*, p. 136). Gaskell portrays Job's ascendance in the debate as a result of his relation to Margaret, the object of Will's desire, thus closely associating Job's intellectual authority with his paternal authority. That even this provincial patriarch could become an arbiter of biological exotica signifies the depth to which imperial notions had already saturated British society during the period in which Gaskell wrote. Thomas Richards describes the trajectory of Linnaean pursuits, such as Job's, as passing 'first from the domain of science into the domain of myth, and last into the domain of ideology. . . . [T]he project of constructing universal taxonomies of form remains very much alive, one of the last surviving emblems of the Victorian imperium, the project of a positive and comprehensive knowledge of the world.'[6] Job's scepticism regarding Mermaidicus in the face of Will's account of an eyewitness testimony enacts the power of rational projection and an attempt to order the natural world that became characteristic of British departmental overseers in the administration of the empire. While Job also serves as a comic figure in his taxonomic pretension (witness that earwigs supply his apparent motive for visiting Jem and Mary in Canada), his role as a representative of the imperial archive underscores the ideological function of 'a positive and comprehensive knowledge' which can command the resources of the British merchant marine from the patriarchal centre of the home. Job's agency throughout the novel emphasizes how his knowledge of the world can be mobilized to serve the domestic interests of the working class, most notably in the assistance he renders to Mary during her attempt to prove Jem's innocence.

Working class poverty and success in *Mary Barton* are thus shown to rely on participation in mechanisms of economic hegemony that reach beyond the confines of both Manchester and England. In relation to the workers' strike, this connectedness results in a double-bind in which both the workers and the industrialists can be seen as responding to forces apparently beyond their control. Since the narrator excuses the industrialists for lowering wages by invoking the need to guarantee foreign demand, she legitimates a world in which workers would always bear the brunt of fluctuating foreign demand. They could escape only by taking their place within the machinery of empire. The clash of the novel's economic and emotive imperatives here leaves Gaskell open to the charge of incoherence, for what the heart seems

6. Thomas Richards, *The Imperial Archive: Knowledge and the Fantasy of Empire* (New York: Verso, 1993), p. 50.

to reveal about the reader's obligation to ameliorate suffering, the mind must reject in favour of economic utility. What Gaskell does not directly state in the novel, but which is implied by the historical period in which she places it, is that foreign demand is not, to borrow de Quincey's wording, the 'panacea . . . for all human woes' that it first appears to be. To observe how the novel comments upon the desirability of world economic hegemony, we must look closely at the sources of economic depression in *Mary Barton*, which can be in part attributed to the disruption of a particular foreign market: China.

Deteriorating British relations with China over the issue of opium smuggling led to the first of the so-called Opium Wars between the two countries in the spring of 1839.[7] From May, 1839, until the treaty of Nanking in August, 1842, British exports of cotton and opium to China were severely curtailed. The loss of revenue from opium sales also led to a modest decrease in Indian demand for cotton products because the smuggled opium was exported from India to China, and a portion of the profits thereof supported Indian opium farmers who were an important market for Manchester cotton.[8] The effects of the Opium War were felt immediately in Manchester. In 1838, Manchester merchants had exported 739,904 pounds sterling worth of cotton manufactures to China through the port of Liverpool. While this represented only 4% of total British exports of cotton goods to foreign countries in 1838, the subsequent decline in exports to China in 1839 and 1840 represents 30% and 35%, respectively, of the total decline in exports to foreign countries during those years.[9] The loss of the China trade was part of the com-

7. See Jack Beeching, *The Chinese Opium Wars* (New York: Harcourt Brace Jovanovich, 1975), p. 19. British demand for Chinese products like tea and porcelain created a dangerous imbalance of trade which led to a net transfer from 1710 to 1759 of nearly 27 million pounds worth of silver specie. By exploiting a modest Chinese market for opium, the East India Company was able to redress the imbalance. British opium exports to China created problems of its own. Under Chinese law, trade in opium was forbidden. After the East India Company's monopoly on the China trade was rescinded in 1834, opium smuggling skyrocketed and Chinese authorities began to take more resolute measures against the smugglers. By 1839, tensions had broken into open hostilities, the first of the Opium Wars between Great Britain and China.

8. For the example of India, which demonstrates that even an indigenous cotton industry could be displaced by Manchester cotton if there were sufficient military and political support for the venture, see Marcus, *op.cit.*, p. 8. India is, however, a complicated case, for as British exports began displacing the indigenous cotton industry, it became necessary to supplement the local economy with a new source of income so that the Lancashire exports could be purchased. Beeching notes that '[t]he opium-growing cultivators of Bengal, paid cash by the government for their crop, were precisely the kind of thriving market Lancashire was looking for. The more opium grown, the more cotton cloth sold.' See Beeching, *Chinese Opium Wars*, p. 33. While Beeching exaggerates the possibilities of prosperity accruing to the peasant farmer, some correlation between cotton sales and opium production can hardly be denied. See Brian Inglis, *The Opium War* (London: Hodder & Stoughton, 1976), pp. 87–89. From a minuscule annual production in the mid-eighteenth century sufficient for local consumption, Indian cultivation of opium exploded from the end of the eighteenth until the early twentieth century.

9. Statistical data derived from table 25 in James A. Mann, *The Cotton Trade of Great Britain* (London: Cass, 1968), p. 124.

plex of factors that led to the unemployment and partial-employment depicted in *Mary Barton*, and it was significant enough to motivate the Manchester merchants to political action. After months of slack business and uncertainty, thirty-nine Manchester merchants petitioned Parliament in September, 1839, for 'prompt, vigorous, and decided measures' to resolve the conflict in China, pleading that the cessation in trade 'may eventually entail very serious losses on us'.[1] The eventuality of this loss, not its present reality, is precisely what John Barton observes in the Manchester industrialists: while the workers starved to death, he saw only idleness and pleasure among the industrialists. Even 'sacrificing capital to obtain a decisive victory over the continental manufacturers' would not result in equivalent material suffering among the industrialist class (*MB*, p. 152).

The historical moment in which the Manchester industrialists petition Parliament for decisive military action to stabilize foreign demand coincides with the fictional moment in which the Manchester industrialists precipitate a strike in their attempt to guarantee foreign demand by lowering wages. Unlike the petition to Parliament carried by John Barton and his fellow Trade Unionists which Gaskell places in the spring of 1839, the industrialists' 1839 petition regarding the China trade was received respectfully and heeded. During the months of the strike, Harry Carson's murder, and the subsequent trial depicted in *Mary Barton*, British warships were forcing their way into Chinese ports to avenge the Chinese government's destruction of British-owned opium contraband and to guarantee the right of the British to demand access to Chinese markets. As a result of the war, the British were able to expand their access to Chinese markets from one port to five, and by 1864 the total value of the trade, including opium, between China, England, and India exceeded 100 million pounds.[2] Consequently Gaskell's choice to set *Mary Barton* during the Opium War not only associates the economic violence of the industrialists against the working class with British imperialism in China, it also highlights the metaphoric possibilities of the economic interdependence of the cotton and opium trade.

As a result of the first Opium War, the relationship between cotton manufacturing and the opium trade became a topic of public debate. The most prominent discussion of the connection between the opium trade and the plight of the English working class occurred in 1843 when Lord Ashley, later the seventh Earl of Shaftesbury, presented petitions from three missionary societies to the House of Commons urging the abolition of the opium trade. In the course of

---

1. *Journals of the House of Commons* Vol. 39, ed. E.L. Erickson (London: HMSO, 1840), p. 639.
2. Exports of cotton piece goods to China increased from 21 million yards in 1838 to 113 million yards in 1856.

condemning the trade on moral grounds, Lord Ashley also appealed to commercial interests. Mary Mason summarizes Lord Ashley's argument as follows: 'The opium traffic was harmful to British trade because a pernicious drug was substituted for the manufactures of Great Britain. . . . The extension of England's commerce and the opening of new markets for British manufacturers would greatly benefit the English working classes'.[3] Though nothing substantive came of Lord Ashley's resolution, speeches for and against it placed the opium trade directly before the British people through the press, and they were among the first public discussions of the connection between working class hunger, opium addiction, and the industrialists' desire for expanding markets. By associating the cotton trade with the opium trade, Manchester industrialism could be portrayed as both a source of plenty and a site of need, for the tremendous productive capacity of the Manchester mills depended upon foreign markets for economic viability. Furthermore, the brazen association of military might and economic right exemplified in the opium trade also underlay the relations between the cotton masters and the workers. The worker's attempt to upend the hierarchy of dependence through their trade unionism depends on an understanding of the relationship between masters and workers as one of reversible need, the same reasoning which led the Chinese to believe that the British would not be willing to sacrifice their addiction to tea and porcelain for the sake of opposing Chinese efforts to rid themselves of an unwanted supply of opium. In both cases, coercion proved the logic faulty.

Gaskell's treatment of addiction and exploitation in *Mary Barton* is both suggestive and involved. Gaskell's recognition of the multiple forms of dependence pervades *Mary Barton*, and one of its prominent forms includes the characterization of the ideal relationship between workers and masters as symbiotic. However, at the heart of *Mary Barton* lies a more ambivalent evocation of dependence and desire: the image of John Barton as an opium-eater. The foreign dependence of the industrialists, which is only fleetingly referenced throughout the novel, is vividly pictured in the body of John Barton, and the consequences of addiction are equally vivid. John Barton's physical decline is presented as both the result of malnutrition and opium: 'No haunting ghost could have had less of the energy of life in its involuntary motions than he' (*MB*, p. 299). His listlessness should not be confused with numbness, as is made evident in the description of John Barton's face when he returns to his home at the end of the novel: 'And as for his face, it was sunk and worn,—like a skull, with yet a

3. Mary G. Mason, *Western Concepts of China and the Chinese, 1840–1876* (New York: Russell & Russell, 1939), p. 109.

suffering expression which skulls have not' (*MB*, p. 306). John Barton's opium addiction and his subsequent recourse to violence can be seen as the representative pattern of how Gaskell weaves the triple strand of physical, commercial, and narcotic desires throughout the narrative as both implicit and explicit stimuli for action. She invokes the reader's sympathy in explaining John Barton's recourse to opium addiction as a means of lessening the hunger pangs of starvation and the intellectual pangs of daily perceiving economic injustice: 'before you blame too harshly this use [of opium], or rather abuse, try a hopeless life, with daily cravings of the body for food. Try, not alone being without hope yourself, but seeing all around you reduced to the same despair' (*MB*, pp. 149–150). Thus, in a novel which does not directly reference the Opium War as a contributing factor to the principal scenes of suffering, we are still presented with an image of the dire consequences of addiction such as the one industrialists had for foreign markets: the tortured and violent addict who, for reasons of interpersonal connections, yet deserves sympathy.

John Barton's addiction functions in multiple ways within the novel. First, it completes his status as the representative sufferer of the Manchester industrialists' greed and ruthlessness. As a leader in the trade union, he is at the centre of the controversy over the industrialists' attempt to guarantee the foreign market. As an opium addict, he also becomes doubly associated with the Chinese, metonymically through the use of opium and metaphorically as a representative of the human suffering that results from the industrialists' efforts to control foreign demand. In the former role, John Barton assumes a complex and pathetic position, for missionary agitation about Chinese opium addicts emphasized the British East India Company's role in sustaining and extending the drug's reach in Chinese society.[4] The anti-opium lobby grew in strength through the latter half of the nineteenth century, and John Barton prefigures the dire consequences for Britain's involvement in the opium trade heralded by this movement: '[T]he Orient (especially China) will enter, colonize, and conquer the English body in the form of a contaminating contagion enabled by Opium.'[5] In the words of Reverend George Piercy, a former missionary to Canton, 'It begins with the Chinese, but it doesn't end there'.[6] By figuring domestic opium addicts as a just revenge for the addiction of the British to unjustly sustaining foreign markets, anti-opium rhetoric suggests how the addiction of a

---

4. Another imperial association with opium is also possible, that of the Ottoman Empire. Turkey accounted for nearly 90% of all British opium imports for most of the nineteenth century. It was reputedly of a higher grade than Indian opium, which was dedicated to mitigating the imbalances of the China trade. See Virginia Berridge and Griffith Edwards, *Opium and the People: Opiate Use in Nineteenth-Century England* (New Haven: Yale UP, 1987), Chapters I and 9.
5. Barry Milligan, *Pleasures and Pains: Opium and the Orient in Nineteenth-Century British Culture* (Charlottesville: UP of Virginia, 1995), p. 83.
6. *Ibid.*

figure like John Barton can become a metaphor for the industrialists' need for stable markets and the colonial relationships which result. Whether or not Gaskell meant John Barton's opium addiction to be seen as a metaphor for British expansionist policies, the thrust of her tale establishes the basis for such a critique of British imperialism.

The imperial dependencies of foreign trade and colonial subjugation appear in the role of an ambiguous *deus ex machina* at crucial junctures in the plot. Gaskell privileges the pursuit of foreign markets and colonies as a panacea for the suffering depicted in the novel. Nonetheless, she also expresses horror at the tremendous human costs associated with industrialism and presents the conflict between the Trade Unionists and the masters as inevitable given the material conditions of the workers. She refuses to pass glibly over the substantial suffering of the working classes and presents their complaints with dignity and humanity. Most significantly, John Barton's decline and final recourse to violence make him a horrifying example of the results of dependencies such as are given some justification by reference to economic exigencies elsewhere in the novel. That the extension of the empire, an assumed good through most of the novel, should be so incongruously paired with the degradations of opium addiction may appear at first contradictory, an inconsistency to be attributed to narrative incoherence. How can a beloved source of nurture also be the foulest ill? Additional clues to Gaskell's attitude towards the ambiguous association of John Barton and the industrialists can be found in Mary Barton's transformed view of her father during her breakdown subsequent to Jem's trial:

> Among the mingled feelings she had revealed in her delirium, aye, mingled even with the most tender expressions of love for her father, was a sort of horror of him; a dread of him as a blood-shedder, which seemed to separate him into two persons,—one, the father who had dandled her on his knee, and loved her all her life long; the other, the assassin, the cause of all her trouble and woe. (*MB*, p. 300)

The bifurcation of consciousness evidenced in Mary's attitude towards her father is attributed to the disjunction between affective ties and the exercise of moral judgment. Mary's ambivalence is not incoherent within the narrative frame of a tale which means to humanize debates about 'theories of trade' by presenting them 'truthfully' through individual lives (*MB*, p. 6).[7] After all, Gaskell's novel deplored a system enabled by and enriching a class of Manchester

---

7. Another interesting association can be found in the name of Will's ship, the *John Cropper*. Cropper has at least two meanings here. First, 'cropper' describes the gathering of crops, the collection of material goods. A secondary meaning of cropper is more enlightening: a misfortune, or a fall. Merchant vessels such as the *John Cropper* were indeed both a means to gather in profits and the stumbling block that could lead to an unfortunate fall.

merchants to whom she was both personally known and occasionally beholden as a consequence of her husband's role as the most prominent Unitarian minister in Manchester. Gaskell is further able to associate Mary's ambivalence towards her father with British imperialism in China by the ingenious move of having Mary express the above sentiments during her recuperation at the Sturgis's house, in a room which normally accommodates a son who is sailing to China. This association is doubly poignant because a British sailor in China during the historical moment in which the novel is placed would inevitably be involved in some fashion with the execution of the first Opium War.

The use of opium addiction as a trope for empire leads one to many and contradictory reflections on the nature of the imperial enterprise and its end result. By constructing John Barton's body, the beloved and reviled site of addiction, violence, and despair, as a metaphor for the English political and economic body, Gaskell provides a bleak vision of the trajectory of empire. She concludes the industrial portion of the novel with the restricted ameliorative agency of the elder Carson, a domestic precursor of the colonial bureaucrat labouring under the White Man's Burden. But the necessarily limited activity of the now-enlightened imperial agent is not able to erase the effects or the memory of the addiction figured in the body of John Barton. The historical period of England's imperial addiction, feverishly alternating between colonial dependence and desire, concludes in much the same manner as the celebrated English Opium-eater ends his confessions:

> [I]f the gentlemen of Surgeons' Hall think that any benefit can redound to their science from inspecting the appearances in the body of an Opium-eater, let them speak but a word, and I will take care that mine shall be legally secured to them . . . I assure them they will do me too much honour by 'demonstrating' on such a crazy body as mine: and it will give pleasure to anticipate this posthumous revenge and insult inflicted upon that which has caused me so much suffering in this life.[8]

The constitutive ideological process which resulted in widespread social and economic support for the British empire can be explored by recourse to such 'crazy' bodies as *Mary Barton*, so full of 'suffering in this life.' By emphasizing the ways in which *Mary Barton* critiques, extends, and assumes the construction of the English social body in the global economy of empire, I have tried to clarify the ways in which Gaskell's engagement with 'theories of trade' merit more careful consideration as a contribution to historical and contemporary

8. Thomas de Quincey, *Confessions of an English Opium Eater*. 1821. intro. William Bolitho (New York: Heritage Press, 1950), p. 77.

debates about the material suffering of workers in a world context. In a global context of economic recolonization, one use of Gaskell's evocation of working class suffering could be to energize movements defending the human rights of foreign workers who are exploited through the addictive demands of western consumers mediated through a globally empowered merchant class not unlike the industrialists of *Mary Barton*.[9] One continuing function of *Mary Barton*, read as both cultural product and culture producer, can be to awaken contemporary readers to the hidden investments and addictions which underlie the ongoing exploitation of foreign people and places by Western nations.[1] Such an unabashedly sentimental and political claim is both an interpretation and reenactment of Gaskell's accomplishment in *Mary Barton*.

9. A unit on *Mary Barton* in an undergraduate literature course could easily include readings about the anti-sweatshop movement in order to emphasize the relevance of this reading strategy. Despite Thomas Recchio's claim that 'emphasiz[ing] how social/political/economic conflict is played out (or not)' in *Mary Barton* enacts a form of 'interpretive violence', I believe that such an exercise would open interpretive possibilities that increase rather than attenuate the intersubjectivity of reader and text. Thomas Recchio, 'A Monstrous Reading of *Mary Barton*: Fiction as "Communitas"', *College Literature*, Vol. 23.3 (1996), pp. 2–22, at p. 4.
1. Nor should this reading be limited to 'foreign' places. For more on the garment industry in the United States, see Lisa Lowe, *Immigrant Acts: On Asian American Cultural Politics* (Durham: Duke UP, 1996), Chapter 7.

Elizabeth Gaskell: A Chronology

1810	Elizabeth Cleghorn Stevenson (later Gaskell) born on September 29 in the Chelsea district of London. Older brother John had been born in 1798.
1811	Her mother, Elizabeth Stevenson, dies. Elizabeth sent to Knutsford, Cheshire, to be raised by her maternal aunt Hannah Lumb.
1814	Her father, William Stevenson, marries Catherine Thompson.
1821–26	Attends boarding school in Barford, Warwickshire; school moves to Stratford-upon-Avon in 1824.
1825	Her father completes a series of articles on political economy.
1828	Disappearance of her brother John at sea. Elizabeth joins her father and stepmother in Chelsea.
1829	William Stevenson dies. Elizabeth leaves to stay with her uncle, the Reverend William Turner, in Newcastle-upon-Tyne.
1831	Thomas Ashton, for reasons related to industrial conflict, murdered in Manchester. Years later the murder was wrongly taken as a source for the murder of Harry Carson in *Mary Barton*.
1832	Passage of the first Reform Bill. Elizabeth marries William Gaskell, junior minister of Cross Street Unitarian Chapel, Manchester. The couple settle in Manchester.
1833	Passage of the Factory Act, which barred children under the age of nine from working in the cotton mills. First child, a daughter, is stillborn.
1834	Marianne Gaskell born.
1837	First publication, "Sketches among the Poor" (a poem) appears in *Blackwood's* xli, 48–50. Margaret Emily Gaskell born. Hannah Lumb dies. Ascension of Queen Victoria.
1838–41	A son born, then dies. No name recorded. Date unclear.

1839	Chartist Petition with more than one million signatures presented to House of Commons and subsequently rejected.
1842	A second Chartist Petition, this one with three million signatures, also refused a hearing in Parliament. Florence Elizabeth Gaskell born.
1844	William (Willie) Gaskell born in October.
1845	Willie dies of scarlet fever in August. Gaskell begins composing *Mary Barton*.
1846	Julia Bradford Gaskell born. Most of *Mary Barton* written after Julia's birth.
1847	*Mary Barton* completed. "Libbie Marsh's Three Eras" published under the pseudonym Cotton Mather Mills in *Howitt's Journal*. Gaskell attends Ralph Waldo Emerson's Manchester lecture, later writing an unsigned review.
1848	*Mary Barton* published on October 18 to mixed reviews and high acclaim for Gaskell.
1850	Charles Dickens asks Gaskell to contribute to the inaugural number of his new journal *Household Words*, marking the beginning of a long and somewhat stormy publishing relationship. Gaskell meets Charlotte Brontë.
1851	*Cranford*, Gaskell's affectionately ironic exploration of village life in the 1830s, begins publication in *Household Words*. Installments run through 1853.
1853	Publication of *Ruth*, her controversial novel about a "fallen woman." Single volume edition of *Cranford* published.
1854	*North and South* begins publication in *Household Words*. Installments run through January 1855.
1855	First book edition (2 volumes) of *North and South*. Charlotte Brontë dies. Gaskell agrees, at the request of Brontë's father Patrick, to write Charlotte's biography.
1857	Travels to Rome in February prior to the publication in March of *The Life of Charlotte Brontë*. Publishers recall unsold copies in response to objections raised about Gaskell's presentation of the scandalous behavior of Charlotte's brother, Branwell, and about the condition of the boarding school Charlotte briefly attended as a child. A retraction of the objectionable passages published in the *Times* and the *Athenaeum*. In September a "Revised and Corrected" edition is released.

1863   *Sylvia's Lovers* published in three volumes. A single-volume edition with illustrations by George du Maurier soon follows. *Cousin Phillis* begins publication in the *Cornhill*. Installments run until February 1864.

1864   *Wives and Daughters* begins publication in the *Cornhill* with illustrations by du Maurier.

1865   While having afternoon tea with her daughters at the "Lawn" in Holybourne, the house in Hampshire that Gaskell had just purchased and refurbished as a southern retreat from Manchester (and as a surprise for her husband that she planned to reveal the next day), Gaskell dies suddenly of heart failure, the final pages of *Wives and Daughters* unwritten.

1866   *Wives and Daughters* published in two volumes.

Selected Bibliography

• Indicates works included or excerpted in this Norton Critical Edition.

Bibliographies

Northrop, Clarke Sutherland. In Gerald de Witt Sanders, *Elizabeth Gaskell*. New Haven: Yale UP for Cornell University; London: Oxford UP for Cornell University, 1929, pp. 163–262.

Selig, Robert L. *Elizabeth Gaskell: A Reference Guide*. Boston: G. K. Hall, 1977.

Smith, Walter E. *Elizabeth Gaskell: A Bibliographical Catalogue*. Los Angeles: Heritage Book Shop, 1998.

Welch, Jeffrey Egan. *Elizabeth Gaskell: An Annotated Bibliography 1929–1975*. New York: Garland, 1977.

Weyant, Nancy S. *Elizabeth Gaskell: An Annotated Bibliography of English-Language Sources, 1976–1991*. Metuchen, N.J.: Scarecrow Press, 1994.

———. *Elizabeth Gaskell: An Annotated Guide to English-Language Sources, 1992–2001*. Metuchen, N.J.: Scarecrow Press, 2004.

Journal

The Gaskell Society Journal, vols. 1–21, 1986–2007. (There are no individual listings below for articles from this journal. Volume 16, 2002, contains author, subject, and book review indexes for volumes 1–16.)

Biographies, Letters, Diaries

Chapple, J. A. V. *Elizabeth Gaskell: A Portrait in Letters*. Manchester: Manchester UP, 1980.

Chapple, J. A. V. and Anita Wilson. *Private Voices: The Diaries of Elizabeth Gaskell and Sophia Holland*. Keele: Keele UP, 1996.

• Chapple, J. A. V. and Arthur Pollard, eds. *The Letters of Mrs. Gaskell*. Manchester: Manchester UP, 1966.

Chapple, John. *Elizabeth Gaskell: The Early Years*. Manchester: Manchester UP, 1997.

Chapple, John, and Alan Shelston, eds. *Further Letters of Mrs. Gaskell*. Manchester: Manchester UP, 2000.

———. *Further Letters of Mrs. Gaskell* [newly updated in paperback]. Manchester: Manchester UP, 2003.

Foster, Shirley. *Elizabeth Gaskell: A Literary Life*. Basingstoke: Palgrave Macmillan, 2002.

Gerin, Winifred. *Elizabeth Gaskell*. Oxford: Oxford UP, 1980.

Handley, Graham. *An Elizabeth Gaskell Chronology*. Basingstoke: Palgrave Macmillan, 2005.

Hopkins, Annette B. *Elizabeth Gaskell: Her Life and Work*. London: John Lehmann, 1952.

Uglow, Jenny. *Elizabeth Gaskell: A Habit of Stories*. London: Faber & Faber, 1993.

Waller, Ross D. "Letters Addressed to Mrs. Gaskell by Celebrated Contemporaries. Now in the Possession of the John Rylands Library." *Bulletin of the John Rylands Library*, 19, 102–69, 1935.

Whitehill, Jane. *Letters of Mrs. Gaskell and Charles Eliot Norton 1855–1865*. London: Humphrey Milford, Oxford UP, 1932.

Monographs and Critical Studies
(With substantial material on *Mary Barton*)

- Altick, Richard. "Dion Boucicault Stages *Mary Barton*." *Nineteenth-Century Fiction* 14.2 (1959), 129–41

Anderson, Amanda. *Tainted Souls and Painted Faces: The Rhetoric of Fallenness in Victorian Culture*. Ithaca: Cornell UP, 1993.

Baldridge, Cates. "Interminable Conversations: Social Concord in *Mary Barton* and *North and South*." *Th=e Dialogics of Dissent in the English Novel*. Hanover and London: Middlebury College P (1994), 119–43.

Billington, Josie. *Faithful Realism: Elizabeth Gaskell and Leo Tolstoy, a Comparative Study*. Lewisburg, Penn.: Bucknell UP, 2002.

- Bodenheimer, Rosemarie. "Private Grief and Public Acts in *Mary Barton*." *Dickens Studies Annual* 9 (1981), 195–216.

Bonaparte, Felicia. *The Gypsy-Bachelor of Manchester: The Life of Mrs. Gaskell's Demon*. Charlottesville: UP of Virginia, 1992.

Cazamian, Louis. *The Social Novel in England, 1830–1850: Dickens, Disraeli, Mrs. Gaskell, Kingsley*. London: Routledge & Kegan Paul, 1973.

Chadwick, Mrs. Ellis H. *Mrs. Gaskell: Haunts, Homes, and Stories*. London: Sir Isaac Pitman & Sons, 1913.

Childers, Joseph W. *Novel Possibilities: Fiction and the Formation of Early Victorian Culture*. Philadelphia: U of Pennsylvania P, 1995.

Colby, Robin. *"Some Appointed Work to Do". Women and Vocation in the Fiction of Elizabeth Gaskell*. Westport, Conn.: Greenwood Press, 1995.

Craik, W. A. *Elizabeth Gaskell and the English Provincial Novel*. London: Methuen, 1975.

- d'Albertis, Deirdre. *Dissembling Fictions: Elizabeth Gaskell and the Victorian Social Text*. New York: St. Martin's Press, 1997.

Duthie, Enid. *The Themes of Elizabeth Gaskell*. Totowa, N.J.: Rowan and Littlefield, 1980.

Easson, Angus. *Elizabeth Gaskell*. London: Routledge & Kegan Paul, 1979.

Easson, Angus, ed. *Elizabeth Gaskell: The Critical Heritage*. London: Routledge, 1991.

Ellison, David. "Glazed Expression: *Mary Barton*, Ghosts and Glass." *Studies in the Novel*, 36.4 (Winter 2004), 484–508.

Felber, Lynette. "Gaskell's Industrial Idylls: Ideology and Formal Incongruence in *Mary Barton* and *North and South*." *CLIO* 18.1 (1988), 55–72.

ffrench, Yvonne. *Mrs. Gaskell*. London: Home & Van Thal, 1949.

Flint, Kate. *Elizabeth Gaskell*. Plymouth: Northcote House, 1995.

Fryckstedt, Monica Correa. *Elizabeth Gaskell's* Mary Barton *and* Ruth: *A Challenge to Christian England*. In *Studia Anglistica Upsaliensia* 43, Uppsala, 1982.

- Gallagher, Catherine. *The Industrial Reformation of English Fiction, 1832–1867*. Chicago: U of Chicago P, 1985.

Ganz, Margaret. *Elizabeth Gaskell: The Artist in Conflict*. New York: Twayne, 1969.

- Guy, Josephine. *The Victorian Social-Problem Novel*. Basingstoke: Macmillan, 1996.

Haldane, Elizabeth. *Mrs. Gaskell and Her Friends*. London: Hodder and Stoughton, 1931.

Hennelly, Mark. "Letters 'All Bordered with Hearts and Darts': Sex, Lies and Valentines in *Mary Barton*, Part 1." *Journal of Evolutionary Psychology* 20 (1999), 140–60.

———. "Letters 'All Bordered with Hearts and Darts': Sex, Lies and Valentines in *Mary Barton*, Part 2." *Journal of Evolutionary Psychology* 21 (2000), 40–48.

Hopkins, Annette B. "*Mary Barton*: A Victorian Best Seller." *Trollopian* 3.1 (1948), 1–18.

Hotz, Mary. "A Grave with No Name: Representations of Death in Elizabeth Gaskell's *Mary Barton*." *Nineteenth-Century Studies*, 15 (2001), 37–56.

Hughes, Linda K. and Michael Lund. *Victorian Publishing and Mrs. Gaskell's Work*. Charlottesville: UP of Virginia, 1999.

Johnson, Patricia E. *Hidden Hands: Working-Class Women and Victorian Social Problem Fiction*. Athens: Ohio UP, 2001.

———. "Art and Assassination in Elizabeth Gaskell's *Mary Barton*." *Victorians Institute Journal*. 27 (1999), 149–64.

Kestner, Joseph. *Protest and Reform: The British Social Narrative by Women, 1827–1867*. Madison: U of Wisconsin P, 1985.

Krueger, Christine L. *The Reader's Repentance: Women Preachers, Women Writers, and Nineteenth-Century Social Discourse*. Chicago: U of Chicago P, 1992.

Lansbury, Coral. *Elizabeth Gaskell: The Novel of Social Crisis*. New York: Barnes & Noble, 1975.

———. *Elizabeth Gaskell*. Boston: Twayne, 1984.

- Lucas, John. *The Literature of Change*. Sussex: Harvester Press, 1980.

- ———. "Mrs. Gaskell and Brotherhood." *Tradition and Tolerance in Nineteenth-Century Fiction.* New York: Barnes & Noble, 1967, 141–205.

  McVeagh, John. *Profiles in Literature: Elizabeth Gaskell.* London: Routledge & Kegan Paul, 1970.

- Nord, Deborah Epstein. *Walking the Victorian Streets: Women, Representation, and the City.* Ithaca: Cornell UP, 1995.

  Pollard, Arthur. *Mrs. Gaskell: Novelist and Biographer.* Cambridge, Mass.: Harvard UP, 1965.

  Poovey, Mary. "Disraeli, Gaskell and the Condition of England." *The Columbia History of the British Novel.* Ed. John Richetti. New York: Columbia UP, (1994), 508–32.

  Recchio, Thomas E. "The Problem of Form in Mrs. Gaskell's *Mary Barton.*" *Studies in English Literature* (Japan, English Number) (1984), 19–35.

  ———. "A Monstrous Reading of *Mary Barton*: Fiction as 'Communitas.'" *College Literature* 23.3 (October 1996), 2–22.

  Rubenius, Aina. *The Woman Question in Mrs. Gaskell's Life and Works.* In *Essays and Studies on English Language and Literature,* V, ed. S.B. Liljegren. The English Institute in the University of Uppsala, 1950.

  Samuelian, Kristen Flieger. "Lost Mothers: The Challenge to Paternalism in *Mary Barton.*" *Nineteenth-Century Studies* 6 (1992), 19–36.

- Schor, Hilary M. *Scheherezade in the Marketplace: Elizabeth Gaskell & the Victorian Novel.* New York: Oxford UP, 1992.

- Sharps, John Geoffrey. *Mrs. Gaskell's Observation and Invention: A Study of Her Non-Biographic Works.* Fontwell, Sussex: The Linden Press, 1970.

  Spencer, Jane. *Elizabeth Gaskell.* New York: St. Martin's Press, 1993.

  Stone, Marjorie. "Bakhtinian Polyphony in *Mary Barton. Dickens Studies Annual* 20 (1991), 175–200.

- Stoneman, Patsy. *Elizabeth Gaskell.* 2nd ed. Manchester: Manchester UP, 2006.

- Tillotson, Kathleen. *Novels of the Eighteen-Forties.* Oxford: Clarendon Press, 1954.

  Unsworth, Anna. *Elizabeth Gaskell: An Independent Woman.* London: Minerva Press, 1996.

  Valverde, Mariana. "The Love of Finery: Fashion and the Fallen Woman in Nineteenth-Century Social Discourse." *Victorian Studies* Winter 32.2 (1989), 169–88.

  Wheeler, Michael. *The Art of Allusion in Victorian Fiction.* London: Macmillan, 1979.

  Whitfield, A. Stanton. *Mrs. Gaskell: Her Life and Work.* George Routledge & Sons, 1929.

- Williams, Raymond. *Culture & Society, 1780–1950.* New York: Harper & Row, 1958.

  Wright, Edgar. *Mrs. Gaskell: The Basis for Reassessment.* London: Oxford UP, 1965.

  Wright, Terence. *Elizabeth Gaskell: 'We are not angels' Realism, Gender, Values.* Basingstoke: Macmillan Press, 1995.

- Zlotnick, Susan. *Women, Writing, and the Industrial Novel.* Baltimore: Johns Hopkins UP, 1998.

Dramatic Adaptations

- Boucicault, Dion, Esq. *The Long Strike: A Drama in Four Acts.* London: Samuel French, 1866. [Opened at the Royal Lyceum, London on September 15, 1866.]

  Munro, Rona. *Mary Barton* [A Play in Two acts]. London: Nick Hern Books, 2006. [Opened at the Royal Exchange Theatre, Manchester on September 6, 2006.]

  Unknown author. *Mary Barton: or, a Tale of Manchester Life.* [Performed at the Victoria Theatre, London February 17–22 and 24–27 and March 1–2, 1851.]

  ———. *The Life's Adventures of Mary Barton.* [Performed at the Effingham Saloon, London from March 16–21, 1863.]

Illustrated Editions

- Gaskell, Mrs. *Mary Barton and Other Tales.* A new edition with four illustrations. London: Smith & Elder, 1881.
- ———. *Cranford and Mary Barton.* Illustrated by Chris Hammond. London: Gresham, 1899.
- ———. *Mary Barton.* [Frontispiece illustration] London and Felling-on-Tyne: Walter Scott, no date, c. 1900.
- ———. *Mary Barton.* Illustrated by Ivor Symes. Illustrated Pocket Classics. London & Glasgow: Collins' Clear-type Press, no date, c. 1905.
- ———. *Mary Barton.* Illustrated by C.M. Relyea. English Comedie Humaine Home Library. New York: Century Company, 1907.